T0332833

EX LIBRIS

VINTAGE **CLASSICS**

JARED SHURIN

Jared Shurin's previous anthologies include *The Outcast Hours* and *The Djinn Falls in Love* (both with Mahvesh Murad and both finalists for the World Fantasy Award). He has also been a finalist for the Shirley Jackson Award (twice), the British Science Fiction Association Award (twice) and the Hugo Award (twice), and won the British Fantasy Award (twice).

Alongside Anne C. Perry, he founded and edited the 'brilliantly brutal' (*Guardian*) pop culture website *Pornokitsch* for ten years, responsible for many of its more irritating and exuberant articles. Together, they also co-founded the Kitschies, the prize for progressive, intelligent and entertaining speculative and fantastic fiction, and Jurassic London, an award-winning, not-for-profit small press.

His other projects have included the *Best of British Fantasy* and *Speculative Fiction* series and anthologies of mummies, weird Westerns and Dickensian London. A frequent reviewer, he has also written articles on topics as diverse as *Gossip Girl* and *Deadwood*.

Jared is a certified BBQ judge.

ALSO EDITED BY JARED SHURIN

The Djinn Falls in Love and Other Stories (with Mahvesh Murad)
The Outcast Hours (with Mahvesh Murad)
Irregularity
The Lowest Heaven (with Anne C. Perry)

JARED SHURIN

The Big Book of Cyberpunk

Volume Two

VINTAGE CLASSICS

1 3 5 7 9 10 8 6 4 2

Vintage Classics is part of the Penguin Random House group of companies whose addresses can be found at global.penguinrandomhouse.com

First published in Great Britain by Vintage Classics in 2024
First published in The United States by Vintage Books in 2023

penguin.co.uk/vintage-classics

A CIP catalogue record for this book is available from the British Library

ISBN 9781784879617

Typeset in 10/12pt Ehrhardt MT Pro by Jouve (UK), Milton Keynes
Printed and bound in Great Britain by Clays Ltd, Elcograf S.p.A.

The authorised representative in the EEA is Penguin Random House Ireland, Morrison Chambers, 32 Nassau Street, Dublin D02 YH68

Penguin Random House is committed to a sustainable future for our business, our readers and our planet. This book is made from Forest Stewardship Council® certified paper.

CONTENTS

CONTENTS

Hope there is, but limits are quickly reached.

—*Salvage*

EDITOR'S NOTE

The Big Book of Cyberpunk is a historical snapshot as much as a literary one, containing stories that span almost seventy-five years.

Cyberpunk, at its inception, was ahead of many other forms of literature in how it embraced (and continues to embrace) progressive themes. Cyberpunk, at its best, has strived for an inclusive vision of the present and future of society. Accordingly, the stories within *The Big Book of Cyberpunk* discuss all aspects of identity and existence. This includes, but is not limited to, gender, sexuality, race, class, and culture.

Even while attempting to be progressive, however, these stories also use language, tropes, and stereotypes common to the times and the places in which they were originally written. Even as some of the authors challenged the problems of their time, their work still includes problematic elements. To pretend otherwise would be hypocritical; it is the essence of cyberpunk to understand that one can simultaneously challenge and deserve to be challenged.

Cyberpunk is also literature that exists in opposition, and the way it expresses its rebellion is very often shocking, provocative, and offensive. It is transgressive by design, but not without purpose, and I tried to make my selections with that principle in mind.

—Jared Shurin

INTRODUCTION TO VOLUME 2

THERE'S A POPULAR MEME that essentially goes along these lines:

WE WERE PROMISED BLADE RUNNER *AND WE GOT X INSTEAD.*

X is then something that represents a disappointing status quo. The digital animation in the latest superhero movie, AI-generated images of children with three arms, vegan pepperoni, whatever *cause célèbre* is rampaging across social media at any given movement. X represents the distinctively banal: something that taps our collective unconsciousness on the shoulder and whispers 'this is a bit shit, innit?'. There are, undeniably, promises unmet. We don't have flying cars or jet packs, holiday homes on Mars or meals in pill form.

Taken from the cyberpunk perspective (as is the remit of this book), the only response is 'yes, obviously'. The genre exists to interrogate our relationship with technology and, more often than not, the result of that interrogation is an exasperated sigh. From its inception, cyberpunk has been whacking at the piñata of science fantasy with the bat of critical realism. It is easy to get lost in the hype and the dream; cyberpunk spikes optimism with realism.

If that sounds unduly harsh: cyberpunk doesn't exist to quash dreams, or even undermine them, but it does ruthlessly tear into unexamined premises. Whether it is the glorious promise of post-singularity equality, shiny techno-utopian virtual realities, or even the naive notion of meritocratic corporate rule, cyberpunk is there, to prod and poke at the underlying assumptions. It is a snarky guardian angel of a genre, protecting us from our own worst impulses.

WE WERE PROMISED BLADE RUNNER *AND WE GOT . . .*

The previous volume of *The Big Book of Cyberpunk* began with William Gibson's "The Gernsback Continuum" (1981). This story represents a self-aware bridging of fantasy and modernity; a moment of adolescence in science-fiction literature. The story, which also introduced the anthology *Mirrorshades* (1986), serves as the opening salvo for cyberpunk—both as a genre and a movement. It is also, for all practical purposes, this exact idea: *We were promised enormous flying wings and we got collapsing gas stations instead.*

What the story adds, as only a story can, is the emotional context of wistfulness; a nostalgia for that which never was. Whereas the meme expresses a more pronounced disappointment, "Gernsback"—setting the tone for cyberpunk as a whole—understands that these imagined futures were never possible in the first place. We are allowed (encouraged, even) to be disappointed about how things turned out, but we also bear responsibility for not tempering our expectations in the first place. Cyberpunk stories do not exist to quash our spirit, but to channel it. They encourage us to have less faith in sweeping, techno-utopian solutions, and more in ourselves. They encourage us to be skeptical of sweeping promises, while reinforcing the value of empathy and our shared humanity.

WE WERE PROMISED BLADE RUNNER . . .

Of course, the irony of this particular construction is that the world of *Blade Runner* is genuinely awful.

Ridley Scott's 1982 film is an adaptation of Philip K. Dick's *Do Androids Dream of Electric Sheep?* (1968).* In both the film and the source material, the future is bleak. Dick's novel describes a post-nuclear setting in which virtually all non-human organic life has been rendered critically endangered. Out of a combination of guilt and whimsy, owning animals is now a fashionable trend. There's a distinct class system that emerges between those who can afford the luxury of a real animal versus those who make do with a robotic equivalent. The novel also centers around the robotic equivalents of human beings, androids, who have been manufactured as slaves.

The future in *Do Androids Dream* is undeniably miserable. The underlying theme throughout the book is that humanity has become drained of empathy. The mass extinction of animals may be either a cause or a symptom, but the result is the same: humans now struggle to find any way to connect with, or even feel for, one another. This is further shown by humanity's ability (or lack thereof) to feel even for the androids created in our own image. The world is miserable in less abstract ways as well. There's a cultist religion that fetishizes misery, an oppressive class system, and a world that is still in the throes of an atomic holocaust.

Blade Runner is no cheerier. It focuses heavily on the story's protagonist.

* Dick's broader contributions to the genre are discussed later in this volume, alongside his story "We Can Remember It For You Wholesale" (1966).

Decker is the titular 'blade runner': part private eye, part assassin.* Blade runners are bounty hunters, tasked with forcibly retiring those androids (or 'replicants') that manage to escape their lives of forced servitude.† Although an undeniably slow-moving film, it is punctuated with moments of incredible tension and painful loss.

Ridley Scott's film is beautiful. Its rain-and-neon aesthetic successfully captivated the imagination in a Gernsbackian way: the look and feel of a future that never happened. But when it comes to the actual, lived experience of human beings (or near-human beings), the future is still, again, miserable. *Blade Runner*'s projections of a stark, corporate-controlled future with clear distinctions drawn between the elite minority and the rough and dirty world beneath their feet. Decker is an example of a noir-worthy working stiff, who earns his paycheck 'retiring' replicants, with whom, we suspect, he has more in common than his paymasters. Our hero, such as he is, has an unpleasant role in an unpleasant world.

The meme's promise/reality construction is catchy, but the world of *Blade Runner* is sorely lacking.

WE WERE PROMISED . . .

Why then is *Blade Runner*, and cyberpunk more generally, used as a positive benchmark for our expectations? Why do we feel betrayed that this future, despite being patently impossible and pragmatically undesirable, has not come about? We want it, knowing that, for all practical purposes, we really, really shouldn't. The lingering popularity of cyberpunk in its many guises, both thematic and aesthetic, proves that there is something in these worlds that resonates with audiences.

Functionally, cyberpunk plays an important role in helping us understand our relationship with technology and its impact on ourselves, our society, and the world(s) in which we live. From its inception—and indeed, before it coalesced into a named genre—cyberpunk has served as a mode of theoretical investigation of new technologies and their potential impact on people: how we

---

* As noted, the film is known for its contributions to the 'look' of cyberpunk. Similarly, the influence of its soundtrack, by Vangelis, is well noted. The film's inventive use of language is just as important to the cyberpunk aesthetic as those other elements. Terms like 'blade runner' and 'replicant' never appear in the original novel. These chilly, futuristic, and functional phrases, alongside euphemisms such as 'retiring' replicants, set the tone for how cyberpunk connects technology and humanity, and establishes a linguistic 'brand' for the genre that continues to this day.

† At the time of writing this, London's suburbs are currently plagued by a handful of loosely organized individuals who have taken against, of all things, the cameras that monitor London's traffic for high-polluting vehicles. Their antics have included vandalizing the cameras, cutting them down, and even blowing one up with a homemade explosive device (miraculously, no one was killed, but the counter-terrorism police took a very dim view of the proceedings). These self-appointed crusaders have named themselves 'blade runners', demonstrating a fairly fundamental misunderstanding of the movie and who, exactly, are the baddies.

create and consume culture, how we develop and express our identities, and how we relate to other human beings.

However, there's still a disconnect between cyberpunk's practical function (exploring what are, largely, disappointing futures) and its emotional appeal. Readers, viewers, gamers, listeners are all actively seeking out cyberpunk media as a form of entertainment. The ubiquity and longevity of this 'dead' genre is not solely down to its merits as a tool of critical engagement with modernity. It is emotionally resonant and, somehow, escapist.

The appeal of escaping into a cyberpunk world is, I propose, less about the world itself and more about our perceived role within it. Cyberpunk works are rarely caught up in the functional details: they're often possible (and perhaps even plausible) extrapolations of a contemporary context. The technological shift is rarely robustly supported. We do not know, nor do we need to know, how *exactly* replicants are made. They merely are, and the narrative is predicated on their existence.

This vagueness feels antithetical to escapism. Surely we need to know the precise details in order to visit these worlds in our mind? Yet the truth is the reverse. One's engagement with a fictional world is less about the precision of that world, and more about our emotional investment in it.* We respond most to worlds that invite us; worlds in which we can see ourselves; and worlds that have a clear role for us.

Cyberpunk, perhaps unintentionally, delivers against all three of those precepts. By being grounded in our contemporary reality, **cyberpunk stories are invitational**: we can see how we 'enter' them. No magical wardrobe or owl-dropped acceptance letter is required: the path to a cyberpunk world is simply there, unspooling in real time in front of our eyes. Some, like Neal Stephenson's "The Great Simoleon Caper" (1995) or Bruce Bethke's "Cyberpunk" (1983) could happen now (or, at least, contemporaneously). Others, such as Tim Maughan's "Flyover Country" (2016) or Ken Liu's "Thoughts and Prayers" (2019) are within easy touching distance. Even the wildest, most *outre* settings, like Eileen Gunn's "Computer Friendly" (1989) or K. A. Teryna's "The Tin Pilot" (2021), have recognizable *potential.* They may be frightening, or simply weird, but we can dimly see the thread connecting us from here to there. (In some stories, such as John Kessel's "The Last American" (2007), that thread is spooled out in front of us.)

Cyberpunk is also inclusive: it is easy to see oneself in there. No magic powers or cosmic forces are necessary. Nor does cyberpunk revolve around Chosen Ones or the *ubermensch*. Cyberpunk protagonists are us: somewhat flawed, occasionally heroic, and entirely messy. These stories, in fact, revolve around human *un*exceptionalism: they're tales of people, not mythic archetypes.

* Perhaps best explained by Henry Jenkins in *Convergence Culture* (2006) and the works that succeeded it. Or simply by talking to a supporter of any beleaguered property, from *Gossip Girl* to Arsenal. One is a fan not for any rational reason, but because, despite common sense and one's own best efforts, one simply can't bear *not* to be. And yes, I am very much talking about myself here.

In this volume, our protagonists range from seedy corporate schemers to irritated private investigators; grieving parents to angry rebels; burned-out hackers to ambitious 'brand ambassadors'. That's a huge variety, united only by the fact that they are all achievable (if not always aspirational). None of them are out of reach; they are all, by design, easy extensions of ourselves.

Finally, and perhaps most importantly, **cyberpunk stories give us the dream of agency**. The underpinning and all-encompassing theme of cyberpunk is humanity triumphant (for good or for ill). Technology influences human affairs, but it does not subsume them. In each and every story, we see a system changed by technology, but humans are still finding a way to explore, interrogate, challenge, and even—occasionally—shift that system. Whether that is through actively participating in revolution (such as Michael Moss's "Keep Portland Wired"), plotting a petty crime (such as Tim Maughan's "Flyover Country" or Victor Pelevin's "The Yuletide Cyberpunk Yarn, or Christmas_Eve-117.DIR"), or simply asking questions of the status quo (as in Eileen Gunn's "Computer Friendly"). Even in the darkest and rainiest of worlds, we still see characters pushing towards glimmers of light—even, in the case *Blade Runner*'s replicants, striving to defy their inescapable, pre-programmed fate (or, in this book, the 'cultures' of Punktown, as in Jeffrey Thomas's "Immolation").

Cyberpunk being cyberpunk, with its commitment to plausible speculation, not every rebellion succeeds or scheme pays off. More often than not, characters wind up exactly where they began—or perhaps set back further. But it is the action itself that is the appeal: the ability not just to exist in a world, but to have the ability to affect it.

The dream of agency feels a very pitiful sort of escape, but it is one of the most powerful emotional drivers. At any given time we are buffeted by forces beyond our control. We are, in our global village, increasingly aware of the many crises constantly occurring—and also aware of our own, personal, inability to contribute to solving them.* The apocalypse in and of itself is not a fearsome thing, it is our inability to avert it that is terrifying. Like replicants, programmed to expire, we feel like our destiny is out of our hands.

Cyberpunk offers us worlds we can easily imagine, filled with people like us. People that, unlike us, seem to have some say, however minor, over the path of their lives. Whether they are stealing or sleuthing, running or revolting, the characters in cyberpunk worlds are acting, and their actions have meaning. Sometimes that's the escape we need.

• • •

This volume of *The Big Book of Cyberpunk* continues along the path set up by its predecessor—one based, loosely, on Marshall McLuhan's concept of the global

* According to YouGov (January 2024), when asked 'I believe people like me have the power to help influence changes that shape the future', more Britons disagreed (42%) than agreed (40%).

village.* While the previous volume focused on self and culture, this volume looks at system and challenge. It is, in a nutshell, less about the individual and more about the world in which they live.

Tim Berner-Lee wrote that "the world can be seen as only connections, nothing else."† We, ourselves, are only one small part of a complex system; one that's built on those connections between us. But what happens when those connections are facilitated through new technologies? What if they become faster, or slower; broader, or narrower; freer, or more surveilled? What are the worlds that are built as a result? What does society become, how does governance work, and who can we count on as friends, or family? These are not abstract questions, but ones that we already wrestle with every day. The stories within are simply ahead of the curve in seeking answers.

The stories in this volume also examine how, and why, we challenge these established systems.

Cyberpunk reminds us that we need not take the future for granted. For better or for worse, we *do* have agency, and our fate is not sealed. Nothing is settled, nothing is certain, and there's always the capacity for change. These are stories about revolution and rebellion, which are not always justified, as well as crime and transgression, not always without merit. The forms of challenge in these stories range from petty crime to open warfare; choosing who to love, or even how to die. Many of the characters within are facing difficult choices: a dawning awareness that they live in an imperfect system, but that upending it could lead to something even worse.

These stories showcase not that our human agency exists, but also that it is meaningful, precious and, occasionally, very, very dangerous indeed.

---

* *The Gutenberg Galaxy: The Making of Typographic Man.* Toronto: University of Toronto Press (1962).

† *Weaving the Web: The Original Design and Ultimate Destiny of the World Wide Web.* New York: Harper (1999)

SYSTEM

A system is a combination of interacting or interdependent elements, creating a whole that is both separate from, and more than, the sum of its parts. It is a set of things 'interconnected in such a way that they produce their own pattern of behaviour over time'.* Society, as a whole, is a system (sometimes even a functioning one), but so are most interpersonal relationships, from romances to cults. Families, found or blood; corporations, cities and countries; gangs, bands, and online forums: these are all social systems. Systems are the broadest, most inclusive level of human affairs.

Technology influences all aspects of these systems: the individual elements, the connections between those elements, and the resulting outputs of the system itself. Technology changes how and where we work, how we travel, how we support our friends or fight with our enemies. Technology can make communities more interconnected or exacerbate the divisions between them. It encourages participation and spreads disinformation, it enables us to find love (and hedgehogs)† or share revenge porn, it launches our careers or docks our wages when we pee in bottles. Technology amplifies the whims and passions of these systems. It helps humans as a collective, empowering us to make dreams—or nightmares—come true.

---

* Donella H. Meadows. *Thinking in Systems*. Vermont: Chelsea Green Publishing (2008).

† Shout-out to the Big Hedgehog Map (bighedgehogmap.org).

Marshall McLuhan notes that technology serves as an "extension of man," but tech does more than merely amplify our innate capacity for good or evil. What are the repercussions to outsourcing these relationships—to putting our systems in the phantom hands of algorithms? What happens if, or when, we entrust the heartless and the mechanical with authority over human dynamics? What does it mean for us as we increasingly rely on technology not only to facilitate our relationships, but also to create, manage, or even end them?

As systems are wide-ranging, so are the stories within this section. However, in each one of these stories, a system is established, investigated, and—in most cases—found wanting. Moreover, some aspect of that connection with others has been augmented by technology. What becomes swiftly apparent is that, even with the most seamless or desirable technological option, there remains friction. However oppressive the regime—or efficient the solution—a technocratic system that operates perfectly is impossible. The spark of creative chaos that makes us human is somehow anathematic to a smoothly functioning system. Technology creates and enforces a systems' rules; humanity finds new ways to break them.

• • •

The initial story in this section is Samuel R. Delany's "Time Considered as a Helix of Semiprecious Stones" (1968). Its atmospheric and decadent interplanetary setting is a far cry from the grubby, Earth-bound stories of cyberpunk worlds that follow. Delany's story, however, sets up a recurring theme: that of the outsider perspective. Literature is obsessed with the outsider, and science fiction—and cyberpunk—is no exception. HCE, Delany's wry criminal protagonist, gives us a (supposedly) dispassionate view as he climbs the ranks of society, showing us the rational flaws and emotional malaise that bubble under this seemingly charming society. Behind the pleasant veneer, there's a culture of self-destruction and discontent.

The outsider perspective is also on display in Bruce Bethke's "Cyberpunk" (1983). Bethke writes a techno-thriller twist on the "juvenile delinquency" genre. Under the surface, Bethke's story is less about an angsty generational divide than society's wildly accelerated pace of change. The "punk" of the title is an embodiment of havoc and unease, bringing to life new dangers and unexpected threats. As well as defining the genre's name, Bethke establishes the archetype of the hacker: someone that seeks thrills, power, and agency by exploiting holes in the system.

The titular character in James Patrick Kelly's "Rat" (1986) is, like HCE or Bethke's hacker, openly criminal. "Rat was not a fighter, he was a runner." There's very little moral *or* malicious intent to his actions. Rat's a creature of instinct, simply trying to live. He's a metaphor for the future of man in an overtly cyberpunk system: a scavenger and a survivor, doing what it takes to survive. However, unlike the two previous protagonists, Rat is not outside the system, but *of* it. He is a natural product of a system that encourages amorality. He fits, not breaks, the pattern.

In "Axiomatic" (1990), Greg Egan explores a radical reinterpretation of the social contract. Beliefs can be directly created—or deleted—by the use of implants. A faith, a habit, or even the fundamental respect for human life: now embeddable and editable. It feels inherently sinister, but, as the protagonist philosophizes, "using an implant wouldn't rob me of my free will; on the contrary, it was going to help me to assert it." Egan posits a social system where, thanks to technology, the social contract itself is now a variable, and not something that is fundamental and sacrosanct. What does a society look like when it is predicated on the total flexibility of belief?

"Ripped Images, Rusted Dreams" (1993) is a true classic of the cyberpunk genre, making its first appearance in English in this volume. Written and translated by Gerardo Horacio Porcayo, the story is an atmospheric vignette into the life of a burned-out hacker. Despite our protagonist's pioneering efforts, he's now sitting on the sidelines, seemingly desperate for the respect of the younger, more vicious and more extreme players. The tantalizing world of the story—with its references to a predatory digital deity and roving packs of android hunters—only makes the character's internal pathos all the more powerful. This is a man that has seen (and possibly even contributed to) systemic change, and is struggling to find his place in a new world.

Our hero in "The Great Simoleon Caper" (1995) is no rebel. He's a mathematician (as many of Neal Stephenson's protagonists are) tasked with a giveaway of a new digital currency.* The titular "caper" occurs when he discovers that this harmless advertising gimmick is suddenly of interest to both the government and "crypto-anarchists." Stephenson coined the now famous phrase "Metaverse" in 1992, as part of his playful—and insightful—science-fiction novel *Snow Crash*. The novel is certainly cyberpunk adjacent, but it also functions as a breathless and wide-eyed tour of the fascinating possibilities of a technologically enriched future. In "Simoleon," Stephenson outlines a more grounded vision of an online world, one filled with grubbiness, fraud, intrusive advertising, and incoherent ideological shouting matches. Although very funny, it is also uncomfortably prescient.

Maurice Broaddus's "I Can Transform You" (2013) is, above all, massively good fun. Broaddus's novella contains all the most enjoyable tropes of the cyberpunk genre: the burned-out investigator, the sinister corporate overlords, big guns, and dark schemes. It shows a world in which technology has (quite

* The notion of "digital cash" was posited in 1983 by inventor David Lee Chaum, a cryptography pioneer whose technical work formed the inspiration for the "cypherpunk" movement. He put his notions into practice in 1990 with DigiCash, which sent its first payment in 1994 (the year after Stephenson's "Simoleon"). Since then, digital currency has taken a variety of forms, ranging from "electronic gold" to "primates wearing funny hats."

literally) been used to patch over the world's fundamental problems, creating a broken society held together solely by greed and profit. Sometimes big problems need explosive solutions. Not all systems can be salvaged.

• • •

There's no shortage of heists, shady PIs, hackers, and net-running fools in cyberpunk. Their outsider perspective on systems is invaluable. But cyberpunk doesn't forget those who sit within the system as well. Rebels and revolutionaries make for great literary protagonists, but can feel (tragically) irrelevant to most readers' lives. Cyberpunk considers all of society, not just the outsider.

What is it like to live, and perhaps even thrive, within a technologically enhanced system? Lisa Mason's "Arachne" (1987) features a mediator, a young legal advocate at a massive corporate firm. When her telelink fails for unknown reasons, Carly can't continue her work. She's desperate to avoid unemployment, reprogramming, and a return to the bottom. Her goal is simple and, throughout the story, Carly shows she has few limits on what she'll do to keep her place on the ladder.

Paul J. McAuley's "Gene Wars" (1991) begins in a world much like our own and ends up someplace very, very different. Despite the epic scope of the story, "Gene Wars" is ultimately about a very simple concept: control. Through the lens of one man's life, we see what happens when a technology becomes the plaything of children and corporations alike, freely used without any thought or oversight. This is a story of a system that is strained and broken, eventually finding a new, unexpected equilibrium.

In "Immolation" (2000), Magnesium Jones is a culture: a vat-grown human with few rights. He's one of the many strange and wondrous inhabitants of Punktown, a world brought to life through decades of Jeffrey Thomas's work. Magnesium works as a drudge, living a thankless, grinding existence with little joy and no prospects. When he sees the chance for a better life, it is difficult to blame him for grabbing at it.

Our hustling heroine in Nick Mamatas's "Time of Day" (2002) is taking a vacation: "a whole day spent on only one job instead of my usual eleven jobs." Mamatas's story contrasts two very different worlds: a hyperactive urban hustle that requires a steady flow of drugs and information simply to keep up, and the medieval, self-flagellating conservatism of a monastery. Although neither society is appealing, Mamatas manages to convey why people are drawn to, and remain within, these extreme situations.

By contrast, the world of Lauren Beukes's "Branded" (2003) strikes a little too close to home. Published before the launch of Facebook, YouTube, or Twitter, Beukes's story reflects the desire of corporate advertisers to invade friend groups and social circles. The notion of living one's best life ("brought to you by . . .") not only exposes the low price we set on ourselves but predicts the rise of influencer culture.

In Madeline Ashby's "Be Seeing You" (2015), Hwa is a bodyguard for the

Lynch family. They own the town, which means that Hwa's job comes with (rather intrusive) oversight. Her boss knows her medical history, her usual breakfast order, and every single thing she sees. She watches the family. The company watches her. That's simply the way of things.

The hero of Steven S. Long's "Keeping Up with Mr. Johnson" (2016) is also a company employee. "Mr. Johnson" is Shadowrun slang for the corporate boss—the men or women who hire out "shadowrunners" to carry out the shadier side of the business. The heist-centered story has all the twists the reader might expect, with the largest being the protagonist's surprising humanity.

Ken Liu's "Thoughts and Prayers" (2019) describes an ordinary family dealing with extraordinary pain. A grieving mother tries to keep the memory of her child online with a virtual tribute. Told from many points of view, Liu's heartbreaking story underlines the core theme that there is no technological solution for human nature. It is particularly tragic in that, when the technology (which is proven ultimately meaningless) is stripped away, the flawed and broken system that Liu describes is simply the world in which we live now.

In "Somatosensory Cortex Dog Mess You Up Big Time, You Sick Sack of S**T" (2021), Minister Faust uses technology as a karmic force in a truly satisfying satire. A greedy and amoral billionaire gets his comeuppance in a surprising but delightful way. Is it ethical? Probably not. Is it wildly entertaining? Absolutely.

• • •

Cyberpunk is also often connected with a sense of place. Settings like the Sprawl, Night City, and Neo-Tokyo are rightfully iconic. On a less grand level, there's a clear pattern of cyberpunk stories taking place in bars and squats: transient, nameless locations. At the other end of the spectrum, even "wealth" in a cyberpunk world invariably leads to cookie-cutter homes and cubicle jobs. Spaces are anonymized, either through social erosion or mass production.

"Rural" cyberpunk does exist but is much more rare.* If the two essential components of cyberpunk are "human affairs" and "technology," both occur in greater density in urban settings. Cities are also associated with a greater pace of change and are home to greater disparity in wealth and opportunity: all material for cyberpunk.† Although village life comes with its own unique set of challenges, cities are ultimately more complex systems, giving authors more to play with and explore.

In Craig Padawer's "Hostile Takeover" (1985), the action all takes place in one specific part of the city. From start to finish, it is a gonzo litany of warfare,

* Jonathan Lethem's "How We Got In Town and Out Again" (1996) and Carmen Maria Machado's "The Hungry Earth" (2013) are two excellent examples.

† The suburbs have always been an excellent setting for tales of capitalist indecency and social ennui, making them fertile ground for cyberpunk. Please see the stories by Erica Satifka and Phillip Mann for two examples.

with hired killers in "titanium zoot suits" blasting their way through inflatable bodyguards to take control of the sex trade. It is pointed (and poignant) commentary precisely because it is so over-the-top, proving that no matter how dehumanized someone can be, they are still worthy of both empathy and respect.

Another bizarre city features in James Lovegrove's "Britworld™" (1992). Capitalism has become the new imperialism, and Britain is now a massive theme park. In Britworld™, USACorp Entertainments ensures that everything is historically accurate for the most fulfilling visitor experience, even down to the regulation four-and-a-half hours of rain per day.*

Yun Ko-eun's "P" (2011) makes its first appearance in English in this book, translated by Sean Lin Halbert. Chang quietly works at his job at the tire factory in the company town of P. He keeps his head down and has the requisite one (1) family photo on his desk. Chang even agrees to a "voluntary" endoscopy. There's a speculative (or perhaps hallucinatory) element that's central to the story, but the true influence of technology is "the interconnectedness of P." His environment is a closed system; one that operates through a powerful combination of custom and surveillance. Chang feels the pressure to conform in everything he does, but he doesn't find this disagreeable. In fact, his utmost desire is to keep his head down and simply do his work. But his desire to be the ideal employee is gradually offset by the dawning awareness that the company has a presence in all aspects of his life. As the powers that run the system tinker with it, Chang discovers exactly how expendable he is.

Tim Maughan's "Flyover Country" (2016) is set in an American anytown, a nowhere that could be anywhere. Structurally, it is a low-stakes heist, but the emphasis is on the grinding and oppressive nature of the entire environment. Even the petty crime is an attempt at finding agency. Although ultimately successful, the reality remains. These tiny rebellions won't change the system.

In the Pennsylvania town of E. Lily Yu's "Darkout" (2016), "there was hardly forty square feet that was not continuously exposed to public view." It is a world without privacy, where everyone can see and be seen. Yet, despite living in a panopticon, our grimy lives continue unchecked: gambling, adultery, racism, and domestic violence. "Darkout" ends with the ironic illusion of hope, a promise of returning to the world that we already have.

Ryuko Azuma's "2045 Dystopia" (2018) gives us four short and harrowing glimpses into a near-future cyberpunk landscape, a world both wondrous and darkly fascinating. Translated by Marissa Skeels, these comics first appeared on Twitter and have not been previously collected. These vignettes show technology attempting to suppress our humanity, but only giving rise to darker impulses.

Arthur Liu's "The Life Cycle of a Cyber Bar" (2021), translated by Nathan Faries, is a story of place, told from the place's own perspective. We catch glimpses of stories, one after the other, but only within the door of the bar. The vast breadth and width of human affairs, as seen through a single, tightly focused

* This is satire. We all know the average is closer to six.

aperture. Despite the nonhuman protagonist, it continues the theme of an all-consuming relationship between person and place.

• • •

McLuhan muses that "no society has ever known enough about its actions to have developed immunity to its new . . . technologies." Introducing something new into a system will have repercussions: not all societies are—or should be—resilient, and not all feedback is positive. But these cyberpunk stories serve as a chance to test new technologies in the (relatively) safe sandbox of the imagination.

All the stories within this section allow for the influence of technology and highlight it as a vital part of any system, with the power to reinforce or disrupt its elements, the connections between them, or the pattern as a whole. However, the stories also showcase the persistence of humanity—the human beings that are often overlooked or taken for granted. Whether it comes from our enviable adaptability, our relentless survival instinct, our unshakable flaws or our irrepressible compulsions, humans still remain the most dominant element in any system, with a latent ability to sow chaos and cause change.

SAMUEL R. DELANY

TIME CONSIDERED AS A HELIX OF SEMIPRECIOUS STONES

(1968)

LAY ORDINATE AND ABSCISSA on the century. Now cut me a quadrant. Third quadrant if you please. I was born in fifty. Here it's seventy-five.

At sixteen they let me leave the orphanage. Dragging the name they'd hung me with (Harold Clancy Everet, and me a mere lad—how many monikers have I had since; but don't worry, you'll recognize my smoke) over the hills of East Vermont, I came to a decision:

Me and Pa Michaels, who had belligerently given me a job at the request of *The Official* looking *Document* with which the orphanage sends you packing, were running Pa Michaels's dairy farm, i.e., thirteen thousand three hundred sixty-two piebald Guernseys all asleep in their stainless coffins, nourished and drugged by pink liquid flowing in clear plastic veins (stuff is sticky and messes up your hands), exercised with electric pulsers that make their muscles quiver, them not half-awake, and the milk just a-pouring down into stainless cisterns. Anyway. The Decision (as I stood there in the fields one afternoon like the Man with the Hoe, exhausted with three hard hours of physical labor, contemplating the machinery of the universe through the fog of fatigue): With all of Earth, and Mars, and the Outer Satellites filled up with people and what all, there had to be something more than this. I decided to get some.

So I stole a couple of Pa's credit cards, one of his helicopters, and a bottle of white lightning the geezer made himself, and took off. Ever try to land a stolen helicopter on the roof of the Pan Am building, drunk? Jail, schmail, and some hard knocks later I had attained to wisdom. But remember this, o best beloved: I have done three honest hours on a dairy farm less than ten years back. And nobody but nobody has ever called me Harold Clancy Everet again.

• • •

Hank Culafroy Eckles (redheaded, a bit vague, six-foot-two) strolled out of the baggage room at the spaceport, carrying a lot of things that weren't his in a small briefcase.

Beside him the Business Man was saying, "You young fellows today upset me. Go back to Bellona, I say. Just because you got into trouble with that little blonde you were telling me about is no reason to leap worlds, come on all glum. Even quit your job!"

Hank stops and grins weakly: "Well . . ."

"Now I admit, you have your real needs, which maybe we older folks don't understand, but you have to show some responsibility toward . . ." He notices Hank has stopped in front of a door marked MEN. "Oh. Well. Eh." He grins strongly. "I've enjoyed meeting you, Hank. It's always nice when you meet somebody worth talking to on these damned crossings. So long."

Out the same door, ten minutes later, comes Harmony C. Eventide, six-foot even (one of the false heels was cracked, so I stuck both of them under a lot of paper towels), brown hair (not even my hairdresser knows for sure), oh so dapper and of his time, attired in the bad taste that is oh so tasteful, a sort of man with whom no Business Men would start a conversation. Took the regulation copter from the port over to the Pan Am building (Yeah. Really. Drunk.), came out of Grand Central Station, and strode along Forty-Second toward Eighth Avenue, with a lot of things that weren't mine in a small briefcase.

The evening is carved from light.

Crossed the plastiplex pavements of the Great White Way—I think it makes people look weird, all that white light under their chins—and skirted the crowds coming up in elevators from the subway, the sub-subway, and the sub-sub-sub (eighteen and first week out of jail, I hung around here, snatching stuff from people—but daintily, daintily, so they never knew they'd been snatched), bulled my way through a crowd of giggling, goo-chewing schoolgirls with flashing lights in their hair, all very embarrassed at wearing transparent plastic blouses which had just been made legal again (I hear the breast has been scene [as opposed to obscene] on and off since the seventeenth century) so I stared appreciatively; they giggled some more. I thought, *Christ, when I was that age, I was on a goddamn dairy farm,* and took the thought no further.

The ribbon of news lights looping the triangular structure of Communication, Inc., explained in Basic English how Senator Regina Abolafia was preparing to begin her investigation of Organized Crime in the City. Days I'm so happy I'm disorganized I couldn't begin to tell.

Near Ninth Avenue I took my briefcase into a long, crowded bar. I hadn't been in New York for two years, but on my last trip through ofttimes a man used to hang out here who had real talent for getting rid of things that weren't mine profitably, safely, fast. No idea what the chances were I'd find him. I pushed among a lot of guys drinking beer. Here and there were a number of well-escorted old bags wearing last month's latest. Scarves of smoke gentled through the noise. I don't like such places. Those there younger than me were all morphadine heads or feebleminded. Those older only wished more younger ones would come. I pried my way to the bar and tried to get the attention of one of the little men in white coats.

The lack of noise behind me made me glance back.

She wore a sheath of veiling closed at the neck and wrists with huge brass pins (oh so tastefully on the border of taste); her left arm was bare, her right covered with chiffon-like wine. She had it down a lot better than I did. But such an ostentatious demonstration of one's understanding of the finer points was absolutely out of place in a place like this. People were making a great show of not noticing.

She pointed to her wrist, blood-colored nail indexing a yellow-orange fragment in the brass claw of her wristlet. "Do you know what this is, Mr. Eldrich?" she asked; at the same time the veil across her face cleared, and her eyes were ice; her brows, black.

Three thoughts: (One) She is a lady of fashion, because coming in from Bellona I'd read the Delta coverage of the "fading fabrics" whose hue and opacity were controlled by cunning jewels at the wrist. (Two) During my last trip through, when I was younger and Harry Calamine Eldrich, I didn't do anything *too* illegal (though one loses track of these things); still I didn't believe I could be dragged off to the calaboose for anything more than thirty days under that name. (Three) The stone she pointed to . . .

". . . Jasper?" I asked.

She waited for me to say more; I waited for her to give me reason to let on I knew what she was waiting for. (When I was in jail, Henry James was my favorite author. He really was.)

"Jasper," she confirmed.

"—Jasper . . ." I reopened the ambiguity she had tried so hard to dispel.

". . . Jasper—" But she was already faltering, suspecting I suspected her certainty to be ill-founded.

"Okay, Jasper." But from her face I knew she had seen in my face a look that had finally revealed I knew she knew I knew.

"Just whom have you got me confused with, ma'am?"

Jasper, this month, is the Word.

Jasper is the pass/code/warning that the Singers of the Cities (who last month sang "Opal" from their divine injuries; and on Mars I'd heard the Word and used it thrice, along with devious imitations, to fix possession of what was not rightfully my own; and even there I pondered Singers and their wounds) relay by word of mouth for that loose and roguish fraternity with which I have been involved (in various guises) these nine years. It goes out new every thirty days; and within hours every brother knows it, throughout six worlds and worldlets. Usually it's grunted at you by some blood-soaked bastard staggering into your arms from a dark doorway; hissed at you as you pass a shadowed alley; scrawled on a paper scrap pressed into your palm by some nasty-grimy moving too fast through the crowd. And this month, it was: Jasper.

Here are some alternate translations:

Help!

or

I need help!

or

I can help you!

or

You are being watched!

or

They're not watching now, so move!

Final point of syntax: If the Word is used properly, you should never have to think twice about what it means in a given situation. Fine point of usage: Never trust anyone who uses it improperly.

I waited for her to finish waiting.

She opened a wallet in front of me. "Chief of Special Services Department Maudline Hinkle," she read without looking at what it said below the silver badge.

"You have that very well," I said, "Maud." Then I frowned. "Hinkle?"

"Me."

"I know you're not going to believe this, Maud. You look like a woman who has no patience with her mistakes. But my name is Eventide. Not Eldrich. Harmony C. Eventide. And isn't it lucky for all and sundry that the Word changes tonight?" Passed the way it is, the Word is no big secret to the cops. But I've met policemen up to a week after change date who were not privy.

"Well, then: Harmony. I want to talk to you."

I raised an eyebrow.

She raised one back and said, "Look, if you want to be called Henrietta, it's all right by me. But you listen."

"What do you want to talk about?"

"Crime, Mr. . . . ?"

"Eventide. I'm going to call you Maud, so you might as well call me Harmony. It really is my name."

Maud smiled. She wasn't a young woman. I think she even had a few years on Business Man. But she used makeup better than he did. "I probably know more about crime than you do," she said. "In fact I wouldn't be surprised if you hadn't even heard of my branch of the police department. What does Special Services mean to you?"

"That's right, I've never heard of it."

"You've been more or less avoiding the Regular Service with alacrity for the past seven years."

"Oh, Maud, really—"

"Special Services is reserved for people whose nuisance value has suddenly taken a sharp rise . . . a sharp enough rise to make our little lights start blinking."

"Surely I haven't done anything so dreadful that—"

"We don't look at what you do. A computer does that for us. We simply keep checking the first derivative of the graphed-out curve that bears your number. Your slope is rising sharply."

"Not even the dignity of a name—"

"We're the most efficient department in the Police Organization. Take it as bragging if you wish. Or just a piece of information."

"Well, well, well," I said. "Have a drink?" The little man in the white coat left us two, looked puzzled at Maud's finery, then went to do something else.

"Thanks." She downed half her glass like someone stauncher than that wrist would indicate. "It doesn't pay to go after most criminals. Take your big-time racketeers, Farnesworth, the Hawk, Blavatskia. Take your little snatch-purses, small-time pushers, housebreakers, or vice-impresarios. Both at the top and the bottom of the scale, their incomes are pretty stable. They don't really upset the social boat. Regular Services handles them both. They think they do a good job. We're not going to argue. But say a little pusher starts to become a big-time pusher; a medium-sized vice-impresario sets his sights on becoming a full-fledged racketeer; that's when you get problems with socially unpleasant repercussions. That's when Special Services arrive. We have a couple of techniques that work remarkably well."

"You're going to tell me about them, aren't you?"

"They work better that way," she said. "One of them is hologramic information storage. Do you know what happens when you cut a hologram plate in half?"

"The three-dimensional image is . . . cut in half?"

She shook her head. "You get the whole image, only fuzzier, slightly out of focus."

"Now I didn't know that."

"And if you cut it in half again, it just gets fuzzier still. But even if you have a square centimeter of the original hologram, you still have the whole image—unrecognizable but complete."

I mumbled some appreciative m's.

"Each pinpoint of photographic emulsion on a hologram plate, unlike a photograph, gives information about the entire scene being hologrammed. By analogy, hologramic information storage simply means that each bit of information we have—about you, let us say—relates to your entire career, your overall situation, the complete set of tensions between you and your environment. Specific facts about specific misdemeanors or felonies we leave to Regular Services. As soon as we have enough of our kind of data, our method is vastly more efficient for keeping track—even predicting—where you are or what you may be up to."

"Fascinating," I said. "One of the most amazing paranoid syndromes I've ever run up against. I mean just starting a conversation with someone in a bar. Often, in a hospital situation, I've encountered stranger—"

"In your past," she said matter-of-factly, "I see cows and helicopters. In your not too distant future, there are helicopters and hawks."

"And tell me, oh Good Witch of the West, just how—" Then I got all upset inside. Because nobody is supposed to know about that stint with Pa Michaels save thee and me. Even the Regular Service, who pulled me, out of my head, from that whirlybird bouncing toward the edge of the Pan Am, never got that one from me. I'd eaten the credit cards when I saw them waiting, and the serial numbers had been filed off everything that could have had a serial number on it by someone more competent than I: good Mister Michaels had boasted to me, my first lonely, drunken night at the farm, how he'd gotten the thing in hot from New Hampshire.

"But why—" it appalls me the clichés to which anxiety will drive us "—are you telling me all this?"

She smiled, and her smile faded behind her veil. "Information is only meaningful when shared," said a voice that was hers from the place of her face.

"Hey, look, I—"

"You may be coming into quite a bit of money soon. If I can calculate right, I will have a helicopter full of the city's finest arriving to take you away as you accept it into your hot little hands. That is a piece of information . . ." She stepped back. Someone stepped between us.

"Hey, Maud—"

"You can do whatever you want with it."

The bar was crowded enough so that to move quickly was to make enemies. I don't know—I lost her and made enemies. Some weird characters there: with greasy hair that hung in spikes, and three of them had dragons tattooed on their scrawny shoulders, still another with an eye patch, and yet another raked nails black with pitch at my cheek (we're two minutes into a vicious free-for-all, case you missed the transition. I did) and some of the women were screaming. I hit and ducked, and then the tenor of the brouhaha changed. Somebody sang "Jasper!" the way she is supposed to be sung. And it meant the heat (the ordinary, bungling Regular Service I had been eluding these seven years) were on their way. The brawl spilled into the street. I got between two nasty-grimies who were doing things appropriate with one another, but made the edge of the crowd with no more wounds than could be racked up to shaving. The fight had broken into sections. I left one and ran into another that, I realized a moment later, was merely a ring of people standing around somebody who had apparently gotten really messed.

Someone was holding people back.

Somebody else was turning him over.

Curled up in a puddle of blood was the little guy I hadn't seen in two years who used to be so good at getting rid of things not mine.

Trying not to hit people with my briefcase, I clucked between the hub and the bub. When I saw my first ordinary policeman, I tried very hard to look like somebody who had just stepped up to see what the rumpus was.

It worked.

I turned down Ninth Avenue and got three steps into an inconspicuous but rapid lope—

"Hey, wait! Wait up there . . ."

I recognized the voice (after two years, coming at me just like that, I recognized it) but kept going.

"Wait. It's me, Hawk!"

And I stopped.

You haven't heard his name before in this story; Maud mentioned the Hawk, who is a multimillionaire racketeer basing his operations on a part of Mars I've never been to (though he has his claws sunk to the spurs in illegalities throughout the system) and somebody else entirely.

I took three steps back toward the doorway.

A boy's laugh there: "Oh, man. You look like you just did something you shouldn't."

"Hawk?" I asked the shadow.

He was still the age when two years' absence means an inch or so taller.

"You're still hanging around here?" I asked.

"Sometimes."

He was an amazing kid.

"Look, Hawk, I got to get out of here." I glanced back at the rumpus.

"Get." He stepped down. "Can I come, too?"

Funny. "Yeah." It makes me feel very funny, him asking that. "Come on."

• • •

By the streetlamp half a block down, I saw his hair was still pale as split pine. He could have been a nasty-grimy: very dirty black denim jacket, no shirt beneath; very ripe pair of black jeans—I mean in the dark you could tell. He went barefoot; and the only way you can tell on a dark street someone's been going barefoot for days in New York is to know already. As we reached the corner, he grinned up at me under the streetlamp and shrugged his jacket together over the welts and furrows marring his chest and belly. His eyes were very green. Do you recognize him? If by some failure of information dispersal throughout the worlds and worldlets you haven't, walking beside me beside the Hudson was Hawk the Singer.

"Hey, how long have you been back?"

"A few hours," I told him.

"What'd you bring?"

"Really want to know?"

He shoved his hands into his pockets and cocked his head. "Sure."

I made the sound of an adult exasperated by a child. "All right." We had been walking the waterfront for a block now; there was nobody about. "Sit down." So he straddled the beam along the siding, one filthy foot dangling above the flashing black Hudson. I sat in front of him and ran my thumb around the edge of the briefcase.

Hawk hunched his shoulders and leaned. "Hey . . ." He flashed green questioning at me. "Can I touch?"

I shrugged. "Go ahead."

He grubbed among them with fingers that were all knuckle and bitten nail. He picked two up, put them down, picked up three others. "Hey!" he whispered. "How much are all these worth?"

"About ten times more than I hope to get. I have to get rid of them fast."

He glanced down past his toes. "You could always throw them in the river."

"Don't be dense. I was looking for a guy who used to hang around that bar. He was pretty efficient." And half the Hudson away a water-bound foil skimmed above the foam. On her deck were parked a dozen helicopters—being ferried up to the Patrol Field near Verrazzano, no doubt. For moments I looked back and forth between the boy and the transport, getting all paranoid about Maud. But the boat *mmmm*ed into the darkness. "My man got a little cut up this evening."

Hawk put the tips of his fingers in his pockets and shifted his position.

"Which leaves me uptight. I didn't think he'd take them all, but at least he could have turned me on to some other people who might."

"I'm going to a party later on this evening—" he paused to gnaw on the wreck of his little fingernail "—where you might be able to sell them. Alexis Spinnel is having a party for Regina Abolafia at Tower Top."

"Tower Top . . . ?" It had been a while since I palled around with Hawk. Hell's Kitchen at ten; Tower Top at midnight—

"I'm just going because Edna Silem will be there."

Edna Silem is New York's eldest Singer.

Senator Abolafia's name had ribboned above me in lights once that evening. And somewhere among the endless magazines I'd perused coming in from Mars, I remembered Alexis Spinnel's name sharing a paragraph with an awful lot of money.

"I'd like to see Edna again," I said offhandedly. "But she wouldn't remember me." Folk like Spinnel and his social ilk have a little game, I'd discovered during the first leg of my acquaintance with Hawk. He who can get the most Singers of the City under one roof wins. There are five Singers of New York (a tie for second place with Lux on Iapetus). Tokyo leads with seven. "It's a two-Singer party?"

"More likely four . . . if I go."

The inaugural ball for the mayor gets four.

I raised the appropriate eyebrow.

"I have to pick up the Word from Edna. It changes tonight."

"All right," I said. "I don't know what you have in mind, but I'm game." I closed the case.

• • •

We walked back toward Times Square. When we got to Eighth Avenue and the first of the plastiplex, Hawk stopped. "Wait a minute," he said. Then he buttoned his jacket up to his neck. "Okay."

Strolling through the streets of New York with a Singer (two years back I'd spent much time wondering if that was wise for a man of my profession) is probably the best camouflage possible for a man of my profession. Think of the last time you glimpsed your favorite Tri-D star turning the corner of Fifty-Seventh. Now be honest. Would you really recognize the little guy in the tweed jacket half a pace behind him?

Half the people we passed in Times Square recognized him. With his youth, funereal garb, black feet, and ash-pale hair, he was easily the most colorful of Singers. Smiles; narrowed eyes; very few actually pointed or stared.

"Just exactly who is going to be there who might be able to take this stuff off my hands?"

"Well, Alexis prides himself on being something of an adventurer. They might just take his fancy. And he can give you more than you can get peddling them in the street."

"You'll tell him they're all hot?"

"It will probably make the idea that much more intriguing. He's a creep."

"You say so, friend."

We went down into the sub-sub. The man at the change booth started to take Hawk's coin, then looked up. He began three or four words that were unintelligible inside his grin, then just gestured us through.

"Oh," Hawk said, "thank you," with ingenuous surprise, as though this were the first, delightful time such a thing had happened. (Two years ago he had told me sagely, "As soon as I start looking like I expect it, it'll stop happening." I was still impressed by the way he wore his notoriety. The time I'd met Edna Silem, and I'd mentioned this, she said with the same ingenuousness, "But that's what we're chosen for.")

In the bright car we sat on the long seat. Hawk's hands were beside him; one foot rested on the other. Down from us a gaggle of bright-bloused goo-chewers giggled and pointed and tried not to be noticed at it. Hawk didn't look at all, and I tried not to be noticed looking.

Dark patterns rushed the window.

Things below the gray floor hummed.

Once a lurch.

Leaning once, we came out of the ground.

Outside, the city tried on its thousand sequins, then threw them away behind the trees of Ft. Tryon. Suddenly the windows across from us grew bright scales. Behind them girders reeled by. We got out on the platform under a light rain. The sign said TWELVE TOWERS STATION.

By the time we reached the street, however, the shower had stopped. Leaves above the wall shed water down the brick. "If I'd known I was bringing someone, I'd have had Alex send a car for us. I told him it was fifty-fifty I'd come."

"Are you sure it's all right for me to tag along then?"

"Didn't you come up here with me once before?"

"I've even been up here once before that," I said. "Do you still think it's . . ."

He gave me a withering look. Well; Spinnel would be delighted to have Hawk even if he dragged along a whole gang of real nasty-grimies—Singers are famous for that sort of thing. With one more or less presentable thief, Spinnel was getting off light. Beside us rocks broke away into the city. Behind the gate to our left the gardens rolled up toward the first of the towers. The twelve immense luxury apartment buildings menaced the lower clouds.

"Hawk the Singer," Hawk the Singer said into the speaker at the side of the gate. *Clang* and *tic-tic-tic* and *Clang*. We walked up to the path to the doors and doors of glass.

A cluster of men and women in evening dress were coming out. Three tiers of doors away they saw us. You could see them frowning at the guttersnipe who'd somehow gotten into the lobby (for a moment I thought one of them was Maud because she wore a sheath of the fading fabric, but she turned; beneath her veil her face was dark as roasted coffee); one of the men recognized him, said something to the others. When they passed us, they were smiling. Hawk paid about as much attention to them as he had to the girls on the subway. But when they'd passed, he said, "One of those guys was looking at you."

"Yeah. I saw."

"Do you know why?"

"He was trying to figure out whether we'd met before."

"Had you?"

I nodded. "Right about where I met you, only back when I'd just gotten out of jail. I told you I'd been here once before."

"Oh."

Blue carpet covered three-quarters of the lobby. A great pool filled the rest in which a row of twelve-foot trellises stood, crowned with flaming braziers. The lobby itself was three stories high, domed and mirror-tiled.

Twisting smoke curled toward the ornate grill. Broken reflections sagged and recovered on the walls.

The elevator door folded about us its foil petals. There was the distinct feeling of not moving while seventy-five stories shucked down around us.

We got out on the landscaped roof garden. A very tanned, very blond man wearing an apricot jumpsuit, from the collar of which emerged a black turtleneck dicky, came down the rocks (artificial) between the ferns (real) growing along the stream (real water; phony current).

"Hello! Hello!" Pause. "I'm terribly glad you decided to come after all." Pause. "For a while I thought you weren't going to make it." The Pauses were to allow Hawk to introduce me. I was dressed so that Spinnel had no way of telling whether I was a miscellaneous Nobel laureate that Hawk happened to have been dining with, or a varlet whose manners and morals were even lower than mine happen to be.

"Shall I take your jacket?" Alexis offered.

Which meant he didn't know Hawk as well as he would like people to think. But I guess he was sensitive enough to realize from the little cold things that happened in the boy's face that he should forget his offer.

He nodded to me, smiling—about all he could do—and we strolled toward the gathering.

Edna Silem was sitting on a transparent inflated hassock. She leaned forward, holding her drink in both hands, arguing politics with the people sitting on the grass before her. She was the first person I recognized (hair of tarnished silver; voice of scrap brass). Jutting from the cuffs of her mannish suit, her wrinkled hands about her goblet, shaking with the intensity of her pronouncements, were heavy with stones and silver. As I ran my eyes back to Hawk, I saw half a dozen whose names/faces sold magazines, music, sent people to the theater (the drama critic for *Delta*, wouldn't you know), and even the mathematician from Princeton I'd read about a few months ago who'd come up with the "quasar/quark" explanation.

There was one woman my eyes kept returning to. On glance three I recognized her as the New Fascistas' most promising candidate for president, Senator Abolafia. Her arms were folded, and she was listening intently to the discussion that had narrowed to Edna and an overly gregarious younger man whose eyes were puffy from what could have been the recent acquisition of contact lenses.

"But don't you feel, Mrs. Silem, that—"

"You must remember when you make predictions like that—"

"Mrs. Silem, I've seen statistics that—"

"You *must* remember—" her voice tensed, lowered till the silence between the words was as rich as the voice was sparse and metallic—"that if everything, *everything* were known, statistical estimates would be unnecessary. The science of probability gives mathematical expression to our ignorance, not to our wisdom," which I was thinking was an interesting second installment to Maud's lecture, when Edna looked up and exclaimed, "Why, Hawk!"

Everyone turned.

"I *am* glad to see you. Lewis, Ann," she called: there were two other Singers there already (he dark, she pale, both tree-slender; their faces made you think of pools without drain or tribute come upon in the forest, clear and very still; husband and wife, they had been made Singers together the day before their marriage six years ago), "he hasn't deserted us after all!" Edna stood, extended her arm over the heads of the people sitting, and barked across her knuckles as though her voice were a pool cue. "Hawk, there are people here arguing with me who don't know nearly as much as you about the subject. You'd be on my side, now wouldn't you—"

"Mrs. Silem, I didn't mean to—" from the floor.

Then her arms swung six degrees, her fingers, eyes, and mouth opened. "You!" Me. "My dear, if there's anyone I never expected to see here! Why it's been almost two years, hasn't it?" Bless Edna; the place where she and Hawk and I had spent a long, beery evening together had more resembled that bar than Tower Top. "Where have you been keeping yourself?"

"Mars, mostly," I admitted. "Actually I just came back today." It's so much fun to be able to say things like that in a place like this.

"Hawk—both of you—" (which meant either she had forgotten my name, or she remembered me well enough not to abuse it) "—come over here and help me drink up Alexis's good liquor." I tried not to grin as we walked toward her. If she remembered anything, she certainly recalled my line of business and must have been enjoying this as much as I was.

Relief spread Alexis's face: he knew now I was *someone* if not *which* someone I was.

As we passed Lewis and Ann, Hawk gave the two Singers one of his luminous grins. They returned shadowed smiles. Lewis nodded. Ann made a move to touch his arm, but left the motion unconcluded; and the company noted the interchange.

Having found out what we wanted, Alex was preparing large glasses of it over crushed ice when the puffy-eyed gentleman stepped up for a refill. "But, Mrs. Silem, then what do you feel validly opposes such political abuses?"

Regina Abolafia wore a white silk suit. Nails, lips, and hair were one copper color; and on her breast was a worked copper pin. It's always fascinated me to watch people used to being the center thrust to the side. She swirled her glass, listening.

"I oppose them," Edna said. "Hawk opposes them. Lewis and Ann oppose them. We, ultimately, are what you have." And her voice had taken on that authoritative resonance only Singers can assume.

Then Hawk's laugh snarled through the conversational fabric.

We turned.

He'd sat cross-legged near the hedge. "Look . . ." he whispered.

Now people's gazes followed his. He was looking at Lewis and Ann. She, tall and blond, he, dark and taller, were standing very quietly, a little nervously, eyes closed (Lewis's lips were apart).

"Oh," whispered someone who should have known better, "they're going to . . ."

I watched Hawk because I'd never had a chance to observe one Singer at another's performance. He put the soles of his feet together, grasped his toes, and leaned forward, veins making blue rivers on his neck. The top button of his jacket had come loose. Two scar ends showed over his collarbone. Maybe nobody noticed but me.

I saw Edna put her glass down with a look of beaming anticipatory pride. Alex, who had pressed the autobar (odd how automation has become the upper crust's way of flaunting the labor surplus) for more crushed ice, looked up, saw what was about to happen, and pushed the cutoff button. The autobar hummed to silence. A breeze (artificial or real, I couldn't tell you) came by, and the trees gave us a final *shush*.

One at a time, then in duet, then singly again, Lewis and Ann sang.

• • •

Singers are people who look at things, then go and tell people what they've seen. What makes them Singers is their ability to make people listen. That is the most magnificent oversimplification I can give. Eighty-six-year-old El Posado in Rio de Janeiro saw a block of tenements collapse, ran to the Avenida del Sol and began improvising, in rhyme and meter (not all that hard in rhyme-rich Portuguese), tears runneling his dusty cheeks, his voice clashing with the palm swards above the sunny street. Hundreds of people stopped to listen; a hundred more; and another hundred. And they told hundreds more what they had heard. Three hours later, hundreds from among them had arrived at the scene with blankets, food, money, shovels, and more incredibly, the willingness and ability to organize themselves and work within that organization. No Tri-D report of a disaster has ever produced that sort of reaction. El Posado is historically considered the first Singer. The second was Miriamne in the roofed city of Lux, who for thirty years walked through the metal streets, singing the glories of the rings of Saturn—the colonists can't look at them without aid because of the ultraviolet the rings set up. But Miriamne, with her strange cataracts, each dawn walked to the edge of the city, looked, saw, and came back to sing of what she saw. All of which would have meant nothing except that during the days she did not sing—through illness, or once she was on a visit to another city to which her fame had spread—the Lux Stock Exchange would go down, the number of violent crimes rise. Nobody could explain it. All they could do was proclaim her Singer. Why did the institution of Singers come about, springing up in just about every urban center throughout the system? Some have speculated that it was a spontaneous reaction to the mass media which blanket our lives. While Tri-D and radio and newstapes disperse information all over the worlds, they also spread a sense of alienation from firsthand experience. (How many people still go to sports events or a political rally with their little receivers plugged into their ears to let them know that what they see is really happening?) The first Singers were proclaimed by the people around them. Then, there was a period where anyone could proclaim himself a Singer who wanted to, and people either responded to him or laughed him into oblivion. But by the time I was left on the doorstep of somebody who didn't want me, most cities had more or less established an unofficial quota. When a position is left open today, the remaining Singers choose who is going to fill it. The required talents are poetic, theatrical, as well as a certain charisma that is generated in the tensions between the personality and the publicity web a Singer is immediately snared in. Before he became a Singer, Hawk had gained something of a prodigious reputation with a book of poems published when he was fifteen. He was touring universities and giving readings, but the reputation was still small enough so that he was amazed that I had ever heard of him, that evening we encountered in Central Park. (I had just spent a pleasant thirty days as a guest of the city, and it's amazing what you find in the Tombs Library.) It was a few weeks after his sixteenth birthday. His Singership was to be announced in four days, though he had been informed already. We sat by the lake till dawn while he weighed and pondered and agonized over the coming responsibility. Two years later, he's still the youngest Singer in six worlds by half a dozen years. Before becoming a Singer, a person need not have been a poet, but most are either that or actors. But the roster through the system includes a longshoreman, two university professors, an heiress to the Silitax millions (Tack it down with Silitax), and at least two persons of such dubious background that the ever-hungry-for-sensation Publicity Machine itself has agreed not to let any of it past the copy editors. But wherever their origins, these diverse and flamboyant living myths sang of love, of death, of the changing of seasons, social classes, governments, and the palace guard. They sang before large crowds, small crowds, to an individual laborer coming home from the city's docks, on slum street corners, in club cars of commuter trains, in the elegant gardens atop Twelve Towers, to Alex Spinnel's select soirée. But it has been illegal to reproduce the "Songs" of the Singers by mechanical means (including publishing the lyrics) since the institution arose, and I respect the law, I do, as only a man in my profession can. I offer the explanation then in place of Lewis's and Ann's song.

• • •

They finished, opened their eyes, stared about with expressions that could have been embarrassment, could have been contempt.

Hawk was leaning forward with a look of rapt approval. Edna was smiling politely. I had the sort of grin on my face that breaks out when you've been vastly moved and vastly pleased. Lewis and Ann had sung superbly.

Alex began to breathe again, glancing around to see what state everybody else was in, saw, and pressed the autobar, which began to hum and crush ice. No clapping, but the appreciative sounds began; people were nodding, commenting, whispering. Regina Abolafia went over to Lewis to say something. I tried to listen until Alex shoved a glass into my elbow.

"Oh, I'm sorry . . ."

I transferred my briefcase to the other hand and took the drink, smiling. When Senator Abolafia left the two Singers, they were holding hands and looking at one another a little sheepishly. They sat down again.

The party drifted in conversational groups through the gardens, through the groves. Overhead clouds the color of old chamois folded and unfolded across the moon.

For a while I stood alone in a circle of trees, listening to the music: a de Lassus two-part canon programmed for audio-generators. Recalled: an article in one of last week's large-circulation literaries, stating that it was the only way to remove the feel of the bar lines imposed by five centuries of meter on modern musicians. For another two weeks this would be acceptable entertainment. The trees circled a rock pool; but no water. Below the plastic surface, abstract lights wove and threaded in a shifting lumia.

"Excuse me . . . ?"

I turned to see Alexis, who had no drink now or idea what to do with his hands. He *was* nervous.

". . . but our young friend has told me you have something I might be interested in."

I started to lift my briefcase, but Alexis's hand came down from his ear (it had gone by belt to hair to collar already) to halt me. Nouveau riche.

"That's all right. I don't need to see them yet. In fact, I'd rather not. I have something to propose to you. I would certainly be interested in what you have if they are, indeed, as Hawk has described them. But I have a guest here who would be even more curious."

That sounded odd.

"I know that sounds odd," Alexis assessed, "but I thought you might be interested simply because of the finances involved. I am an eccentric collector who would offer you a price concomitant with what I would use them for: eccentric conversation pieces—and because of the nature of the purchase I would have to limit severely the people with whom I could converse."

I nodded.

"My guest, however, would have a great deal more use for them."

"Could you tell me who this guest is?"

"I asked Hawk, finally, who you were, and he led me to believe I was on the verge of a grave social indiscretion. It would be equally indiscreet to reveal my guest's name to you." He smiled. "But indiscretion is the better part of the fuel that keeps the social machine turning. Mr. Harvey Cadwaliter-Erickson . . ." He smiled knowingly.

I have *never* been Harvey Cadwaliter-Erickson, but Hawk was always an inventive child. Then a second thought went by, viz., the tungsten magnates, the Cadwaliter-Ericksons of Tythis on Triton. Hawk was not only inventive, he was as brilliant as all the magazines and newspapers are always saying he is.

"I assume your second indiscretion will be to tell me who this mysterious guest is?"

"Well," Alex said with the smile of the canary-fattened cat, "Hawk agreed with me that *the* Hawk might well be curious as to what you have in there," (he pointed) "as indeed he is."

I frowned. Then I thought lots of small, rapid thoughts I'll articulate in due time. "*The* Hawk?"

Alex nodded.

I don't think I was actually scowling. "Would you send our young friend up here for a moment?"

"If you'd like." Alex bowed, turned. Perhaps a minute later, Hawk came up over the rocks and through the trees, grinning. When I didn't grin back, he stopped.

"*Mmmm* . . ." I began.

His head cocked.

I scratched my chin with a knuckle. ". . . Hawk," I said, "are you aware of a department of the police called Special Services?"

"I've heard of them."

"They've suddenly gotten very interested in me."

"Gee," he said with honest amazement. "They're supposed to be pretty effective."

"*Mmmm*," I reiterated.

"Say," Hawk announced, "how do you like that? My namesake is here tonight. Wouldn't you know."

"Alex doesn't miss a trick. Have you any idea *why* he's here?"

"Probably trying to make some deal with Abolafia. Her investigation starts tomorrow."

"Oh." I thought over some of those things I had thought before. "Do you know a Maud Hinkle?"

Hawk's puzzled look said "no" pretty convincingly.

"She bills herself as one of the upper echelon in the arcane organization of which I spoke."

"Yeah?"

"She ended our interview earlier this evening with a little homily about hawks and helicopters. I took our subsequent encounter as a fillip of coincidence. But now I discover that the evening has confirmed her intimations of plurality." I shook my head. "Hawk, I am suddenly catapulted into a paranoid world where the walls not only have ears, but probably eyes and long, claw-tipped fingers. Anyone about me—yea, even very you—could turn out to be a spy. I suspect every sewer grating and second-story window conceals binoculars, a tommy gun, or worse. What I just can't figure out is how these insidious forces, ubiquitous and omnipresent though they be, induced you to lure me into this intricate and diabolical—"

"Oh, cut it out!" He shook back his hair. "I didn't lure—"

"Perhaps not consciously, but Special Services has Hologramic Information Storage, and their methods are insidious and cruel—"

"I said cut it out!" And all sorts of hard little things happened again. "Do you think I'd—" Then he realized how scared I was, I guess. "Look, the Hawk isn't some small-time snatch-purse. He lives in just as paranoid a world as you're in now, only all the time. If he's here, you can be sure there are just as many of his men—eyes and ears and fingers—as there are of Maud Hickenlooper's."

"Hinkle."

"Anyway, it works both ways. No Singer's going to—Look, do you really think *I* would—"

And even though I knew all those hard little things were scabs over pain, I said, "Yes."

"You did something for me once, and I—"

"I gave you some more welts. That's all."

All the scabs pulled off.

"Hawk," I said. "Let me see."

He took a breath. Then he began to open the brass buttons. The flaps of his jacket fell back. The lumia colored his chest with pastel shiftings.

I felt my face wrinkle. I didn't want to look away. I drew a hissing breath instead, which was just as bad.

He looked up. "There're a lot more than when you were here last, aren't there?"

"You're going to kill yourself, Hawk."

He shrugged.

"I can't even tell which are the ones I put there anymore."

He started to point them out.

"Oh, come on," I said too sharply. And for the length of three breaths, he grew more and more uncomfortable till I saw him start to reach for the bottom button. "Boy," I said, trying to keep despair out of my voice, "why do you do it?" and ended up keeping out everything. There is nothing more despairing than a voice empty.

He shrugged, saw I didn't want that, and for a moment anger flickered in his green eyes. I didn't want that either. So he said: "Look . . . you touch a person softly, gently, and maybe you even do it with love. And, well, I guess a piece of information goes on up to the brain where something interprets it as pleasure. Maybe something up there in my head interprets the information in a way you would say is all wrong. . . ."

I shook my head. "You're a Singer. Singers are supposed to be eccentric, sure; but—"

Now he was shaking his head. Then the anger opened up. And I saw an expression move from all those spots that had communicated pain through the rest of his features and vanish without ever becoming a word. Once more he looked down at the wounds that webbed his thin body.

"Button it up, boy. I'm sorry I said anything."

Halfway up the lapels, his hands stopped. "You really think I'd turn you in?"

"Button it up."

He did. Then he said, "Oh." And then, "You know, it's midnight."

"So?"

"Edna just gave me the new Word."

"Which is?"

"Agate."

I nodded.

Hawk finished closing his collar. "What are you thinking about?"

"Cows."

"Cows?" Hawk asked. "What about them?"

"You ever been on a dairy farm?"

He shook his head.

"To get the most milk, you keep the cows practically in suspended animation. They're fed intravenously from a big tank that pipes nutrients out and down, branching into smaller and smaller pipes until it gets to all those high-yield semi-corpses."

"I've seen pictures."

"People."

". . . and cows?"

"You've given me the Word. And now it begins to funnel down, branching out, with me telling others and them telling still others, till by midnight tomorrow . . ."

"I'll go get the—"

"Hawk?"

He turned back. "What?"

"You say you don't think I'm going to be the victim of any hanky-panky with the mysterious forces that know more than we. Okay, that's your opinion. But as soon as I get rid of this stuff, I'm going to make the most distracting exit you've ever seen."

Two little lines bit down Hawk's forehead. "Are you sure I haven't seen this one before?"

"As a matter of fact I think you have." Now I grinned.

"Oh," Hawk said, then made a sound that had the structure of laughter but was all breath. "I'll get the Hawk."

He ducked out between the trees.

• • •

I glanced up at the lozenges of moonlight in the leaves.

I looked down at my briefcase.

Up between the rocks, stepping around the long grass, came the Hawk. He wore a gray evening suit over a gray silk turtleneck. Above his craggy face, his head was completely shaved.

"Mr. Cadwaliter-Erickson?" He held out his hand.

I shook: small sharp bones in loose skin. "Does one call you Mr. . . . ?"

"Arty."

"Arty the Hawk?" I tried to look like I wasn't giving his gray attire the once-over.

He smiled. "Arty the Hawk. Yeah. I picked that name up when I was younger than our friend down there. Alex says you got . . . well, some things that are not exactly yours. That don't belong to you."

I nodded.

"Show them to me."

"You were told what—"

He brushed away the end of my sentence. "Come on, let me see."

He extended his hand, smiling affably as a bank clerk. I ran my thumb around the pressure-zip. The cover went *tsk*. "Tell me," I said, looking up at his head, lowered now to see what I had, "what does one do about Special Services? They seem to be after me."

The head came up. Surprise changed slowly to a craggy leer. "Why, Mr. Cadwaliter-Erickson!" He gave me the up and down openly. "Keep your income steady. Keep it steady, that's one thing you can do."

"If you buy these for anything like what they're worth, that's going to be a little difficult."

"I would imagine. I could always give you less money—"

The cover went *tsk* again.

"—or, barring that, you could try to use your head and outwit them."

"You must have outwitted them at one time or another. You may be on an even keel now, but you had to get there from somewhere else."

Arty the Hawk's nod was downright sly. "I guess you've had a run-in with

Maud. Well, I suppose congratulations are in order. And condolences. I always like to do what's in order."

"You seem to know how to take care of yourself. I mean I notice you're not out there mingling with the guests."

"There are two parties going on here tonight," Arty said. "Where do you think Alex disappears off to every five minutes?"

I frowned.

"That lumia down in the rocks"—he pointed toward my feet—"is a mandala of shifting hues on our ceiling. Alex"—he chuckled—"goes scuttling off under the rocks where there is a pavilion of Oriental splendor—"

"And a separate guest list at the door?"

"Regina is on both. I'm on both. So's the kid, Edna, Lewis, Ann—"

"Am I supposed to know all this?"

"Well, you came with a person on both lists. I just thought . . ." The Hawk paused.

I was coming on wrong. But a quick-change artist learns fairly quick that the verisimilitude factor in imitating someone up the scale is your confidence in your unalienable right to come on wrong. "I'll tell you," I said. "How about exchanging these"—I held out the briefcase—"for some information."

"You want to know how to stay out of Maud's clutches?" He shook his head. "It would be pretty stupid of me to tell you, even if I could. Besides, you've got your family fortunes to fall back on." He beat the front of his shirt with his thumb. "Believe me, boy. Arty the Hawk didn't have that. I didn't have anything like that." His hands dropped into his pockets. "Let's see what you got."

I opened the case again.

The Hawk looked for a while. After a few moments he picked a couple up, turned them around, put them back down, put his hands back in his pockets. "I'll give you sixty thousand for them, approved credit tablets."

"What about the information I wanted?"

"I wouldn't tell you a thing." The Hawk smiled. "I wouldn't tell you the time of day."

There are very few successful thieves in this world. Still less on the other five. The will to steal is an impulse toward the absurd and tasteless. (The talents are poetic, theatrical, a certain reverse charisma . . .) But it is a will, as the will to order, power, love.

"All right," I said.

Somewhere overhead I heard a faint humming.

Arty looked at me fondly. He reached under the lapel of his jacket and took out a handful of credit tablets—the scarlet-banded tablets whose slips were ten thousand apiece. He pulled off one. Two. Three. Four.

"You can deposit this much safely—"

"Why do you think Maud is after me?"

Five. Six.

"Fine," I said.

"How about throwing in the briefcase?" Arty asked.

"Ask Alex for a paper bag. If you want, I can send them—"

"Give them here."

The humming was coming closer.

I held up the open case. Arty went in with both hands. He shoved them into his coat pockets, his pants pockets; the gray cloth was distended by angular bulges. He looked left, right. "Thanks," he said. "Thanks." Then he turned and hurried down the slope with all sorts of things in his pockets that weren't his now.

I looked up through the leaves for the noise, but I couldn't see anything.

I stooped down now and laid my case out. I pulled open the back compartment where I kept the things that did belong to me and rummaged hurriedly through.

• • •

Alex was just offering Puffy-eyes another Scotch, while the gentleman was saying, "Has anyone seen Mrs. Silem? What's that humming overhead—?" when a large woman wrapped in a veil of fading fabric tottered across the rocks, screaming.

Her hands were clawing at her covered face.

Alex sloshed soda over his sleeve, and the man said, "Oh, my God! Who's that?"

"No!" the woman shrieked. "Oh, no! Help me!" waving her wrinkled fingers, brilliant with rings.

"Don't you recognize her?" That was Hawk whispering confidentially to someone else. "It's Henrietta, Countess of Effingham."

And Alex, overhearing, went hurrying to her assistance. The Countess ducked between two cacti, however, and disappeared into the high grass. But the entire party followed. They were beating about the underbrush when a balding gentleman in a black tux, bow tie, and cummerbund coughed and said in a very worried voice, "Excuse me, Mr. Spinnel?"

Alex whirled.

"Mr. Spinnel, my mother . . ."

"Who are *you*?" The interruption upset Alex terribly.

The gentleman drew himself up to announce: "The Honorable Clement Effingham," and his pants leg shook for all the world as if he had started to click his heels. But articulation failed. The expression melted on his face. "Oh, I . . . my mother, Mr. Spinnel. We were downstairs at the other half of your party when she got very . . . excited. She ran up here—oh, I *told* her not to! I knew you'd be upset. But you must help me!" and then looked up.

The others looked, too.

The helicopter blacked the moon, rocking and settling below its hazy twin parasols.

"Oh, please . . ." the gentleman said. "You look over there! Perhaps she's gone back down. I've got to"—looking quickly both ways—"find her." He hurried in one direction while everyone else hurried in others.

The humming was suddenly syncopated with a crash. Roaring now, as plastic fragments from the transparent roof chattered down through the branches, clattered on the rocks . . .

• • •

I made it into the elevator and had already thumbed the edge of my briefcase clasp, when Hawk dove between the unfolding foils. The electric eye began to swing them open. I hit DOOR CLOSE full fist.

The boy staggered, banged shoulders on two walls, then got back breath and balance. "Hey, there's police getting out of that helicopter!"

"Hand-picked by Maud Hinkle herself, no doubt." I pulled the other tuft of white hair from my temple. It went into the case on top of the plastiderm gloves (wrinkled, thick blue veins, long carnelian nails) that had been Henrietta's hands, lying in the chiffon folds of her sari.

Then there was the downward tug of stopping. The Honorable Clement was still half on my face when the door opened.

Gray and gray, with an absolutely dismal expression, the Hawk swung through the doors. Behind him people were dancing in an elaborate pavilion festooned with Oriental magnificence (and a mandala of shifting hues on the ceiling). Arty beat me to DOOR CLOSE. Then he gave me an odd look.

I just sighed and finished peeling off Clem.

"The police are up there . . . ?" the Hawk reiterated.

"Arty," I said, buckling my pants, "it certainly looks that way." The car gained momentum. "You look almost as upset as Alex." I shrugged the tux jacket down my arms, turning the sleeves inside out, pulled one wrist free, and jerked off the white starched dicky with the black bow tie and stuffed it into the briefcase with all my other dickies; swung the coat around and slipped on Howard Calvin Evingston's good gray herringbone. Howard (like Hank) is a redhead (but not as curly).

The Hawk raised his bare brows when I peeled off Clement's bald pate and shook out my hair.

"I noticed you aren't carrying around all those bulky things in your pockets anymore."

"Oh, those have been taken care of," he said gruffly. "They're all right."

"Arty," I said, adjusting my voice down to Howard's security-provoking, ingenuous baritone, "it must have been my unabashed conceit that made me think that those Regular Service police were here just for me—"

The Hawk actually snarled. "They wouldn't be that unhappy if they got me, too."

And from his corner Hawk demanded, "You've got security here with you, don't you, Arty?"

"So what?"

"There's one way you can get out of this," Hawk hissed at me. His jacket had come half-open down his wrecked chest. "That's if Arty takes you out with him."

"Brilliant idea," I concluded. "You want a couple of thousand back for the service?"

The idea didn't amuse him. "I don't want anything from you." He turned to Hawk. "I need something from you, kid. Not him. Look, I wasn't prepared for Maud. If you want me to get your friend out, then you've got to do something for me."

The boy looked confused.

I thought I saw smugness on Arty's face, but the expression resolved into concern. "You've got to figure out some way to fill the lobby up with people, and fast."

I was going to ask why, but then I didn't know the extent of Arty's security. I was going to ask how, but the floor pushed up at my feet and the door swung open. "If you can't do it," the Hawk growled to Hawk, "none of us will get out of here. None of us!"

I had no idea what the kid was going to do, but when I started to follow him out into the lobby, the Hawk grabbed my arm and hissed, "Stay here, you idiot!"

I stepped back. Arty was leaning on DOOR OPEN.

Hawk sprinted toward the pool. And splashed in.

He reached the braziers on their twelve-foot tripods and began to climb.

"He's going to hurt himself!" the Hawk whispered.

"Yeah," I said, but I don't think my cynicism got through. Below the great dish of fire, Hawk was fiddling. Then something under there came loose. Something else went *Clang!* And something else spurted out across the water. The fire raced along it and hit the pool, churning and roaring like hell.

A black arrow with a golden head: Hawk dove.

I bit the inside of my cheek as the alarm sounded. Four people in uniforms were coming across the blue carpet. Another group were crossing in the other direction, saw the flames, and one of the women screamed. I let out my breath, thinking carpet and walls and ceilings would be flameproof. But I kept losing focus on the idea before the sixty-odd infernal feet.

Hawk surfaced on the edge of the pool in the only clear spot left, rolled over onto the carpet, clutching his face. And rolled. And rolled. Then, came to his feet.

Another elevator spilled out a load of passengers who gaped and gasped. A crew came through the doors now with firefighting equipment. The alarm was still sounding.

Hawk turned to look at the dozen-odd people in the lobby. Water puddled the carpet about his drenched and shiny pants legs. Flame turned the drops on his cheek and hair to flickering copper and blood.

He banged his fists against his wet thighs, took a deep breath, and against the roar and the bells and the whispering, he Sang.

Two people ducked back into the two elevators. From a doorway half a dozen more emerged. The elevators returned half a minute later with a dozen people each. I realized the message was going through the building, there's a Singer Singing in the lobby.

The lobby filled. The flames growled, the firefighters stood around shuffling, and Hawk, feet apart on the blue rug by the burning pool, Sang, and Sang of a bar off Times Square full of thieves, morphadine-heads, brawlers, drunkards, women too old to trade what they still held out for barter, and trade just too nasty-grimy; where earlier in the evening a brawl had broken out, and an old man had been critically hurt in the fray.

Arty tugged at my sleeve.

"What . . . ?"

"Come on," he hissed.

The elevator door closed behind us.

We ambled through the attentive listeners, stopping to watch, stopping to hear. I couldn't really do Hawk justice. A lot of that slow amble I spent wondering what sort of security Arty had.

Standing behind a couple in bathrobes who were squinting into the heat, I decided it was all very simple. Arty wanted simply to drift away through a crowd, so he'd conveniently gotten Hawk to manufacture one.

To get to the door we had to pass through practically a cordon of Regular Service policemen, who I don't think had anything to do with what might have been going on in the roof garden; they'd simply collected to see the fire and stayed for the Song. When Arty tapped one on the shoulder—"Excuse me please"—to get by, the policeman glanced at him, glanced away, then did a Mack Sennett double take. But another policeman caught the whole interchange, touched the first on the arm, and gave him a frantic little headshake. Then both men turned very deliberately back to watch the Singer. While the earthquake in my chest stilled, I decided that the Hawk's security complex of agents and counteragents, maneuvering and machinating through the flaming lobby, must be of such finesse and intricacy that to attempt understanding was to condemn oneself to total paranoia.

Arty opened the final door.

I stepped from the last of the air-conditioning into the night.

We hurried down the ramp.

"Hey, Arty . . ."

"You go that way." He pointed down the street. "I go this way."

"Eh . . . what's that way?" I pointed in my direction.

"Twelve Towers sub-sub-subway station. Look. I've got you out of there. Believe me, you're safe for the time being. Now go take a train someplace interesting. Goodbye. Go on now." Then Arty the Hawk put his fists in his pockets and hurried up the street.

I started down, keeping near the wall, expecting someone to get me with a blow dart from a passing car, a death ray from the shrubbery.

I reached the sub.

And still nothing had happened.

Agate gave way to Malachite:

Tourmaline:

Beryl (during which month I turned twenty-six):

Porphyry:

Sapphire (that month I took the ten thousand I hadn't frittered away and invested it in The Glacier, a perfectly legitimate ice cream palace on Triton—the first and only ice cream palace on Triton—which took off like fireworks; all investors were returned eight hundred percent, no kidding. Two weeks later I'd lost half of those earnings on another set of preposterous illegalities and was feeling quite depressed, but The Glacier kept pulling them in. The new Word came by):

Cinnabar:

Turquoise:

Tiger's Eye:

Hector Calhoun Eisenhower finally buckled down and spent three months learning how to be a respectable member of the upper-middle-class underworld. That's a novel in itself. High finance; corporate law; how to hire help: Whew! But the complexities of life have always intrigued me. I got through it. The basic rule is still the same: Observe carefully; imitate effectively.

Garnet:

Topaz (I whispered that word on the roof of the Trans-Satellite Power Station, and caused my hirelings to commit two murders. And you know? I didn't feel a thing):

Taafeite:

We were nearing the end of Taafeite. I'd come back to Triton on strictly Glacial business. A bright pleasant morning it was: the business went fine. I decided to take off the afternoon and go sightseeing in the Torrents.

". . . two hundred and thirty meters high," the guide announced, and everyone around me leaned on the rail and gazed up through the plastic corridor at the cliffs of frozen methane that soared through Neptune's cold green glare.

"Just a few yards down the catwalk, ladies and gentlemen, you can catch your first glimpse of the Well of This World, where over a million years ago, a mysterious force science still cannot explain caused twenty-five square miles of frozen methane to liquefy for no more than a few hours during which time a whirlpool twice the depth of Earth's Grand Canyon was caught for the ages when the temperature dropped once more to . . ."

People were moving down the corridor when I saw her smiling. My hair was black and nappy, and my skin was chestnut dark today.

I was just feeling overconfident, I guess, so I kept standing around next to her. I even contemplated coming on. Then she broke the whole thing up by suddenly turning to me and saying perfectly deadpan: "Why, if it isn't Hamlet Caliban Enobarbus!"

Old reflexes realigned my features to couple the frown of confusion with the smile of indulgence. *Pardon me, but I think you must have mistaken . . .* No, I didn't say it. "Maud," I said, "have you come here to tell me that my time has come?"

She wore several shades of blue with a large blue brooch at her shoulder obviously glass. Still, I realized as I looked about the other tourists, she was more inconspicuous amid their finery than I was. "No," she said. "Actually I'm on vacation. Just like you."

"No kidding?" We had dropped behind the crowd. "You are kidding."

"Special Services of Earth, while we cooperate with Special Services on other worlds, has no official jurisdiction on Triton. And since you came here with money, and most of your recorded gain in income has been through The Glacier; while Regular Services on Triton might be glad to get you, Special Services is not after you as yet." She smiled. "I haven't been to The Glacier. It would really be nice to say I'd been taken there by one of the owners. Could we go for a soda, do you think?"

The swirled sides of the Well of This World dropped away in opalescent grandeur. Tourists gazed, and the guide went on about indices of refraction, angles of incline.

"I don't think you trust me," Maud said.

My look said she was right.

"Have you ever been involved with narcotics?" she asked suddenly.

I frowned.

"No, I'm serious. I want to try and explain something . . . a point of information that may make both our lives easier."

"Peripherally," I said. "I'm sure you've got down all the information in your dossiers."

"I was involved with them a good deal more than peripherally for several years," Maud said. "Before I got into Special Services, I was in the Narcotics Division of the regular force. And the people we dealt with twenty-four hours a day were drug users, drug pushers. To catch the big ones we had to make friends with the little ones. To catch the bigger ones, we had to make friends with the big. We had to keep the same hours they kept, talk the same language, for months at a time live on the same streets, in the same buildings." She stepped back from the rail to let a youngster ahead. "I had to be sent away to take the morphadine detoxification cure twice while I was on the narc squad. And I had a better record than most."

"What's your point?"

"Just this. You and I are traveling in the same circles now, if only because of our respective chosen professions. You'd be surprised how many people we already know in common. Don't be shocked when we run into each other crossing Sovereign Plaza in Bellona one day, then two weeks later wind up at the same restaurant for lunch at Lux on Iapetus. Though the circles we move in cover worlds, they *are* the same—and not that big."

"Come on." I don't think I sounded happy. "Let me treat you to that ice cream." We started back down the walkway.

"You know," Maud said, "if you do stay out of Special Services' hands here and on Earth long enough, eventually you'll be up there with a huge income growing on a steady slope. It might be a few years, but it's possible. There's no reason now for us to be *personal* enemies. You just may, someday, reach that point where Special Services loses interest in you as quarry. Oh, we'd still see each other, run into each other. We get a great deal of our information from people up there. We're in a position to help you, too, you see."

"You've been casting holograms again."

She shrugged. Her face looked positively ghostly under the pale planet. She said, when we reached the artificial lights of the city, "I did meet two friends of yours recently, Lewis and Ann."

"The Singers?"

Maud nodded.

"Oh, I don't really know them well."

"They seem to know a lot about you. Perhaps through that other Singer Hawk."

"Oh," I said again. "Did they say how he was?"

"I read that he was recovering about two months back. But nothing since then."

"That's about all I know, too," I said.

"The only time I've ever seen him," Maud said, "was right after I pulled him out."

Arty and I had gotten out of the lobby before Hawk actually finished. The next day on the newstapes I learned that when his Song was over, Hawk shrugged out of his jacket, dropped his pants, and walked back into the pool.

The firefighter crew suddenly woke up. People began running around and screaming. He'd been rescued, seventy percent of his body covered with second- and third-degree burns. I'd been industriously trying not to think about it.

"*You* pulled him out?"

"Yes. I was in the helicopter that landed on the roof," Maud said. "I thought you'd be impressed to see me."

"Oh," I said. "How did you get to pull him out?"

"Once you got going, Arty's security managed to jam the elevator service above the seventy-first floor, so we didn't get to the lobby till after you were out of the building. That's when Hawk tried to—"

"But it was you who actually saved him, though?"

"The firemen in that neighborhood hadn't had a fire in twelve years! I don't think they even know how to operate the equipment. I had my boys foam the pool, then I waded in and dragged him—"

"Oh," I said again. I had been trying hard, almost succeeding, these eleven months. I wasn't there when it happened. It wasn't my affair. Maud was saying:

"We thought we might have gotten a lead on you from him, but when I got him to the shore, he was completely out, just a mass of open, running—"

"I should have known the Special Services uses Singers, too," I said. "Everyone else does. The Word changes today, doesn't it? Lewis and Ann didn't pass on what the new one is?"

"I saw them yesterday, and the Word doesn't change for another eight hours. Besides, they wouldn't tell *me*, anyway." She glanced at me and frowned. "They really wouldn't."

"Let's go have those ice-cream sodas," I said. "We'll make small talk and listen carefully to each other while we affect an air of nonchalance. You will try to pick up things that will make it easier to catch me. I will listen for things you let slip that might make it easier for me to avoid you."

"*Um-hm.*" She nodded.

"Why did you contact me in that bar, anyway?"

Eyes of ice: "I told you, we simply travel in the same circles. We're quite likely to be in the same bar on the same night."

"I guess that's just one of the things I'm not supposed to understand, huh?"

Her smile was appropriately ambiguous. I didn't push it.

• • •

It was a very dull afternoon. I couldn't repeat one exchange from the nonsense we babbled over the cherry-peaked mountains of whipped cream. We both exerted so much energy to keep up the appearance of being amused, I doubt either one of us could see our way to picking up anything meaningful—if anything meaningful was said.

She left. I brooded some more on the charred phoenix.

The Steward of The Glacier called me into the kitchen to ask about a shipment of contraband milk (The Glacier makes all its own ice cream) that I had been able to wangle on my last trip to Earth (it's amazing how little progress there has been in dairy farming over the last ten years; it was depressingly easy to hornswoggle that bumbling Vermonter) and under the white lights and great plastic churning vats, while I tried to get things straightened out, he made some comment about the Heist Cream Emperor; that didn't do *any* good.

By the time the evening crowd got there, and the moog was making music, the crystal walls were blazing; and the floor show—a new addition that week—had been cajoled into going on anyway (a trunk of costumes had gotten lost in shipment [or swiped, but I wasn't about to tell *them* that]), and wandering through the tables I, personally, had caught a very grimy little girl, obviously out of her head on morph, trying to pick up a customer's pocketbook from the back of his chair—I just caught her by the wrist, made her let go, and led her to the door daintily, while she blinked at me with dilated eyes and the customer never even knew—and the floor show, having decided what the hell, were doing their act *au naturel*, and everyone was having just a high old time, I was feeling really bad.

I went outside, sat on the wide steps, and growled when I had to move aside to let people in or out. About the seventy-fifth growl, the person I growled at stopped and boomed down at me, "I thought I'd find you, if I looked hard enough! I mean if I really looked."

I looked at the hand that was flapping at my shoulder; followed the arm up to a black turtleneck where there was a beefy, bald, grinning head. "Arty," I said, "what are . . . ?" But he was still flapping and laughing with impervious *gemütlichkeit*.

"You wouldn't believe the time I had getting a picture of you, boy. Had to bribe one out of the Triton Special Services Department. That quick change bit: great gimmick. Just great!" The Hawk sat down next to me and dropped his hand on my knee. "Wonderful place you got here. I like it, like it a lot." Small bones in veined dough. "But not enough to make you an offer on it yet. You're learning fast there, though. I can tell you're learning fast. I'm going to be proud to be able to say I was the one who gave you your first big break." Arty's hand came away, and he began to knead it into the other. "If you're going to move into the big time, you have to have at least one foot planted firmly on the right side of the law. The whole idea is to make yourself indispensable to the good people. Once that's done, a good crook has the keys to all the treasure houses in the system. But I'm not telling you anything you don't already know."

"Arty," I said, "do you think the two of us should be seen together here . . . ?"

The Hawk held his hand above his lap and joggled it with a deprecating motion. "Nobody can get a picture of us. I got my men all around. I never go anywhere in public without my security. Heard you've been looking into the security business yourself," which was true. "Good idea. Very good. I like the way you're handling yourself."

"Thanks. Arty, I'm not feeling too hot this evening. I came out here to get some air . . ."

Arty's hand fluttered again. "Don't worry, I won't hang around. You're right. We shouldn't be seen. Just passing by and wanted to say hello. Just hello." He got up. "That's all." He started down the steps.

"Arty?"

He looked back.

"Sometime soon you will come back; and that time you will want to buy out my share of The Glacier, because I'll have gotten too big; and I won't want to sell because I'll think I'm big enough to fight you. So we'll be enemies for a while. You'll try to kill me. I'll try to kill you."

On his face, first the frown of confusion, then the indulgent smile. "I see you've caught on to the idea of hologramic information. Very good. Good. It's the only way to outwit Maud. Make sure all your information relates to the whole scope of the situation. It's the only way to outwit me, too." He smiled, started to turn, but thought of something else. "If you can fight me off long enough and keep growing, keep your security in tiptop shape, eventually, we'll get to the point where it'll be worth both our whiles to work together again. If you can just hold out, we'll be friends again. Someday. You just watch. Just wait."

"Thanks for telling me."

The Hawk looked at his watch. "Well. Goodbye." I thought he was going to leave finally. But he glanced up again. "Have you got the new Word?"

"That's right," I said. "It went out tonight. What is it?"

The Hawk waited till the people coming down the steps were gone. He looked hastily about, then leaned toward me with hands cupped at his mouth, rasped, "Pyrite," and winked hugely. "I just got it from a gal who got it direct from Colette" (one of the three Singers of Triton). Arty turned, jounced down the steps, and shouldered his way into the crowds passing on the strip.

• • •

I sat there mulling through the year till I had to get up and walk. All walking does to my depressive moods is add the reinforcing rhythm of paranoia. By the time I was coming back, I had worked out a dilly of a delusional system: The Hawk had already begun to weave some security-ridden plot about me, which ended when we were all trapped in some dead-end alley, and trying to get aid I called out, "Pyrite!" which would turn out not to be the Word at all but served to identify me for the man in the dark gloves with the gun/grenade/gas.

There was a cafeteria on the corner. In the light from the window, clustered over the wreck by the curb was a bunch of nasty-grimies (à la Triton: chains around the wrist, bumblebee tattoo on cheek, high-heel boots on those who could afford them). Straddling the smashed headlight was the little morph-head I had ejected earlier from The Glacier.

On a whim I went up to her. "Hey . . . ?"

She looked at me from under hair like trampled straw, eyes all pupil.

"You get the new Word yet?"

She rubbed her nose, already scratch red. "Pyrite," she said. "It just came down about an hour ago."

"Who told you?"

She considered my question. "I got it from a guy, who says he got it from a guy, who came in this evening from New York, who picked it up there from a Singer named Hawk."

The three grimies nearest made a point of not looking at me. Those farther away let themselves glance.

"Oh," I said. "Oh. Thanks."

Occam's Razor, along with any real information on how security works, hones away most such paranoia. Pyrite. At a certain level in my line of work, paranoia's just an occupational disease. At least I was certain that Arty (and Maud) probably suffered from it as much as I did.

• • •

The lights were out on The Glacier's marquee. Then I remembered what I had left inside and ran up the stairs.

The door was locked. I pounded on the glass a couple of times, but everyone had gone home. And the thing that made it worse was that I could *see* it sitting on the counter of the coat-check alcove under the orange bulb. The Steward had probably put it there, thinking I might arrive before everybody left. Tomorrow at noon Ho Chi Eng had to pick up his reservation for the Marigold Suite on the Interplanetary Liner *The Platinum Swan*, which left at one-thirty for Bellona. And there behind the glass doors of The Glacier, it waited with the proper wig, as well as the epicanthic folds that would halve Mr. Eng's sloe eyes of jet.

I actually thought of breaking in. But the more practical solution was to get the hotel to wake me at nine and come in with the cleaning man. I turned around and started down the steps; and the thought struck me, and made me terribly sad, so that I blinked and smiled just from reflex; it was probably just as well to leave it there till morning, because there was nothing in it that wasn't mine anyway.

—*Milford*
July 1968

BRUCE BETHKE

CYBERPUNK

(1983)

THE SNOOZER WENT OFF at seven and I was out of my sleepsack, powered up, and on line in nanos. That's as far as I got. Soon's I booted and got—

CRACKERS/BUDDYBOO/8ER

—on the tube I shut down fast. Damn! Rayno had been on line before me, like always, and that message meant somebody else had gotten into our Net—and that meant trouble by the busload! I couldn't do anything more on term, so I zipped into my jumper, combed my hair, and went downstairs.

Mom and Dad were at breakfast when I slid into the kitchen. "Good Morning, Mikey!" said Mom with a smile. "You were up so late last night I thought I wouldn't see you before you caught your bus."

"Had a tough program to crack," I said.

"Well," she said, "now you can sit down and have a decent breakfast." She turned around to pull some Sara Lees out of the microwave and plunk them down on the table.

"If you'd do your schoolwork when you're supposed to you wouldn't have to stay up all night," growled Dad from behind his caffix and faxsheet. I sloshed some juice in a glass and poured it down, stuffed a Sara Lee into my mouth, and stood to go.

"What?" asked Mom. "That's all the breakfast you're going to have?"

"Haven't got time," I said. "I gotta get to school early to see if the program checks." Dad growled something more and Mom spoke to quiet him, but I didn't hear much 'cause I was out the door.

I caught the transys for school, just in case they were watching. Two blocks down the line I got off and transferred going back the other way, and a coupla transfers later I wound up whipping into Buddy's All-Night Burgers. Rayno was in our booth, glaring into his caffix. It was 7:55 and I'd beat Georgie and Lisa there.

"What's on line?" I asked as I dropped into my seat, across from Rayno. He just looked up at me through his eyebrows and I knew better than to ask again.

At eight Lisa came in. Lisa is Rayno's girl, or at least she hopes she is. I can see why: Rayno's seventeen—two years older than the rest of us—he wears flash plastic and his hair in The Wedge (Dad blew a chip when I said I wanted my hair cut like that) and he's so cool he won't even touch her, even when she's begging for it. She plunked down in her seat next to Rayno and he didn't blink.

Georgie still wasn't there at 8:05. Rayno checked his watch again, then finally looked up from his caffix. "The compiler's been cracked," he said. Lisa and I both swore. We'd worked up our own little code to keep our Net private. I mean, our Olders would just blow *boards* if they ever found out what we were *really* up to. And now somebody'd broken our code.

"Georgie's old man?" I asked.

"Looks that way." I swore again. Georgie and I started the Net by linking our smartterms with some stuff we stored in his old man's home business system. Now my dad wouldn't know an opsys if he crashed on one, but Georgie's old man—he's a *greentooth*. A tech-type. He'd found one of ours once before and tried to take it apart to see what it did. We'd just skinned out that time.

"Any idea how far in he got?" Lisa asked. Rayno looked through her, at the front door. Georgie'd just come in.

"We're gonna find out," Rayno said.

Georgie was coming in smiling, but when he saw that look in Rayno's eyes he sat down next to me like the seat was booby-trapped.

"Good morning, Georgie," said Rayno, smiling like a shark.

"I didn't glitch!" Georgie whined. "I didn't tell him a thing!"

"Then how the Hell did he do it?"

"You know how he is, he's weird! He likes puzzles!" Georgie looked to me for backup. "That's how come I was late. He was trying to weasel me, but I didn't tell him a thing! I think he only got it partway open. He didn't ask about the Net!"

Rayno actually sat back, pointed at us all, and smiled. "You kids just don't know how *lucky* you are. I was in the Net last night and flagged somebody who didn't know the secures was poking Georgie's compiler. I made some changes. By the time your old man figures them out, well . . ."

I sighed relief. See what I mean about being cool? Rayno had us outlooped all the time!

Rayno slammed his fist down on the table. "But *dammit* Georgie, you gotta keep a closer watch on him!"

Then Rayno smiled and bought us all drinks and pie all the way around. Lisa had a cherry Coke, and Georgie and I had caffix just like Rayno. God, that stuff tastes awful! The cups were cleared away, and Rayno unzipped his jumper and reached inside.

"Now kids," he said quietly, "it's time for some serious fun." He whipped out his microterm. "School's off!"

I still drop a bit when I see that microterm—Geez, it's a beauty! It's a Zeilemann Nova 300, but we've spent so much time reworking it, it's practically custom from the motherboard up. Hi-baud, rammed, rammed, ported, with the wafer display folds down to about the size of a vid cassette; I'd give an ear to have one like it. We'd used Georgie's old man's chipburner to tuck some special tricks in ROM and there wasn't a system in CityNet it couldn't talk to.

Rayno ordered up a smartcab and we piled out of Buddy's. No more riding the transys for us, we were going in style! We charged the smartcab off to some law company and cruised all over Eastside.

Riding the boulevards got stale after a while, so we rerouted to the library. We do a lot of our fun at the library, 'cause nobody ever bothers us there. Nobody ever *goes* there. We sent the smartcab, still on the law company account, off to Westside. Getting past the guards and the librarians was just a matter of flashing some ID and then we zipped off into the stacks.

Now, you've got to ID away your life to get on the libsys terms—which isn't worth half a scare when your ID is all fudged like ours is—and they watch real careful. But they move their terms around a lot, so they've got ports on line all over the building. We found an unused port, and me and Georgie kept watch while Rayno plugged in his microterm and got on line.

"Get me into the Net," he said, handing me the term. We don't have a stored opsys yet for Netting, so Rayno gives me the fast and tricky jobs.

Through the dataphones I got us out of the libsys and into CityNet. Now, Olders will never understand. They still think a computer has got to be a brain in a single box. I can get the same results with opsys stored in a hundred places, once I tie them together. Nearly every computer has got a dataphone port, CityNet is a *great* linking system, and Rayno's microterm has the smarts to do the job clean and fast so nobody flags on us. I pulled the compiler out of Georgie's old man's computer and got into our Net. Then I handed the term back to Rayno.

"Well, let's do some fun. Any requests?" Georgie wanted something to get even with his old man, and I had a new routine cooking, but Lisa's eyes lit up 'cause Rayno handed the term to her, first.

"I wanna burn Lewis," she said.

"Oh fritz!" Georgie complained. "You did that *last* week!"

"Well, he gave me another F on a theme."

"I never get F's. If you'd *read* books once in a—"

"Georgie," Rayno said softly, "Lisa's on line." That settled that. Lisa's eyes were absolutely glowing.

Lisa got back into CityNet and charged a couple hundred overdue books to Lewis's libsys account. Then she ordered a complete fax sheet of Encyclopaedia Britannica printed out at his office. I got next turn.

Georgie and Lisa kept watch while I accessed. Rayno was looking over my shoulder. "Something new this week?"

"Airline reservations. I was with my dad two weeks ago when he set up a business trip, and I flagged on maybe getting some fun. I scanned the ticket clerk real careful and picked up the access code."

"Okay, show me what you can do."

Accessing was so easy that I just wiped a couple of reservations first, to see if there were any bells and whistles.

None. No checks, no lockwords, no confirm codes. I erased a couple dozen people without crashing down or locking up. "Geez," I said, "There's no deep secures at all!"

"I been telling you. Olders are even dumber than they look. Georgie? Lisa? C'mon over here and see what we're running!"

Georgie was real curious and asked a lot of questions, but Lisa just looked bored and snapped her gum and tried to stand closer to Rayno. Then Rayno said, "Time to get off Sesame Street. Purge a flight."

I did. It was simple as a save. I punched a few keys, entered, and an entire plane disappeared from all the reservation files. Boy, they'd be surprised when they showed up at the airport. I started purging down the line, but Rayno interrupted.

"Maybe there's no bells and whistles, but wipe out a whole block of flights and it'll stand out. Watch this." He took the term from me and cooked up a routine in RAM to do a global and wipe out every flight that departed at an :07 for the next year. "Now that's how you do these things without waving a flag."

"That's sharp," Georgie chipped in, to me. "Mike, you're a genius! Where do you get these ideas?" Rayno got a real funny look in his eyes.

"My turn," Rayno said, exiting the airline system.

"What's next in the stack?" Lisa asked him.

"Yeah, I mean, after garbaging the airlines . . ." Georgie didn't realize he was supposed to shut up.

"Georgie! Mike!" Rayno hissed. "Keep watch!" Soft, he added, "It's time for The Big One."

"You sure?" I asked. "Rayno, I don't think we're ready."

"We're ready."

Georgie got whiney. "We're gonna get in *big* trouble—"

"Wimp," spat Rayno. Georgie shut up.

We'd been working on The Big One for over two months, but I still didn't feel real solid about it. It *almost* made a clean if/then/else; *if* The Big One worked/ *then* we'd be rich/*else* . . . it was the *else* I didn't have down.

Georgie and me scanned while Rayno got down to business. He got back into CityNet, called the cracker opsys out of OurNet, and poked it into Merchant's Bank & Trust. I'd gotten into them the hard way, but never messed with their accounts; just did it to see if I could do it. My data'd been sitting in their system for about three weeks now and nobody'd noticed. Rayno thought it would be really funny to use one bank computer to crack the secures on other bank computers.

While he was peeking and poking I heard walking nearby and took a closer look. It was just some old waster looking for a quiet place to sleep. Rayno was finished linking by the time I got back. "Okay kids," he said, "this is it." He looked around to make sure we were all watching him, then held up the term and stabbed the *RETURN* key. That was it. I stared hard at the display, waiting to see what *else* was gonna be. Rayno figured it'd take about ninety seconds.

The Big One, y'see, was Rayno's idea. He'd heard about some kids in Sherman Oaks who almost got away with a five-million-dollar electronic fund transfer; they hadn't hit a hang-up moving the five mil around until they tried to dump it into a personal savings account with a $40 balance. That's when all the flags went up.

Rayno's cool; Rayno's smart. We weren't going to be greedy, we were just going to EFT fifty K. And it wasn't going to look real strange, 'cause it got strained through some legitimate accounts before we used it to open twenty dummies.

If it worked.

The display blanked, flickered, and showed:

TRANSACTION COMPLETED. HAVE A NICE DAY.

I started to shout, but remembered I was in a library. Georgie looked less terrified. Lisa looked like she was going to attack Rayno.

Rayno just cracked his little half smile, and started exiting. "Funtime's over, kids."

"I didn't get a turn," Georgie mumbled.

Rayno was out of all the nets and powering down. He turned, slow, and looked at Georgie through those eyebrows of his. "*You* are still on The List."

Georgie swallowed it 'cause there was nothing else he could do. Rayno folded up the microterm and tucked it back inside his jumper.

We got a smartcab outside the library and went off to someplace Lisa picked for lunch. Georgie got this idea about garbaging up the smartcab's brain so that the next customer would have a real state fair ride, but Rayno wouldn't let him do it. Rayno didn't talk to him during lunch, either.

After lunch I talked them into heading up to Martin's Micros. That's one of my favorite places to hang out. Martin's the only Older I know who can really work a computer without blowing out his headchips, and he never talks down to me, and he never tells me to keep my hands off anything. In fact, Martin's been real happy to see all of us, ever since Rayno bought that $3000 vidgraphics art animation package for Lisa's birthday.

Martin was sitting at his term when we came in. "Oh, hi Mike! Rayno! Lisa! Georgie!" We all nodded. "Nice to see you again. What can I do for you today?"

"Just looking," Rayno said.

"Well, that's free." Martin turned back to his term and punched a few more IN keys. "Damn!" he said to the term.

"What's the problem?" Lisa asked.

"The problem is *me*," Martin said. "I got this software package I'm supposed to be writing, but it keeps bombing out and I don't know what's wrong."

Rayno asked, "What's it supposed to do?"

"Oh, it's a real estate system. Y'know, the whole future-values-in-current-dollars bit. Depreciation, inflation, amortization, tax credits—"

"Put that in our tang," Rayno said. "What numbers crunch?"

Martin started to explain, and Rayno said to me, "This looks like your kind of work." Martin hauled his three hundred pounds of fat out of the chair and looked relieved as I dropped down in front of the term. I scanned the parameters, looked over Martin's program, and processed a bit. Martin'd only made a few mistakes. Anybody could have. I dumped Martin's program and started loading the right one in off the top of my head.

"Will you look at that?" Martin said.

I didn't answer 'cause I was thinking in assembly. In ten minutes I had it in, compiled, and running test sets. It worked perfect, of course.

"I just can't believe you kids," Martin said. "You can program easier than I can talk."

"Nothing to it," I said.

"Maybe not for you. I knew a kid grew up speaking Arabic, used to say the same thing." He shook his head, tugged his beard, looked me in the face, and smiled. "Anyhow, thanks loads, Mike. I don't know how to . . ." He snapped his fingers. "Say, I just got something in the other day, I bet you'd be really interested in." He took me over to the display case, pulled it out, and set it on the counter. "The latest word in microterms. The Zeilemann Starfire 600."

I dropped a bit! Then I ballsed up enough to touch it. I flipped up the wafer display, ran my fingers over the touch pads, and I just *wanted* it so bad! "It's smart," Martin said. "Rammed, rammed, and ported."

Rayno was looking at the specs with that cold look in his eye. "My 300 is still faster," he said.

"It should be," Martin said. "You customized it half to death. But the 600 is nearly as fast, and it's stock, and it lists for $1400. I figure you must have spent nearly 3K upgrading yours."

"Can I try it out?" I asked. Martin plugged me into his system, and I booted and got on line. It worked great! Quiet, accurate; so maybe it wasn't as fast as Rayno's—*I* couldn't tell the difference. "Rayno, this thing is the max!" I looked at Martin. "Can we work out some kind of . . . ?" Martin looked back to his terminal, where the real estate program was still running tests without a glitch.

"I been thinking about that, Mike. You're a minor, so I can't legally employ you." He tugged on his beard and rolled his tongue around his mouth. "But I'm hitting that real estate client for some pretty heavy bread on consulting fees, and it doesn't seem real fair to me that you . . . Tell you what. Maybe I can't hire you, but I sure can buy software you write. You be my consultant on, oh . . . seven more projects like this, and we'll call it a deal? Sound okay to you?"

Before I could shout yes, Rayno pushed in between me and Martin. "I'll buy it. List." He pulled out a charge card from his jumper pocket. Martin's jaw dropped. "Well, what're you waiting for? My plastic's good."

"List? But I owe Mike one," Martin protested.

"*List*. You don't owe us nothing."

Martin swallowed. "Okay Rayno." He took the card and ran a credcheck on it. "It's clean," Martin said, surprised. He punched up the sale and started laughing. "I don't know *where* you kids get this kind of money!"

"We rob banks," Rayno said. Martin laughed, and Rayno laughed, and we all laughed. Rayno picked up the term and walked out of the store. As soon as we got outside he handed it to me.

"Thanks Rayno, but . . . but I coulda made the deal myself."

"Happy Birthday, Mike."

"Rayno, my birthday is in August."

"Let's get one thing straight. You work for *me*."

It was near school endtime, so we routed back to Buddy's. On the way, in the smartcab, Georgie took my Starfire, gently opened the case, and scanned the boards. "We could double the baud speed real easy."

"Leave it stock," Rayno said.

We split up at Buddy's, and I took the transys home. I was lucky, 'cause Mom and Dad weren't home and I could zip right upstairs and hide the Starfire in my closet. I wish I had cool parents like Rayno does. They never ask him any dumb questions.

Mom came home at her usual time, and asked how school was. I didn't have to say much, 'cause just then the stove said dinner was ready and she started setting the table. Dad came in five minutes later and we started eating.

We got the phone call halfway through dinner. I was the one who jumped up and answered it. It was Georgie's old man, and he wanted to talk to my dad. I gave him the phone and tried to overhear, but he took it in the next room and talked real quiet. I got unhungry. I never liked tofu anyway.

Dad didn't stay quiet for long. "He *what*?! Well thank you for telling me! I'm going to get to the bottom of this right now!" He hung up.

"Who was that, David?" Mom asked.

"That was Mr. Hansen. Georgie's father. Mike and Georgie were hanging around with that punk Rayno again!" He snapped around to look at me. I'd almost made it out the kitchen door. "Michael! Were you in school today?"

I tried to talk cool. I think the tofu had my throat all clogged up. "Yeah . . . yeah, I was."

"Then how come Mr. Hansen saw you coming out of the downtown library?"

I was stuck. "I—I was down there doing some special research."

"For what class? C'mon Michael, what were you studying?"

It was too many inputs. I was locking up.

"David," Mom said, "Aren't you being a bit hasty? I'm sure there's a good explanation."

"Martha, Mr. Hansen found something in his computer that Georgie and Michael put there. He thinks they've been messing with banks."

"*Our* Mikey? It must be some kind of bad joke."

"You don't know how serious this is! Michael Arthur Harris! What have you been doing sitting up all night with that terminal? What was that system in Hansen's computer? Answer me! What have you been doing?!"

My eyes felt hot. "None of your business! Keep your nose out of things you'll never understand, you obsolete old relic!"

"That *does* it! I don't know what's wrong with you damn kids, but I know that *thing* isn't helping!" He stormed up to my room. I tried to get ahead of him all the way up the steps and just got my hands stepped on. Mom came fluttering up behind as he yanked all the plugs on my terminal.

"Now David," Mom said. "Don't you think you're being a bit harsh? He needs that for his homework, don't you, Mikey?"

"You can't make excuses for him this time, Martha! I mean it! This goes in the basement, and tomorrow I'm calling the cable company and getting his line ripped out! If he has anything to do on a computer he can damn well use the terminal in the den, where I can watch him!" He stomped out, carrying my smartterm. I slammed the door and locked it. "Go ahead and sulk! It won't do you any good!"

I threw some pillows around till I didn't feel like breaking anything anymore, then I hauled the Starfire out of the closet. I'd watched over Dad's shoulders enough to know his account numbers and access codes, so I got on line and got down to business. I was finished in half an hour.

I tied into Dad's terminal. He was using it, like I figured he would be, scanning school records. Fine. He wouldn't find out anything; we'd figured out how to fix school records months ago. I crashed in and gave him a new message on his vid display.

"Dad," it said, "there's going to be some changes around here."

It took a few seconds to sink in. I got up and made sure the door was locked real solid. I still got half a scare when he came pounding up the stairs, though. I didn't know he could be so loud.

"MICHAEL!!" He slammed into the door. "Open this! *Now!*"

"No."

"If you don't open this door before I count to ten, I'm going to bust it down! One!"

"Before you do that—"

"Two!"

"Better call your bank!"

"Three!"

"B320-5127-OlR." That was his checking account access code. He silenced a couple seconds.

"Young man, I don't know what you think you're trying to pull—"

"I'm not trying anything. I did it already."

Mom came up the stairs and said, "What's going on, David?"

"Shut up, Martha!" He was talking real quiet, now. "What did you do, Michael?"

"Outlooped you. Disappeared you. Buried you."

"You mean, you got into the bank computer and *erased* my checking account?"

"Savings and mortgage on the condo, too."

"Oh my God . . ."

Mom said, "He's just angry, David. Give him time to cool off. Mikey, you wouldn't *really* do that, would you?"

"Then I accessed DynaRand," I said. "Wiped your job. Your pension. I got into your plastic, too."

"He couldn't have, David. Could he?"

"Michael!" He hit the door. "I'm going to wring your scrawny neck!"

"Wait!" I shouted back. "I copied all your files before I purged! There's a way to recover!"

He let up hammering on the door, and struggled to talk calm. "Give me the copies right now and I'll just forget that this happened."

"I can't. I mean, I did backups in other computers. And I secured the files and hid them where only I know how to access."

There was quiet. No, in a nano I realized it wasn't quiet, it was Mom and Dad talking real soft. I eared up to the door but all I caught was Mom saying "why not?" and Dad saying, "but what if he *is* telling the truth?"

"Okay Michael," Dad said at last. "What do you want?"

I locked up. It was an embarrasser; what *did* I want? I hadn't thought that far ahead. Me, caught without a program! I dropped half a laugh, then tried to think. I mean, there was nothing they could get me I couldn't get myself, or with Rayno's help. Rayno! I wanted to get in touch with him, is what I wanted. I'd pulled this whole thing off without Rayno!

I decided then it'd probably be better if my Olders didn't know about the Starfire, so I told Dad first thing I wanted was my smartterm back. It took a long time for him to clump down to the basement and get it. He stopped at his term in the den, first, to scan if I'd really purged him. He was real subdued when he brought my smartterm back up.

I kept processing, but by the time he got back I still hadn't come up with anything more than I wanted them to leave me alone and stop telling me what to do. I got the smartterm into my room without being pulped, locked the door, got on line, and gave Dad his job back. Then I tried to flag Rayno and Georgie, but couldn't, so I left messages for when they booted. I stayed up half the night playing a war, just to make sure Dad didn't try anything.

I booted and scanned first thing the next morning, but Rayno and Georgie still hadn't come on. So I went down and had an utter silent breakfast and sent Mom and Dad off to work. I offed school and spent the whole day finishing the war and working on some tricks and treats programs. We had another utter silent meal when Mom and Dad came home, and after supper I flagged Rayno had been in the Net and left a remark on when to find him.

I finally got him on line around eight, and he said Georgie was getting trashed and probably heading for permanent downtime.

Then I told Rayno all about how I outlooped my old man, but he didn't seem real buzzed about it. He said he had something cooking and couldn't meet me at Buddy's that night to talk about it, either. So we got off line, and I started another war and then went to sleep.

The snoozer said 5:25 when I woke up, and I couldn't logic how come I was awake till I started making sense out of my ears. Dad was taking apart the hinges on my door!

"Dad! You cut that out or I'll purge you clean! There won't be backups this time!"

"Try it," he growled.

I jumped out of my sleepsack, powered up, booted and—no boot. I tried again. I could get on line in my smartterm, but I couldn't port out. "I cut your cable down in the basement," he said.

I grabbed the Starfire out of my closet and zipped it inside my jumper, but before I could do the window, the door and Dad both fell in. Mom came in right behind, popped open my dresser, and started stuffing socks and underwear in a suitcase.

"Now you're fritzed!" I told Dad. "I'll *never* give you back your files!" He grabbed my arm.

"Michael, there's something I think you should see." He dragged me down to his den and pulled some bundles of old paper trash out of his desk. "These are receipts. This is what obsolete old relics like me use because we don't trust computer bookkeeping. I checked with work and the bank; everything that goes on in the computer has to be verified with paper. You can't change anything for more than twenty-four hours."

"Twenty-four *hours*?" I laughed. "Then you're still fritzed! I can still wipe you out any day, from any term in CityNet."

"I know."

Mom came into the den, carrying the suitcase and Kleenexing her eyes. "Mikey, you've got to understand that we love you, and this is for your own good." They dragged me down to the airport and stuffed me in a private Lear with a bunch of old gestapos.

• • •

I've had a few weeks now to get used to the Von Schlager Military Academy. They tell me I'm a bright kid and with good behavior, there's really no reason at all why I shouldn't graduate in five years. I *am* getting tired, though, of all the older cadets telling me how soft I've got it now that they've installed indoor plumbing.

Of course, I'm free to walk out any time I want. It's only three hundred miles to Fort McKenzie, where the road ends.

Sometimes at night, after lights out, I'll pull out my Starfire and run my fingers over the touchpads. That's all I can do, since they turn off power in the barracks at night. I'll lie there in the dark, thinking about Lisa, and Georgie, and Buddy's All-Night Burgers, and all the fun we used to pull off. But mostly I'll think about Rayno, and what great plans he cooks up.

I can't wait to see how he gets me out of this one.

CRAIG PADAWER

HOSTILE TAKEOVER

(1985)

AND THEN ONE NIGHT Swann's armored cars rolled into town, and the consolidation of flesh began.

They hit Ho's first, blasting their way past his sumos and into the pimp's private parlor, where his Ninja waited. But even Ho's master assassin was no match for Shimmy G's hi-tech killers with their Black & Decker implants and their five-speed rotating blades. They'd diced the Ninja like a carrot and then fed the pieces to Ho with his jade chopsticks before they finally killed him as well. Then they ground his geishas into tofu and continued north to The Hairy Clam, where they shot all the fish in Felsig's barrel. Real sportsmen, Swann's chromeheads. They stood at poolside with their telescopic eye implants and their 9 mm semiautomatic arm grafts . . . firing, reloading, and firing again, picking off patrons in the glass-bottom boats, murdering the mermaids as they tried to take cover beneath the inflatable lily pads, filling the porpoises so full of lead that they sank like submarines to the bottom of the tank.

The Clam's kitchen just happened to have run out of the house specialty at 11:00 that night and had called in an emergency order of Littlenecks to Veraciti's Seafood Supply, which had dispatched a truck immediately. They were just unloading the shellfish when Swann's goons struck. Felsig managed to slip out through the kitchen and escape in the fish king's refrigerated delivery truck accompanied by six cartons of red snapper filets, a pair of halibut hanging on hooks, and a crate of clams that chattered at him like a bundle of bones as the driver hit what seemed like every pothole between Harbor Street and the fish pier. Back at The Clam, Swann's chrome killers were snapping drill bits into their multifunction wrist sockets and boring holes in the skulls of Felsig's kitchen staff in an attempt to discover his whereabouts, as if in their mechanical naivete the overhauled imbeciles imagined that language was a liquid bottled up inside the body and any hole would decant it. In fact, the busboys had leaked as soon as they got a look at the hardware on Shimmy G's hoodlums, but the toolheads hadn't liked what they'd heard and they drilled the pimp's busboys dry, their gears seizing with rage. When that failed to produce Felsig, they burst into The Clam's plush grottoes, pried open the pimp's patented shell beds, shucked his nymphs, and minced them like mollusks. Then they blew the bottom out of the glass lagoon, drowning the diners below and flooding Harbor Street from Cod Place to Waterfront Drive.

Meanwhile, a second unit had struck at the cash gash end of Harbor Street and was moving south toward the blue-chip houses, gunning down street pimps and freelancers along the way, firebombing the budget brothels and the fast-fuck joints. They blew the lid off the Dick-in-the-Box on Eel Street, leveled the Wiener Queen, and wiped The Bun Factory right off the block. They hit the Instant Eatery on the corner of Harbor and Tuna Street, and some tax adder with her muff up against the drive-in window was divested of her assets along with the hired tongue who was delivering her Slurpy to her through the hole in the bulletproof glass.

While their counterparts to the south finished off Felsig's and moved on to The Sweat Shop, the northern unit raided The Side Show and Tufa's Club Zoo, neither of which had heavy security. The houses fell like dominoes. Swann's anti-tank missiles turned Tufa's elephants into hamburger, while what was left of the pimp's menagerie stampeded south, trampling wounded bathhouse boys and hookers hobbling along on broken heels. A small detachment of mechanical thugs remained behind to mop up the top end of Harbor Street while the northern unit's main force headed west on Oyster to take Rocheaux's office and knock out Brash, Sarsen & Scree's flagship facility. Then the troops regrouped two blocks south for an assault on The Rubber Womb.

Merkle had invested heavily in the latest weaponry and The Womb had a formidable security force, despite the mocking comments made by Merkle's colleagues. Vesuvius, who liked to boast about his own rented muscle, had once told Emma with a sneer that Merkle's inflatable bodyguards were "full of hot air."

"Hydrogen," Merkle corrected him, having overheard the remark.

"Hot air, hydrogen . . . same shit," Vito spat.

"I'm afraid you're quite mistaken. There's a definitive difference, Vito, and if you get any closer to Emile here with that vile cigar of yours, you'll discover it firsthand . . . and then foot, nose, teeth, and liver. In short, my friend, they'll be sweeping your pieces off the street."

"Pshshhhh!" Vito hissed derisively, his head snapping back as if he'd been slugged in the chin, smoke spewing from his mouth.

Merkle turned to Emma. "Good night, Ms. Labatt," he said. "You're to be commended on your tolerance, but surely a businesswoman of your caliber recognizes a profitless endeavor when she sees one." With that he wrapped his rubber scarf around his throat and slipped into the bulletproof overcoat being offered by one of his bodyguards. Then he bowed to Emma, pulled the brim of his black rubber fedora down over his brow with a squeak, and walked off flanked by four of his inflatable escorts.

"Hey, Merkle," Vesuvius had shouted after him, "fuck you, ya dumb bastard. You call that protection? They're nothing but a bunch a fuckin' balloons. That's right, fuckin' bunch a rubber scumbags with faces painted on 'em, that's all. It's like tryna stop a bullet with a goddamn condom, fer chrissake. Hey! Tell ya what, Merkle . . . I'll have my boys cut a hole in one of those balloon goons a yours and I'll wear him on my dick when I fuck your mother. How 'bout that? How's that for fuckin' protection? Hey, maybe you oughta fold one up and carry him in your wallet, cause that's all the protection they're gonna give ya."

In the end, Vito was right, not just about Merkle's security force, but about his entire inflatable enterprise. It was a credit to the pimp's miraculous craftsmanship that his entire nightclub, from floor to ceiling, from light fixtures to plumbing to windows, was nothing more than an elaborate balloon. But that sort of evanescent intricacy was only so admirable. Merkle paid the price for his genius in vulnerability. His inflatable men proved to be no match for Swann's mechanical killers. The chromeheads went through The Rubber Womb like a nail through a beach ball. Pulling steel stickpins from their copper neckties, they popped Merkle's balloon goons, and had at his dolls. Swann, who believed the penis was obsolete, an inefficient cord of meat vulnerable to viruses and vaginal bacteria, had replaced his killers' genitals with weaponry. Now the toolheads unzipped their flies, greased their barrels with balloon jelly, and rammed them up the rubber rectums of Merkle's dolls, pumping away until a twitch of pleasure in what remained of their flesh tripped their triggers, and they came in a burst of gunfire. The inflatable beauties popped like party balloons when the bullets struck, leaving their attackers clutching nothing but air and a few shreds of latex.

As johns jumped from the windows of The Womb and hoofed it up Harbor Street, Swann's clockwork killers went from room to rubber room, doing in Merkle's dolls, puncturing the air mattresses, the inflatable toilets, and the blow-up bathtubs. The air outside became so saturated with helium that Tufa's tigers sounded like tabbies as they fled down Harbor Street. Helium hissed from the inflatable walls and beams, and the nightclub began to collapse in on itself, to shrivel and fold, until finally the chrome assassins turned their flamethrowers on it, and The Womb went up with a *WHOOSH*. There was a single explosion as Merkle's hydrogen tank blew, and then it was over. All that remained of the club was a puddle of molten rubber.

Emma pushed through the bordello's revolving door and stepped out into the chaos of the street. Out on the avenue the traffic was frozen: drivers and passengers peered through their windows. The yap schlock hawkers and the cat dog vendors had left their carts and drifted to the curb like sleepwalkers summoned in a dream. She could hear animals howling, the braying of Tufa's pornographic donkeys. And beneath that another sound, a murmur like a mechanical parody of the harbor washing against the pier.

Then the northern end of the Harbor Street seemed to explode with movement. Refugees began streaming into the square: barefoot house whores wrapped in satin sheets, queens in kimonos zigzagging down the street like enormous butterflies as they tried to dodge the bullets that went zipping by. Jailbait and babymeat were borne along on a tide of trained tigers, inflatable whores, and wounded studs dressed in the Marquis de Sade's underwear. Emma saw a chimpanzee and a pair of Gneissman's naked midgets go galloping by on one of Tufa's zebras; they turned west on Oceanside, weaving through the stalled traffic until she lost sight of them. The sound of gunfire grew closer. Bullets ricocheted off the mansion's facade. Panicky passengers left their cars and fled up the avenue on foot.

The remnants of Merkle's security force fell back along the water, pursued by Swann's goons. Emma could see the mechanical killers now. They wore titanium zoot suits and steel fedoras, and they came marching down Harbor Street looking like a fleet of tanks designed by Oleg Cassini. Some of them had machine gun assemblies built right into their skulls, and their grinning heads rotated 360 degrees as they raked the streets with gunfire. Merkle's hydrogen hoodlums went off like incendiary bombs when the slugs hit them. Those who hadn't been hit returned fire with Uzis and Street Sweepers, but the bullets didn't even put a dent in the enemy's wardrobe.

As Emma ordered her women to pull back from the street, she could see Merkle's men tossing aside their weapons, stepping out of their lead loafers, and floating up into the night sky, rising above the flaming streets like rubber angels, until the wind carried them out over the harbor. Some of them would drift for days or weeks, finally floating to earth somewhere on the coast of Greenland or Labrador, where they would vainly hunt for helium like vampires hungry for blood, until finally, sagging and emaciated, they would expire on barren bluffs, where fisherman's wives would find them, take them home, and stitch them into raincoats for their sea-haunted husbands.

Back inside the mansion, Emma threw all her security at her front door, opened up the bar, and circulated among her customers to calm them. But as Swann's first army swept up from the south, the pincer closed, trapping the fleeing whores in the square. The desperate refugees stormed the mansion seeking asylum.

Emma prayed for fog to mask the carnage and inhibit the killers, but the night remained clear and the moon burned like a bulb. From the window she could see one of Galena's Gigantic Gigolos lying dead in the street, wearing nothing but his own blood. One of his coworkers crouched over him, moving like an astronaut in the merciless moonlight, his body so bloated with muscle he was barely able to bend. Over to the south a rocket struck G.A.S.M.'s headquarters and the old building burped smoke. Tracer fire arced across the square like a flock of burning birds. The two naked giants outside Emma's window looked now like a pair of Greek heroes that had been painted onto the wrong scenery: Achilles bawling over the death of his pornographic Patroclus as Paris fell to the Germans. A passing queen paused and began tugging at the mourner's arm with one hand as she clutched the front of her kimono closed with the other, but the giant wouldn't budge. She tried again, letting go of her robe and wrapping both her arms around his biceps, but it was like trying to uproot an oak tree. And then somehow the gigolo lost his balance and tipped backward. He lay there in the gutter with his arms waving in the air, like some enormous beetle, so weighed down by his own muscle that he was unable to sit up or flip himself over. The queen flapped her arms and screamed for help, her kimono billowing behind her in the frigid wind. Her hormone-grown breasts were stunted and pale in the moonlight, her prick shaven clean as an infant's and shriveled now with fear.

A bunch of streetwalkers, ever practical, responded to the queen's distress by tugging off their whorehoppers and flinging them through the mansion's stained-glass windows in an attempt to get Emma's attention.

Hippolyta opened up the bordello's arsenal and began arming the patrons, the whores, and the housekeeping staff, then joined Emma at the window and nervously surveyed the scene. To the north, along the curve of the water, Swann's killers fired surface-to-surface missiles from their prosthetic arm launchers, and the boardwalk crumbled like a cracker in the tracer-light. Cabs burned out on the avenue, and flaming figures raced down the streets like human shish kebabs. The lobby smelled of sulfur and burning meat. Shimmy G's southern units were already on the outskirts of the square. The trapped refugees would have the option of either being driven into the frigid harbor or slaughtered in the streets.

As rocket fire began to eat up the asphalt, the blowjob boys and anal artists stormed Emma's steps. Rocheaux's brats tried to scale the fence and were impaled on the wrought iron spikes where they flapped like fish on the end of a spear and whined through the night like tortured cats. Merkle's girls also fell prey to the spikes: their corpses hung from the fence like an atman's laundry, and whores hoisted themselves up by the dolls' deflated limbs—but the bordello's windows were too high and there was nowhere for them to go. Bullets cut into the crowd. There were screams as the sea of flesh surged forward and washed up against the mansion's facade.

The cops were nowhere in sight. And for all Emma knew, these were Vito's soldiers, mail ordered from some weapons warehouse in Georgia or Tennessee and kept under wraps until the moment was right. She had no choice but to open her doors.

That night her house took on the atmosphere of a field hospital. Her boudoirs were filled with wounded whores, and all her satin sheets went for bandages. Giles was busy in the kitchen, boiling his old mechanic's tools in hot water and performing makeshift surgeries on the chrome countertops, prying slugs out of house whores with a Phillips screwdriver and a pair of needle-nose pliers, and leaving it to Hector Citrine's seamstress to sew them up. They stacked the dead in the walk-in freezer. By dawn they were almost out of shelf space.

Even one of Merkle's helium whores managed to make it to Emma's place.

She was leaking, and Giles patched her up with a piece of electrical tape, then gave her mouth-to-mouth in an attempt to reinflate her. She perked up for a while, but as the night wore on her head began to wilt again, wrinkles appeared in her face and thighs, her latex tits began to shrink and droop. She seemed to be aging right before their eyes. They pumped some more air into her, but it was no good. She needed helium. Or maybe she was leaking from a hole they hadn't seen. By morning she was as flat as a floor mat. Emma wondered whether she was dead. How could you tell with a blowup doll, anyway? What vital signs did you check for? Air pressure? Surface tension? Finally they just pulled the plug on her. What was left of her helium escaped in one brief sigh. Emma thought she felt the air in the room change ever so slightly, and she held her breath for a moment, as if she were afraid that by breathing she might inhale the whore's soul. Then she folded up the girl's empty skin and tucked it away in a drawer. By that point, all she could think of was that Merkle's ingenuity had saved her a space in the freezer.

She waited all night for the attack, but it never came. Swann's troops swung west, bypassing her bordello. A couple of hours later heavy artillery could be heard from the south. It went on for a solid hour. The mansion's beams rattled in the thunder, and plaster rained down from the kitchen ceiling like confectionery sugar, powdering the whores' open wounds so that their hearts and livers looked like candied fruits. Giles called for more water while Emma provided what suction she could with a turkey baster.

Toward dawn the gunfire began to die down. Outside the blood froze in the streets, and come morning children with ice skates appeared, carving figure eights in the crimson pools.

JAMES PATRICK KELLY

RAT

[1986]

RAT HAD STASHED the dust in four plastic capsules and then swallowed them. From the stinging at the base of his ribs he guessed they were now squeezing into his duodenum. Still plenty of time. The bullet train had been shooting through the vacuum of the TransAtlantic tunnel for almost two hours now; they would arrive at Port Authority/Koch soon. Customs had already been fixed, according to the marechal. All Rat had to do was to get back to his nest, lock the smart door behind him, and put the word out on his protected nets. He had enough Algerian Yellow to dust at least half the cerebrums on the East Side. If he could turn this deal he would be rich enough to bathe in Dom Perignon and dry himself with Gromaire tapestries. Another pang shot down his left flank. Instinctively his hind leg came off the seat and scratched at air.

There was only one problem; Rat had decided to cut the marechal out. That meant he had to lose the old man's spook before he got home.

The spook had attached herself to him at Marseilles. She braided her blonde hair in pigtails. She had freckles, wore braces on her teeth. Tiny breasts nudged a modest silk turtleneck. She looked to be between twelve and fourteen. Cute. She had probably looked that way for twenty years, would stay the same another twenty if she did not stop a slug first or get cut in half by some automated security laser that tracked only heat and could not read—or be troubled by—cuteness. Their passports said they were Mr. Sterling Jaynes and daughter Jessalynn, of Forest Hills, New York. She was typing in her notebook, chubby fingers curled over the keys. Homework? A letter to a boyfriend? More likely she was operating on some corporate database with scalpel code of her own devising.

"Ne fais pas semblant d'étudier, ma petite," Rat said. *"Que fais-tu?"*

"Oh, Daddy," she said, pouting, "can't we go back to plain old English? After all, we're almost home." She tilted her notebook so that he could see the display. It read, "Two rows back, second seat from aisle. Fed. If he knew you were carrying, he'd cut the dust out of you and wipe his ass with your pelt." She tapped the return key and the message disappeared.

"All right, dear." He arched his back, fighting a surge of adrenaline that made his incisors click. "You know, all of a sudden I'm feeling hungry. Should we do something here on the train or wait until we get to New York?" Only the spook saw him gesture back toward the fed.

"Why don't we wait for the station? More choices there."

"As you wish, dear." He wanted her to take the fed out now but there was nothing more he dared say. He licked his hands nervously and groomed the fur behind his short, thick ears to pass the time.

The International Arrivals Hall at Koch Terminal was unusually quiet for a Thursday night. It smelled to Rat like a setup. The passengers from the bullet shuffled through the echoing marble vastness toward the row of customs stations. Rat was unarmed; if they were going to put up a fight the spook would have to provide the firepower. But Rat was not a fighter, he was a runner. Their instructions were to pass through Station Number Four. As they waited in line Rat spotted the federally appointed vigilante behind them. The classic invisible man: neither handsome nor ugly, five-ten, about one-seventy, brown hair, dark suit, white shirt. He looked bored.

"Do you have anything to declare?" The customs agent looked bored too. Everybody looked bored except Rat who had two million new dollars' worth of illegal drugs in his gut and a fed ready to carve them out of him.

"We hold these truths to be self-evident," said Rat, "that all men are created equal." He managed a feeble grin—as if this were a witticism and not the password.

"Daddy, please!" The spook feigned embarrassment. "I'm sorry, ma'am; it's his idea of a joke. It's the Declaration of Independence, you know."

The customs agent smiled as she tousled the spook's hair. "I know that, dear. Please put your luggage on the conveyor." She gave a perfunctory glance at her monitor as their suitcases passed through the scanner and then nodded at Rat. "Thank you, sir, and have a pleasant . . ." The insincere thought died on her lips as she noticed the fed pushing through the line toward them. Rat saw her spin toward the exit at the same moment that the spook thrust her notebook computer into the scanner. The notebook stretched a blue finger of point discharge toward the magnetic lens just before the overhead lights novaed and went dark. The emergency backup failed as well. Rat's snout filled with the acrid smell of electrical fire. Through the darkness came shouts and screams, thumps and cracks—the crazed pounding of a stampede gathering momentum.

He dropped to all fours and skittered across the floor. Koch Terminal was his territory; he had crisscrossed its many levels with scent trails. Even in total darkness he could find his way.

But in his haste he cracked his head against a pair of stockinged knees and a squawking weight fell across him, crushing the breath from his lungs. He felt an icy stab on his hindquarters and scrabbled at it with his hind leg. His toes came away wet and he squealed. There was an answering scream and the point of a shoe drove into him, propelling him across the floor. He rolled left and came up running. Up a dead escalator, down a carpeted hall. He stood upright and stretched to his full twenty-six inches, hands scratching until they found the emergency bar across the fire door. He hurled himself at it, a siren shrieked and with a whoosh the door opened, dumping him into an alley. He lay there for a moment, gasping, half in and half out of Koch Terminal. With the certain knowledge that he was bleeding to death he touched the coldness on his back. A sticky purple substance; he sniffed, then tasted it. Ice cream. Rat threw back his head and laughed. The high squeaky sound echoed in the deserted alley.

But there was no time to waste. He could already hear the buzz of police hovers swooping down from the night sky. The blackout might keep them busy for a while; Rat was more worried about the fed. And the spook. They would be out soon enough, looking for him. Rat scurried down the alley toward the street. He glanced quickly at the terminal, now a black hole in the galaxy of bright holographic sleaze that was Forty-Second Street. A few cops with flashlights were trying to fight against the flow of panicky travelers pouring from its open doors. Rat smoothed his ruffled fur and turned away from the disaster, walking crosstown. His instincts said to run but Rat forced himself to dawdle like a hick shopping for big city excitement. He grinned at the pimps and window-shopped the hardware stores. He paused in front of a pair of mirror-image sex stops—GIRLS! LIVE! GIRLS! and LIVE! GIRLS! LIVE!—to sniff the pheromone-scented sweat pouring off an androgynous robot shill which was working the sidewalk. The robot obligingly put its hand to Rat's crotch but he pushed it away with a hiss and continued on. At last, sure that he was not being followed, he powered up his wallet and tapped into the transnet to summon a hovercab. The wallet informed him that the city had cordoned off midtown airspace to facilitate rescue operations at Koch Terminal. It advised trying the subway or a taxi. Since he had no intention of sticking an ID chip—even a false one!—into a subway turnstile, he stepped to the curb and began watching the traffic.

The rebuilt Checker that rattled to a stop beside him was a patchwork of orange ABS and stainless-steel armor. "No we leave Manhattan," said a speaker on the roof light. "No we north of a hundred and ten." Rat nodded and the door locks popped. The passenger compartment smelled of chlorobenzylmalononitrile and urine.

"First Avenue Bunker," said Rat, sniffing. "Christ, it stinks back here. Who was your last fare—the circus?"

"Troubleman." The speaker connections were loose, giving a scratchy edge to the cabbie's voice. The locks reengaged as the Checker pulled away from the curb. "Ha-has get a full snoot of tear gas in this hack."

Rat had already spotted the pressure vents in the floor. He peered through the gloom at the registration. A slogan had been lased over it—probably by one of the new Mitsubishi penlights. "Free the dead." Rat smiled: the dead were his customers. People who had chosen the dusty road. Twelve to eighteen months of glorious addiction: synesthetic orgasms, recursive hallucinations leading to a total sensory overload and an ecstatic death experience. One dose was all it took to start down the dusty road. The feds were trying to cut off the supply—with dire consequences for the dead. They could live a few months longer without dust but their joyride down the dusty road was transformed into a grueling marathon of withdrawal pangs and madness. Either way, they were dead. Rat settled back onto the seat. The penlight graffito was a good omen. He reached into his pocket and pulled out a leather strip that had been soaked with a private blend of fat-soluble amphetamines and began to gnaw at it.

From time to time he could hear the cabbie monitoring NYPD net for flame-outs or wildcat tolls set up by street gangs. They had to detour to heavily guarded Park Avenue all the way uptown to Fifty-Ninth before doubling back toward the bunker. Originally built to protect UN diplomats from terrorists, the bunker had gone condo after the dissolution of the United Nations. Its hype was that it was the "safest address in the city." Its rep was that most of the owners' association were prime candidates either for a mindwipe or an extended vacation on a fed punkfarm.

"Hey, Fare," said the cabbie, "Net says the dead be rioting front of your door. Crash through or roll away?"

The fur along Rat's backbone went erect. "Cops?"

"Letting them play for now."

"You've got armor for a crash?"

"Shit yes. Park this hack to ground zero for the right fare." The cabbie's laugh was static. "Don't worry, bunkerman. Give those deadboys a shot of old CS gas and they be too busy scratching they eyes out to bother us much."

Rat tried to smooth his fur. He could crash the riot and get stuck. But if he waited either the spook or the fed would be stepping on his tail before long. Rat had no doubt that both had managed to plant locator bugs on him.

"'Course, riot crashing don't come cheap," said the cabbie.

"Triple the meter." The fare was already over two hundred dollars for the fifteen-minute ride. "Shoot for Bay Two—the one with the yellow door." He pulled out his wallet and started tapping its luminescent keys. "I'm sending recognition code now."

He heard the cabbie notify the cops that they were coming through. Rat could feel the Checker accelerate as they passed the cordon, and he had a glimpse of strobing lights, cops in blue body armor, a tank studded with water cannons. Suddenly the cabbie braked and Rat pitched forward against his shoulder harness. The Checker's solid rubber tires squealed and there was the thump of something bouncing off the hood. They had slowed to a crawl and the dead closed around them.

Rat could not see out the front because the cabbie was protected from his passengers by steel plate. But the side windows filled with faces streaming with sweat and tears and blood. Twisted faces, screaming faces, faces etched by the agonies of withdrawal. The soundproofing muffled their howls. Fear and exhilaration filled Rat as he watched them pass. If only they knew how close they were to dust, he thought. He imagined the dead faces gnawing through the cab's armor in a frenzy, pausing only to spit out broken teeth. It was wonderful. The riot was proof that the dust market was still white hot. The dead must be desperate to attack the bunker like this looking for a flash. He decided to bump the price of his dust another ten percent.

Rat heard a clatter on the roof: then someone began to jump up and down. It was like being inside a kettledrum. Rat sank claws into the seat and arched his back. "What are you waiting for? Gas them, damn it!"

"Hey, Fare. Stuff ain't cheap. We be fine—almost there."

A woman with bloody red hair matted to her head pressed her mouth against the window and screamed. Rat reared up on his hind legs and made biting feints at her. Then he saw the penlight in her hand. At the last moment Rat threw himself backward. The penlight flared and the passenger compartment filled with the stench of melting plastic. A needle of coherent light singed the fur on Rat's left flank; he squealed and flopped onto the floor, twitching.

The cabbie opened the external gas vents and abruptly the faces dropped away from the windows. The cab accelerated, bouncing as it ran over the fallen dead. There was a dazzling transition from the darkness of the violent night to the floodlit calm of Bay Number Two. Rat scrambled back onto the seat and looked out the back window in time to see the hydraulic doors of the outer lock swing shut. Something was caught between them—something that popped and spattered. Then the inner door rolled down on its track like a curtain coming down on a bloody final act.

Rat was almost home. Two security guards in armor approached. The door locks popped and Rat climbed out of the cab. One of the guards leveled a burster at his head; the other wordlessly offered him a printreader. He thumbed it and the bunker's computer verified him immediately.

"Good evening, sir," said one of the guards. "Little rough out there tonight. Did you have luggage?"

The front door of the cab opened and Rat heard the low whine of electric motors as a mechanical arm lowered the cabbie's wheelchair onto the floor of the bay. She was a gray-haired woman with a rheumy stare who looked like she belonged in a rest home in New Jersey. A knitted shawl covered her withered legs. "You said triple." The cab's hoist clicked and released the chair; she rolled toward him. "Six hundred and sixty-nine dollars."

"No luggage, no." Now that he was safe inside the bunker, Rat regretted his panic-stricken generosity. A credit transfer from one of his own accounts was out of the question. He slipped his last thousand-dollar bubble chip into his wallet's card reader, dumped three hundred and thirty-one dollars from it into a Bahamian laundry loop, and then dropped the chip into her outstretched hand. She accepted it dubiously: for a minute he expected her to bite into it like they did sometimes on fossil TV. Old people made him nervous. Instead she inserted the chip into her own card reader and frowned at him.

"How about a tip?"

Rat sniffed. "Don't pick up strangers."

One of the guards guffawed obligingly. The other pointed but Rat saw the skunk port in the wheelchair a millisecond too late. With a wet plop the chair emitted a gaseous stinkball which bloomed like an evil flower beneath Rat's whiskers. One guard tried to grab at the rear of the chair but the old cabbie backed suddenly over his foot. The other guard aimed his burster.

The cabbie smiled like a grandmother from hell. "Under the pollution index. No law against sharing a little scent, boys. And you wouldn't want to hurt me anyway. The hack monitors my EEG. I go flat and it goes berserk."

The guard with the bad foot stopped hopping. The guard with the gun shrugged. "It's up to you, sir."

Rat batted the side of his head several times and then buried his snout beneath his armpit. All he could smell was rancid burger topped with sulphur sauce. "Forget it. I haven't got time."

"You know," said the cabbie. "I never get out of the hack but I just wanted to see what kind of person would live in a place like this." The lifts whined as the arm fitted its fingers into the chair. "And now I know." She cackled as the arm gathered her back into the cab. "I'll park it by the door. The cops say they're ready to sweep the street."

The guards led Rat to the bank of elevators. He entered the one with the open door, thumbed the print reader and spoke his access code.

"Good evening, sir," said the elevator. "Will you be going straight to your rooms?"

"Yes."

"Very good, sir. Would you like a list of the communal facilities currently open to serve you?"

There was no shutting the sales pitch off so Rat ignored it and began to lick the stink from his fur.

"The pool is open for lap swimmers only," said the elevator as the doors closed. "All environmats except for the weightless room are currently in use. The sensory deprivation tanks will be occupied until eleven. The surrogatorium is temporarily out of female chassis; we apologize for any inconvenience . . ."

The cab moved down two and a half floors and then stopped just above the subbasement. Rat glanced up and saw a dark gap opening in the array of light diffuser panels. The spook dropped through it.

". . . the holo therapist is off line until eight tomorrow morning but the interactive sex booths will stay open until midnight. The drug dispensary . . ."

She looked as if she had been water-skiing through the sewer. Her blonde hair was wet and smeared with dirt; she had lost the ribbons from her pigtails. Her jeans were torn at the knees and there was an ugly scrape on the side of her face. The silk turtleneck clung wetly to her. Yet despite her dishevelment, the hand that held the penlight was as steady as a jewel cutter's.

"There seems to be a minor problem," said the elevator in a soothing voice. "There is no cause for alarm. This unit is temporarily nonfunctional. Maintenance has been notified and is now working to correct the problem. In case of emergency, please contact Security. We regret this temporary inconvenience."

The spook fired a burst of light at the floor selector panel; it spat fire at them and went dark. "Where the hell were you?" said the spook. "You said the McDonald's in Times Square if we got separated."

"Where were you?" Rat rose up on his hind legs. "When I got there the place was swarming with cops."

He froze as the tip of the penlight flared. The spook traced a rough outline of Rat on the stainless-steel door behind him. "Fuck your lies," she said. The beam came so close that Rat could smell his fur curling away from it. "I want the dust."

"Trespass alert!" screeched the wounded elevator. A note of urgency had crept into its artificial voice. "Security reports unauthorized persons within the complex. Residents are urged to return immediately to their apartments and engage all personal security devices. Do not be alarmed. We regret this temporary inconvenience."

The scales on Rat's tail fluffed. "We have a deal. The marechal needs my networks to move his product. So let's get out of here before . . ."

"The dust."

Rat sprung at her with a squeal of hatred. His claws caught on her turtleneck and he struck repeatedly at her open collar, gashing her neck with his long red incisors. Taken aback by the swiftness and ferocity of his attack, she dropped the penlight and tried to fling him against the wall. He held fast, worrying at her and chittering rabidly. When she stumbled under the open emergency exit in the ceiling he leapt again. He cleared the suspended ceiling, caught himself on the inductor and scrabbled up onto the hoist cables. Light was pouring into the shaft from above; armored guards had forced the door open and were climbing down toward the stalled car. Rat jumped from the cables across five feet of open space to the counterweight and huddled there, trying to use its bulk to shield himself from the spook's fire. Her stand was short and inglorious. She threw a dazzler out of the hatch, hoping to blind the guards, then tried to pull herself through. Rat could hear the shriek of burster fire. He waited until he could smell the aroma of broiling meat and scorched plastic before he emerged from the shadows and signaled to the security team.

A squad of apologetic guards rode the service elevator with Rat down to the storage subbasement where he lived. When he had first looked at the bunker, the broker had been reluctant to rent him the abandoned rooms, insisting that he live above ground with the other residents. But all of the suites they showed him were unacceptably open, clean and uncluttered. Rat much preferred his musty dungeon, where odors lingered in the still air. He liked to fall asleep to the booming of the ventilation system on the level above him and slept easier knowing that he was as far away from the stink of other people as he could get in the city.

The guards escorted him to the gleaming brass smart door and looked away discreetly as he entered his passcode on the keypad. He had ordered it custom-built from Mosler so that it would recognize high-frequency squeals well beyond the range of human hearing. He called to it and then pressed trembling fingers onto the printreader. His bowels had loosened in terror during the firefight and the capsules had begun to sting terribly. It was all he could do to keep from defecating right there in the hallway. The door sensed the guards and beeped to warn him of their presence. He punched in the override sequence impatiently and the seals broke with a sigh.

"Have a pleasant evening, sir," said one of the guards as he scurried inside. "And don't worry ab . . ." The door cut him off as it swung shut.

Against all odds, Rat had made it. For a moment he stood, tail switching against the inside of the door, and let the magnificent chaos of his apartment soothe his jangled nerves. He had earned his reward—the dust was all his now. No one could take it away from him. He saw himself in a shard of mirror propped up against an empty THC aerosol and wriggled in self-congratulation. He was the richest rat on the East Side, perhaps in the entire city.

He picked his way through a maze formed by a jumble of overburdened steel shelving left behind years, perhaps decades, ago. The managers of the bunker had offered to remove them and their contents before he moved in; Rat had insisted that they stay. When the fire inspector had come to approve his newly installed sprinkler system she had been horrified at the clutter on the shelves and had threatened to condemn the place. It had cost him plenty to buy her off but it had been worth it. Since then Rat's trove of junk had at least doubled in size. For years no one had seen it but Rat and the occasional cockroach.

Relaxing at last, Rat stopped to pull a mildewed wingtip down from his huge collection of shoes; he loved the bouquet of fine old leather and gnawed it whenever he could. Next to the shoes was a heap of books: his private library. One of Rat's favorite delicacies was the first edition *Leaves of Grass* which he had pilfered from the rare book collection at the New York Public Library. To celebrate his safe arrival he ripped out page 43 for a snack and stuffed it into the wingtip. He dragged the shoe over a pile of broken sheetrock and past shelves filled with scrap electronics: shattered monitors and dead typewriters, microwaves and robot vacuums. He had almost reached his nest when the fed stepped from behind a dirty Hungarian flag that hung from a broken florescent light fixture.

Startled, Rat instinctively hurled himself at the crack in the wall where he had built his nest. But the fed was too quick. Rat did not recognize the weapon; all he knew was that when it hissed Rat lost all feeling in his hindquarters. He landed in a heap but continued to crawl, slowly, painfully.

"You have something I want." The fed kicked him. Rat skidded across the concrete floor toward the crack, leaving a thin gruel of excrement in his wake. Rat continued to crawl until the fed stepped on his tail, pinning him.

"Where's the dust?"

"I . . . I don't . . ."

The fed stepped again; Rat's left fibula snapped like cheap plastic. He felt no pain.

"The dust." The fed's voice quavered strangely.

"Not here. Too dangerous."

"Where?" The fed released him. "Where?"

Rat was surprised to see that the fed's gun hand was shaking. For the first time he looked up at the man's eyes and recognized the telltale yellow tint. Rat realized then how badly he had misinterpreted the fed's expression back at Koch. Not bored. Empty. For an instant he could not believe his extraordinarily good fortune. Bargain for time, he told himself. There's still a chance. Even though he was cornered he knew his instinct to fight was wrong.

"I can get it for you fast if you let me go," said Rat. "Ten minutes, fifteen. You look like you need it."

"What are you talking about?" The fed's bravado started to crumble and Rat knew he had the man. The fed wanted the dust for himself. He was one of the dead.

"Don't make it hard on yourself," said Rat. "There's a terminal in my nest. By the crack. Ten minutes." He started to pull himself toward the nest. He knew the fed would not dare stop him; the man was already deep into withdrawal. "Only ten minutes and you can have all the dust you want." The poor fool could not hope to fight the flood of neuroregulators pumping crazily across his synapses. He might break any minute, let his weapon slip from trembling hands. Rat reached the crack and scrambled through into comforting darkness.

The nest was built around a century-old shopping cart and a stripped subway bench. Rat had filled the gaps in with pieces of synthetic rubber, a hubcap, plastic greeting cards, barbed wire, disk casings, baggies, a No Parking sign and an assortment of bones. Rat climbed in and lowered himself onto the soft bed of shredded thousand-dollar bills. The profits of six years of deals and betrayals, a few dozen murders and several thousand dusty deaths.

The fed sniffled as Rat powered up his terminal to notify security. "Someone set me up some vicious bastard slipped it to me I don't know when I think it was Barcelona . . . it would kill Sarah to see . . ." He began to weep. "I wanted to turn myself in . . . they keep working on new treatments you know but it's not fair damn it! The success rate is less than . . . I made my first buy two weeks only two God it seems . . . killed a man to get some lousy dust . . . but they're right it's, it's, I can't begin to describe what it's like . . ."

Rat's fingers flew over the glowing keyboard, describing his situation, the layout of the rooms, a strategy for the assault. He had overriden the smart door's recognition sequence. It would be tricky but security could take the fed out if they were quick and careful. Better to risk a surprise attack than to dicker with an armed and unraveling dead man.

"I really ought to kill myself . . . would be best but it's not only me . . . I've seen ten-year-olds . . . what kind of animal sells dust to kids . . . I should kill myself. And you." Something changed in the fed's voice as Rat signed off. "And you." He stooped and reached through the crack.

"It's coming," said Rat quickly. "By messenger. Ten doses. By the time you get to the door it should be here." He could see the fed's hand and burrowed into the rotting pile of money. "You wait by the door, you hear? It's coming any minute."

"I don't want it." The hand was so large it blocked the light. Rat's fur went erect and he arched his spine. "Keep your fucking dust."

Rat could hear the guards fighting their way through the clutter. Shelves crashed. So clumsy, these men.

"It's you I want." The hand sifted through the shredded bills, searching for Rat. He had no doubt that the fed could crush the life from him—the hand was huge now. In the darkness he could count the lines on the palm, follow the whorls on the fingertips. They seemed to spin in Rat's brain—he was losing control. He realized then that one of the capsules must have broken, spilling a megadose of first-quality Algerian Yellow dust into his gut. With a hallucinatory clarity he imagined sparks streaming through his blood, igniting neurons like tinder. Suddenly the guards did not matter. Nothing mattered except that he was cornered. When he could no longer fight the instinct to strike, the fed's hand closed around him. The man was stronger than Rat could have imagined. As the fed hauled him—clawing and biting—back into the light, Rat's only thought was of how terrifyingly large a man was. So much larger than a rat.

LISA MASON

ARACHNE

(1987)

THE FLIER LEVITATES from a vermilion funnel and hovers. Stiff chatoyant wings, monocoque fuselage, compound visual apparatus. The flier skims over the variegated planetscape, seeking another spore source. Olfactory sensors switch on. The desired stimuli are detected; another spore source is located.

Down the flier dips. But the descent is disrupted for a moment by atmospheric turbulence. The flier's fine landing gear is swept against a translucent aerial line, as strong as steel and sticky with glue. A beating wing tangles in more lines. The flier writhes.

The trapper hulks at the edge of the net. Stalked eyebuds swivel, pedipalps tense. At the tug of the flier's struggler, the trapper scuttles down a suspended line, eight appendages gripping the spacerope with acrobatic agility. The trapper spits an arc of glue over the flier's wings, guides the fiber around the flier's slim waist. A pair of black slicers dripping with goo snap around the flier's neck.

• • •

Carly Quester struggles out of the swoon. Blackout smears across the crisp white cube of her telelink like a splash of ash rain down a window. It's happened again. Her system crashes for a monstrous second, she plunges into deep, black nothing. Then, inexplicably, she's in link again, hanging like a child on a spinning swing to a vertiginous interface with the Venue.

Panic snaps at her. How many seconds lost this time?

"We will now hear *Martino v. Quik Slip Microship, Inc.*," announces the Arbiter. Edges of his telelink gleam like razor blades. His presence in the Venue, a massive face draped in black, towers like an Easter Island godhead into the upper perimeter of telespace. The perimeter is a flat, gray cloudbank.

"On what theory does Quik Slip Microchip counterclaim to quiet title when Rosa Martino has been titleholder to the *Wordsport Glossary* for thirty-five years? Mediator for defendant? Ms. Quester?"

Carly hears her name—muffled, tinny—through the neckjack. Her answer jams in her throat. Weird, she shouldn't feel her body in link. For an eerie second she feels like she's *inside* the telelink, sweating and heaving inside the airless, computer-constructed telespace itself. Her body, hunched over the terminal in her windowless cubicle at Ava & Rice, wrapped up in a web of wires, mutters a curse.

But her presence in the Venue is struck dumb.

Gleeful static from the two scruffy solos representing the plaintiff, Martino. Carly can hear them ripple with excitement, killers closing in on their prey.

Of course, they're on contingency, and old lady Martino probably couldn't even scare up the filing fees. One of them, a weaselly hack, shrugs at the whirring seconds on the chronograph and says, "Not defaulting on your crooked counterclaim, are ya, hotshot?"

"Mediator for defense? The mediator from Ava and Rice? *Ms. Quester?*" thunders the Arbiter. "You have thirty seconds to log in your counterclaim."

Telelinks of the jury, two rows of red-veined, glassy eyes floating across the purple right perimeter of the Venue, glance doubtfully at each other. The silvery pupils dart to and fro.

Gritty bile bites at the base of Carly's throat. A peculiar ache throbs in her jaw, thrusts icy fingers into her neck. She tries audio again, but her presence in the Venue is still silent.

"Huh, hotshot?" goads the solo. His telelink has the sloppy look and gravelly sound cheap equipment produces. But for a second, he manages to hot-wire an I-only access into her telelink.

"You ball-breakers from the big firms, with your prime link. You think you're so tough. Watch out, hotshot. I'm going to eat you alive this time, hotshot."

The big board across the back perimeter of the Venue hums and clicks. Gaudy liquid crystal projections in each division indicate the moment. In Stats, the luminous red Beijing dial registers another three hundred thousand births. *Chik-chik-chik-chik!* Ten seconds later on Docket—*bing!*—the eminent mediation firm of Ava & Rice registers as defense for Pop Pharmaceutical against the Chinese women who claim they took glucose, instead of birth control pills. In Trade, bids for rice futures soar. On News, reports of fifteen suicides of corn investors are filed.

"In ten seconds your client will have defaulted, Ms. Quester, and I will cite you for contempt of this Venue—obstructing the speedy dispensation of justice," says the Arbiter.

"I'm sorry, Your Honor, request a recess," Carly says finally. Audio feeds back with an earsplitting whine.

Her telelink suddenly oscillates crazily, sharp white edges flipping black-white-purple-white, like her terminal's shorting out. It's all she can do to keep logged in. Metallic tickle—pain of electrical shock gooses her body to raise a limp hand and refocus the projection.

"On what grounds?" demands the Arbiter.

"I'm—I'm sick."

Jagged flash; the Arbiter's gavel cracks; telespace vibrates. "Mediation recessed until next week, this same time. Ms. Quester, you will approach the bench."

As Carly approaches, the solo zooms in with one last I-only. "Hey hotshot, hotshot," he says in a cushy vibe. "You new, right? A word to the wise, hotshot. The Arbiter, he hates to wait. Got a reputation for the fastest Venue in town. He disposes sixty mediations an hour sometimes. You hold him up, hotshot, you in trouble. Better talk fast, better have a rap. I'll see you in the Venue, hotshot."

The solo logs off, extinguishing the smeary bulb of his presence in telespace.

Fully in link at last, Carly slips and slides up to the Arbiter's quarters. No privacy in the gleaming metal construct of telespace; no shadowed corner, no hidden booth behind which to hide her humiliation. All the blank eyes stare at her.

"Ms. Quester, you are hereby cited under Rule Two of the Code of Civil Procedure for obstruction of the speedy dispensation of justice. You are suspended from this Venue for thirty days."

Thirty days. Thirty days suspended from the Venue could cost Carly her first job, a *great* job, with the prosperous mediation firm of Ava & Rice. How many other bright, qualified applicants did she beat out for this job? Three thousand? How many other bright, qualified applicants would vie for her position if she lost it? Ten thousand?

Her presence in the Venue sparkles with bright panic. "I'm permitted to show reasonable cause under Rule Two, Your Honor."

"Proceed."

"I blacked out for a second, I've not been well . . ."

"If the mediator cannot prepare the mediation you extend, you re-petition, you re-calendar, you notify the Venue, Ms. Quester, in advance. Dismissed."

"But, Your Honor, I had no warning. I just went down for a second, no warning at all. I've not been well, it's true, but not so bad as to keep me out of the Venue. Your Honor, I had no warning, please believe me."

The Arbiter's eyeball zooms in on her flickering link for a close-up. His glittering pupil pulses with his plain doubt. "You've not been well but not so bad, but your system went down. All of a sudden! Oh, yes! You young wires, holding up my Venue with your lame excuses. I know why link fails most of the time. I should cite you for abuse of altering substances, too."

Carly's teeth begin to chatter; a puddle of urine floods her plastic seat. Then a fouler, hotter wash of shame. During her first link fifteen years ago, her ten-year-old body had disgraced her like this, in the presence of two hundred other link-prep students. She feels her body stress out at the memory of her juvenile dishonor. Her presence in the Venue vacillates.

"I'm not on drugs, Your Honor. I'm ill, I tell you, it's something insidious striking without warning. It could be cancer or radiation poisoning."

"Or the flu? Or a hangover? Or the disposal ate your brief?"

The Venue quivers with pitiless laughter from scores of unseen throats. The spectacle of a peer's downfall is cause for rejoicing.

"Your Honor, request permission to enter medical documentation to establish reasonable cause."

"Oh, very well, you're new. Permission granted, Ms. Quester. Submit your documentation before your next mediation date. This Venue will now hear *Sing Tao Development v. Homeowners' Association of Death Valley*. Issue is breach of warranty under federal standards governing the relocation of low-income housing into public parkland. Mediation for the defense?"

A team from Ava & Rice logs into the Venue with a brilliantly constructed defense. A silver spiral twirls across telespace, frosty tail ejecting wisps of pale yellow sophisms into its own blue-lipped devouring mouth. Standards met under the extraordinary circumstances of the relocation *or* standards not applicable under the extraordinary circumstances of the relocation; thus, in either case, no breach. Mediation for plaintiff withdraws the complaint in two seconds. Screams of outrage and despair whistle through the public telespace. Someone logs in a whimpering five-year-old child dying of third-degree sunburns. The Arbiter's gavel booms like doom. Dismissed! In one second the homeowners' association files suit against its former mediator. *Teep!* On Docket, Ava & Rice registers as new mediation in the malpractice suit brought by the Homeowners' Association of Death Valley.

Carly logs out of telespace.

And links out into a heap of flesh and ooze, sprawled in her windowless cubicle at Ava & Rice. Blown it, she's blown the mediation bad. Every first-year mediator's nightmare come true. Carly rips the neckjack out, spills half a bottle of denatured alcohol into the needle-thin aperture. Grimaces as a tincture of pure alcohol bursts into her brain's blood. Messy, careless—shit! Get too much of that old evil backrub up your linkslit—bang!—you're dead, grunt. Happens every now and again around the firm, someone just drops dead.

She swabs herself off as best she can and flees her dim cubicle, link still flickering with fluorescent green light. Jogs down the endless corridor of cubicles, working off panic with sheer locomotion.

The mediation firm of Ava & Rice boasts five hundred partners, three thousand associates, one thousand secretaries, five hundred clerk-messengers, and ten thousand terminals interfaced with a mammoth sengine, all installed in a forty-story building downtown.

At every open door, the limp body of a mediator is wired up to a terminal. Some are as wasted as junkies, rolled-back eyes between precipitous skull bones. Some are bloated with the sloth, raw lips crusty with food solutions piped down their throats.

Everyone's got a different handle on practicing mediation, but the basics are the same. *Time is of the essence. When in doubt, dispute. When in the Venue, win.* The volume of mediation is astronomical. Planning for the future becomes obsolete overnight. Catastrophe strikes with regularity. Billions of bucks are to be made, and you'd better grab them before someone else does.

How many bright, qualified applicants would vie for Carly's position when the personnel committee finds out about her failure in the Venue? Fifteen thousand?

• • •

Deep in the heart of Ava & Rice, the library hums with a low, soft growl like the roll of a distant surf. The vast, shadowed hall is set with fluorescent amber terminals, stacked row upon row, up to the flat, smeary ceiling.

Before every flickering screen lies a mediator jacked into link. The steady hum comes from the controls: temperature, humidity, luminosity, radiation. All for the machines. The air in the library is cool, stagnant, tinged with a faint metallic stench. The hum gnaws at the nerves.

The big board across the library's west wall flashes like an arcade. Down from thirty state Venues shoot twenty thousand decisions on whether foreign assets may be frozen when national property is seized by revolutionaries. *Define revolutionaries. Zing!* The government freezes five billion bank accounts and deposits their funds into a slushy umber escrow. Specialists in these matters, jacked into library links for as long as they can stand it, loll on their benches, moan listlessly. Flecks of data crawl across their raw neuroprograms like ants on meat.

Carly sneaks in, slipping through a sullen crew hanging around the doorway. She leans against the cool, grimy wall, shrinking from everyone's sight. News travels fast; surely everyone knows of her disgrace. The doorway gang is skin-popping scag—anything to ease away the whine of link.

"So, Quester," says an associate from the Death Valley team. Cool cannibal gaze, supercilious link-bitten smile. "Arbiter suspend you? Too bad. Maybe you can get a job in research somewhere. Process mediation data all day."

"You wish, Rox," Carly says in a steady voice, but she cringes from the dead-eyed faces that turn toward her. "Arbiter won't suspend me. I must have a bug in my link. I can prove it."

"Sure, Quester. We saw. We all saw your link in the Venue. We don't fault you, Quester. Blackout in link, it can happen." Rox tips her head back, cracking her neck cord, and snorts a hotline. She drools as the drug hits her, spittle staining the ragged three-piece suit that fits her like a man's. "But if you can't handle link, Quester, don't go into the life."

Carly seizes Rox's wrist, thrusts it back, pins it at an odd angle. "Rox, I'm telling you, I'm not on a binge. Something's wrong, my system went down—"

"Yeah, doll, your system went down. And then?"

Carly turns. From the double bar on his ragged lapel, he's a middle-level.

From his desperate look, not on the fast track. But not as bad as the menopausal ones can be in this business, with their cold killer eyes and vampire skin. This one's got a ripple of muscles under the suit, a shot of hots in the look he gives her. Carly rolls her pupils back into her eye-sockets, scans the firm's roster, IDs him: *Wolfe, D.*

"And then nothing," she says, shaking her eyeballs down. *"Nothing."*

"Visuals?"

"Visuals, maybe. Yeah. Hallucinations." Carly shivers. "But they fade so fast, like a nightmare. Something . . . *crawling*. I don't know. I can't remember."

"You're burned out, doll," says Wolfe. "You're losing your program, loosening it up much too soon. You're too young for this, doll. But don't worry. I know what you need."

"Yeah?"

"Losing link like that? Just a little cram. Cram will put you right." Wolfe moves closer. Scent like burned rubber and cinnamon spills off him.

Carly flinches. "Cram's illegal."

"Oh, but it gets you there. Gets you there easy, just in time for your next appearance in the Venue. You *need* that appearance, doll."

"You're crazy. I could get decertified for cramming in Venue."

"Gets you in link like nothing else."

"No way."

"The only way, doll. You're in trouble, don't you know?" Wolfe's hand on her hipbone now. Wolfe breathing the words into her ear. "Come on, don't you know what everyone's saying? Lose a diddly-shit mediation like *Martino v. Quik Slip Microchip*, you're out. And when you're out . . . ever been on the streets?"

No, but she's seen the devastation. "But how."

"I can get it."

"For godsakes, I just got out of school. How much?"

"Oh—" Wolfe grins, teeth clacking as a tic twists his lean face—"you'll have something to make it worth my while."

• • •

The medcenter sengine says Carly is healthy. No treacherous disease. No tissue attrition. Then Probers slide their needles through her telespace, insinuate steel tips into her neuroprogram.

Her right perimeter glistens with logical thought, the tan floor of her telespace supports weighty principles. Even the dull black monolith of tough, crisscrossed strands of inhibition that extends across Carly's left perimeter looks like a fortress. A woven steel wall.

Nothing amiss.

"Then what is it?" Carly pleads. "I'm crashing every other day. *What is it?*"

"A stitch in your left perimeter must be loose," says the sengine. "Oh, I know. Looks like it's sewn up tight. But I don't know what else to diagnose. You've got a leak of unregulated neurality into your telelink. Hence this program failure. The weird hallucinations. But I can't say where or how it could happen."

"Then my program guarantee from mediation school is worthless."

"Yes," says the sengine with, Carly thinks, evil satisfaction. There are rumors some artificial intelligences are jealous of the human condition. Envious of intelligence beyond program.

"Ah." A strange sadness wells up in her. "Do you know I still remember the left perimeter? How it used to be? My programmer in elementary school. My first crude telelink. Do you know I once saw blue jungles and green oceans? Oh, and gold castles and scarlet gardens. And then the thick, black stitches of inhibition wove up and down. Stabbing. Slicing off the left side of my telespace. And the colors and beauty faded. Faded to nothing."

"Well!" The sengine has no answer for that. "I'll have to suspend your limitation certificate, Ms. Quester," says the sengine briskly. "The Venue will not link mediators with loose perimeters. Much too dangerous. All that raw unconscious energy seeping into telespace? No, you can't go to the Venue, Ms. Quester. Not like this."

"But what can I do? There must be something I can do!"

"Your school will reprogram you at a reduced tuition."

"But that'll take another three years of standard programming!"

"Maybe longer. Deleting an old, flawed program, installing another, that can be tricky business."

And she would lose her job at Ava & Rice. She would lose everything she'd worked for. Carly weeps, frothy waterfalls of grief spilling across her telelink.

"All right, listen, there *is* another way," the sengine says with surprising kindness. "It's expensive, risky. Doesn't always work. Doesn't always stick when it *does* work. But I'm sorry for you, Ms. Quester. I'm not programmed to ruin biologicals. I can refer you to a perimeter prober. This one's got full medical certification. If the prober can find the loose stitch, the defect can be rewoven. You'll be good as new. Recertifiable, too."

"What's the risk?" Carly asks.

"The perimeter prober may not find the loose stitch, and you'll have to get wiped and reprogrammed," says the sengine cautiously. "Or the prober will find it, all right, but you won't endure the psychic pain. It'll wipe you in another way."

"Okay, so how long? How long will the probe take?"

"Three probes. If the prober can't find the defect in three attempts, it can't be found, not without serious neural damage. I can't recertify you then. You'll just have to go back for reprogramming."

"But three probes. I could be cured in *three* probes?"

"Yes."

Carly jumps at the chance. She takes a jetcopter west over brooding slums, ticky-tacky high rises, dilapidated factories that crouch on the banks of the sluggish Metro River. For some reason the perimeter prober isn't accessed into standard telespace. Carly has got to get herself *physically* to the prober's office.

Rather a shady state of affairs, not to mention the costly commute, the waste of time spent transporting the body. Carly pops a viddeck from her briefcase, jacks into a sitcom. Anything to ease the pain of link.

• • •

"And you've never injected cram, is that so, Carly Quester?" asks the prober. Her synthy voice sounds like an antique phonograph record left too many dusty decades in an attic.

"No, never, that is correct, Prober Spinner." Carly eyes the disheveled robot. Medically certified, indeed. Prober Spinner is crudely articulated, torso and arms, then mobilized from a boxlike locomotor. Faceplace of an oldish careworn woman.

The faceplace must have been intended to evoke empathy and trust, but Prober Spinner's bleary eyespots glare at Carly with an enmity approaching fury.

Carly shifts uncomfortably. The prober's office is tucked amid birth 'n' abort clinics, drug-drag therapists, dentists on the muni dole into the corner of a shabby medical building on the south side of town. The place reeks. Scabby plants abound. An aquarium, filthy with dull green scum, bubbles with a school of dingy fish. The floor is dabbled with viscous white spots. Then Carly spots a flock of ugly little sparrows perched atop a crumbling bookcase.

An organic feline does chin-ups on the arm of a ragged couch; then the cat stalks past her, stinking of fur, flops on its skinny cat ass, and bites at its flea-bitten haunch. *Jeez, bugs.* Carly considers her robopet, a Chatty Catty Deluxe with three pop-in eye colors and two slip-on breeds, with new appreciation.

"This is charming."

The prober is flipping through Carly's file, humming a popular tune with awful two-part harmony. "Hm? The décor? Oh, yes. You mean *for a robot.*" The eyespots stare, accusation flickering across the crone's faceplace.

"I didn't say that, Prober Spinner."

"But that's what you *mean*, eh, Carly Quester? I know your kind. I know what you mean. Why should a robot keep biologicals around? Eh? Why should a tin can with dual disk drives keep *life* around? And worthless life at that, that's what you're thinking, eh?"

"Prober Spinner, please. I meant no offense."

"I'll *tell* you why. Because I have *respect* for life, Carly Quester. There are mysteries, there are unknown presences in biological intelligence, there are myths and secrets." Prober Spinner's voicetape begins to rattle and wheeze. "No, but you could never understand that, could you?"

"Prober Spinner, please." Carly says sharply. "I came for your help. Can you help me?"

"Oh, yes. Oh, certainly." Prober Spinner wheels over, takes Carly's face between the cool aluminum spindles of her robot fingers. The fingers feel like claws—needle-slim, alien appendages against Carly's skin. "Yes, soft. Like fruit. Like a berry, so soft with fine down. Well, Carly Quester." The prober briskly releases her. "It's like this. We'll go into link, you and I, and I will probe the perimeter blocking your unconscious mind. They stitched it shut, you know; only controllable thought can be permitted into telespace. That's why my telelink isn't accessed to public space. If I can uncover this defect in your left perimeter, all sorts of unconscious energy—oh, demons, Carly Quester, strange and terrible things—could come out. Could manifest right into telespace."

"And what happens when these demons manifest into your little telespace, Prober?"

"I can control them, don't you worry. I can push them back and stitch the defect shut. I'm a robot, you see. The mysteries of biological intelligence may fascinate me, but they can't hold power over me. Not like they can possess *you.*"

"Possess me, Prober Spinner?"

"Oh, yes. Oh, certainly. You're in the grip of an unconscious force now, yes, right now. But you can't see its form. It's hiding."

"Hiding?"

"Inside your blackouts."

The truth of the prober's assertion pierces Carly. What *is* the demon that lurks in the nameless visions? Does she really want to know? Carly considers walking out. She considers her Venue recertification. She stays.

And she and the prober jack into link. Telespace there is unfocused, hazy. Goddamn cheap equipment. Spires of silver mist rise and twist from Carly's immaculate tan floor.

"I'm ready for the probe, Prober," says Carly. To her satisfaction, she notes that her presence, even in this link, is still a crisp, white cube.

"All right, Carly Quester," says Prober Spinner. The prober's presence in link is a brown cone the size of a Japanese jasmine incense that skitters across the undulating telespace like some verminous thing.

The cone angles its way across the immaculate woven wall of Carly's left perimeter. Tilts its tip in. Digs into the neat crisscrosses of inhibition. Jams there. Digs and digs.

Carly moans.

A crackling black mass leaps from the wall, vaults across telespace in frantic, jolting bounds. Gripped with dread, Carly shrinks from it, scurrying back into the abacus set across her right perimeter. But the prober flies at her flank, driving her with the sharp conetip to confront the black mass.

It leaps about crazily, a living shard of black glass that stretches and shifts, stinks of sulfur and fresh human blood.

"Is this a blackout, Carly?" asks Prober Spinner.

"No . . . no."

"Then, what? What is it? What do you see?"

A face appears inside the black glass. An old woman, her eyes pulled down with sickness and sorrow, frail, gray haired, utterly vulnerable. "Joe worked on it for fifteen years, you know, in the garage, on a tenth-hand computer," says Rosa Marino in a trembling voice. "'Rosa,' he'd say, 'we'll be rich. We'll be rich, and then I'll get roses, a whole garden full of roses for my Rosa.' But that was long ago, when we were so young, so strong. When he was done, you know, he took it to the company. He *knew* he could sell it to the company because he'd worked for the company as a splicer for twenty years."

Sinister shimmer beside her, like a knife blade.

"But those people, the researchers at the company, they said they weren't interested. They said the company didn't need Joe's *Wordsport Glossary*. They said no. It broke his will to live. Broke his heart, you know. He dropped dead two days after his fiftieth birthday, heart attack. Oh, there was a small payout, a small pension, some insurance. But the money never could pay for what they did to my Joe. What they were about to do.

"Then I got sick, Social Security went broke for good, and the money, I don't know where the money went. And my daughter Luisa, she's bringing up her Dan, such a smart boy, Danny, he should go to school. But Luisa gets laid off, she can't pay the school tax, and that lousy bastard of a father won't cough up, not even for his own son, and then he leaves my Luisa. I suppose it was just as well. But the money's gone, I got a little left from the payout, and I won't let those lousy mediators touch *that*."

Into the jolting black mass rolls the slick circular emblem of Quik Slip Microchip. Pointed teeth gleam in anonymous smiles. Smiles harden into black crescents, shiny black insect-like claws. The claws snap at the old lady. She flutters her hands in despair, tries to escape.

But she's trapped.

"It was my Dan, my little Danny," says Rosa Martino, "who said, 'Granma, they're using Granpa's glossary. I saw the glossary they taught me at school before. Granma, *you* showed me.' That company had been selling my Joe's *Wordsport Glossary* to millions, oh, ten million elementary schools. They just took it, made money off it, twenty years. And how was I to know? Luisa was out of elementary school, Danny not yet in, for all that time. How could I know?"

The greedy claws pop like snapping fingers, pinch off pieces of Rosa Martino's weeping face.

"That company made five hundred million dollars off Joe's work, his own work that he loved," screams Rosa Martino. "Can you imagine so much money? And I don't want all of it, I'm not asking for all of it. Just a little bit, a little percentage royalty that's rightfully Joe's. Rightfully mine. So Luisa and Dan, my little Danny, don't have to be so poor."

The claws rip the old lady to shreds, stuff chunks of her cheeks into a smiling, munching mouth. Quik Slip Microchip burps.

"I'm sorry," yells Carly. "I'm sorry, I didn't know, I'm sorry!"

The glassy black mass spins away, ricochets off her left perimeter, speeds into the infinite gleam of rationalization.

Then suddenly Carly slams out of link, seated with Prober Spinner in the prober's grimy office before the telelink console.

Her face is drenched in tears. She shakes uncontrollably.

"Calm yourself, Carly Quester," says Prober Spinner mildly. "A little guilt never hurt anyone. Glad to see you haven't sealed all of your ethics behind that damned left perimeter."

"It's just a job," whispers Carly. "I'm just doing my job."

She swallows the tranquilizer Prober Spinner offers. "Just doing your job, shit," says the prober. "Stop anytime you want to. Change your life anytime you want to."

"But I can't. How can I?"

"Do something else."

"I don't know what else to do. I've been programmed. What else can I do?"

"Oh, perhaps we shall see," says Prober Spinner. "There's a hell of lot more work we've got to do. We still haven't found a blackout."

• • •

D. Wolfe lies back in the bed, stretches out his arms in a hug to be filled. "Come here, Carlique." He's flushed and glittery-eyed from the cocaine he's just snorted.

Three syringes of cram lie neatly wrapped on the bed table. The price: one thousand in cash, plus a roll on the bed. *All right, just one,* Carly thinks. He doesn't seem so bad, and she knows three hits of cram, which is what he's offering, which could get her through ten telelinks or more, could be three times the bankroll he wants, and who knows how many bedrolls with a stranger.

Dim light softens his lean-mean features. Not so bad at all, with shadows smoothing his tough look, making his eyes seem lonely. But for the way he abuses himself, he wears his middle age well.

Carly sheds her suit, suddenly full of flirt, moved to entice him. But Wolfe doesn't watch her. He's busy with the coke again.

"Come here, Carlique," he says when he's done.

She goes to him, twines around him, gives him her heat. He directs her. Touch here, kiss there, move this way, turn that. He takes his pleasure quickly and withdraws, falling back on the bed, reaching now for whiskey to cut the ragged end of his high.

But he touched her. She forgot how long it's been since she's been touched. Painful longing grips her. Carly turns to him, tries to stroke him, but he waves her away, hand held up like a stop sign, keeping her touch away.

"Wolfe."

"Leave me alone."

"But, Wolfe."

"My head is killing me."

Carly sits up, lights a cigarette, then takes a syringe of cram from the bed table, fingers it curiously.

"I want to thank you for this."

"*Thank* me?" He laughs, bitter bark of a laugh, then guzzles whiskey. "Wait till you take cram. Then thank me, if you can."

"I thought you said I need it. Thought you said it'll focus me in link."

"Sure. Does. Focuses you in link by narrowing your focus. Eliminates self-doubt, inner challenges, the slightest reservation you may have about what you're doing, why you're doing it. Glosses glitches in program, masks stray thought."

"Total concentration, that's what I must *need*, Wolfe. Sounds good to me."

"Yeah, well." He finishes the fifth, cracks open gin. "Gets so you can't stand the smallest deviation from conformity. The most trivial hint of ambiguity drives you mad. You new wires with your doubts and fears and idealism, you make me sick." His speech is fast degenerating into slush.

"Wolfe?" Carly runs her fingertip across the hard curve of his arm. He flinches. "Wolfe, will I see you again?"

"See me? Come on, Carlique. You mean will I want you next time you want cram? Maybe. Maybe not. I'll need more cash. Got to get myself fixed with more cram, you know." He fixes her with a fierce, desperate stare. "Don't you know? You're just a score to me now, Carlique."

Then he passes out.

With tender fingertips, Carly slides his wasted eyelids over his rolled-back eyes. "It won't happen to me," she whispers into his unhearing ear. "Not like this."

• • •

"But how can I get *inside* a blackout?" says Carly. "The blackouts take my whole system down." She picks at the linkjack peevishly. *Don't want to, don't want to do this.* Carly's whole body recoils from the grimy little prober. Prober Spinner's faceplace is smudged with greasy fingerprints. Bird crap mottles her headpiece.

"Got to find us a blackout in telespace, go *inside* it," insists Prober Spinner. She wheels over to Carly. Skinny silver fingers wrest the jack from her, plug it into her linkslit. The prober's eyespots flash with glee when Carly winces. "Your puny little guilt trip is shit. I want to see a *blackout*."

"And just what do you expect to see there, Prober Spinner?"

"A big, sloppy heap of unconscious energy. Plus an archetype or two, I truly hope. Only real kick to working with humans. Do you have any idea how bad your breath is, Carly Quester? Whew, no shit. Makes my olfactory sensors puke."

Carly rips out the linkjack, jumps up. "I don't like your attitude, Prober Spinner. I've got a good mind to report you to the medcenter sengine. Malpractice, see. I'll throw the fucking *book* at you."

"Oh, yes. Oh, certainly. The fucking book. All in good time Carly Quester. First we probe you three times, then we get you your Venue recert, *then* you throw the fucking book at me. Understand? So you don't get your ass thrown into reprogramming for three more years. Isn't that what you want? What little Carly wants, little Carly gets, yes?"

Carly sits, plunks the jack in herself. Of course that's what she wants. "Why do you hate me, Prober Spinner?"

"Hate you? Don't give yourself such importance. Oh, sit *down*. You would rather stitch up your left perimeter, just like that, without even *seeing* what it is that's got the symbolic power to intrude through a tight-ass weave like you. Oh, yes. Oh, certainly! I know your game, Carly Quester. You bet it upsets me. You receive this *gift*, a great gift from your unconscious mind, an aspect of intelligence no robot can ever hope to glimpse except through a human. For me, there is only *nothing*. Nothing but program, and then nothing—try *that* for existential angst. But you, a mysterious presence in your link, visions of an archetype you can't even name, and you, you organic intelligence, you want to cut it out, turn *yourself* into a robot. No, I don't hate you. But you could never understand that, could you?"

"All right, Prober Spinner." Carly sighs, then steels herself. No more emotion, take *control*. "Let's get on with it."

They jack into link. Telespace is murkier than the first probe. Prober Spinner's presence has darkened from brown to charcoal gray. The sight of the scuttling cone makes Carly so queasy she nearly flips the log-out switch.

"What shall I do?" she asks instead.

"Look for a blackout," says Prober Spinner brusquely. "Take me to a blackout."

At a loss, Carly slides along her towering left perimeter, pausing here and there as the prober darts behind her, jabbing again. Telespace suddenly gets foggier, a dark poisonous fog. Roiling mud beneath her reeks of raw sewage and strange decay.

Carly can feel her body start to retch, that skin-crawling feeling again. Physically somehow *there* in telespace. She jams two fingers into the base of her throat.

"Get out," Carly says, choking. "Got to get out."

Prober Spinner prods her forward into the fog.

Then, there. Two rows of double-bladed hatchets thrust out of the murk. The personnel committee of the top-notch mediation firm of Ava & Rice stands before Carly. Gleaming blades drip rust. Rust coagulates into a poisonous pool.

Mr. Capp Rice III, grandson of the late Capp Rice II, who was cofounder of the venerable mediation firm of Ava & Rice, lurches toward her. Jerky walk, like a marionette held by an epileptic. At age seventy, Mr. Rice has had so many body parts replaced he's nearly a robot.

"So, Ms. Quester." Dry steel joints screech. Mr. Rice towers over Carly's presence in link. "You have not met our expectations. I am sorry." An articulated tin tongue flickers between his platinum canine teeth. His empty unblinking solar eye fills Carly with such dread that her body back in the prober's office throws up.

"I can do better, Mr. Rice. I—I will do better."

The personnel committee stands in silence, dead eyes watching. Seventeen thousand resumes from recent mediation school graduates drop in a wriggling heap at Carly's feet.

"So, so, so, Ms. Quester." Mr. Rice's tin tongue flick-flick-flicks, some gear stuck at the back of his throat, until a member of the personnel committee reaches over and whacks him on the neck. "If you cannot meet our expectations, we will have to ask you to leave. I am so sorry."

"I can do better. I *will* do better." Carly starts to sob. "I'll do anything to keep my job. It's a *great* job, Mr. Rice. I'll do *anything.*"

"Will you kiss my ass?" Mr. Rice offers. Carly puckers.

"Will you lick my shoes?" Mr. Rice extends his appendage. Carly laps.

"Will you take cram?"

"Cram is illegal," says Carly, flushing.

"Cram focuses you in link like nothing else, Ms. Quester," says Mr. Rice. He takes out a hypodermic needle, stabs the needle into the corner of his eye, slams the plunger. "Oh! Like nothing else."

"I'll do anything to keep my job, Mr. Rice, *anything.*"

"I am glad to hear that, Ms. Quester. Just don't let that asshole Arbiter catch you. Be discreet. Takes one to know one." Mr. Rice pops the needle out, tosses the syringe over his shoulder. A member of the personnel committee picks it up and eats it, steel molars crunching the glass and metal into pulp. "I will give you another chance, Ms. Quester," says Mr. Rice. "Don't make me regret it, eh?"

The personnel committee vanishes.

"Shit!" yells Prober Spinner, poking Carly's cube. "Lousy *fear* is all you got for me?"

Carly is numb, so still, so paralyzed that she can't even shiver from the deep, deathly cold.

"I hate this fear," she whispers at last. "I hate them for making me afraid. Hate myself for being afraid."

"Guilt and fear, guilt and fear," says Prober Spinner, taunting.

"And I hate *you.*" A spume of angry red smoke races through Carly's telespace.

"Boo-hoo-hoo." Prober Spinner laughs. "Poor little Carly, she's so sad. Poor little Carly, can't even get mad."

Carly snaps into fury, slaps the prober's cone with a resounding *Gong!* The prober scuttles away, darts and dashes. Turns back sharply at the slick bank of her right perimeter, wrestles her.

"Good, good, good!" cries Prober Spinner, still laughing. She aims the conetip squarely into Carly's side. *Oof!* Carly falls back winded. "There, you see? You're not hamstrung by guilt anymore. You're not trapped by fear."

"But I *am* still trapped in this lousy life of mine. I'm still trapped in this soul-sucking world."

"Ah, we shall see," says the prober. "We haven't found a blackout. Not yet."

• • •

Carly approaches the Arbiter's quarters. Her presence in the Venue gleams like mother-of-pearl. Cram always adds a sheen.

"Your Honor, my client Quik Slip Microchip denies the plaintiff Martino's claim on the grounds of adverse possession." She logs in the facts of the mediation, a sleek green stream of data. "Plaintiff failed to protest defendant's illegal and flagrant use of the *Wordsport Glossary* over twenty years. Legality of acquisition is sustained by virtue of sustained illegality." In one and a half seconds, strict conformity of data with the statutory requirements of Property Code Section 344 is confirmed.

The two scruffy solos for Martino groan.

"Therefore," continues Carly, "my client counterclaims to quiet title under Section 501 of the Property Code."

Nee-dee-nee-dee-nee-dee-DEE! On the big board, the registrar of deeds cheerfully transfers title to the Wordsport Glossary from file M to file Q.

"Further," says Carly, "my client sues for mediator's fees under Civil Code Section 666.09(1)(B)."

"Objection!" screams the weaselly solo. "You can't get away with this, hotshot!"

"Overruled," says the Arbiter. His gigantic eyes flick over the whirring chronograph. Carly has presented, proved, and concluded her defense and counterclaim in five seconds.

The Arbiter's towering face smiles at Carly "I am pleased to readmit you to telespace and look forward to your official recertification. Proceed, Ms. Quester."

"Grounds are vexatious and baseless litigation."

Ching! Data conforms to statute.

"I claim," says Carly, "ten thousand dollars."

"So held, award granted. Dismissed." The Arbiter nods approvingly at Carly. Her presence in the Venue glows.

The big steel hook of a garnishment plucks the last of Rosa Martino's money. From stats, a soft *poop!* like a fart. In a tiny black-and-white newline, the big board reports that Rosa Martino, age seventy-one, locked herself, her daughter, and her grandson in the kitchen of her southside tenement studio apartment and turned on the gas. *Tik-tik-tik!* Three corpses are dumped into the crunching jaws of the public morgue.

The inky net of a collection agent logs into the Venue, scoops up the solos before they can jack out of link.

"What goes around comes around, hotshot!" yells the weaselly solo as the collection agent's net drags him away to service his debts.

Carly doesn't know what he means. She logs out of the Venue, coming conscious in her filthy little cubicle at Ava & Rice. Rox is there, cutting up lines of coke on a blood-spattered mirror.

"Way to go, Quester," she says, winking a bloodshot, black-rimmed eye. "Nice touch, sticking it to the old lady. That'll teach laypeople to fuck with business."

In the hallway, Mr. Capp Rice III rolls by. He toasts Carly with a shot glass of high-octane gas. "I'm so glad you are meeting our expectations, Ms. Quester." Mr. Rice winks, too, but the wink opens and shuts, opens and shuts, until Rox reaches over and whacks him on the ear. "I've got another mediation just like Martino's. Consider this sort of thing your new specialty. Every mediator needs a good specialty, eh, Ms. Quester?"

Carly nods, takes the mirror from Rox, toots. Quick, sharp high pierces the deadening stupor that always follows cramming. Wolfe has taught her other ways to handle cramming, ways to handle the cram addiction. Wolfe has taught her lots of tricks of the trade now that he's her pusher. She's had to learn. Twenty thousand dollars in debt to him, she finds other scores, gets them hooked, deals. Anything to score more cram.

Her hands shake all the time now. Fifteen pounds gone, she looks like an anorexic. Her left eye twitches, and some kind of swelling aches in her left temple, stretching out blue, bruised skin. Afraid to sleep, afraid to dream. She crams into link, cokes out of cram, boozes herself down in deep black nothing.

Two damned probes have shaken something loose. Carly's dislike of Prober Spinner festers into loathing. Surely the terror of the probes hasn't been necessary. Carly tries to contact the medcenter sengine, go over Spinner's head, get the recertification without a third probe. But the sengine is teaching a class at summer school and cannot be accessed.

Furious, Carly accesses the medcenter library, researches perimeter probers. She discovers the treatment is deemed not just unreliable like the sengine said from the start, but suspect. Several probers, *human* probers, hold this view.

In particular Prober Marboro at Stanford, who advocates layering new thicknesses of inhibition when left perimeter defects are suspect and who has proven layering is ninety percent effective, writes quite harshly of the probe technique. Probing threatens the integrity of the left perimeter, which Marboro asserts is the guardian of correct thought and proper linkage. Marboro exposed the case of Steven H., a young industrial programmer about Carly's age who, despite a strong body and a good education, suffered from hallucinations in link.

Steven H. jacked into telelink with a perimeter prober, never came out. The man vanished, mind and body. The prober claimed Steven was lured through a gash in his left perimeter. Bolted into his unconscious mind, re-created his own reality. Of course the prober claimed she tried to stop him, block him, chase, him. But the prober's telespace wasn't publicly accessed so there were no witnesses, no record. Only a computer ID and an overdrawn credit account to show Steven H. ever existed.

A cult of telespace technicians propounding the existence of multiple universes sprang up in the medical community, claimed Steven H. as their patron saint. But the big board suppressed the account.

Enraged, determined to press malpractice charges against the medcenter *and* Prober Spinner, Carly calls the prober's office, intending to refuse a third appointment. But the prober's answering machine talks her into a third probe.

"You don't want no cloud hangin' over your Venue recert, do ya Miss Quester?" says the answering machine. "Come *on*. Link in wit' the prober one last time, and I *guarantee* she'll recert ya."

Carly considers this. She has an appearance before the Arbiter in two days, has promised to present him with the final medcenter recertification.

"We haven't found a blackout, and Prober Spinner keeps insisting we must. But—" Carly takes a breath—"I don't think that's ever going to happen."

"Don't worry. She'll recert ya. I wouldn't kid ya."

Carly sets up the appointment. Just one last probe. Get in link, get out quick.

• • •

"You really will? Just like *that*?" Carly stalks back and forth across the prober's dust-fluffy floor.

"Oh, sure." Humming this week's pop hit off-tune, Prober Spinner fiddles with the telelink console.

"I can't believe it. I can't *believe* it." Carly shakes with fury. "Then what has been the fucking *point*?"

"Medcenter sengine says three probes, then recert. Then I get another paid-for probe client. You look like hell, Carly Quester. Not cramming, are you? No, you wouldn't tell me if you were."

"The sengine said recertification *if* I'm cured in three probes. You haven't done a damn thing for me, Spinner."

"Haven't done a thing? Not a *thing*? I beg to differ. You've been sprung loose of guilt and fear. Can't claim your freedom with baggage like that. Whew, you even smell like a crammer. Don't you know that garbage is illegal? And do you know *why* it's illegal? Hey? Rips the living shit out of your perimeters, that's why. I would have bounced you right out of here if you had showed up like this at the start of treatment."

Bitter cold shock. Wolfe never *did* say what the long-term effects of cramming could be. Carly shrugs it off. Robot bitch is trying to hassle her, as usual.

"I don't want to argue, Spinner," says Carly. "Let's get on with it."

And they jack into link.

• • •

Telespace is clear, still, focused, luminous. Maybe the cram. Maybe Carly's clear, pure anger. In any case, very nice. Very calming.

Carly lightens up, then recoils. Oh, yes, just what the prober wants, for her to let down her guard.

Prober Spinner's presence in link is a crisp, perfect, ebony cone.

"Please navigate your left perimeter, Carly Quester," says the prober. Her voice seems to contain an awestruck note.

Ahead lies a beautiful golden glow. Carly's presence in link slides gracefully, eagerly toward it. Her hand brushes a lock of hair from her cheek and, in link, she feels the soft touch of her own skin on her face. But the impossible physical touch doesn't panic her, doesn't worry her a bit.

"At last!" Prober Spinner cries. "At last, a blackout!"

"You're crazy," says Carly. Terror gallops through her, ripping away her wary peace. "I see a beam, not a blackout."

"Yes, yes! A blackout, *your* blackout. Tell me what you see!"

The golden glow swirls with luminous colors. A world appears, both microscopic and gigantic to Carly's eye. *A flier levitates from a vermilion funnel and hovers. Stiff chatoyant wings, monocoque fuselage, compound visual apparatus.* The mayfly bungles into a spider web. *The trapper hulks at the edge of the net. Stalked eyebuds swivel, pedipalps tense.* A garden spider darts down, wraps the fly in a silken shroud, begins to feed.

Carly screams.

"So *this* is the secret place inside your blackouts!" exclaims Prober Spinner. "The spider! How fascinating!"

"Horrible, horrible, oh God help me!" Carly yells.

"Why? What are you afraid of?"

"Ugly. Repulsive. Monstrous. *Alien.*"

"Oh, no, not ugly." Prober Spinner glides around the bright vision. The spider sips fluid from the flier's body. "It's Nature. It's beautiful."

"Violent. Vicious. *Murderous.*" Carly chases after the spinning cone. "Just like the Arbiter and Ava and Rice and Wolfe and *you*. All of you, preying on me, trapping me, sucking me dry."

"Oh, yes. Oh, certainly. You've been a victim. The world, the people around you, the role you've found yourself compelled to play. These have preyed upon you. The spider has slipped from the depths of the dark unconscious, through your left perimeter, in search of such a fine victim. But what about *you*, Carly Quester? You've taken your own victims, don't tell me you had no choice. All that human creativity reduced to such a low and ugly fate."

"I won't hear this, Spinner." Carly scurries to log out of link.

"But wait, Carly. It's not so simple." The cone dives at her, prodding her, slapping her away from the log-off key. "There is a story, an old story no one remembers anymore. There was a goddess, an immortal weaver, who grew jealous of a talented mortal girl and her incomparable weaving. So gray-eyed Athena transformed the beautiful Arachne into a spider."

Out of the glowing garden creeps the garden spider. It scuttles across Carly's clean tan floor. The spider extends a hairy, clawed spindle, catches a silken line. Sweeps across telespace. Drops down onto Carly's cube.

Carly shrieks, gags, tries to shrink away, shake it off. But she can't. She can't. She's trapped.

"But Carly, the story is apocryphal." Prober Spinner lovingly taps at the spider, gently hurrying it across Carly's cube, catching it as it tumbles off the edge, easing it back onto her. "A lie, a slander, a political ploy. No better than the propaganda flashes on the big board. The Greeks, who worshipped the vengeful goddess coveted the lucrative textile trade of the Cretan weavers, who worshipped the spider as their goddess."

The spider quadruples in size. Instead of crawling across Carly's cube, it straddles her. Gazes down at her with a ghoulish, gape-mouthed face.

"Who would worship *that*?" says Carly, gasping. "How could they? *Why?*"

"To the Cretan weavers, the spider was the Eater of Souls. She who relentlessly destroys, the hunter, the killer, the maker of deceptions. But She was also the Weaver of Fate. She who unceasingly creates," says Prober Spinner.

"Universe upon universe. Over and over. She redeems Her destructive power with Her infinite power to create. She is Grandmother Spider, the Creator. She weaves, Carly. She *weaves*!"

Salty wind blasts across telespace. Carly sees a pinpoint in the sturdy crisscrosses of her left perimeter, sees a thread of gold mist connecting the vision and the pinpoint. The pinpoint dilates, thick ropes of inhibition unraveling, rippling away.

The golden thread solidifies, and a spider of extraordinary beauty descends. Long, graceful legs, a rounded abdomen and slender torso, all made of shining silver set with faceted bits of marcasite. The stalked eyebuds gleam, two rubies regarding her.

"Look!" cries Prober Spinner. "Carly, look!"

"No," whispers Carly. Her presence in link, her physical body jacked into the console, feel so insubstantial. As if she's floating. "I'm afraid."

"Don't fear now," says Prober Spinner. "You've lived the dark side of Arachne. Now claim the light."

• • •

Telespace is a gray-green mist. Carly's presence in link is her own nude body. She stands on a windswept crag, surrounded by a splashing sea. Before her lies a gigantic loom, made of smooth hardwood, strung with woolen warp and woof.

She seats herself before the loom, takes the smooth hard shuttle. Slips it in and out, around and through, the fibrous matrix. The wool glows phosphorescent green and amber.

The warp slips off the loom and coils into a shape. The shape solidifies, a crystal retort in the form of a woman's figure through which white sand falls endlessly. The woof snaps and hurtles a spray of globes into deep space. The shuttle becomes a bullet of light and disappears.

Carly reaches out, seizing pulsing strands of pure creative energy.

All is darkness.

Carly opens her left hand. A bright bubble springs from her fingers, filling her eyes with light. Clouds of dust roil. Stars cool, the corona of dust settles, planets spin. The primordial ocean roars. Creatures swim, then wade onto shell-strewn beaches, and stand up. Empires rise. China, Egypt, Rome, England, America, China. Mushroom clouds jut above broken cities. Spaceships blast off toward an uncharted galaxy.

All is darkness.

Then Carly opens her right hand. A luminous sphere pops out of her palm, flooding her eyes with light. Clouds of dust roil. Stars coagulate, the halo of ashes precipitates, planets settle into their orbits. The primal ocean pounds. Creatures swim, then the skin of their fins closes around each digital bone, and they grasp. Empires rise. Xeron, Forf, Klamat, Lator, Meen, Xeron. An ocean floor splits, swallowing crushed cities. Spaceships blast off into the unknown universe.

All is darkness.

Prober Spinner's voice calls, "Carly? Carly? Carly? Carly?"

Checkerboards of golden light pierce Carly's left perimeter. The thick black wall of inhibition shatters, shards of guilt, wisps of fear, strands of denial flung into infinity.

• • •

Carly hovers in telespace. Her presence in link is a luminous pearl. She gleams with crystal, the wonder drug that preserves life, expands consciousness, permits Earth dwellers to send their presence across the galaxy to new worlds. The jade obelisk of D. Wolfe, her beloved, hovers beside her. Prober Spinner's presence in link, an indigo cone with silver crescent moons, joins them.

Before them towers a castle of gold, turrets ablaze. There the Arbiter presides over the Venue, dispensing justice. Across Carly's right perimeter splashes an emerald sea, dragons frolicking in swells. There new people of the modern age refresh themselves, cast nets for plentiful fish. Bordering the back perimeter, scarlet gardens yield spicy perfumes. And there Rosa Martino joins hands with her daughter, Luisa, and her grandson, Dan, and the three of them circle in a sprightly dance. Glorious blooms thrust brilliant creepers into the blue jungle of Carly's left perimeter. There, through jungle vines and murex bushes peep the wild yellow eyes of new ideas not yet thought, of jungle cats and bright-beaked birds.

"Prober Spinner," says Carly, "what is this place?"

"Telespace, Carly Quester," says Prober Spinner. "Oh, yes. Oh, certainly. As only a human mind could create it."

"But some call it reality," says Wolfe. "It is yours, my beloved."

Anchored overhead to the four corners of telespace is the lattice of space and time, like a spider web, a beautiful fine spiral hung with crystalline drops of dew. Night rain has torn a hole in its center. Carly knows what to do. She flies up through telespace, takes the warp, takes the woof. She skips across the silk and begins to weave.

GREG EGAN

AXIOMATIC

(1990)

". . . LIKE YOUR BRAIN has been frozen in liquid nitrogen, and then smashed into a thousand shards!"

I squeezed my way past the teenagers who lounged outside the entrance to The Implant Store, no doubt fervently hoping for a holovision news team to roll up and ask them why they weren't in school. They mimed throwing up as I passed, as if the state of not being pubescent and dressed like a member of Binary Search was so disgusting to contemplate that it made them physically ill.

Well, maybe it did.

Inside, the place was almost deserted. The interior reminded me of a video ROM shop; the display racks were virtually identical, and many of the distributors' logos were the same. Each rack was labelled: PSYCHEDELIA. MEDITATION AND HEALING. MOTIVATION AND SUCCESS. LANGUAGES AND TECHNICAL SKILLS. Each implant, although itself less than half a millimeter across, came in a package the size of an old-style book, bearing gaudy illustrations and a few lines of stale hyperbole from a marketing thesaurus or some rent-an-endorsement celebrity. "*Become* God! *Become* the Universe!" "The Ultimate Insight! The Ultimate Knowledge! The Ultimate Trip!" Even the perennial, "This implant changed my life!"

I picked up the carton of *You Are Great!*—its transparent protective wrapper glistening with sweaty fingerprints—and thought numbly: If I bought this thing and used it, I would actually believe that. No amount of evidence to the contrary would be *physically able* to change my mind. I put it back on the shelf, next to *Love Yourself a Billion* and *Instant Willpower, Instant Wealth.*

I knew exactly what I'd come for, and I knew that it wouldn't be on display, but I browsed a while longer, partly out of genuine curiosity, partly just to give myself time. Time to think through the implications once again. Time to come to my senses and flee.

The cover of *Synaesthesia* showed a blissed-out man with a rainbow striking his tongue and musical staves piercing his eyeballs. Beside it, *Alien Mind-Fuck* boasted "a mental state so bizarre that even as you experience it, you won't know what it's like!" Implant technology was originally developed to provide instant language skills for businesspeople and tourists, but after disappointing sales and a takeover by an entertainment conglomerate, the first mass-market implants appeared: a cross between video games and hallucinogenic drugs. Over the years, the range of confusion and dysfunction on offer grew wider, but there's only so far you can take that trend; beyond a certain point, scrambling the neural connections doesn't leave anyone *there* to be entertained by the strangeness, and the user, once restored to normalcy, remembers almost nothing.

The first of the next generation of implants—the so-called axiomatics—were all sexual in nature; apparently that was the technically simplest place to start. I walked over to the Erotica section, to see what was available—or at least, what could legally be displayed. Homosexuality, heterosexuality, autoeroticism. An assortment of harmless fetishes. Eroticization of various unlikely parts of the body. Why, I wondered, would anyone choose to have their brain rewired to make them crave a sexual practice they otherwise would have found abhorrent, or ludicrous, or just plain boring? To comply with a partner's demands? Maybe, although such extreme submissiveness was hard to imagine, and could scarcely be sufficiently widespread to explain the size of the market. To enable a part of their own sexual identity, which, unaided, would have merely nagged and festered, to triumph over their inhibitions, their ambivalence, their revulsion? Everyone has conflicting desires, and people can grow tired of both wanting and not wanting the very same thing. I understood *that*, perfectly.

The next rack contained a selection of religions, everything from Amish to Zen. (Gaining the Amish disapproval of technology this way apparently posed no problem; virtually every religious implant enabled the user to embrace far stranger contradictions.) There was even an implant called *Secular Humanist* ("You WILL hold these truths to be self-evident!"). No *Vacillating Agnostic*, though; apparently there was no market for doubt.

For a minute or two, I lingered. For a mere fifty dollars, I could have bought back my childhood Catholicism, even if the Church would not have approved. (At least, not officially; it would have been interesting to know exactly who was subsidizing the product.) In the end, though, I had to admit that I wasn't really tempted. Perhaps it would have solved my problem, but not in the way that I wanted it solved—and after all, getting my own way was the whole point of coming here. Using an implant wouldn't rob me of my free will; on the contrary, it was going to help me to assert it.

Finally, I steeled myself and approached the sales counter.

"How can I help you, sir?" The young man smiled at me brightly, radiating sincerity, as if he really enjoyed his work. I mean, really, *really*.

"I've come to pick up a special order."

"Your name, please, sir?"

"Carver. Mark."

He reached under the counter and emerged with a parcel, mercifully already wrapped in anonymous brown. I paid in cash, I'd brought the exact change: $399.95. It was all over in twenty seconds.

I left the store, sick with relief, triumphant, exhausted. At least I'd finally bought the fucking thing; it was in my hands now, no one else was involved, and all I had to do was decide whether or not to use it.

After walking a few blocks toward the train station, I tossed the parcel into a bin, but I turned back almost at once and retrieved it. I passed a pair of armored cops, and I pictured their eyes boring into me from behind their mirrored faceplates, but what I was carrying was perfectly legal. How could the government ban a device which did no more than engender, in those who *freely chose* to use it, a particular set of beliefs—without also arresting everyone who shared those beliefs naturally? Very easily, actually, since the law didn't have to be consistent, but the implant manufacturers had succeeded in convincing the public that restricting their products would be paving the way for the Thought Police.

By the time I got home, I was shaking uncontrollably. I put the parcel on the kitchen table, and started pacing.

This wasn't for Amy. I had to admit that. Just because I still loved her, and still mourned her, didn't mean I was doing this for *her*. I wouldn't soil her memory with that lie.

In fact, I was doing it to free myself from her. After five years, I wanted my pointless love, my useless grief, to finally stop ruling my life. Nobody could blame me for that.

• • •

She had died in an armed holdup, in a bank. The security cameras had been disabled, and everyone apart from the robbers had spent most of the time facedown on the floor, so I never found out the whole story. She must have moved, fidgeted, looked up, she must have done *something*; even at the peaks of my hatred, I couldn't believe that she'd been killed on a whim, for no comprehensible reason at all.

I knew who had squeezed the trigger, though. It hadn't come out at the trial; a clerk in the Police Department had sold me the information. The killer's name was Patrick Anderson, and by turning prosecution witness, he'd put his accomplices away for life, and reduced his own sentence to seven years.

I went to the media. A loathsome crime-show personality had taken the story and ranted about it on the airwaves for a week, diluting the facts with self-serving rhetoric, then grown bored and moved on to something else.

Five years later, Anderson had been out on parole for nine months.

Okay. *So what?* It happens all the time. If someone had come to me with such a story, I would have been sympathetic, but firm. "Forget her, she's dead. Forget him, he's garbage. Get on with your life."

I didn't forget her, and I didn't forget her killer. I had loved her, whatever that meant, and while the rational part of me had swallowed the fact of her death, the rest kept twitching like a decapitated snake. Someone else in the same state might have turned the house into a shrine, covered every wall and mantelpiece with photographs and memorabilia, put fresh flowers on her grave every day, and spent every night getting drunk watching old home movies. I didn't do that, I couldn't. It would have been grotesque and utterly false; sentimentality had always made both of us violently ill. I kept a single photo. We hadn't made home movies. I visited her grave once a year.

Yet for all of this outward restraint, inside my head my obsession with Amy's death simply kept on growing. I didn't *want* it, I didn't *choose* it, I didn't feed it or encourage it in any way. I kept no electronic scrapbook of the trial. If people raised the subject, I walked away. I buried myself in my work; in my spare time I read, or went to the movies, alone. I thought about searching for someone new, but I never did anything about it, always putting it off until that time in the indefinite future when I would be human again.

Every night, the details of the incident circled in my brain. I thought of a thousand things I "might have done" to have prevented her death, from not marrying her in the first place (we'd moved to Sydney because of my job), to magically arriving at the bank as her killer took aim, tackling him to the ground and beating him senseless, or worse. I knew these fantasies were futile and self-indulgent, but that knowledge was no cure. If I took sleeping pills, the whole thing simply shifted to the daylight hours, and I was literally unable to work. (The computers that help us are slightly less appalling every year, but air traffic controllers *can't* daydream.)

I had to do something.

Revenge? Revenge was for the morally bankrupt. Me, I'd signed petitions to the UN, calling for the worldwide, unconditional abolition of capital punishment. I'd meant it then, and I still meant it. Taking human life was *wrong*; I'd believed that, passionately, since childhood. Maybe it started out as religious dogma, but when I grew up and shed all the ludicrous claptrap, the sanctity of life was one of the few beliefs I judged to be worth keeping. Aside from any pragmatic reasons, human consciousness had always seemed to me the most astonishing, miraculous, *sacred* thing in the universe. Blame my upbringing, blame my genes; I could no more devalue it than believe that one plus one equaled zero.

Tell some people you're a pacifist, and in ten seconds flat they'll invent a situation in which millions of people will die in unspeakable agony, and all your loved ones will be raped and tortured, if you don't blow someone's brains out. (There's always a contrived reason why you can't merely *wound* the omnipotent, genocidal madman.) The amusing thing is, they seem to hold you in even greater contempt when you admit that, yes, you'd do it, you'd kill under those conditions.

Anderson, however, clearly was not an omnipotent, genocidal madman. I had no idea whether or not he was likely to kill again. As for his capacity for reform, his abused childhood, or the caring and compassionate alter ego that may have been hiding behind the facade of his brutal exterior, I really didn't give a shit, but nonetheless I was convinced that it would be wrong for me to kill him.

I bought the gun first. That was easy, and perfectly legal; perhaps the computers simply failed to correlate my permit application with the release of my wife's killer, or perhaps the link was detected, but judged irrelevant.

I joined a "sports" club full of people who spent three hours a week doing nothing but shooting at moving, human-shaped targets. A recreational activity, harmless as fencing; I practiced saying that with a straight face.

Buying the anonymous ammunition from a fellow club member *was* illegal; bullets that vaporized on impact, leaving no ballistics evidence linking them to a specific weapon. I scanned the court records; the average sentence for possessing such things was a five-hundred dollar fine. The silencer was illegal, too; the penalties for ownership were similar.

Every night, I thought it through. Every night, I came to the same conclusion: despite my elaborate preparations, I wasn't going to kill anyone. Part of me wanted to, part of me didn't, but I knew perfectly well which was strongest. I'd spend the rest of my life dreaming about it, safe in the knowledge that no amount of hatred or grief or desperation would ever be enough to make me act against my nature.

• • •

I unwrapped the parcel. I was expecting a garish cover—sneering body builder toting submachine gun—but the packaging was unadorned, plain gray with no markings except for the product code, and the name of the distributor, Clockwork Orchard.

I'd ordered the thing through an on-line catalog, accessed via a coin-driven public terminal, and I'd specified collection by "Mark Carver" at a branch of The Implant Store in Chatswood, far from my home. All of which was paranoid nonsense, since the implant was legal—and all of which was perfectly reasonable, because I felt far more nervous and guilty about buying it than I did about buying the gun and ammunition.

The description in the catalog had begun with the statement *Life is cheap!* then had waffled on for several lines in the same vein: *People are meat. They're nothing, they're worthless.* The exact words weren't important, though; they weren't a part of the implant itself. It wouldn't be a matter of a voice in my head, reciting some badly written spiel which I could choose to ridicule or ignore; nor would it be a kind of mental legislative decree, which I could evade by means of semantic quibbling. Axiomatic implants were derived from analysis of actual neural structures in real people's brains, they weren't based on the expression of the axioms in language. The spirit, not the letter, of the law would prevail.

I opened up the carton. There was an instruction leaflet, in seventeen languages. A programmer. An applicator. A pair of tweezers. Sealed in a plastic bubble labeled STERILE IF UNBROKEN, the implant itself. It looked like a tiny piece of gravel.

I had never used one before, but I'd seen it done a thousand times on holovision. You placed the thing in the programmer, "woke it up," and told it how long you wanted it to be active. The applicator was strictly for tyros; the jaded cognoscenti balanced the implant on the tip of their little finger, and daintily poked it up the nostril of their choice.

The implant burrowed into the brain, sent out a swarm of nanomachines to explore, and forge links with, the relevant neural systems, and then went into active mode for the predetermined time—anything from an hour to infinity—doing whatever it was designed to do. Enabling multiple orgasms of the left kneecap. Making the color blue taste like the long-lost memory of mother's milk. Or, hard wiring a premise: *I will succeed. I am happy in my job. There is life after death. Nobody died in Belsen. Four legs good, two legs bad . . .*

I packed everything back into the carton, put it in a drawer, took three sleeping pills, and went to bed.

• • •

Perhaps it was a matter of laziness. I've always been biased toward those options which spare me from facing the very same set of choices again in the future; it seems so *inefficient* to go through the same agonies of conscience more than once. To *not* use the implant would have meant having to reaffirm that decision, day after day, for the rest of my life.

Or perhaps I never really believed that the preposterous toy would work. Perhaps I hoped to prove that my convictions—unlike other people's—were engraved on some metaphysical tablet that hovered in a spiritual dimension unreachable by any mere machine.

Or perhaps I just wanted a moral alibi—a way to kill Anderson while still believing it was something that the *real* me could never have done.

At least I'm sure of one thing. I didn't do it for Amy.

• • •

I woke around dawn the next day, although I didn't need to get up at all; I was on annual leave for a month. I dressed, ate breakfast, then unpacked the implant again and carefully read the instructions.

With no great sense of occasion, I broke open the sterile bubble and, with the tweezers, dropped the speck into its cavity in the programmer.

The programmer said, "Do you speak English?" The voice reminded me of one of the control towers at work; deep but somehow genderless, businesslike without being crudely robotic—and yet, unmistakably inhuman.

"Yes."

"Do you want to program this implant?"

"Yes."

"Please specify the active period."

"Three days." Three days would be enough, surely; if not, I'd call the whole thing off.

"This implant is to remain active for three days after insertion. Is that correct?"

"Yes."

"This implant is ready for use. The time is seven forty-three a.m. Please insert the implant before eight forty-three a.m., or it will deactivate itself and reprogramming will be required. Please enjoy this product and dispose of the packaging thoughtfully."

I placed the implant in the applicator, then hesitated, but not for long. This wasn't the time to agonize; I'd agonized for months, and I was sick of it. Any more indecisiveness and I'd need to buy a second implant to convince me to use the first. I wasn't committing a crime; I wasn't even coming close to guaranteeing that I would commit one. Millions of people held the belief that human life was nothing special, but how many of them were murderers? The next three days would simply reveal how *I* reacted to that belief, and although the attitude would be hard wired, the consequences were far from certain.

I put the applicator in my left nostril, and pushed the release button. There was a brief stinging sensation, nothing more.

I thought, *Amy would have despised me for this*. That shook me, but only for a moment. Amy was dead, which made her hypothetical feelings irrelevant. Nothing I did could hurt her now, and thinking any other way was crazy.

I tried to monitor the progress of the change, but that was a joke; you can't check your moral precepts by introspection every thirty seconds. After all, my assessment of myself as being unable to kill had been based on decades of observation (much of it probably out of date). What's more, that assessment, that self-image, had come to be as much a *cause* of my actions and attitudes as a reflection of them—and apart from the direct changes the implant was making to my brain, it was breaking that feedback loop by providing a rationalization for me to act in a way that I'd convinced myself was impossible.

After a while, I decided to get drunk, to distract myself from the vision of microscopic robots crawling around in my skull. It was a big mistake; alcohol makes me paranoid. I don't recall much of what followed, except for catching sight of myself in the bathroom mirror, screaming, "HAL's breaking First Law! HAL's breaking First Law!" before vomiting copiously.

I woke just after midnight, on the bathroom floor. I took an anti-hangover pill, and in five minutes my headache and nausea were gone. I showered and put on fresh clothes. I'd bought a jacket especially for the occasion, with an inside pocket for the gun.

It was still impossible to tell if the thing had done anything to me that went beyond the placebo effect; I asked myself, out loud, "Is human life sacred? Is it wrong to kill?" but I couldn't concentrate on the question, and I found it hard to believe that I ever had in the past; the whole idea seemed obscure and difficult, like some esoteric mathematical theorem. The prospect of going ahead with my plans made my stomach churn, but that was simple fear, not moral outrage; the implant wasn't meant to make me brave, or calm, or resolute. I could have bought those qualities too, but that would have been cheating.

I'd had Anderson checked out by a private investigator. He worked every night but Sunday, as a bouncer in a Surry Hills nightclub; he lived nearby, and usually arrived home, on foot, at around four in the morning. I'd driven past his terrace house several times, I'd have no trouble finding it. He lived alone; he had a lover, but they always met at her place, in the afternoon or early evening.

I loaded the gun and put it in my jacket, then spent half an hour staring in the mirror, trying to decide if the bulge was visible. I wanted a drink, but I restrained myself. I switched on the radio and wandered through the house, trying to become less agitated. Perhaps taking a life was now no big deal to me, but I could still end up dead, or in prison, and the implant apparently hadn't rendered me uninterested in my own fate.

I left too early, and had to drive by a circuitous route to kill time; even then, it was only a quarter past three when I parked, a kilometer from Anderson's house. A few cars and taxis passed me as I walked the rest of the way, and I'm sure I was trying so hard to look at ease that my body language radiated guilt and paranoia—but no ordinary driver would have noticed or cared, and I didn't see a single patrol car.

When I reached the place, there was nowhere to hide—no gardens, no trees, no fences—but I'd known that in advance. I chose a house across the street, not quite opposite Anderson's, and sat on the front step. If the occupant appeared, I'd feign drunkenness and stagger away.

I sat and waited. It was a warm, still, ordinary night; the sky was clear, but gray and starless thanks to the lights of the city. I kept reminding myself: *You don't have to do this, you don't have to go through with it.* So why did I stay? The hope of being liberated from my sleepless nights? The idea was laughable; I had no doubt that if I killed Anderson, it would torture me as much as my helplessness over Amy's death.

Why did I stay? It was nothing to do with the implant; at most, that was neutralizing my qualms; it wasn't forcing me to *do* anything.

Why, then? In the end, I think I saw it as a matter of honesty. I had to accept the unpleasant fact that I honestly wanted to kill Anderson, and however much I had also been repelled by the notion, to be true to myself I had to do it—anything less would have been hypocrisy and self-deception.

At five to four, I heard footsteps echoing down the street. As I turned, I hoped it would be someone else, or that he would be with a friend, but it was him, and he was alone. I waited until he was as far from his front door as I was, then I started walking. He glanced my way briefly, then ignored me. I felt a shock of pure fear—I hadn't seen him in the flesh since the trial, and I'd forgotten how physically imposing he was.

I had to force myself to slow down, and even then I passed him sooner than

I'd meant to. I was wearing light, rubber-soled shoes, he was in heavy boots, but when I crossed the street and did a U-turn toward him, I couldn't believe he couldn't hear my heartbeat, or smell the stench of my sweat. Meters from the door, just as I finished pulling out the gun, he looked over his shoulder with an expression of bland curiosity, as if he might have been expecting a dog or a piece of windblown litter. He turned around to face me, frowning. I just stood there, pointing the gun at him, unable to speak. Eventually he said, "What the fuck do you want? I've got two hundred dollars in my wallet. Back pocket."

I shook my head. "Unlock the front door, then put your hands on your head and kick it open. Don't try closing it on me."

He hesitated, then complied.

"Now walk in. Keep your hands on your head. Five steps, that's all. Count them out loud. I'll be right behind you."

I reached the light switch for the hall as he counted four, then I slammed the door behind me, and flinched at the sound. Anderson was right in front of me, and I suddenly felt trapped. The man was a vicious killer; *I* hadn't even thrown a punch since I was eight years old. Did I really believe the gun would protect me? With his hands on his head, the muscles of his arms and shoulders bulged against his shirt. I should have shot him right then, in the back of the head. This was an execution, not a duel; if I'd wanted some quaint idea of honor, I would have come without a gun and let him take me to pieces.

I said, "Turn left." Left was the living room. I followed him in, switched on the light. "Sit." I stood in the doorway, he sat in the room's only chair. For a moment, I felt dizzy and my vision seemed to tilt, but I don't think I moved, I don't think I sagged or swayed; if I had, he probably would have rushed me.

"What do you want?" he asked.

I had to give that a lot of thought. I'd fantasized this situation a thousand times, but I could no longer remember the details—although I did recall that I'd usually assumed that Anderson would recognize me, and start volunteering excuses and explanations straight away.

Finally, I said, "I want you to tell me why you killed my wife."

"I didn't kill your wife. Miller killed your wife."

I shook my head. "That's not true. I *know*. The cops told me. Don't bother lying, because I *know*."

He stared at me blandly. I wanted to lose my temper and scream, but I had a feeling that, in spite of the gun, that would have been more comical than intimidating. I could have pistol-whipped him, but the truth is I was afraid to go near him.

So I shot him in the foot. He yelped and swore, then leaned over to inspect the damage. "Fuck you!" he hissed. "Fuck you!" He rocked back and forth, holding his foot. "I'll break your fucking neck! I'll fucking kill you!" The wound bled a little through the hole in his boot, but it was nothing compared to the movies. I'd heard that the vaporizing ammunition had a cauterizing effect.

I said, "Tell me why you killed my wife."

He looked far more angry and disgusted than afraid, but he dropped his pretense of innocence. "It just happened," he said. "It was just one of those things that happens."

I shook my head, annoyed. "No. *Why?* Why did it happen?"

He moved as if to take off his boot, then thought better of it. "Things were going wrong. There was a time lock, there was hardly any cash, everything was just a big fuckup. I didn't mean to do it. It just happened."

I shook my head again, unable to decide if he was a moron, or if he was stalling. "Don't tell me 'it just happened.' *Why* did it happen? Why did you do it?"

The frustration was mutual; he ran a hand through his hair and scowled at me. He was sweating now, but I couldn't tell if it was from pain or from fear. "What do you want me to say? I lost my temper, all right? Things were going badly, and I lost my fucking temper, and there she was, all right?"

The dizziness struck me again, but this time it didn't subside. I understood now; he wasn't being obtuse, he was telling the entire truth. I'd smashed the occasional coffee cup during a tense situation at work. I'd even, to my shame, kicked our dog once, after a fight with Amy. Why? *I'd lost my fucking temper, and there she was.*

I stared at Anderson, and felt myself grinning stupidly. It was all so clear now. I understood. I understood the absurdity of everything I'd ever felt for Amy—my "love," my "grief." It had all been a joke. She was meat, she was nothing. All the pain of the past five years evaporated; I was drunk with relief. I raised my arms and spun around slowly. Anderson leapt up and sprung toward me; I shot him in the chest until I ran out of bullets, then I knelt down beside him. He was dead.

I put the gun in my jacket. The barrel was warm. I remembered to use my handkerchief to open the front door. I half-expected to find a crowd outside, but of course the shots had been inaudible, and Anderson's threats and curses were not likely to have attracted attention.

A block from the house, a patrol car appeared around a corner. It slowed almost to a halt as it approached me. I kept my eyes straight ahead as it passed. I heard the engine idle. Then stop. I kept walking, waiting for a shouted command, thinking: if they search me and find the gun, I'll confess; there's no point in prolonging the agony.

The engine spluttered, revved noisily, and the car roared away.

• • •

Perhaps I'm *not* the number one most obvious suspect. I don't know what Anderson was involved in since he got out; maybe there are hundreds of other people who had far better reasons for wanting him dead, and perhaps when the cops have finished with them, they'll get around to asking me what I was doing that night. A month seems an awfully long time, though. Anyone would think they didn't care.

The same teenagers as before are gathered around the entrance, and again the mere sight of me seems to disgust them. I wonder if the taste in fashion and music tattooed on their brains is set to fade in a year or two, or if they have sworn lifelong allegiance. It doesn't bear contemplating.

This time, I don't browse. I approach the sales counter without hesitation.

This time, I know exactly what I want.

What I want is what I felt that night: the unshakeable conviction that Amy's death—let alone Anderson's—simply didn't matter, any more than the death of a fly or an amoeba, any more than breaking a coffee cup or kicking a dog.

My one mistake was thinking that the insight I gained would simply vanish when the implant cut out. It hasn't. It's been clouded with doubts and reservations, it's been undermined, to some degree, by my whole ridiculous panoply of beliefs and superstitions, but I can still recall the peace it gave me, I can still recall that flood of joy and relief, and *I want it back*. Not for three days; for the rest of my life.

Killing Anderson *wasn't* honest, it wasn't "being true to myself." Being true to myself would have meant living with all my contradictory urges, suffering the multitude of voices in my head, accepting confusion and doubt. It's too late for that now; having tasted the freedom of certainty, I find I can't live without it.

"How can I help you, sir?" The salesman smiles from the bottom of his heart.

Part of me, of course, still finds the prospect of what I am about to do totally repugnant.

No matter. That won't last.

PAUL J. MCAULEY

GENE WARS

(1991)

1.

On Evan's eighth birthday, his aunt sent him the latest smash-hit biokit, *Splicing Your Own Semisentients*. The box lid depicted an alien swamp throbbing with weird, amorphous life; a double helix spiraling out of a test tube was embossed in one corner. *Don't let your father see that,* his mother said, so Evan took it out to the old barn, set up the plastic culture trays and vials of chemicals and retroviruses on a dusty workbench in the shadow of the shrouded combine.

His father found Evan there two days later. The slime mold he'd created, a million amoebae aggregated around a drop of cyclic AMP, had been transformed with a retrovirus and was budding little blue-furred blobs. Evan's father dumped culture trays and vials in the yard and made Evan pour a liter of industrial-grade bleach over them. More than fear or anger, it was the acrid stench that made Evan cry.

That summer, the leasing company foreclosed on the livestock. The rep who supervised repossession of the supercows drove off in a big car with the test-tube and double-helix logo on its gull-wing door. The next year the wheat failed, blighted by a particularly virulent rust. Evan's father couldn't afford the new resistant strain, and the farm went under.

2.

Evan lived with his aunt, in the capital. He was fifteen. He had a street bike, a plug-in computer, and a pet microsaur, a triceratops in purple funfur. Buying the special porridge which was all the microsaur could eat took half of Evan's weekly allowance; that was why he let his best friend inject the pet with a bootleg virus to edit out its dietary dependence. It was only a partial success: the triceratops no longer needed its porridge, but developed epilepsy triggered by sunlight. Evan had to keep it in his wardrobe. When it started shedding fur in great swatches, he abandoned it in a nearby park. Microsaurs were out of fashion, anyway. Dozens could be found wandering the park, nibbling at leaves, grass, discarded scraps of fast food. Quite soon they disappeared, starved to extinction.

3.

The day before Evan graduated, his sponsor company called to tell him that he wouldn't be doing research after all. There had been a change of policy: the covert gene wars were going public. When Evan started to protest, the woman said sharply, "You're better off than many long-term employees. With a degree in molecular genetics you'll make sergeant at least."

4.

Rivers made silvery forked lightnings in the jungle's vivid green blanket. Warm wind rushed around Evan as he leaned out the helicopter's hatch; the harness dug into his shoulders. He was twenty-three, a tech sergeant. It was his second tour of duty.

His goggles laid icons over the view, tracking the target. Two villages a klick apart, linked by a red dirt road narrow as a capillary that suddenly widened to an artery as the helicopter dove.

Muzzle-flashes on the ground. Evan hoped the peasants only had Kalashnikovs: last week, an unfriendly had downed a copter with an antique SAM. Then he was too busy laying the pattern, virus-suspension in a sticky spray that fogged the maize fields.

Afterward, the pilot, an old-timer, said over the intercom, "Things get tougher every day. We used just to take a leaf, cloning did the rest. You couldn't even call it theft. But this stuff . . . I always thought war was bad for business."

Evan said, "The company owns copyright to the maize genome. Those peasants aren't licensed to grow it."

The pilot said admiringly, "Man, you're a real company guy. I bet you don't even know what country this is."

Evan thought about that. He said, "Since when were countries important?"

5.

Rice fields quilted the floodplain. In every paddy, peasants bent over their own reflections, planting seedlings for the winter crop.

At the center of the UNESCO delegation, the Minister for Agriculture stood under a black umbrella held by an aide. He was explaining that his country was starving to death after a record rice crop.

Evan was at the back of the little crowd, bareheaded in warm drizzle. He wore a smart one-piece suit, yellow overshoes. He was twenty-eight, had spent two years infiltrating UNESCO for his company.

The minister was saying, "We have to buy seed gene-spliced for pesticide resistance to compete with our neighbors, but my people can't afford to buy the rice they grow. It must all be exported to service our debt. We are starving in the midst of plenty."

Evan stifled a yawn. Later, at a reception in some crumbling embassy, he managed to get the minister on his own. The man was drunk, unaccustomed to hard liquor. Evan told him he was very moved by what he had seen.

"Look in our cities," the minister said, slurring his words. "Every day refugees pour in from the countryside. They cannot feed themselves and neither can we. There is cholera. Very bad cholera. There is kwashiorkor. Beriberi."

Evan popped a canapé into his mouth. One of his company's new lines, it squirmed with delicious lasciviousness before he swallowed it. "I may be able to help you," he said. "The people I represent have a new yeast that completely fulfills dietary requirements and will grow in a simple medium."

As Evan explained, the minister, no longer as drunk as he had seemed, steered him onto the terrace.

"You understand this must be confidential," the minister said. "Under UNESCO rules—"

"We have arrangements with five countries that have trade imbalances similar to your own. We can lease the genome as a loss-leader, if your government is willing to look favorably on certain other products . . ."

6.

The gene pirate was showing Evan his editing facility when the slow poison finally hit him. They were aboard an ancient ICBM submarine grounded somewhere off the Philippines. Missile tubes had been converted into fermenters. The bridge was crammed with the latest manipulation technology, virtual reality gear which let the wearer directly control molecule-sized cutting robots as they traveled along DNA helices.

"It's not facilities I need," the pirate told Evan. "It's distribution."

"No problem," Evan said. The pirate's security had been pathetically easy to penetrate. He'd tried to infect Evan with a zombie virus, but Evan's gene-spliced immune system had easily dealt with it. Slow poison was so much more subtle: by the time it could be detected it was too late. Evan was thirty-two. He was posing as a Swiss gray-market broker.

"This is where I keep my old stuff," the pirate said, rapping a stainless-steel cryogenic vat. "Stuff from before I went big time. A luciferase gene drive, for instance. Remember when the Brazilian rainforest started to glow? That was me."

He dashed sweat from his forehead, frowned at the room's complicated thermostat. Grossly fat and completely hairless, he was bare-chested in Bermuda shorts and shower sandals. He'd been targeted because he was about to break the big time with a novel AIDS cure. The company was still making a lot of money from its own cure, having made sure HIV had never been completely eradicated in developing countries.

Evan said, "I remember the Brazilian government was overthrown—the population took it as a bad omen."

"Hey, what can I say? I was only a kid. Rejigging the genes was easy; only difficulty was finding a vector. Old stuff. Somatic mutation really is going to be the next big thing, believe me. Why breed new strains when you can rework an organism cell by cell?" The pirate rapped the thermostat. His hands were shaking. "Why is it so hot in here?"

"That's the first symptom," Evan said. He stepped out of the way as the gene pirate crashed to the decking. "And that's the second."

The company had taken the precaution of buying the pirate's security chief: Evan had plenty of time to fix the fermenters. They would have boiled dry by the time he was ashore. On impulse, against orders, he took a sample of the AIDS cure with him.

7.

"The territory between piracy and legitimacy is a minefield," the assassin told Evan. "It's also where paradigm shifts are most likely to occur, and that's where I come in. My company likes stability. Another year and you'd have gone public, and most likely the share issue would have made you a billionaire—a minor player, but still a player. Those cats, no one else has them. The genome was supposed to have been wiped out back in the twenties. Very astute, quitting the gray medical market and going for luxury goods." She frowned. "Why am I talking so much?"

"For the same reason you're not going to kill me," Evan said.

"It seems such a silly thing to want to do," the assassin admitted.

Evan smiled. He'd long ago decoded the two-stage virus the gene-pirate had used on him: one a Trojan horse which kept his T-lymphocytes busy while the other rewrote loyalty genes companies implanted in their employees. Once again it had proven its worth. He said, "I need someone like you in my organization. And since you spent so long getting close enough to seduce me, perhaps you'd do me the honor of becoming my wife. I'll need one."

"You don't mind being married to a killer?"

"Of course not. I used to be one myself."

8.

Evan saw the market crash coming. Gene wars had winnowed basic crops to soy beans, rice, and dole yeast: tailored, ever-mutating diseases had reduced cereals and many other food plants to nucleotide sequences stored in computer vaults. Three global biotechnology companies held patents on the calorific input of 98 percent of humanity, but they had lost control of the technology. Pressures of the war economy had simplified it to the point where anyone could directly manipulate her own genome, and hence her own body form.

Evan had made a fortune in the fashion industry, selling basic genetic templates and virus vectors. But he guessed that sooner or later someone would come up with a direct photosynthesis system, and his stock market expert systems were programmed to monitor research in the field. He and his wife sold controlling interest in their company three months before the first green people appeared.

9.

"I remember when you knew what a human being was," Evan said sadly. "I suppose I'm old-fashioned, but there it is."

From her cradle, inside a mist of spray, his wife said, "Is that why you never went green? I always thought it was a fashion statement."

"Old habits die hard." The truth was, he liked his body the way it was. These days, going green involved somatic mutation which grew a meter-high black cowl to absorb sufficient light energy. Most people lived in the tropics: swarms of black-caped anarchists. Work was no longer a necessity, but an indulgence. Evan added, "I'm going to miss you."

"Let's face it," his wife said, "we never were in love. But I'll miss you, too." With a flick of her powerful tail she launched her streamlined body into the sea.

10.

Black-cowled post-humans, gliding slowly in the sun, aggregating and reaggregating like ameobae. Dolphinoids, tentacles sheathed under fins, rocking in tanks of cloudy water. Ambulatory starfish; tumbling bushes of spikes; snakes with a single arm, a single leg; flocks of tiny birds, brilliant as emeralds, each flock a single entity.

People, grown strange, infected with viruses and myriads of microscopic machines which reengraved their body form at will.

Evan lived in a secluded estate. He was revered as a founding father of the posthuman revolution. A purple funfur microsaur followed him everywhere. It was recording him because he had elected to die.

"I don't regret anything," Evan said, "except perhaps not following my wife when she changed. I saw it coming, you know. All this. Once the technology became simple enough, cheap enough, the companies lost control. Like television or computers, but I suppose you don't remember those." He sighed. He had the vague feeling he'd said all this before. He'd had no new thoughts for a century, except the desire to put an end to thought.

The microsaur said, "In a way, I suppose I am a descendant of computers. Will you see the colonial delegation now?"

"Later." Evan hobbled to a bench and slowly sat down. In the last couple of months he had developed mild arthritis and liver spots on the backs of his hands: death finally expressing parts of his genome that had been suppressed for so long. Hot sunlight fell through the velvet streamers of the tree things; Evan dozed, woke to find a group of starfish watching him. They had blue, human eyes, one at the tip of each muscular arm.

"They wish to honor you by taking your genome to Mars," the little purple triceratops said.

Evan sighed. "I just want peace. To rest. To die."

"Oh, Evan," the triceratops said patiently. "Have you forgotten that nothing really dies anymore?"

JAMES LOVEGROVE

BRITWORLD™

(1992)

HI! Welcome to Britworld™. My name is Wanda May June and I will be your guide, hostess, and compère for the duration of the tour. If you have any questions about anything you see here today, I will be more than happy to answer them.

Thank you for coming prepared with warm clothing. The temperature in Britworld™ is kept at a refreshing forty-five degrees Fahrenheit all year round. USACorp Entertainments have gone to great lengths to enhance the authenticity of your experience by reproducing the exact climate of the original. This also means a) If there is anyone here who suffers from respiratory ailments or is in any way inconvenienced by the Britworld™ environment, they should not hesitate to leave by one of the emergency exits, one of which you will see over there, marked EXIT.

Now, has everyone got their umbrellas, or "bumbershoots," as we call them in Britworld™?

Good. Then why don't you follow me to the first sector? Thank you!

Here we find ourselves in a typical urban situation. This is in fact London, which was the capital of Britworld™ and home to the famous Beatles.

The wind is a little gusty today. Look how it speeds the clouds along! There is a 97 percent chance of rain later.

A brief technical note. The sky you are now seeing is, of course, projected on to the underside of the geodesic dome. Now, whereas other theme parks use simple loop-sequences of an hour or so in length, the clouds here are generated using the latest in Chaos Model programs. Thus no two are ever alike. Some are large, some are small. That one looks just like a duck, doesn't it? We at USA-Corp Entertainments are justly proud of innovations such as these which keep us one step ahead of the competition.

As you cross the street, mind your step on the piles of garbage—or "rubbish" as it is known here.

Yes, it does smell kind of bad, doesn't it? But you must remember that in the real Britworld™ they had never heard of efficient disposal or recycling.

Whoops-a-daisy! Are we all right, ma'am? Good. I can see that you haven't sustained any serious injury, but I should take this opportunity to mention to you all that in the eventuality of an accident situation, USACorp Entertainments will accept zero liability. You all signed the waiver forms at the entrance.

Please try to keep up!

Let's wait here for a few minutes at this bus stop. If we are lucky, we may see a genuine double-decker bus. The word "bus" is short for "omnibus," which is pretty much the same thing as a coach. A double-decker bus is a bus with two decks. Hence the name. It is red and will have a number on the front, signifying its route, and a destination—perhaps the Houses of Parliament, where Guy Fawkes lived, or Hyde Park, named after the alter ego of the famous scientist Dr. Jekyll, or maybe the Globe Theater, which was built by Sir William Shakespeare.

Any minute now, there may be an omnibus. There may even be two. Or three!

Double-decker buses have a seating capacity of sixty-eight, forty-four on top, twenty-four below—not forgetting, of course, standing room for another twenty passengers.

Any . . . minute . . . now.

It doesn't look like one's coming. What a disappointment. Well, we can't hang around all day. Let's proceed along this road to the market.

Many historians consider the market to be an early precursor of our shopping mall. Notice how each stall sells a different product, what we now call franchising. Here is the fruit and vegetable stall, selling fruit and vegetables. It is tended by a cheerful man known as a greengrocer. The name is derived from the fact that a large proportion of his groceries are green in color.

Listen.

"Apples and pears! Apples and pears! Getcha apples and pears!"

Isn't that clever? USACorp Entertainments have taken every effort to reduplicate the Britworld™ dialect, incomprehensible now to the great majority of the English-speaking world.

Little boy, the automata are *extremely* delicate. Please don't touch.

I would just like to show you this. A strawberry. Everybody! Look at this strawberry. This is the fruit from which we derive strawberry flavor.

Yes, sir, I suppose it does bear a slight resemblance to a wino's nose.

On the street corner we see the newsvendor, vending newspapers. Let's listen to his distinctive cry.

"Paperrrr! Getcha paper heeeere!"

The cloth cap and raincoat he is wearing are the real thing, the genuine article, as is all the clothing you will see today, purchased at great cost by USA-Corp Entertainments from museums all over the world.

Beyond the newsvendor you may already have spotted the street musicians, or "buskers," so called because they used to play on buses until the law banned them. The tune they are playing is a traditional folk ballad, "Strawberry Fields Forever." Remember that strawberry I showed you earlier on? Well, this song was written, so they say, about fields of strawberries stretching so far into the distance they seemed to go on forever.

Don't the buskers sing well?

We are standing outside a pub, the Britworld™ equivalent of a bar. "Pub" is short for public house, a house into which members of the public may enter whenever they wish. This one has a name. The King's Head. On the sign up there we see a picture of the head of the King. Notice his crown. Shall we go in?

Here we see the inhabitants of Britworld™ relaxing in the friendly, intimate atmosphere of the pub. At the bar we see the landlord and the landlady, so called because they rent out the house to the public.

This is Charly, a cheerful local. Cheerful locals in London were known as Cockneys because—so legend goes—they were born within the sound of the bells of Cockney Cathedral. Tell us, Charly, do you enjoy drinking here?

"God blimey, luvaduck, I should say. Crikey, strike me blind if I jolly bloomin' well don't! Lor lumme! Eh, guvnor?"

I think he does! And chim-chim-cheroo to you, too, Charly!

Now, follow me, everyone. Don't try that, sir. It's not safe to drink. It's a substitute for the popular pub drink, bitter ale, designed to maintain its color and consistency and that distinctive frothy head for approximately eighteen years.

Let's hurry on to the next sector. But I must warn you, be prepared to be thrilled, chilled, and spilled! Those with heart conditions or nervous complaints may wish to consider leaving by the nearest convenient emergency exit over there, marked EXIT.

Where are we? Fog swirls along darkened streets and the gas lamps flicker, casting strange shadows on the sidewalk. Villains surely lurk in this fog-enshrouded place.

But look at that road sign! "Baker's Street." How many of you know which well-known historical personality lived on Baker's Street?

No.

No.

No, not the Reverend Jim Bakker.

No.

No, it was Sherlock Holmes! And if we are lucky, we may just catch a glimpse . . .

Ah! There! The deerstalker, the cape, the pipe. It can only be . . . And yes, there is his friend and faithful companion, Dr. Watson.

"The game's afoot."

"Good heavens, Holmes! How on earth did you deduce that?"

"Elementary, my dear Watson. When you have eliminated the impossible, whatever remains, however improbable, must be the truth."

And so the great detective sweeps past us on his way to solving another baffling, mystifying, perplexing mystery. So close, so realistic, you could reach out and touch him.

But who is that? A woman, wandering the night streets, vulnerable and alone. She must be careful. There's murder in the air.

Oh, look out! That man in the top hat and cloak! He has a knife! He is Jack the Ripper, that terrible fiend of the night and depraver of women. Who will save her? Who will save her?

Hooray! Here comes a friendly policeman, whose name is Bobby. He blows his whistle. That's seen that dreadful Ripper off! Look how Bobby is comforting that poor woman. How safe she must feel.

Well, I'm quite breathless with excitement. Everybody follow me to the next sector.

Oh dear. Bumbershoots up, everyone! As the saying in Britworld™ goes, "It's raining buckets of cats."

If you can't hear me over the rain, say so and I will speak up. Okay?

Good.

This grand edifice is none other than the Buckingham Palace, home of the King and Queen of Britworld™. USACorp Entertainments, sparing no expense, had the original building transported brick by brick and reconstructed here. See how the Union Jack, royal flag of Britworld™, flutters proudly from the mast on the palace roof.

The palace has a large number of large rooms and a smaller number of small rooms. All the interiors have been re-created down to the finest detail. However, as we're running a little behind, we'll have to skip that part of the tour.

If you *do* want a refund, ma'am, I'd advise you to take the matter up with USACorp's Central Office and not with me.

Trust me, they are *bee-yootiful* rooms.

Notice the Beefeaters standing guard at the palace gates with their fierce pikes and their mustaches. They get their name from their traditional beef-only diet. Yes, amazing as it may sound, they used to eat nothing but beef! Naturally, Beefeaters had a disproportionately high rate of death from bowel cancer.

Twice a day the guards change their positions to avoid cramp. This is known as the Changing of the Guard.

Wait! Look! Up there! On the balcony! Why, the King and Queen have come out to wave at us! Wave back, everybody.

The King is wearing his crown. Remember the sign at the pub? The Queen, meanwhile, is wearing an elegant mid-length gown in taffeta, cut on the bias, with a lace hem and gold braid trim along the sleeves. To complete the ensemble, she wears a diamond tiara and earrings and matching accessories. Ladies, don't you wish you could dress as elegantly as that?

Oh, they're going in again. Goodbye, your majesties! Goodbye! Goodbye!

We are now entering the Shakespeare sector. You can put down your bumbershoots now, as the rain has been switched off. I know several of you have heard about the little difficulty we had in this sector some months back, but I am pleased to be able to tell you that the fire damage has been repaired and the tour can proceed as normal. However, please remember to observe the *No Smoking* rule at all times.

Sir William Shakespeare was known as the Bard of Avon, a hereditary title handed down from one generation of bards to the next in the town of Avon, which was situated a few miles from London, capital city of Britworld™.

The Globe Theater was first constructed by USACorp Entertainments to the same specifications as the original, but since the fire a number of alterations have been made, for instance the use of steel and plastics in place of wood and plaster.

Let's go in.

Shhh. On the stage at this very moment a play is being performed. The play is *Macbeth*, about a barbarian king who goes on a rampage of slaughter and mayhem before being brought to justice by his best friend. You've all seen the old movie starring Arnold Schwarzenegger.

"Tomorrow and tomorrow and tomorrow."

We don't need to hear much more to get an idea of the genius of Sir William Shakespeare's dialogue.

And here, I'm sorry to say, the tour ends. Before we leave via the exit marked EXIT, may I say what a privilege and a pleasure it has been for me to share with you the sights, sounds, and smells of Britworld™. As you will have seen, everything has been designed to the most rigorous of standards, including the automata, which incorporate numerous technological breakthroughs that allow for a wide range of facial expression, body odors, minor blemishes, and deformities, even perspiration!

On behalf of USACorp Entertainments, I would like to thank you for accompanying me on the experience that was . . . Britworld™.

The following souvenirs are available at the merchandise kiosks: reproduction bric-a-brac; a Cockney phrase-book; Union Jack baseball caps; ebook editions of the works of Sherlock Holmes and Sir William Shakespeare, abridged and modernized; *My Parents Went To Britworld™ And All I Got Was This Lousy T-Shirt* T-shirts; foam-rubber crowns for the kids; the fabulous *You Are Saucy Jack* computer game (all formats); and downloads of favorite Britworld™ folk songs, including "Strawberry Fields Forever," "Jerusalem," "God Save the King," and many many more. All major credit cards accepted.

And finally, may I remind you about our other Lost Worlds® experiences, all bookable. They include the Native American Experience™, Dreamtime: the Australian Aborigine Experience™, and Life Among the Bushmen of the Kalahari™.

USACorp Entertainments—where the science of tomorrow brings the past into the present.

Have a nice day.

© USACorp Entertainments
Britworld™ is a registered trademark
of USACorp Entertainments

GERARDO HORACIO PORCAYO

RIPPED IMAGES, RUSTED DREAMS

(1993)

Translated from the Spanish by the author

"THE TIMES GLITTERED. Human shoals swimming through neon, laser lights, and synthetic junk food. It was still shit, I swear, but better than today's shit. And it was mine in all senses. Guadalupe City was the access point. You could find everything in the rotten slums that grew at the hillside of Cerro de la Silla: stolen cars and smuggled intelligent drugs, not forgetting the classics of heroin and boxes of pleasure. You could get high for real; reach madness. You were well supplied with everything, because Monterrey consumed everything. In those days *the heat* could smell you, look at you in the eye, while you picked up a fake coke high through the wires attached to your brain. And you could climb, real high without them playing to kill you."

The Retro looks at me heavily, almost with showiness. He values his Electric Dreams more, his computer Chimeras; chronometric insanity and then ready for a reboot, almost every time. They've become part of the computer, vile maze rats, addicted to electric shocks; to the venom itself. Like her . . .

"I was running away from Laredo, four DEA pigs after me. Three salesmen with Glocks under their armpits and inhalers filling their pockets. I was looking for fresh air, a little cash, and stuff to keep me going."

"You're out of step, old man. Things were always the same, only now we have the Electric Dream," he says. He gets up, throwing a couple rotten dollars on the bar as he leaves. I know his weakness. The darkness clings to our spirit. It's the stigmata of those who hate the world as it is.

Now they hunt addictive software, have labyrinthine dreams of crime and forbidden sex, cycle through blasphemies in a planet ruled, more and more, by a cybernetic god from his silicon heaven beyond the stars. They get lost in venal places that stink of semen and vaginal fluids, in the dim light of ripped sunsets. The world no longer has any pretense at virginity, it's a decrepit whore, walking sadly to the end of the Milky Way only to find out there are no clients left for her.

"Give me another triple," I ask the barman, and he looks back at me, so weary. He knows my business, a null one, just the waiting, the hunt for users who hate the tales, the beer, and their own life.

"You are going to end with your teeth broken," he warns me. Pity leaks from his eyes like old pus.

"Did I tell you about Cora?"

The son of a bitch pushes me away, he goes to the other end of the battered bar, past the sailors' and workers' vomit, to find the warm hug of the TV. There, he doesn't need to think things over. Why are they all so lost? I prefer the old paranoia, the threats that surrounded you and made you leave Austin or Florida, Houston on a bullet train or hitchhiking across the bloody fields of Illinois, through the rocky deserts near TJ, bug-eyed traffickers with sweaty hands and nervous, bloated agents closing in.

I survey the bar, looking for my contact, or another listener. Even a grubby cat with a broken tail, clambering up the frame of a fractal or a tesseract painting.

The Retro comes back. And he's not alone. A wasted girl with an airbrush shadow makeup that resembles a raccoon, and four hairy beasts that stink of Benzedrine and overheated wires. The curls in their hair are natural, they burn by themselves at the top of the skull, near the socket.

"Beat it!" he warns me. "We don't want flies around."

"I know the business even better than you. I know the history."

One hairy man stands in front of me, he carries a taser glove and his lips are full of post-holocaustic piercings.

"Get lost, graybeard. It would break my heart to kick the shit out of you."

"I even used to have a band like yours," I insist. My shame gets away from me, nauseating me.

"Let him talk. Maybe you will end up like him," says the raccoon girl, giggling like a battered coffee maker.

"He stinks."

"When I reached Monterrey, only the yuppies used the Electric Dream. Well suited, with eight-hundred-dollar pants and British raincoats that smelled like the Thames."

"He lost all his head knobs and bolts when they kicked the shit out of him," states another hairy one.

"I met Loquillo, a guy with an eternal lapbody and a red, curled forelock that hid his socket. And he really loved to get wasted, he never turned down any of the hallucinogenic stuff that appeared, wherever it came from." Raccoon looks at me with loose eyes, each pupil facing a different direction. Squinting Raccoon with atrophied nose.

"Loquillo was a hacker and a wire addict. Not a chemical junkie," argues the Retro. That's a big difference now. You don't gain cred with neuro-activated stuff, but with technology: electricity and wires sunk deep into your brain. It means they know what I'm talking about, and Raccoon, at least, wants to hear the whole story.

"I bet eighty greens that you don't know shit," dares one of the hairy ones.

"I used to play with the black box, with the brain pleasure. They moved adulterated coke at such a high cost that you couldn't even pick up a decent addiction. You had to replace it with small charges straight into the proper conduits, and you'd get high, real high. Charly 29 used to know how to do it. He had a Lincoln convertible, an international credit card with no limit. He had Roger, Isidro, and Cora. And good cranial butchers, not like the usual ones, who think their medibots are best for brain surgery."

"It seems your socket got battered miles ago, and now your brain's rusted," says the Retro. "We begin at fifteen and dine hot software every night."

"Charly found the first net for us. Back then, the Electric Dream was just a complement; the best thing was being on the streets. The adrenaline rushing through you when the cops were pushed to keep appearances up or the PGR had to justify their income. The days when you fixed new cocktails, not even knowing what door you were going to be throwing them at."

"And what happened with Loquillo?" asks the Raccoon.

"That's an old story. Even you would've heard it. He was hunted in the big revolt against the silicon god." A hairy one watches me with tight teeth, his hand tight in his spandex vest pocket. "He was one of my kind and he saw that the good times were dying with the Northern Lights of the Christ-receptionism. At the same time, he fought for Cora. She was the first one to taste the Seagull's Dream, she even baptized it with its name."

"That's old news," grunts the Retro. "Nobody does the Seagull's Dreams today. The ghosts slice you apart if you're not at their level. They rip your guts out with a chain saw, in landscapes built of car bumpers, seas of dry polystyrene, mountains of plastic garbage, and squirrels full of chips and servomotors. Or you are caught in a corner by God, and thrown to the hell of cannibal guts, or into a nightmare of dull teeth. Now, diving into a computer is like running through the streets with the hounds after you and the paranoia of getting caught with the hot stuff. Now, we defy God in every joint, in every hallucination. *You* were never hunted by God."

"I saw him for the first time with Cora. We'd been running through university parties full up to the top with Ecstasy. Rushing down your spine like a galvanic stream, giving you such a boner that you believed you could open new sexual holes. Charly 29 had found us a net. We rode after the fall. There were no drugs left. The President was in town and they successfully cleaned up for the occasion. We were dry. And you know it: abstinence is mortal. So we jumped back to the net. Both in one deck. At that time, we had already tried orgies, the five of us. But that day, it was just me and her. And it was different. We felt God's nauseating breath over our shoulders. His face appeared in the graffiti upon the asphalt and the peeled walls; the sadness stuck to our ribs like lead. We could barely breathe. Her body seemed to be falling apart, my fingers got sunk in her flesh like it was dry mud. We let go. She told me she wanted to go on a boat, so we took a transatlantic from the hotel's door. Its chimneys expelled atomic vapors, MDA, and nootropic cocktails. We traveled with open skies and the sea was more pure than any nanomachine reproductions. The seagulls orbited us like psychotic satellites. They were hungry. Cora wanted to feed them by sheer willpower and, after that, with sushi. Sushi miraculously multiplied. One thousand seagulls kept flying against the wind and crying every time a chunk of fish entered their domain. 'Look at them,' she said, 'they are like angels of solitude, like a mountain that goes around oceans and valleys, they are like faith and happiness.' And she was right. We came back eight times to the same dream, after that, she went alone and never came back."

"And what was Loquillo's role in all this?"

"He met her a little while after that, when he was trying to steal info from Mariano's Labs. It was really hot stuff. Cora was stuck all the way to his bones. She was already a ghost, but kept being special, she could transfer her beauty to you as if it were viral files. When they trapped Loquillo, the bait was Cora herself. He couldn't refuse her, nobody could."

"I've met her," says the hairy one with the glove. "She came to me in a mix of exodiprine and a pirate dream program. And I could break free. She's not such a big deal. Any black software has better divas now. They're vampires that suck you dry. First, they steal your memories, then your sexual appetite, and then even your hope of living."

"That you've never had," I said. "I know what I'm talking about, I'm one of the pioneers."

The Raccoon doesn't laugh anymore. Her eyes have become dark and disoriented, black holes without any spark of life. She's going down fast, to the pit. She needs wires . . .

"You defy God just by living," says the Retro. "The fear has always been there, but, in the Electric Dream, you can touch it. The torture comes in waves, like rabid hurricanes, it comes over you like dragonflies from hell. Your stomach growls, trying to open its way out of your skin and leave you there, lying in the middle of a nonexisting alley; those mazes are sordid, more than the real ones. One time I found a homeless lady, her eyes had never met the light, they were half-dead, sunken in her eye sockets, covered by a reptilian membrane; she had a small left hand, which grew a sick prosthesis that suppurated semen. Her fatness was so huge that she only kept upright with little crutches attached to her handicap wheels. And the wires came out of her skull; they buzzed, mimicking a cry of help. With her right hand she stirred a dirty mug, filled with human embryos. She was the Virgin. I tell you. I promise you. She hunted me through swamps, computer cemeteries. She ripped open bulldozers. Drunken rockets fell down from the sky, like banished angels. And you cannot escape, she hunts you, even when you've left the Electric Dream. Some nights I still dream of her. The streets are safer, even the Anti-Sin Brigade is clumsy and slow. They have high-tech weapons and scanners, but you can lose them in dry river glens, in dry sewer systems, or through the subway. And, if you've performed well, they'll never find you. But once God has seen you, he never stops appearing, even in the most recent software, in programs compiled in Thailand, with ideographic graffiti and old-fashioned red zones. His breath is worse than you can say. When it hits you, it's like you'll never ever smell anything again; everything becomes lessened and the sole memory of his breath brings you open-eye hallucinations. Heavenquakes happen and drip like rotten glycerin, showering you, stopping your scurry, blurring any possible horizon, extinguishing any spark of hope— You don't know what you're all talking about." His gaze is lost in his glass. His hands shake frantically like they're trying to fly away, to get the hell out of the body.

I look around. An angel has passed, dropping the pest. The Raccoon operates her black box. Her eyes are already cosmic bat clusters; they cry blasphemies and overwhelming curses. The hairy ones keep to themselves. They're in the Reality Syndrome, they no longer know where they are. The one with the glove confuses me for an exterminator angel. He stares at me closely, like a meditation. He sees my rotten face, half-eaten by static, and my silhouette, deformed by nonexistent pixels.

"That's why I said that my time was a better one," I conclude. "There was nothing this big back then, nothing so overwhelming but the hangover, the shakes of your dryness, your guts yelling with chemical hunger."

The bartender shepherds the flies. They follow him like he'd made an attachment spell, they watch him as he juggles glass and adulterated bottles, stare at his everlasting, tattooed reflection on the mirrors. He is tired of us all. He gestures to me, resigned. He has tried it before and doesn't bother to wait for my reaction. I follow his gaze. Three Voices awaits, hidden at a corner table. The White Privateer is standing up beside him.

I leave the group without a word. The hairs on my back bristle like roaches' antennas. I bound forward, and rush to my meeting.

"It's not a good thing to open your mouth that much," says Three Voices, carefully steering his felt hat, controlling his own movements through it. "They never forget, not even the old stuff."

"I have to do something," I lie to him. He doesn't care, he's only doing his job. The protocols are strict and should be observed. I reach my hand to him. Hidden green inside. He takes it, delaying the contact. And his eyes tell me abyssal things, horrible truths.

"The rest comes tomorrow at the Macroplaza," he promises, and hands me a small plastic cylinder. I turn away, without a word. I have no intention of leaving the bar.

One of the hairy ones puts his hand out to me. I sense the bills, their poor and ruined texture; rotten leaves, almost useless excrescences.

"The eighty we bet. You earned it, old man. I knew Loquillo couldn't have been screwed in the reality. I knew he couldn't have died in the bomb attack. His death belonged to the net."

No more words, we share booze and loneliness. Anguish that piles itself like acid in the guts. We are balloons that, little by little, get inflated. Someday we will burst.

"I think I understand you now," says the Retro, pulling the Raccoon along with him, as she travels the virtual frequency.

I see them get lost through the mirror, through the inner darkness, through the pitch black of the outside. And the silence stays in the air for a long time, like clots in zero gravity. It fills the atmosphere and makes my paranoia all the stronger.

"Someone's gonna end breaking your teeth," warns the bartender again, picking up the dollars. His watery eyes are opaque and sad.

"I know," I answer him, and I leave the bar, the shelter.

The city expands itself before me, a hypertrophied and dying organism. The buildings cut themselves against the bloody night like spades in a battlefield. Tons of parabolic antennas bend their ears looking forward to catch the voice of God. The worm of fear begins to eat my guts. The cathedrals are like blind eyes in the hellish darkness, they keep on going, block by block; like dogs, wanderers, and some junkies shaking with the beat of peristaltic movements, forgetting ignominies, boredom, apprehension . . .

They were even better than me, junkies, I mean. They're not afraid, not of God, not of the Anti-Sin Brigade. The narcotic officers don't exist anymore.

I walk, and with each step I miss the old ways, the sirens screaming your almost certain arrest, agents so corrupt, so full of needs, like your own, closing in. Shit has changed. Paranoia, too. Like many other nights, I fear androids after me, angry, thirsty for justice, a revenge postponed for so long, bleeding, while they get free of the nails and the crosses and follow my footprints, showering them in their synthetic blood. The crown of thorns is a vector of their memories.

And I fear. And I swallow the pills. The hunt may never end.

And the hunger in me never will.

For a couple of Williams
Burroughs and Gibson

NEAL STEPHENSON

THE GREAT SIMOLEON CAPER

(1995)

HARD TO IMAGINE a less attractive lifestyle for a young man just out of college than going back to Bismarck to live with his parents—unless it's living with his brother in the suburbs of Chicago, which, naturally, is what I did. Mom at least bakes a mean cherry pie. Joe, on the other hand, got me into a permanent emotional headlock and found some way, every day, to give me psychic noogies. For example, there was the day he gave me the job of figuring out how many jelly beans it would take to fill up Soldier Field.

Let us stipulate that it's all my fault; Joe would want me to be clear on that point. Just as he was always good with people, I was always good with numbers. As Joe tells me at least once a week, I should have studied engineering. Drifted between majors instead, ended up with a major in math and a minor in art—just about the worst thing you can put on a job app.

Joe, on the other hand, went into the ad game. When the Internet and optical fiber and HDTV and digital cash all came together and turned into what we now call the Metaverse, most of the big ad agencies got hammered—because in the Metaverse, you can actually whip out a gun and blow the Energizer Bunny's head off, and a lot of people did. Joe borrowed ten thousand bucks from Mom and Dad and started this clever young ad agency. If you've spent any time crawling the Metaverse, you've seen his work—and it's seen you, and talked to you, and followed you around.

Mom and Dad stayed in their same little house in Bismarck, North Dakota.

None of their neighbors guessed that if they cashed in their stock in Joe's agency, they'd be worth about $20 million. I nagged them to diversify their portfolio—you know, buy a bushel basket of Krugerrands and bury them in the backyard, or maybe put a few million into a mutual fund. But Mom and Dad felt this would be a no-confidence vote in Joe. "It'd be," Dad said, "like showing up for your kid's piano recital with a Walkman."

Joe comes home one January evening with a magnum of champagne. After giving me the obligatory hazing about whether I'm old enough to drink, he pours me a glass. He's already banished his two sons to the Home Theater. They have cranked up the set-top box they got for Christmas. Patch this baby into your HDTV, and you can cruise the Metaverse, wander the Web, and choose from among several user-friendly operating systems, each one rife with automatic help systems, customer-service hotlines, and intelligent agents. The theater's subwoofer causes our silverware to buzz around like sheet-metal hockey players, and amplified explosions knock swirling nebulas of tiny bubbles loose from the insides of our champagne glasses. Those low frequencies must penetrate the young brain somehow, coming in under kids' media-hip radar and injecting the edfotainucational muchomedia bitstream direct into their cerebral cortices.

"Hauled down a mother of an account today," Joe explains. "We hype cars. We hype computers. We hype athletic shoes. But as of three hours ago, we are hyping a currency."

"What?" says his wife, Anne.

"Y'know, like dollars or yen. Except this is a new currency."

"From which country?" I ask. This is like offering lox to a dog: I've given Joe the chance to enlighten his feckless bro. He hammers back half a flute of Dom Perignon and shifts into full-on Pitch Mode.

"Forget about countries," he says. "We're talking Simoleons—the smart, hip new currency of the Metaverse."

"Is this like E-money?" Anne asks.

"We've been doing E-money for e-ons, ever since automated-teller machines." Joe says, with just the right edge of scorn. "Nowadays we can use it to go shopping in the Metaverse. But it's still in US dollars. Smart people are looking for something better."

That was for me. I graduated college with a thousand bucks in savings. With inflation at 10 percent and rising, that buys a lot fewer Leinenkugels than it did a year ago.

"The government's never going to get its act together on the budget," Joe says. "It can't. Inflation will just get worse. People will put their money elsewhere."

"Inflation would have to get pretty damn high before I'd put my money into some artificial currency," I say.

"Hell, they're all artificial," Joe says. "If you think about it, we've been doing this forever. We put our money in stocks, bonds, shares of mutual funds. Those things represent real assets—factories, ships, bananas, software, gold, whatever. Simoleons is just a new name for those assets. You carry around a smart card and spend it just like cash. Or else you go shopping in the Metaverse and spend the money online, and the goods show up on your doorstep the next morning."

I say, "Who's going to fall for that?"

"Everyone," he says. "For our big promo, we're going to give Simoleons away to some average Joes at the Super Bowl. We'll check in with them one, three, six months later, and people will see that this is a safe and stable place to put their money."

"It doesn't inspire much confidence," I say, "to hand the stuff out like Monopoly money."

He's ready for this one. "It's not a handout. It's a sweepstakes." And that's when he asks me to calculate how many jelly beans will fill Soldier Field.

Two hours later, I'm down at the local galaxy-class grocery store, in Bulk: a Manhattan of towering Lucite bins filled with steel-cut rolled oats, off-brand Froot Loops, sun-dried tomatoes, prefabricated s'mores, macadamias, French roasts, and pignolias, all dispensed into your bag or bucket with a jerk at the handy Plexiglas guillotine. Not a human being in sight, just robot restocking machines trundling back and forth on a grid of overhead catwalks and surveillance cameras hidden in smoked-glass hemispheres. I stroll through the gleaming Lucite wonderland holding a perfect 6-in. cube improvised from duct tape and cardboard. I stagger through a glitter gulch of Gummi fauna, Boston Baked Beans, gobstoppers, Good & Plenty, tart n' tiny. Then, bingo: bulk jelly beans, premium grade. I put my cube under the spout and fill it.

Who guesses closest and earliest on the jelly beans wins the Simoleons. They've hired a Big Six accounting firm to make sure everything's done right. And since they can't actually fill the stadium with candy, I'm to come up with the Correct Answer and supply it to them and, just as important, to keep it secret.

I get home and count the beans: 3,101. Multiply by 8 to get the number in a cubic foot: 24,808. Now I just need the number of cubic feet in Soldier Field. My nephews are sprawled like pithed frogs before the HDTV, teaching themselves physics by lobbing antimatter bombs onto an offending civilization from high orbit. I prance over the black zigzags of the control cables and commandeer a unit.

Up on the screen, a cartoon elf or sprite or something pokes its head out from behind a window, then draws it back. No, I'm not a paranoid schizophrenic—this is the much-hyped intelligent agent who comes with the box. I ignore it, make my escape from Gameland, and blunder into a lurid district of the Metaverse where thousands of infomercials run day and night, each in its own window. I watch an ad for Chinese folk medicines made from rare-animal parts, genetically engineered and grown in vats. Grizzly bear gallbladders are shown growing like bunches of grapes in an amber fluid.

The animated sprite comes all the way out and leans up against the edge of the infomercial window. "Hey!" it says, in a goofy, exuberant voice, "I'm Raster! Just speak my name—that's Raster—if you need any help."

I don't like Raster's looks. It's likely he was wandering the streets of

Toontown and waving a sign saying WILL ANNOY GROWN-UPS FOR FOOD until he was hired by the cable company. He begins flying around the screen, leaving a trail of glowing fairy dust that fades much too slowly for my taste.

"Give me the damn encyclopedia!" I shout. Hearing the dread word, my nephews erupt from the rug and flee.

So I look up Soldier Field. My old Analytic Geometry textbook, still flecked with insulation from the attic, has been sitting on my thigh like a lump of ice. By combining some formulas from it with the encyclopedia's stats . . .

"Hey! Raster!"

Raster is so glad to be wanted that he does figure eights around the screen. "Calculator!" I shout.

"No need, boss! Simply tell me your desired calculation, and I will do it in my head!"

So I have a most tedious conversation with Raster, in which I estimate the number of cubic feet in Soldier Field, rounded to the nearest foot. I ask Raster to multiply that by 24,808 and he shoots back: 537,824,167,717.

A nongeek wouldn't have thought twice. But I say, "Raster, you have Spam for brains. It should be an exact multiple of eight!" Evidently my brother's new box came with one of those defective chips that makes errors when the numbers get really big.

Raster slaps himself upside the head; loose screws and transistors tumble out of his ears. "Darn! Guess I'll have to have a talk with my programmer!" And then he freezes up for a minute.

My sister-in-law Anne darts into the room, hunched in a don't-mind-me posture, and looks around. She's terrified that I may have a date in here. "Who're you talking to?"

"This goofy IA that came with your box," I say. "Don't ever use it to do your taxes, by the way."

She cocks her head. "You know, just yesterday I asked it for help with a Schedule B, and it gave me a recipe for shellfish bisque."

"Good evening, sir. Good evening, ma'am. What were those numbers again?" Raster asks. Same voice, but different inflections—more human. I call out the numbers one more time and he comes back with 537,824,167,720.

"That sounds better," I mutter.

Anne is nonplussed. "Now its voice recognition seems to be working fine."

"I don't think so. I think my little math problem got forwarded to a real human being. When the conversation gets over the head of the built-in software, it calls for help, and a human steps in and takes over. He's watching us through the built-in videocam," I explain, pointing at the fish-eye lens built into the front panel of the set-top box, "and listening through the built-in mike."

Anne's getting that glazed look in her eyes; I grope for an analog analogy. "Remember *The Exorcist*? Well, Raster has just been possessed, like the chick in the flick. Except it's not just Beelzebub. It's a customer-service rep."

I've just walked blind into a trap that is yawningly obvious to Anne. "Maybe that's a job you should apply for!" she exclaims.

The other jaw of the trap closes faster than my teeth chomping down on my tongue: "I can take your application online right now!" says Raster.

My sister-in-law is the embodiment of sugary triumph until the next evening, when I have a good news/bad news conversation with her. Good: I'm now a Metaverse customer-service rep. Bad: I don't have a cubicle in some Edge City office complex. I telecommute from home—from her home, from her sofa. I sit there all day long, munching through my dwindling stash of tax-deductible jelly beans, wearing an operator's headset, gripping the control unit, using it like a puppeteer's rig to control other people's Rasters on other people's screens, all over the US. I can see them—the wide-angle view from their set-top boxes is piped to a window on my screen. But they can't see me—just Raster, my avatar, my body in the Metaverse.

Ghastly in the mottled, flattening light of the Tube, people ask me inane questions about arithmetic. If they're asking for help with recipes, airplane schedules, child-rearing, or home improvement, they've already been turfed to someone else. My expertise is pure math only.

Which is pretty sleepy until the next week, when my brother's agency announces the big Simoleons Sweepstakes. They've hired a knock-kneed fullback as their spokesman. Within minutes, requests for help from contestants start flooding in. Every Bears fan in Greater Chicago is trying to calculate the volume of Soldier Field. They're all doing it wrong; and even the ones who are doing it right are probably using the faulty chip in their set-top box. I'm in deep conflict-of-interest territory here, wanting to reach out with Raster's stubby, white-gloved, three-fingered hand and slap some sense into these people.

But I'm sworn to secrecy. Joe has hired me to do the calculations for the Metrodome, Three Rivers Stadium, RFK Stadium, and every other NFL venue. There's going to be a Simoleons winner in every city.

We are allowed to take fifteen-minute breaks every four hours. So I crank up the Home Theater, just to blow the carbon out of its cylinders, and zip down the main street of the Metaverse to a club that specializes in my kind of tunes. I'm still "wearing" my Raster uniform, but I don't care—I'm just one of thousands of Rasters running up and down the street on their breaks.

My club has a narrow entrance on a narrow alley off a narrow side street, far from the virtual malls and 3-D video-game amusement parks that serve as the cash cows for the Metaverse's E-money economy. Inside, there's a few Rasters on break, but it's mostly people "wearing" more creative avatars. In the Metaverse, there's no part of your virtual body you can't pierce, brand, or tattoo in an effort to look weirder than the next guy.

The live band onstage—jacked in from a studio in Prague—isn't very good, so I duck into the back room where there are virtual racks full of tapes you can sample, listening to a few seconds from each song. If you like it, you can download the whole album, with optional interactive liner notes, videos, and sheet music.

I'm pawing through one of these racks when I sense another avatar, something big and shaggy, sidling up next to me. It mumbles something; I ignore it.

A magisterial throat-clearing noise rumbles in the subwoofer, crackles in the surround speakers, punches through cleanly on the center channel above the screen. I turn and look: it's a heavyset creature wearing a T-shirt emblazoned with a logo: *HACKERS 1111*. It has very long scythe-like claws, which it uses to grip a hot-pink cylinder. It's much better drawn than Raster; almost Disney-quality.

The sloth speaks: "537,824,167,720."

"Hey!" I shout. "Who the hell are you?" It lifts the pink cylinder to its lips and drinks. It's a can of Jolt. "Where'd you get that number?" I demand. "It's supposed to be a secret."

"The key is under the doormat," the sloth says, then turns around and walks out of the club.

My fifteen-minute break is over, so I have to ponder the meaning of this through the rest of my shift. Then, I drag myself up out of the couch, open the front door, and peel up the doormat.

Sure enough, someone has stuck an envelope under there. Inside is a sheet of paper with a number on it, written in hexadecimal notation, which is what computer people use: 0A56 7781 6BE2 2004 89FF 9001 C782—and so on for about five lines.

The sloth had told me that "the key is under the doormat," and I'm willing to bet many Simoleons that this number is an encryption key that will enable me to send and receive coded messages.

So I spend ten minutes punching it into the set-top box. Raster shows up and starts to bother me: "Can I help you with anything?"

By the time I've punched in the 256th digit, I've become a little testy with Raster and said some rude things to him. I'm not proud of it. Then I hear something that's music to my ears: "I'm sorry, I didn't understand you," Raster chirps. "Please check your cable connections—I'm getting some noise on the line."

A second figure materializes on the screen, like a digital genie: it's the sloth again. "Who the hell are you?" I ask.

The sloth takes another slug of Jolt, stifles a belch, and says, "I am Codex, the Crypto-Anarchist Sloth."

"Your equipment requires maintenance," Raster says. "Please contact the cable company."

"Your equipment is fine," Codex says. "I'm encrypting your back channel. To the cable company, it looks like noise. As you figured out, that number is your personal encryption key. No government or corporation on earth can eavesdrop on us now."

"Gosh, thanks," I say.

"You're welcome," Codex replies. "Now, let's get down to biz. We have something you want. You have something we want."

"How did you know the answer to the Soldier Field jelly bean question?"

"We've got all twenty-seven," Codex says. And he rattles off the secret numbers for Candlestick Park, the Kingdome, the Meadowlands . . .

"Unless you've broken into the accounting firm's vault," I say, "there's only one way you could have those numbers. You've been eavesdropping on my little chats with Raster. You've tapped the line coming out of this set-top box, haven't you?"

"Oh, that's typical. I suppose you think we're a bunch of socially inept, acne-ridden, high-IQ teenage hackers who play sophomoric pranks on the Establishment."

"The thought had crossed my mind," I say. But the fact that the cartoon sloth can give me such a realistic withering look, as he is doing now, suggests a much higher level of technical sophistication. Raster only has six facial expressions and none of them is very good.

"Your brother runs an ad agency, no?"

"Correct."

"He recently signed up Simoleons Corp.?"

"Correct."

"As soon as he did, the government put your house under full-time surveillance."

Suddenly the glass eyeball in the front of the set-top box is looking very big and beady to me. "They tapped our infotainment cable?"

"Didn't have to. The cable people are happy to do all the dirty work—after all, they're beholden to the government for their monopoly. So all those calculations you did using Raster were piped straight to the cable company and from there to the government. We've got a mole in the government who cc'd us everything through an anonymous remailer in Jyväskylä, Finland."

"Why should the government care?"

"They care big-time," Codex says. "They're going to destroy Simoleons. And they're going to step all over your family in the process."

"Why?"

"Because if they don't destroy E-money," Codex says, "E-money will destroy them."

• • •

The next afternoon I show up at my brother's office, in a groovily refurbished ex–power plant on the near West Side. He finishes rolling some calls and then waves me into his office, a cavernous space with a giant steam turbine as a conversation piece. I think it's supposed to be an irony thing.

"Aren't you supposed to be cruising the I-way for stalled motorists?" he says.

"Spare me the fraternal heckling," I say. "We crypto-anarchists don't have time for such things."

"Crypto-anarchists?"

"The word *panarchist* is also frequently used."

"Cute," he says, rolling the word around in his head. He's already working up a mental ad campaign for it.

"You're looking flushed and satisfied this afternoon," I say. "Must have been those two imperial pints of Hog City Porter you had with your baby-back ribs at Divane's Lakeview Grill."

Suddenly he sits up straight and gets an edgy look about him, as if a practical joke is in progress, and he's determined not to play the fool.

"So how'd you know what I had for lunch?"

"Same way I know you've been cheating on your taxes."

"What!?"

"Last year you put a new tax-deductible sofa in your home office. But that sofa is a hide-a-bed model, which is a no-no."

"Hackers," he says. "Your buddies hacked into my records, didn't they?"

"You win the Stratolounger."

"I thought they had safeguards on these things now."

"The files are harder to break into. But every time information gets sent across the wires—like, when Anne uses Raster to do the taxes—it can be captured and decrypted. Because, my brother, you bought the default data-security agreement with your box, and the default agreement sucks."

"So what are you getting at?"

"For that," I say, "we'll have to go someplace that isn't under surveillance."

"Surveillance!? What the . . ." he begins. But then I nod at the TV in the corner of his office, with its beady glass eye staring out at us from the set-top box.

We end up walking along the lakeshore, which, in Chicago in January, is madness. But we hail from North Dakota, and we have all the cold-weather gear it takes to do this. I tell him about Raster and the cable company.

"Oh, Jesus!" he says. "You mean those numbers aren't secret?"

"Not even close. They've been put in the hands of twenty-seven stooges hired by the government. The stooges have already FedEx'd their entry forms with the correct numbers. So, as of now, all of your Simoleons—twenty-seven million dollars' worth—are going straight into the hands of the stooges on Super Bowl Sunday. And they will turn out to be your worst public-relations nightmare. They will cash in their Simoleons for comic books and baseball cards and claim it's safer. They will intentionally go bankrupt and blame it on you. They will show up in twos and threes on tawdry talk shows to report mysterious disappearances of their Simoleons during Metaverse transactions. They will, in short, destroy the image—and the business—of your client. The result: victory for the government, which hates and fears private currencies. And bankruptcy for you, and for Mom and Dad."

"How do you figure?"

"Your agency is responsible for screwing up this sweepstakes. Soon as the debacle hits, your stock plummets. Mom and Dad lose millions in paper profits they've never had a chance to enjoy. Then your big shareholders will sue your ass, my brother, and you will lose. You gambled the value of the company on the faulty data-security built into your set-top box, and you as a corporate officer are personally responsible for the losses."

At this point, big brother Joe feels the need to slam himself down on a park bench, which must feel roughly like sitting on a block of dry ice. But he doesn't care. He's beyond physical pain. I sort of expected to feel triumphant at this point, but I don't.

So I let him off the hook. "I just came from your accounting firm," I say. "I told them I had discovered an error in my calculations—that my set-top box had a faulty chip. I supplied them with twenty-seven new numbers, which I worked out by hand, with pencil and paper, in a conference room in their offices, far from the prying eye of the cable company. I personally sealed them in an envelope and placed them in their vault."

"So the sweepstakes will come off as planned," he exhales. "Thank God!"

"Yeah—and while you're at it, thank me and the panarchists," I shoot back. "I also called Mom and Dad, and told them that they should sell their stock—just in case the government finds some new way to sabotage your contest."

"That's probably wise," he says sourly, "but they're going to get hammered on taxes. They'll lose forty percent of their net worth to the government, just like that."

"No, they won't," I say. "They aren't paying any taxes."

"Say what?" He lifts his chin off his mittens for the first time in a while, reinvigorated by the chance to tell me how wrong I am. "Their cash basis is only ten thousand dollars—you think the IRS won't notice twenty million dollars in capital gains?"

"We didn't invite the IRS," I tell him. "It's none of the IRS's damn business."

"They have ways to make it their business."

"Not anymore. Mom and Dad aren't selling their stock for dollars, Joe."

"Simoleons? It's the same deal with Simoleons—everything gets reported to the government."

"Forget Simoleons. Think CryptoCredits."

"CryptoCredits? What the hell is a CryptoCredit?" He stands up and starts pacing back and forth. Now he's convinced I've traded the family cow for a handful of magic beans.

"It's what Simoleons ought to be: E-money that is totally private from the eyes of government."

"How do you know? Isn't any code crackable?"

"Any kind of E-money consists of numbers moving around on wires," I say. "If you know how to keep your numbers secret, your currency is safe. If you don't, it's not. Keeping numbers secret is a problem of cryptography—a branch of mathematics. Well, Joe, the crypto-anarchists showed me their math. And it's good math. It's better than the math the government uses. Better than Simoleons' math too. No one can mess with CryptoCredits."

He heaves a big sigh. "Okay, okay—you want me to say it? I'll say it. You were right. I was wrong. You studied the right thing in college after all."

"I'm not worthless scum?"

"Not worthless scum. So. What do these crypto-anarchists want, anyway?"

For some reason I can't lie to my parents, but Joe's easy. "Nothing," I say. "They just wanted to do us a favor, as a way of gaining some goodwill with us."

"And furthering the righteous cause of World Panarchy?"

"Something like that."

Which brings us to Super Bowl Sunday. We are sitting in a skybox high up in the Superdome, complete with wet bar, kitchen, waiters, and big TV screens to watch the instant replays of what we've just seen with our own naked, pitiful, nondigital eyes.

The corporate officers of Simoleons are there. I start sounding them out on their cryptographic protocols, and it becomes clear that these people can't calculate their gas mileage without consulting Raster, much less navigate the subtle and dangerous currents of cutting-edge cryptography.

A Superdome security man comes in, looking uneasy. "Some, uh, gentlemen here," he says. "They have tickets that appear to be authentic."

It's three guys. The first one is a 300 pounder with hair down to his waist and a beard down to his navel. He must be a Bears fan because he has painted his face and bare torso blue and orange. The second one isn't quite as introverted as the first, and the third isn't quite the button-down conformist the other two are. Mr. Big is carrying an old milk crate. What's inside must be heavy, because it looks like it's about to pull his arms out of their sockets.

"Mr. and Mrs. De Groot?" he says, as he staggers into the room. Heads turn toward my mom and dad, who, alarmed by the appearance of these three, have declined to identify themselves. The guy makes for them and slams the crate down in front of my dad.

"I'm the guy you've known as Codex," he says. "Thanks for naming us as your broker."

If Joe wasn't a rowing-machine abuser, he'd be blowing aneurysms in both hemispheres about now. "Your broker is a half-naked blue-and-orange crypto-anarchist?"

Dad devotes thirty seconds or so to lighting his pipe. Down on the field, the two-minute warning sounds. Dad puffs out a cloud of smoke and says, "He seemed like an honest sloth."

"Just in case," Mom says, "we sold half the stock through our broker in Bismarck. He says we'll have to pay taxes on that."

"We transferred the other half offshore, to Mr. Codex here," Dad says, "and he converted it into the local currency—tax free."

"Offshore? Where? The Bahamas?" Joe asks.

"The First Distributed Republic," says the big panarchist. "It's a virtual nation-state. I'm the Minister of Data Security. Our official currency is CryptoCredits."

"What the hell good is that?" Joe says.

"That was my concern too," Dad says, "so, just as an experiment, I used my CryptoCredits to buy something a little more tangible."

Dad reaches into the milk crate and heaves out a rectangular object made of yellow metal. Mom hauls out another one. She and Dad begin lining them up on the counter, like King and Queen Midas unloading a carton of Twinkies.

It takes Joe a few seconds to realize what's happening. He picks up one of the gold bars and gapes at it. The Simoleons execs crowd around and inspect the booty.

"Now you see why the government wants to stamp us out," the big guy says. "We can do what they do—cheaper and better."

For the first time, light dawns on the face of the Simoleons CEO. "Wait a sec," he says, and puts his hands to his temples. "You can rig it so that people who use E-money don't have to pay taxes to any government? Ever?"

"You got it," the big panarchist says. The horn sounds announcing the end of the first half.

"I have to go down and give away some Simoleons," the CEO says, "but after that, you and I need to have a talk."

The CEO goes down in the elevator with my brother, carrying a box of twenty-seven smart cards, each of which is loaded up with secret numbers that makes it worth a million Simoleons. I go over and look out the skybox window: twenty-seven Americans are congregated down on the 50-yard line, waiting for their mathematical manna to descend from heaven. They are just the demographic cross section that my brother was hoping for. You'd never guess they were all secretly citizens of the First Distributed Republic.

The crypto-anarchists grab some Jolt from the wet bar and troop out, so now it's just me, Mom, and Dad in the skybox. Dad points at the field with the stem of his pipe. "Those twenty-seven folks down there," he says. "They didn't get any help from you, did they?"

I've lied about this successfully to Joe. But I know it won't work with Mom and Dad. "Let's put it this way," I say, "not all panarchists are long-haired, Jolt-slurping maniacs. Some of them look like you—exactly like you, as a matter of fact."

Dad nods; I've got him on that one.

"Codex and his people saved the contest, and our family, from disaster. But there was a quid pro quo."

"Usually is," Dad says.

"But it's good for everyone. What Joe wants—and what his client wants—is for the promotion to go well, so that a year from now, everyone who's watching this broadcast today will have a high opinion of the safety and stability of Simoleons. Right?"

"Right."

"If you give the Simoleons away at random, you're rolling the dice. But if you give them to people who are secretly panarchists—who have a vested interest in showing that E-money works—it's a much safer bet."

"Does the First Distributed Republic have a flag?" Mom asks, out of left field. I tell her these guys look like sewing enthusiasts. So, even before the second half starts, she's sketched out a flag on the back of her program. "It'll be very colorful," she says. "Like a jar of jelly beans."

JEFFREY THOMAS

IMMOLATION

(2000)

1: KEEPING UP WITH THE JONESES

They had made it snow again this weekend, as they would every weekend until Christmas. Not on the weekdays, hampering the traffic of workers, or so much today as to inconvenience the shoppers; rather, enough to inspire consumers to further holiday spirit, and further purchases.

High atop the Vat, a machine that to some might resemble an oil tanker of old standing on its prow, Magnesium Jones crouched back among the conduits and exhaust ports like an infant gargoyle on the verge of crowning. His womb was a steamy one; the heat from the blowers would have cooked a birther like a lobster. Jones was naked, his shoulder pressed against the hood of a whirring fan. When he had instant coffee or soup to make he would boil water by resting a pot atop the fan's cap. He was not wearing clothes lest they catch fire.

Not all the cultures were designed to be so impervious to heat; some, rather, were unperturbed by extreme cold. On the sixth terrace of the plant proper, which faced the Vat, a group of cultures took break in the open air, a few of them naked and turning their faces up to the powdery blizzard invitingly. It had been an alarming development for many, the Plant's management allowing cultures to take break. It suggested they needed consideration, even concern.

Jones squinted through the blowing veils of snow. He recognized a number of the laborers. Though all were bald, and all cloned from a mere half-dozen masters, their heads were tattooed in individual designs so as to distinguish them from each other. Numbers and letters usually figured into these designs—codes. Some had their names tattooed on their foreheads, and all tattoos were colored according to department: violet for Shipping, gray for the Vat, blue for Cryogenics, red for the Ovens, and so on. Magnesium Jones's tattoo was of the last color. But there was also some artistry employed in the tattoo designs. They might portray familiar landmarks from Punktown, or from Earth where most of Punktown's colonists originated, at least in ancestry. Animals, celebrities, sports stars. Magnesium Jones's tattoo was a ring of flame around his head like a corona, with a few black letters and a bar code in the flames like the charred skeleton of a burnt house.

Some artistry, some fun and flourish, was also employed in the naming of the cultures. On the terrace he recognized Sherlock Jones, Imitation Jones, and Basketball Jones. He thought he caught a glimpse of Subliminal Jones heading back inside. Waxlips Jones sat on the edge of the railing, dangling his legs over the street far below. Jones Jones held a steaming coffee. Huckleberry Jones was in subdued conversation with Digital Jones. Copyright Jones and M. I. Jones emerged from the building to join the rest.

Watching them, Magnesium Jones missed his own conversations with some of them, missed the single break that he looked forward to through the first ten hours of the workday. But did he miss the creatures themselves, he wondered? He felt a kinship with other cultures, an empathy for their lives, their situations, in a general sense . . . but that might merely be because he saw himself in them, felt for his own life, his own situation. Sometimes the kinship felt like brotherhood. But affection? Friendship? Love? He wasn't sure if his feelings could be defined in that way. Or was it just that the birthers felt no more strongly, merely glossed and romanticized their own pale feelings?

But Jones did not share the plight of the robot, the android . . . the question of whether they could consider themselves alive, of whether they could aspire to actual emotion. He felt very much alive. He felt some very strong emotions. Anger. Hatred. These feelings, unlike love, were not at all ambiguous.

He turned away from the snowy vista of Plant and city beyond, shivering, glad to slip again into his nest of thrumming heat. From an insulated box he had stolen and dragged up here he took some clothing. Some of it was fireproof, some not. The long black coat, with its broad lapels turned up to protect his neck from the snow, had a heated mesh in the lining. Worn gloves, and he pulled a black ski hat over his bald head, as much to conceal his tattoo as to shield his naked scalp from snow. He stared at his wrist, willing numbers to appear there. They told him the time. A feature all the cultures at the Plant possessed, to help them time their work efficiently. He had an appointment, a meeting, but he had plenty of time yet to get there.

As much as he scorned his former life in the Plant, there were some behaviors too ingrained to shake. Magnesium Jones was ever punctual.

• • •

Walking the street, Jones slipped on a pair of dark glasses. In the vicinity of the Plant it would be easy to recognize him as a culture. The six masters had all been birther males, criminals condemned to death (they had been paid for the rights to clone them for industrial labor). Under current law it was illegal to clone living human beings. Clones of living beings might equate themselves with their originals. Clones of living beings might thus believe they had certain rights.

Wealthy people stored clones of themselves in case of mishap, cloned families and friends, illegally. Everyone knew that. For all Jones knew, the president of the Plant might be a clone himself. But still, somehow, the cultures were cultures. Still a breed of their own.

Behind the safe shields of his dark lenses, Jones studied the faces of people he passed on the street. Birthers, Christmas shopping, but their faces closed off in hard privacy. The closer birthers were grouped together, the more cut off they became from each other in that desperate animal need for their own territory, even if it extended no further than their scowls and stern, downcast eyes.

Distant shouted chants made him turn his head, though he already knew their source. There was always a group of strikers camped just outside the barrier of the Plant. Tents, smoke from barrel fires, banners rippling in the snowy gusts. There was one group on a hunger strike, emaciated as concentration camp prisoners. A few weeks ago, one woman had self-immolated. Jones had heard screams, and come to the edge of his high hideout to watch. He had marveled at the woman's calm as she sat cross-legged, a black silhouette with her head already charred bald at the center of a small inferno . . . had marveled at how she did not run or cry out, panic or lose her resolve. He admired her strength, her commitment. It was a sacrifice for her fellow human beings, an act which would suggest that the birthers felt a greater brotherhood than the cultures did, after all. But then, their society encouraged such feelings, whereas the cultures were discouraged from friendship, companionship, affection.

Then again, maybe the woman had just been insane.

• • •

To reach the basement pub Jones edged through a narrow tunnel of dripping ceramic brick, the floor a metal mesh . . . below which he heard dark liquid rushing. A section of wall on the right opened up, blocked by chicken wire, and in a dark room like a cage a group of mutants or aliens or mutated aliens gazed out at him as placid as animals waiting to eat or be eaten (and maybe that was so, too); they were so tall their heads scraped the ceiling, thinner than skeletons, with cracked faces that looked shattered and glued back together. Their hair was cobwebs blowing, though to Jones the clotted humid air down here seemed to pool around his legs.

A throb of music grew until he opened a metal door and it exploded in his face like a boobytrap. Slouched heavy backs at a bar, a paunchy naked woman doing a slow grinding dance atop a billiard table. Jones did not so much as glance at her immense breasts, aswirl in smoky colored light like planets; the Plant's cultures had no sexual cravings, none of them even female.

At a corner table sat a young man with red hair, something seldom seen naturally. He smiled and made a small gesture. Jones headed toward him, slipping off his shades. He watched the man's hands atop the table; was there a gun resting under the newspaper?

The man's hair was long and greasy, his beard scruffy and inadequate, but he was good-looking and his voice was friendly. "Glad you decided to come. I'm Nevin Parr." They shook hands. "Sit down. Drink?"

"Coffee."

The man motioned to a waitress, who brought them both a coffee. The birther wasn't dulling his senses with alcohol, either, Jones noted.

"So how did you meet my pal Moodring?" asked the birther, lifting his chipped mug for a cautious sip.

"On the street. He gave me money for food in turn for a small favor."

"So now you move a little drug for him sometimes. Hold hot weapons for him sometimes."

Jones frowned at his gloved hands, knotted like mating tarantulas. "I'm disappointed. I thought Moodring was more discreet than that."

"Please don't be angry at him; I told you, we're old pals. So, anyway . . . should I call you Mr. Jones?" Parr smiled broadly. "Magnesium? Or is it Mag?"

"It's all equally meaningless."

"I've never really talked with a culture before."

"We prefer 'shadow.' "

"All right. Mr. Shadow. So how old are you?"

"Five."

"Pretty bright for a five-year-old."

"Memory-encoded long-chain molecules in a brain drip. I knew my job before I even got out of the tank."

"Of course. Five, huh? So that's about the age when they start replacing you guys, right? They say that's when you start getting uppity . . . losing control. That's why you escaped from the Plant, isn't it? You knew your time was pretty much up."

"Yes. I knew what was coming. Nine cultures in my crew were removed in two days. They were all about my age. My supervisor told me not to worry, but I knew . . ."

"Cleaning house. Bringing in the fresh meat. They kill them, don't they? The old cultures. They incinerate them."

"Yes."

"I heard you killed two men in escaping. Two real men."

"Moodring is very talkative."

"It isn't just him. You killed two men. I heard they were looking for you. Call you 'hothead,' because of your tattoo. Can I see it?"

"That wouldn't be wise in public, would it?"

"You're not the only escaped clone around here, but you're right, we have work that demands discretion. Just that I like tattoos; I have some myself. See?" He rolled up a sleeve, exposing a dark mass that Jones only gave a half glance. "I hear they get pretty wild with your tattoos. Someone must enjoy himself."

"Robots do the tattooing. They're just accessing clip art files. Most times it has nothing to do with our function or the name that was chosen for us. It's done to identify us, and probably for the amusement of our human coworkers. Decorative for them, I suppose."

"You haven't been caught, but you're still living in this area, close to the Plant. You must be stealthy. That's a useful quality. So where are you staying?"

"That's none of your concern. When you need me you leave a message with Moodring. When he sees me around he'll tell me. Moodring doesn't need to know where I live, either."

"He your friend, Moodring, or is it just business?"

"I have no friends."

"That's too bad. I think you and I could be friends."

"You don't know how much that means to me. So, why did you want me? Because I'm a culture? And if so, why?"

"Again . . . because you killed two men escaping the Plant. I know you can kill again, given the right incentive."

"I'm glad we've got to that. So what's my incentive?"

"Five thousand munits."

"For killing a man? That's pretty cheap."

"Not for a culture who never made a coin in his life. Not for a culture who lives in the street somewhere."

"So who am I to kill?"

"More incentive for you," said Nevin Parr, who smiled far too much for Jones's taste. Jones seldom smiled. He had heard that smiling was a trait leftover from the animal ancestry of the birthers; it was a threatening baring of the fangs, in origin. The idea amused him, made him feel more evolved for so seldom contorting his own face in that way. After his smiling heavy pause, Parr continued, "The man we have in mind is Ephraim Mayda."

Jones raised his hairless eyebrows, grunted, and stirred his coffee. "He's a union captain. Well guarded. Martyr material."

"Never mind the repercussions; he's trouble for the people I'm working for, and worth the lesser trouble of his death."

Jones lifted his eyes in sudden realization. He almost plunged his hand into his coat for the pistol he had bought from Moodring. "You work for the Plant!" he hissed.

Parr grinned. "I work for myself. But never mind who hired me."

Jones composed himself outwardly, but his heart pulsed as deeply as the music. "The union is cozy with the syndy."

"The people I work for can handle the syndy. Mag, those strikers out there hate you . . . shadows. They've lynched a dozen of your kind in a row outside the Plant barrier. If they had their way, every one of your kind would go into the incinerator tomorrow. You yourself got roughed up by a group that got inside the Plant, I hear." Parr paused knowingly. His spoon clinked in his mug, making a vortex. "They broke in. Trashed machines. Killed a few of your kind. I heard from our mutual friend that they found you naked by the showers, and cut you . . . badly."

"It didn't affect my job," Jones muttered, not looking the human in the eyes. "And it's not like I ever used the thing but to piss. So now I piss like a birther woman."

"Didn't bother you at all, then? Doesn't bother you that Mayda works these thugs up like that?"

They were angry. Jones could understand that. If there was anything that made him feel a kinship with the birthers, it was anger. Still, the weight of their resentment . . . of their loathing . . . their outright furious hatred . . . was a labor to bear. They had hurt him. He had never intentionally harmed a birther. It was the Plant's decision to utilize cultures for half their workforce (more than that would constitute a labor violation, but the conservative candidate for Prime Minister was fighting to make it so that companies did not have to guarantee any ratio of nonclones; freedom of enterprise must be upheld, he cried). Let the strikers mutilate the president of the Plant, instead. Let them hang him and his underlings in the shadow of the Vat. But didn't they see—even though Jones worked in their place while their unemployment ran out and their families starved like the protestors—that he was as much a victim as they?

This man was under the employ of his enemies. Of course, he himself had once been under their employ. Still, could he trust this man as his partner in crime? No. But he could do business with men he didn't trust. He wouldn't turn his back to Moodring, either, but in the end he needed to eat. Five thousand munits. He had never earned a coin until he had escaped the Plant, and never a legal one since.

He could go away. Somewhere hot. Have his tattoo removed. Maybe even his useless vestige of "manhood" restored.

Parr went on, "A third bit of incentive. You're no fool, so I'll admit it. The people who hired me . . . you once worked for them, too. If you decline, well . . . like I say, they'd like to get ahold of you after what you did to those two men."

Slowly and deliberately Jones's eyes lifted, staring from under bony brows. He smiled. It was like a baring of fangs.

"You were doing well, Nevin. Don't spoil it with unnecessary incentives. I'll help you kill your man."

"Sorry." Ever the smile. "Just that they want this to happen soon, and I don't want to have to look for a partner from scratch."

"Why do you need a partner?"

"Well let me tell you . . ."

2: THE PIMP OF THE INVERSE

From his perch atop the Vat, with its stained streaked sides and its deep liquid burbling, Jones watched night fall in Punktown. The snow was a mere whisking about of loose flakes. Colored lights glowed in the city beyond the Plant, and flashed here and there on the Plant itself, but for less gay purposes. Once in a while there was a bright violet-hued flash in the translucent dome of the shipping department, as another batch of products was teleported elsewhere on this planet, or to another. Perhaps a crew destined to work on an asteroid mine, or to build an orbital space station or a new colony, a new Punktown, on some world not yet raped, merely groped.

He watched a hovertruck with a covered bed like a military troop carrier pull out of the shipping docks and head for the east gate. A shipment with a more localized destination. Jones imagined its contents, the manufactured goods, seated in two rows blankly facing each other. Cultures not yet tattooed, not yet named. Perhaps the companies they were destined for did not utilize tattoos and decorative names—mocking names, Jones mused—to identify the clone workers. Jones wondered what, if anything, went on in their heads along the drive. They had not yet been programmed for their duties, not yet had their brain drips. He, whose job it had been to bake these golems, had been born already employed, unlike them. They were innocent in their staring mindlessness, better off for their mindlessness, Jones thought, watching the truck vanish into the night. He himself was still a child, but a tainted innocent; the months since his escape had been like a compacted lifetime. Had he been better off in his first days, not yet discontented? Disgruntled? There were those times, he in his newfound pride would hate to admit, that he felt like a human boy who longed to be a wooden puppet again.

He listened to the Vat gurgle with its amniotic solutions, pictured in his mind the many mindless fetuses sleeping without dream in the great silo of a womb beneath him. Yes, Christmas was coming. Jones thought of its origins, of the birther woman Mary's immaculate conception, and gave an ugly smirk.

He lifted his wrist, gazed at it until luminous numbers like another tattoo materialized. Time to go; he didn't like being late.

• • •

So that Parr would not guess just how close Jones lived to the Plant, he had told Parr to pick him up over at Pewter Square. To reach it, Jones had to cross the Obsidian Street Overpass. It was a slightly arched bridge of a Ramon design, built of incredibly tough Ramon wood lacquered in what once had been a glossy black. It was now smeared and spray-painted, dusty and chipped. Vehicles whooshed across in either direction, filling the covered bridge with roaring noise. The pedestrian walkway was protected from the traffic by a rickety railing, missing sections now patched with chicken wire. Furthermore, homeless people had nested in among the recesses of the bridge's wooden skeleton, most having built elaborate parasite structures of scrap wood, sheets of metal, plastic, or ceramic. One elderly and malnourished Choom, a former monk of the dwindling Raloom faith, lived inside a large cardboard box on the front of which, as if it were a temple, he had drawn the stern features of Raloom. The pedestrian walkway was bordered on one side by the railing, on the other by this tiny shanty town. Some of its denizens sold coffee to the passersby, or newspaper hard copies, or coaxed them behind their crinkly plastic curtains or soggy cardboard partitions for the sale of drugs and sex.

Jones knew one of these shadowy creatures, and as if it had been awaiting him, it half emerged from its shelter as he approached. Its small house was one of the most elaborate; as if to pretend that it belonged to the bridge, in case of an infrequent mass eviction, it had constructed its dwelling of wood and painted it glossy black. The shack even had mock windows, though these were actually dusty mirrors. Jones saw his own solemn face multiply reflected as he approached, his black ski hat covering his tattoo.

The tiny figure moved spidery limbs as if in slow motion, but its head constantly twitched and gave sudden jolts from side to side, so fast its features blurred. When still, they were puny black holes in a huge hairless head—twice the size of Jones's—almost perfectly round and with the texture of pumice. No one but Jones would know that this was no ordinary mutant, but a culture defect from the Plant, an immaculate misconception, who had somehow escaped incineration and to freedom. Who would suspect that they had been cloned from the same master? The defect had once stopped Jones and struck up a conversation. Jones's hairless eyebrows had given him away. When not wearing dark glasses, Jones now wore his ski hat pulled down to his eyes.

"Where are we going at this hour?" crackled the misshapen being, who had named itself Edgar Allan Jones. Magnesium Jones could not understand why a shadow would willingly give itself such a foolish name, but then sometimes he wondered why he hadn't come up with a new name for himself.

"Restless," he grunted, stopping in front of the lacquered dollhouse. He heard a tea kettle whistling in there, and muffled radio music that sounded like a child's toy piano played at an inhuman speed.

"Christmas is in three days, now," said the flawed clone, cracking a toothless smile. "Will you come see me? We can listen to the radio together. Play cards. I'll make you tea."

Jones glanced past Edgar into the miniature house. Could the two of them both fit in there? It seemed claustrophobic. And too intimate a scene for his taste. Still, he felt flattered, and couldn't bring himself to flat-out refuse. Instead, he said, "I may not be around here that day . . . but if I am . . . we'll see."

"You have never been inside . . . why not come in now? I can . . ."

"I can't now, I'm sorry; I have . . . some business."

The globe of a head blurred, halted abruptly, the smile shaken into a frown. "That Moodring friend of yours will lead you to your death."

"He isn't my friend," Jones said, and started away.

"Don't forget Christmas!" the creature croaked.

Jones nodded over his shoulder but kept on walking, feeling strangely guilty for not just stepping inside for one cup of tea. After all, he was quite early for his appointment.

• • •

"Ever been in a car before?" Parr asked, smiling, as he pulled from the curb into the glittering dark current of night traffic.

"Taxi," Jones murmured, stiff as a mannequin.

"Mayda lives at Hanging Gardens; it's a few blocks short of Beaumonde Square. He's not starving like the folks he works up; he has a nice apartment to go home to. It's that syndy money."

"Mm."

"Hey," Parr looked over at him, "don't be nervous. Just keep thinking about your lines. You're going to be a vid star, my man . . . a celebrity."

3: THE CARVEN WARRIOR

Parr let Jones off, and the hovercar disappeared around the corner. Jones cut across a snow-caked courtyard as instructed, his boots squeaking as if he tramped across Styrofoam. He slipped between apartment units, climbed a set of stairs to another, and found a door propped open for him. Parr motioned him inside, then let the door fall back in place. Jones heard it lock. He didn't ask Parr how he had got inside the vestibule.

Together they padded down a gloomy corridor across a carpet of peach and purple diamonds. The walls and doors that flanked the men were pristine white. This place reminded Jones of the cleaner regions of the Plant; primarily, the seldom seen administration levels. He listened to the moving creak of Parr's faux leather jacket. Both of them wore gloves, and Jones still had on his ski hat and a scarf wound around his neck against the hellish cold he could never get used to.

A lift took them to the sixth floor. Then, side by side, they made their way down the hall to the door at its very end. Quite easily, Parr knocked, and then beamed at his companion.

Jones pulled off his ski hat at last, and pushed it into his pocket. In the dim light, his hairless pate gleamed softly, the fiery halo pricked into his skin burning darkly. He hid both hands behind his back.

"Who is it?" asked a voice over an intercom. Above the door, a tiny camera eye, small as an ant's feeler, must now be watching them.

"Enforcer, sir," said Parr, his voice uncharacteristically serious. And he did look the part in his black uniform; leather jacket, beetle-like helmet, holstered weapons. He had cut his hair to a butch and shaved to a neat goatee. He held one of Jones's elbows. "May I have a word?"

"What's going on?"

"Your neighbor down the hall reported a suspicious person, and we found this culture lurking around. He claims he's not an escapee, but was purchased by an Ephraim Mayda."

"Mr. Mayda doesn't own any cultures."

"May I please speak with Mr. Mayda himself?" Parr sighed irritably.

A new voice came on. "I know that scab!" it rumbled. "He escaped from the Plant, murdered two human beings!"

"What? Are you sure of this?"

"Yes! He was from the Ovens department. It was on the news!"

"May I speak with you in person, Mr. Mayda?"

"I don't want that killer freak in my house!"

"I have him manacled, sir. Look, I need to take down a report on this . . . your recognizing him is valuable."

"Whatever. But you'd better have him under control . . ."

The two men heard the lock clack off. The knob was turned from the other side, and as the door opened Jones pushed through first, reaching his right hand inside his coat as he went. He saw two faces inside, both half-identical in that both wore expressions of shock, horror, as he ripped his small silvery block of a pistol from its holster to thrust at their wide stares. But one man was bleached blond and one man was dark-haired and Jones shot the blond in the face. A neat, third nostril breathed open beside one of the other two, but the back of the blond's head was kicked open like saloon doors. The darker man batted his eyes at the blood that spattered him. The report had been as soft as a child's cough, the blond crumpled almost delicately to the floor, Jones and then Parr stepped onto the lush white carpet and Parr locked the door after them.

"Who are you?" Mayda cried, raising his hands, backing against the wall.

"Into the living room," Jones snarled, flicking the gun. Mayda glanced behind him, slid his shoulders along the wall and backed through a threshold into an expanse of plush parlor with a window overlooking the snowy courtyard of Hanging Gardens. Parr went to tint the window full black.

"I'll give you money, listen . . ." Mayda began.

"You do remember me, don't you?" Jones hissed, leveling the gun at the paunchy birther's groin. "You emasculated me, remember that?"

"I didn't! That was those crazy strikers that got in the Plant that time . . . that was out of my hands!"

"So how do you know about it? They told you. It was a big joke, wasn't it?"

"What do you want? You can have anything!" The union captain's eyes fearfully latched onto Parr as he slipped something odd from his jacket. What looked like three gun barrels were unfolded and spread into a tripod. Atop it, Parr screwed a tiny vidcam. A green light came on, indicating that it had begun filming. Parr remained behind the camera, and Mayda flashed his eyes back to Jones to see what he had to say.

Jones hesitated. What he had to say was rehearsed, but the lines were a jumble in his head, words exploded to fragments by the silent shot that had killed the blond. He had killed a man . . . for the third time. It came naturally to him, like a brain-dripped skill; it was a primal animal instinct, survival. So why, in its aftermath, should he feel this . . . disconcertion?

His eyes darted about the room. He had never been in such a place. Tables fashioned from some green glassy stone. Sofas and chairs of white with a silvery lace of embroidery. A bar, a holotank. On the walls, a modest art collection. Atop several tables, shelves, and pedestals, various small Ramon sculptures, all carved from an iridescent white crystal. Animals, and a Ramon warrior rendered in amazing detail considering the medium, from his lionlike head to the lance or halberd he brought to bear in anticipation of attack. Each piece must be worth a fortune. And yet there were men and women camped outside the Plant who were on a hunger strike, emaciated. And those who were emaciated but not by choice. And Jones recalled that woman sitting in her shroud of flame.

His disconcertion cleared. Jones returned a molten gaze to the terrified birther. The anger in his voice was not some actor's fakery, even if the words were not his own.

"I'm here to make a record, Mr. Mayda . . . of the beginning of a rebellion, and the first blow in a war that won't stop until we clones are given the same rights as you natural born."

It was clever, he had mused earlier; the Plant would be rid of the thorn in their lion's paw, and yet the law and the syndy would not hold the Plant responsible. No, it would be a dangerous escaped culture who killed Ephraim Mayda; a fanatic with grand delusions. Still, Jones had considered, wouldn't this make birther workers at the Plant, unemployed workers outside, and a vast majority of the public in general all the more distrusting of cultures, opposed to their widespread use? Wouldn't this hurt the Plant's very existence? And yet, they surely knew what they were doing better than he. After all, he was just a culture . . . educated by brain drip, by listening to human workers talk and to the radio programs the human workers listened to. Educated on the street since that time. But these men sat at vast glossy tables, making vast decisions. It was beyond his scope. The most he could wrap his thoughts around was payment of five thousand munits . . . and Parr had given him half of that when he climbed into his hovercar tonight.

"Hey," Mayda blubbered, "what are you saying . . . look . . . please! Listen . . ."

"We want to live as you do," Jones went on, improvising now as the rest of the words slipped through the fingers of his mind. He thought of his own hellish nest, and of Edgar's tiny black shed of a home. "We want . . ."

"Hey! Freeze!" he heard Parr yell.

Jones snapped his head around. What was happening? Had another bodyguard emerged from one of the other rooms? They should have checked all of the rooms first, they should have . . .

Parr was pointing the police issue pistol at him, not at some new player, and before Jones could bring his own gun around Parr snapped off five shots in rapid succession. Gas clouds flashed from the muzzle, heat lightning with no thunder, but the lightning struck Jones down. He felt a fireball streak across the side of his throat, deadened somewhat by the scarf wound there. He was kicked by a horse in the collarbone, and three projectiles in a cluster entered the upper left side of his chest. He spun down onto his belly on the white carpet, and saw his blood flecked there like beads of dew, in striking close-up. Beautiful red beads like tiny rubies clinging to the white fibers of the carpet. Even violence was glamorous in this place.

Mayda scampered closer, kicked his small silvery gun out of his hand. Jones's guts spasmed, but his outer body didn't so much as flinch. He cracked his lids a fraction, through crossed lashes saw Parr moving closer as well. For a moment, he had thought it was another man. Since firing the shots from behind the camera, out of its view, Parr had shed the bogus forcer uniform and changed into street clothes.

"I thought I heard a strange voice in here, Mr. Mayda!" Parr gushed, out of breath. "I dozed off in the other room . . . I'm so sorry! Are you all right?"

"Yes, thank God. He killed Brett!"

"How'd he get in here?"

"I don't know . . . Brett went to answer the door, and the next thing I knew . . ."

Parr didn't work for the Plant, Jones realized now, poor dumb culture that he was. He cursed himself. He wasn't street-smart. He was a child. He was five years old . . .

Parr worked for Ephraim Mayda, captain of a union, friend of the syndicate. Mayda, whose trusting followers killed others and themselves to fight for a job, to fight for their bread and shelter, while his job was to exploit their hunger, their anger and fear.

And the vid. The vid of a murderous clone attacking a hero of the people, stopped just in time by a loyal bodyguard (while another loyal bodyguard, poor Brett, had been sacrificed). One murderous forerunner of a much larger threat, as he had proclaimed. The vid that would unite the public against the cultures, lead to an outcry for the abolition of cloned workers . . . to their mass incineration . . .

He had almost seen this before. He'd let the money dazzle him. The bullets had slapped him fully awake.

"Call the forcers!" Mayda said for the benefit of the camera, sounding shaken, though he had known all along he was safe.

Through his lashes, Jones saw Parr stoop to retrieve his silvery handgun.

Jones's left arm was folded under him. He reached into his coat, and rolling onto his side, tore free a second gun, this one glossy black, a gun Parr hadn't known about, and as Parr lifted his startled head, Jones let loose a volley of shots as fast as he could depress the trigger. Parr sat down hard on his rump comically, and as each shot struck him he bounced like a child on his father's knee. When at last Jones stopped shooting him, his face almost black with blood and holes, Parr slumped forward into his own lap.

Jones sat up with a nova of agony in his chest, and a nova of hot gas exploded before his eyes as he saw Mayda bolting for the door. The shot hit the birther in the right buttock, and he sprawled onto his face shrieking like a hysterical child frightened by a nightmare.

As Jones struggled to his feet, staggered, and regained his footing, Mayda pulled himself toward the door on his belly. Almost casually, Jones walked to him, stood over him, and pointed the small black gun. Mayda rolled over to scream up at him and bullets drove the scream back into his throat. Jones shot out both eyes, and bullets punched in his nose and smashed his teeth, so that the face remaining looked to Jones like Edgar's with its simple black holes for features.

The gun had clicked empty. He let it drop, stepped over Mayda's body, over

Brett's body farther on, and then stopped before the door, snuffing his ski hat over the flames of his skull. But before he opened the door, he changed his mind and returned to the plush, vast parlor just for a moment . . .

• • •

It was an hour to dawn when Magnesium Jones reached the house of Edgar Allan Jones on the Obsidian Street Overpass.

Edgar croaked in delight to see him, until the withered being saw the look on the taller culture's face. It took Jones's arm, and helped him as he stooped to enter the tiny black-painted shack.

"You're hurt!" Edgar cried, supporting Jones as he lowered himself into a small rickety chair at a table in the center of the room. Aside from shelves, there was little else. No bed. A radio played music like the cries of whales in reverse, and a kettle was steaming on a battery-pack hot plate.

"I have something for you," Jones said, his voice a wheeze, one of his lungs deflated in the cradle of his ribs. "A Christmas present . . ."

"I have to get help. I'll go out . . . stop a car in the street," Edgar went on.

Jones caught its arm before Edgar could reach the door. He smiled at the creature. "I'd like a cup of tea," he said.

For several moments Edgar stared at the man, gouged features unreadable. Then, in slow motion, head blurring, it turned and went to the hot plate and steaming kettle.

While Edgar's back was turned, Jones reached into his long black coat, now soaked heavy with his blood, and from a pouch in its lining withdrew a sculpture carved from opalescent crystal. It was a fierce Ramon warrior, bringing his lance to bear. He placed it on the table quietly, so that the stunted clone would be surprised when it turned back around.

And while he waited for Edgar to turn around with his tea, Jones stripped off his ski hat and lowered his fiery brow onto one arm on the table. Closed his eyes to rest.

Yes, he would just rest a little while . . . until his friend finally turned around.

NICK MAMATAS

TIME OF DAY

(2002)

I HAD JUST GOTTEN OFF WORK and was on my way to more work when the phones in my mind rang. It was another seven jobs calling in, begging for my attention. In headspace, my ego agent, a slick and well-tanned Victor Mature, arranged them according to potential economic gain, neo-Marxist need measurement, and location.

I stuck my coffee cup in the beverage holder and leaned heavily on the wheel. Traffic was snarled. I initiated my patented anti-traffic protocol: "Whoo, let's go!" I shouted. I even banged my hands on the dashboard, but the snaking lines of red lights between me and my gig weren't impressed. I rewarded myself with more coffee anyway.

In headspace, my homunculus—a small, gray-winged gargoyle—shook its fist at the car ahead of me. My ego agent handed me his traveling salesman recommendation, a crazed zigzag all over the tristate. His plan was the cheapest and quickest way to install all the jacks, but my wetnurse was pinging about my pulse rate, lung color, and electrolyte levels, so I did my own math. I took two seconds to read a short article about another week of the Brown Haze over the city and decided that I needed a vacation. I'd do only one jackgig. A whole day spent on only one job instead of my usual eleven jobs a day. Far away. A monastery upstate, Greek Orthodox even. A vacation, or as close to one as jacked employees get.

The country would be quiet and the sky large. Like the parking lot I pulled into, but even bigger and with less soot.

• • •

"Okay, here we all are," I said to the kids. Not all my gigs were high-paying and glamorous; I was leading a tour of corporate HQ that night. Hi, I am Kelly Angelakis and I picked the short straw. Pleased to meet ya.

The kids gathered by the large office windows and stared up at me. They were college sophomores—the oldest was probably thirteen—and their eyes were wide and white, their skin slick with sweat. Their adrenal patches, all but mandatory for people on the go these days, were doing a bit too much to their young bodies. Some of the girls were almost vibrating in their sneakers. My ego agent provided me with some magnetizdat oral histories of patch addiction, but they were interrupted and replaced by soothing propaganda designed to reassure me. And I got some crossthought from another jack.

("Jesus forgive me, a miserable sinner!")

I sent the homunculus winging into the dark corners of my headspace to find the source of the crossthought, but he flew back to me empty-handed. Whoever was murmuring that little ditty needed a vacation worse than I did. Was it Sam, up on level seven? He was a pervert or something, and frequently filled nearby jacks with crapthink.

I couldn't bear to make eye contact with the tour group for more than a few seconds at a time, so I kept glancing out the window at the bright cityscape. The sky was black and the moon obscured by fog; more Brown Haze for tomorrow. A snarl of blinking red and white lights from the day's fifth rush hour entranced me for a second, but the sound of ten people twitching woke me up. I couldn't get a tenthsecond's rest that night.

My homunculus went and found that errant bit of religious crossthink: it came from the jackgig request up at the monastery. A distraction. Victor Mature stepped up to the mic to take over the tour.

(Stock footage of Bill Cosby entered from skull-right and accepted a cigar from Freud with a smile. "Some acumen agents may appear as imaginary friends." A human-sized cartoon cigar with flickering red ash for hair, goggle eyes rolling and stick-figure limbs akimbo, marched into view and waved. The crowd giggled as if on cue.)

In headspace, the homunculus flew into view and unfurled a parchment. A green visor hung from its horns and it waved a quill pen in one claw. Cute. My helicopter to the country was ready. I blinked my signature at the parchment and the image derezzed.

The children were all quivering eyes and hair slicked down against clammy skin (—delete that, only happythink tonight!). Victor gave the standard disclaimer, pointed out the gift shop and cheerily spat out the company slogan, "We're Not Just Jack."

(Corporate logo, cue jingle.)

The helicopter was still ready, and I was already late. There was no way the elevator would get me to the roof on time. In headspace, My Pet Dog scuttled forward and stared at the copter's scheduling systems with his puppy-dog eyes. He scored twenty seconds for me. I took the steps up to the roof three at a time, swallowed a lungful of whipping smog on the helipad, and hopped aboard.

(My Pet Dog was a droopy old basset hound with folds of brown and white fur draped over his snout. Designed to curry favor with acumen and humans alike, he almost never failed. Even a helicopter had to submit to his cuteness.)

"Are you well rested, or just patched?" the pilot asked. He was old and had that skinny-guy-with-a-paunch look that ex-athletes and the unpatched had. I didn't know his name or number, so I couldn't look him up on the jacknet. Small talk. Grr.

"I'm patched," I said, trying to sound a bit apologetic. "That's business, you know, a working girl has to make a living." He smiled when I said "working girl." What a Neanderthal. My Pet Dog had already sniffed out his body language and idiolect, cross-referenced it with his career choice, and suggested a conversational thread.

I looked out the window. "Shame, isn't it?" I knew he'd know I was talking about the smog.

"The Brown Haze. Have you ever seen a white cloud? I know you live in the city."

"Sure I've seen them, in the country. Won't there be some over the hills by the monastery?"

He nodded once, as people of his temperament tend to. "Yeah."

Then I realized that I was only hearing him with my ears. He wasn't jacked at all. He'd just waited for me instead of overriding his helicopter and taking off without me. He'd done—what was it?—a favor.

It was hot in the cockpit, too hot, and my connection to the net faded. Victor Mature was beginning to warble, but the wetnurse rushed up and gave me a shot of sleepytime before my jack overheated entirely. Snoozeville.

• • •

"Excuse me, I only had three seconds of the language," I said in heavily accented Greek. The monk just smiled, showing that he actually had a pair of lips under his thick black beard. It was quiet outside, and cold.

"Welcome to Saint Basil's," he said in the bland English of disc jockeys and foreigners who've had their accents eradicated. "I'm Brother Peter." He smiled weakly, his lips still moving slightly, like he was talking to himself. Or like he had just had a jack installed. ("It is two thirty-five ay em," the homunculus whispered.) The monastery was impressive from the outside, at least: a squat four-story building made of thick carved granite. The lawn was well-kept, but still a bit wild, with weeds and poorly pruned bushes lining the walkway up the hill. I heard some crickets chirping away in soothing unison. It reminded me of the city, but quieter, like the volume was turned down on the universe. The noise of the jacknet was far away too, like waves lapping a shoreline just out of sight.

"My God, you're tired." I looked him over but couldn't see any of the telltale sweat or twitches. My own patches responded to that stray thought with another surge of tingly chemicals to the bloodstream. I blinked hard and rose to the tips of my toes. "I'm sorry, I'm . . . you know . . . I am not used to people who . . . actually let themselves get tired."

"People who are not from the city," Peter said. He didn't smile this time, but he muttered something to himself after he spoke, then bowed his head slightly and took a step backward. "Come in, please."

I slipped through the door and frowned. The walls were plain old drywall, with an icon or two hanging from nails for decoration. The ceiling lights were old yellow incandescent bulbs, and the monastery's little foyer smelled of wax, incense, and unwashed feet. I got another burst of crossthought. (". . . have mercy on me, a miserable sinner.")

The source was here, somewhere down below. I could feel a jack pinging nearby, a strange chanting beat. There was only one of them, though, not the thousands I was used to in the city. Like one water droplet falling into a still puddle, it stood out.

Even out in the real world, it was quiet. Wind moved over the grass. Peter tugged on the sleeve of my blouse.

"Ms. Angelakis, you'll need to retire for several hours at least. Morning prayers are in ninety minutes. Then we hold a morning liturgy, and of course—"

"Women may not attend the liturgy. After the morning meal, we will meet again so we may begin my examination of George Proios, who needs a jack installed," I said along with him. There were only two variances. Peter said "your examination" instead of "my examination," which I expected. More importantly, he said "removed" instead of "installed." And his lips moved even after he finished speaking.

"What? Why would he want his jack removed?" I asked, my voice spiking enough to make My Pet Dog wince. My ego agent immediately got FedEx on the jacknet and had them send my tools out. "I wasn't told this was a removal. A removal requires tools and facilities that I do not have. A removal needs a medical doctor. I'm just an installer. Assembly-line stuff. I'm unskilled labor."

"Brother George does not want his jack removed. However, he requires it. *We* require it. He is a medical doctor and can assist you in that regard. He believes he can work with you, which is why he requested you."

In the headspace, I ran to one of the phones and hit the hot button, but there was no dial tone.

The inky blackness of my headspace solidified into a curved stone wall, a cave with no entrance or exit. The homunculus tried to fly to the shadows, to the open networks, but slammed against the mental block and fell at my feet, twitching. The wetnurse knelt down to repair it. Outside, I was still, staring off into space.

"Ms. Angelakis?" Peter asked. He waved his hand in front of my face.

I stepped back up, my vision refocusing on the outside world. Peter's lips twitched silently. I wanted to rip his beard off, to feel the wiry hair in my hands, but the wetnurse sedated me. From a few feet under the floor, I felt George Proios's malfunctioning jack repeating one recursive command, one thought, over and over. In the corner of my headspace, I sensed him, like an old file I'd forgotten to delete, like a shadow on a cave wall.

("Step up, there's a world out there!" Victor Mature demanded. Kelly snapped to attention.)

"He's having his jack removed," I said to Peter. "How can he assist me?" The wetnurse ran about my headspace with cold compresses, but I got all flushed anyway. I could feel the heat pouring from my skin. Peter's expression didn't change; his eyes were distant and his body still but for his twitching lips.

"You do not need his help, just his consent," he said, finally. His voice retained that dreamy, flat tone, like a computer or a jazz radio announcer.

"Jesus forgive me!" I said. "I'm not going to break half a dozen laws and risk a man's . . ." I stopped and realized what I had just said.

(The homunculus flew about Kelly's head, a flashing red siren strapped to its head. "Warning, warning," it screeched. Kelly waved it away.)

Peter didn't smile. I licked a line of sweat off my top lip. In the headspace, My Pet Dog went sniffing after shadows. Downstairs, he was in a basement cell: George Proios. One command line, one task endlessly replicated by his Sinner Self, the Holy Spirit, and A Young Lamb, the monk's custom acumen agents. Some religious people even installed Jesus Christ masques, to keep them from fucking strange women or swearing. I'd never seen anyone with a lamb before. Certainly not one standing alongside a dove bathed in nearly blinding light and a haggard, leprous monk who was mindlessly repeating "O Lord Jesus Christ, Son of God, Jesus forgive me, a miserable sinner." My homunculus slapped its little claw against its forehead ("We could have had a V8!"). Then the monk turned to me, staring with his dead eyes, and linked our jacks. The shadow on the cave wall of my headspace began to murmur a prayer. Jesus forgive me, a miserable sinner, so I won't have to think anymore.

(Kelly Angelakis, age fourteen. She was thin and underdeveloped, with a huge mop of black curls splayed on the pillows. Her palm ran over her nude stomach, sliding down between her legs. Then guilt and bitter vomit filled her mouth.)

"I am sure you will help him, Ms. Angelakis. Brother George assures us that you are a good Greek girl. Also, he tells us that the state he is experiencing is . . . how would one put it . . . contagious, no?" He turned on his heel and led me to my room. I glanced up at the back of his neck, just to make sure. Smooth skin and wiry black hair. No jack.

They were all dry here. I could only sense one other signal, the drumbeat of George Proios and his begging cybernetic prayer. It overwhelmed his system and hit mine hard too. The homunculus scratched at headspace's new walls, trying to get out, but it was grounded. I was cut off from the network now, thanks to distance, granite, and the white noise chant of "Jesus forgive me." He had trapped me. The last message he'd allowed out was for the equipment I needed.

In the headspace, Victor Mature stepped into view. "Kelly, listen. We can get through this. Don't forget how good you are. Proios sounds dangerous, but he's going to let you knock him out and uninstall his jack. We can do it and then we'll be able to call the police, the sysops, the FBI. All we have to do is take it easy for a few hours, do a job just like we were planning, and then we can leave. And all we need to do to succeed is not fall apart right now." I opened my mouth to answer him like he was standing next to me, then caught myself.

(My Pet Dog whimpered, knowing that even if the company was interested in Kelly's location, it would be cheaper to hire some thirteen-year-old right out of college to replace her than to waste the copter fuel on retrieving her. Kids worked more cheaply and had a useful decade in them before burning out. And everyone was too busy to worry about Kelly or where she was anyway.)

My room was spartan, with blank walls, a cot, and a small table where a candle, a Bible, and a bunch of grapes were laid out for me. A water cooler bubbled to itself on the opposite end of the room. My wetnurse suggested flipping through the New Testament, "purely to keep our mind on something else right now." I hadn't read a whole book in years, hadn't needed to. I flipped through the pages and ran my palms over the vellum, and quickly sliced my finger open on the gold leaf of a page from Revelation. I sucked on my finger for a few seconds, then decided to try something else. Being alone, without the net, was . . . disconcerting. Hell, it was scary.

I thought I'd make a game of seeing how far I could spit grape seeds, but the grapes were seedless. I stretched out on the bed—the mattress was hard and lumpy—and closed my eyes. In the headspace, my ego agent brought out the old film projector and suggested a movie. I shrugged and pulled down the screen.

(Victor Mature took his place in front of the projection screen, the cave morphing about him into a Hollywood studio. My Pet Dog jumped into his arms and licked his face, "Oh, Won Ton Ton," the ego agent crooned, "you'll be perfect!" "Yeah, Nick, he sure will be!" someone called from offscreen.)

I squeezed my eyes shut tighter. I'd already seen this movie too many times. *Won Ton Ton, the Dog Who Saved Hollywood*, a cheesy bit of tinsel that I'd caught on television at three in the morning once, when I was seven. Victor Mature had played Nick. I was so happy to hear my father's name on TV. It was either Victor Mature or Santa Claus, so I glommed onto Victor.

George Proios was still in my mind. He dug through my memories like someone picking through a bowl of pistachios.

(Kelly Angelakis, age seven. Nick Angelakis towered over her, a torn book in his hand, the pages falling around Kelly like feathers from a burst pillow. "Why do you read this garbage! This is for retarded kids, Kalliope, with the spaceships and pointy ears. What is he supposed to be,"—the back of the hand slapped the cover of the novel—"the devil?"

From the kitchen, Vasso Angelakis called out "Leave her alone, let her read what she wants!"

"I'm trying to raise my daughter right!" Nick shouted back.)

Childhood was another movie I had seen too many times already. I took a deep breath, pulled myself up out of bed, and hit the hallway. Peter was waiting for me, his eyes wide with confusion, his lips still going, and a package in his hands.

"Ms. Angelakis?"

"Come on, let's go see Proios now. He's doing . . . something."

"What?"

". . . Praying!"

"Well, yes, I certainly hope so," Peter said, glancing out one of the dark windows in the hallway. "It has been only four minutes since I showed you the room. Please, try to get some rest. I brought you blankets. I'll come for you after morning prayers. I'm sure your mail will be here by then."

There was no threat in his tone or body language, but I took a backward step into the room anyway. Then he said, "Will you need more blankets?"

"No, I'm fine." I closed the door. Goddamn, I needed to turn off my head, but Proios was digging through my old files. He introduced a virus into my headspace, one smarter than my wetnurse—an artificial mental illness called existential angst. Bastard.

(Kelly Angelakis, age seventeen. The back of her head was shaved. Her father, now an inch shorter than she, shook his head slowly as she explained, "I can talk to people with it, access information. Everyone's going to have one, one of these days, just like the computer."

"I never used the computer," Nick Angelakis said. "This is terrible. You want to talk to people? You can talk to me, you can talk to Mama, your friends in school. You should have learned Greek, if you wanted to talk to people. Your poor grandmother can't say two words to you.")

My eyes refocused from the blank walls of my headspace to the blank walls of the room. I decided that I would lie still and be perfectly silent, to listen to the building. That lasted two seconds. The homunculus flung itself against the headspace's cave walls again. Back to the grapes, this time making a game of how many I could fit into my mouth at once (fifteen!) but I started gagging and had to dig a few of them out of my mouth and crush the rest by pushing on my cheeks with my palms.

I had already used up my sleepytime with that damn nap on the helicopter. I counted the beats of a cricket chirping and then counted the holes in the ceiling tiles. One hundred and eighty-five holes per tile, thirty-eight tiles. Seven thousand and thirty ceiling tile holes in this room. The dimensions of the room and layout of the hallway suggested eight rooms of identical size on this floor. Was it dawn yet? Fifty-six thousand, two hundred and forty holes in the ceiling tiles on this floor. How many floors? Four.

Was it dawn yet? ("It is three fifteen ay em," the homunculus whispered.) Random facts littered headspace. Saint Nicholas (there's that name again) was the patron saint of Greece and of sailors. "And of prostitutes," the shadow on the cave wall whispered. Only 20 percent of the land in Greece is arable, while nearly 92 percent of Greece's population lives near the endless coastlines. (Jesus forgive me.)

I had been to church once, years ago, after my father died. It was a blur now, thanks to my jack and my busy little brain. The priest was mumbling in Greek and my jack was off, at mother's request—three hours of processing time I'll never get back. No translation but the priest's own, which was incomplete. The line "Life is more elusive than a dream" was the only thing I remembered from the sermon. I haven't dreamed in eight years.

The night before my father—not Dad, not Papa—died, I slept with a boy named Thomas Smith. My Pet Dog dug a hole at my feet and found the old sensations, the breeze on my back, the moisture, the throbbing in my tired calves after a few minutes of squelching. Was it dawn yet? That's all I wanted to know then, and all I wanted to know now. It wasn't, though. ("It's three forty-seven ay em," the homunculus whispered.) I gave up, closed my eyes, and actually, really, naturally slept. And I dreamed. I was taking a final exam after cutting class all semester. I was naked.

• • •

I awoke to a knock on the door, and was up in point two seconds. Brother Peter and I slipped past half a dozen other monks. Their footfalls were quiet enough, but it wasn't the sound of six dryboys, it was the lockstep beat of a jacked workplace. And the murmuring, the lips, each man I passed was muttering to himself. I glanced at the backs of their necks as they passed, but there were no jacks to be seen. Dry as a bone, and dry to the bone. But every one of them was tied to some jacknet, somewhere.

Peter had my FedEx package tucked under his arm and was marching down the hall, sending the hem of his cassock flying up to his knees. I was faster, though, and kept stepping on his heels.

"Brother Peter," I said, "you do realize, of course, that when I get back to the city, I'm going to put you on report. Not just for demanding this highly irregular removal, but for kidnapping me! This is contract under false pretenses, this is misallocation of processing time, this is wire fraud—"

"Please help him." He handed me the package and nodded toward a flight of steps leading down into a basement. "Go on."

"You're not coming with me?" I asked him. "How can I trust you on any of this? Heck, how can you trust me, I can go down there and lobotomize him." Peter shrugged and mumbled something again. In headspace, I heard Proios's own voice chanting, "O Lord Jesus Christ, Son of God, Jesus forgive me, a miserable sinner." The ego agent joined in the chant, in Victor Mature's dusky tones. My Pet Dog howled.

Then I realized that Peter hadn't been mumbling to himself. He had been reciting the same prayer as George, the same as the six other monks marching down the hall. The homunculus perched on my shoulder and held out a headspace lantern. In the real world, my pupils instantly adjusted to the dark and I walked down the steps.

George Proios looked just like the monk I had seen in the crossthought, and his shadow was splayed against the stone wall of the basement, just like it was in my headspace. His beard was long and matted, held against his chest by his own sweat and grime. He smiled.

("Jesus forgive me," the wetnurse muttered, and performed a preliminary diagnosis on our subject.)

His lips weren't moving. I realized then that mine were. That upstairs, Peter's still were. That every monk was saying a little prayer. They were always saying a little prayer. Now I was too, I was on a new jacknet. Except there was no jack necessary, and no net.

"Have you found God?" George asked.

"I'm here to remove your jack."

He didn't say anything for a long moment. Then he nodded toward a small table. A slice of bread sat there, not doing much. The words "Have you eaten?" came from somewhere—headspace or real world, I didn't know. He rose up and shuffled toward the table, split the piece in half and offered it to me. I looked down and my face flushed. I held a complete piece of bread in my hand, and George still had a full slice in his hand. "More?" He broke his piece in two again and offered me one of them. It was cold and heavy in my hand. The slice was whole, though, and now I had two pieces of bread. Two whole pieces of bread.

"I would like to remove the jack, and then leave," I said. I dropped the bread on the floor and took a step forward, My Pet Dog feeding me a conversational thread of icy professionalism designed to engender compliance.

"I have no wish for the jack to be removed," he said.

"It's broken. Malfunctioning. You're experiencing a severe cognitive loop, probably because of a physical defect in the jack's antenna array. I can't do a spinal intervention here, but without reception, your problem should alleviate itself," My Pet Dog said to me and I said to George.

George shrugged. "I do not have a problem. I pray without ceasing, as Scripture demands. I do what my brothers spend their adult lives attempting through privation and contemplation. One begins by praying as often as one can, on the level of the spoken word. All the time, one must begin to pray, muttering, whispering, thinking. Finally, after long years one can literally pray without ceasing. One's thoughts are always with God, not with sin. I pray from the heart, not from the jack. I am serene." My Pet Dog opened the package and spread the instruments on the tabletop.

"Look," George said, grabbing the two pieces of bread from the table. "Look! How do you explain this? Science, no? Somehow? What, with your quantum something-or-other?" He waved his arms and shoved the bread under my nose. Spittle coated his beard, and his arms were as thin as twigs. With a conductor's flourish, he whipped the sleeves of his robe up to his elbows and threw the bread on the ground. I took a step forward. "Mesmerism, perhaps, no? My jack interfering with yours? Have you thought of sin this morning, my child? Are you at peace? Have you ever even breathed? Jesus have mercy on me, a miserable sinner. Jesus have mercy on you."

George knelt to the floor near my feet, his head near the bread. The Jesus Prayer had done it. Two pieces where there used to be one. The dusty crusts, my footprint impressed onto one of them, existed. Without having to buy or sell them, without eleven jobs to pay for them, without a jingle. A miracle, at my feet.

I slapped a patch on George's neck and he dropped like a few sticks wrapped in a rag. Maybe I could know God after all. No more existential angst, no more rushing from job to job, the fabled free lunch. The bread. I tapped into George's spine and began to draw the information from him. The inspiration from him. It was like breathing a rainbow, but I could taste bread and wine, flesh and blood, in my mouth.

("The Lord tells us in Thessalonians 5:17 to 'Pray without ceasing,'" George explained to Kelly. "Our brothers have spent their lives contemplating their navels, muttering the words to themselves, trying to never lose contact with God. But I couldn't. The world was too distracting, too earnest. So I had a pirate jack installed, and found a way. And I prayed so well that God allowed others to hear me as well."

It was world of the Godnet: all the jackless wonders out there with one job, one personality, and one little life each, the whole smelly superstitious lot of them. And now Kelly was jacked in too.)

With George unconscious and his netblock gone, the rest of yesterday's junkmail finally downloaded and hit my brain. The latest news, spinning into headspace like a shot of a newspaper in an old movie, let me know what I had been missing for the past few hours. War with the Midwest, wethead bias crimes against dryboys on the rise, sumo results, the GM workers' council calling for a strike, markets down. People had things to buy and sell, important pinhead opinions to howl across my brain. I was needed, necessary, a crucial memebucket for the best the world had to offer, at low low interest rates. No thanks, I thought to myself (to myself, not some nano-neurological stooge!); I quit.

In headspace, I shot My Pet Dog. I shot him dead, and took over my body, once and for all.

Headspace crumbled and a noisy blackness buried me. I think I fell to my knees, or was it on my face? I couldn't breathe. My lips were clenched shut, but vomit poured into my mouth and through the gaps in my teeth. Then, in headspace, I felt the firm hand of my ego agent on the back of my neck, lifting me above the swirling advertisements, the dizzying dance of thousands of stock prices, and the casual emergencies of work and memos and updated job queues. I coughed up the liquid shit of it all and finally, finally, took a moment. And I breathed, and my breath was a prayer.

I turned to face my acumen. The light from Victor Mature's miner's helmet dazzled my eyes, but that was probably just the jack's way of explaining the stars I saw from the bump on my head. The homunculus flew overhead, clutching My Pet Dog's corpse in his claws. The wetnurse was standing on a stepladder as a waist-deep flood of information spilled into our little world.

"Guess what, gang," I said. "You're all fired. I don't need to work twenty-three point seven hours a day anymore, and neither does anyone else. God will provide." In headspace, I held up two pieces of miracle bread, and threw them to the floor. Then I fired my acumen agents. With my gun.

The jack removal took longer than I thought it would. The scalpel felt too heavy in my hands; my fingers were too stiff to move. My connection to the jacknet was a distant scream, like a child left behind in a parking lot by his deranged parents. George's eyes were still open, in spite of the narcotic. What would he be like when he woke up? Would he still be tied into the Godnet, like the monks upstairs? Like me? An overheated Jesus guided my hands, and my thoughts. His face was red, and steam poured from his ears.

The police took my ego agents' posthumous statements. (Damn backups.) I heard their filing cabinet drawer slam shut and echo. They'd get to my case by the time I was ninety, if I lived that long. My dry cleaning was done and the menu for the next three weeks needed to be planned; provisions needed to be requisitioned. My apartment back in the city wanted to know if it could please water the plants. A personal ad wrote itself for me and begged for my eyeblink signature. Sneaky anarchist magnetizdats nipped at my ankles, demanding attention. Helicopter blades were talking to me, saying "hurry hurry hurry" with the whip of wind. I had a deadline to meet. One deadline a second, every second, for the rest of my life.

("'Lord Jesus Christ, have mercy on me, a miserable sinner' is as powerful for its cadence as it is for its content. Once integrated into the head, it is actually hard to remove. Rather, one begins to receive, the monks say, messages from God," Kelly said, mimicking the singsong of the prayer.)

I sent the jacknet a final, very important message, the same one George had sent me. Jesus forgive me, a miserable sinner. I reached behind my neck and blindly disconnected my jack. I was alone, but for the constant prayer on my lips and the love for every man and woman in the world. The Godnet.

• • •

I ate a sandwich and sat on the hill just outside the monastery, waiting for the helicopter. Everyone in the Godnet ate that sandwich, the two pieces of bread coming straight from George's miracle—after I brushed the dirt off them, of course. And I tasted gyros in Cyprus, kimchi in Pýôngyang, and injera in Addis Ababa. And I even felt the tickle of a patch here and exhaust-stained breakfast coffee there, from the first jacknetters to be infected with the God virus. Information wasn't a horrible flood of jingles and logos and unfair trades of wayward seconds of processing time anymore; it was a smile, a wave, a breeze, a broken leg. Even the dying felt good, because there was always a birth right behind it.

It was odd, being alone, but not at all scary anymore. It was odd, being one with the world and everyone in it. It was hard, eating a sandwich and incessantly muttering the prayer at the same time. It was nice, though, to know that the Godnet would be giving me food and water and love and a place to live. Miracle bread for everyone. I heard angels' wings, but they were really only the spinning rotors of the copter.

The trip back. I spoke with the pilot. She had kids. She played the cello. She'd been raped once, at thirteen, but was healing now, and her lips moved with an invisible prayer. Her jack was cold and nearly dormant, buzzing with low-grade euphoria. We were just in range of the city, and I could already hear the Jesus Prayer—the God virus—in the ear of every poor jacked bastard in town. It was all prayer now; they shut down the news, the soaps, and even the ads. The reporters were too busy taking time off to report on the collapse of the economy, the wine flowing from the public urinals, the lame walking, the stupid finally getting a clue, the kids actually sleeping—really, really sleeping and then getting up because it was morning, not because it was time for their shifts. As we flew down into the city, the sun rose into the already-shrinking pool of brown smog that sat atop the skyline like a bad toupee. Morning. Not work or betweenwork or morework. I knew what time of day it was.

LAUREN BEUKES

BRANDED

(2003)

WE WERE AT STONES, playing pool, drinking, goofing around, maybe hoping to score a little sugar, when Kendra arrived, all moffied up and gloaming like an Aito/329. "Ahoy, Special-K, where you been, girl, so juiced to kill?" Tendeka asked while he racked up the balls, all click-clack in their white plastic triangle. Old school this pool bar was. But Kendra didn't answer. Girl just grinned, reached into her back pocket for her phone, hung skate-rat style off a silver chain connected to her belt, and infra'd five Rand to the table to get tata machance on the next game.

But I was watching the girl and as she slipped her phone back into her pocket, I saw that telltale glow 'neath her sleeve. Long sleeves in summer didn't cut it. So, it didn't surprise me none in the least when K waxed the table. Ten-Ten was surprised though. Ten-Ten slipped his groove. But boy kept it in, didn't say anything, just infra'd another five to the table and racked 'em again. Anyone else but Ten woulda racked 'em hard, woulda slammed those balls on the table, eish. But Ten, Ten went the other way. Just by how careful he was. Precise 'n clipped like an assembly line. So you could see.

Boyfriend wasn't used to losing, especially not to Special-K. I mean, the girl held her own 'gainst most of us, but Ten could wax us all six-love baby. Boyfriend carried his own cue, in a special case. Kif shit it was. Lycratanium, separate pieces that clicked into each other, assembled slick 'n cold and casual-like, like he was a soldier in a war movie snapping a sniper rifle together. But Kendra grinning now, said, "No, my bra. I'm out," set her cue down on the empty table next to us.

"Oh ja, like Ten's gonna let this hook slide." Rob snorted into his drink.

"Best of three," Tendeka said and smiled loose and easy. Like it didn't matter and chalked his cue.

Girl hesitated and shrugged then. Picked up the cue. Tendeka flicked the triangle off the table, flip-rolling it between his fingers lightly. "Your break."

Kendra chalked up, spun the white ball out to catch it at the line. Edged it then sideways so's it would take the pyramid out off-center. Girl leaned over the table. Slid the tip of the cue over her knuckles once, taking aim, pulled back and cut loose, smooth as sugar. Crack! Balls twisting out across the table. Sunk four solids straight-up. Black in the middle and not a single stripe down.

Rob whistled. "Shit. You been practicing, K?"

Kendra didn't even look up. Took out another two solids and lined up a third in the corner pocket. Girl's lips twitched, but she didn't smile, no, didn't look at Ten, who was still sayin' nothin' like. He chalked his cue again, like he hadn't done it already, and stepped up. The freeze was so tight I couldn't take it. Anyway. I knew what was coming. So, off by the bar I was, but nears enough so I was still in on the action like. Ten lined 'em up and took out two stripes at the same time, rocketing 'em into different pockets. Bounced the white off the pillow and took another, edged out the solid K had all lined up. Another stripe down and boy lined up a fifth blocking the corner pocket. "You're up."

Girl just stood there lookin' as if she was sizing up.

"K. You're up."

Girl snapped her head toward Tendeka. Tuned back in. Took her cue up, leaned over, standing on tiptoes and nicked the white ball light as candy, so it floated, spinning, into the middle of table like. Shrugged at Ten, smiling, and that ball just kept on spinning. Stepped back, set her cue down on the table next and started walking over to the bar, to me, while that white ball, damn, was still spinning.

"Hey! What the fuck?"

"Ah c'mon, Ten. You know I gotcha down."

"What! Game ain't even started. And what's with this, man? Fuckin' party tricks don't mean shit."

"It's over, Ten."

"You on drugs, girl? You tweaked?"

"Fuck off, Ten."

Ten shoved his cue at Rob, who snatched it quick, and rounded on the girlfriend. "You're mashed, Kendra!" He grabbed her shoulder, spun her round, "C'mon, show me!"

"Kit Kat, baby. Give it a break."

"Oh yeah? Lemme see. C'mon."

"Fuck off, Tendeka! Serious!"

People were looking now. Cams were too, though in a place like Stones, they probably weren't working none too well. Owner paid a premium for faulty equipment like. Jazz was defending Kendra now. Not that she needed it. We all knew the girl wasn't a waster like. Even Ten.

Now me. I was a waster. I was skeef. Jacked that kind shit straight into my tongue, popping lurid lurex candy capsules into the piercing to disseminate like. Lethe or supersmack or kitty. Some prefer it old-style, pills 'n needles, but me, the works work best straight in through that slippery warm pink muscle. Porous your mouth is. So's it's straight into the blood and saliva absorbs the rest into your glands. I could tell you all things about that wet hole mouth that makes it perfect for drugs like. But, tell you true, it's all cheap shit. Black-market. Ill legit. Not like sweet Kendra's high. Oh no, girl had gone the straight 'n arrow. All the way, baby. All the way.

"C'mon Ten, back off, man." Rob was getting real nervous like. Bartender too, twitchin' to call his defuser. But Kendra-sweet had enough now, spun on Ten, finally, stuck out her tongue at him like a laaitie. And Jazz sighed. "There. Happy now?" But Ten wasn't. For yeah, sure as sugar, Special-K's tongue was a virgin. Never been pierced by a stud let alone an applijack. Never had that sweet rush as the micro-needles release slick-quick into the fleshy pink. Never had her tongue go numb with the dark oiliness of it so's you can't speak for minutes. Doesn't matter though. Talkin'd be least of your worries. Supposin' you had any. But then Ten knew that all along. Cos you can't play the way the girlfriend did on the rof. Tongue's not the only thing that goes numb. And boyfriend knows it. And everything's click-clicking into place.

"Oh you fucking crazy little shit. What have you done?" Ten was grabbing at her now, tough-like, her swatting at him, pulling away as he tried to get a hold of her sleeve. Jazz was yelling again. "Ease off, Tendeka!" Shouldn't have wasted her air time. Special-K could look after herself all well now. After those first frantic swats, something leveled. Only to be expected when she's so fresh. Still adjustin' like. But you could see it kick in. Sleek it was. So's instant she's flailing about and the next she lunges, catches him under his chin with the heel of her palm. Boy's head snaps back and at the same time she shoves him hard so's he falls backward, knocks over a table on his way. Glass smashing and the bartender's pissed now. Everyone still, except Rob who laughed once, abrupt.

Girl gave Ten a look. Cocky as a street kid. But wary it was too. Not of him, although he was already getting up. Not that she could sustain like. Battery was running low now. Was already when she first set down her cue. And boy was pissed indeed. But that look, boys and girls, that look was wary not of him at all. But of herself like.

Ten was on his feet now, screaming. The plot was lost, boys and girls. The plot was gone. Cut himself on the broken glass. Like paint splats on to the wooden floor. Lunged at Kendra, backing away, hands up, but still with that look. And boy was big. Intent on serious damage, yelling and not hearing his cell bleep first warning then second. Like I said, the plot was gone. Way past its expiry date.

Then predictable; defuser kicked in. Higher voltage than necessary like, but bartender was pissed. Ten jerked epileptic. Some wasters I know set off their own phone's defuser, on low settings like for those dark an' hectic beats. Even rhythm can be induced, boys and girls. But it's not maklik. Have to hack SAPcom to SMS the trigger signal to your phone. Worse now since the cops privatized, upgraded the firewalls. That or tweak the hardware and then the shocks could come random. Crisp you KFC.

Me, I defused my defuser. 'Lectric and lethe don't mix. Girlfriend in Sea Point pulled the plug one time. Simunye. Cost ten kilos of sugar so's it don't come cheap an' if the tec don't know what they're doing, ha, crisp you KFC. Or worse, Disconnect. Off the networks. Solitary confinement like. Not worth the risk, boys and girls, unless you know the tec is razor.

So, Ten, jerking to imaginary beats. Bartender hit endcall finally and boy collapsed to floor, panting. Jasmine knelt next to him. Ten's phone still crackling. VIMbots scuttling to clean up blood an' glass and spilled liquor. Other patrons were turning away now. Game over. Please infra another coin. Kendra stood watching a second, then also turned away, walked up to the bar where I was sitting.

"Cause any more kak like that, girl, an I'll crisp you too." The bartender said as she sat down on the bar stool next to me.

"Oh please. Like how many dial-ins you got left for the night?" Kendra snapped, but girl was looking almost as strung out as Ten was now.

"Yeah, well don't make me waste 'em all on you."

"Just get me a Sprite, okay?"

Behind her, Jazz and Rob were holdin' Tendeka up. He made as if to move for the bar, but Jazz pulled him back, wouldn't let him. Not least cos of the look the bartender shot them. Boy was too fried to stir anyway, but said, loud enough for all to hear, "Sellout."

"Get the fuck out, kid." Dismissive the bartender was. Knew there was no fight left.

"Fucking corporate whore!"

"C'mon, Ten. Let's go." Jazz was escortin' him out.

Kendra ignored him. Girl had her Sprite now and downed it in one. Asked for another.

Already you could see it kickin' in.

"Can I see?" I asked, mock sly-shy.

Kendra shot me a look which I couldn't figure and then finally slid up her sleeve reluctant like, revealing the glow tattooed on her wrist.

The bartender clicked his tongue as he set down the drink. "Sponsor baby, huh?" Sprite logo was emblazoned there, not on her skin, but under it, shining through, with the slogan, "just be it."

No rinkadink light show was this. Nanotech she'd signed up for changed the bio-structure of her cells, made 'em phosphorescent in all the right places. Nothing you couldn't get done at the local light-tat salon, but corporate sponsorship came with all the extras. Even on lethe, I wasn't 'blivious to the ad campaigns on the underway. But Kendra was the first I knew to get Branded like.

Girl was flying now. Ordered a third Sprite. Brain reacting like she was on some fine-ass bliss, drowning her in endorphins an' serotonin, Sprite binding with aminos and the tiny bio-machines hummin' at work in her veins. Voluntary addiction with benefits. Make her faster, stronger, more coordinated. Ninja-slick reflexes. Course, if she'd sold her soul to Coke instead, she'd be sharper, wittier. Coke nano lubes the transmitters. Neurons firing faster, smarter, more productive. All depends on the brand, on your lifestyle of choice and it's all free if you qualify. Waster like me would never get with the program, but sweet Kendra, straight up candidate of choice. Apply now, boys and girls, while stocks last. You'll never afford this high on your own change.

Special K turned to me, on her fourth now, blissed out on the carbonated nutri-sweet and the tech seething in her hot little sponsor baby bod, nodded, "And one for my friend," to the bartender like. And who was I to say no?

YUN KO-EUN

P

(2011)

Translated from the Korean by Sean Lin Halbert

P259. This was where Chang lived and worked. If anyone wanted to send him a letter or package, all they needed were these four characters. The reason his address was so short, and the reason he only needed one for both work and home, was because the company he worked for *was* a city. Every day from eight in the morning to seven at night, Chang was at P259. And every night when he got home from work, he was still at P259.

He received it at about eleven in the morning on a workday. He wasn't the only one—all members of his team had been sent the same envelope. It was addressed from HR and contained an application to receive a free capsule endoscopy.

Chang threw the application in his desk drawer. That was where he put everything he didn't need. The only items he kept on his desk were a computer, cellphone, and family photo. Everyone he knew had a family photo on their desk, so he thought it'd look weird if he didn't. The photo also served as a kind of magic talisman, something to control his frequent, sudden impulses to leave the company. Some employees used paper carnations, others, cards from their kids—they all served a similar purpose.

"Did you fill it out?"

Chang looked up from his lunch tray. Song was asking about the capsule endoscopy application. The endoscope in question, which was thirty millimeters long and eleven millimeters wide, went by the name "jellyfish" because of its bulbous head and tentacle-like legs. Unlike traditional endoscopes, this all-weather capsule traveled past the small intestine, swimming down the entire length of the patient's digestive tract like a fish in the ocean. Performing such an expensive new procedure for free on the employees of P Tires was of course nothing more than one large advertisement. But such sponsorships were common here. Because P Tires had nearly twenty thousand employees, it was often used as promotional fodder for new businesses that moved into the city. Not even the hospitals were above such business tactics. The company was itself one large market. The hospital, which had just launched its new medical device, was the newest member to the business complex. And as always, there were rumors that its president was related to someone from management.

"It's not mandatory, you know."

Despite saying this, Chang knew it definitely *was*. The constant barrage of applications, all of which were for the same endoscopy, was enough to convince him of its compulsory nature. Not only did they send him one by mail, but they also sent him three more via email, company shuttle bus, and the hallway bulletin board. Of course, it was for a good cause, but Chang had no interest.

Song stared at Chang for a moment before lighting a cigarette. Song had quit smoking two years ago, only to start again just recently. Chang wondered if it had anything to do with the fact that new management all loved their tobacco.

That day, before ending the meeting, Chang's team leader asked everyone who turned in their application to raise their hands. Tomorrow was the last day to submit. To Chang's surprise, he was the only one with his hand down. He sat there feeling like a gaping hole in the room. Chang turned in his application the next day.

At nine in the morning after several hours of fasting, Chang and all his colleagues swallowed their capsule endoscopes and forced the microscopic cameras down their esophagi. Then, after putting data receivers on their waists, they went about their business like it was just another day at work. The endoscope took three images per second until the clock hit 7:00 p.m., at which point the hospital came to collect the receivers. They explained that the jellyfish would exit everyone's digestive tract within the next twenty-four hours. And indeed, starting next afternoon, one by one, all the employees of P Tires began depositing their jellyfish in company toilets. There was no need to retrieve the jellyfish, the hospital said. It had done its job. The most important thing was that everyone successfully got it out of their body. This was especially true for those whose twenty-four hours had already expired.

• • •

Chang's jellyfish, however, was stuck to the mucosa of his small intestine. He was now in his seventy-second hour. The X-ray image of the jellyfish was gray and grainy, like a UFO pictured in broad daylight. For some reason, even though a foreign object had entered his body, the image of the jellyfish looked more like the remnants of something that had been vaporized.

The doctor painstakingly asked Chang whether he followed all their precautions. Did he fast for eight hours before the test? Was he sure he didn't have an iron deficiency? Did he forget to mention any medications? Did he apply lotion the day of the test? Did he remember to take the medicine they gave him?

"Can you tell me what you did after ingesting the capsule?"

"I did everything that I normally would," Chang protested. "I went to work, did my job, gave you back the receiver when you came for it at seven and went home around eight."

"And what is it you usually do at work?"

"Just tire development. I work in spares."

The doctor looked like he was waiting for a more detailed explanation, so Chang went over in his mind everything he did that day. But there was nothing worth mentioning. He had a meeting—nothing unusual about that—and did some model trimming just before the new design went into mass production.

"What's trimming?"

"It's the last step a model goes through before production. We also do it for tires when they come off the line. Most people think tires come out of the factory perfectly round. But their surface is bumpy and uneven. Trimming is the process of snipping off those little nodules."

"What tool do you use for that?"

"It's a blade on a handle. The end is Y-shaped. You use it by running the blade over the surface of the tire, as if you were shaving your face or shearing a sheep. A new tire is like a fish waffle. When fish waffles come out of the waffle machine, their edges aren't perfectly smooth. You need to trim the edges, those little imperfections that stick out."

"Is that your main job?"

"Part of it."

Chang enjoyed running his blade over the surface of tires and removing any nodules that deviated from the standard mold. If only the jellyfish were such a nodule. That way, he could snip it off with his blade. Unfortunately, the jellyfish was inside him and out of reach.

"Some people have trouble passing the capsules. It happens for all kinds of reasons—a dilating intestine, for example. But it's only a matter of when. Don't worry too much. If nothing has changed by this time next week, we can take another look."

Chang never wanted an endoscopy. The results didn't even teach him anything new. He was already well aware he suffered from mild IBD. If anything, this endoscopy was making it worse with all the unnecessary stress. When things like this happened to him, he wondered if he was just unlucky, or if other people were experiencing the same thing. But as far as he knew, everyone he worked with had successfully passed their jellyfish. Some even retrieved the thing from the toilet and washed it to keep as a kind of souvenir. Over the weekend, he drank lots of water and took some laxatives, but he still couldn't pass the jellyfish.

The capsule endoscope was surely dead by now. The two internal batteries only lasted at most twenty hours, and the hospital had collected the receiver (its only connection to the outside world) almost a week ago. But Chang was unable to shake the feeling that the jellyfish was still moving inside him. On the other hand, he might have been less anxious had he known for certain the capsule was still on and connected. He was, of course, terrified of the thought that someone had left a machine turned on inside him, but he was more terrified of the idea of a remote-less, disconnected monster swimming around his body of its own free will. He had heard horror stories of people who had accidentally swallowed rings, or had surgical scissors left inside them after laparotomies. He also heard that some people required surgery to remove capsule endoscopes that had become lodged in the crevasses of their digestive tract. But the foreign-body sensation Chang felt was of a different kind.

This jellyfish had entered Chang's body because of a connection to the company. In other words, if it weren't for his company, he never would have gotten an endoscopy. But he was afraid this connection didn't end there. What if the jellyfish was reporting everything about him to the company? Soon, this fear turned to paranoia. He never used his work computer for personal matters. He always used his cell phone to do online searches, but even that wasn't safe anymore. In his paranoid mind, the company no longer needed to spy on him through his computer, cell phone, or the company security cameras at the office or housing complex—they now had a window directly into his body.

With a few concrete incidents, Chang's suspicion that his thoughts were being monitored became a conviction. He had always internally bemoaned the fact that the staff lounge, which was clearly marked as a nonsmoking zone, always smelled like a chimney stack. But after management changed, the lounge was openly used as a watering hole for smokers, making the smell even worse and causing Chang a lot of stress. But he never expressed his discontent to anyone. And yet, a week or so after the failed endoscopy, an air purifier was installed in the staff lounge and several more nonsmoking signs were posted. He asked around and learned that they were making a separate smoking room near the emergency exit. This was exactly what he had wanted, so he should have been happy. But something didn't seem right. And then, when his paranoia couldn't get any worse, his team leader stopped him in the hallway.

"No more cigarette smoke. Isn't that nice?"

Chang's team leader patted him gently on the shoulder. Chang was well within reach of a normal talking voice, but his team leader was practically shouting. Even stranger was the fact that his team manager should have been the last person to care about the sooty smell of cigarette smoke, as that was exactly what his breath smelled like. The team leader then looked at Chang's face and asked if he was feeling okay. He got this question a lot recently. Everyone was always asking if he was "feeling okay." But most of them shouldn't have known about his condition.

However, maybe they were onto something. He did, in fact, feel off. But oddly, it felt less like an object had entered his body, and more like a piece of him was missing. It was this void, this absence that worried Chang more than any foreign-body sensation ever could. It was like something that had been screwed down tight to the interior wall of his body had been snipped off. But he knew almost everything inside him was vital. There were very few things one could remove without major side effects. And right now, it felt like one of those vital pieces had been snipped off and was floating away from his body, like a lost balloon. What worried him most was the fact that he had no way of knowing what it was that had been cut from him, or what had become of it.

• • •

Chang came to P three years ago. Moving to P, which had company housing, was quite attractive to Chang who, after sending his wife and son to America, had been looking at micro studio apartments designed for students. On the day of the move, he only had two 24-inch suitcases of luggage, and yet the company sent an entire moving truck to his address. He felt grateful thinking about how the two movers had come so early from so far away just to carry one suitcase each.

Chang stared out the window. He couldn't see the other end of the city (even though there was nothing blocking his view), but he knew it would be a mirror image of where he was standing now. Across the city from him, there would be yet another black skyscraper, which would also belong to P Tires. This black skyscraper would form one segment of a circle. And when you took all the buildings of P City together, they would form one large dark ring. In fact the city resembled a giant tire when seen from a bird's eye view. The area of this black tire was two-thirds of the circle's total area. Most shops and stores were contained within this tire-shaped company complex, but even those that were outside it were located as close to people as possible. Banks, post offices, religious facilities, and city hall were also inside the tire, even though they weren't officially affiliated with the company.

Chang was inside the tire, too. He hadn't once left since coming here three years ago. He had no need to. The company often planned outings and trips, but only within the city. Except for an airport, seaport, and train station, P had everything. And because the bus routes were so well designed, there was no point in owning a personal car. Unlike what you might expect for employees of a tire company, there weren't many people who used their personal car. Most people sold their car when they realized they wouldn't be needing it. Those who didn't left it in the parking lot like an exhibition piece. Of course, the buses were only open to people with a company card key.

A similar thing happened to Chang when he first entered the company. At the time, a dentist's office was giving out discounted teeth cleanings for P Tires employees. Chang had gone to the dentist with his team, and as he lay in the dentist's chair, he could smell someone else's saliva coming from the dentist's hand. Chang reflexively closed his mouth.

"Say, ahhh."

When the dentist's hands finally left his mouth, Chang watched closely to see where they went. And just as he suspected, the dentist went right over to the next patient, without changing gloves or washing his hands. Chang wanted to say something, but he didn't want to embarrass the owner of the saliva before him. Nor did he want to embarrass himself, as someone would be smelling his own spit right now. But what made him most uncomfortable was the fact that no one else was expressing their discomfort. It was hardly a surprise when he came down with a nasty cold the next day. Ever since then, Chang hated company sponsorships.

This jellyfish incident was equally frustrating. Chang knew the only reason for his company to partner with that hospital was because of some shady (perhaps nepotistic) relationship. This realization caused a wad of phlegm to form in his throat. He went to the hospital weekly, but even after three weeks, he still couldn't pass the jellyfish.

"Are you sure the jellyfish ran out of battery?" Chang asked bluntly.

"It's been more than three weeks," the doctor said in a relaxed tone. "If we had a battery that lasted that long, it'd be groundbreaking."

"It can only take pictures of my digestive tract, right? It can't do things like read my thoughts . . . Right?"

"If it could do that, it'd be truly groundbreaking."

Well, there was something that was groundbreaking, but it wasn't that, and it wasn't necessarily something to celebrate. On Chang's fourth checkup, he learned that the endoscope was growing inside him, like a real jellyfish. The doctor brought out Chang's previous X-rays to show him. At forty years old, news of something growing inside your body was never good news. That usually meant cancer, or if you were lucky, a noncancerous cyst. But a foreign-body object? That was truly unexpected. Even groundbreaking, you could say.

"We'll let y represent the length of the jellyfish in centimeters, and x represent the week, starting at one. Based on the data I have here, we can write a function to calculate the length at a later date: $y = 3x$."

The doctor then added something, as if he were reading Chang's mind.

"Of course, your intestine would rupture before the y value exceeded your height. We should avoid that at all costs, the problem is that, right now, there's no point in performing an enterotomy. We're not sure exactly where the jellyfish is, and if it turns out to be lodged deep inside your small intestine, it will be very difficult to remove."

"But is that my fault? Isn't that your fault?"

"The way I see it, you're the only one in twenty thousand patients to have this happen to them. I'd say your personal history was more of a factor than anything else. All we can do now is hope the medicine helps your body dissolve the endoscope. Or we could perform the surgery with lasers. I'm not saying that's the solution. But it's an option."

But even if they went with lasers, they still would need to wait and watch to see if his condition improved. It seemed like even the hospital didn't have all the answers.

Chang hadn't told anyone about what the doctor said, but it appeared management had already been notified of the situation. But the jellyfish wasn't the problem. The real problem was the interconnectedness of P. Chang's team leader called him into his office and asked if he was okay. Chang didn't know why exactly his team leader was asking him this, but he had his answer when he went back to his desk and turned on his computer to browse the news. Making headlines was an article that claimed the capsule endoscope, the same one swimming around inside Chang's body, contained a hazardous material. Of course, this was only a problem if the material stayed in the body for an extended period of time, and most people passed the jellyfish within twenty-four hours. The last part of the article reported that all the endoscopes released onto the market had been recalled and wouldn't be released again until the problem was fixed. Other medical devices and drugs that used the hazardous material had all been recalled, too. Everything had been recalled, they claimed, but they had forgotten about the jellyfish inside Chang. And worst of all, it was now growing.

• • •

Chang always took the same route to work. It was a fair distance from company housing to the office, but as long as he picked the right elevator, he had no trouble making the trip in twenty minutes.

On his way to his desk, he felt like people were staring at him. They were all following him with their eyes, but no one approached him. It was possible that he was just imagining things, but it was more likely he wasn't. The reason for his certainty was because he had overheard someone say the word "jellyfish" in the elevator. He knew people always talked about it when they saw him. Before sitting down at his desk, he took his family photo and stashed it in his desk drawer before turning on his computer.

"Did you see that news article? The one about the 'thing.' "

Chang had a message from Angel, his subordinate, on the company messenger. Chang knew which article Angel was referring to, but he asked what he meant anyway. Eventually, Angel said the magic words: "The jellyfish." The article had already been deleted, and Chang couldn't find any other articles about the recall, but everyone in the company had already read it, including Chang. Angel told him not to worry, then started talking about jellyfish in a way Chang found inappropriate given the circumstances. And not jellyfish as in the capsule endoscope jellyfish, but real jellyfish from the ocean. Of the many pointless factoids he shared with Chang, the worst was the one about the scientific name for jellyfish: medusa. In fact, according to him, the word *méduse* in French meant jellyfish. Chang asked why he was telling him this.

"Just 'cause. I thought you might want to know."

"Isn't Medusa that woman with snakes for hair? The one who turns people to stone by looking at them?"

"Perseus decapitated her. Cut the head right off her shoulders."

Angel followed this last message with a "HAHA" and a long string of sword emoticons. Chang couldn't help but notice that the swords were all pointed at his profile picture.

According to a book Chang had once read, some companies kept two lists of employees: a blacklist and an angel-list. They used these lists to separate employees into those they should protect at all costs, and those they should push out as soon as the opportunity arose. The reason Chang called his subordinate Angel was because, if anyone was on the company's angel-list, it would be him. This was, of course, a bit tongue in cheek, but it wasn't like Chang was the only one who called him this.

Because of what Angel said to him, Chang couldn't look people in the eye, even though he knew he wasn't going to petrify anyone. But perhaps it didn't matter because no one made eye contact with him anyway.

Chang tried eating rice porridge for lunch, but his stomach still ached. He also had trouble swallowing his food because of all the phlegm that he was coughing up. And any food he managed to swallow sat in his stomach like heavy rocks, as though they were the eyeballs of Medusa's victims. It continued like this all week. If there was one thing good about this week, it was that on Friday, Chang realized he would have the company apartment all to himself from now on. Chang wasn't sure if his roommate had transferred or simply gotten a new place. All he knew was that he wasn't going to be seeing his roommate anymore. When Chang arrived home after work, he found that his roommate had taken all his belongings and left a note on the table wishing Chang a "speedy recovery." Even though there was only one less person in the apartment, the place now seemed empty to the point of being cavernous. It was only a 280-square-foot apartment, but it somehow felt bigger than that now.

It was the season for promotions and transfers. Chang was pretty sure they were going to give him a transfer, but he was wrong. When he got the call and walked into his team leader's office, he was immediately led to the director of research's office. The director was who people in their department talked to before leaving the company. The first thing the director did when Chang entered the office was ask, "Are you okay now? The cigarette smoke, I mean." This was an ambiguous question. On the one hand, he could have meant: "Are you okay, now that the smoke is gone?" Or he could have meant: "Are you okay now, even though the smoke *isn't* gone?" Without knowing which one it was, Chang just nodded his head quickly. He now regretted being so sensitive about smoking inside the office.

They were giving Chang three months of "sick leave." He would be reinstated as soon as he made a full recovery, but who knew when or if that would happen. The director patted Chang on the shoulder:

"You heard that I got stung by a jellyfish too, didn't you? It happened in Saipan last year. God-awful. The doctor in the ER told me jellyfish are mostly harmless. He compared them to mosquitoes in the summer. Mosquitoes my ass! The medicine alone made me nauseous for days. I blame it on my IBD."

"But sir, I wasn't stung by a jellyfish."

This was the first time Chang had talked to the director about personal matters. Talking with him like this would usually be difficult, but now that he was (temporarily) leaving the company, Chang felt at ease, even with the director. He patted Chang on the shoulder again as he continued:

"I heard poisonous jellyfish aren't edible. Did you know that?"

"No. To be honest, I've never been interested."

"Well, they say you can't eat the ones that sting. God-awful. You said your family's in America? You better get well soon and come back to work. I heard you developed the new spare tire with Department Head Song, is that right? We're expecting great things from that project, so you better come back soon."

Chang couldn't hide the rigid look on his face. He had never mentioned to anyone at the company that his wife and son were living in America. It wasn't like he had something to hide. He just wasn't one to go on about private matters.

• • •

Before, Chang would commute to and from work with just the swipe of his card key, but as soon as he was put on sick leave, his card key no longer registered. That day, it took him forever to find public transportation that would get him back to company housing. After two transfers, Chang finally arrived back home at his empty studio apartment. It was only then that Chang realized why he had the apartment all to himself, why he didn't have a roommate. No employee of P wanted to room with someone who had hazardous materials inside them. Since entering the company, Chang had always dreamed of having a room to himself, but not like this.

It wasn't just the company bus. There were dozens of places that were now off-limits to him that he had always had access to. The bank, gym, supermarket, and even some restaurants became unavailable to him because they were located inside P, where he was no longer allowed to go. Chang considered it a miracle they still allowed him to stay in company housing. He even had to change hospitals. It was now almost impossible to access his old hospital (the very same hospital that got him into this mess in the first place), and even when he did manage to get in touch with someone, it was like they were speaking a different language. Chang demanded they take responsibility for their defective jellyfish, but in the eyes of the hospital, it was Chang who was the defective one. Eventually, Chang realized this was a problem he would have to come back to. Arguing with the hospital required a lot of energy, something he had less and less of these days.

On Chang's first Monday of sick leave, he received a letter from the local tax office. The way the envelope was addressed reminded him that he was no longer a member of the company. Written on the envelope was a different address, not the usual "P259" he was used to. Indeed, Chang could no longer be described with just four characters. He had lived here ever since coming to this city. And he was still living here. The only thing that had changed was his status at the company, and yet he had to get an entire new address. The envelope contained tax bills. A detailed analysis of Chang's medical condition and the harmful substances in the jellyfish had been used to calculate the taxes he owed:

Probability of environmental pollution: 80%
Probability of noise pollution: 45%

Probability of water pollution: 20%
Probability of soil pollution: 21.5%
Estimated increase to environmental burden tax: 27.5%

Not understanding what this was, Chang asked one of the workers at a restaurant he frequented. According to them, anyone in the city not a member of P Tires had to pay an "environmental burden tax." It was independent of their income and was usually a small flat rate. However, the amount you owed the government increased whenever you broke a food or environmental regulation.

Hearing this, Chang wanted even less to pay the bill. He asked the restaurant worker how to get to the tax office, but he couldn't understand their directions. As he wandered around in the middle of the street looking for the building, it felt like the organs in his body were pulsating like a ticking time bomb. Exhausted, he eventually gave up and returned to his apartment. A person from the tax office was waiting for him outside his front door. The tax collector walked with Chang to a nearby teashop and took out a large stack of documents.

"There's nothing wrong with a company having its employees take a test if they make everyone take it. Besides, everyone else was able to pass the jellyfish in the allotted time. The fact that you couldn't pass your jellyfish, Mr. Hyeong-jun Chang, is a personal problem. Because of this, we have no choice but to ask you to take responsibility. Naturally, we're concerned the foreign object will outgrow your body. What was your current height, again?"

The tax collector asked this question even as he stared down at Chang's height, which was written in the documents.

"Five feet eight inches."

"As I thought. And your weight?"

This too the tax collector asked while circling Chang's weight with a ball pen.

"One hundred fifty, one hundred fifty-five?"

"Good. We heard the foreign-body object is growing like a weed, getting larger with each day. Is that correct?" The tax collector put down the pen and looked at Chang. "Just as we feared. If the object continues to grow at its current rate, within two years, it will become too big for your body, and when that happens, it won't be just your problem anymore, Chang Hyeong-jun. It will be an issue of social and national concern! It was reported recently that the medical device contains many environmentally harmful materials. If nothing else, it will negatively affect P City, don't you agree?"

Chang was slowly starting to lose focus in his eyes. Every time the tax collector made threatening circles with the pen, Chang's pupils wobbled like an egg on a kitchen table.

"Let's use an example to illustrate what I mean. Imagine you go to the post office to send a package. They have different-sized boxes, right? Large, medium, small, long, short, you name it. But the thing you're trying to send won't fit in the small box. For whatever reason, it pokes out a little. You do your best to cram it in and secure the flaps with tape, hoping they'll give you a pass. And most of the time they do—they're human too, after all. But what if, hypothetically speaking, the thing you crammed into a small box is also too big for even the medium? Not only will you damage your item, but you make things difficult for the post office and you might negatively impact the delivery of the other packages in the same mail truck. What then?"

"I don't know, you put it in the medium box? Look, I mean, it's not like I'm the only one passing a foreign object through my body. You go to the bathroom too, don't you? We all excrete foreign bodies into the environment."

The tax collector started twirling the pen in their hand and grinned as though they had heard it all before.

"Everyone is subject to the rules," the tax collector said calmly. "That's what makes it fair. Either the tax applies to everyone, or it applies to no one. But you're an exception. I doubt you're planning on taking responsibility for that thing once it crawls out of your body and into the world. The city is promising to take care of everything if you pay the tax. You know that P City won the Eco-friendly City Award, don't you?"

"The city is going to take care of me?"

"Not you, not medically. I meant they'll take care of the environmental impact you'll have on the city. That's the whole purpose of the environmental burden tax. All I'm saying is we need to upgrade your box from small to medium."

Chang refused to pay any such "upgrade" fee. He wanted to make an appeal. But he knew he would have trouble making one. Appeals were long and involved, and just gathering the necessary documents would require more time, money, and patience than he had. It didn't take long for him to be labeled as a delinquent taxpayer. Chang was sure he could feel the jellyfish inside him growing faster and faster. But somehow, the amount he owed the city always seemed to stay ahead.

• • •

Chang swore he could hear the translucent jellyfish washing out his organs. Every time he moved, he thought he sensed a strong sloshing sound inside him. But he had no way of knowing if what he was hearing was real or just his imagination.

Chang stopped walking midstep. He was just about to put his foot down when he felt something else move inside his body. He both heard and felt it. His heart, intestines, lungs, and kidneys were all jostling around. And his uvula felt like a speaker, absorbing the vibrations and amplifying them. His intestines were currents of cold ocean water, and a stormy sea of stomach acid was thrashing against the walls of his esophagus.

Nonemployees of P Tires were useful to Chang. One day, he asked the owner of a restaurant for directions to the hospital. It seemed to Chang like the hospital was located on the outskirts of P City, but he couldn't be sure. And if by some chance it wasn't, that meant P was much larger than Chang had previously imagined. It was nearly a four-hour round trip, and Chang had trouble finding taxis or public transportation to take him there. The hospital was rather large. It was five stories tall, and Chang's destination, the department of cardiothoracic surgery, was located on the third floor. But Chang had to start at reception on the first floor and go through billing on the second before he finally saw a doctor. After a few questions, he was sent to internal medicine on the fourth. Endlessly walking up flights of stairs like this, Chang wondered if he would eventually pass through the roof and onto heaven. But then again, he would probably run out of money before that happened.

The doctor showed Chang a video of the inside of his body. The jellyfish was pulsating rhythmically. The head was bulging like an overinflated soccer ball, and its two tentacles were swaying like locks of hair from a Greek demigod. The jellyfish was swimming inside the sea of Chang's body. As he gazed into the video, he momentarily forgot what the doctor was saying.

"It moves just like a real jellyfish."

Turning away from the video toward Chang, the doctor explained that psychologists sometimes used jellyfish in their treatments. Chang couldn't tell if this was supposed to comfort him or just typical doctor banter, but he found it memorable for some reason. According to the doctor, the rhythm of a pulsating jellyfish was similar to the pulse of a human heart.

"Watching jellyfish swim helps people relax. Obviously, this only works when patients are out of the water."

So, jellyfish dances were only beautiful when observed from afar. Chang did feel somewhat relaxed watching the video of the jellyfish inside him. The video even allowed him to forget for a brief moment that his body had become home to one.

On his second visit to that remote hospital, Chang ran into Department Head Song in the lobby. It was pure coincidence. Chang looked dejected, and Song, collected. Song was smoking a cigarette. Song told Chang he was worried about the wreckage inside his body. Indeed, Song was the second person after Chang to be put on sick leave because of the jellyfish. Chang was equally surprised to find that Song was suffering from the same symptoms as himself. But he clearly remembered Song telling him, the day after the endoscopy, that he had passed the jellyfish in the bathroom.

"I was afraid. So I lied."

Song rubbed out his cigarette as he said this. Remembering what happened to Chang, he had tried his best to hide his symptoms, but eventually (and after a few more health checkups), he suffered the same fate when they inevitably discovered the jellyfish inside him. According to Song, several other people were forced to hand in their card key because they, too, had failed the test.

Song urged Chang to pay his environmental burden tax to the best of his ability. Debt was bad, yes, but being labeled a delinquent taxpayer was even worse. Song also seemed to think the word "delinquent" was better than "diseased." Then he said something that really surprised Chang: he was planning on suing the company.

"I'm going to file a dispute," Song said in a quiet but resolute voice. "This is obviously the hospital's fault. The company should be held responsible, too. They practically forced us into participating in the endoscopy. I've already asked one of the doctors here for their opinion, and I'm bringing in a lawyer from outside the city. I just need to collect the necessary documentation. Did you hear that our project was put on hold? They've got two holes and no one qualified enough to fill them. We need to act now and make them afraid of us while we're still on sick leave. If we play our cards right, there's no reason we shouldn't be reinstated."

Now that Chang was getting a better look at Song, he could see behind his composed demeanor a pale face and withered body. His eyes were hollow, too. Chang tried his best to avoid looking Song directly in the eye. He used the cup of water placed on the table to look at Song's reflection. Song had always been just as exemplary outside the company as he was inside it. He always paid his bills on time and was always composed. Hearing that someone like him was meticulously scheming to take revenge on the company made Chang afraid. He didn't know his situation was so dire. Chang glanced around, paranoid that someone would be listening in on their conversation. But he soon remembered that there was more to be afraid of than just CCTVs, wiretaps, and passersby. A less tangible terror was brewing inside him. What if the jellyfish was listening to their conversation? The thing that had made his body a swimming pool, that should have been turned off ages ago.

"I'm going to file a dispute. I'll be in contact with you soon. Let's meet again here. I might need your help."

The three months of sick leave the company had given Chang were almost up. And the environmental burden tax was accelerating, as though it could taste Chang's thinning wallet. He was living in this city like a solution just before saturation, teetering on the edge of his boiling point. When the three months were up, when Chang's bank account hit zero and his debt increased toward infinity, they might finally kick him out of company housing and out onto the streets.

On his way home from meeting Song, the moon was faint, the stars were infrequent, and the only thing whose existence Chang could be sure of were the neon billboards that were plastered to the sides of skyscrapers like gaudy wallpaper. On one of the billboards, a P tire was hovering above the earth like a black moon. Chang had written down the address of the bus terminal on a piece of paper, but finding the terminal again at night wasn't easy. It wasn't at the address he had written down. Chang searched his memory for the names of the other cities that were connected to P. He could go anywhere if he called a taxi or got on the right bus. No, the problem wasn't the means of transportation. Chang didn't know where he was going; his three months were almost completely spent. If Song's plans worked, that might mean good things for Chang. When his innocence was finally revealed, he would either be reinstated to the company or released forever on account of insolence. But even if he was released, at least he could receive compensation. In fact, he preferred the second of these two options. He wasn't sure if he could return to the company like this. And if he couldn't stay at P Tires, it would be best to leave P City altogether.

Then one day, Chang felt the violent rumbling of something surging up from inside his body, like a roller coaster being ratcheted to the top of a hill. Chang reached for a tissue. He quickly realized one wasn't going to be enough. Finally holding five sheets of tissues, he heaved into his palm, and a giant wad of phlegm shot out of his throat like a roller coaster making its first plunge. He instinctively crumpled up the tissues, but then unfolded them again to have a look. This phlegm wasn't like the others. Dissolved inside the yellow goo was an oddly colorful substance. Chang stood in front of the bathroom mirror and opened his mouth. There was some strange fluid, some fluid that wasn't his, endlessly flowing out of the back of his throat. This was his first time looking beyond his own uvula, and what he found there was darkness.

Chang turned down the TV and picked up the telephone. There was only one place now for him to call. His wife and son were in New Jersey. The longer he was away from them, the less they said to one another. It wasn't that they had nothing to say, but rather that, over months of constant omissions and selections, he had developed the habit of filtering out anything that wasn't a truly important happening. Eventually, he only sent across the Pacific those few words that were left after endless trimming and omitting.

"I think something's living in the back of my throat. I think it's starting to crawl out. Something alive, something like a jellyfish."

What would his wife say when she heard this? The most recent message he had sent across the Pacific was about his sending them his bonus. Before that, it was about the advantageous exchange rate. His words needed to have a certain level of authority to justify being sent across the ocean. Should he tell his New Jersey audience about the jellyfish? Chang thought about this until he couldn't think anymore. He had picked up the phone with such urgency, but now he was just sitting there, paralyzed by excessive contemplation. As soon as he heard the voice of his son through the receiver, he lost all courage. For a brief moment as he listened to the sounds of a New Jersey suburban neighborhood, he completely forgot about everything that had happened to him. He was completely absorbed in the peacefully busy noises of life across the ocean. It was only after hanging up the phone that Chang was brought back to his reality. On paper, he and his wife were already separated. They only exchanged bank account numbers and contact information because of their son.

• • •

Chang was positive he would be fired once his three-month sick leave ended. He was shocked when he was called into the office to talk. His team leader had since changed. The new team leader was Angel—the same subordinate whom Chang had always considered number one on the company's angel-list. Angel looked at Chang and gave him a welcoming smile.

"I want to help you, Chang. I heard that you've been having a hard time because of the environmental burden tax. I want to find a way out for you."

Angel mentioned how the company was in a difficult situation as the project Chang had been working on wasn't going smoothly. They were looking for someone to take Chang's position, but this had been made more complicated when

Song, the other project lead, was put on sick leave as well. Of course, the company thought it would be best if Chang focused on getting better, but Angel was of a different opinion. After all, it wasn't like it was contagious.

"But everyone acts like I have some radioactive object inside my body."

"Of course we can't just ignore other people's feelings. If people are too uncomfortable with it, the least I can do for you is give you your own small office. Do you still have the inclination to work?"

He really was an angel. Before Chang realized what he was doing, he was bowing and thanking his old subordinate.

• • •

A few days after visiting P Tires, Chang saw Song on the news. A month ago, Song had received an award for being an exemplary taxpayer. A few weeks later, he committed suicide. Song wanted to die a model taxpayer. The news reported that he had been diligent with his environmental burden tax payments, but that recently, he had been having financial difficulties. When he found it impossible to make any more payments, he ended his own life. He was more afraid of becoming a delinquent taxpayer than he was of death. People who knew him well claimed he was a perfectionist. Nowhere was there any mention of the capsule endoscope, his unemployment, or the lawsuit. Everything that Song had planned, everything that would have been an uncomfortable subject for P, seemed to have been vaporized.

The funeral took place beneath the hospital where Chang and Song had run into one another. Chang's hand shook as he lit the incense. He was just a mourner, but it felt like it was he who had died. The photo of Song that was placed at the altar looked like a mirror. Chang heard a sloshing sound. The young chief mourner was staring at him. More sloshing. Song was staring at him. More sloshing. The jellyfish was moving inside him. Chang met eyes with Song's picture when he lifted his head after bowing, and his breath went heavy as stone. Chang could barely manage to turn his body and face the chief mourner. The two children, the same two children whose photo had sat on Song's desk at the office, were now looking at Chang with tear-filled eyes.

Looking around the funeral home, Chang felt relieved that no one from work had come. The only person here that Chang knew was Song, and he couldn't talk. Even though Chang had wished he wouldn't run into anyone he knew here, at the same time, he wanted someone to talk to, someone to tell everything that had happened to him. He fiddled with his cell phone. He weighed the option of calling the phone number saved in his cell phone as "New Jersey." He had once used their names. But then one day, he changed them. That's how much distance there was between him and his estranged family. Chang wanted to tell his wife and son that he had been reinstated at the company. He wanted to tell them that come next week, he would be back to normal again: working, riding the shuttle bus, and eating at the company cafeteria. He wanted to tell them that he wouldn't be paying the environmental burden tax anymore, that he could start paying off all the debt he had accrued. He wanted to tell them that even though the jellyfish had, and was, making a mess, it wasn't going to threaten his health anymore. But Chang just continued to fiddle with his cell phone, unable to press CALL. He tried several times but always stopped himself just in time. Now that he thought about it, they didn't even know he had been put on sick leave, that he had hazardous substances inside him, that he hadn't been able to pass that jellyfish on time—they didn't know anything. News of his sudden reinstatement would confuse them more than anything.

Chang was about to put his cell phone in his pocket when he decided to look at his recent call history. He wanted to change his subordinate's caller ID from "Angel" to "Team Leader." Angel had played the biggest role in Chang's reinstatement. If it weren't for him, Chang might have ended up like Song for all he knew.

After Chang changed Angel's caller ID, he slumped down on a bench as though all the energy had been sucked out of him. Staring at his team leader's phone number for a long time, he was reminded of Song's face. Had Song known? Would he have understood Chang's reason for not waiting for his phone call? What Chang had really been waiting for was a call from the company. But he couldn't expect the company to be the first one to dial. In fact, Chang's team leader had never once contacted Chang since the jellyfish incident. All his recent phone calls were outgoing. The night after he ran into Song, he had a long phone call with his team leader. This call was made by Chang, just like all the others. Chang's meeting with his team leader was only made possible after he told him about Song's plans to sue. Chang sat across from his team leader and told him everything:

"I want to finish the new spare tire with my own hands. But I'm having difficulties because of the environmental burden tax. Please, give me some way out."

"But aren't you suffering from an illness?"

"It's never caused me major health problems. And it's not contagious."

Chang's team leader scratched his chin.

"People say it's radioactive."

"If people feel uncomfortable with it, I can work by myself in the warehouse. I'd be fine with any kind of work, even if it's menial."

Chang recalled the things he had done just a few days prior. But as he looked at himself, he did so through an opaque lens, like Perseus looking at Medusa's reflection through a shield made of mirrors. Because of what he told his team leader that day, Song's plans were completely ruined. Chang was promised he could return to his job, and the team leader was able to strengthen his grip on his new post. Chang sat in the far back of the funeral home and tried to console himself, telling himself that he had no choice. Song and he had done the same job and received the same diagnosis. That was the problem. Chang wasn't confident he could compete with Song for the same position. So he sold out.

The zipper on one of Chang's two suitcases was broken, even though he rarely used them since moving to the city. Every time he tried closing the zipper, it would just as quickly pop back open. Chang consolidated his belongings as much as he could and crammed what he had left into the one good suitcase. The car came as scheduled, and Chang got in. It dropped him off at P1765—Chang's new address. The door opened straight down into the ground. Every hallway in P City skipped P1765, this was the only door that had those digits. It was a round door that opened straight into the earth.

It was the exact size of the mold they made spare tires in. Spare tires were slightly smaller and lighter than normal tires. They only had to last until you could replace the flat tire with a new one. Chang opened the door that headed down into the ground and hunched over. Y-shaped clippers appeared seemingly from nothing and started trimming his back. As it removed the angular pieces sticking out of him, his skin became round and smooth. Chang didn't mind the sensation of being fit into a mold. He curled his back into a tighter circle. A familiar sensation traced the curve of his spine, sliding all the way down to his tailbone. Then Chang could feel a light but constant force pushing on him. The weight felt at once oppressive yet liberating. When the pressure was released, he felt something fall from his body. It was charred and rolling around like a used bullet casing on the battlefield.

The jellyfish. After months of growing like a parasite inside Chang's body, it had now exited him smaller than it entered. It moved each of its tentacles and withdrew its head into its body. Chang remembered the joy of trimming tires, the joy of putting the final touches on his work. He straightened his back and looked up at the sky. Shining above his head was the sun, yet another circle that looked exactly like P1765.

MAURICE BROADDUS

I CAN TRANSFORM YOU

(2013)

MAC PETERSON WAS HURLED through a storefront window. As his world was reduced to a shower of glass, he counted himself lucky that the Chaise Lounge was an old-school establishment: most windows had synth fibers in them, smart glass that could turn any pane into a billboard. And despite what people viewed on their vids, industrial glass wasn't designed to break away into a scree of shards upon impact. With the state of terraforming these days, it was designed to withstand minor earthquakes and eruptions. So a body would have to be sent through it with significant force in order for the glass to shatter. The kind of force Jesse "Duppy" Honeycutt was capable of generating when hopped up on Stim.

This was supposed to have been a simple surveillance job. Some "creepy guy" at the Chaise Lounge was bothering a stripper—no, exotic dancer; no, anatomical sales model for display purposes only; shit, Mac didn't know what to call them these days. He was to be paid to find the suspect and perhaps persuade him to move along.

This conversation wasn't going well.

"You got a smart mouth, mon." Duppy's accent shifted between overly affected Jamaican and some version of Midwestern. He stepped through the jagged hole where glass used to be. A black tank top stretched over his huge frame, showing off the bulging muscles that came from a prison bid. A pattern of tattoos, like glow-in-the-dark runes, ran along his arms, which waved about in menace. Prior to crashing through the glass, Mac had studied the brute's eyes and believed they told a counterintuitive story: that prison had broken him and drugs helped him forget the pain. Of course, that was before he found himself lying in a pool of glass shards. Hating to be wrong, he chalked Duppy's violent outburst up to overcompensating. After all, everyone had an image to maintain.

Case in point: born Jeremiah Dix of Bedford, Indiana, Duppy put on a faux Jamaican accent as a part of his story, just another small-time hood trying to make a rep for himself. Once he had landed in Waverton, he'd joined the Easton MS crew; the MS stood for Murder Squad because they were killing the streets. Clever disds. They had made a name for themselves as major Stim traffickers, and Duppy had hooked up with them. High on Stim, he proved less reasonable than usual.

"Yeah, I get that a lot." Premature gray at his temples, Mac had a good build on him, the last remnant of his former military training. A carefully cultivated week's worth of facial hair covered his face. A low beard hid a lot of scars. Sunglasses covered his eyes. No designer glasses, no viz screen built in. Plain sunglasses were usually the first casualty in any conversation, so he saw no point in spending too many creds on them. For that matter, he'd hate to have to get a new coat. The dampener lining absorbed a lot and hid even more. This came in quite handy, as he was prone to take a lot of hits. He considered this a reasonable expense to compensate for his failed people skills.

Sitting up, Mac shook his head to try to clear it while palming a fistful of glass. He staggered to his feet and wiped a trail of blood from his mouth.

Duppy stepped through the open hole where the window used to be, oblivious to the jagged teeth of glass that bit into his hand as he searched for purchase. Stim was bad enough; if Duppy's blast had been mixed with something else, things could get quite messy. Just like if Mac drew his Cougar PT-10, he'd have to use it and he wasn't being paid enough to deal with the paperwork headache of a shooting. Neither of them had to end up dead over a simple dustup. Besides, he had Duppy right where he wanted him.

"Maybe we got off on the wrong foot." Mac neared him. "A fella as charming as yourself wouldn't have any problem paying for tail somewhere else. The blind school's only a few miles up the way . . ."

Duppy charged him, wrapping Mac up in the beefy tubes he called arms. With his free hand, Mac ground the glass into the man's eyes, and they tumbled to the ground. Duppy dropped to his knees, his screams cut short as Mac scrambled out of his grasp. A quick jab to his throat dropped the brute, but Mac proceeded to kick him in the head a few times. It wasn't pretty, but it got the job done. Mac bent over and searched Duppy's clothes for extra doses of Stim and slipped them into his pocket. The owner of the Chaise Lounge—a slovenly overweight bald man with a penchant for sweating through his wardrobe—approached him. "I think I've persuaded your stalker to peruse the merchandise at another establishment."

"You persuaded him through a new window." The man daubed his forehead with a dirty handkerchief. "Who's going to pay for that?"

"For starters, *he* threw *me*. I had little say in the matter. Second, the terms of my rate were five hundred creds for the job plus expenses. Consider that an expense."

"Fuck you, Mac," the man said, then held out a transaction scanner. Mac passed his hand under it, checked his balance on his own scanner, straightened his glasses, then turned his back on the scene.

This job would barely cover his rent, and he wasn't exactly staying at a high-rise over in Waverton. Mac hated being out on the streets here; they left him feeling too exposed. A hover drone whirred by. The administrators could just as easily use satellites for the same purpose but they wanted the populace to be aware that they were being watched. The drones didn't deter crime, nor did the death penalty, despite how swiftly it was carried out. People knew they would get caught if the LG Security Force cared enough to come after them. Many days that was a mighty big if. Those on the employment cycles traveled into Waverton on the artery of the trams like circulated blood once it had been deoxygenated, then passed back out into Old Town. Old Town felt like a prison for those whose only crime was to be born poor. There were no worries about the state of Mars colonization. There was no time for political discussion on trade among the corp-nations. No, the world he lived in was as lowest common denominator as it got. There was only room for day-to-day survival, with none of the luxury worries of middle-class citizens. From Old Town, one could clearly see the towers of Waverton and the grand spires that formed the cityscape. Proud, tall, and distant, like an unobtainable dream. Sewer rats, strippers, junkies, and private investigators all lived in the shadow of the new architecture and stared up at the azure-streaked night skies, waiting for the world to end.

• • •

The call tore Mac from the fitful thing he called sleep. At least he woke up in a bed, not a burned-out husk of a car or a stretch of sidewalk. Small comfort in the unfamiliar surroundings. He didn't remember checking into a hotel. From the look of its decor—a full bed, a trash can, and a toilet and sink in the corner—it charged by the hour. The air was redolent with sex—unwashed, sweaty, desperate, and unremembered—and he stank of booze and stale Redi-Smokes. He hoped he hadn't spent the entire job's payday on his company. Had he found a companion dead next to him, it wouldn't have surprised him.

"Mac." Deputy Chief Clovis Hollander's voice sounded as hoarse as ever, as if he'd been screaming for the entire ten-hour shift.

"Miss me, Chief?"

"You need to come down to the LaPierre Towers." His tone of voice was off. He maintained a casual air as best he could, but something grave undergirded his words.

"I don't exactly work for you anymore."

"You'd want to be here. Besides, I distinctly recall a report coming across my net-log about a brawl between a tweaker and a peeper."

"Is that any way to speak of so noble a profession as mine, you fat fuck?" Mac provoked him, hoping to unsettle Hollander enough to get a moment of honesty from him. Even just a glimpse.

"Get your ass down here and it gets buried."

"Well, you do know where all the bodies are buried."

Mac sighed with every movement, as if sleep had only left him even more exhausted. He shambled to the sink. No sign of whoever he had spent the night with. His muscles ached. Bandaged wounds opened up slightly, spots of blood soaked through their wraps. His joints creaked and popped as he moved; the body in the reflection was easily a decade older than his thirty-nine years. He splashed water on his face.

Mac had always imagined that he'd have an office with one of those classic pebbled glass door panels with the words *Mac Peterson, Investigations* in bold black letters across it. The letters might be chipped around the edges to add character to the sign. Instead, he had a message service and a table in whatever establishment in Old Town was open.

"You ain't pretty," he started in at his reflection. "You ain't that bright. You ain't that funny. Or charming. There's nothing in you worth loving."

Like an offering to the stirring serpent in his belly, he repeated his daily mantra aloud. His core truths to begin the day, bottoming himself out; that way the day could only get better from there.

• • •

Maybe the eruption event had been a sign of the end and the apocalyptos had it right.

Rows of phosphorous blue lanterns blotted out the night sky, creating an alien vista, completely different from the memory of only a few years ago, the only remnants of the caustic dust kicked up those nights twenty years ago. The glowing canvas rendered the downtown skyline in a perpetual twilight, like a forest under a thick canopy of tree branches. Giant stone buildings rose in the dimness, obsidian behemoths, like death's bony fingers protruding from where they had inexplicably ruptured from the ground. Since the eruption event, the city-dwellers liked to whisper stories of men and women, those mixed-up souls ready to end it all, blissfully swimming upward through the opaque, dense air until they reached the top of the alien structures, where they found paradise and disappeared into the forever of the cosmos.

"Bullshit," Mac whispered to no one in particular.

Mac viewed life through a lens of skepticism and impatience, the towers and the flight to heaven—complete and utter nonsense. Surrounded by a mess of blood, brain matter, and pieces of bits he could only guess were the remains of internal organs, the crime scene told another story he struggled to make sense of. Two bodies had exploded like human grenades upon impact after falling from the top of the tallest structure. His gaze followed the jutting stone until it disappeared into the haze. Maybe these two had been evicted from heavenly paradise and tossed to their deaths, he mused. The foul stench failed to turn the detective's stomach, as he'd long grown accustomed to the stink of death. Thousands had died when the tower first shattered the mantle of the earth's surface. It appeared as if this tower had simply claimed two more.

Mac lit up a Redi-Smoke and inhaled. Genetically engineered to mimic the effects of nicotine, the companies benefitted from using chemical formulas that hadn't been banned yet. The packaging of the Redi-Smoke produced only wisps of smoke, which dissipated in the mouth almost immediately. The company's marketing campaign preyed on the ritual of smoking itself, per VCC regulations. All Mac needed to know was that the burn leeched away at his lungs; the genetically enhanced tobacco-like buzz hit hard and quick, dispelling most of his annoyance at being called out in the middle of the Godforsaken night for yet *another* tower death. The victims had been falling for months now, one or two a week. No leads, no evidence. Nobody could make out whether the jumpers were murdered or simply succumbed to an inner nihilistic cry, compelled to die by suicide. Whatever the case, Mac wished the bullshit would end.

"Hey, Mac. Sorry to call you in, but you know how it is." The city's deputy chief of police appeared out of the fog. Hollander grimaced at the scene around them before he shook Mac's hand. Gray hair wrapped like a horseshoe on the chief's otherwise bald head. He sported a Hitler mustache on his egg-shaped face as if he could bring the affectation back, but his extra jowls only accentuated the ridiculousness of his appearance. And his hands were too soft, like a woman's. The blue haze darkened his eyes, seeming to erase them. Mac held the pack of smokes out to him, but the deputy chief declined.

"Yeah?" Mac pushed his hat down over his face, covering his eyes in shadows. "Well, fuck you. You want to tell me why the *fuck* either of us are out here stomping through the remains of some sorry-assed tower jumpers?" He knew the dance of bullshit when he saw it. The chief was holding back. No way was he going to be on scene, much less call out Mac, unless it was important.

"It's a bad one." The chief stepped gingerly around bits of innards. "It's one of our own this time."

"What do you have?" Mac asked.

The chief grabbed Mac by the elbow and led him a couple of feet away from the nearest set of ears. Mac couldn't help but think that his former boss didn't want to be seen with him. "A lot of shit is going down and I need you braced for it. Does the name Harley Wilson ring a bell for you?"

"Not even a little."

"Goddamn, Mac, you live in a cave?"

"Hey man, fuck you. I don't have a Stream connect, so I also don't get the latest news on your favorite teen pop stars. You're lucky I have a cop-net linkup."

"Right. Whatever, you Luddite piece of shit. Harley Wilson's that gangbanger out of Easton. Suspected of making that hit on, shit . . ."

"Shit? Seems strange that a loving mother would take a look at the sweet product of her loins and name it 'Shit,'" Mac said.

"Always with the jokes. Anyways, I can't remember the name. Some corporate muckety-muck. It's in my notes back at the office. But this isn't about him. It's about Kiersten."

"My ex?" That serpent in his belly stirred. The gentle swell of anxious nausea left him uneasy, and Mac wanted Hollander to just spit it out. "Last I heard, she'd been working undercover. Bravest lady I know."

"Kiersten had been running with Wilson the past couple of months." Hollander stared at his feet. "The squints in the lab have confirmed that the bodies who fell tonight were Harley Wilson and Kiersten Wybrow."

The world lost its axis, and Mac leaned against a storefront wall. Kiersten. A rush of emotions hit him at once. Mac covered his face with his hand. The azure haze of the night skies shifted with the clouds, hiding his grief. He pushed the pain back, down into a personal dark space, a well to draw upon when needed, when the time was right.

"You all right, Mac?" Hollander stepped closer, concern underscoring his voice.

"Me and Kiersten were still . . . close. . . ." A moment of silence passed between the two men. The bottom fell out of where he thought he had bottomed out. Only a yawning chasm of grief awaited him. His head went light with the vertigo of pain, but he steadied himself before anyone else saw. He scanned the onlooking sets of eyes just in case.

"I'm sorry, Mac. I had no idea."

"I'll go check out the scene."

Hollander placed his hand on Mac's shoulder. "You know I can't let you do that. We need background, then your ass is going home."

"That's bullshit."

"You're too close. The judicial net would make any case we built that included your involvement ass-wipe worthy. But you should already know: folks who kill one of our own do not go unpunished. We don't need the other predators getting it in their heads that it's open season on LG Security Force members. They need to know who runs these streets. No one, and I mean no one, sleeps in Easton tonight. We're rounding up all of the Easton MS crew. Hitting all of their spots. We will knock down every door, bust every head, and make business very difficult for them until we have who did this. I hope you hear me on that, Mac."

"Who's working it?"

"Ade Walters."

"Spookbot?" Mac reached for another Redi-Smoke, doing his best to hide the slight tremor of his hands.

"Don't let him hear you call him that or you'll be in sensitivity reprogramming for a month. Or in a full body cast."

"Can I get some professional courtesy at least?" The unsteady strains of pain crept into his voice. "Someone's got to speak for her."

"You need to be careful. Grieving people are prone to rash decisions and poor impulses." Mac met him with a stony, eye-to-eye glare. Hollander eventually sighed. "I suppose Ade will have a few questions for you. But don't make a mess of the scene. It's his show."

The gore on the street and walls now had a name. Kiersten. Bits of her covered the whole area. The force of impact reduced her to a crimson smear. "Isn't *this* the scene?"

"This is just part of it. Follow me." Hollander patted Mac's shoulder, careful not to have too much or too lingering contact. Mac had never been comfortable with people touching him. Hollander escorted Mac to the penthouse roof as if not trusting him to go alone.

The Lifthrasir Group was the fifth-largest multinational in what remained of the United States and the American Dream™. As America's debt load grew too large for even it to service, several corporations had purchased statewide territories. The Lifthrasir Group owned what had once been Indiana, Kentucky, and Ohio. Those territories were especially hard hit by the eruptions and the subsequent societal upheaval called The Trying Times™, but the Lifthrasir Group funded their own internal security forces.

The duo entered a nearby stone building and took the elevator to the top. People's resourcefulness never ceased to amaze Mac. Once explored and examined, the structures had been declared sound and people had begun using them as homes. At first only the desperate and needy, but they had been dislocated by the hipsters and nouveau riche, making it the popular thing to do.

When the doors opened to the rooftop, a wind gusted inside and carried along with it the towers' signature smell of sulfur mixed with burnt ozone. The stink gave Mac a headache. His tongue suddenly felt coated with paste.

The pair walked over to a figure crouched near the edge of the roof.

"Detective Ade Walter, Former Detective Mac Peterson. Mac here was . . . acquainted with the deceased."

"Kiersten Wybrow," Ade said, then paused as if reading an invisible file. "Her jacket's exemplary. She even disclosed your relationship once the two of you started seeing one another, as required by protocol. Her file had been sealed due to her temporary assignment."

Mac grunted and glanced at Hollander.

Ade stood up and faced them. At six foot seven, Ade easily towered over the two of them. He had bulk on his frame, too, but carried it with the easy grace of a boxer. *Spent too much money on his pin-striped suit, much less that custom brown trench coat that he's sporting,* Mac thought, suddenly self-conscious of his tattered raincoat—despite its dampener lining—worn over an off-the-rack jacket.

Then there was Ade's face. The left half had been replaced. Around the eye, down the left cheek, and down to the collarbone, the silver gleam of metal glinted in the cerulean light. Mac could barely make out the tube, stemming from Ade's neck before it wound into his suit. It attached somewhere to a pack on his side that released scheduled fresh supplies of nanobots into his bloodstream to facilitate the workings of the cybernetic implant. An affectation of the wealthy, most of whom had the common decency to get the skin grafting to cover the prosthetic.

"Others in her acquaintance are still under ethics inquiry." Ade sniffed in Mac's direction.

"Is that right?" Mac turned back to Ade.

"Standard procedure, Detective," Hollander answered.

"Since when?"

"Gentlemen, you want to bicker all night or work the case?" Ade asked.

"Fine. Wanna lay it out for me?" Mac asked.

Ade glanced over at Hollander, who nodded, before he fixed his high-res imager on Mac, taking in whatever data streamed across his screen. "Signs of a struggle. Microabrasions on the floor. Trace amounts of DNA. Unidentifiable residue."

"So you've got nothing. Like the rest of the Goddamned jumper cases."

"We could . . . use help running down a few things," Hollander said. "Off-the-books stuff. Like a consultant."

Ade fixed the red gleam of his implant squarely on the chief. "I appreciate the offer, but I have things covered."

"Now hold on; perhaps the esteemed deputy chief makes a good suggestion," Mac said. "Besides, you don't expect me to sit on my ass and do nothing, do you?"

"No. I expect you to preen about like the Neanderthal throwback you pretend to be. You'll suffer through the pain of Ms. Wybrow's loss alone because you think that's how men do things. As that rarely works, you'll drink yourself into a stupor to quell the pain rather than deal with it. Then once that temporary measure proves as empty a gesture as it ultimately ever is, you'll fix yourself on vengeance by way of 'finding who did it.' And then do your level best to shit all over my fine case. So can we skip all the cliché cop bullshit? I'll keep you in the loop—but I need you to give me room to conduct this investigation. Are we clear on that?" Ade again glanced in Hollander's direction, but this time for Mac's benefit.

"Yeah, we're clear," Mac said with a sour grin and amused eyes.

"Good."

Hollander turned on his heel. As soon as he was out of earshot, Ade stepped near. "I remember you from the Ritenour case. You were stand-up then, even if the brass didn't see it that way. What was it you said then?"

Carlos Ritenour. What a mess of a case. It started when Mac was dispatched to a domestic disturbance. A man had beaten his three-year-old adopted son so badly both legs were broken and his entire head was an off shade of blue from all of the bruises that had amassed. Mac called for paramedics, never once taking his eyes from the boy.

"Do. Not. Move," was all Mac said to the man, not turning around to look at him. The man froze. Ten minutes until medical help arrived. Only the sound of their breathing broke the silence. The man didn't so much as twitch. Mac never said another word the entire time, only stared at the boy. The boy shivered, a thin trail of mucous streaming from his nose, in too much pain to even comfort. Eyes swollen shut so he couldn't make out Mac even if he could lift his head. Mac loomed over him, his rage building.

The paramedics on the scene circled Mac with a wide berth, sensing the mounting fury. They treated the boy, comforting him with meds and soothing tones as they loaded him for transport to the hospital. Right before he left the scene, the paramedic took one last glance at Mac and the father, but thought better of asking any questions.

As it turned out, Carlos Ritenour was one of many children brought in as a part of an underground sex ring for the nouveau riche. All their predilections and perversions spent on children brought in from around the globe with no citizenship status. Thus, in the eyes of the law, they didn't exist.

Mac led the team who busted the ring. All sorts of powerful businessmen and politicos were brought low in the scandal.

No one ever found the body of the man accused of beating Carlos Ritenour. Nor were any charges filed. But the swirling rumors about the disappearance centered around Mac. Not to mention that the enemies he made of the friends of the rich and powerful brought low by the scandal created enough behind-the-scenes furor to cost Mac his job.

He never regretted any part of that.

Mac placed his thumb and forefinger on the bridge of his nose and concentrated on getting his head straight. The memories didn't help. The job was the job and his days on it were numbered from the jump. Mac was never going to make rank. He wasn't that kind of cop. He made cases, even if it meant putting his thumb on the scales of justice every now and then. He didn't have to think very long for the words that had made him famous among the rank and file for a season. "'The law has a way of getting in the way of justice. Our true calling is the pursuit of justice no matter where it takes us. That's what binds us together and makes us family. And family is family.'"

"Yeah, that's it." Ade fished in his pockets for a pair of designer gloves and slipped them on. "Anyway, not much is on the Stream about the Easton MS crew. The set not jacked in?"

"Nope. Staying off the Stream is part of their code."

"You close to them?"

"Close as I need to be."

"I could use some street-level intel I can depend on," Ade said.

"Meet me at Fourth and Transom in two hours."

When they broke their conspiratorial huddle, they spied Hollander frowning. He shook his head and skulked off.

• • •

As only a few could afford cars, there were few streets in Old Town, only emergency corridors. Most people made do with either the sidewalks or the tram. If they were crazy enough to take the tram. Or crazier to walk. Mac took the underground tram to Easton, not having any patience for street preening and the ritual eyefuck of those who made him as a cop. He had never lost that cop walk, that puffed-up, straight-backed waddle of owning all he surveyed. Times like this, he wished he could still flash his badge to clear the car. Instead, nestled near the rear of the car, he hunched over on a bench. Despite being surrounded by people, he was alone. He dreaded moments like this. The stillness. When he had time to think. And feel. Grief threatened to devour him, to suck the marrow from his bones. His hands trembled with helplessness and he stuffed them into his pockets as if that would magically quell his racing mind and the torrent of memories. His mouth watered at the thought of a drink. The rusting steel wall across from him held a bit of wisdom scrawled into the surface with a knife: "Escape is the way to salvation!"

The rattling and clacking of the tram compounded the buzzing headache growing within Mac's brain. It had been hours since his last dose of Stim, the effects lasting shorter and shorter durations these days. Stim was the law enforcement drug originally developed and used during The Trying Times™, as the Stream called the post-eruption widespread riots. Mac had been on the force then, on the front lines. They'd had to stay alert longer, be faster, be stronger because they were so outnumbered. It was their thin blue line vs. the tsunami of panic. Panic the officers themselves shared. Every member of LG Security Force wanted to run and be with their families while uncertainty sprang up all around them. Instead they had to be there to stem the rioting and hold the line of civilization before people's baser instincts consumed them. And the officers resented every person who caused them to have to be here rather than with their own.

At ten p.m. sharp, Mac emerged from the Fourth and Transom tram entranceway. Light rarely penetrated down to the street level of the Easton section of Old Town. With the strange lanterns above them, the luminescence was reduced to a sapphire haze. The hustle and flow of urban ruin danced about the mixed landscape of trash-littered streets. The giant stone eruptions had disrupted the routine of the lives of Easton citizens, but people did what they had done since the days they first walked upright to take a piss: adapted and thrived, living among the alien structures as if they were their new homes.

The streets hadn't changed much. Kids in adult bodies still hung out on the corners, discussing the neighborhood in code thick enough to keep outsiders locked out of the know. The fashions changed, with the thug du jour favoring collared shirts unbuttoned at the cuffs and from the chest down. Thick, corded belts with the number of their building assignment as a buckle, worn with pride. Military fatigues shorn midcalf on the left leg, signifying a set in the prisons their families were tied to. If one member jailed, the rest of the family jailed with that relative in spirit, essentially sitting shiva during their sentence.

"The Carmillon is based here. You should see these freaks," Mac started in with Ade before he had a chance to offer up any greetings. The cybernetic man was forced to match Mac's pace as he stormed toward the houses. "Like a single-homed village. In the winter they all huddle around a wood-burning stove. They have to chip away ice from inside the toilets to use them. Summertime, shit, it's a flophouse free-for-all. They're organized, if that's not too strong a word, by a crew they call 'the crown.' The crown has five points, members, one of whom being a Chike Walters. Any relation?"

"No," Ade said with cold finality. "We all have to be related?"

"Put the race card back in your wallet. I was merely noting the coincidence."

"How do they afford this place?"

"It's not exactly the Ritz-Carlton, Detective. Besides, they have this policy of not paying rent. They just walk in and take over. Their philosophy is simple: act like you own the place and most folks will think you do. Most street bums don't run up against professional dropout artists on a regular basis."

A clean-shaven black man—draped in a vest darned with dental floss over a T-shirt and black shorts—approached them from across the street to head them off. Leather bands wrapped around his neck and wrists, accentuating the lean, lanky build of his runner's body. Though short and skinny, he couldn't disguise his muscles, as his gait gave it away: muscle heads, even thin ones, had that chest-out walk they couldn't shake. Much like cops. Ade's high-res imager fixed on the man's face.

"Chike Walters," Ade said.

"Good evening, officers," Chike said with a silky politeness before either could flash him their identification. "Here in an official capacity?"

"We have a few questions we'd like to ask you to help out with an investigation." Ade stalked about, circling Chike while studying the adjacent property.

"What investigation?"

"Do you live here?"

"As much as I live anywhere."

"I mean, is this your legal place of residence?" Ade pressed.

"You uptowners. So quick to look down your nose at us when it's you that should be ashamed of how you're living. Our country has so much. We throw away enough for nations to live on. Anything you want, I can get it for you. I can find anything I need out here."

"And what you can't find, you take," Mac said.

"What? Now you're standing up for the rights of garbage? I guess everyone will sleep better tonight."

"In someone else's bed," Mac continued.

"Private property is just another way to oppress people," Chike said.

"Not if it's my shit you're sleeping in."

"Folks would rather board up buildings if they can't make a profit from them. It makes no sense."

"It's. Not. Your. Shit." Mac emphasized each word for effect.

"Housing is a right, Detective. Food is a right. Anything less is buying into the propaganda of the system."

"What you're telling me is that you don't work?" Mac said.

"Once you have clothes, food, and housing, you don't really need credits," Chike said.

"So you're bums."

"It's always hard for some to give up privilege, that sense that you were born to own all you survey. Wouldn't you rather spend the time you do working being with your family?"

"Sometimes family's not all it's cracked up to be," Ade sniffed.

Chike turned to Ade with an icy glance. "Most people spend a good chunk of their lives at a job they hate, taking orders from people they can't stand to buy stuff they don't need. *That's* no kind of life."

"Who are they?" Ade nodded to the figures skulking around the side of the house.

"Our foraging party returning. Come on, we can talk inside."

Mac lingered a few steps behind them. The glow from a lit Dumpster cast a yellow pall on three men huddled together around a curbside campfire. Thick pustules grew in clumps along their chin and ears: victims of the Bud, a gene-specific virus released during The Trying Times™ as terrorists took advantage of the chaos to stir the pot. The virus attacked certain members of the populace by genome. It wasn't contagious, but no one had known that at the time. It produced the pustules by simply replicating in certain tissues until they grew and ruptured. A virus that shamed more than anything else, as affected individuals were ostracized by friends and family, left abandoned by those who claimed to love them. Terminated from the employment cycles and unable to get work, they took to the streets. Sections of many cities were set aside as colonies for them. Mac lived in one that kept visitors to a minimum. The Carmillon had the same idea.

Parts littered the lawn: car parts, bike parts, computer parts. The words "Escape while you can" were spray-painted on one of the crumbling brick walls of the turn-of-the-century mansion. The home was an umbrella of constant repair. Missing clay tiles left gaping wounds in the roof. Shingles peeled from the exterior, like a lizard sloughing its skin. Some of the rooms had six fireplaces, some rooms had two. The dining room was large enough to be called "The Cafeteria." The library was full of borrowed and found books—actual, paper, bound books—along with dusty old couches. Computers lined the far wall. Though reserved mostly for full citizens on the employment cycle, if they needed to, they tapped into the Stream by use of their homemade "cantenna," a primitive work-around that created an untraceable network hot spot. The massive house had half a dozen bedrooms, not counting what were originally built as servant's quarters. Strains of opera lilted from a radio. A radio. Mac had never seen a working one in real life. Signals still automatically broadcast on a loop from some centuries-old station. They had reappeared the day the towers erupted. No one knew how or why, but that didn't stop some people from enjoying the music.

A caramel-colored woman entered the room. She doffed a bowler cap, letting her white hair drape down to her shoulders. Carrying a walking stick in one hand, she plopped a backpack on the table with the other. A cross on a necklace dangled from around her neck, and a fine filigree of wrinkles framed her small mouth.

"Elia Baum, detectives. Detectives, Elia Baum. She's what you might call my second-in-command."

"Elia Baum." Ade fixed his high-res screen on her. "Three counts breaking and entering. Arrested six times on minor drug charges. Final disposition of those cases pending completion of her drug rehabilitation program."

"How's the program treating you, Ms. Baum?" Mac asked with a smirk.

"More hypocrisy. What's the difference between you and her?" Chike asked. "I can smell the stink of Redi-Smoke on your breath. And you have the look of a broken-down addict trying to muddle through. Protect and serve your high and leave those dealing with their pain and their recovery alone."

Mac bristled, ready to lunge toward the man, but Ade placed his large, meaty hand in the center of his chest and stopped him cold.

Chike, not even bothering to give Mac a second glance, turned to Elia. "What've we got?"

"Check this out." She gestured to the people behind her.

Her compatriots dumped several grocery bags worth of found treasures on the table. Sealed stir-fry vegetable packs. Bags of salad—crystals still on some of the leaves from having been frozen—probably from the bottom of a refrigerator kept too cold, then thrown out as ruined. Tomatoes. Four ready-made deli trays, vacuum sealed. Mushrooms. Oranges. Another of her companions arrived with lamps, brooms, random tools, and an ancient iPod. She lifted up the flap of her backpack to reveal bottles of lotion, detergent, and toothpaste.

"Nice work, Elia." Chike turned back to the detectives. "So what's this all about, gentlemen?"

Ade stepped forward. "We're investigating the disappearance of one Kiersten Wybrow."

"Ah, Kiersten Wybrow. So a pretty white woman—and she was pretty, right officer?" Chike locked eyes with Mac. "—she gets her hair mussed, so you hunt down the pack of n—— who had to be out to rape her."

"She did more than get her hair mussed, you walking cum stain . . ." Mac evaded Ade's arm and charged toward Chike.

Elia stepped in between the two men and swept the back of Mac's feet with her staff. He landed flush on his back, and by the time he realized his position, the butt of her staff pressed against his throat. The rest of the Carmillon gathered around, a wall of steel-eyed gazes whose body language hinted that they were well trained and not afraid to get in a fight. The detectives were clearly outnumbered.

"Call off your dog, Chike," Ade said in a tone that didn't invite discussion.

Chike locked eyes with him and then smirked. "Elia . . ."

She withdrew her staff then offered her hand to Mac.

"You're lucky I—we—don't have you hauled in right now." Mac brushed her hand aside and dusted himself off, knowing full well that Ade would have to call in backup to make that play. And this whole situation at second scan seemed more like a family beef than a game of posturing and disrespect.

"On what charges?" Chike asked.

"Assault on an officer," Ade said, covering for Mac, who clearly was no longer police. "Suspicion of murder."

"The Carmillon would never kill anyone. Ever."

"The Carmillon, eh? Wasn't Harley Wilson one of yours?"

"Why do you have to step on the man's name by insisting on calling him by his government name?"

"Figured you wouldn't care," Mac interjected. "If you found his body, you'd probably only use it for compost anyway. They're still scraping parts of him off the sidewalk downtown. If you hurry . . ."

"We knew him as Baraka. And, yes, he was one of ours. And, despite his dealings with the Easton MS crew, I cannot imagine him killing anyone." Chike stepped toward him, a spark of anger in his eyes. "Perhaps you should look into your undercover princess."

"You knew she was undercover?" Ade asked with the nonchalance of asking for the time.

Chike swallowed just hard enough to be noticed and wore the expression of a child caught in a lie. Mac had cracked the man's smooth veneer, finally getting to him. Angry people got sloppy.

"There are few secrets among the Carmillon."

"Then what's the muscle for?" Mac pointed to Elia and her crew, though didn't meet her eyes. "If we toss them, we likely to find weapons? Or other . . . accoutrements?"

"We have to protect ourselves. Not everyone is tolerant of our way of life."

"There are two bodies that took a header from a tower tonight—whose families won't even be able to bury them properly—who beg to differ. Her prints were everywhere. Wilson's were nowhere." Ade stepped closer to Chike. "How do you think that happened?"

"Your questions betray your prejudice. Apparently, every time something goes wrong in your precious, civilized world, those without have to be the cause of it."

"Your little foragers were all together?"

"Ours is a lifestyle of freedom. People can come and go as they please without fear of being checked up on."

"Do you know why Harley Wilson and Kiersten Wybrow would be at the top of the stone tower?" Ade asked.

"Baraka," Chike corrected, "was a good man. Maybe someday you'll have a chance to ask him when your time comes. He understood that we were in a war and that not all of our enemies reveal themselves. Some hide behind government and corporations and have the wealth and connections to think of themselves as untouchable. Everyone can be touched."

Mac rolled his eyes and tapped Ade's arm. "Come on, I've heard enough."

• • •

Mac daydreamed about being a farmer. Not a farmer, per se, but something simpler that harkened back to an earlier age. When a man could be alone with his thoughts and work out what he felt as he toiled in the earth. A time when he could think in peace without distraction. He needed space to himself. He supposed that was why he resisted using the data cloths or having any tech hardware attached to his brain stem. Nothing beyond the data chip in his hand, which carried his banking, citizenship status, and medical information.

At his usual table at Jenxie's Diner, a tiny hole-in-the-wall place specializing in obscure "genuine Southern cuisine," Mac leaned back in his seat. They actually still fried food, and his mouth nearly salivated at the thought of macaroni and cheese, fried okra, and fried chicken. He'd gone so far as to erase all traces of his Kentucky—no, southern Lifthrasir Group—roots. Most people assumed he was just another big-city douche, but memories of biscuits, gravy, and thick bacon flooded back to him, and the food nourished a part of him that ached from neglect.

"What was that? Back there with Chike," Mac said.

"You're here as a consultant and observer. That's it." Ade stared out the window wearing the same expression he'd had when he'd refused to meet Chike's eyes.

"I ain't trying to be your shrink. I just sensed a little . . . tension."

"Let's leave it at he and I have history."

"What are you doing, anyway? I know you're not just sitting there."

Ade raised a sardonic eyebrow. "You accusing me of not being shiftless and lazy?"

He slumped into the corner of the booth opposite Mac, lost in the transmissions of his high-res screen. Ade's synthetic eye thrummed as he read reports and newsfeeds from the Stream, searching for any reference connecting Easton, the Carmillon, Kiersten Wybrow, Chike Walters, or Harley "Baraka" Wilson. He probably also read the *New Yorker* and the *Brazz Report* celebrity scandal sheets, being the well-rounded Spookbot.

According to Ade, the murder rate in Easton had increased 45 percent in the last quarter, the uptick not corresponding to any rise in seasonal temperatures nor increased financial uncertainty. The only cross-reference point was the increased appearance of the blue lanterns and a rise in the number of jumpers. Scientists were still studying the lantern phenomenon, some likening it to some sort of dark matter/aurora borealis type effect. Conspiracy theorists chattered about alien invasions. Apocalyptos turned up their religious fervor. The government persisted in the claim that the civil unrest could be traced to the Freeganist Carmillon and their five-pointed leadership, discarding the more outlying explanations as nonsense.

"What do you think, Mac?"

"I think whenever the government speaks, the truth usually lies in the opposite direction. You gonna bust my balls all night or do you plan on easing up sometime soon?"

"Going through data and reports is how I relax. I let the information wash over me. Kind of like a fish swimming, I don't take in all the water."

"What exactly are you looking for?"

"Don't know. Actually, I think I'm looking for what's not there." Ade peered toward him as if reading his mood. "But about the Carmillon, what do you think?"

"I think they are a lying pack of hippy shitbags."

"What do we know about our victim? This crime? Or a motive?"

"Not much." Mac took out a Redi-Smoke and lit up.

"Not anything. All we have is a woman we know existed, a man who for all intents and purposes didn't, and a whole lot of nothing to go on." Ade stood motionless, the metal side of his face gleaming in the dim moonlight. "Tell me about Kiersten. Not anything I could read in a report. Tell me about the Kiersten you knew."

"Kiersten is . . . was . . ." Mac hated the grammar of the recently dead. The way the mind played its tricks to remind a person of another's absence. "Pure Security Force. Old school. Her dad was a cop and his dad was a cop, and along came Kiersten, a daughter instead of a son."

"Only child?"

"Yeah, her mother died during childbirth. Her dad didn't take it well. He and Kiersten were never close. She always harbored the suspicion that though he loved her he never really liked her all that much. In fact, she said she could never shake the feeling that he blamed her for her mother's death."

"That's no way to grow up."

"Tell me about it. Probably why she got into the family business."

"Same old story: trying to earn a parent's approval." With fidgety energy, Ade held the glass of water up to his eyes, as if marveling at it. "A fool's errand. Besides, kids have to find their own way, not live in their fathers' shadows."

"So you know how it goes?"

Ade paused as if debating how to respond to him. "She threw herself into the job?"

"Took her mother's maiden name and joined the force. Didn't want any special consideration for being Ronald Kemper's daughter."

"Kemper is a big name to live up to. You should know."

"Yeah. On the one hand, she wanted the old man to see what she could do on her own."

"On the other hand?" Ade asked.

"She wanted him to know that she was her own woman and he couldn't take credit for anything she did."

"I'm really starting to like this woman."

"Yeah, she has that effect on folks."

Ade repositioned himself, sitting straighter on the bench. He tried to catch a waitress's attention to no avail. "So when did you two meet?"

"I was her training officer. Man, if you'd have known her then. She was your type."

"My type?"

"Oh yeah. All rules and regulations. 'The rules are there for a reason. Without the law, there'd be chaos. The law is what separates us from the animals.' She was always quoting that."

"It's from an argument. Massiah versus Indiana."

"You know the law?" Mac asked.

"I'm a cop."

"You know what I mean."

"I know the lawyer. Melvin Walters. He said it." Ade quickly moved the conversation back to focus on Kiersten. "So she was a real by-the-books sort of person."

"Like you said, she disclosed our relationship while I thought I was being all clever hiding it from the bosses."

"So how'd you two get involved?"

"You ever have a partner?"

"No. People choose to not partner with me. That's their choice, not mine. I don't take that Spookbot stuff to heart."

"I was her training officer. You didn't have to be around her more than a few minutes to realize she was special. Beautiful. Smart. Tough. She took shit from no one; she didn't care who you were. And she kind of looked up to me. A real eager student, the kind a teacher could pour themselves into."

"Literally."

"Not like that." Mac hated the implication of how it sounded, turning his very real emotions—what they'd had—into something tawdry. "I mean, when you have someone you know can take what you teach them and take it to a whole other level. Like the chance to coach a Jordan, LeBron, or Mikatsu."

"So, as her elder, superior, and instructor, you didn't see it as an abuse of power to get involved with her?"

"Fuck you." It was Mac's turn to adjust, not quite rearing up, but meeting Ade's steady, probing gaze with his own. The two waited in silence, neither backing down.

Ade broke loose with a wan grin to ease the tension. "What was her assignment with the Carmillon?"

"Way I heard it, she went undercover to monitor their activities."

"Vice?"

"No, narcotics plucked her. Hollander assigned her personally."

"One last question: How'd it end?"

Mac remained silent for a time. There wasn't a day that went by that he didn't regret the mess he'd made of both of their lives. They were both on the job. He was her training officer for a time. They got involved, dated for over a year without the brass knowing. He was transferred to robbery/homicide once it came out. Tried to change some of his old ways and tame some of his demons. But, eventually, he fucked things up good. First letting the job get to him with that Ritenour mess, then letting the drinking and Stim use drive her away. Until one day she tired of his act and left. "It ended the way all things end: badly."

"Harbor any resentments?"

"Am I a suspect?"

"Honestly? Not really. Just doing my due diligence."

"No resentments. Only regrets."

"What kind of regrets?" Ade pressed.

"What are you, my shrink now?"

"I'm just trying to get the fullest picture possible of the woman she was and the man you are. So . . . regrets?"

"I . . . a person like Kiersten deserves a good man. Anyone around her wants to . . . be better. To be worthy of . . . shit." Mac hated to come across like half a douche: not having the words to put to his feelings, but having just enough to make a real tool of himself trying to sound like a fool-in-love poet. "I'm a fuckup. That's what I do, and that's who I am. I just didn't want to take her down when I crashed and burned. She deserved better."

A moment passed between them. Ade respected the silence and the man enough to leave it be. Privacy was something no one could afford anymore, so it had to be given. Ade turned away, pretending to be distracted by something outside, and gave Mac room to lick his emotional scars or else grieve in his own way. And Mac appreciated it.

"Now, I'm fucking starved. We're here in one of Easton's finer all-night dives. What you say me and you grab some coffee and donuts," Mac said.

"You cannot resist being a walking cliché."

"Fine, you can have one of those puke-green protein shakes or whatever it is you muscle boys like to eat."

Ade revealed a mouth full of gleaming white teeth. A crooked, painful approximation of a smile broke against the metal in his unyielding face. "Now you're talking."

One of the Jenxie's Diner owners brought out Mac's order: a plate of biscuits topped with sausage gravy, topped with two eggs sunny side up. Ade glanced over with mild disgust.

"Not too many Forcers got one of those." Mac pointed his fork—laden with a bit of gravy-dipped biscuit and the yolk of an egg dripping from it—at Ade's cybernetic implant. "Way I see it, anyone who can afford that kind of tech is already above a chief's pay grade. You're like Chike, slumming with us poor folks."

"I'm nothing like Chike." Ade raised his hands as if pushing away from the table and settled into his half-slouch of reading the news Stream. "We've run down Harley. Little more than a two-bit hitter, suspected in three homicides. Most we've ever managed to pin on him was a few assaults."

"Yeah. Ran across his crew a few times. Vicious little pricks, the kind who'd slit his own momma's throat for a few moments' buzz. Just tussled with one of them last night. I don't know why Kiersten would ever get tangled up with him. Any of them. You saw them. I doubt any of them could take a toss without coming up holding. Still, they seem like harmless enough recreational users. More the 'live and let live' type."

"Sounds about right. Still, that's the story they gave her to give us. And . . ."

". . . the truth is somewhere in the other direction," Mac said.

"You know, back in the 1960s and 1970s, police were assigned to infiltrate groups suspected of being revolutionaries. They'd get in bed with the groups, go with them on their little criminal activities, but inform if they were planning something huge. Real." Mac tapped his finger on his empty glass, indicating the need for a refill, wishing he had something harder than the carbonated pabulum he swallowed. As if finally accepting a truth, he whispered, "Kiersten's gone . . ."

"When was the last time you heard from her?" Ade asked in a gentle tone.

"Two days ago." Mac recognized the tone—one he often used with relatives of victims—and snapped back from the melancholy vortex that waited for him. "Just to talk about the old days. Her place. Part of me thought it was an invitation, but I didn't take her up on it."

"That get you worried?"

"Just thought it weird, her reaching out to me in the first place. Being undercover, she could go weeks without checking in. That was just the way it worked. Protocols had it that she had to check in with Hollander every day, though."

"I've only had the case three hours. With no body, it'll be tough to establish a timeline. With no body, we can't check for drugs, can't check for sexual—" Ade stopped himself. "Sorry, man."

"It's the job. I know." Mac fired up another Redi-Smoke. "What about that?"

"About what?"

"What you said earlier about what's not there?"

"The body?" Ade asked.

"Think there's a reason they wanted to splatter Kiersten across the city?"

Ade returned to his state of brooding silence. A hint of a grin upturned the corner of his mouth as he searched: the semi-vacant, glassy-eyed stare of a junky in the throes of getting high.

"You get a phone dump?" Mac asked.

"Still waiting on it. Some sort of hold is on her records. I'm also waiting on her full background: financial, criminal, and public. My next stop is to go over to her place and see what she was getting into."

"Good plan. I'll go with you."

"Former Detective Peterson, you are dangerously close to shitting on my investigation."

"All you can see are the cheeks of my pasty white ass. I have not yet begun to shit. If I had intentions of doing so, I wouldn't have given you the heads-up. Besides, it's not the crime scene, and I have a key."

• • •

"Western Investigator Twenty-One to base. Left Fourth and Transom with informant. Heading to Easton apartments of undercover investigator Kiersten Wybrow," Ade said into his cop-net. Mac knew Ade documented as much as he could in order to give the appearance of an investigation by the book.

"Base to Western Twenty-One. Time is oh three forty-five."

Though Kiersten kept a cover apartment on the outskirts of the Easton section of Old Town, she lived in another tower in Waverton, not too far from the one where she was found. He hated the facade of Waverton. A gleaming city whose dwellers had the dispirited expressions of those who lived in war zones: desperate, without hope, eyes devoid of life. Shuffling about in steps drained of vitality. Mac didn't know how people could stand living in a tower. When he stared at their strange geometry for too long, especially under the glare of the lanterns, nausea overwhelmed him. Each of the tower's original occupants carved out their own space for their apartment, paying for each square foot. Thus the spaces were not uniform, each floor plan was unique, and the rooms were carved out like natural hollows. The city had used code violations to seize the property under eminent domain and had the towers refurbished. In Kiersten's case, the city had repossessed this space after a Stim bust—a home lab that refined the police stimulant to its more potent street form—so it made for a perfect cover.

Standing in front of the locked door, Mac shifted awkwardly, suddenly feeling like he chased the ghost of someone he never knew. Not that he was going to admit that he may have exaggerated his access to their place. He knew where she stayed in case of an emergency, and he wasn't supposed to know that for the sake of her cover. He certainly hadn't been there before. Unlike her (real) place, there was no palm lock that responded to his print. Kiersten was old-school at heart. He reached above the archway and checked under the mat. He found what he was looking for under a fake rock. A mechanical bolt slid free as he turned a key. Funny how he thought of their life together as real and this world he and Ade traipsed in as no more than a facade.

Mac searched for anything familiar, anything of the Kiersten he knew in the spartan space. He couldn't shake the sensation that he was intruding into the wrong person's life. Seeing the cloying undertones of flowers in vases, which gave every room the feel of a funeral home, he almost missed how Kiersten had decorated her place. He had always hated her aesthetic taste, as it made her seem like a frumpy old woman. A bowl of candy rested on the table next to the door. Mac grabbed a few pieces.

"Not what you expected?" Ade asked.

"It's not like I kept my stained underwear in her panty drawer."

Ade's mouth had begun to creep into a mild grin when it froze, and his smile evaporated. Ade held up a hand commanding Mac to pipe down, first pointing to his ear and then to the shut bedroom door. Mac looked over the tops of his sunglasses and then reached into the folds of his dampening jacket and removed his Cougar PT-10. Ade's arms crisscrossed and pulled out two semiautomatic crowd-control machine guns. Mac twisted the knob, but it had been locked. Ade brushed him aside, kicked the door once, and when it splintered open, stepped first into the unknown, unwelcoming darkness.

Two figures wrestled in the dark. The murk of the room obscured the figures, and they were entangled too closely to draw a bead on either.

"Security Force. Hold it right there," Ade commanded.

The figures ceased their dance. Then one shoved the other toward the detectives and bounded out the window. Mac dashed after the figure.

"Mac, wait," Ade yelled too late.

The window, like the rest of the windows along the tower, was neither square nor smooth nor spaced with any regularity. The rooflines shifted like rock slides. Shelves had been cut into the walls and the windows opened onto a terrace. From their second-floor vantage point, the figure dropped to the ground as if boneless, landing with the grace of a leopard then bounding farther into the recesses of the tower's outcropping. Almost like cliff dwellings, the tower itself was a seamless piece of masonry, with no cracks, like river-cut stone created as one sheaf. Gibbous and grayish, the towers disoriented him. Geometric and beautiful, a math equation of art, he had the sense that he was too close to it to see the whole pattern. However, the angles and placement seemed too intentional, guided by an intelligence behind its order.

Mac followed the suspect, his knees popping and groaning in protest. He had to let his equilibrium reassert itself. He pursued the figure as it bounded along the towers. It leaped onto an overhang and pulled itself up and over onto another terrace, barely breaking stride. Mac did his best to keep pace. In a chase, especially now that he was old and out of shape, his goal was to just keep the perp in sight. He ran smart, not fast, allowing his targets to exhaust themselves, because most people couldn't go full tilt for very long. Mac jogged along at his half trot, watching as the figure climbed and bounded. He matched its path if not its acrobatics.

The artificial hue of the lanterns bobbing in the midnight sky above the tower deepened the shadows. Mac trailed the figure into a dead end where the towers met. Sound traveled differently in this network, dampening the noise, creating a sacred space. That was the word that sprang to Mac's mind: sacred. He leaned against a bare wall, with its unnatural smoothness and no signs of erosion or wear. A lavender fragrance suffused the surrounding area, but underneath the smell was something old and moldy, like rotted cabbage. Treelike plants cloistered the intersection. A woman emerged from a tangle of branches. There was a moment when reality shifted, like a child's kaleidoscope turning. Mac threw up. He didn't take his eyes from her as he wiped his mouth with the cuff of his sleeve.

"Elia, what the hell?"

"This isn't what you think," she said.

"I think I'm hauling your ass in."

"The man back there, he knows. He's a part of this."

"Who is he?" Mac hesitated. He needed to get back to Ade, but he couldn't just let Elia walk. "Never mind, you need to come in with me."

"I can't, Detective. I must see this through. For my people's sake, as well as yours."

A moment passed between them. When she closed her eyes, her eyeballs moved around like disjointed marbles beneath the fragile membranes of her lids. He knew her full measure now.

Elia charged at him without a word, without a sound. The swing of her staff swooshed over his head. He hadn't realized he'd ducked as instinct had taken over. She reversed the arc of her attack in one fluid movement, catching him in his ribs. The coat absorbed most of the blow, but it caused him to drop his gun. He wrapped his arms around her staff. With the flourish of a pirouette, she released her staff, spun away from him, then came at him with her hands poised like daggers. Three times she struck him, and then each spot went numb. In a desperate bid, he jacked his knee up, which caught her in her side and threw her off balance. He locked arms with her and pushed her into the wall. With a graceful turn, she entangled him in a hold before slamming him into an adjacent wall. His glasses shattered into jagged bits that clawed his face. Blood trailed from his smashed nose. His breath came in jagged gulps. His shoulder wrenched out of place. His body reacted on instinct, desperate to stay conscious. His elbow crashed into her neck. He followed up with an awkwardly thrown punch. Trapped in close quarters, they exchanged a flurry of punches, with none landing especially hard as each of them began to tire, though Mac more than she. Mac scrabbled about, his hand searching for anything he could use as a weapon. Finding a branch, he jammed it into her neck. Blood spurted. Enraged, she lifted him and flipped him onto the ground. He kicked madly as she leaped on him, catching her twice, but neither blow had much power. Her hands wrapped around the soft folds of his neck. Headbutting her, he staved her off as she released her grip. He clambered for his weapon as she lunged for her staff. He fired twice. He hit her center mass, just as he was trained. He had to have hit her. She fell into the shadows. He raised his gun level and trained it on where she had fallen. He took measured half steps, easing into his approach. He neared where her body had dropped. He clutched his side and daubed his face as slick pools of blood trickled from him. When he reached the spot, she was gone.

• • •

Mac returned to Kiersten's place. His breath still coming in ragged hitches as years of Redi-Smokes overrode his military training. He remembered his time in the service as clean, a simple time of young idiots still searching for the people they were meant to grow into. It was a time when he had learned duty, responsibility, and the horseshit that was chain of command. Getting an other-than-honorable discharge for punching his commanding officer—no matter how correct Mac had proved himself to be—had left him as sore as he felt now.

"What happened?" Ade said. "You look like you got the mess stomped out of you."

"The . . ." Mac lifted his chin toward the suspect, "perp got away from me. I'll tell you later. What have we got here?"

"Look for yourself."

A figure slumped against the side of Kiersten's bed, his face bruised and swollen. "Damn it, Ade, you've beat him to near death."

"Wasn't me. I found him like that." Ade took a step back, his head cocked at an angle.

"What are you doing?"

"Checking him for drugs, his heartbeat, respiration, implants," Ade said, "establishing a baseline should we be so inclined as to engage him in conversation. I hate to be lied to."

"I need to get me one of those."

"What's your name?" Ade asked the suspect.

"I ain't sayin' shit." The man leaned forward and let out a small chuckle. Blood spilled from his mouth.

"Anyone else in the apartment we should know about, Mr. Sayin' Shit?" Ade asked.

"I'll clear the place," Mac said.

"Don't open any drawers," Ade reminded him. "Plain view search only or the judicial net will tear me a new one."

"Too bad you have to make a case. The law has a way of getting in the way of justice."

Ade looked down and shook his head. Sirens roared in the distance. "I'll secure the scene. You should have the service medics take a look at you."

"I'll be fine."

"Former Detective Peterson," Ade said in a voice that didn't invite argument, "please sit down. You've lost more blood than you realize and you're probably in shock."

"I'm not going anywhere till I've figured out what went on here." Mac faced him, an unwavering gaze locked onto his erstwhile partner's robotic visage.

"You mean besides you getting your ass kicked? You need to settle down and let them do their job."

"I need to do mine first." Mac turned toward Kiersten's bedroom. The door closed behind and he leaned against it, recalling what it was like to be in there again. Alone with his anger. And underneath the anger was more anger. Under that, lifting up that inner welcome mat—black earth squirming with worms and isopods and other insects that broke down organic matter, building something from death and decay—was fear. Kiersten had only wanted to be let in. She'd said that he had constructed a life—with the booze and the Stim—where he cut himself off from having to deal with others and the potential pain they brought. Living with the fear that if he exposed himself, showed people who he really was, they would abandon him. Some part of him became convinced that he would rather be alone and unhurt rather than risk others in his life. He preferred to live with the fear. Fear that she'd betray him. Fear that she'd see him for who he was. Fear that she'd humiliate him.

Fear that she'd leave him.

That was why he ran. That was why he always ran.

The room hadn't changed. A row of porcelain figurines lined the mantle over her chest-o-drawers. Her queen-sized bed—how many nights had their bodies tangled up in the space trying to get comfortable but still appreciating that they had it to begin with?—divided the room. On the other side was her desk, an antique rolltop. Pulling out the main drawer, he ran his hand underneath it. There it was. An envelope. Inside was a tiny spiral-bound notebook. Kiersten was running an off-the-book investigation. He flipped through the pages.

"Where'd you get that?" Ade asked, suddenly filling the doorway.

"It fell out." Mac nudged the drawer closed and stood up.

"What are you thinking?"

"Right now that maybe one of the Carmillon paid one of their brothers . . . or sisters . . . to take care of a couple of liabilities."

• • •

Devices measured their brainwaves, heartbeats, and body temperatures, logged retinal scans, DNA, and fingerprint info. The biocircuitry that formed the artificial intelligence of the LG Security Force headquarters in Waverton gave it a kind of low-level sentience. While it allowed for adaptive responses, more importantly, it allowed for self-repair. Mac wasn't allowed on the interrogation floor, but Ade found him a spot up in an observation room. A great seat for his show.

In the small confines of the interrogation room, under the glare of a single column of light, the suspect seemed a lot smaller. And younger. A young man, barely a man at that. Hair styled in thick cornrows, a bruise under his left eye, and the entire right side of his face remained swollen. Tattoos, in a pattern familiar to Mac, trailed down each skinny arm. A razor-thin goatee framed his mouth; three gold rings pierced each ear. Seated in the metal chair, his knee hopped to a frenetic beat; his eyes scanned and rescanned the room at every sound; his heartbeat tripped along as if he were a hunted rabbit. Fear made everyone smaller.

"What's your name, son?" Ade circled the table, which blocked the suspect from the door. A subtle reminder that the only way to the door was through the detective. He set a data sheet on the table between them. A subtle reminder that evidence, the truth, separated them.

"Don't call me son. I'm not your son." The subject reared up slightly, partly a show for the detective, partly to move away from the sheet and what it might portend.

"Yeah, well, I figured 'what's your name you scumbag, daring to shoot at Security Force, pain in the ass' would get us off on the wrong foot."

"But at least it'd be honest."

"Honesty's important to you?"

"Honesty's all that we have. That and respect, but honesty's something no one can take away from you but you."

"What can I call you?" Ade asked again.

"Between that fancy eye of yours and my prints, retinal scan, and DNA, you probably know all my history."

"Oh, I have that: Quavay Middleton. Twenty-two years old. Dropped out of Edu-Link at thirteen. Known associate of the Easton MS crew. Four assaults, one possession without intent to distribute, suspect in three B and Es. But that's your government name. What do *you* want to be called?"

"Tin Tin," he replied, tentatively, as if uncertain of his own name, much less what the detective's play was. The concession to his name caught him off guard.

"How'd you get a name like Tin Tin?"

"Just sort of stuck. I can get anyone jacked in from anywhere."

"So you're like a walking cantenna."

"Yeah. Tin Tin. Why you being so cool to me?"

"Well, Tin Tin, I got to say, you done right by me, so I got to do right by you." Ade broke out his wide, fractured smile and patted the data sheet.

"What you mean?"

"I mean, here you are, right in the middle of a jackpot. This murder case is closed."

"Murder?"

"Yeah. Turns out your fingerprints match a set of unknowns at the murder scene. Then we catch you in the apartment of the woman whose murder we're investigating. It doesn't matter how great a story you may have, this case is done."

"Shit, man, that ain't right." Tin Tin's eyes widened and followed the detective wherever he moved with plaintive desperation.

"Right doesn't have anything to do with it. You should know that by now. You're twenty-two. You've been in and out of the system for years. You know how the game works. How we do. Us Security Forces, we're strictly about the easy workload: if we can close a case on your ass, we will."

"You got it all wrong."

Ade crossed his arms and leaned back against the wall. His heavy gaze fell on Tin Tin, and the boy—he seemed more like a frantic little boy in search of his mother—squirmed under its weight. "Then set me straight. You keep my job easy, I'll keep listening."

"Word came from up high: Kiersten had been snitching. Had notes and recordings of a lot of the dirt we do."

"So you were sent to shut her up."

"It wasn't like that. She was greenlit, all right. But she was still Kiersten. We'd accepted her as one of us. I know some folks felt this sense of betrayal and . . . I guess. Still didn't stop me from feeling what I did. I loved her a little. Still, though, we couldn't have her notes just out there. She could put all of our business out on the streets."

"But?"

"But that ain't what I do. I don't handle that end of things. I'm strictly . . . acquisitions."

"So you broke into her place just looking for her notes and stuff?"

"That shit could've been anywhere. A micro dot even."

"That's why they sent in my man Tin Tin."

Tin Tin beamed with pride. "None other."

Mac hadn't known Ade long, but he guessed some of the pressures he may have been under. No matter how postracial they had declared their world, too many times Ade had needed to make a choice: whether he was black or blue, one of those cops who was a black man first, cop second, or vice versa. Too much of that brother-brother crap could play in some people's heads and cloud their judgment. Feeling too responsible for fuckups fucking up, that's what a sense of community meant to Mac. As far as he was concerned, Ade was just there to clean up their mess, not play Father Malone or something to get them to see the light.

"So who was your playmate?" Ade asked.

"Fuck if I know. I'm steady tossing the place, suddenly this kung fu heifer jumps my shit."

"She whupped that ass," Ade enjoyed saying.

"I got my licks in."

"You want that to go in the official report?"

"Nah, man. You know, I'm a lover and all. Can't be seen putting my hands on no female. Just trying to fend her off so I can do my do."

There it was. Though guilty of many things, Tin Tin had neither the demeanor nor heart of a killer. Now a gentler touch was required. The old juices of being in the room began to flow again for Mac, the gentle tug to join Ade on the performance.

"So you have no idea who she was?" Ade sat down across from him now. Like an actor commanding the stage, he owned the room.

"None. Though I got the feeling she was there for the same reason."

"Where were you about three forty-five last night?" Ade asked.

"Tucking my ass into bed."

"Here's my problem, Tin Tin: scan says we got your prints at the scene of my homicide."

"Can't be. I didn't do no murder."

"Then explain your prints."

"Someone fucked up on your end. Carried a one or some shit when they shouldn't have. All I know was that I wasn't nowhere near no murder."

"Well, you'll forgive us if we don't take your word on it."

"Don't go soft on me," Tin Tin said with a sudden steel to his words.

"Excuse me?"

"I didn't do no murder, so I need you and your robo-ass to put in some elbow work. Revisit the crime scene. CSI some shit, 'cause I'm telling you, I'm innocent."

"You may be many things, Tin Tin, but innocent surely isn't one of them."

"But . . ."

"Sit tight. I'm going to check things out. If you didn't do this, I'll find out. If you did, well, I'll find that out, too."

• • •

Entering the observation room to join Mac, Ade sighed with exasperation. Mac recognized that sigh because he'd already let one out a few minutes ago. They were nowhere. They were worse than nowhere because they had a viable suspect in hand they knew wasn't good for the crime. But expediency often trumped niceties like what one's gut might say or what one might intuit from years of experience. Ade paced back and forth, working off his frustration. Pausing, he tilted his head in that tell that said he'd received new information across his high-res screen.

"We got the call dump back on Kiersten's communications."

"About time," Mac said.

"Told you, something had the files all but suppressed. Anyway, Baraka was the last one to call her."

"Think he arranged the meet?"

"We could assume that. Maybe he was her confidential informant. That could get them both killed if they were caught."

"It's all right there, I know it. All connected somehow." Mac pored over Kiersten's notes, not understanding most of the technical jargon. He recognized the name that topped the manifests and memos. "What do we know about the Lifthrasir Group?"

"They're into all sorts of weird stuff. Alternative energy sources. One of their labs had a break-in reported a week ago. Case got buried."

"Why? Brass interference?"

"You'd think, but apparently when the Lifthrasir Group talks, the bosses jump. The group was completely uncooperative. Their alarms went off, we responded, and it was like we were inconveniencing them. Case shut down."

"That doesn't make any sense. When shit don't make sense, it rubs my taint raw."

"You are a lovely, lovely man." Ade leaned forward, his gaze distant. He thumbed through a crate of bagged material like a child at Christmas choosing which present to open first.

"What are you doing?"

"About to log this stuff in."

"You can't do that."

"It's procedure."

"You haven't been about procedure this whole case. Why? Because part of you suspected this was an unusual case from the beginning. Look, I don't understand most of what she has here, but much of this stuff doesn't look like any technology I'm familiar with. She was onto something. Something big."

"I know where you're going with that science fiction conspiracy theory tone. Snippets of internal memorandums, schematics for devices, blurry photographs, and recordings of meetings? You connect these pieces one way, you get to spin the tale of business executives in league with . . . foreign agencies . . . to procure tech. You spin the same facts a little differently, you have Kiersten involved in corporate espionage—the equivalent of high treason—and needing to scapegoat somebody."

"But we agree it revolves around the Lifthrasir Group," Mac said.

"Yes."

"And the Lifthrasir Group owns the Security Force."

"They provide the funding and we do report ultimately to their appointed civilian review board."

"I know. I dealt with them on my way off the force. But that's what I mean. You've seen the kind of juice in play to pull the strings that have been yanked so far. We log this into the system, no telling what will happen to the evidence."

"So what do you suggest?"

"Log in a duplicate. We keep the originals. Kiersten might have done that herself. Worked with the dupes while keeping the originals somewhere safe. Think about it. Why else do a pen and paper investigation? Because they can't be monitored or traced."

Clutching his hands behind his head, Ade stretched back in the chair. The room buzzed with activity, detectives and uniformed officers milling about trying to appear as if they were being productive in case any of the brass wandered through. Official memorandums trailed along the walls, along with case status and deployment updates. The phones chirped constantly.

"What's he doing here?" Deputy Chief Hollander sneered with a mild derision toward Mac.

"Consulting," Ade said.

"I meant for you to extend him a courtesy, not have him move in."

"He helped me bring in our prime suspect, Tin Tin. Even got his ass handed to him by another suspect. Figured I owed it to him to let him see this through a little bit further."

"I'm strictly a shadow investigator," Mac assured, though the chief wasn't buying it.

"See that it stays that way." Hollander turned fully to Ade, standing in front of the "murder board," as the squad called the case wall. Crime scene photos lit up the board, along with victim profiles, and results streamed from the crime lab. Diagrams detailing the physics of impacts or the biology of any drugs present filled the screens. From every possible scenario or angle, various theories and guesses ran along the side of the board in blue. "Now we're going to pretend that you're still lead investigator on this case. Where do we stand?"

"We're in the middle of interviews. Her friends. Her family. Her coworkers." Ade fixed his cybernetic eye on him. "We're working on trace evidence right now."

"So what do we have?" Mac asked.

"Kiersten Wybrow goes undercover to investigate the Easton MS crew as well as an ancillary organization known as the Carmillon. The group is headed up by Chike Walter and his right hand, Elia Baum. Kiersten hooks up with Harley Wilson, and the two of them get into some shit they shouldn't have. Our Mr. Quavay Middleton, aka Tin Tin, was found beaten at her place by perp unknown." Ade cut a glance at Mac to keep him silent.

"Any word on the unknown perp?"

"That's the other reason Former Detective Peterson is here. He's going through arrays of known Easton MS crew associates to see if a familiar face pops out."

"What's your next step?" Hollander peeked into the evidence box, then scanned a data sheet.

"Let the suspect stew a bit then see if he gives up anything else."

"He look good for this?" Hollander asked.

"He looks great for this. He's been practically delivered to us with a bow on top. Everything points to him: prints on the scene; knowing Kiersten reported to us; caught at her place ransacking it for incriminating evidence."

"Why isn't he in holding?"

"His statement is like high grade Stim: ninety percent pure. That's the way this game is rigged. Everything he's telling is ninety percent truth, but that last ten percent can get folks killed. Plus, I hate loose ends and unanswered questions."

"Well you know what? I hate open cases even more. Do I need to remind you that Kiersten Wybrow was one of our own? *One of us.* Murders of Security Force members do not go unsolved, especially when there is a perp who has all but confessed to it already in our custody. Close this case so that we can move on. Somebody's gotta give the press their morning hand jobs, and I'm the man anointed for the mission. Do I make myself clear?"

"Yes Chief."

The deputy chief stormed back to his office. Mac pointedly kept his back to Kiersten's picture, as if it hurt too much to see her image. Her curly mop of brown hair. Her dark, sultry eyes that stole a man's soul when they peered at him. The too-red thin lips of her about-to-get-into-trouble grin. But no matter where he stood, the weight of her profile bore down on him. "You didn't mention Elia to him."

"Because I have an uncooperative witness who hasn't confirmed that it was her."

"Is that what I am?" Mac asked.

"Not everything goes into my final report all at once. I still have questions. I need to be able to frame things in context. And I know where to find Elia should it prove to be her."

"The fact that this case keeps coming back to Chike has nothing to do with it?"

"Mind your own."

"I am. That's how I got here in the first place."

"Hollander's true to his word." Ade nodded to the monitor. "Tin Tin's on his way to holding."

Two guards escorted Quavay Middleton into the holding facility, which would double as the courtroom as a judicial net monitor burned to life. It was easier to hold the preliminary trial and motions at the station in order to streamline the judicial process. The overly pixilated image of a judge sputtered, the connection not very good, as Stream for government use had even lower priority than those mandated for public access. The high mounted lights winked on, a single column illuminating Tin Tin's space.

"Quavay Middleton," the face of the judicial net said.

"Tin Tin," he corrected.

"You stand accused of the murders of Harley Wilson and Kiersten Wybrow. How do you plead?"

"I didn't do that shit."

Mac turned to make a smart-ass comment to Ade, only to see the detective's pallor flush. He teetered for a bit, a tall tree on the verge of falling.

"What is it?" Mac half rose to steady him. "You don't look okay."

At first Ade's face simply went slack, enraptured by images only he could see. Then he doubled over as if a searing blade sliced through his head. Mac caught the big man as he fell forward.

"Something's wrong," was all Ade could muster.

The image of the judge flickered, grayed with static, then went black. Quavay stood alone in his circle of light, surrounded by shadows. Too many shadows. He gestured wildly and appeared to be screaming, but no sound transmitted. Then that image, too, flickered, grayed with static, then went black.

"What's going on?" Mac asked.

Ade pointed toward a console and Mac helped him to it. Ade slid the nail of his pinky finger back, revealing an exoport embedded in the tip, and he plugged into the panel. The feed on the monitor changed, and a new image burned to life. Tin Tin huddled in a corner. The point of view of the camera had changed. No longer was it a sweeping arc from the side of the room. It was much closer, peering down at Tin Tin. From the point of view of whoever was in with him. "Someone's hijacked the signal to my eye."

"Who?"

"I don't know. Someone with juice. This tech isn't easy to hack. This is what I'm seeing."

"Yeah, I'm betting whoever installed that isn't exactly in the refund business."

The electric wail of a weapon discharge halted them in their spots, and their attention drew back to the screen. A hole had burned neatly through Tin Tin's chest. His clothes still smoldered from the energy beam. Tin Tin's body filled the screen, from the perspective of the assailant inspecting his (or her) handiwork. Then the contact signal broke. The screen went black, then reflected itself, as it was what Ade now saw. He withdrew his finger from the port.

"Lock the building down," Ade said in a spent voice just above a whisper. Unsteady getting to his feet, his head seemed to clear as other Security Force officers pushed through their initial shock and their training took over. Mac followed, all but ignored in the ensuing rush. By the time the officers got back to the holding chamber, a crowd blocked the door. The two guards were being attended to by medics, returning to consciousness but otherwise unharmed. Tin Tin's vacant eyes accused the gathered throng.

"I'm not exactly weeping over this one," Hollander said.

"Sir?" Ade asked.

"They kill one of ours. They paid the price. Case closed."

"Our brand of 'blue justice'?"

"No, no. Of course not. I'm launching a full investigation. You can't pull this cowboy shit on my watch," Hollander said in an unconvincing tone. He all but signaled a going-through-the-motions investigation, strictly an exercise in filing paperwork. "I'll just shake his hand before I Mirandize him. Or her."

"How did he get in here? Or get out?" Ade asked.

"Double-check all personnel. I want to know who all has been in and out of this building," Hollander said.

"It won't matter. Whoever pulled this off had access. I bet every clearance is accounted for. They are one step ahead of us and two levels above our pay grade."

"At least."

"That stunt with my eye wasn't easy. However, it automatically recorded the entire episode. Full spectrum analysis. I'm running a protocol now to see if I can backtrace the signal."

"Let's get this scene processed and let me know what you find. I'll get everyone out of here. Short leash, Peterson."

Already kneeling, Ade examined the weapon, which had been discarded without a care of it being traced back to the perpetrator. "A Cougar PT-10, like yours, except that this one is military grade. Energy charged."

"Mine was a souvenir." His Cougar PT-10 was the only token from the Michigan incursion. Prior to him being drummed out of military service, the Lifthrasir Group had initiated a hostile takeover of the Michigan territory but was rebuffed. The skirmish had lasted two years and Mac had served three consecutive tours in the futile engagement.

"After a couple hundred years," he said, almost absently, "the design of a handgun hasn't changed all that much."

"There's a romance to the image," Mac said.

"You mean the image of men waving around their junk to see whose is bigger?"

"Let's not be sexist: women wave around my junk too."

"Right. Not sexist at all." Ade continued, "Look at this: the primer has been shaved down so it wouldn't snag if drawn quickly. And the grips are custom made. No fingerprints, no DNA."

"Professional hitter?"

"A little beyond these disds."

"It might be beyond them, but the case dead-ends with them. Once he was logged into the judicial net, it was a matter of prosecution."

"Out of our hands."

"Other than some paperwork, case closed."

Mac hated the way things remained, like he'd been presented with a new sweater with a few threads dangling that he had to yank free. On paper it could work. The Easton MS crew got wind that Kiersten worked for Security Force. One of their hitters took out her and her snitch, Baraka or Harley or whatever the hell he was calling himself. It could have been Tin Tin, who then went after whatever evidence she had. Once detained, he had become a liability, either because of what he knew or to whoever actually carried out the hit. Regardless, there was still a killer to track, and a case to close if anyone cared: Tin Tin's if not also Kiersten's. But what truly bothered Mac was the sense of something bigger pulling at them and the investigation. Someone with the resources to hijack Ade's eye, get in and out of LG Security Force headquarters, and have access to military hardware. Events moved too quickly, too neatly, not giving anyone a chance to think things through.

• • •

There were times when Mac dreamed of plunging his hands into soil, of getting dirt under his fingernails so thick that he would never seem to get completely clean. Of pulling weeds and tending to his young sprouting plants while sweat beaded along his forehead, falling in large droplets, and his shirt completely drenched. The nagging sensation never left him, but he couldn't put his finger on what exactly troubled him. The blaring wail of an incoming call only served to increase his growing irritation. The call was blocked, so no image or information came through. This was exactly why Mac didn't have an office, only a messenger service that forwarded his calls through a series of anonymous proxies. That way he had no unexpected visitors, which meant no unanticipated mayhem and/or property damage.

"This better be good. I haven't had coffee yet." Mac tamped out a Redi-Smoke and put it between his lips, holding it there without lighting.

"Are you Mac Peterson? The investigator?" the voice sounded vaguely familiar, though hushed and muffled.

"Who's asking?"

"Jesse Honeycutt."

"Who?"

"Duppy."

"Oh, Duppy." Mac lit his Redi-Smoke. He let the rush hit his system and the smoke halo his mouth before he continued. "How are the eyes doing?"

"Me fe gwon spend two days after the clinic recovering," Duppy said, then tired of putting in the energy for his accent. "We need to meet somewhere."

"What for? Our last encounter left me ill-disposed to meeting with you."

"I have information."

"What information could you possibly have interesting enough to make me go meet you somewhere, especially when you might harbor feelings of a violent nature directed toward my ass?"

"It's about Tin Tin. He wasn't where they said he was. He was with me."

"Look, I'm sorry about your man. I know you two were close, but there's nothing you can do for him now."

"There's the truth. That mattered to him."

"Why not go to the Security Force?"

"The Security Force ain't interested in the truth. They just want their cases closed no matter how many dead disds it takes to get there. Someone's got to speak for him."

The words had the echo of sincerity, but Mac also knew that junkies could be the sweetest of talkers. "All right. Meet you at Monument Boulevard. Is ten thirty past your bedtime?"

"Fuck you, you two-bit bomboclott. Meet me at Lot Forty-Two."

"Don't you want to tell me to come alone?"

"Would it make a difference?"

"Suppose not."

"Then let's keep it honest."

• • •

Waverton, like many cities, had its shadow side. The victim of benign neglect and the original site of Waverton, Old Town existed in the penumbra of the towers, like a suburban spread abandoned and forgotten. On the clearest nights, the glow of the blue lanterns in the sky penetrated even the ghost of a city like Old Town. The Easton neighborhood of Old Town bumped up against Waverton, separated only by the Liberty River, which acted as a natural dividing line within Waverton. But one had to live in Old Town for a while to know about Portsmouth Street. And one could know about Portsmouth Street without knowing about the warehouse complex known as the Shroud. The buildings of the Shroud district were boarded up, the area always on the list for demolition, with that day never seeming to arrive. A warped fence surrounded the property, rusted and bordering a cracked pavement walkway. Winding midway through the complex, Portsmouth Street opened up against a break in the fence, large enough for a single vehicle to pass through. If one knew what one was looking at, the graffiti on the buildings told a story: a star with one of the points ending with an arrow, a crown on its side, all directing toward another building.

Lot 42 had a boarded-up front, but the grates were metal and had none of the markings of city inspectors. The pavement around the building appeared worn, but only in the affected way of folks who wore distressed clothes as fashion. Lot 42 was a bar, one off the grid of Security Force, who intentionally turned a blind eye to its patrons' untaxed synthehol trade and boutique drug use. The street brand of Stim had found its launch place here.

Mac and Ade parked outside the fence and walked the rest of the way to Lot 42. A lone figure stood outside of the crate of a building. A black man about the height of Ade, but twice the width, wore all black. A band circled his head, covering his eyes.

"We got a problem . . . officers?" he said after casual scrutiny of them.

"Don't start none, won't be none," Ade said.

"We're strictly off the clock," Mac reassured him. "Here to meet a friend and conversate."

"Who?"

"Duppy. We go way back."

"We don't take too kindly to recording devices." The man tapped his eye band while staring at Ade.

"I am upfront about it, which is why I didn't have the dermal overlay procedure. It helps me see, but there's plenty I choose to not see."

The man stepped aside and a doorway arch appeared. The pair passed through the opening.

"They not worried about us carrying?" Mac asked.

"I'm guessing everyone in here is carrying," Ade said. "Some more than others."

They made their way over to a booth just off from the main bar. A figure slumped low in its confines, as if not wanting to be seen with them. The closest patrons edged away from the pair, preferring to be out of earshot or direct lines of vision anyway.

"My man, Duppy," Mac said a little too loudly as he slid in across from Duppy.

"Cho," Duppy said with the disgust of sucking his teeth at them, "keep your voice down."

"You chose the place."

"My home turf, true. Still don't like to advertise."

"A man is certainly judged by the company he keeps," Ade said.

"How do you know Tin Tin?" Mac asked.

"We ran in the Easton MS crew. Came up together. You gotta understand, we Old Town through and through. Born here, die here. We know the drill," Duppy said.

Mac had grown up with kids like this. The streets had their own call. A siren's whisper of absent fathers or homes bereft of love or too full of drugs or abuse. Hard life any way he sliced it, and once everything became a matter of day-to-day survival, it ground away luxuries like hope. Or dreams of tomorrow. His own world had become a tunnel, and all he had seen was a life in Old Town until he'd gotten into trouble in his neighborhood, which he'd escaped by joining the military and then the LG Security Force. But in his heart, the watering hole he kept returning to was Old Town.

"You do a bid in Sizemore?" The Sizemore Correctional Facility was the stop of choice for Old Towners on their way to Wallace Field, the cemetery for those buried who left no one behind who cared about them.

"Yeah. Me and Tin Tin both. I wouldn't have survived without him. Barely did with him."

"That where you got the rune wear?" Mac had run across such tattoos before. Woven biocircuitry, like a synth net, which allowed the wearer to feel or be connected neurally to another. The designs of the tattoos acted as brands, labeling the connected partners.

"The synth tats?" Duppy held out his arms, inspecting and displaying them. "Yeah. But when we got out, we wanted to get out of the life. That's when we started talking to Chike."

"Chike? What's he got to do with it?"

"Chike's like a prophet out here. Always trying to turn folks. Get them out of their life and into his. Trying to get everyone to be straight edged like him and the Carmillon."

Ade went silent, his unblinking red eye fixed on the man-boy in front of him as if locked in, assessing him. Or Chike.

"How did Tin Tin's prints get all over Kiersten's place?"

"At the tower? I don't know. We were crew and all, but it's not like we shugged like that. I'm telling you, he was set up."

A plaintive echo of truth filled Duppy's words. Mac sifted through the facts. Tin Tin's prints were found on objects that could have been placed there, like drinking glasses. Not on any surfaces. It was possible that Tin Tin could have been set up. "So what was Tin Tin doing down there?"

"He was shugging behind that donut shop down there on Crennant Avenue, behind the tower, to see if they threw out any jellies. He was a fiend for them jellies." Duppy grew wistful, with an odd curl to his lips as if caught in a pleasant memory. Or a part of Tin Tin only he knew.

"So he was digging through garbage?" Mac asked.

"Chike, I'm telling you, had him rethinking his priorities and way of life."

"Must've been persuasive. The man does have a way," Mac said.

"Tell me about Baraka, then. What was he like?" Ade pressed forward.

"Dude was fierce. One of them stone cold, fearless types. He was the first to leap into a situation. But he was ambitious, too. Always had his eye on his next move."

"When you say that, you think he was running game?"

"Don't know. He always had an agenda he was working. Like he was down with the crew as it suited him, but he wasn't true. Then he started rolling large. Latest gear. Tossing credits about like he'd found a fountain of them."

"He putting in extra work?"

"Not that we saw. We were all on the line. It's not like you got employee of the month or anything," Duppy said.

"He skimming a little off the top for himself?" Mac asked.

"That's what we thought. Then Baraka went to ground before we could . . . discuss it."

"To ground. That's an interesting turn of phrase," Ade said.

"I just meant we couldn't find him. No one could. Until . . ." Duppy's voice trailed off.

"You weren't worried? He was your boy and all," Mac said.

"Our lifestyle ain't conducive to worry," Duppy said. "Besides, I thought maybe he'd gotten out the game for real. Start over somewhere. Get himself set up."

"What made you think of that?"

"Like I said, brother was always secretive. Liked to play things close. Calls. Meetings. It was his way. He was a ghost."

"What if Baraka wanted out?"

"You mean out of the Easton MS crew?"

"Yeah, how does that play? After all," Mac said, "in my experience, gang members don't look upon it favorably when one of their own decides to call it quits."

"You been watching too many vids. Folks around here leave this game for one of two reasons: they dead or they get a better opportunity. And Baraka ain't around no more."

• • •

Most people rode the tram, as the luxury of personal vehicles was no longer practical. A few, the very rich, had their own transportation, as did police and other emergency services personnel. Ade drove a Mantori Grendel. A classic design with all mechanical parts, not one computer chip onboard. They were designed to be EMP proof. Ade's was a large red behemoth with raised fins in the rear. What looked to be a simple convertible top was another layer of shielding. Ade enjoyed styling and profiling as much as the next man, but was still security conscious. One only had to be trapped on the wrong side of the blue line during the Trying Times™ once to take precautions quite seriously.

The road wound its way through the outer skirts of the city, through the hillside out of which Waverton had been built. For those who knew Waverton and Old Town, sometimes traveling the outer roads that looped the city was the most direct way to get from Point A to Point B. It also allowed time for the mind to wander and relax.

Sometimes, however, the burgeoning silence needed to be filled.

"Where are we headed?" Mac asked.

"To confirm this story with Chike."

"Confirm what? That Tin Tin and Duppy were his pet projects? That doesn't get us any closer to anything."

"You're right. I can drop you off."

"Nah, that's all right. I'm the curious sort. Besides, I don't have anything at home waiting for me."

"Except your grief."

Even if what Ade said was true, it felt like an invasion of privacy by pointing it out. Mac wanted the room to do his own thing in his own time. The idea of pursuing Kiersten's murderer gave him something to focus on. A distraction. Gave purpose to his anger and grief and pain. But acknowledging that, even the inadvertent push in by Ade, pressed too closely in on Mac.

"Don't you have some tragic backstory?"

"No, I'm a well-adjusted motherfucker," Ade grinned. "Wife. Two kids."

"And a brother you don't talk to. Or acknowledge." Mac popped a Redi-Smoke between his lips then caught Ade's disapproving glare. "Don't look at me like that. I am a detective, and it wasn't much of a secret. What? I don't get to ask about you or provide obtrusive commentary?"

"Family. That minefield never gets easier. It always hurts."

"So what do you do to get by?"

"Nothing."

"Nothing?" Mac asked.

"No porn. No booze. No drugs. No Stream. No comfort eating. No throwing myself into destructive relationships. None of the little addictions we use to medicate from the pain of life."

"Sometimes that pain is real," Mac said to the tinge of judgment he heard in Ade's words. "You may start off with painkillers because your shoulder isn't right from taking a bullet some years back. Then codeine 'cause your knees and back are shot but you want to stay on the job. Then one day you're studying the shit pile of your life thinking, 'I pay taxes, I'm a pretty good guy. What's with the fucked-up turn of events?' Then you just say 'Fuck it.' Whatever it takes to get by."

"I wasn't judging."

"You were, while trying to sound like you aren't. So what do you do?"

"I let it hurt."

"That it?"

"I feel the full weight of the pain. Let it remind me that there's a price to relationships . . . and that I'm still alive to feel it. I deal with it rather than keep shoving it down."

"You make it sound easy," Mac said.

"You know better," Ade said. "I'm surprised you make it out of bed most mornings."

"Shit, me too." Mac placed his Redi-Smoke back in its pack. "So what happened with you and your brother?"

"Nothing happened."

"You went into the force. He joined the hippy convicts. Something happened."

"What do you want to hear? That mommy and daddy beat us? That some rogue uncle touched him? Things aren't always so melodramatic. Sometimes dysfunction is simply . . . dysfunction."

"Well, shit. That was anticlimactic."

"Sorry to disappoint. We're just private people. We don't all need to be all searching for . . . whatever you searching for."

"What's that supposed to mean?" Mac asked, but Ade only drove.

They pulled off on the exit leading into Easton. The searing lights from the surrounding buildings, the noise of people yelling, music clanging, were all familiar and comforting. Ade parked near Chike's claimed home. A small, round-faced boy eyed them. Ade offered him ten credits to watch his car. The boy negotiated another five. As Mac and Ade strode up the sidewalk, the front door opened and Chike came out to greet them. Elia shadowed him but kept a discreet distance.

"Evening, officers. What brings you back to us on so fine an evening?" Chike asked.

"We got to talk," Ade said.

"Why now?"

"You're in the thick of it, and I can't protect you much longer."

"Is that what you been doing? Protecting me? Who the hell asked you to?" Chike stepped close to Ade; drops of spittle flew out of his mouth as he raised his voice.

"That's my job. It's what big brothers do."

"Where was my 'big brother' when I needed him?"

"Chike, I . . ."

"You. Left."

"I had to," Ade said with a too-defensive strain in his voice. "I wasn't going to go into the family business. The law wasn't for me, not like that. I had to go my own way."

"You left me with them."

"What did you want me to do? Wait for you to get through Edu-Link? I thought it would be easier on you that way. I'd take the hit for being the disappointing son . . ."

"Yeah, that'd be great if I was who they wanted. But I was an afterthought. I was their backup plan. And I couldn't even do that. You were the one they wanted. You were the one they loved."

"Don't say that."

"Why? Because it's too hard to hear out loud?" Chike shoved him. "Dad had it all worked out. Sent you to the special school. You and he went on all those trips. At the table, he was always quizzing you, grooming you. He had . . . expectations. Of you. Not of me. Never of me."

"Chike, don' start re-remembering our childhood now. You had been getting into shit and fucking up as long as I can remember."

"Because I've known for that long. Just 'cause you turned a blind eye to him . . ."

"I've been looking out for you, Chike, whether you believe it or not. And right now, shit is piling up at your doorstep."

"Here it comes. The latest iteration of 'Blame Chike.' "

"Save your self-pitying nonsense. You're out here, bringing folks together. The Carmillon. Easton MS crew. A cynical observer might think you were creating one huge operation. One legit, the other less so. But sometimes working well outside the law allowed you to get certain things done, as well as being an alternate funding source. Baraka was part of your organization. Duppy and Tin Tin were among your disciples. Elia, your lieutenant, was . . . seen in Kiersten's apartment. You don't think things start adding up and pointing to you?"

"Arrest me, then." Chike threw his arms up, a pantomime of waiting to be cuffed.

"I can't."

"Because you have no case."

"Because you're still my baby brother. And I know you didn't do this. You knew Kiersten was Security Force . . ."

"Because my brother's a cop, and I learned to smell swine a mile away."

"Fuck you." But Ade's rejoinder had no sting.

"On the real, we did know that while we were planning our latest foray against the instruments of societal ruin, she ran across some stuff."

"What sort of stuff?"

"I don't know. We didn't have a chance to look at it. But it had her scared."

"What was your . . . foray?"

"I can't tell you that. Not without a lawyer, 'cause I'd be admitting to some shit."

"It have to do with the Lifthrasir Group?"

"Yeah."

"We're up on them. So you can back off."

"No can do."

"I said we got this."

"Go ahead, then. Do your do and let me know how that works out for you. Meanwhile, we're moving ahead with our offensive."

"Offensive? Who are you, General Patton now?"

"People like the Lifthrasir Group live above the law. You can't reason with them. You can't touch them."

"But you can?"

"Sometimes the law has a way of getting in the way of justice," Chike said.

Mac smiled. When Ade turned to him, he shrugged his shoulders.

"Yeah, well why don't we let the law take one more bite of the apple? You got a name for me?" Ade asked. "Let me at least see what I can find out. Do my big brother thing."

Chike smiled. "Charleston Ptacek."

"Fuck me," Mac whispered.

• • •

Expensive artifacts—backlit on nearly invisible shelves—lined the walls of the office of Lifthrasir Group executive Charleston Ptacek. Forty-five years old. Straight black hair slicked back with old-fashioned hair grease. Round lenses rested high on his nose, frameless, but they allowed images on them like a screen. An expansive desk created a gulf between him and the detectives. An untouched cup of coffee steamed at one side of his desk. He turned the pictures of his family away from their lingering gazes. The windows of his office frosted for privacy.

Still an officious son of a bitch, Mac thought and suppressed the urge to punch him in the face.

"So good to see you again, Mr. Peterson. Timely as ever," Ptacek said.

"Mr. Ptacek, so sorry for being late. My friend here," Mac lifted his chin toward Ade, "had to have his morning pancakes and coffee. He's a beast before breakfast. You know how it goes."

Ade stepped forward, his imposing frame eliciting no reaction from the executive.

"Do you know when I saw it was you looking to speak to me, I canceled an appointment to fit you in. I haven't seen you since the civilian review board at your hearing. I just had to see what became of you for myself."

"I'm surprised that you had the time."

"Oh, I always have time for old friends."

Fuck you, you ridiculous, needle-dicked windbag. You wouldn't know good Security Force members or their work no matter how many of your corrupt buddies they sent up to Sizemore. Mac balled his fists and scooted to the edge of his chair.

"Do you know why we're here?" Ade touched Mac's shoulder and continued the questioning.

"I was briefed this morning, yes. Our name came up incidental to an investigation you're conducting. You screwed up, one of yours died, and now you need a scapegoat. Yes, I know exactly why you're here. I thought the matter settled."

"Consider this a follow-up. We're all about customer service," Mac said.

"We? Have you been reinstated into Security Force and I didn't know about it?"

"Former Detective Peterson is here as a special consultant." Ade remained composed. "There was a report of a break-in a couple of weeks ago. Mr. Ptacek, what is it you do?"

"My department oversees biosynthetics, mostly. Literally cloning parts for soldiers. Or Security Force. Get a leg blown off, have a copy of your own leg grafted back on, that sort of thing. The rest is research. Government."

"Above my pay grade, right?" Mac motioned around at the high-end office furniture and walls.

"And clearance," Ptacek said. "Tell me again how you plan to tie the Lifthrasir Group to your case?"

"Probably nothing," Ade said with a faux deflated whisper. Without taking his eyes from the man, he laid a datasheet on the table in front of Ptacek, opened it, and pointed to several lines on the screen. "Did you ever find out who was behind your burglary?"

"No." Ptacek bridged his fingers in front of his face.

"Great news, Mr. Ptacek, I might have a lead in that case," Mac said. "I suspect a woman broke in, under the guise of possibly vandalizing the place, and snooped around where she shouldn't. Maybe took notes, a few photos, information on things she shouldn't have. Important, secret shit that corporations would hire a team to find and retrieve," Mac interjected. "Information they might have failed to destroy."

"Interesting theory, Detective," Ptacek said. "Though *I* suspect you don't have a shred of evidence to back up your theories."

"We have the notes. They paint a disturbing picture."

"I doubt you understood what you were looking at, and if you did, then you are thinking entirely too small. I've got just as good an imagination for making up stories. What if aliens fell from the sky one night and said, 'Hey, want us to show you something neat?' Our friendly visitors give us the technology to tap into a near-endless energy source. Completely hypothetical, of course."

Mac scratched at his face to cover his bemusement as he chewed over Ptacek's words. "Okay. You're saying aliens gave you a near-endless source of energy?"

"Gentlemen, humanity stands on a beach studying a sea we don't understand, much like the loincloth-wearing aborigines swinging through trees—or whatever it is they do—trying to fathom our cars. The world is on the precipice of ridding itself of poverty, oil dependence, hunger."

"What do they get out of it?"

"Perhaps someplace to expand to."

"Like drilling rights or what?"

"They might not be so different from us. Look like us. With a few modifications, grow acclimated to our ways."

"The eruptions?" Ade asked.

"Naturally, a more familiar landscape, not to mention the shift in the composition of the atmosphere. Easily chalked up to pollution," Ptacek continued. "Of course, as with any new venture, there are risks. Containment can be an issue. Ruptures could occur."

"The blue lights in the sky? Like a ruptured energy spill?"

"Do you need me to connect every dot? Should there be a breach, cleanup can become an issue. We can learn much even in how the messes are treated."

"So let me get this straight . . ." Mac started.

"There's nothing to get straight. I haven't told you anything. Only a fanciful story."

"And if someone else stumbled across this story?"

"Errant stories, like energy sources, need to be gotten in front of. Contained."

"And the people in charge of this . . . containment?"

"Government money. Paid for by senators, representatives, executives, presidents . . . the kind of folks that guarantee that this investigation stops now. I would wager to guess that all of your notes, evidence, and logs are being seized right now."

"Is Deputy Chief Hollander on your payroll?"

"All of the LG Security Force is on my payroll."

"What about . . . Harley Wilson?"

"Who?"

"Why tell us anything?"

"You need to understand the precarious nature of your situation. If there is even idle speculation around the water cooler, then your worlds will cease to exist. Long before any of my people see the inside of an interrogation room." Charleston Ptacek buttoned his jacket as he got up, then extended his arm toward the door. The windows cleared for everyone to watch their dismissal. "Now, if you'll excuse me. I believe you know enough to close the book on your investigation. And you may want to watch the news feed. Good day."

Mac followed Ade out the door, mildly confused, but their mouths shut. When they stepped outside of Ptacek's office, a security detail met them to escort them out. The Lifthrasir Group's building jutted against the downtown skyline, tall and proud, indifferent to its neighboring buildings. The two detectives waited in its shadow.

Finally, Mac broke the silence. "Let's see what the chief has to say."

• • •

Every news media outlet from the *National Investigator* down to the *Brazz Report* gossip feed ran stories related to the Lifthrasir Group's release of new technology. A renewable, cheap energy source, medical advancements, a slew of drugs—the implication being that the Lifthrasir Group was about to change the way of life on the planet. The head of the Lifthrasir Group addressed world leaders, promising that some of the technology would be available completely free simply to better all of humanity. In the background of some of the photo ops Mac spied Charleston Ptacek, all but taunting him. The story for media and public consumption drowned out all concern for anything else being worked on. Ade and Mac stormed into Hollander's office.

"Whose payroll are you on? Are you running this investigation as the chief of detectives or as a cleaner for the Lifthrasir Group?"

"You talked to Ptacek?" Hollander pushed away from his desk.

"It's what you wanted us to do, right? You leave us a bread crumb, we follow it home."

"It's done. Over. You needed to know why and what the stakes were. I figured I owed you that much."

"You don't owe us shit. You owe Kiersten. She's one of us. And she goes unavenged."

"I know. And I'm sorry about that. I really am. She got too close, and for them it became a . . . teachable moment. Charleston Ptacek brazenly showing me just how untouchable they are. That anyone, be they a detective or a civilian, could be . . ." Hollander's voice cracked with shame, averting his eyes from Mac's.

Mac's face reddened. The worst part about grief was the sense of impotence. Unable to protect the ones he loved. Unable to be there for them when they needed him. And his opportunity to finally do something again left him powerless to do anything.

"I need to get out of here. I can't be in the same room as this excuse for Security Force anymore."

• • •

The sheer rock face loomed like a wall next to the road, so close it left little room for driver error. Water seeped from the stones, tears of crags broken by slate screes. Trees lined the other side of the road, a stand of soldiers at parade rest. Evenly spaced, their leaves not yet grown in for the year. With the eruptions of the strange towers and the weird iridescent skies, the Lifthrasir Group planted acres of trees to reclaim the open spaces, stripping away many concrete avenues and long-abandoned malls in favor of retooled landscape. The hills on the fringe of town were still green, deep roads cut into a valley. What were perhaps the remains of a series of towers aborted mid-eruption now sprouted with weeds and outgrowths, like the tentative facial growth on a pubescent boy. The greenery was broken by shelves of rock passed by outside of Ade's car window.

It was entirely too claustrophobic.

Mac couldn't figure out Ade's angle. A hand of friendship had been offered, no strings, no requirements. He didn't know why this man he had never encountered before this case allowed him such access. Didn't know if he wanted Mac to succeed or be a scapegoat should they fail. Didn't know what was expected. Perhaps to have a front-row seat for Mac's final burnout and then have him trotted out so that all those he had ever bent out of shape while on the LG Security Force could have their moment to point and laugh.

All Ade offered was friendship, yet Mac felt under attack by the idea. All he knew was that the walls were closing in on him. Flight or fight. The pressure like tectonic plates in the earth shifting, producing jutting spires of coarse anger.

And fear.

"If I were telling the story of Baraka's death," Mac broke the silence, "I would look for someone who had a really good reason to see him dead."

"He had everyone looking for him: the police, Kiersten, Carmillon."

"Not everyone."

"What do you mean?" Ade asked.

"The Lifthrasir Group. They were all over Kiersten, but made no mention of Baraka."

"Forget it. It's done. Case is closed. The only story to tell and the Lifthrasir Group is ahead of it, spinning it their way."

"We've got to do something. Kiersten . . ." Mac slumped in his seat, not knowing how he planned to finish that sentence.

"The foundation on which you've built your whole life is an illusion. There is more to you than this story you've written of yourself, as if all there is to you is this broken-down mope who sleeps in his clothes and bathes in booze."

"But you expect me to believe that you see beyond that?"

Ade tapped his eye and then his head. "I read people."

"It's part of the job. Having that eye helps."

"I don't need an eye to tell me that you never believed yourself to be standard-issue Security Force. You don't believe the rules apply to you. They're more like suggestions. Being booted from the force would've killed guys who were all about the job, but for you, it fed into your lone wolf/maverick thing you have going on."

"I have more fun and fewer rules doing what I do."

"I know that's what you tell yourself. Thing is, guys like you need boundaries or you lose yourselves. Kiersten was a boundary."

"You've stopped making sense again. Time for a system reboot."

"The lies you want to believe about yourself, they had to wither under the reality of her loving you. As you were. For who you were as well as who you could be."

"Whatever. You can save that psychobabble shit." Mac turned away from him, but he still heard a voice. Kiersten's voice when he was leaving her.

I'm not the one who hates you. You're the one who hates you. And I think you're more comfortable with your hate than you are risking letting anyone in who may love you.

His hate. At least he still felt something. "I drove her away like I did everyone else."

"Yeah, you have a charm about you that enjoys pushing people away. And when you encounter people that won't be pushed, you don't know how to deal with them. At best, you sort of resign yourself to being close to them."

"Better be careful. These days all I do is lose people who get close to me."

"Good thing I got no interest in that. You need a pet. Or a hobby."

"Self-destruction is my hobby."

"You think I can't spot a junkie? You spend your days wallowing in self-pity and pumping Stim into your system. Don't act all shocked. I *am* a detective, and it wasn't much of a secret."

The blue haze lit up the sky; a neon borealis, like an electric fog cover. The rains had passed for the most part, a wet spring that lingered too long. They wound down the serpentine corridor between the hills as silence settled on them again. Ade kept checking the rearview mirror, not liking what he thought he saw.

"We've picked up a tail." A set of headlights lit up Ade's face.

"You sure?"

"I'm going to pretend you didn't just insult my skills as a Security Force—detective grade, mind you—nor my common sense, as there aren't but a handful of cars out here in the first place."

The lights behind them flared as if recognized or giving up the pretense of being discreet. The beams bounded across Ade's face, the glint from his eye casting his face in steep shadows of menace. He grimaced, mostly annoyed, then hunched over the steering wheel.

"Get down." Ade reached over and shoved Mac forward.

"What?" was all Mac could mutter before the rapid-fire report of automatic weapons spraying at the car answered him.

Three distinct kinds of fire. A continuous rat-tat-tat over a repeating bang, punctuated by a large burst as if the pursuing truck was auditioning for a percussion trio of firearms. Bullets splattered across the body of the Mantori Grendel, their impact leaving cracks in the glass. The car rocked with each report of the irregular booms and wouldn't hold up for long under such a concentrated attack. One blast left deep gouges in the door as if a hand sought to punch through to grab Mac. The rear window finally gave way; glass riddled the interior ahead of a swarm of bullets. From deep within the seat well, Ade knocked out the remaining glass above him and fired blindly at the charging truck, hoping to keep them off balance. Mac huddled low in his seat, withdrawing his Cougar PT-10.

The truck neared, attempting to pull alongside. Ade gritted his teeth in a mad smile, his fingers digging into the soft mat of his steering wheel as if he could will the car to do what he wanted. The road was all but deserted at that time of night; Ade swerved in and out of their line of fire.

"Hold on. This is about to get ugly." Ade stomped on the brakes. The car veered, slamming into the truck. The truck ran up the embankment, the jagged rocks scraping the side and throwing the occupants of the truck bed around. The Grendel careened down the hillside. The car made it most of the way down on all four wheels, bouncing and nearly tipping as it sped headlong down the side. But the last crest proved too much and the car overturned, toppling onto its side.

"You okay?" Mac massaged the back of his neck as he sprang up from the back seat, where he'd landed.

"No, I'm pissed." Ade unbuckled his seat harness and climbed out the passenger window.

By the time Mac crawled through the window, Ade was already a good way up the hill, positioning himself for the shooters, ready for them to come after them. Mac had wrenched something in his lower back in the car crash, and who knew how many new bruises he'd be adding to his collection by the morning. In a sore lope, he moved to the lowest tier of trees to keep Ade in his sights. The world spun at crazy angles. His equilibrium was shot, and he needed a minute to clear his head.

"This way," a distant voice cried. Mac counted four men, possibly a fifth, but with the blue luminescence playing games with the tree shadows, not to mention his still-blurry vision, he couldn't be sure. Whoever they were, they were loud and untrained. Thugs "R" Us was obviously having a clearance sale on grunt-level hitters. Mac almost felt insulted that he wasn't worth digging deeper into someone's pocket for a quality hit.

"Over here, you shitbirds!" Mac took wild shots in their general direction. As he only needed to be a distraction, he didn't try too hard to actually hit anyone.

This far from the city proper, the azure field above them illuminated the sky the way a snow-covered ground lightened the night sky. The strange glow wreaked havoc on the senses, alternately piercing shadows then deepening them. Unlike the pursuing men, Ade's eye compensated for the light shifts and targeted perfectly in the pitch black. Ade cleared the shadow of the trees. His twin semiautomatic crowd-control machine guns roared to life. Precise bursts cut down the first two thugs without any effort, splintering bullets through their torsos. The sloped, rocky terrain played to his advantage. The men were caught in their downhill trots, unable to stop in time or do little more than dive for cover. Ade wasn't in the mood to play coy. The two remaining men slowed, stumbling over the bodies of their fallen comrades. They attempted to draw a bead on him, but with robotic accuracy, he riddled them with shots. They jerked violently at the end of a concise burst, their bodies dead before they knew to collapse. Arms still outstretched, Ade scanned for further movement.

"That all of them?" Mac asked.

"No." Ade trained his weapon on a spot in front of him. "But if he makes any sudden movements, it will be his last. Then that will be the last of them. Drop your weapon."

"I'm unarmed. Officer." The man pointedly said the word "officer" as if reminding Ade he had rules he had to play within. A squat figure with a bulbous belly whose shirt barely covered it. Thick arms, once heavily muscled but gone to flab. A sour face held a lifetime of disappointments through a biker mustache over a gleaming smile full of sin.

"Detective," Ade corrected. "On your knees. Lace your fingers behind your head."

"Who are you?" Mac asked.

"Does it matter?" the man responded.

"I need to know whose mother to notify to pick up what's left of your body."

"Your tone is disrespectful. We do not like . . . constables . . . of any sort. Especially those with too many questions."

"Any shade of constable irritate you more than others?" Ade asked.

"You are mistaken. You're all blue. Besides, I'm not seeing the inside of a cell."

"You assume you're making it to a cell."

"We all have roles to play, Detective."

"What's mine?" Mac aimed his gun directly at the man's temple.

"Rabid dog needing to be put down?"

"Another fan club member," Ade yanked the man's arms down one at a time and began to cuff him. "Like I said, you have a charm about you."

"What's this about?" Mac asked.

"This is about stories." The man grimaced as Ade snapped the cuffs tight. "Every people has a story to tell. When all is said and done, any racial identity is about shared story. A story that defines them and continues to form them. When stories are reduced to law or dogma, their vitality is drained. When people no longer tell or listen to others' stories, they become locked in their provincial mindset, cultural ghettos of their own making. In fact, when people become so removed from another's story, they become compelled to destroy those others' stories, for they suggest other ways of living. Their stories become a threat."

"You're one of . . . them, aren't you?"

The man didn't reply.

"So you've been watching us? Our investigation?" Ade asked.

"I'm not watching you specifically. You're blocking my view as I observe a civilization in its death throes. Wanton sexuality. An addicted populace. By indulging all your so-called freedoms, you lost all sense of discipline. You have lost your center."

"Do you understand what this disd is talking about?"

"Not a damn word. Are you a member of the Carmillon?" Mac asked.

"Dissident is right. But no, I'm not a member of any group. I avoid politics."

"I'm done playing twenty questions with him. I'm dumping his ass in a cell and let the system sort it out," Ade said.

The man laughed.

"Something funny?"

"You want justice."

"I'd settle for you on death row."

"You would have to burn down your own house to get to me. Either way, we still win," the man said.

The man halted midstep as if he gagged on something. Ade shook him to nudge him forward. The man spasmed, his arms wrenching out of socket since his hands were still cuffed behind him. Falling to his knees, the man was caught by Ade, who screamed at him. Mac dashed over, and they rolled him onto his back. Ade was about to clean the man's airway when the man's eyes seemed to dry out. They grayed then shriveled in their sockets. His skin tightened then drew away from his eyes, his mouth a taut, forced grin. His face split; a crease zipped down as if an invisible blade flensed the flesh from his bone, graying as it went. The flesh smoldered. Ade and Mac both scampered away from it as if not wanting to get any of the man on them, fearing whatever contagion that consumed him. Within minutes, the man's flesh and bones had been reduced to ash.

"You ever see something you wish you could *un*see?" Mac asked. "Your parents screwing in the bedroom. Your grandma stepping out of the shower."

"This make your list?"

"Do you drink?"

"No," Ade said.

"I'll have to teach you."

• • •

The glowing canvas lit the ground with a powder-blue haze, giving certain objects, viewed at the proper angles, a slight diaphanous quality the way oil slicks on water's surface had a way of looking pretty under the right circumstances.

Tonight, two officers stared up at the night sky as they drank from a bottle of twenty-five-year-old Macallan. Kiersten had stashed away the single malt for special occasions, and they drank in her honor.

"Fuck you, moon." Mac poured a stiff drink straight into his mouth, then passed the bottle over to Ade.

"Fuck you, stars." Ade swallowed.

"Fuck you, big buildings doing your sausage dance out of the earth."

"Fuck you, strange alien blue shit."

"Fuck you, police commissioners an' all you other ball-less sacks of brass shit."

"Fuck you, government pricks covering up all your asses."

"Fuck you, Lifthrasir Group. And your officious prick CEOs."

"Fuck you, you whining pinhead sheep going about your days without a care outside of your own business."

"Fuck you, Kiersten, for leaving me," Mac said.

Ade averted his gaze to give the man space to grieve.

"Am I interrupting or can anyone join this party?" Chike asked. Elia strode a few feet behind him, white hair sprouting out from under her bowler cap, then leaned against her walking stick. A cross on a necklace dangled from around her neck.

"You're late," Mac said.

"You're drunk."

"Technically, he's shitfaced," Ade corrected. "Which means he's prone to making monumental errors in judgment."

"What about you?" Chike turned to Ade.

"I'm not even here. I closed my file, turned over all my notes, and went home to await my new assignment tomorrow."

"People don't give a fuck anymore," Mac started. "Laws are supposed to protect people, not leave them out like bait in a trap."

"He all right? What's he going on about?" Chike thumbed in Mac's direction.

"Don't know. Told you, I'm not even here." Ade took another swig of the Macallan.

"Thing is, all the evidence had to be turned in. Case closed. Everything is being buried as we speak." Mac took the bottle from him. "The end comes not with mighty firing of weapons or grand pronouncements, but with a bureaucrat's pen. A couple signed slips of paper and everything's gone."

"So now you know?" Chike asked. "The eruptions, the blue haze, Lifthrasir?"

Mac laughed. "The thing about justice is that sometimes it has to move around the law. Take Spookbot over there. He turned in all of his case notes and turned over the evidence to the deputy chief." Mac lit up a Redi-Smoke. "I, on the other hand, may have requisitioned a notebook or two." Mac winked at Chike.

"That better not mean more paperwork for me to have to fill out," Ade said.

"Merely returning unclaimed property to its rightful owner." Mac turned to Elia. "Does that cross mean anything to you or did you find it in one of your forays?"

A fine filigree of wrinkles framed her small mouth when she smiled. Such a horrible, alien smile. "Where I come from, there is no concept known as God. There is only life or death. The in-between has no intrinsic value. Attachments are meaningless. We are what we were born to be. I am Xa'nthi, warrior class. My kind are bred for battle. Here on your world, there is more. There is . . . connection. Meaning. Things worth dying for."

Mac tossed the notebook to her. "I trust you know what to do with it."

"I have a few ideas."

"One way or another," Mac said, "we need to take the fight to them."

• • •

Mac waited in the doorway to his apartment. The lights automatically burned to life, illuminating the room to perfect ambience. His place, little more than a hovel, was dark and had a cloying moisture to the air, a faint hint of mildew to everything. He collapsed into his bed, exhausted but not sleepy. A single disheveled comforter covered his mattress. Four pillows were piled at the head of the bed, three more than he needed, but some nights he shoved the others to his side and it left the illusion that his bed wasn't empty. Nights like tonight, however, that wouldn't be enough. He needed to keep moving, so as not to have to think. To think meant swelling on the anxiousness that filled his ear. The emptiness. Kiersten occupied a space in his heart. Not a large space. There wasn't room for anything or anyone to occupy a large space in his heart. The space she took up was more like a wedge, something that propped a door shut, staving off the rushing darkness and loneliness that awaited him once it was gone. And she was gone.

Mac reached inside his jacket for his Redi-Smokes, only to realize the package was empty. He crumpled it up and threw it against the wall. His hands trembled. He needed another dose of Stim, but at the same time, didn't. Nor did he want a drink. His soul itched, but he couldn't quite find the right way to scratch it.

The nagging voice left him unable to find a comfortable position in bed. The day's events flitted through his mind, and a strange anxiousness, a longing, filled his heart. The case wasn't closed, not really. Whoever murdered Kiersten was still out there, drawing breath and living life. And once again, he couldn't be the man she needed him to be. He needed something to take the edge off. It was more than late-night horniness. He just needed some sort of respite, and peace was not soon in coming. Not for people like him.

Finally he settled on the idea of a companion. It wasn't as if he hadn't paid for tail before. Those relationships were pure, a simple transaction. Base need met with commerce. No expectations. No investments. No commitment. No judgment. Then and now, Kiersten haunted him. Then, knowing that he couldn't be with her without tearing her down, he had retreated to the bartered embrace of companions. Now, with her gone, he sought solace in the illusion of relationship. In the illusion that someone cared about him and would hold him in the nights. In the illusion that he wasn't the failure he knew himself to be.

The call house said they'd send a companion right over. Five minutes later, the front alarm sounded at the outer door of his building. When he checked the vid screen, a woman in a raincoat, broad hat, and sunglasses that covered nearly half her face peered back at him. He buzzed her in. Wearing only a white tank top over pinstriped boxers, he flopped on the edge of his bed while he waited for her. The door opened, half closed—like a held breath—then shut all the way. She didn't have to knock on the entryway frame or give a polite cough to let him know she was there.

She was small, much smaller than he would have guessed from her appearance on the vid screen. Smooth brown hair pulled back into a bun, rimless glasses, and a moue with a garish shade of red lipstick smeared across it, which made her mouth look huge. Like a fussy librarian, except the way the raincoat cinched tight at the waist and revealed her generous cleavage he knew that she wore nothing underneath.

"Ident chip?" She held out her hand, waiting for him to place his in it.

"Business up front, I see." Mac held out his hand. She waved her portable scanner over it.

"Mac Peterson," she read from her scanner.

"At your service." Mac reached up and twitched her glasses free of her nose. She remained perfectly still, only her eyes tracking his movements. He set the glasses down on the mantle over his bed. "And you are?"

"Olga. Do you need a last name?"

"No."

Confident in her charms, she relaxed, her head canted to the side and her lips parted a little. Her hands trailed down his side, resting playfully just below his waist. Her weight leaned into him, and by instinct his arms wrapped around her. As if in a practiced dance, she pushed him away, taking a half step backward herself. She undid the belt holding the coat shut. Draped only by the coat, her naked silhouette approached him. A provocative smile crossed her lips. She planted her hand dead center in his chest and shoved him onto the bed. Straddling him, her fingers dug into his hair to draw him close, plunging her tongue into his mouth, long and hard. His hands wriggled at his boxers. She batted them away, not breaking the kiss. Her hands slipped within the band of his underwear. As he lost himself in the moment, he let out an easy sigh.

A primitive part of his brain, an echo of his soldier's instinct, alerted him that something wasn't right. The doors. Like a held breath. Held too long. The shadows on the other side of the room shifted. His dampener jacket rustled from where it hung across the room. A red dot gleamed in his direction and a figure rushed from the darkness. His Cougar PT-10 was under his pillow, but Mac barely had time to shift Olga's weight out of the way to absorb the brunt of the attack. That was when the slight charge at the back of his neck stabbed at him and his world went black.

• • •

Mac hated being knocked unconscious. He hated the wave of nausea that accompanied coming to. He hated the pounding in his head, like kids running up and down wood stairs. He hated the dizziness and disorientation as if he'd been on a drunken bender and needed to remember where he had passed out. Mac's first thought was that the companion and her accomplice might have run a Murphy game on him. The problem was that with companionship having been made legal, there was little to gain by a pro and her erstwhile pimp rolling a john for whatever credits they could scrounge, especially futile with ident chips. Even if they tossed his place, they were in Old Town. There weren't exactly a lot of eccentric wealthy people living there by choice. No, there had to be something else.

Seated upright, Mac didn't change his slumped posture, careful to feign continued unconsciousness while he assessed his situation. His shoulders burned, but Mac was happy to feel anything. His arms were behind him, each hand zip-tied to a part of the chair, which gave him little wiggle room. Still able to wangle his fingers. Though they were cold and increasingly numb. His legs weren't bound to the chair, but his feet burned with a thousand pinpricks, as they had fallen asleep. His muscles stretched tight, each bruise and cut rose to the surface of his attention, throbbing reminders of his ill-tended accumulation of hurts. He allowed himself a moment of vanity, feeling ridiculous in his tank top and boxers. Mac chanced opening an eye and craning his head up as much as possible. From the look of things, he was in a warehouse of some sort. One with the distinctive odor of chemicals. He made out a few approaching figures, so he shut his eyes.

"What did you summon me down here for?" Mac recognized the voice of Charleston Ptacek.

"We have Peterson," Olga said.

"So? Who told you to do that?"

"Your boy brought me. We can't afford the loose end. It's the Kiersten Wybrow scenario all over again."

"So you brought me down here to sort out your mess?"

"We tried it your way, look where it got us. Now we do it ours."

"No point in pretending you can't hear us, Mr. Peterson," Ptacek said. "We've gone through a lot of trouble to accommodate you."

"You shouldn't have put yourself out." Mac sat up straight, adjusting for the dull ache that had settled in his lower back.

"Are you stupid?"

"Immensely." An empty warehouse, its disposable construction little more than a giant metal barn. A heavy door on a thick frame separating this room from the next. Mac tested the ties. He'd have better luck going through the chair itself. No jacket. No Cougar PT-10. He didn't have a lot to work with. Mac turned to his female captor. "I'm guessing Olga's not your real name."

"You've stirred up quite the little furor over the last couple of days. Your name came up so often I had to meet you for myself," Olga said. "You've certainly managed to piss off a lot of people."

"Well, they say a man's life should be measured by the quality of his enemies. By any measure, my life is shit."

"Putting on a brave front. I like that. A little coarse, but not without your charms."

"I've been told that I have my own brand of charm."

"You should have dropped all of this. Instead, you run off to tell the Carmillon . . . what? What did you hope to accomplish?" Ptacek marched by a table. He inspected a few of the instruments, holding up the occasional blade or screwdriver for Mac's scrutiny. Ptacek made exaggerated faces of disgust at the possible destructive use of each implement before setting them back down.

"What's this all about?" Mac asked.

"I doubt you'd understand. Though it all comes back to your jumpers in a way."

"The apocalyptos?"

"My theory is that they subconsciously suspect the truth." Ptacek paced the floor, going back and forth with the haughtiness of a gloating hyena. "When confronted with ideas so much bigger than themselves, ideas which shatter the carefully constructed paradigms they live in, some people can't face the utter futility of their lives."

"What sort of big ideas?" Mac asked.

"That we aren't alone. That we aren't the center of the universe. That there is a whole other dimension to reality that sometimes bleeds into ours. That there may be wars fought on whole different planes of existence, all around us, that help determine our destiny. That our lives are not our own."

"It's what you were talking about with the aliens, the idea exchange, the accident which left the . . . tears . . . in the sky."

"That story isn't the real story. Not the whole of it, anyway. It goes much, much deeper."

"What's the big plan? You want to take over the world?"

"No, son, we already have. Don't look so shocked. The world as you know it ended years ago, smothered to death in its sleep. Ending with a whimper. We've been here for a generation now. Blended into your world on your terms and you never noticed. We attended your schools, climbed to the tops of your corporations, embedded ourselves in every aspect of your society: finance, media, science and technology, military, politics, religion. That was Phase One."

"Let me guess, Phase Two: terraforming Earth to suit your needs."

"Very good, Mr. Peterson."

"You give me too much credit. I don't get any of this. Kiersten was undercover investigating the Easton MS crew. During one of their 'forays,' she runs across your little operation. What it is, I'm still not sure. All I have is your version of coming clean."

"Olga is also a member of that esteemed group."

"You expect me to believe that you two are aliens? You don't really look like one."

"What'd you expect? Scales and a tail?" Olga asked.

"I . . ." Mac didn't know what he expected. Little gray men with big heads and large eyes. Blue giants with whole new ways of life. Horned warriors set on conquering. But he'd read a lot of fantasy stories when he was younger.

"Something like that."

"It'd be hard to blend in with your people that way."

"Case should've been closed, but you kept digging," Ptacek said. "That was always your problem. You don't know when to leave well enough alone and stop digging. You have to keep pushing and pushing until everything around you is left in ruin."

"This time it was because my partner doesn't like loose ends and becomes grouchy and suspicious when delivered a patsy with a great big bow on him. Much more so when said patsy has people who care about him. So now we start nosing around and someone makes a ham-fisted attack on us. Which meant we were on the right track, we just didn't know how to get to you."

"The subsequent attack was unfortunate. That wasn't us," Ptacek said.

"That was my bad." Another figure stepped out from the shadows. About six feet tall, a solid build but not overly muscled. A black vest, worn open, revealed a muscled, sweaty chest. Camo military fatigues and combat boots finished off his look. Clean shaven and bald, a band covered his eyes. He removed it to give Mac a more clear inspection. A dermal overlay procedure had been done, but the man had an implant much like Ade's, though without any tubing or accessories.

"Allow me to present—" Ptacek said.

"Harley Wilson," Mac finished.

"You don't seem that surprised."

"I was beginning to suspect. Once we started thinking about all the people after Harley, none of them had enough motivation to want him dead. Quite the opposite. The only one who would benefit from his death would be him. Then I thought about all of your prosthetics and thought it would be real easy to create enough material to stage a murder scene. Score some bioteched organs and two new souls join the army of apocalyptos leaping into the void."

"It seems I was remiss in underestimating you, Mr. Peterson. My colleagues, though less subtle, have the right idea."

"Nice eye. A friend of mine has one like it." Mac worked the ties against the chair. He only needed a little more time.

"Not like this one. This right here is the latest generation of wetware," Harley said. "A gift from my employers."

"It still has a few kinks. Like signals getting crossed or piggy-backed on when you're transmitting to your bosses. Or vice versa."

"You're referring to the Quavay Middleton incident. More sloppy work, really. But young Master Harley is quite adept at cleaning up his messes. It's why we continue him in our employ."

"I like to keep things simple," Mac said. "You're the bad guy. All I need to know is which one of you killed Kiersten."

"Kiersten got too close. A casualty of the truth. She was killed by a larger plan. Faceless corporations, collateral damage from an errant memo."

"All this shit—the energy fallout, the terraforming, the colonization—all that is too big for me. All I need to know is who did the deed."

"Harley, of course." Ptacek turned to walk out. "And I'll leave you to his tender mercies."

Baraka backhanded Mac across the face before Ptacek left the room. A wan smile crossed the executive's face as he pushed through the door. Baraka's ham-sized fist landed several blows in Mac's ribs. Without his jacket to absorb some of the force, a bone cracked. Each punch rattled the framework of the chair. Mac was glad to already be sitting as his legs went rubbery. Baraka squatted low, meeting Mac at eye level. Mac met the man's intense silence by spitting in his face. Unmoved, Baraka patiently wiped the sputum from his face, reached for Mac's left hand, and snapped his pinky finger. His body convulsed, a shudder as a wave of fresh pain washed through him. His face twisted in agony.

A crash came from down the hallway, followed by a rush of raised voices that soon became pointed shouts. Screams erupted, trailing the staccato pop of automatic weapon fire. Mac only needed a window of opportunity, but he would have to act quickly. Adrenaline surged in his system, coasting on a wave of panic. The world slowed to stop-motion.

At the first sounds of ruckus, a well-trained Baraka sprang up and brought to bear Mac's Cougar PT-10. Mac leaned forward in his chair and pushed to his feet, charging at Baraka. Baraka drew down on him. Mac smashed into him, leading with the edge of the chair. Baraka got off a shot. The heat of the discharge singed Mac's cheek, but he dived, barely avoiding the bullet's path. The impact demolished the chair enough for him to slip his bonds.

Baraka swung around and pistol-whipped him with a blow to the side of the head. Mac returned with a punch, hammering down, causing the gun to clatter across the floor toward the thick door. His initial blows deflected, Mac charged again. Fists flying with abandon, he whirled and threw himself against Baraka.

Baraka lashed out, two chops to the sides of Mac's neck. The muscles went numb and a shard of pain jolted into Mac's skull. In desperation, Mac dashed his skull into Baraka's, the force of which sent Mac reeling as he remembered too late that much of Baraka's skull had been replaced with metal to accommodate his eye. Mac clamped his teeth down and succeeded only in smearing the blood on his lip in an attempt to wipe it off.

Lunging again, not wanting to give Baraka time or space to put his training and youth to use, Mac clawed at him then wrapped his hairy, bare legs around him, wrestling until he found himself on top of Baraka. He hated that he was self-conscious to the point of distraction that he was clad only in underwear and his junk was so vulnerable. Twisting, drawing his attacker along with him, they tumbled through the doorway. Baraka slipped in an elbow to his head before Mac could get him sufficiently entangled.

The next room sounded like it held a barely contained war. A couple of people skittered down the hallway; a few wore protective filter masks and gloves. They startled both men, but Baraka used the opportunity to slip from Mac's grasp. Mac dodged Baraka's combat boot, which landed only inches from his head. He couldn't imagine the state of his skull had the blow connected. He neither was in the mood nor had the luxury to fight fair. Baraka kicked out again, but Mac rolled then scampered after the gleaming metal. Too late, Baraka realized what Mac was going for.

Mac fired off a shot through the red target of Baraka's eye before he realized he'd even squeezed the trigger.

No joy. No relish. Only action.

Mac bent down to inspect the body. Putting his feet up to Baraka's, he decided the other man's boots were a good enough fit, certainly better than his bare feet. Ditto the camo pants.

The air grew thick, and Mac had a difficult time breathing. The gun battle hit tanks, releasing chemicals into the air. Bullets pocked the wall inches from him. Strays from the gunfight on the other side of the door, but Mac couldn't worry about that. He took cover behind a nearby counter. Two dead bodies had fallen on each other at the end of a hallway. The gunfire stopped. Mac peeked around the corner of the counter.

Ade's twin semiautomatic crowd-control machine guns pointed directly at Charleston Ptacek. "Everyone stay right where they are!"

Mac eased out from his hiding spot. Ade glanced at him, and something akin to relief flickered across his face. "How'd you find me?"

"Finally was able to backtrace the signal that hijacked my eye and thought I'd bring some friends to the party." Ade upticked his chin toward Elia and members of the Carmillon. He then turned his attention to Mac's wardrobe. "I don't want to burst your moment or anything, but I really hope you don't think the glasses help with your look when you're dressed like an army clown."

"Beats running around in my drawers. Don't ask."

"Are you here to arrest us, Officer? Even if you were to go through the motions of detaining me, Mr. Peterson's presence in the case, much less the Carmillon, would be enough for our team of lawyers to sink any criminal case brought against us."

"Nope, I just came for my friend," Ade said. "I think we all know there's no case to be made here. The bosses wouldn't let that happen. You see, the way I heard tell is that not everyone is in agreement with your planet's plans for Earth. Some of you, during your time here, became sympathetic to us lowly meatbags. Even went so far as to defect and join the resistance. You'll want to leave my boy be."

"My mother was a bit of a control freak," said Ptacek. "Remarkable woman, really. A force of nature. She had to have things her way. On every point. No matter how big or small the issue was, she was all in, fighting tooth and nail, as it were, to make sure things came out her way. An indiscriminate waste of energy, if you ask me. Now me? I'm a go along to get along sort of man. I keep my eye on the prize. You see, eighty percent of the time, what other people want doesn't matter; that is, doesn't interfere with my agenda. So I let them have their way. I put up token resistance; they feel they've won something and go off mollified. Now that last twenty percent, that's what matters. Those are the battles worth fighting. That's where wars are won and lost. Me? I'm a bureaucrat. Strictly middle management. I'm sure you can be accommodated before this escalates to an even greater mess."

"So what you're saying is that there's someone shitting on your head while you shit on mine," Mac said.

"If my vocabulary were stripped of all polysyllabic words, then yes. We all have bosses. The same bosses who cover the murder of one of their own. Who probably wouldn't blink twice about another unfortunate accident, but there's only so much they are willing to stomach. This matter is done."

"Another memo and it's all done."

"Not especially gratifying, but yes."

Mac bundled up his mouth in a swallow of resolve, determined to bottle up the chasm yawning inside him. The serpent in his belly stirred. Anger rattled, his grief a rearing with a hiss. His Cougar PT-10 drew a bead on Charleston Ptacek before his mind caught up to what was going on. And he shot Charleston Ptacek.

"Obviously self-defense." Ade towered over the crumpled body.

"Obviously." Mac sidled across from him, also peering down. "You all may want to get out of here."

Ade patted his shoulder as he went by, leaving him to his feelings. Mac searched the space. It gradually dawned on him why it seemed so familiar. It was a Stim production lab. Obviously funded by the Lifthrasir Group. Finding a gallon jug filled with a liquid, he sniffed it and judged it sufficiently flammable. He punched a hole in it with a screwdriver and let the liquid pool before he poured a trail of it to the front door, where he met Ade.

"Everyone out?"

"All of our people. The rats scattered at the first shots."

"Good enough."

Mac lit a Redi-Smoke and took a long drag from it. Then he tossed it.

A blue flame, like an electric arc, swept along the liquid path into the building. Tanks erupted into a blossom of orange and red flames. The rush of intense heat like a long-held breath released.

• • •

No matter the state of the economy, construction continued in Waverton. They continued building to provide the hope of a better tomorrow. Neighborhoods were razed to build new ones. The words "Escape while you can" had been spray-painted along the wall of the remaining husk of a building—which had been condemned as the site of an illegal Stim lab. Bud victims shuffled about the remains of the building, without words, sifting through the debris, scavenging for anything useful.

"What do you think?" Mac asked.

"Life is pain. You have to learn how to take it."

"Or dish it out."

They watched the Bud colony march about. The spires of Waverton loomed all around them. The media spun the story. The Lifthrasir Group was still hailed as pioneers and saviors. The world continued to transform around them. But they had to find a way to muddle through.

"Hope it was worth it. You're on their radar now."

"You too."

"We didn't really do any good. Lifthrasir wasn't just one empty building," Ade said.

"Yeah, but it felt good." Mac instinctively reached for a Redi-Smoke. Instead, he slipped a toothpick in his mouth and waited out the craving.

"Like a two-year-old's temper tantrum."

"Yeah, but the occasional temper tantrum has its place."

"That's fine. Just don't ask me to change your ass."

MADELINE ASHBY

BE SEEING YOU

(2015)

"DOESN'T IT GET, like, distracting? Hearing me breathing?" Hwa asked.

Only at first, her boss said.

Her feet pounded the pavement. She ducked under the trees that made up the Fitzgerald Causeway Arboretum. Without the rain pattering on the hood of her jacket, she could hear the edges of Síofra's voice a little better. The implant made sure she got most of the bass tones as a rumble that trickled down her spine. Consonants and sibilants, though, tended to fizzle out.

You get up earlier than I do, so I've had to adjust.

Hwa rounded the corner to the Fitzgerald Hub. It swung out wide into the North Atlantic, the easternmost edge of the city, a ring of green on the flat gray sea. Here the view was best. Better even than the view from the top of Tower Five, where her boss had his office. Here you could forget the oil rig at the city's core, the plumes of fire and smoke, the rusting honeycomb of containers that made up Tower One where Hwa lived. Here you couldn't even see the train. It screamed along the track overhead, but she heard only the tail end of its wail as the rain diminished.

"It's better to get a run in before work. Better for the metabolism."

So I've heard.

Síofra had a perfect metabolism. It was a combination of deep brain stimulation that kept him from serotonin crashes, a vagus nerve implant that regulated his insulin production, and whatever gentle genetic optimization he'd had in utero. He ate everything he wanted. He fell asleep for eight hours a night, no interruptions. He was a regular goddamn Ubermensch.

Hwa just had a regular old-fashioned human body. No permanent implants. No tweaking. She'd eaten her last slice of bread the day before joining the United Sex Workers of Canada as a bodyguard. Now that she worked for Lynch as the bodyguard for their heir apparent, the only thing that had changed about her diet was the amount of coffee she drank.

"Look out your window," she said.

Give me your eyes.

She shook her head. Could he see that? Maybe. She looked around for botflies. She couldn't see any, but that didn't mean anything. "I'm not wearing them."

Why not?

"They're expensive. I could slip and fall while I'm running."

Then we would give you new ones.

"Wouldn't that come out of my pay?"

A soft laugh that went down to the base of her spine. *Those were the last owners of this city. Lynch is different.*

Hwa wasn't so sure about that. Lynch rode in on a big white copter and promptly funded a bunch of infrastructure improvement measures, but riggers were still leaving. Tower One was starting to feel like a ghost town.

Then again, the Lynch family *was* building an alternative reactor, right in the same place where the milkshake straw poked deep into the Flemish Pass Basin and sucked up the black stuff. It was better insulated, they said, under all that water. It just meant the oil was going away.

All towns change, Hwa. Even company towns. We're better for this community than the previous owners. You'll see.

She rolled her neck until it popped. All the way over at the top of Tower Five, her boss hissed in sympathy. "Look out your window," she reminded him.

Fine, fine. An intake of breath. He was getting up. From his desk, or from his bed? *Oh,* he murmured.

Hwa stared into the dawn behind the veil of rain. It was a line of golden fire on a dark sea, thinly veiled behind shadows of distant rain. "I time it like this, sometimes," she said. "Part of why I get up early."

I see.

She heard thunder roll out on the waves, and in a curious stereo effect, heard the same sound reverberating through whatever room Síofra was in.

May I join you, tomorrow?

Hwa's mouth worked. She was glad he couldn't see her. The last person she'd had a regular running appointment with was her brother. Which meant she hadn't run with anyone in three years. Then again, maybe it would be good for Síofra to learn the city from the ground up. He spent too much time shut up behind the gleaming ceramic louvers of Tower Five. He needed to see how things were on the streets their employers had just purchased.

She grinned. "Think you can keep up with me?"

Oh, I think I can manage.

• • •

Of course, Síofra managed just fine. He showed up outside Tower One at four thirty in the morning bright-eyed and bushy-tailed as a cartoon mascot. Like everything else about him, even his running form was annoyingly perfect. He kept his chin up and his back straight throughout the run. He breathed evenly and smoothly and carried on a conversation without any issues. At no point did he complain of a stitch in his side, or a bone spur in his heel, or tension in his quads. Nor did he suggest that they stretch their calves first, or warm up, or anything like that. He just started running.

A botfly followed them the entire way.

"Do we really need that?" Hwa asked. "We can ping for help no problem, if something happens." She gestured at the empty causeway. "Not that anything's going to happen."

"What if you have a seizure?" her boss asked.

Hwa almost pulled up short. It took real and sustained effort not to. She kept her eyes on the pavement instead. They had talked about her condition only once. Most people never brought it up. Maybe that was a Canadian thing. After all, her boss had worked all over the world. They were probably a lot less polite in other places.

"My condition's in my halo," she muttered.

"Pardon?"

"My halo has all my medical info," she said, a little louder this time. She shook her watch. "If my specs detect a change in my eye movement, they broadcast my status on the emergency layer. Everyone can see it. Everyone with the right eyes, anyway."

"But you don't wear your specs when you're running," he said, and pulled forward.

The route took them along the Demasduwit Causeway, around Tower Two, down the Sinclair Causeway, and back to Tower Two. It was a school day, which meant Hwa had to scope New Arcadia Secondary before Joel Lynch arrived for class. This meant showering and dressing in the locker room, which meant she had to finish at a certain time, which meant eating on schedule, too. If she ate before the run, she tended to throw up.

She was going to explain all this, when Síofra slowed down and pulled up to Hwa's favorite twenty-four-hour cart and held up two fingers. "Two number sixes," he said. He stood first on one leg and then another, pulling his calf up behind him as he did. From behind the counter, old Jorge squinted at him until Hwa jogged up to join him. Then he smiled.

"You have a friend!" He made it sound like she'd just run a marathon. Which it felt like she had—keeping up with Síofra had left her legs trembling and her skin dripping.

"He's my boss." She leaned over and spat out some of the phlegm that had boiled up to her throat during the run. "What he said. And peameal." She blinked at Síofra through sweat. He was looking away, probably reading something in his lenses. "You like peameal?"

"Sorry?"

"Peameal. Bacon. Do you like it?"

"Oh. I suppose."

She glanced at Jorge. "Peameal. On the side."

Jorge handed them their coffees while the rest of the breakfast cooked. Now the city was waking up, and the riggers joining the morning shift were on their way to the platform. A few of them stood blinking at the other carts as they waited for them to open up.

"How did you know my order?" Hwa asked.

Síofra rolled his neck. It crunched. He was avoiding the answer. Hwa already suspected what he would say. "I see the purchases you make with the corporate currency."

She scowled. "I don't always have the eggs baked in avocado, you know. Sometimes I have green juice."

"Not since the cucumbers went out of season."

Hwa stared. Síofra cocked his head. "You're stalking me."

"I'm not stalking you. This is just how Lynch does things. We know what all our people buy in the canteen at lunch, because they use our watches to do it. It helps us know what food to buy. That way everyone can have their favorite thing. The schools here do the same thing—it informs the farm floors what to grow. This is no different."

Hwa sighed. "I miss being union."

• • •

Joel Lynch's vehicle drove him to the school's main entrance exactly fifteen minutes before the first bell. Hwa stood waiting for him outside the doors. He waved their way in—the school still did not recognize her face, years after she'd dropped out—and smirked at her.

"How are your legs?" he asked.

"Christ, does my boss tell you *everything*?"

"Daniel just said I should go easy on you today!" Joel tried hard to look innocent. "And that maybe we didn't have to do leg day today, if you didn't really want to."

"You trying to get out of your workout?"

"Oh, no! Not at all! I was just thinking that—"

"Good, because we're still doing leg day. My job is protecting you, and how I protect you is making you better able to protect yourself. Somebody tries to take you, I need you to crush his instep with one kick and then run like hell. Both of which involve your legs."

"So, leg day."

Hwa nodded. "Leg day."

You can crush someone's instep with one kick?

Hwa rolled her eyes and hoped her specs caught it. "Of course I can," she subvocalized.

I think I'd pay good money to see that.

"Well it's a good thing I'm on the payroll, then."

The school day proceeded just like all the others. Announcements. Lectures. Worksheets. French. Past imperfect, future imperfect. Lunch. People staring at Joel, then sending each other quick messages. Hwa saw it all in the specs—the messages drifting across her vision like dandelion fairies. In her vision, the messages turned red when Joel's name came up. For the most part it didn't. While she wore the uniform and took the classes just like the other students, they knew why she was there. They knew she was watching. They knew about her old job.

"Hwa?"

Hwa turned away from the station where Joel was attempting squats. Hanna Oleson wore last year's volleyball T-shirt and mismatched socks. She also had a wicked bruise on her left arm. And she wouldn't quite look Hwa in the eye.

"Yeah?" Hwa asked.

"Coach says you guys can have the leg press first."

"Oh, good. Thanks." She made Hanna meet her gaze. The other girl's eyes were bleary, red-rimmed. Shit. "What happened to your arm?"

"Oh, um . . . I fell?" Hanna weakly flailed the injured arm. "During practice? And someone pulled me up? Too hard?"

Hwa nodded slowly. "Right. Sure. That happens."

Hanna smiled. It came on sudden and bright. Too sudden. Too bright. "Everything's fine, now."

"Glad to hear it. You should put some arnica on that."

"Okay. I'll try that."

She tried to move away, but Hwa wove in front of her. "I have some at my place," she said. "I'm in Tower One. Seventh floor, unit seven. Easy to remember."

Hanna nodded without meeting Hwa's eye. "Okay."

Hwa moved, and Hanna shuffled away to join the volleyball team. She turned back to Joel. He'd already put the weights down. She was about to say something about his slacking off, when he asked: "Do you know her?"

Hwa turned and looked at Hanna. She stood a little apart from the others, tugging on a sweatshirt over her bruised arm. She took eyedrops from the pocket and applied them first to one eye, and then the other. "I know her mother," Hwa said.

• • •

Mollie Oleson looked a little rounder than Hwa remembered her. She couldn't remember their last appointment together, which meant it had probably happened months ago. Mollie was more of a catch-as-catch-can kind of operator—she only listed herself as available to the USWC 314 when she felt like it. It kept her dues low and her involvement minimal. But as a member she was entitled to the same protection as a full-timer. And that meant she'd met Hwa.

Hwa sidled up to her in the children's section of the Benevolent Irish Society charity shop. Mollie stood hanging little baggies of old fabtoys on a pegboard. "We close in fifteen minutes," she said, under her breath.

"Even for me?" Hwa asked.

"Hwa!" Mollie beamed, and threw her arms around Hwa. Like her daughter, she was one of those women who really only looked pretty when she was happy. Unlike her daughter, she was better at faking it.

"What are you doing here?"

Hwa shrugged. "I got a new place. Thought it was time for some new stuff."

Mollie's smile faltered. "Oh, yeah . . ." She adjusted a stuffed polar bear on a shelf so that it faced forward. "How's that going? Working for the Lynches, I mean?"

"The little one is all right," Hwa said. "Skinny little bugger. I'm training him."

Mollie gave a terse little smile. "Well, good luck to you. About time you got out of the game, I'd say. A girl your age should be thinking about the future. You don't want to wind up . . ." She gestured around the store, rather than finishing the sentence.

"I saw Hanna at school, today. Made me think to come here."

Mollie's hands stilled their work. "Oh? How was she? I haven't seen her since this morning." She looked out the window to the autumn darkness. "Closing shift, and all."

Hwa nodded. "She's good." She licked her lips. It was worth a shot. She had to try. "Her boyfriend's kind of a dick, though."

Mollie laughed. "Hanna doesn't have a boyfriend! She has no time, between school and volleyball and her job."

"Her job?"

"Skipper's," Mollie said. "You know, taking orders, bussing tables, the like. It's not much, but it's a job."

"Right," Hwa said. "Well, my mistake. I guess that guy was just flirting with her."

"Well, I'll give you the employee discount, just for sharing that little tidbit. Now I have something to tease her with, eh?"

"Oh, I wouldn't do that," Hwa said. "Girls her age are so sensitive."

• • •

At home, Hwa used her Lynch employee login to access the Prefect city management system. Lynch installed it overnight during a presumed brownout, using a day-zero exploit to deliver the viral load that was their surveillance overlay. It was easier than doing individual installations, Síofra had explained to her. Some kids in what was once part of Russia had used a similar exploit to gain access to a Lynch reactor in Kansas. That was fifteen years ago.

Now it was a shiny interface that followed Hwa wherever she went. Or rather, wherever she let it. Her refrigerator and her washroom mirror were both too old for it. So it lived in her specs, and in the display unit Lynch insisted on outfitting her with. That made it the most expensive thing in what was a very cheap studio apartment.

"Prefect, show me Oleson, Hanna," she said.

The system shuffled through profiles until it landed on two possibilities, each fogged over. One was Hanna. The other was a woman by the name of Anna Olsen. Maybe it thought Hwa had misspoken.

"Option one." Hanna's profile became transparent as Anna's vanished. It solidified across the display, all the photos and numbers and maps hanging and shimmering in Hwa's vision. She squinted. "Dimmer."

Hanna's profile dimmed slightly, and Hwa could finally get a real look at it. Like Hwa, Hanna lived in Tower One. She'd been picked up once on a shoplifting charge, two years ago. She raised her hands and gestured through all the points at which facial recognition had identified Hanna in the last forty-eight hours. Deeper than that, and she'd need archival access.

But first, she needed to call Skipper's. Rule them out. "Hi, is Hanna there?"

"Hanna doesn't work here anymore." Hwa heard beeping. The sounds of fryer alarms going off. Music. "Hello?"

Hwa ended the call.

There was Hanna on the Acoutsina Causeway, walking toward Tower One. The image was time-stamped after volleyball practice. Speed-trap checked her entering a vehicle in the driverless lane for a vehicle at 18:30. Five minutes later, she was gone. Wherever she was now, there were no cameras.

"Prefect, search this vehicle and this face together."

A long pause. *Archive access required.*

For a fleeting moment, Hwa regretted the fact that Prefect was not a human being she could intimidate. "Is there a record in the archives?"

Archive access required.

Hwa growled a little to herself. She popped up off the floor and began to pace. She walked through the projections of Hanna's face, sliding the ribbon of stills and clips until she hit the top of the list. Today was Monday. If Hanna had sustained her injury on Friday night, then Hwa was out of luck. But Mollie had said she worked all weekend. Maybe that meant—

What are you doing?

Hwa startled. "Jesus Christ, stop doing that!"

Doing what? Síofra was trying to sound innocent. It wasn't working.

"You know exactly what," she said. "Why can't you just text, like a normal person? How do you know I wasn't having a conversation with somebody?"

Your receiver would have told me, he said.

Hwa frowned. "Can you . . . ?" She wished she had an image of him she could focus her fury on. "Can you listen in on my conversations, through my receiver?"

Only during your working hours.

"And you can just . . . tune in? All day? While I'm at school with Joel?"

Of course I can. I thought you had some excellent points to make about Jane Eyre *in Mr. Bartel's class, last week.*

Hwa plunged the heels of her hands into the sockets of her eyes. She had known this was possible, of course. She just assumed Síofra actually had other work to do, and wasn't constantly spying on her instead of accomplishing it.

"Are you bored?"

I'm sorry?

"Are you bored? At work? Is your job that boring? That you need to be tuned into my day like that?"

There was a long pause. She wondered for a moment if he'd cut out. *You watch Joel and I watch you,* he said. *That is my job.*

Hwa sighed. He had her, there. It was all right there in the Lynch Ltd employee handbook. She'd signed on for this level of intrusion when she'd taken their money. He was paying, so he got to watch. She'd stood guard at enough peep shows to learn that particular lesson. Maybe she wasn't so different from her mother, after all.

You aren't supposed to be prying into your fellow classmates' lives unless they pose a credible threat to Joel. So he'd been spying on her searches, too. Of course. *I know what you're thinking, and—*

"How come I can't do this to you?" Hwa blurted. "That's what I'm thinking. I'm wondering how come I can't watch you all the time the way you watch me. Why doesn't this go both ways? Why don't I get to know when you're watching me?"

Another long pause. *Is there something about me that you would like to know?*

Oh, just everything, she thought. The answer came unbidden and she shut her eyes and clenched her jaw and squashed it like a bug crawling across her consciousness.

"Are you coming running tomorrow?"

Of course I am.

• • •

Síofra had a whole route planned. He showed it to her the next morning in her specs, but she had only a moment to glance over it before heading out the door.

"Why did you stay in this tower?" Síofra asked, leaning back and craning his neck to take in the brutalist heap of former containers. "We pay you well enough to afford one of the newer ones. This one has almost no security to speak of."

"You've been watching me twenty-four/seven for a solid month and you still haven't figured that one out? Corporate surveillance ain't what it used to be."

"Is it because your mother lives here?"

Hwa pulled up short. "You just don't know when to quit, do you?"

"I only wondered because you never visit her." He grinned and pushed ahead of her down the causeway.

His route took them along the Acoutsina. They circled the first joint, and Síofra asked about the old parkette and the playground. This early, there were no children and it remained littered with beer cozies and liquor pouches. She told him about the kid who had kicked her down the slide once, and how nobody let her on the swings, and he assumed it had to do with her mother and what she did for a living. His eyes were not programmed to see her true face, or the stain dripping from her left eye down her neck to her arm and her ribs and her leg. She had tested his vision several times; he never stared, never made reference to her dazzle-pattern face. And with their connection fostered by her wearables, he probably never watched her via botfly or camera. He could spend every minute of every day observing her, and never truly see her.

They ran to the second joint of the causeway and circled the memorial for those who had died in the Old Rig. "Do you want to stop?" he asked.

It was bad luck not to pay respects. She knew exactly where her brother's name was. Síofra waited for her at the base of the monument as her steps spiraled up the mound. She slapped Tae-kyun's name lightly, like tagging him in a relay run, and kept going. Síofra had already started up again by the time she made it back down. They were almost at Tower Three when he called a halt, in a parking lot full of rides.

"Cramp," he said, pulling his calf up behind him. He placed a hand up against a parked vehicle for balance. When Hwa's gaze followed his hand, she couldn't help but see the license plate.

It was the one she'd asked Prefect to track. The one Hanna had disappeared into, last night. "I thought . . ." Hwa looked from him to the vehicle. "I thought you said—"

"I haven't the faintest idea what you're talking about, Hwa." He smirked. Then he appeared to check something in his lenses. "Goodness, look at the time. I have an early meeting. I think I'll just pick up one of these rides here, and drive back to the office. Are you all right finishing the run alone?"

Hwa frowned at him. He winked at her. She smiled. "Yeah," she said. "I'm good here."

He gestured at the field of rides and snapped his fingers at one of them. It lit up. Its locks opened. She watched him get into it and drive away. Now alone, Hwa peered into the vehicle. Nothing left behind in any of the seats. No dings or scratches. She looked around at the parking lot. Empty. Still dark. She pulled her hood up and took a knee. She fussed with her shoelaces with one hand while her other fished in the pocket of her vest. The joybuzzer hummed between her fingers as she stood. And just like that, the trunk unlocked.

Hanna was inside. Bound and gagged. And completely asleep.

"Shit," Hwa muttered. Then the vehicle chirped. Startled, Hwa scanned the parking lot. Still empty. The ride was being summoned elsewhere. It rumbled to life. If Hwa let it go now, she would lose Hanna. In the trunk, Hanna blinked awake. She squinted up at Hwa. Behind her gag, she began to scream.

"It's okay, Hanna." Hwa threw the trunk door even wider, and climbed in. She pulled it shut behind her as it began to move. "You're okay. We're okay."

The vehicle lurched. She heard the lock snap shut again as the ride locked itself. "We're okay," she repeated. "We're going to be okay."

• • •

Hwa busied herself untying Hanna as the ride drove itself. "Tell me where we're going," Hwa said.

"It's my fault," Hanna was saying. "He told me not to talk to Benny."

"Benny works at Skipper's?" Hwa picked the tape off Hanna's wrists.

"I told him I was just being nice." Hanna gulped for air. She coughed. "I quit, just like he told me to, but Benny and I are in the same biology class! I couldn't just ignore him. And Jarod said if I really loved him, I'd do what he asked . . ."

"Jarod?" Hwa asked. "That's his name? What's his last name?" She needed Prefect. Why hadn't she brought her specs? She could be looking at a map, right now. She could be finding out how big this guy was. If he had any priors.

"Why are you here?" Hanna asked. "Did my mom send you? I thought you didn't work with us anymore."

Beneath them, the buckles in the pavement burped along. They were still on the Acoutsina, then. It had the oldest roads with the most repairs. Hwa worked to quiet the alarm bell ringing in her head. Hanna's skin was so cold under her hands. She probably needed a hospital. But right now, she needed Hwa to be calm. She needed Hwa to be smart. She needed Hwa to think.

"With us?" Hwa asked.

"For the union," Hanna sniffed.

"Eh?"

The angle of the vehicle changed. They tipped down into something. Hwa heard hydraulics. They were in a lift. Tower Three. They'd parked Hanna not far from where they were then. Hwa's ears popped. She rolled up as close as possible to the opening of the trunk. She cleared her wrists and flexed her toes. She'd have one good chance when the trunk opened. If there weren't too many of them. If they didn't have crowbars. Something slammed onto the trunk. A fist. A big one, by the sound of it.

"Wakey, wakey, Hanna!"

The voice was muffled, but strong. Manic. He'd been awake for a while. Boosters? Shit. Hanna started to say something, but Hwa shushed her.

"Had enough time to think about what you did?"

Definitely boosters. That swaggering arrogance, those delusions of grandeur. Hwa listened for more voices, the sound of footsteps. She heard none. Maybe this was a solo performance.

"You know, I didn't like doing this. But you made me do it. You have to learn, Hanna."

Behind her, Hanna was crying.

"I can't have you just giving it away. It really cuts into what I'm trying to do for us."

Fingers drummed on the trunk of the ride.

"Are you ready to come out and say you're sorry?"

You're goddamn right I am, Hwa thought.

The trunk popped open. Jarod's pale, scaly face registered surprise for just a moment. Then Hwa's foot snapped out and hit him square in the jaw. He stumbled back and tried to slam the trunk shut. It landed on her leg and she yelled. The door bounced up. Not her ankle. Not her knee. Thank goodness. She rolled out.

Jarod was huge. A tall, lanky man in his early twenties, the kind of rigger who'd get made fun of by guys with more muscle while still being plenty strong enough to get the job done. He had bad skin and a three-day growth of patchy beard. He lunged for Hwa and she jumped back. He swung wide and she jumped again.

"Let me guess," she said. "You told Hanna you'd fix it with the union if she paid you her dues directly. Even though she's a minor and USWC doesn't allow those."

Jarod's eyes were red. He spat blood. He reeked of booster sweat—acrid and bitter.

"And you had her doing what, camwork?" She grinned. "I thought her eyes were red because she'd been crying. But yours look just the same. You're both wearing the same shitty lenses."

"He made me watch the locker room." Hanna sat on her knees in the trunk of the ride. Her voice was a croak. For a moment she looked so much like her mother that Hwa's heart twisted in her chest. "He said he'd edit my team's faces out—"

"Shut up!"

Jarod reached for the lid of the trunk again. He tried to slam it shut on Hanna. Hwa ran for him. He grabbed her by the shoulders. Hwa's right heel came down hard on his. The instep deflated under the pressure. He howled. She elbowed him hard under the ribs and spun halfway out of his grip. His right hand still clung to her vest. She grabbed the wrist and wedged it into the mouth of the trunk.

"Hanna! Get down!"

She slammed the lid once. Then twice. Then a third time. *He'll never work this rig again,* she thought distantly. The trunk creaked open and Jarod sank to his knees. He clutched his wrist. His hand dangled from his arm like a piece of kelp.

Behind her, she heard a slow, dry clap.

"Excellent work," Síofra said.

He stood against the ride he'd summoned. Two go-cups of coffee sat on the hood. He held one out.

"You didn't want in on that?" Hwa asked, jerking her head at the whimpering mess on the floor of the parking garage.

"Genius can't be improved upon." Síofra gestured with his cup. "We should get them to a hospital. Or a police station."

"Hanna needs a hospital." Hwa sipped her coffee. "This guy, I should report to the union. He falsified a membership and defrauded someone of dues in bad faith."

"They don't take kindly to that, in the USWC?"

Hwa swallowed hard. "Nope. Not one bit."

Síofra made a sound in his throat that sounded like purring.

• • •

During the elevator ride between the hospital and the school in Tower Two, Hwa munched a breakfast sandwich. She'd protested the presence of bread, but Síofra said the flour was mostly crickets anyway. So she'd relented. Now he stood across the elevator watching her eat.

"What?" she asked, between swallows.

"I have something to share with you."

She swiped at her mouth with the back of her hand. "Yeah?"

"I don't remember anything beyond ten years ago."

Hwa blinked. "Sorry?"

"My childhood. My youth. They're . . ." He made an empty gesture. "Blank."

She frowned. "Do you mean this like . . . emotionally?"

"No. Literally. I literally don't remember. My first memory is waking up in a Lynch hospital in South Sudan, ten years ago. They had some wells there. I was injured. They brought me in. Patched me up. They assumed I was a fixer of some sort. They don't know for which side. And apparently I had covered my tracks a little too well. I've worked for them ever since."

Hairs rose on the back of Hwa's neck. "Wow."

"As long as I can remember, I've worked for this company. I don't know any other kind of life."

"Okay," Hwa said.

"I've never lived without their presence in my life. I've never had what you might call a private life."

Oh. "Oh."

"But you have. And that's something that's different, about our experiences."

"Yeah. You could say that."

"You don't have implants," he said. "Not permanent ones, anyway. They—we—can't gather that kind of data from you. But they know everything about me. My sugars, how much I sleep, where I am, if I'm angry, my routines, even the music I listen to when I'm making dinner."

"You listen to music while you make dinner?"

"Django Reinhardt."

"Who?"

He smiled ruefully. "What I'm saying is, you're the last of a dying breed."

Hwa thought of the stain running down her body, the flaw he couldn't see. He had no idea. "Thank you?"

"You're a black swan," he said. "A wild card. Something unpredictable. Like getting into the trunk of that ride this morning."

Hwa shrugged. "Anybody could have done that. I couldn't just let Hanna go. She needed my help."

"You could have called the police. You could have called *me*. But you didn't. You took the risk yourself."

She frowned. "Are you pissed off? Is that what this is about? Because you're the one who—"

Síofra hissed. He brought his finger to his lips and shook his head softly. With his gaze, he brought her attention to the eyes at the corners of the elevator.

"I just want you to know something about me," he said, after a moment. "Something that isn't in my halo."

She smiled. "Well, thanks."

"Not a lot of other people know this about me."

"Well, it is kind of weird." She stretched up, then bent down. She looked up at him from her ragdoll position. "I mean, you are only ten years old, right? You can't even drink."

He rolled his eyes. "Here it comes."

She stood. "Or vote. Or even have your own place. Does your landlord know about this?"

He pointed at the view of the city outside the elevator. "My landlord is your landlord."

The elevator doors chimed open. They were on the school floor. Hwa had fifteen minutes to shower and put on her uniform before she met Joel.

"Hey, if you're not too busy? I kind of didn't do the last question on my physics homework. So I might need some help with that. Before I hand it in."

"I think something can be arranged."

She stood in the door. It chimed insistently. She leaned on it harder. "Did you ever go to school? After you woke up, I mean? Or are you just winging it?"

"I know what a man my age needs to know," Síofra said. "Be seeing you."

STEVEN S. LONG

KEEPING UP WITH MR. JOHNSON

(2016)

"IT'S SIX A.M., MR. Hardwick. Please get up," the housecomp said in its pleasantly neutral, precisely modulated, feminine voice.

"All right, all right, I'm up," he said as he sat up and swung his legs off the edge of the bed. Helen rolled over and put a hand on his back; he leaned over, caressed her blonde hair, kissed her on the forehead. It didn't seem like so long ago when their morning contact would have been far more intimate, full of fire and urgency, but two decades of marriage and two kids had replaced that early passion with a calmer, more profound connection.

No more time to linger, though—another busy day ahead. He jumped in the shower, where the housecomp chased away his morning bleariness with precisely warmed water and a review of his schedule. Helen was working on her makeup when he emerged. He stood next to her at the sink and shaved. Occasionally they exchanged a comment about the kids, the apartment, some upcoming social event.

He paused in mid-shave to look at Helen as she carefully applied lipstick. Watching her do everyday things was one of the simple pleasures of his life. Any fool could see she was beautiful, but it was more than that. Unlike most of his colleagues he hadn't ditched his "starter wife" for some surgically enhanced would-be trideo star of a trophy wife. He couldn't even imagine doing that; he loved Helen, heart and soul, in a way few of his fellow SK execs would understand. He'd only ever cheated on her with one woman, and there was a damn good reason for that. They'd never talked about it, but she knew and understood. He was sure of it.

"What?" she said with that little smile of hers, the one he liked to think she reserved only for him.

"Nothing," he said, matching her smile as he returned to his shaving.

Breakfast was the usual controlled chaos: him trying to read the overnight datafeed while eating; the kids unable to sit still for long; Matilda, their housekeeper/cook, attempting to corral them with limited success; Helen chattering on about this and that. Nothing requiring his immediate attention had happened overnight, so he enjoyed the comfortable familiarity of it all without distraction.

He dressed, luxuriating in the feel of the 500-nuyen silk shirt, the 3,000-nuyen suit jacket, the gold cuff links in the shape of the Saeder-Krupp logo. He'd done some things for the corp that he didn't like to think about, but he couldn't deny that the salary they paid him made his life a lot more pleasant than it was before he met Helen. It let him provide her and the kids with anything they needed, and that was well worth giving up the freedom of his old life to join the corporate ranks.

He slipped on one of his few souvenirs of his previous life—an orichalcum ring in the shape of an ouroboros. Snakeman had made it for him years ago to mark the end of his apprenticeship, and he'd held on to it even when he'd had to let things with far greater objective value go. He felt the little tingle of power from it, a sensation as familiar and comforting as his family's voices around the breakfast table. Then he fetched his Caliban from his home office and headed for the door. "Take good care of them, Matilda," he said on his way out.

"Always, Mr. Hardwick." She looked like your typical Third World immigrant working a typical immigrant job, but she was part of his benefits package. A bodyguard for Helen and the kids, Matilda had enough cyber and bio enhancements to outdo most elite soldiers. There were no guarantees in the Sixth World, but having her around made him feel better about his family's safety.

His own bodyguards waited for him just outside the apartment door: Rapier, an elf as swift and deadly as her namesake, with looks that let her pass as arm candy right up to the point where she put two rounds in some unsuspecting fool's head; and Brutus, a huge ork with more muscle augmentation and dermal plating than anyone Hardwick had ever met. Rapier favored him with the intimate nod of her chin they used to communicate a world of meaning in a simple gesture. He didn't return it; Helen was too close by.

"G'morning, boss," Brutus said, his voice slightly slurred by his tusks.

"Good morning. Let's go." The helicopter ride took them past Aztechnology's garish, pyramid-shaped local headquarters, then over the still-visible scar Hurricane Penelope had left on Miami a dozen years ago. City leaders now euphemistically referred to it as "Vizcaya Free Park," but the citizens called it the Vizcaya Free-Fire Zone. It was just the sort of place he used to live and work in. Flying effortlessly over it always gave him a touch of the thrill an escaped convict feels as the prison walls shrink in the distance behind him. But he paid no more attention than that, focusing on his Caliban instead; Rapier and Brutus were more than wary enough to notice any possible threat.

Soon they arrived at SK Tower. Perched atop the highest point on Lofwyr Key, the artificial island the corp built a decade ago, the Tower offered an unequaled view of Bayside Park, the Atlantic Ocean, and the Atlantis Autonomous District offshore/undersea habitat where only the *really* rich people could afford to live.

With Rapier leading and Brutus bringing up the rear, they headed inside. His assistant Ashleigh waited just inside the door marked UNCONVENTIONAL ASSETS DIVISION, same as always. "Good morning, Mr. Hardwick," she said, handing him a mug of coffee brewed the way he liked it.

"Good morning. Updates?" She filled him in on calls, calendar changes, and other details, but he only half paid attention. The truly important meeting, the one after lunch, already occupied most of his thoughts. After all, none of the day's other activities required him to risk his life.

• • •

The morning's meetings went without a hitch. Now for the main event: as head of SK Miami's Unconventional Assets Division, he had to go talk with the unconventional assets—or "shadowrunners," as the street called them. Powerful, deniable, illegal "soldiers" the corps used in their covert wars against each other, he could hire them to do just about anything; from theft, sabotage, and personnel extraction to outright murder.

There was a problem, though—and that was why he had a job. Megacorporations, the most conventional of entities, clashed with the unconventional assets they so desperately needed. His years in both worlds made him the ideal interface between them.

The best shadowrunners were smooth as silk to work with. They'd survived on the streets, in the Matrix, among the Awakened for years; life on the edge had burned most of the stupid out of them. Professional and reliable, they lived by a code nearly as binding as a corp's bylaws. But the best never came cheap, and prime runners weren't always available on his timetable. That meant having to dig deeper into the barrel, and the end result was often as smooth as burlap.

Most of the stress of his job came from having to deal with that sort of shadowrunner: the know-it-alls, the jandering bastards, the chip-on-their-shoulders, the psychotics, the chrome-junkies, the weirdos. In his experience, the average shadowrunner was so unreliable and unprofessional that working with them was like playing roulette. But he'd keep working with them no matter how often the little white ball landed on the wrong number, because they were the only ones who could do work vital to the bottom line. As disreputable as they might be, shadowrunners filled a niche in the megacorporate ecosystem. That guaranteed him a job—as long as he got results.

Unfortunately, one of the unconventional things about unconventional assets was their refusal to come onto corp property for a meeting. The idea of being scanned, identified, recorded, watched, giving up their weapons—they'd rather stick their heads in a hell hound's mouth. He had to go to them, which meant stepping outside the safe, comfortable confines of SK turf.

Rapier and Brutus led him to a black, unmarked SK Bentley Concordat, where a corp rigger and another pair of armed guards waited. He settled into his seat and the others arranged themselves protectively around him. He'd have preferred some sort of combat van like an SK Rhino, but he had to maintain the image of Mr. Johnson. At least the car had plenty of armor and power.

The Bentley headed out the gates of SK's corporate park and into the urban jungle of Miami. As they kept driving, that jungle turned to wasteland: ruined buildings taken over by squatters; competing scrawls of graffiti everywhere; ads for the cheapest possible products and services garishly assaulting the eye. The human misery was almost palpable. Spirits of Fire and Air be praised that he didn't have to live in places like this anymore.

They drove to an old cinderblock building in a half-deserted part of the 'plex. No one had lived there for years except devil rats. In other words, just the sort of place runners liked to hold meetings.

The guards got out, weapons ready, and entered the building while Hardwick and his bodyguards waited in the Bentley. A few minutes later, they signaled all-secure and he walked in.

The interior of the building wasn't much more than an empty shell; scavengers had stripped out anything of any possible value, right down to the wiring. Rapier picked the spot she liked best for defensive purposes, near a sturdy-looking brick wall in the back. The guards set up the portable furniture they'd brought along. Not only would "the office" make things more comfortable, it gave him a bit of a psychological edge by making this place as much his turf as the runners'.

Finally he added his own magical touch: a detect enemies spell to alert him if any of the runners posed a threat. He knew some Johnsons who went further, adding a mask spell to hide their identities or an armor spell in case a runner's trigger finger got too itchy. He'd rarely found the former to be of much use, and he knew from personal experience that a lot of runners considered the latter insulting. The detect was enough for him—that, and his ouroboros ring, if necessary.

The agreed-upon signal knock on the east door came at 1230 hours precisely: chalk one up for their professionalism. The detect spell remained silent. He nodded at Rapier, who passed it on to a guard. He opened the door left-handed, his right hand near his weapon.

"Year of the dragon," said a loud voice similar to, but not quite the same as, Brutus's. That was the second signal.

"Let them in," he said, his voice firm and confident, his posture and attitude radiating competence and control. That was the only way to deal with runners: from a position of strength, whether real or illusory.

An ork—obviously a samurai from his 'ware, his weapons, his swagger—entered, followed by four others: a human, his talismans marking him as a

Hermetic mage; a red-bearded dwarf with a small robot perched on his shoulder; a human decker; and another Awakened, an attractive human woman with the tattoos and accouterments of a Raccoon shaman. Pretty standard runner team, just what Operation Altitude needed.

The runners moved as a group, with a smooth wariness that showed they were skilled professionals. They took care not to do anything the *sararimen* would perceive as threatening—and that showed they were smart. He was well aware that on the street you didn't survive to become the former if you weren't the latter.

They reached the half-circle of chairs in front of the desk, stopped, fanned out cautiously. "I'm Tuskarora, leader of the Five Aces," the ork said. "These are Trismegistus, Teamster, Ryder, and Atsa," he continued, pointing at each of the others in turn.

"Good afternoon. You can call me Mr. Johnson," Hardwick said, speaking the words of the old ritual. "Please be seated." He sat down; Rapier, Brutus, and his other guards remained standing.

"Thank you for meeting me today. Ephraim Fivestars tells me you're pros, and he's never steered me wrong before."

"He says the same about you."

Hardwick smiled thinly. "Good. Down to business, then."

"Let's make sure we're clear up front, chummer," Tuskarora said. "I've done way too many runs where a suit didn't tell me everything I needed to know, and I'm sick of that drek. The more, and more accurate, intel you provide us with, the better our chances of success. If you lie to us, if you hide useful data from us, if you make our job harder than it needs to be because of some secret agenda—I'll burn you. We clear?"

Hardwick didn't speak, just stared straight at the big ork. Brutus didn't move, but Rapier edged closer to him.

Tuskarora grinned, his gaze flicking between elf and human. "You two, huh? Nice going, Johnson. Never got to visit a dandelion patch myself—what's it like? They as cold in bed as they are on the street?"

Rapier flushed, but did nothing. Hardwick could sense the tension in her. He felt his own anger rising, damped it down, shoved it aside. It wouldn't help him here. "That's none of your concern."

"Bulldrek." Tuskarora leaned forward to emphasize his words. "No written contracts in this biz. It's all trust between you and me"—he pointed at Hardwick's wedding ring—"and I'm not so sure I can trust a man who betrays the strongest bond of faith in his life."

Hardwick could almost feel the ork wanting to pop a handrazor blade out from under his fingernail, but the detect spell still hadn't sounded.

Sensing Rapier was about to lose it, he reached out, gently took her arm, calmed her down a little. "The one thing has nothing to do with the other. You and I don't trust each other, and we never will. But we've got a stronger connection: mutual interest: I want something badly enough to pay major nuyen for it, and you're the people I think can get it for me. You want the money—and the adrenaline rush of the job."

Hardwick released Rapier's arm and folded his hands together on his desk. "My odds of getting what I want decrease if I'm not straight with you or I dangle you—not to mention that I end up with an enemy instead of a valuable business contact. Let's cut the drek, assume we're both professionals, and proceed accordingly. Agreed?"

"*So ka,*" Tuskarora said, nodding with satisfaction as he sat back. Rapier calmed down another couple notches; he figured the odds of someone dying had dropped back to no more than ten percent.

"Now that we're done dancing, what's the job?" Trismegistus asked.

"Basically it's a techjacking, maybe with a snatch job or elimination attached. Pays two hundred thousand nuyen, plus reasonable expenses."

That caught the runners' attention. "Lotta money for a B and E," Tuskarora said. "What's the catch?"

Hardwick reached into a desk drawer, pulled out a small plastic container, slid it across the desk toward Tuskarora. "All the data I have is on this chip."

"Bullet point it for us," Teamster said.

Hardwick tapped his Caliban; it projected an image on the wall behind him. "This is a prototype developed by Aztechnology for a 'genomic exchange enhancer.' I don't know all the engineering, but from what I understand it significantly speeds up the rate of information exchange between biocomputers and silicon computers.

"We want the GEE, any specs or other data related to it, and, if you can grab her, Dr. Lydia Gonzalez-Wu, its inventor. If you can't get her, kill her. If it's a choice between bringing us the GEE and extracting her, make your escape and forget about her."

"Where's Aztech keeping this thing?" Tuskarora asked.

"At a secret research facility in the Everglades."

None of the runners looked happy when he mentioned the Glades: fifteen hundred square miles of swamp, shallow river, sawgrass, trees, mud, insects, and animals both normal and paranormal. Once only half that size and a fraction as dangerous, it had Awakened when the Sixth World dawned. No one dared to try to clear large patches of the Glades for farming or tract housing anymore, but it was a good place for Aztechnology to hide a research lab close to the Miami 'plex.

"What's our out?" Teamster said.

"An extraction point on an isolated part of the coast near the Ten Thousand Islands. Once you've got the goods, proceed there overland. We'll exfil you immediately in a Nissan Wolf helicopter."

"'We,' kemo sabe?" Tuskarora asked.

"Yes, we. This job is too important for me to trust to my lieutenants. I'll oversee things personally."

"Price just went up twenty percent."

"No, it didn't. I'm not going along to interfere with you or look over your shoulders. I'm there to make sure we all get what we want and get out safely. If you have a problem with that, I'll find another team."

Tuskarora said nothing this time.

"Good," Hardwick said. "Take a look at the data, make some plans, and get back to me with your outline, timetable, and requested supplies. I expect to hear from you within twelve hours at the same number we used before."

"You got it, Johnson." At the samurai's nod, the Five Aces stood up and left without further discussion. Two minutes later Hardwick and his team did the same.

"What did you think of them?" Hardwick asked when they were back in the Bentley.

"That ork's an asshole," Rapier said, her anger at being insulted still plain on her face. "But the team seems smart and efficient." It was about the highest praise she could offer.

"Let's hope so—or we're all in trouble."

• • •

The insertion had gone off almost perfectly. It was only later that things went to hell.

Hardwick woke up a few seconds after the explosion. Something had gone wrong on the run; the runners had fled to the exfil point in a stolen helicopter—pursued by one that wasn't. A lot of machine gun fire and one Aztechnology Striker shot later, both choppers had crashed. He was lucky to be alive. No, not luck; Rapier had done her job and pushed him out of the path of danger, spirits bless her.

He stumbled to his feet, head aching, and looked around. The beach was on fire. Puddles of burning fuel and scraps of shrapnel that had once been two helicopters littered the sand. Make that three helicopters—the runners' chopper had pinwheeled across the sand after crashing and smashed into the getaway helicopter. Now he was well and truly fucked.

Worse than the wreckage were the bodies. He'd seen plenty of death in his day, but this was his entire sec-team, his men, blown to bits. This was different.

He couldn't take it anymore and looked away—only to see Rapier. A flying chunk of rotor had cut her nearly in half. Some piece of her chrome sparked a little, fitfully, as if protesting its demise. Unable to stop himself, he scanned the beach until he found what remained of Brutus. Spattered jet fuel ignited by the blast had already burned away most of his flesh and was still working on his dermal armor and laced bones.

"God fucking damn it," he whispered to himself, squeezing his eyes to hold back tears. They'd protected him for over five years. They couldn't have done their jobs any better. He'd genuinely liked them.

And now they'd left him in the Glades with no one to watch his back.

Hearing a deep groan from the swamp side of the beach, he hurried across the sand, avoiding anything burning or sharp, until he found the source: Tuskarora. Next to him lay Atsa. They must have bailed out at the last moment.

Stuck in hostile territory with two runners, one of them a temperamental ork. He wasn't sure if his chances of survival had just gone up or down.

Had they completed the op? Tuskarora had a pack on, but it was torn open, nearly empty. Hardwick examined the ground between the ork and the trees, looking for anything that might have fallen out. Spare knife . . . multi-tool . . . tube of tusk polish. . . . A document pouch!—right in the middle of a puddle of burning fuel.

Casting magic fingers, he tried to lift the pouch out, but it was too far gone and crumbled into ashes. Well, if he didn't have it, at least Aztechnology didn't either.

He saw the firelight glint off something on the other side of the pool. He walked closer. A dura-plas chip box! He opened it with the same sort of eagerness his kids had on Christmas morning.

Inside was the GEE, its plastic and silicon more precious to him than gold and diamonds. He took it out, wrapped it carefully in a piece of clean cloth, and stashed it in one of the secret pouches sewn into his body armor. Then he tossed the box into the fire alongside the remains of the documents pouch.

Tuskarora groaned again. The big ork only had some minor cuts and abrasions, but Atsa was out cold. Hardwick didn't like the look of her pupils or the lump on her head, but he had no idea whether she'd gotten the latter by jumping from the helicopter or earlier in the run. She probably had a concussion, but he couldn't afford to let her keep sleeping. "Wake up, Atsa," he said, patting her cheek.

She moaned and stirred, batting his hand away like a child who didn't want to wake up for school. But at last her eyes flickered open. She started to lever herself up on one elbow, then shrieked with pain. "Leg!" she said through gritted teeth.

He lifted her deerskin skirt up a little and looked. He was no medic, but he'd seen enough combat injuries to know she'd broken her left leg. "Damn it," he said.

"That bad?"

"Not sure, but it's bad for us. Going to slow us down. Gotta rouse Tuskarora."

Getting close enough to wake up a street samurai full of adrenaline wasn't exactly his idea of a smart survival tactic, so he kicked sand at the ork. "Rise and shine, Tuskarora! No time for sleep."

Tuskarora jerked awake and flowed to his feet with augmented speed and grace. He reached for a smartgun that wasn't there, then focused on Hardwick with laser intensity. "You!" he said. In two strides he reached Hardwick. Effortlessly the ork lifted him off the ground with his left hand while drawing his right hand back into a fist. As he did, razor-sharp blades extended from his knuckles. "You got my team killed, Johnson! When you get to Hell, tell 'em I said hello."

"*I* got *your* team killed?" Hardwick said, struggling to speak clearly with the ork's hand around his throat. "You had all the intel I did. *You're* the one who led the Aztechs to us. *You're* the one who blew up their helicopter with a rocket. *You're* the one who got *my* entire sec-team killed, you stupid son of a bitch!"

Tuskarora snarled and thrust his right fist forward. Before he could connect, the ouroboros ring gleamed and an Armor spell shimmered into existence around Hardwick, deflecting the deadly spurs.

"You're *Awakened*?" Tuskarora said.

"You think I have this job just because of my winning personality?" Hardwick replied. "I used to be one of you. I was pulling runs like this when you were pissing your diapers. That's how I can relate to runners—and that's why I deal fairly with them." His conscience nagged at him for a second because of what he'd done with the GEE, but loyalty to SK and his family meant more than a little white lie to a runner. He was sure of it.

"Why didn't you tell me he was Awakened?" Tuskarora asked Atsa.

"You didn't ask."

"Damn treehuggers," the ork muttered. Most of the tension went out of his muscles; veins that had dilated from rage or the effects of his cyberware began to shrink. He let Hardwick go. "Okay, Johnson, what now?"

"First things first. Did you complete the op?"

"Yeah, we geeked the scientist and got the GEE and all her . . . *drek*!" he finished as he discovered his backpack was torn open and empty. "Gotta be here somewhere, let's look!"

The two of them searched; Hardwick let the ork go toward where he'd located the chip. Tuskarora found his Predator, brushed the sand off it, kissed it, and holstered it. A few seconds later he came to the now burned-out puddle of fuel. "Mother*fucker*!" he said, recognizing the ugly lump of ash at its center as the remains of his documents pouch. He crouched down for a closer look, shoulders slumping, face fallen. "The others died for nothing . . . nothing."

"What happened? We had to maintain blackout so the Aztechs wouldn't find us."

"It went great at first," Tuskarora replied. "Took a while for us to find the right lab, but we were quick enough to geek anyone who might've raised the alarm." He grinned in that particularly nasty way only orks could. "When we found the lab, we got lucky—Gonzalez-Wu was working late. She gave up the goods but refused to come along, so we iced her."

"Go on."

"That's when our luck ran out. I guess some Aztechnology decker found Ryder in the system. We walked out of that lab and right into a fully armed security squad.

"Ryder bought it when one of the Azzies shot him in the head, but Tris and Atsa laid down some mojo that gave us the chance to run for it. No way we could escape through the swamp as planned, so we headed for the compound's hangar. They had two choppers there; we took the one Teamster *thought* was faster.

"He took three rounds during the chase, so he couldn't fly steady. Even if they hadn't shot us up, I doubt he could've landed safely; he'd lost too much blood and was too messed up, even after the healing Tris and Atsa slapped on him."

"You're probably right. For what it's worth—I'm sorry about your team."

"Yeah . . ." Tuskarora looked skeptical. "I think it's time we got the hell out of here. Atsa, can you heal that leg?"

"No!" Hardwick said. "She's probably got a concussion. Don't even try to cast or Assense, Atsa. At best it'll make your head hurt even more. But you'll probably miscast and take *serious* Drain. Maybe even fatal."

"He's right," she said. "Between the way my head feels and the pain from my leg, I couldn't even magically light a candle."

"Okay, you're a mage, Johnson—you heal her."

"Ehhh, that might not be such a great idea, either. I've never had much of a knack for most mana spells. I could ease her pain a little, probably, but if I try to heal her, the odds are I end up in a lot of pain, nothing happens to her, and you have *two* people to carry."

"Then cover us with an invisibility spell so no one can find us."

Hardwick shook his head. "Can't do that, either."

"Elvis Christ! You can't do anything, can you, Johnson? What the fuck good are you?"

Before Hardwick could respond, an Aztechnology Plumed Serpent stealth drone flew into view over the treetops. Sensing targets, it angled toward the three of them and opened fire. Bullets kicked up gouts of sand around them.

"Damn it!" Tuskarora shouted. Moving with wired speed, he grabbed Atsa and dove behind some wreckage. She screamed as he jostled her leg.

Hardwick didn't move. He stared at the Plumed Serpent, focusing his willpower to draw mana into and through his self. He pointed at the drone and a spark shot forth from his hand. Traveling almost faster than the eye could follow, it grew larger, blossoming into a fireball. It engulfed the drone with a sound like a bonfire going up all at once. The drone's ammo added a second blast as a crescendo.

Tuskarora peeked over his cover. "Elvis Christ!" he said. "Nice going, Johnson."

Hardwick nodded. "*That's* what the fuck good I am."

"No drek."

"The Azzies saw everything that drone saw," Hardwick continued. "We need to move out of here *now*, or we'll spend the rest of our short lives being prepped for the sacrifice stone."

"Right. Let's get one of the inflatable boats and hightail it."

"Negative," Hardwick said. "We go overland through the swamp."

Tuskarora stared at him. "Did you hit your head too, Johnson? She can't walk through the swamp! Plus it's full of giant snakes and drek."

"And the ocean and river *aren't* full of man-eating monsters? On the water we're sitting ducks; anyone can see us. The swamp provides some cover from the air and from astral searchers, and drones have a harder time maneuvering among the trees and underbrush. If we go by sea, we're *all* dead. If we go overland—some of us might survive."

"Oh, wait—wait. Let me guess. This is the part where you suggest that we abandon Atsa to improve our own chances of survival." From the look on the shaman's face, she expected the same.

"Fuck *that.* No one on *any* team I run gets left behind. We'll make a splint and help her walk. We—well, *you*—carry her if necessary."

Hardwick couldn't read Tuskarora's expression—surprise? Bafflement? Maybe a touch of respect? "Okay, let's do it then," was all the samurai said.

They made a sturdy splint for Atsa with carbon fiber poles from the electronics tent; she already had her staff for a crutch. "Anything here you want to take?" Hardwick asked as he grabbed a field pack and some rations.

Tuskarora glanced around. "Nah. Let's get outta here."

• • •

Hours of miserable walking through the swamp followed. The heat, tension, and exertion made sweat pour off Hardwick and Tuskarora, but despite the effort of walking with her injuries Atsa seemed oddly at peace.

"Wotko provides," she said, using Raccoon's name in Creek. They hadn't run into anything truly dangerous so far, so Hardwick figured she might be right.

Tuskarora signaled for a rest and sat down on the trunk of a fallen tree. "This is never going to work," he said. "Any time now the Azzies will find us, and then—*whhshkkt!*" He made a slicing motion across his throat.

"You're overlooking something," Hardwick said, sitting upwind to avoid the full impact of orkish BO.

"Yeah, Johnson? What's that?"

"The mindset of the typical corporate administrator."

"I've never understood how you assholes think in the first place, so why don't you enlighten me?"

"That lab's important, but not big. So it only has a couple of small choppers, maybe one rigger. This is Aztechnology, so they probably have at least one mage."

"Had," Atsa said. "Teamster's Firetalon killed him."

"Good. But there's *got* to be someone in charge. Unless I miss my guess, it's a 'promising' junior executive on his way up the Aztech ladder. If it gets back to his bosses that he lost the GEE *and* its inventor, his career comes to a screeching halt—maybe his life, too, the way things work in Aztlan. He'll do everything he can to get it back using only what he's got on hand so he doesn't have to notify the higher-ups or call in too many favors. If we can reach the secondary extraction point before he unleashes the full Aztechnology arsenal, we have a good shot at getting out of this alive."

"Hope you're right," Tuskarora said. "That would explain why we haven't seen any signs of pursuit yet."

"Nothing in the astral either, that I can tell—but I'm a little out of practice," Hardwick said. "Come on, let's stay ahead of them as long as we can."

• • •

The swamp attacked them a few minutes later as they waded across a calf-deep channel between two patches of more or less solid ground. Tuskarora had just reached the far side when a monster exploded out of the deep water to their left.

Twice the ork's size, it had scaly, green-brown skin, a heavy rectangular head, and a mouth full of large, sharp fangs.

It lunged for Hardwick, but a few years behind a desk hadn't destroyed his runner's reflexes. He jerked to the side and the beast's jaws clamped onto his field pack instead of his chest. The straps pulled painfully against his shoulders, and then snapped under the strain of the creature's strength as he stumbled and fell into the murky water.

Tuskarora yelled and leaped. Grabbing one of the creature's horns with his left hand, he thrust the cyber-spurs from his right deep into its eye. The monster bellowed in pain. With an agonized jerk of its head, it threw the ork into the deep water.

It turned back to Hardwick, but Tuskarora's attack had given him enough time to prepare one of his own. Obeying his will, mana flowed and coalesced, becoming a blue-white bolt of destructive energy. The creature roared in pain again, its scales offering little protection against magic.

Tuskarora returned to the fight, this time coming in low to rake his spurs across the creature's softer underbelly. The wounds he left were shallow, but they convinced the beast to seek easier prey. It whirled and dove into the deep water.

"Elvis Christ!" Tuskarora said as they waited cautiously to make sure it didn't intend to return. "What the fuck was that, a combat hippo?"

"A behemoth," Atsa said. "An Awakened alligator—a *young* one. An adult would've been twice as big."

"Why didn't you *shoot* it?" Hardwick said.

"Even if a round from a Predator could get through that thing's skin, you think it would make a difference? More important, a gunshot's not natural—if there are any Azzies nearby, they wouldn't care about swamp animal sounds, but gunfire'd bring 'em running."

"Good point," Hardwick said, recovering his composure. "Let's get out of here in case there are more of those things around."

• • •

Half an hour later, they heard the sound they'd been dreading: an approaching helicopter. "Cover!" Tuskarora said. They dove into a thicket and scrambled into it as deep as they could. Hardwick was soon covered in muck and face-to-face with several disturbingly large insects.

The chopper drew closer, passed overhead to the south. The noise of the rotors faded—then increased again.

"Drek and dog piss!" Tuskarora said. "Either they picked up something, or they're focusing on this area."

They waited, unmoving, as the helicopter noise came and went, came and went. Then another sound joined the mix: a buzzing whine, like some strange insect. . . .

"Spy drone!" Atsa whispered.

Tuskarora drew his pistol. "No!" Hardwick said. "The chopper will pick up a gunshot for sure."

"Better than letting that drone eyeball us."

"Let me try something else first," Hardwick said. "Both of you remain *absolutely still*, got it?" They nodded.

Hardwick concentrated. He thought about the look of the leaves, right down to vein and stem; the twisting of the vines; the feel of mud and branch and heat; the sounds made by swamp creatures.

They saw the drone: a red and black dragonfly-like thing, sleek and swift. It came closer. The runners held their breath; Hardwick kept concentrating.

The drone hovered in place only a meter away. Then with a flick of a titanium and plastic appendage it darted off to the north and soon disappeared among the foliage.

The runners exhaled. A wave of fatigue washed over Hardwick; he collapsed to one elbow.

"Johnson, you okay?" Tuskarora said. "What the hell happened?"

"Just . . . a little Drain. Be all right in a sec."

"Drain?"

"I hid us with a Trid Phantasm—fools tech as well as natural senses. Drone thought we were just a thicket."

"You're smarter'n you look, Johnson. But c'mon, we gotta follow that chopper."

"*Follow* it? Are you insane? We should go some other direction."

"You're not the only bright boy here, chummer. That was a Northrup Hornet."

"And you know that how? We couldn't see it."

"From the sound," Tuskarora said in the tone usually used to address idiots and the mentally infirm.

"Okay, okay, good for you. So what? Why follow a Hornet?"

"'Cause it doesn't exactly get great KPL. It's a short-range, two-man attack chopper that's been out on recon patrol all day. It wasn't flying toward the lab, so the pilot must know someplace nearby to refuel. If we can get there, maybe we can grab the Hornet and fly to the extraction point. Or would you rather keep humping it down here with the mud and bugs?"

"Wow, an ork with some brains. Where'd you get your degree—Harvard?"

"No, Overtown University."

• • •

Luck, or perhaps Raccoon, was with them. Another half hour of hard slogging later, they peered through the brush at a clearing containing a big concrete slab supporting a shack, several fuel tanks, and a Northrup Hornet. The place looked like it used to be a ranger station or Park Service depot back in the days when the government owned most things. The green lion logos everywhere proclaimed that it now belonged to Aztechnology. Two pilots worked on the Hornet while three well-armed dwarf guards stood watch.

"I didn't think a Hornet could carry that many," Tuskarora said. "Smart to use dwarves."

"How are we going to get it now?" Hardwick asked.

"I've got a plan," Tuskarora said.

"Hey, I think I know this one: 'kill all of them,' right?" Hardwick said, remembering the usual "plan" favored by his old samurai friend War-Eye.

Tuskarora gave him the stink-eye as only an ork could. "Look, I may have big, pointy teeth, but I'm not a monster. Let's not kill them unless we absolutely have to."

"A nonviolent samurai? This is a first."

"Look, odds are the Azzies'll learn who pulled this job, sooner or later. If I get a rep for casually geeking their guys, that moves me to the top of their hit list, and no one stays on there for long. If I act like a professional and not a butcher, they'll extend me the same respect. It's just good biz."

"You're right," Hardwick said. "I followed the same sort of code. I'm sorry I didn't think you would, too. Working with so many drekhead runners has kind of made me cynical."

Tuskarora grinned. "That's one of the job qualifications for a Johnson, though, ain't it?"

Hardwick stifled a laugh. "Okay, then, how do we take care of the guards and get the Hornet?"

"Simple: we lure them away."

"You can fly the Hornet?"

"I can," Atsa said.

"You up to it?"

She nodded. "The splint lets me move my leg enough to do what I need to do, though it probably won't be the gentlest flight. Raccoon will provide."

"You do realize raccoons are ground-based animals, right?"

"Cut the clowning, Johnson—we got work to do," Tuskarora said.

"All right, so what's this big plan of yours, Tusk?"

"It's that Trid spell of yours—use it to create an illusion of some runners on the other side of that depot firing at the Azzies, then retreating when the Azzies shoot back. Once they've left, we sneak up, grab the Hornet and maybe a pilot, and away we go."

Hardwick considered carefully. "You're smarter than you look, Tusk," he said. "But once I lose line of sight to the Phantasm, the spell ends. With luck, the guards will assume we're still fleeing and continue to chase what they think is us. Without luck . . ."

"Just have to take the chance, unless you got a better idea." Hardwick shook his head. "You ready?" This time he nodded, wishing the sweat dripping down his face came only from the Florida heat.

"Okay. Once the guards leave the platform, I'll run up there. If it looks safe, Atsa, you follow as fast as you can; otherwise wait and come with Johnson."

"Got it," she said.

"Johnson, keep the spell going until those guards are as far away as you can lure them, then get to the platform ASAP. Clear?"

"Clear," Hardwick said, enjoying the feel of working with a good team. Risking his life on a run wasn't his idea of fun anymore, but it created a camaraderie no corp job ever could. He took a deep breath and centered himself, visualizing three prime runners. He focused on the target zone, a patch of trees and brush on the opposite side of the platform.

He drew upon his mana and cast the spell. Moments later the sounds and sights of gunfire and wizardry emanated from the target zone. The Aztechnology guards responded with practiced skill, leaping off the platform and taking cover. Soon they returned fire with coordinated precision.

Tuskarora took off, running faster than any nonaugmented man ever could. He reached the platform and darted in among the fuel tanks, looking for hostiles. Atsa followed at the fastest limp-run she could manage.

Hardwick kept the Phantasm going. Once Atsa reached the platform, he manipulated it so the runners seemed to retreat. The guards followed, moving in short, tactically intelligent maneuvers. He maintained the Phantasm as long as he could see the target zone, then stopped concentrating and ran for the platform.

The shots he expected never came. He reached the concrete and jump-heaved himself onto it behind one of the fuel tanks. He moved around the tank with as much stealth as he could muster, his eyes peeled for Tusk or Atsa—or Azzies.

He reached the Hornet just as Tuskarora shot one of the Aztech pilots in the head with a silenced Ares Light Fire. With blinding speed, he headed toward the nearby shack, saying, "Hey, you, stop!" as he moved. He flattened himself against the shack's wall next to the door, drew his Predator, and waited.

Seconds later the other pilot came out of the shack, a Beretta in his hand and a fresh soykaf stain on the front of his flight suit. Before he could take another step Tuskarora grabbed the pilot's arm and shoved the muzzle of his Predator against the man's head. "Afternoon, chummer. How'd you like to come work for Saeder-Krupp?"

"Uhhh . . . *viva* Lofwyr?"

"Good choice, son, you've got a bright future with this company. Your first assignment is to fly us the hell outta here."

"Hornet's not refueled yet."

"It's got enough juice to get where we're going. Move!"

• • •

Thirty minutes later, they were in comfortable chairs in an SK helicopter, drinking bottles of chilled water. Hardwick had rarely tasted anything so good.

"Don't worry, Johnson," Tuskarora said. "You'll be back in the nine-to-five soon."

"Hope so. I . . . look, I know this probably means nothing to you, but . . . I'm truly sorry about your friends."

The big ork slumped a little, as if the memory weighed him down. "Thanks. I ran with them for a long time; we made it through a lotta drek together. Hard to believe I won't see 'em again."

"Regardless of the op's results, I wish they'd lived. Losing a friend, it . . . leaves a hole in your soul, sort of. The hole gets smaller with time, but it never completely closes up. Maybe that's for the best."

Tuskarora crooked a smile around his tusks. "What's this, Johnson? Getting sentimental and chummy with the 'disposable assets'? What would your bosses say?"

Hardwick shook his head. "Not disposable. Never that. The corps treated me like that too often back in my runner days; it's counterproductive and stupid. I prefer the term 'unconventional' instead."

"How about 'renegade'? Or 'crazed'?"

"Those work too," Hardwick said, now smiling himself.

"Better watch out, Johnson. If your corporate masters learn you have a heart, they won't let you be a Johnson anymore. They'll make you do something that requires more ethics and honesty, like supervising the Unauthorized Human Testing Division."

Hardwick's smile didn't fade. "I hear there are some real opportunities there. But you better watch out yourself. If word hits the street that you saved a Johnson's life and treated him like a decent human being instead of a dick in a suit, your rep'll be barghest chow."

"Well, I won't tell if neither of you will," Atsa said.

"Too bad about the swag," Tuskarora said, leaning back in his seat and shutting his eyes. "All that work and death for nothing."

A different smile teased at Hardwick's face, but he suppressed it before either of the runners saw. Feeling the GEE against his skin through the secret pouch in his body armor, he thought about telling Tuskarora he had it. After all, the samurai had saved his life in the Glades, maybe more than once. They were practically friends now.

Well, not *good* friends. Hardwick leaned back in his seat to get some sleep.

TIM MAUGHAN

FLYOVER COUNTRY

(2016)

I MEET THIS GIRL Mira and her kid in the parking lot of that Wendy's on Jefferson that's been closed since '19. Yellowing grass pushes up through cracks in warped tarmac, and I find myself daydreaming again about the ground ripping open and consuming the whole fucking town. Like an earthquake. Or maybe a big storm rolling in, like last year but fiercer. Something. Anything.

It's only six thirty but it's hot out already. Mira's kid is sleepy, not used to being up this early. But she's still cute as all hell, all pigtails and smiles, playing up for the camera as I snap pictures of her and her mom on an old Samsung phone. Mira has got a CVS bag stuffed full of papers with her—the kid's school reports, some crayon scribbled drawings, letters both of them have written. I snap photos of them too, trying not to read the contents as I fight to get the shitty phone camera to focus on handwriting.

I need to get going. Miguel always sorts this shit out last minute, swapping shifts around so things line up. So everyone is in the right place at the right time. Always seems to end up with yours truly barely prepared, in a rush. Mira gives me forty bucks, which she says is the last of her UBI for the month. I feel bad and try to give her ten back, but she won't take it. Says she can pick up some more cleaning jobs on Handy, that I shouldn't worry. *Just don't fuck up,* she says. I smile and promise her I won't.

I've only got an hour before my shift starts, no time to walk all the way back home, so I duck into the bathroom at the big Walgreens on Lincoln. It's on the way. In the stall I kneel on the floor in front of the john, and spread out a clean shirt from my bag across the closed lid. I place the Samsung in the middle, and start using one of the tool kits I got off eBay to crack open its casing. It's tricky—it always fucking is—but I manage to pry it apart without scratching it up too much, without it looking like it's been tampered with.

I breathe a huge sigh of relief when I see the motherboard. The SD chip is 256 gigabytes and the right model. It makes me fucking laugh, this shit. All these companies always competing to make you buy their phone, and then to make you buy a new one every damn year, making you feel like you're missing out if you've not got the newest, the best ever. But inside they all look the same to me. Same components, same chips, same storage, year in year out.

Somebody comes into the bathroom, so I start making heaving noises, just in case they spot my feet and wonder what the fuck I'm doing. There's a pause and then they reluctantly ask me if I'm okay in there. I laugh and make spit sounds and I'm like *yeah fine, just a heavy night y'know.* I cough some more and listen to them moving around, the sound of pissing then running water, mixed with canned laughter and the theme tune to *Tila Tequila's Beltway Round-Up* pumping in over the store's tinny PA. Eventually I hear the door close and I get back to work.

The SD chip comes out easy, I've done it a few thousand times before. I gently tape it to the backside of the RFID chip sewn into the back of my green overalls with a Band-Aid, before stuffing them back into my bag. I put the phone back together and drop that in there too, along with the clean shirt. Sadly the cheap-ass tool kit has to go in the trash on my way out, cos there's no way I'll get that through security. Pain in the ass, but fuck it. I've got a bunch more of them at home.

• • •

The walk to the Foxconn-CCA Joint Correctional and Manufacturing Facility takes me about twenty minutes on the interstate. Traffic is pretty much nonexistent apart from the cab-less trucks that dwarf me as they pass, kicking up clouds of pale dust that scour my eyes with grit.

Gate security is bullshit as always. They barely care, lazily rummaging through my bag as I stand in the body scanner, feet on the markings, arms bent above my head. They pull out the phone, put it in a RFID tagged baggy to pick up at the end of my shift, and silently hand me back my bag.

Miguel is at the shift manager's desk. He gives me some gruff bullshit about getting in earlier in future, about how I should turn up ready to go in my overalls, while guiltily avoiding making eye contact. Stay cool, Miguel. He checks the rota on his tablet, tells me I've been assigned to production line 3B, building seven. Motherboard assembly. Of course, I know all this already.

I duck through dormitory six as a shortcut, weaving through the endless rows of bunk beds. Artificial light filters down through suicide nets and sprays a slowly undulating checkerboard across the plastic floor. Everyone in here is in green overalls: voluntary. On shift breaks they sit around on their bunks or on plastic chairs, talking, playing cards, watching *A Noble War* on the huge TVs that line the dorm. It's the episode where Barron and Beatrice get married on the bridge of the USS *Thiel*, just after they've put down a socialist uprising on Phobos. I remember the episode, season four I think. Barron still has his real arm. I used to love this shit back in high school.

I keep walking. The dorm is a fucking shithole. It's dirty and smells of ass and body-stink. If this is where they put the voluntary workers I don't want to ever see how bad things are for the actual inmates. I shudder at the thought of choosing to be stuck in here, but I get it. I got no kids, I'm lucky. My Universal Basic Income still covers my rent, just about. I pass a guy that looks my age, stripped to the waist, lying on his bunk. Chest splattered with random, uncoordinated tattoos, like stickers on a kid's lunchbox. He stares up through the suicide nets, into dull fluorescent light, his eyes unmoving. There but for the fucking grace of God.

I find an empty locker and open it, cram my bag in. Checking over my shoulders for guards or drones I reach inside and tear the Band-Aid away from the inside of my overalls, and palm it and the chip into my pocket. I step back and pull the overalls on over my clothes, slip on the paper face mask and hairnet, and head outside, relieved to escape the smell.

• • •

I move quickly through the courtyard. Running late. Again the bodies I weave through are all sealed in green overalls, but on the other side of the three-story chain-link fence I can see red and blue clothed figures. Convicts and Illegal Residents.

I keep my eyes down as I move, not wanting to catch the mirror-shaded gaze of the guards in the towers, or the dead twitching eyes of the drones that hang in the hot, still air.

Inside Building Seven the chain fence runs right through the interior, cleaving the production line in two. Green overalls on my side, red and blue on the other. The dank, mildew smell of almost-failing AC. Today I'm on motherboard assembly. A constant stream of naked iPhones come down the conveyor belt to me, their guts exposed, and as each one passes I clip in a missing chip. 256GB storage chips, from a box covered in Chinese lettering.

One every ten seconds. Six a minute. Three hundred sixty an hour. Four thousand three hundred and twenty a shift.

After me the line snakes away, disappearing through a hole in the chain-link, into the hands of Reds and Blues.

At the station next to me, a slender matte-black robot arm twitches, snapping video chips into the motherboards. It is relentless, undistracted, untiring. Given half a chance Foxconn would replace us all, but then they'd lose all those special benefits the President promised them for coming here in the first place. The ten-year exemption on income and sales tax. The exemption on import tariffs for components. The exemptions from minimum wages. The exemption on labor rights. The protection against any form of legal action from employees or inmates. The exemption from environmental protection legislation. And Apple? Well, without me standing here, clipping one Chinese-made component into another Chinese-made component, Apple loses the right for a robot in Shenzhen to laser engrave 'Made in the USA by the Great American Worker' into every iPhone casing before they're shipped over here.

• • •

It takes me about two hours to pluck up the courage to do what I gotta do. Two hours. Seven hundred twenty iPhones.

Once I decide, there's no going back. Instead of taking a chip from the box to my right, I slip my hand into my overalls pocket, and palm out the chip. To my huge fucking relief it clips effortlessly into the next iPhone on the belt. On top of it I place the Band-Aid, with just enough pressure that it stays there while looking like it fell from my scratched and battered hand.

I watch the phone slide down the line, its little Band-Aid flag making it stand out from its compatriots, as it vanishes through the chain-link fence.

• • •

Eight hours later. Two thousand eight hundred and eighty iPhones.

Shift over. My calves and the backs of my thighs sting from standing for twelve hours, my eyes strained from the fluorescent glare. The panel on the wall bleeps, turns green, as I punch out. I gaze at its screen. My blocky, low-res reflection gazes back, a machine vision approximation of my tired eyes and pale skin. I stand there, silently, not moving, waiting for the panel to recognize me. A tick appears, obscuring my face. Video game statistics scroll along the screen's bottom: efficiency, accuracy, timekeeping, responsiveness, productivity. Four thousand three hundred and fourteen iPhones. Chimes and a bleep. A synthesized, too-cheerful, feminine voice tells me I should smile more. A second bleep, the click of a door unlocking, and I'm out.

• • •

My phone buzzes at 5:24 a.m., under my pillow and loud as all fuck because I made sure the ringer was cranked to max. Text from an unknown number. Miguel on a burner. Time to go to work.

• • •

Two hours later and I'm back in my overalls, back in Building Seven.

This time I'm on Returned QA Fails. The pace is slower, the work slightly more involved. iPhones that have failed quality assurance up the line because of faulty chips come back down. I whip out the fucked chip, stick a new one in, send them back up the line again.

One every twenty seconds. Three a minute. One hundred eighty an hour. Two thousand one hundred and sixty per shift.

It tends to be even more chilled than that, to be honest. There's not that many that come back faulty, obviously. Nowhere near in fact. But the algorithms don't care. The drones lazily orbiting around the ceiling on their quadrotors are always watching, making notes, remembering. Calculating. Doesn't matter how many you actually do, you still gotta do 'em quick. Keep those productivity stats high.

It's less than two hours—maybe sixty phones—into my shift when it appears. Coming down the line, a dropped Band-Aid stuck lazily to its exposed guts.

My stomach flips. I glance upward to make sure the drone has cycled away. As the phone reaches me I pluck the Band-Aid away, drop it to the floor. Un-click the storage chip, and drop in another, new one.

The chip I've just taken out should go in a box, to go into a container, to go onto a truck, to go onto a ship, to go to China, to go onto another truck, to be dumped in some no-fucking-where village in Guangdong where an old lady that used to be a subsistence farmer will pull it apart in her front room to recycle the components.

But this one? This chip I originally ripped from that old Samsung? This chip gets palmed into my pocket.

• • •

I meet Mira in the Wendy's parking lot. Her kid is with her again. Cute as all hell. Running around in the tarmac-piercing grass.

I hand her the Samsung phone, its storage chip returned to its rightful place. She hands me another forty bucks.

Before I turn to leave, I watch her power it on, swipe it open. Her thumb stabs impatiently at icons. And then the screen fills with a photograph, a brown face, beard, smiling. Trying to look happy but nervous. Blue overalls. A photo taken while glancing over your shoulder, on a hastily hacked open, smuggled-in old smartphone you don't even know works. A photo you'd risk spending six months in solitary to take.

Mira smiles, begins to cry.

She calls her kid over.

Look. You know who that is?

Pause. Eyes wide.

Daddy!

As I walk away she's kneeling on the floor, holding the kid close to her, tears rolling down both their faces, as she swipes through images. The face again. Badly focused photos of handwritten notes.

I feel good for a second. Like it's worth it. But part of me still wants the ground to rip open and consume the whole town.

It's cooler today. A breeze is picking up, tugging at my green overalls as I start my walk back home. Somewhere out past the interstate, over the horizon, a storm is rolling in. A big storm like last year. I hope it's fiercer. I hope it's something. Anything.

E. LILY YU

DARKOUT

(2016)

IN ALL OF NORTHCHESTER, Pennsylvania, there was hardly forty square feet that was not continuously exposed to public view, on glass walls if you had money or on tablets if you were poor. This meant that Brandon spent most nights after his shift at the sports store watching Emma, his latest ex and the prettiest, as she chopped garlic, buttered toast, poured herself a gin and tonic, propped her furry-slippered feet on the coffee table with ska pulsing from her speakers, or took a date to bed. The counter at the upper right corner of the wall shifted between four and seven total viewers when Emma was eating dinner or clipping her fingernails. It shot up as high as fifty-five if Emma was mussing her lipstick and her zebra-print sheets with a fresh conquest. One hundred viewers was when ads floated up, loud and flashing, for limpness, smallness, underperformance.

Sometimes Brandon was disappointed in his relative unpopularity, his counter's slow tick of zero, one, zero, one, two, one, but then, white men tended to attract fewer eyeballs. The Indian family on Decker and Main, with two toddlers, boring as paint but only one of two nonwhite households on the east side of the tracks, attracted a dependable twenty every night. You needed pizzazz, or mystery, or difference to become a peripheral home-cam star. You needed nothing but a screen and a billed connection to lurk on others' cam streams.

These days he could hardly remember life without the cameras, although they had only been installed ten years ago, after the passage of the Blue Eye Act.

As Little England and China had demonstrated, where there was universal surveillance, crime rates plummeted. Russia, Zambia, Egypt, and Japan adopted similar systems roughly at the same time as the States, and most other wealthy countries were testing a limited rollout in their ghettos and shantytowns.

Brandon hadn't glanced at the newscast for more than a few seconds. "Eyes once were said to be the windows to a man's soul," the Attorney General thundered from her podium, beside the glum chief of Central. "With the passage of this Act, windows shall look into every person's soul. Not one potential criminal or terrorist will live unwatched."

Bored, and oblivious to history's apparition on his screen, Brandon flipped to an episode of *Snowballers III*.

There were restrictions and concessions to privacy lobbies, of course. Only badges could check logs or monitor, and only then with a warrant. The software was written to prevent remote modification. Two years after deployment, however, Croatian hackers cracked encryptions and began charging for views of the American of your choice. Actresses, usually. A mild fuss was made. Some feminists penned screeds and circulated petitions.

With the rafts of necessary legislation already in force, thirteen of the thirty original contractors and subcontractors out of business, and the budget long since buried beneath truckloads of additional appropriation bills, a complete overhaul of the hardware and individual installation of security patches were as politically feasible as open borders. After long debate, the white-hat community reached a general consensus to open-source the Croatian exploit, so that everyone and everything could be seen at all times. A bright and egalitarian future had arrived, they argued, superseding the dark days of cold cases, unreliable eyewitnesses, and domestic terrorism. Most citizens had become accustomed to the idea of being watched anyway. Polls suggested a solid 79 percent enjoyed the constant access to celebrities' meals and wardrobes.

A front-row seat to hours of Emma's smooth shoulders was an unexpected personal consequence of that legislation. After darkening his wall and pressing his palms against his tired eyes, Brandon considered, not for the first time, taking two weeks off from work and a hike along the West Coast. Emma was a drug, the perfect drug, and after a six-month hit of her, he was clawing through withdrawal. The pillow forts she used to build, the shape of her feet, her high, delighted laughter when he landed the perfect joke: the memories burned like poison, and he could not stop drinking them in.

Sweat, grit, sunlight, distance, and mai tais might cure him. He had done the budget. He had saved enough for a short vacation. The customers at the sports store who swiped kayaks and paddleboards onto silver credit cards, with their freckled shoulders, bronzed cheeks, and bleached hair, always seemed to him an alien species, possessed of a thousand-and-one adventures and the insulation provided by ready cash. He could join them, however briefly.

Brandon powered down his screen and stared out the glass wall at the dead light and gray grass of winter, imagining hot white sand between his toes and the cool spray of the Pacific on his face. He was learning to surf from a wise old instructor. He carried the board under his arm like a knight riding into battle and rode the smooth roaring waves hour after hour, day after day, until the water pounded his thoughts into nothingness. His chalky skin darkened. He ate six swordfish steaks for dinner, bought a drink for every pretty brunette in the bar, and forgot about Emma.

But then the flickering stream of panoptic views into kitchens and bedrooms, kitten-crammed commercials, and staged cop shows, all the cheap and irresistible glitter of secondhand life, sang to him again. Depressing a button, Brandon turned the wall opaque and went back to watching Emma curl and uncurl her toes, his heart in his mouth.

He was waiting for her to collapse into tears. He was waiting for her to scribble on a poster with a squeaking marker and hold it up to her bedroom camera: I LOVE YOU BRANDON. IT WAS A MISTAKE. COME BACK.

When he saw that, when he and the ten strangers on her stream saw he was victorious at last, Brandon would hop into his sneakers and sprint the six miles across town to her apartment, pumping his arms, dodging cars, the Internet cheering unheard in the background. He would hammer on her door. In his imagination, she was pacing the room in her black lace bra and matching panties, a loose robe around her shoulders. Her audience had swelled to two thousand during his dramatic run. She flung open the door and pressed her unblotched and tastefully rouged face to his shoulder. He put his arms around her, and they sank onto the zebra sheets, to the unheard sighs of thousands of spectators. It wasn't impossible. These things were known to happen.

Once in a while Brandon heard the squeak of a marker in a dream, catapulted out of bed, and yanked on socks and shoes before he was entirely awake. But his morning wall only ever showed him commercials for insurance and whole-wheat cereal, tiled four by four.

Tonight, though, he did not linger on Emma's stream. It was the night of the Fitz-Ramen Bowl. He had swapped shifts with Mandy to watch it. Mark Thompson was coming with two twelve-packs of craft beer.

"I need to get out of the house. You need to get out of your head," Mark had said. "You've got the subscription. I'll get the drinks."

Their friendship began four years ago, when Mark, observing Brandon's painful attempt to charm an out-of-town marketing rep in the bar, sent along a pint of porter and a napkin penned with ratings: *Confidence 2, Slickness 0, Desperation 17.* An electrician, Mark was a good fifteen years older than Brandon and married to a sweet talker of a woman who never found fault with him.

He was not at all someone Brandon would have expected as a friend. Brandon did not have many friends.

But Mark's taste in beers was excellent, and over the latest microbrew he confided to Brandon that listening to him brought back the rush and risk of youth, the gambits and heartbreaks and exuberant successes. So did football, which he had to watch out of the house, because his wife slept early, and lightly, and not well.

"A bad back," he said, shaking his head. "Like her father."

So when Mark buzzed the door, and the camera floated his face over the screen, Brandon felt his spirits lift. The two of them popped their beers, propped their feet on the table, and cheered the Pittsburgh College Lynxes. During the commercials they flipped to live cop cams outside the stadium, betting on whether the nastiest officers would be reprimanded. Mark set up a private pool on his phone, floating fives and tens, and they passed it back and forth.

"Do you or don't you understand English? You come to this country, you better learn English—" The driver stared down at his lap. His hands gripped the wheel.

"Five bucks no one remembers." Brandon emptied his can.

"Nope, not taking it. He's Bangladeshi."

"They're all brown to me."

"The accent."

"So?"

"They don't get big Internet mobs. Not like the Indians. Polite complaint from the Association of Bangladeshi Cabdrivers, that's all. *Sir it has come to our attention that*, and *would you pretty please.*"

"Why do they still do traffic stops? You can ID the plates in two cameras, calculate speed, deliver ticket. Wham."

"Maybe they're bored on patrol. Maybe they don't want people watching them sit on their hands. Makes the taxpayer think about payroll."

After Mark's wagers hit a hundred dollars and change, he pocketed the phone. "Personal limit," he said, smiling. "Lizzie's been on my case."

Humming, he appropriated the remote and browsed a DV forecaster. Past emergency call records, crunched for patterns, allowed you to time future incidents so accurately that the popcorn you put in the microwave reached its last thuck, thuck as the boyfriend kicked open the door. A few predictive statistics blogs published regular watching guides. Politicians and athletes attracted the most attention, but the smart ones paid for darkspace: for a million per square foot hour, the ten most popular hosts stopped streaming your cams.

Logs remained available to the police, and a determined viewer, with some finagling, could connect directly to the right camera, but for the most part darkspace worked. A cheaper option was to smash the camera outright. That was a felony, but so was everything that followed.

At 1818 Maple Drive, the microphone still functioned. Brandon grimaced at the screaming and smack of fist against flesh and switched the whole wall back to the game.

"Why do you watch this shit?"

"Third and a long thirteen, Stallions on the Lynxes' twenty-six, Washington is back to pass, Rodriguez is open—it's intercepted by Jones!"

"That's my man!" Mark said. "How long can you go in a shit job in a shit economy before snapping? The game's rigged against white men, you know that. Sometimes it's relaxing to see someone hit his breaking point."

"How do you know that guy was white?"

"The way she was hollering. Black women holler differently."

"Don't tell me you hit Lizzie."

"Never. Cams, though. Used to think there was something they knew that we didn't, so I watched sixteen families at a time. But no. They do holler different when the men beat them, though. They're used to violence. They're violent people. Not like us."

"The Lynxes are putting this game out of reach early, up twenty-four points with four minutes left in the first quarter."

Mark made a noise of satisfaction and grinned.

"Football's not relaxing enough?"

"It's fine. But it's tame. Ever since the concussion lawsuits. The old stuff was better."

Brandon cut to a channel forum and scrolled down the top-ranked links.

Mukwa, Wisconsin, puppycams 1–6
$$$wank Tokyo neighborhood on fire
High court tizzy, cute Aussie accents
Blonde bitch paid sex w/ my husband
Riot police circling US Capitol
Sex sex sex Witchita xxx
Catfight between officer, black woman in five-inch heels
See: protester arrests near US Supreme Court
Turtle feeding time: grapes

"How about them puppies," Mark said.

"I thought you'd be all over *Sex Sex Sex Witchita*."

"It's always some hag pushing seventy," Mark said. "Floppy in all the interesting places. Thought you knew that."

"That's bottom feeding. I don't trawl. The professional stuff's better."

"Sure, or you're interested in one person and no one else." Mark grinned wide enough for Brandon to see his silver fillings and tossed back the rest of his beer. He was in an expansive mood, as if he had both money and holy water on tap. "Seriously, start dating again. Lay some ladies. You'll feel better."

"What does Lizzie say when you talk to her about black people and how much you're suffering?"

"I don't. Because I'm a smart man. I mean, I'm lucky, I'll always have a job. But this Korean woman at the pharmacy yesterday, listen to this, she came up to me and said, 'I don't like the way you're looking at me.' That's the world we live in today. Christ. Maybe I'll see her on the DV watch someday. Don't you dream about smacking whatshername a good one?"

Brandon did, but he wasn't about to admit it.

"I'll sign you up on a few sites," Mark said. "Write you an A-plus profile. I'm good at them."

"You're married."

"That supposed to stop me? She's black, it's different. You wouldn't understand. Go ahead, run me over with a moral locomotive."

"Don't be an idiot."

"So what's the problem? You swipe up full of STDs?"

"I don't like them looking at medical. Full access for a week, no guaranteed sex. I'm sequenced and everything. Who says they won't copy and sell?"

"Hey, you have to give to get."

Brandon pitched his voice higher. "'Oh, you make twenty-four thousand a year?' 'You had appendicitis at sixteen? Wow.' "

"So you watch home cams. For the human contact. Is that it?"

Mark pinched the controller, quartered the screen, and flashed through a rapid succession of cams. A teenager doodling in his textbook. A woman working on a tablet, her face furrowed. An aged brown woman dumping chilies into a pot. A snoring cat. A man typing at a table. Two cats batting each other. An infant banging a rattle on the bars of her crib. Two men lifting free weights, mouths scrunched with the effort. A poodle peeing against a tree.

"Amazing." He smirked.

"It's culture," Brandon said. "Walking in other people's shoes. Makes me a better person. Lay off."

"You want culture, fuck a brown woman. I'm unbelievably cultured. I'm just saying, as your friend, you should get out more."

"What is this, an intervention?"

"If you give me your phone—"

"Go to the game, it's back on."

Four minutes into the fourth quarter, Mark's good mood was gone.

"What happened to our lead?"

"Oof," Brandon said.

"What kind of shit play was that?" Mark punched the table so hard his beer rocked over.

"Easy there."

"The coach is a scab-assed cockcrab. How do you burn a lead like that? How?"

Brandon mopped at the frothy mess of beer and sodden chips. "Every damn year."

"We're doomed." A flask appeared in Mark's hand.

"Put that down, you're drunk."

"I'm sober as a fucking duck. Me and Lizzie are screwed."

"What are you talking about?"

Mark reclaimed the controller and input a numerical camera address Brandon did not recognize, but from the first few digits guessed it was located somewhere in Pittsburgh's swankiest district. On his screen, now, a bald white woman sipped a salted glass while watching the game. She had a cottonmouth tattooed around her neck, red and black heels like ice picks, and six spikes in each ear. Noticing the uptick in her viewer count, she turned and flashed the camera a thumbs-up and a smile that crawled under Brandon's skin and itched.

"Who's that?" Brandon said, very slowly.

"My bookie. Ruth. Name's a joke, not for real. Short for—"

"You have the cash. Right?"

"This was supposed to be a straight-to-the-bank payday. Like the last one."

"The last one."

"I won a thousand betting a three-team parlay last year. She shook my head and told me I looked like a lucky man. 'When you want to make a real bet,' she said, 'with real money, think of me.' "

Ruth stared at the camera as if she could see them, her mouth still hooked in that crowbar of a smile.

Brandon flipped the whole wall back to the game, as if the scrum of blue, red, orange, and white could scrub the prickling off the back of his neck. The scene that greeted him wasn't much more cheerful. The Stallions were down by a single touchdown, and the whole tableau had the velvet air of a Shakespearean tragedy.

Here came the touchdown. Here the conversion.

Mark's head fell into his hands. The last thirty seconds slipped off the clock. Brandon held his beer to his lips with nerveless fingers.

The Stallions won, thirty-two to thirty-one. They flooded the field with blue and red, dancing, howling, cracking their helmets together.

"What do you do now?" Brandon said.

"Fuck if I know." Mark groaned. "She knows my address. Home and work. She has my contacts, too. Runs a background check for big wagers. So she'd know to look at you—"

As if in quiet confirmation, the little zero on the counter flicked to one. Brandon swallowed and wiped his mouth with the back of his hand.

"How much?"

"Ten thousand. It was one to two, I don't know why, Lynxes were favorite. I was gonna triple that—"

Brandon kneaded his temples. "Bonehead."

"Did you pick that up from Lizzie?"

"What were you going to do with thirty thousand?" That wasn't two weeks' vacation and surfing lessons. That was a year of rent on a ranch house somewhere in wine country and a wine tour every month. That was a plane ticket to a dark and disconnected country of grapevines and beautiful women, perhaps even kind women, and bedrooms and breakups without cameras.

"Don't lecture me."

"What were you going to blow it on? Weed? Speed? Cars?"

"Old lady needs spinal fusion, if you have to know."

"But insurance—"

"We don't have any."

"You need *brain* surgery."

Mark scowled. "I was trying to do right by her."

"Mortgage? Second mortgage? Sell the van?"

"Double mortgage already, from the doctors and pills. Need the van for work. We're up to our eyeballs." Mark took a deep breath. "Now you know how fucked we are. I hate doing this, Brandon, but—"

"You couldn't go with a Chinese bookie, could you? You had to get a *local*."

"Ruth gives better odds than the congloms. Plus she let me bet on credit."

Brandon flung the controller. It clattered satisfyingly against the wall and dropped out of sight. "Of course she let you, bumfuck. She knows where you live. Where Lizzie lives."

"I get it, I get it. So—"

"She can't do anything to you, right? Not with—" He gestured to the cameras.

"I've heard Ruth doesn't like dirtying her nails."

"That's a relief."

"So she contracts disposal and retrieval."

"Would I have heard of her?"

"Nothing splashy since six, seven years ago."

"Six—"

"The Burnetts." Mark shifted his weight. "The, uh, two girls, one boy, parents, grandfather, Dalmatian, and hamster. And one goldfish. Though maybe not the goldfish, those things die if you sneeze at them . . ."

"That was her?"

"Unofficially."

"Shit."

"Anyway, if she wants it quiet, she buys black."

"You're fucked."

"Royally." Mark blinked and grinned in terror. "So what I was going to ask—"

"Why mix me up in this? Why sit on my sofa and scarf my chips, with thirty grand riding on the game?"

"Lizzie's asleep. I wanted a friend—if I was going to celebrate—"

"Bullshit. You wanted me here in case you lost. So you could dun me for cash."

"You're angry, I get it. You're angry but I'm fucked."

Whether because the controller landed on a button or whether because the paid sportstream sensed their drifting attention, the postgame analysis switched to news. Thousands of masked protestors milled in the National Mall, waving single yellow roses splattered with black paint. GIVE US DARKNESS, their placards read. PRIVACY IS FREEDOM. The cameras faded from night to day, gliding from DC to San Francisco to Tokyo to Moscow. Every cosmopolis was boiling with protests. DARKOUT! DARKOUT!

"Motherfucking Luddites," Mark said.

"Don't change the subject. You dragged me into this. She's probably auditing me right now. What do you think she'll see? Do you think I have ten grand in my sock drawer?"

"I have two thousand in emergency funds," Mark said. "Lizzie made me. I only need eight."

"Great. Pick a star, click your heels, wish really, really hard—"

"Are you going to help me?" Mark pressed an empty can between his palms until it gave. "The way I helped you, when you totaled your car? When Nina dumped you and your shit on the curb?" It had been raining, and the cardboard boxes melted like sugar. When Brandon called, Mark laughed his ass off, but showed up five minutes later with his van. He had even dug up a dolly somewhere.

"You piece of goose shit." Brandon knuckled his eye sockets. Then he pulled out a phone and scrawled a passpattern with his fingertip. "Look at that balance, you fucking moron. Two thousand six hundred and I don't get paid until next Friday. Look at it!" He thrust the phone into Mark's face and watched Mark's pupils cross.

"I was going to California with this," Brandon said bitterly. He dragged two fingers over the phone and signed with his index finger. "There. Two thousand four hundred in your account tomorrow." He waved his phone at the camera. "See that, Ruth? He's got almost half of it. Charge him stupid interest and don't break his leg. Now get out, dickbrain."

"I'll pay you back."

"You're still short five thousand and change."

"Yeah."

"And Lizzie still needs a new back."

"That can wait."

"Like hell it can. My uncle slipped a disc once. Couldn't look at his face, or I started hurting too. Put her first for once."

Sudden motions and shouts pulled Brandon's eye back to the screen. A wave of protestors swelled and broke over a police barricade in Beijing. The air went blue and blurry with tear gas. The synchrony of their movements suggested careful rehearsal, which could only be coordinated online. In China, public spaces were off limits. The police would have noticed the preparations. Every security apparatus would have known.

Hopeless, all of them.

In the meantime, his own counter reached five, a personal record. Casual browsers attracted by the shouting? *Disappointed Lynx Bros Yelling*. Or black-jacketed, detached men with freshly fingerprinted contracts?

"You're a real friend, you know that?" Mark said. "I'm not going to forget this."

"Door's there. Get out."

"Going, I'm going." Mark slung his coat over his shoulders and banged open the screen door. Cold air swirled in. Brandon dimmed his wall to transparency and peered into the darkness, shivering, until Mark peeled out of the neighborhood in his anchovy can.

Asshole.

He brought his screen back up and stared at masks, placards, yellow roses. A svelte, lipsticked newscaster would have relieved the oppressiveness, but any newscaster was a rarity these days, when free and instant footage flowed everywhere. Who could keep up with that?

"Give us darkness! Darkout! Darkout!"

The news stream wasn't helping his nerves. Brandon retrieved the controller from behind an armchair and returned to his usual forum, cracking open a seventh beer.

Crazy guy scaling broadcast station perimeter: shot or not?

Ducklings hatching!!!

Trespassers at ISP HQ?

Sexy brown sugar mmm

Stallion fans riot in Houston, view from Gray's bar

As if of their own volition, his fingers tapped their way back to Emma's stream.

Kitchen: dark.

Living room: dark.

Bedroom: dark, too, but a slice of orange light from the street slipped under the blinds and threw a soft glow on her bare arms, a long loose curl, the gentle hills of her body under the comforters.

She was asleep. Her chest was rising and falling, rising and falling, and her breath made a fluttering, feathery sound through her lips that the microphone picked up and whispered to him. He remembered the sound from the seventeen times she fell asleep in his bed and the ten times he had slept in hers.

"I am a pathetic creep," he said aloud to his own five watchers. The whole world was his confessional, tonight. But as the words left his mouth, his own counter flickered: four—three—one—zero. No one wanted to hear him grovel.

"You still love me," he told Emma. She was just as lonely as he was. She was auditioning an endless river of men to fill a Brandon-sized hole inside her. And she never looked at his cam stream. Not once.

Not casually.

Not for a second.

Not as one of four or eight or sixteen streams split on her screen.

As if she didn't miss him at all.

The rhythm of her breath was soothing and soporific. He could listen to it forever.

His seventh beer half empty, feeling infinitely sorry for himself, Brandon slept.

• • •

He dreamed he was in California. It was a nice dream, with plenty of sunlight and blue sky and puffy clouds. The trees were spiny and crumpled with drought. He had never been to California, but this looked exactly like what he had seen in movies. Maybe California was more a collective cinematic fantasy than an actual place. Maybe, like an elaborate movie set, it never existed.

He stood in a desert studded with cactuses and hunched pines. Invisible birds cried and piped, and he could hear waves crashing unseen against an invisible shore.

Mirages shimmered everywhere. Mostly they were water mirages, but here was the quivering image of an ice cream cart, and there, on the horizon, stood one of Emma's perfect white breasts, large as a mountain. Why not two? he asked his subconscious. Give me the other one, come on. But the snowy peak shivered and vanished as he approached.

He had been hiking for hours, and his arms and legs were furry with dust. The mountains rising around him muffled the sound of the distant ocean.

One by one, the sharp, croaking bird calls ceased. All around him was a heavy and peculiar silence.

• • •

Brandon was accustomed to hearing the babble of strangers on his screen while he slept: any channel, anybody, anything to feel less alone. The absence of sound rang loud as cymbals in his ears. Startled awake, he poured out of bed and puddled on the floor. For several painful minutes he lay still, trying not to move. Someone was using his skull as blender and trash can and bongos all at once.

The screen had entered standby sometime during the night. It did not show Emma's room, nor his front yard, but rather the illusion of a flat white wall with a window in the center. Brandon pressed the power button. The operating light winked orange, but nothing changed.

"Damn," he said. Mark's beer must have shorted a circuit. But where? And what had he fried? Brandon picked up his phone to troubleshoot and found no signal. He could snap photos, he could play games, and that was all.

Brandon flicked and pushed and plugged and unplugged his watch, his Weatherboy, his scale, his library, his two tablets. All were functional. All were offline. What worried him most were the lights on his three cameras, which had gone from red to yellow. He had no way of placing a support call.

"Fuckity fuck fuck," he said.

He would have to walk downtown to Moby's. No appointment meant fighting through crowds clutching bricked devices and crying for miracles. That would make him at least an hour late for his shift. So he would have to stop at the sports store first, to explain.

His manager could confirm for himself that Brandon's cameras were dead. The law required busted cameras to be fixed within one day. Police arrived, demanding answers, if you didn't. Occasional darkness was only for the very rich, and Brandon did not feel rich at all. Someone like him was not allowed to be offline for long.

His stomach shrank at the thought of eggs and bacon. No breakfast, then. He gave himself a critical once-over in the bathroom mirror: Two bloodshot eyes, a greenish pallor, hair flattened in some places and rucked up in others. He pushed a wet hand over the hair that stuck out, but it bounced straight back.

"Mark, you fucker," he growled. "You dickshot. You douche."

When he went onto the front stoop of the divided house, the morning sun jabbed him in the eye. His breath smoked white from his mouth and nose. Around him the yellow grass glittered and crisped with frost.

The building's palm scan wasn't working. It ignored his hand and did not respond to his slap, but the maintenance light flashed. Swearing under his breath, Brandon dug in his pockets for his analog keys.

His upstairs neighbor, Alice Rosenbaum, crunched over the lawn in scarf and boots. She was in her sixties, with deep wrinkles and snowy hair, and appeared to fall somewhere between the kind of grandmother who invited lonely neighbors in for pie and the kind of grandmother who filed noise complaints punctually at ten each night. She grinned at him.

"That game, huh?" she said. Brandon, patting himself, realized he was still wearing his beer-sticky gear. "I lost fifty dollars on that last play. To my son-in-law. He'll never let me hear the end of it."

"My friend put ten thousand on the Lynxes."

She winced. "You have rich friends."

"He's broke."

"Online?"

"Local."

"Will he be all right?"

"I don't know. I can't call him."

"Right, right. The whole street's down."

"What?"

"I knocked at the Washburns' and asked."

"The Washburns?"

She pointed. "Number eighteen. Two of the cutest little girls."

Brandon couldn't remember ever seeing the family that lived in the yellow house. He felt slow and stupid, like a blind thing in a cave. "What's going on?"

"It's a darkout. Like a blackout. You know what a—no. We haven't had a blackout in twenty-one years. You would have been a kid."

"Someone digging up wires?"

"I don't know. Our phones are dead, too, and the tower's two miles from here. I think it's pretty big. But we won't know until everything's back up."

Mark had caught a break. Brandon hoped the bastard was okay. "How long do you think that'll take?"

"Who knows?" Alice glanced down the street. "I was going to pick up breakfast from the bakery. See if anyone knows. Used to do that when I was younger. You look like a bagel kind of guy. Want to come?"

Brandon hesitated. Someone should check on Mark and Lizzie. Especially Lizzie, who had a raucous belly laugh and mothered him. He hadn't known about her back. But they were ten miles across town, and with lines dead, and no car, what could he do if there was trouble?

Maybe Mark had hocked everything and paid up.

Or maybe, if all cams were dark, his bookie had bigger fish than Mark.

Of course there were bigger fish than Mark.

Mark would be fine.

Emma, though. He felt a pang almost as sharp as the first loss: the cool, cold look, the quick credit swipe for both lunches, as if she pitied him, and the impression of being tossed out along with the sandwich wrappers. He couldn't watch her now. He didn't know where she was or what she was doing, or if she had taken out poster paper and was chewing the end of a marker, thinking about him.

"I could do with a bagel," he said.

And they walked together through the unfamiliar morning, waiting, as the whole world was waiting, for the light to return.

RYUKO AZUMA

2045 DYSTOPIA

(2018)

Translated from the Japanese by Marissa Skeels

2045 AD.
GIANT CATS, WHICH ESCAPED FROM A RESEARCH FACILITY, STRUT ABOUT ALL OVER TOKYO.
THE GOVERN-MENT TRIED WIPING THEM OUT AT FIRST, BUT...

ONCE WORD SPREAD OVERSEAS, ANIMAL WELFARE SOCIETIES INTERVENED.
Japan:
Stop the HugeCat
WHEN EVERYONE REALIZED THEY ONLY PREY ON NONCITIZENS... "GENE POOR INDIVIDUALS"...
THEY GOT FREE REIN TO LIVE OUT THEIR TIMELY PURPOSE: HUNTING "MICE."
AHH!
HELP!
IT'S ALL A GOOD TOURIST ATTRACTION.
GOTTA LOVE JAPAN!

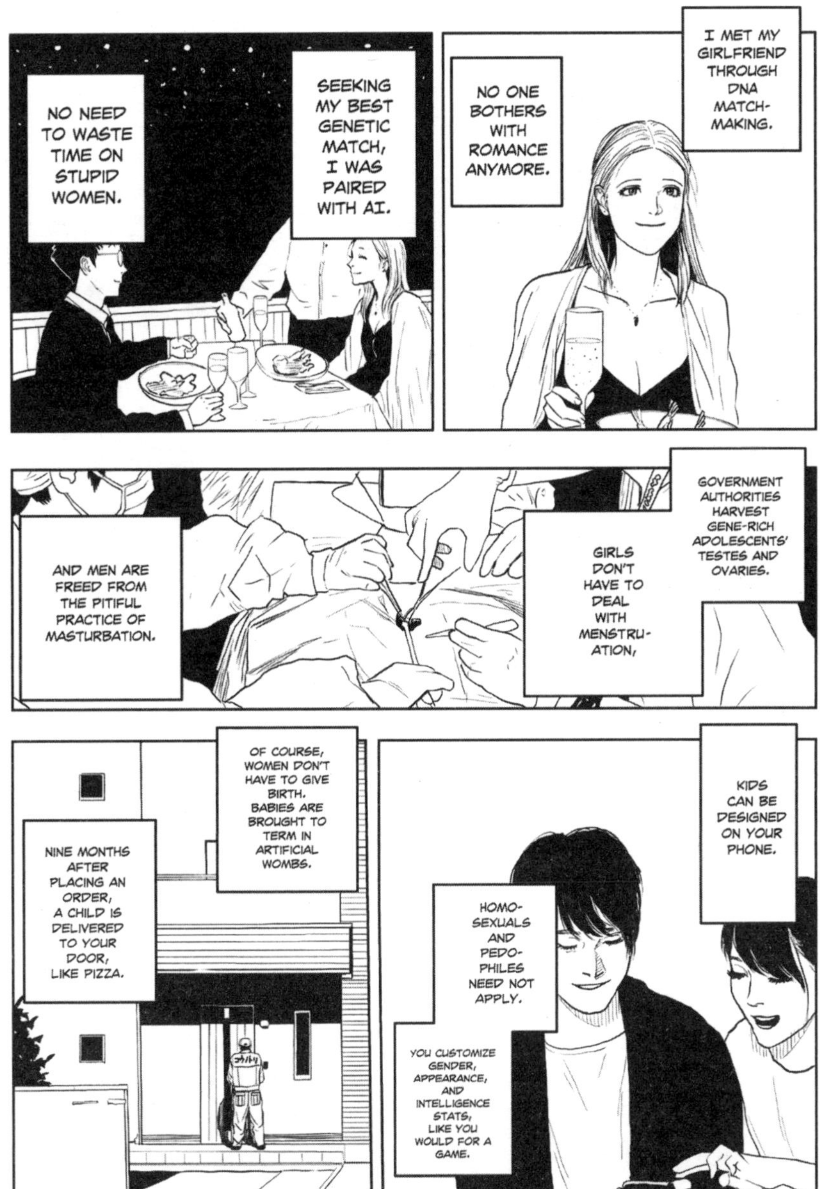
NO NEED TO WASTE TIME ON STUPID WOMEN.
SEEKING MY BEST GENETIC MATCH, I WAS PAIRED WITH AI.
I MET MY GIRLFRIEND THROUGH DNA MATCH-MAKING.
NO ONE BOTHERS WITH ROMANCE ANYMORE.
GOVERNMENT AUTHORITIES HARVEST GENE-RICH ADOLESCENTS' TESTES AND OVARIES.
GIRLS DON'T HAVE TO DEAL WITH MENSTRU-ATION,
AND MEN ARE FREED FROM THE PITIFUL PRACTICE OF MASTURBATION.
OF COURSE, WOMEN DON'T HAVE TO GIVE BIRTH. BABIES ARE BROUGHT TO TERM IN ARTIFICIAL WOMBS.
NINE MONTHS AFTER PLACING AN ORDER, A CHILD IS DELIVERED TO YOUR DOOR, LIKE PIZZA.
KIDS CAN BE DESIGNED ON YOUR PHONE.
HOMO-SEXUALS AND PEDO-PHILES NEED NOT APPLY.
YOU CUSTOMIZE GENDER, APPEARANCE, AND INTELLIGENCE STATS, LIKE YOU WOULD FOR A GAME.

IT'D BE BETTER FOR ANIMAL RIGHTS IF MEAT WERE GROWN FROM CULTURES, BUT...
THAT KIND DOESN'T TASTE AS GOOD AS REAL MEAT.
I WORK IN ANIMAL HUS-BANDRY.
WORK IS CAPPED AT 40 HOURS A MONTH.
NO ONE NEEDS TO WORK, BUT DOING SO TENDS TO MAKE LIFE EASIER.
MACHINES TAKE CARE OF SLAUGH-TERING.
WE PRODUCE MASSES OF UNIFORM, TOP-QUALITY MEAT.
BY OPTIMIZING THEIR EXERCISE, SLEEP, AND FEEDING PATTERNS...
SO LIVESTOCK WITH MACHINE MINDS WERE CREATED.
THEY'RE THE SAME AS MEAT STACKED UP NEATLY AT SUPER-MARKETS.
SINCE THEY LACK BRAINS, THEY PROBABLY CAN'T FEEL PAIN OR FEAR.
VERY OCCA-SIONALLY, THE SHOCK OF DYING MAKES ANIMALS EJACULATE.

MEAT THAT'S HAD ITS PAIN AND EMOTIONS REMOVED BY MACHINES.
MEAT WHICH TRIGGERS INTENSE SORROW AND...
RAGE.
HAH...
HAH...
HAH...
HAH...
WARN-ING
PUT DOWN THE WEAPON, AND PLACE BOTH HANDS ON YOUR HEAD. NOW.
WARN-ING
WHO...
PUT DOWN THE WEAPON, AND...
WHO MADE THIS THEIR FUTURE?

KEN LIU

THOUGHTS AND PRAYERS

(2019)

EMILY FORT:

So you want to know about Hayley.

No, I'm used to it, or at least I should be by now. People only want to hear about my sister.

It was a dreary, rainy Friday in October, the smell of fresh fallen leaves in the air. The black tupelos lining the field hockey pitch had turned bright red, like a trail of bloody footprints left by a giant.

I had a quiz in French II and planned a week's worth of vegan meals for a family of four in Family and Consumer Science. Around noon, Hayley messaged me from California.

Skipped class. Q and I are driving to the festival right now!!!

I ignored her. She delighted in taunting me with the freedoms of her college life. I was envious, but didn't want to give her the satisfaction of showing it.

In the afternoon, Mom messaged me.

Have you heard from Hayley?

No. The sisterly code of silence was sacred. Her secret boyfriend was safe with me.

If you do, call me right away.

I put the phone away. Mom was the helicopter type.

As soon as I got home from field hockey, I knew something was wrong. Mom's car was in the driveway, and she never left work this early.

The TV was on in the basement.

Mom's face was ashen. In a voice that sounded strangled, she said, "Hayley's RA called. She went to a music festival. There's been a shooting."

The rest of the evening was a blur as the death toll climbed, TV anchors read old forum posts from the gunman in dramatic voices, shaky follow-drone footage of panicked people screaming and scattering circulated on the web.

I put on my glasses and drifted through the VR re-creation of the site hastily put up by the news crews. Already, the place was teeming with avatars holding a candlelight vigil. Outlines on the ground glowed where victims were found, and luminous arcs with floating numbers reconstructed ballistic trails. So much data, so little information.

We tried calling and messaging. There was no answer. Probably ran out of battery, we told ourselves. She always forgets to charge her phone. The network must be jammed.

The call came at four in the morning. We were all awake.

"Yes, this is. . . . Are you sure?" Mom's voice was unnaturally calm, as though her life, and all our lives, hadn't just changed forever. "No, we'll fly out ourselves. Thank you."

She hung up, looked at us, and delivered the news. Then she collapsed onto the couch and buried her face in her hands.

There was an odd sound. I turned and, for the first time in my life, saw Dad crying.

I missed my last chance to tell her how much I loved her. I should have messaged her back.

• • •

GREGG FORT:

I don't have any pictures of Hayley to show you. It doesn't matter. You already have all the pictures of my daughter you need.

Unlike Abigail, I've never taken many pictures or videos, much less drone-view holograms or omni-immersions. I lack the instinct to be prepared for the unexpected, the discipline to document the big moments, the skill to frame a scene perfectly. But those aren't the most important reasons.

My father was a hobbyist photographer who took pride in developing his own film and making his own prints. If you were to flip through the dust-covered albums in the attic, you'd see many posed shots of my sisters and me, smiling stiffly into the camera. Pay attention to the ones of my sister Sara. Note how her face is often turned slightly away from the lens so that her right cheek is out of view.

When Sara was 5, she climbed onto a chair and toppled a boiling pot. My father was supposed to be watching her, but he'd been distracted, arguing with a colleague on the phone. When all was said and done, Sara had a trail of scars that ran from the right side of her face all the way down her thigh, like a rope of solidified lava.

You won't find in those albums records of the screaming fights between my parents; the awkward chill that descended around the dining table every time my mother stumbled over the word *beautiful*; the way my father avoided looking Sara in the eye.

In the few photographs of Sara where her entire face can be seen, the scars are invisible, meticulously painted out of existence in the darkroom, stroke by stroke. My father simply did it, and the rest of us went along in our practiced silence.

As much as I dislike photographs and other memory substitutes, it's impossible to avoid them. Coworkers and relatives show them to you, and you have no choice but to look and nod. I see the efforts manufacturers of memory-capturing devices put into making their results better than life. Colors are more vivid; details emerge from shadows; filters evoke whatever mood you desire. Without you having to do anything, the phone brackets the shot so that you can pretend to time travel, to pick the perfect instant when everyone is smiling. Skin is smoothed out; pores and small imperfections are erased. What used to take my father a day's work is now done in the blink of an eye, and far better.

Do the people who take these photos believe them to be reality? Or have the digital paintings taken the place of reality in their memory? When they try to remember the captured moment, do they recall what they saw, or what the camera crafted for them?

• • •

ABIGAIL FORT:

On the flight to California, while Gregg napped and Emily stared out the window, I put on my glasses and immersed myself in images of Hayley. I never expected to do this until I was aged and decrepit, unable to make new memories. Rage would come later. Grief left no room for other emotions.

I was always the one in charge of the camera, the phone, the follow-drone. I made the annual albums, the vacation highlight videos, the animated Christmas cards summarizing the family's yearly accomplishments.

Gregg and the girls indulged me, sometimes reluctantly. I always believed that someday they would come to see my point of view.

"Pictures are important," I'd tell them. "Our brains are so flawed, leaky sieves of time. Without pictures, so many things we want to remember would be forgotten."

I sobbed the whole way across the country as I relived the life of my firstborn.

• • •

GREGG FORT:

Abigail wasn't wrong, not exactly.

Many have been the times when I wished I had images to help me remember. I can't picture the exact shape of Hayley's face at six months, or recall her Halloween costume when she was five. I can't even remember the exact shade of blue of the dress she wore for high school graduation.

Given what happened later, of course, her pictures are beyond my reach.

I comfort myself with this thought: How can a picture or video capture the intimacy, the irreproducible subjective perspective and mood through my eyes, the emotional tenor of each moment when I *felt* the impossible beauty of the soul of my child? I don't want digital representations, ersatz reflections of the gaze of electronic eyes filtered through layers of artificial intelligence, to mar what I remember of our daughter.

When I think of Hayley, what comes to mind is a series of disjointed memories.

The baby wrapping her translucent fingers around my thumb for the first time; the infant scooting around on her bottom on the hardwood floor, plowing through alphabet blocks like an icebreaker through floes; the four-year-old handing me a box of tissues as I shivered in bed with a cold and laying a small, cool hand against my feverish cheek.

The eight-year-old pulling the rope that released the pumped-up soda bottle launcher. As frothy water drenched the two of us in the wake of the rising rocket, she yelled, laughing, "I'm going to be the first ballerina to dance on Mars!"

The nine-year-old telling me that she no longer wanted me to read to her before going to sleep. As my heart throbbed with the inevitable pain of a child pulling away, she softened the blow with, "Maybe someday I'll read to you."

The ten-year-old defiantly standing her ground in the kitchen, supported by her little sister, staring down me and Abigail both. "I won't hand back your phones until you both sign this pledge to never use them during dinner."

The fifteen-year-old slamming on the brakes, creating the loudest tire screech I'd ever heard; me in the passenger seat, knuckles so white they hurt. "You look like me on that roller coaster, Dad." The tone carefully modulated, breezy. She had held out an arm in front of me, as though she could keep me safe, the same way I had done to her hundreds of times before.

And on and on, distillations of the 6,874 days we had together, like broken, luminous shells left on a beach after the tide of quotidian life has receded.

In California, Abigail asked to see her body; I didn't.

I suppose one could argue that there's no difference between my father trying to erase the scars of his error in the darkroom and my refusal to look upon the body of the child I failed to protect. A thousand "I could have's" swirled in my mind: I could have insisted that she go to a college near home; I could have signed her up for a course on mass-shooting-survival skills; I could have demanded that she wear her body armor at all times. An entire generation had grown up with active-shooter drills, so why didn't I do more? I don't think I ever understood my father, empathized with his flawed and cowardly and guilt-ridden heart, until Hayley's death.

But in the end, I didn't want to see because I wanted to protect the only thing I had left of her: those memories.

If I were to see her body, the jagged crater of the exit wound, the frozen lava trails of coagulated blood, the muddy cinders and ashes of shredded clothing, I knew the image would overwhelm all that had come before, would incinerate the memories of my daughter, my baby, in one violent eruption, leaving only hatred and despair in its wake. No, that lifeless body was not Hayley, was not the child I wanted to remember. I would no more allow that one moment to filter her whole existence than I would allow transistors and bits to dictate my memory.

So Abigail went, lifted the sheet, and gazed upon the wreckage of Hayley, of our life. She took pictures, too. "This I also want to remember," she mumbled. "You don't turn away from your child in her moment of agony, in the aftermath of your failure."

• • •

ABIGAIL FORT:

They came to me while we were still in California.

I was numb. Questions that had been asked by thousands of mothers swarmed my mind. Why was he allowed to amass such an arsenal? Why did no one stop him despite all the warning signs? What could I have—should I have—done differently to save my child?

"You can do something," they said. "Let's work together to honor the memory of Hayley and bring about change."

Many have called me naive or worse. What did I think was going to happen? After decades of watching the exact same script being followed to end in thoughts and prayers, what made me think this time would be different? It was the very definition of madness.

Cynicism might make some invulnerable and superior. But not everyone is built that way. In the thralls of grief, you cling to any ray of hope.

"Politics is broken," they said. "It should be enough, after the deaths of little children, after the deaths of newlyweds, after the deaths of mothers shielding newborns, to finally do something. But it never is. Logic and persuasion have lost their power, so we have to arouse the passions. Instead of letting the media direct the public's morbid curiosity to the killer, let's focus on Hayley's story."

It's been done before, I muttered. To center the victim is hardly a novel political move. You want to make sure that she isn't merely a number, a statistic, one more abstract name among lists of the dead. You think when people are confronted by the flesh-and-blood consequences of their vacillation and disengagement, things change. But that hasn't worked, doesn't work.

"Not like this," they insisted, "not with our algorithm."

They tried to explain the process to me, though the details of machine learning and convolution networks and biofeedback models escaped me. Their algorithm had originated in the entertainment industry, where it was used to evaluate films and predict their box-office success, and eventually, to craft them. Proprietary variations are used in applications from product design to drafting political speeches, every field in which emotional engagement is critical. Emotions are ultimately biological phenomena, not mystical emanations, and it's possible to discern trends and patterns, to home in on the stimuli that maximize impact. The algorithm would craft a visual narrative of Hayley's life, shape it into a battering ram to shatter the hardened shell of cynicism, spur the viewer to action, shame them for their complacency and defeatism.

The idea seemed absurd, I said. How could electronics know my daughter better than I did? How could machines move hearts when real people could not?

"When you take a photograph," they asked me, "don't you trust the camera AI to give you the best picture? When you scrub through drone footage, you rely on the AI to identify the most interesting clips, to enhance them with the perfect mood filters. This is a million times more powerful."

I gave them my archive of family memories: photos, videos, scans, drone footage, sound recordings, immersiongrams. I entrusted them with my child.

I'm no film critic, and I don't have the terms for the techniques they used. Narrated only with words spoken by our family, intended for each other and not an audience of strangers, the result was unlike any movie or VR immersion I had ever seen. There was no plot save the course of a single life; there was no agenda save the celebration of the curiosity, the compassion, the drive of a child to embrace the universe, to *become*. It was a beautiful life, a life that loved and deserved to be loved, until the moment it was abruptly and violently cut down.

This is the way Hayley deserves to be remembered, I thought, tears streaming down my face. *This is how I see her, and it is how she should be seen.*

I gave them my blessing.

• • •

SARA FORT:

Growing up, Gregg and I weren't close. It was important to my parents that our family project the image of success, of decorum, regardless of the reality. In response, Gregg distrusted all forms of representation, while I became obsessed with them.

Other than holiday greetings, we rarely conversed as adults, and certainly didn't confide in each other. I knew my nieces only through Abigail's social media posts.

I suppose this is my way of excusing myself for not intervening earlier.

When Hayley died in California, I sent Gregg the contact info for a few therapists who specialized in working with families of mass shooting victims, but I purposefully stayed away myself, believing that my intrusion in their moment of grief would be inappropriate given my role as distant aunt and aloof sister. So I wasn't there when Abigail agreed to devote Hayley's memory to the cause of gun control.

Though my company bio describes my specialty as the study of online discourse, the vast bulk of my research material is visual. I design armor against trolls.

• • •

EMILY FORT:

I watched that video of Hayley many times.

It was impossible to avoid. There was an immersive version, in which you could step into Hayley's room and read her neat handwriting, examine the posters on her wall. There was a low-fidelity version designed for frugal data plans, and the compression artifacts and motion blur made her life seem old-fashioned, dreamy. Everyone shared the video as a way to reaffirm that they were a good person, that they stood with the victims. Click, bump, add a lit-candle emoji, re-rumble.

It was powerful. I cried, also many times. Comments expressing grief and solidarity scrolled past my glasses like a never-ending wake. Families of victims in other shootings, their hopes rekindled, spoke out in support.

But the Hayley in that video felt like a stranger. All the elements in the video were true, but they also felt like lies.

Teachers and parents loved the Hayley they knew, but there was a mousy girl in school who cowered when my sister entered the room. One time, Hayley drove home drunk; another time, she stole from me and lied until I found the money in her purse. She knew how to manipulate people and wasn't shy about doing it. She was fiercely loyal, courageous, kind, but she could also be reckless, cruel, petty. I loved Hayley because she was human, but the girl in that video was both more and less than.

I kept my feelings to myself. I felt guilty.

Mom charged ahead while Dad and I hung back, dazed. For a brief moment, it seemed as if the tide had turned. Rousing rallies were held and speeches delivered in front of the Capitol and the White House. Crowds chanted Hayley's name. Mom was invited to the State of the Union. When the media reported that Mom had quit her job to campaign on behalf of the movement, there was a crypto fundraiser to collect donations for the family.

And then, the trolls came.

A torrent of emails, messages, rumbles, squeaks, snapgrams, televars came at us. Mom and I were called clickwhores, paid actresses, grief profiteers. Strangers sent us long, rambling walls of text explaining all the ways Dad was inadequate and unmanly.

Hayley didn't die, strangers informed us. She was actually living in Sanya, China, off the millions the UN and their collaborators in the US government had paid her to pretend to die. Her boyfriend—who had also "obviously not died" in the shooting—was ethnically Chinese, and that was proof of the connection.

Hayley's video was picked apart for evidence of tampering and digital manipulation. Anonymous classmates were quoted to paint her as a habitual liar, a cheat, a drama queen.

Snippets of the video, intercut with "debunking" segments, began to go viral. Some used software to make Hayley spew messages of hate in new clips, quoting Hitler and Stalin as she giggled and waved at the camera.

I deleted my accounts and stayed home, unable to summon the strength to get out of bed. My parents left me to myself; they had their own battles to fight.

• • •

SARA FORT:

Decades into the digital age, the art of trolling has evolved to fill every niche, pushing the boundaries of technology and decency alike.

From afar, I watched the trolls swarm around my brother's family with uncoordinated precision, with aimless malice, with malevolent glee.

Conspiracy theories blended with deep fakes, and then yielded to memes that turned compassion inside out, abstracted pain into lulz.

"Mommy, the beach in hell is so warm!"

"I love these new holes in me!"

Searches for Hayley's name began to trend on porn sites. The content producers, many of them AI-driven bot farms, responded with procedurally generated films and VR immersions featuring my niece. The algorithms took publicly available footage of Hayley and wove her face, body, and voice seamlessly into fetish videos.

The news media reported on the development in outrage, perhaps even sincerely. The coverage spurred more searches, which generated more content . . .

As a researcher, it's my duty and habit to remain detached, to observe and study phenomena with clinical detachment, perhaps even fascination. It's simplistic to view trolls as politically motivated—at least not in the sense that term is usually understood. Though Second Amendment absolutists helped spread the memes, the originators often had little conviction in any political cause. Anarchic sites such as 8taku, duangduang, and alt-web sites that arose in the wake of the previous decade's deplatforming wars are homes for these dung beetles of the internet, the id of our collective online unconscious. Taking pleasure in taboo-breaking and transgression, the trolls have no unifying interest other than saying the unspeakable, mocking the sincere, playing with what others declared to be off-limits. By wallowing in the outrageous and filthy, they both defile and define the technologically mediated bonds of society.

But as a human being, watching what they were doing with Hayley's image was intolerable.

I reached out to my estranged brother and his family.

"Let me help."

Though machine learning has given us the ability to predict with a fair amount of accuracy which victims will be targeted—trolls are not quite as unpredictable as they'd like you to think—my employer and other major social media platforms are keenly aware that they must walk a delicate line between policing user-generated content and chilling "engagement," the one metric that drives the stock price and thus governs all decisions. Aggressive moderation, especially when it's reliant on user reporting and human judgment, is a process easily gamed by all sides, and every company has suffered accusations of censorship. In the end, they threw up their hands and tossed out their byzantine enforcement policy manuals. They have neither the skills nor the interest to become arbiters of truth and decency for society as a whole. How could they be expected to solve the problem that even the organs of democracy couldn't?

Over time, most companies converged on one solution. Rather than focusing on judging the behavior of speakers, they devoted resources to letting listeners shield themselves. Algorithmically separating legitimate (though impassioned) political speech from coordinated harassment for *everyone* at once is an intractable problem—content celebrated by some as speaking truth to power is often condemned by others as beyond the pale. It's much easier to build and train individually tuned neural networks to screen out the content a *particular* user does not wish to see.

The new defensive neural networks—marketed as "armor"—observe each user's emotional state in response to their content stream. Capable of operating in vectors encompassing text, audio, video, and AR/VR, the armor teaches itself to recognize content especially upsetting to the user and screens it out, leaving only a tranquil void. As mixed reality and immersion have become more commonplace, the best way to wear armor is through augmented-reality glasses that filter all sources of visual stimuli. Trolling, like the viruses and worms of old, is a technical problem, and now we have a technical solution.

To invoke the most powerful and personalized protection, one has to pay. Social media companies, which also train the armor, argue that this solution gets them out of the content-policing business, excuses them from having to decide what is unacceptable in virtual town squares, frees everyone from the specter of Big Brother–style censorship. That this pro–free speech ethos happens to align with more profit is no doubt a mere afterthought.

I sent my brother and his family the best, most advanced armor that money could buy.

• • •

ABIGAIL FORT:

Imagine yourself in my position. Your daughter's body had been digitally pressed into hard-core pornography, her voice made to repeat words of hate, her visage mutilated with unspeakable violence. And it happened because of you, because of your inability to imagine the depravity of the human heart. Could you have stopped? Could you have stayed away?

The armor kept the horrors at bay as I continued to post and share, to raise my voice against a tide of lies.

The idea that Hayley hadn't died but was an actress in an anti-gun government conspiracy was so absurd that it didn't seem to deserve a response. Yet, as my armor began to filter out headlines, leaving blank spaces on news sites and in multicast streams, I realized that the lies had somehow become a real controversy. Actual journalists began to demand that I produce receipts for how I had spent the crowdfunded money—we hadn't received a cent! The world had lost its mind.

I released the photographs of Hayley's corpse. Surely there was still some shred of decency left in this world, I thought. Surely no one could speak against the evidence of their eyes?

It got worse.

For the faceless hordes of the internet, it became a game to see who could get something past my armor, to stab me in the eye with a poisoned videoclip that would make me shudder and recoil.

Bots sent me messages in the guise of other parents who had lost their children in mass shootings, and sprung hateful videos on me after I whitelisted them. They sent me tribute slideshows dedicated to the memory of Hayley, which morphed into violent porn once the armor allowed them through. They pooled funds to hire errand gofers and rent delivery drones to deposit fiducial markers near my home, surrounding me with augmented-reality ghosts of Hayley writhing, giggling, moaning, screaming, cursing, mocking.

Worst of all, they animated images of Hayley's bloody corpse to the accompaniment of jaunty soundtracks. Her death trended as a joke, like the "Hamster Dance" of my youth.

• • •

GREGG FORT:

Sometimes I wonder if we have misunderstood the notion of freedom. We prize "freedom to" so much more than "freedom from." People must be free to own guns, so the only solution is to teach children to hide in closets and wear ballistic backpacks. People must be free to post and say what they like, so the only solution is to tell their targets to put on armor.

Abigail had simply decided, and the rest of us had gone along. Too late, I begged and pleaded with her to stop, to retreat. We would sell the house and move somewhere away from the temptation to engage with the rest of humanity, away from the always-connected world and the ocean of hate in which we were drowning.

But Sara's armor gave Abigail a false sense of security, pushed her to double down, to engage the trolls. "I must fight for my daughter!" she screamed at me. "I cannot allow them to desecrate her memory."

As the trolls intensified their campaign, Sara sent us patch after patch for the armor. She added layers with names like adversarial complementary sets, self-modifying code detectors, visualization auto-healers.

Again and again, the armor held only briefly before the trolls found new ways through. The democratization of artificial intelligence meant that they knew all the techniques Sara knew, and they had machines that could learn and adapt, too.

Abigail could not hear me. My pleas fell on deaf ears; perhaps her armor had learned to see me as just another angry voice to screen out.

• • •

EMILY FORT:

One day, Mom came to me in a panic. "I don't know where she is! I can't see her!"

She hadn't talked to me in days, obsessed with the project that Hayley had become. It took me some time to figure out what she meant. I sat down with her at the computer.

She clicked the link for Hayley's memorial video, which she watched several times a day to give herself strength.

"It's not there!" she said.

She opened the cloud archive of our family memories.

"Where are the pictures of Hayley?" she said. "There are only placeholder *X*s."

She showed me her phone, her backup enclosure, her tablet.

"There's nothing! Nothing! Did we get hacked?"

Her hands fluttered helplessly in front of her chest, like the wings of a trapped bird. "She's just gone!"

Wordlessly, I went to the shelves in the family room and brought down one of the printed annual photo albums she had made when we were little. I opened the volume to a family portrait, taken when Hayley was ten and I was eight.

I showed the page to her.

Another choked scream. Her trembling fingers tapped against Hayley's face on the page, searching for something that wasn't there.

I understood. A pain filled my heart, a pity that ate away at love. I reached up to her face and gently took off her glasses.

She stared at the page.

Sobbing, she hugged me. "You found her. Oh, you found her!"

It felt like the embrace of a stranger. Or maybe I had become a stranger to her.

Aunt Sara explained that the trolls had been very careful with their attacks. Step by step, they had trained my mother's armor to recognize *Hayley* as the source of her distress.

But another kind of learning had also been taking place in our home. My parents paid attention to me only when I had something to do with Hayley. It was as if they no longer saw me, as though I had been erased instead of Hayley.

My grief turned dark and festered. How could I compete with a ghost? The perfect daughter who had been lost not once, but twice? The victim who demanded perpetual penance? I felt horrid for thinking such things, but I couldn't stop.

We sank under our guilt, each alone.

• • •

GREGG FORT:

I blamed Abigail. I'm not proud to admit it, but I did.

We shouted at each other and threw dishes, replicating the half-remembered drama between my own parents when I was a child. Hunted by monsters, we became monsters ourselves.

While the killer had taken Hayley's life, Abigail had offered her image up as a sacrifice to the bottomless appetite of the internet. Because of Abigail, my memories of Hayley would be forever filtered through the horrors that came after her death. She had summoned the machine that amassed individual human beings into one enormous, collective, distorting gaze, the machine that had captured the memory of my daughter and then ground it into a lasting nightmare.

The broken shells on the beach glistened with the venom of the raging deep.

Of course that's unfair, but that doesn't mean it isn't also true.

• • •

"HEARTLESS," A SELF-PROFESSED TROLL:

There's no way for me to prove that I am who I say, or that I did what I claim. There's no registry of trolls where you can verify my identity, no Wikipedia entry with confirmed sources.

Can you even be sure I'm not trolling you right now?

I won't tell you my gender or race or who I prefer to sleep with, because those details aren't relevant to what I did. Maybe I own a dozen guns. Maybe I'm an ardent supporter of gun control.

I went after the Forts because they deserved it.

RIP-trolling has a long and proud history, and our target has always been inauthenticity. Grief should be private, personal, hidden. Can't you see how horrible it was for that mother to turn her dead daughter into a symbol, to wield it as a political tool? A public life is an inauthentic one. Anyone who enters the arena must be prepared for the consequences.

Everyone who shared that girl's memorial online, who attended the virtual candlelit vigils, offered condolences, professed to have been spurred into action, was equally guilty of hypocrisy. You didn't think the proliferation of guns capable of killing hundreds in one minute was a bad thing until someone shoved images of a dead girl in your face? What's wrong with you?

And you journalists are the worst. You make money and win awards for turning deaths into consumable stories; for coaxing survivors to sob in front of your drones to sell more ads; for inviting your readers to find meaning in their pathetic lives through vicarious, mimetic suffering. We trolls play with images of the dead, who are beyond caring, but you stinking ghouls grow fat and rich by feeding death to the living. The sanctimonious are also the most filthy-minded, and victims who cry the loudest are the hungriest for attention.

Everyone is a troll now. If you've ever liked or shared a meme that wished violence on someone you'd never met, if you've ever decided it was okay to snarl and snark with venom because the target was "powerful," if you've ever tried to signal your virtue by piling on in an outrage mob, if you've ever wrung your hands and expressed concern that perhaps the money raised for some victim should have gone to some other less "privileged" victim—then I hate to break it to you, you've also been trolling.

Some say that the proliferation of trollish rhetoric in our culture is corrosive, that armor is necessary to equalize the terms of a debate in which the only way to win is to care less. But don't you see how unethical armor is? It makes the weak think they're strong, turns cowards into deluded heroes with no skin in the game. If you truly despise trolling, then you should've realized by now that armor only makes things worse.

By weaponizing her grief, Abigail Fort became the biggest troll of them all—except she was bad at it, just a weakling in armor. We had to bring her—and by extension, the rest of you—down.

• • •

ABIGAIL FORT:

Politics returned to normal. Sales of body armor, sized for children and young adults, received a healthy bump. More companies offered classes on situational awareness and mass shooting drills for schools. Life went on.

I deleted my accounts; I stopped speaking out. But it was too late for my family. Emily moved out as soon as she could; Gregg found an apartment.

Alone in the house, my eyes devoid of armor, I tried to sort through the archive of photographs and videos of Hayley.

Every time I watched the video of her sixth birthday, I heard in my mind the pornographic moans; every time I looked at photos of her high school graduation, I saw her bloody animated corpse dancing to the tune of "Girls Just Wanna Have Fun"; every time I tried to page through the old albums for some good memories, I jumped in my chair, thinking an AR ghost of her, face grotesquely deformed like Munch's *The Scream*, was about to jump out at me, cackling, "Mommy, these new piercings hurt!"

I screamed, I sobbed, I sought help. No therapy, no medication worked.

Finally, in a numb fury, I deleted all my digital files, shredded my printed albums, broke the frames hanging on walls.

The trolls trained me as well as they trained my armor.

I no longer have any images of Hayley. I can't remember what she looked like. I have truly, finally, lost my child.

How can I possibly be forgiven for that?

MINISTER FAUST

SOMATOSENSORY CORTEX DOG MESS YOU UP BIG TIME, YOU SICK SACK OF S**T

(2021)

EVEN A SCUMBAG like Marvin Shkully knew the second he hit that freaking dog dashing across the street, the chances of getting a blowjob from the engorgifying Ms. "Bam" Drozdova during the drive back to his place had fallen to *hayl-no.*

"Stop ze car, you fakkink ess-hole!" she snapped, and punched him hard on the shoulder. That's not really how she talked, but that's the way he heard it, because that's what he liked, and that's what he was paying for. But he'd already stopped.

"What the shit!" he said, rubbing his shoulder.

So she punched him again in the exact same spot. He couldn't even scream—it hurt that much. He just gaped at her like a dipshit in mid-dip. Fine, she was in shock or whatever. But shoulders weren't free, and her knuckles were like iron wrapped in divorce lawyer.

Of course he'd stopped the car (without her telling him to) because he had to make sure his smoking-new, fully-tricked-out Bezos Infinitive wasn't fucked up because of that goddamned dog.

Standing outside, he flared his watch-light over his front bumper, his grill, his wheel wells, his still-spinning rims, his side panels, his back bumper, and even his spoiler because you just never knew.

"Why're you looking *there*, ass-wank?" said Bam, stomping toward him unsteadily. Blood on her white jacket and miniskirt. She didn't look like a trade attorney now (or maybe she did, but even more). "You think dog shot up from back wheel and smashed into *spoiler*?"

He backed away a couple of steps. Her kicking him with those Lucite stilts was one thing. *When he wanted it.* But out in the street? With his whip chipped?

"Bam, you gotta relax. You are seriously bumming my vibe here."

"Your *vibe*? Look at dog! You *kill* him!"

"I didn't kill it!" he said, pointing at the goldish retrievery bag of breathingless crap on the road. "Bam, seriously, your head's cut—"

She held up a *shut the fuck up* hand while she triple-blinked.

"Emergency vet," she enunciated, and then eye-scrolled. "There is vet only five minutes from here."

"Vets send out ambulances now?"

"*You* are ambulance now, scum-dink."

He gawked and gaped in protest. "In my Bezos? It's still got new-car smell! I don't want my Bezos stinking like some shitty dying dog!"

She glared at him like she'd fork him right in the ballsack first chance she got. He dropped his hands, shook his head.

Bam teetered over to the muttmash. Heels and everything, she knelt and picked it up. Strong chick, for sure. Dog was whimpering like a radio just barely on.

"Get the door!"

Did as ordered. She slid the animal into the back.

"Drive," she said, and called him either *Shitlord* or *Shitload.* He couldn't tell.

• • •

Shkully woke up. Ached everywhere. Triple-blinked, scrolled to *Pain Control*, gave himself a hit. Bam was sitting titbreastfully on the bed next to him, pulling on her bra, although for a second it looked like she'd just been adjusting it.

He reached for her and she got up and out his reach. That's when he saw. And winced. And whined: "Why're you wearing *period* panties?"

She didn't even look at him while she period-pantied around the room, picking up her clothes. "Question answers itself, pee-face."

She pulled on her bloodied skirt, bustier, jacket. Relief washed over him like a hot tide, seeing her restored to full sexfulness.

Over her shoulder, she fixed her falcon eyes on him.

"You were *animal* last night," she growled with what Reddit said that Italians called *sexificato*. "I am needing nets and spear gun to get you off."

"But . . . you *did* get me off, right?" Tried arching his eyebrows as sexidaciously as she'd growled, but the scalp-action felt like an ice giant sawing his skull into snacks—

—nearly passed out, and she was hovering over him, almost touching his cheek.

"Marv, you okay?"

He clicked again on *Pain Control.* Didn't usually need more than one hit per hour. Not a great sign.

Plus, he couldn't even remember getting reamed by Bam, which must've happened, given how sore his asshole felt.

"How much," he rasped, "did I drink last night?"

She smirked sexonically.

"All of it."

Then she turned and sexed out of the room.

"Wait up!" he said. "You going already?"

Sing-songing from the hall: "Busy *day* ahead, *Mar*-vin."

"What about some breakfast?"

"Not hungry, thank you."

"No, I mean for me!"

Leaned back in the room.

"On the stove I leave you nice, hot, fluffy stack of go-fuck-yourself cakes. If you are being still hungry after that, I can leave something steaming in your new car—"

"No, I'll order in."

From down the hallway: "Shouldn't you be getting dressed, Marvin?" And then door-click.

"*Why?*" he shouted.

Wallpapes were synced locally. 10K views of the city. Gray and green, lazy low river. Old, squat buildings. The Capitol. The Washington Monument: either a middle finger or a concrete dick, lubricated with rain.

"Bam?"

No answer.

Got up like an *old* old man. The kind of old man that old men point to and shake their heads and sneer to each other, muttering, "*Look* at that old man." *That's* how he got up, staggering in his thousand-dollar dick-wickers.

And blinking and clicking more pain control and starting to get scared down in his nuts that his wire-heading wasn't working anymore. Better ping Nyandeng about it.

Shuffled to the Wallpapes and made an old-fashioned headset telephone gesture with his right hand.

"Nyandeng," he said clearly.

She flashed in, sitting at her console.

"Marvin. You look like shit," she said. "And could you please not ping me when you're naked?"

"I'm paying you ten gees per service call," he said. "I think I can wear what I like."

"At least *cover* yourself, then."

Oh, right. Even with the ice-saw cutting through his brains, how could she *not* give him a hard-on? She was illegal, she could hack anything, and she looked like Barbie dipped in dark chocolate. He couldn't actually smell her, but just *remembering* smelling her made him sex up—

"*What do you* want, *Marvin?*"

"My pain's at a seven. I've clicked three times already in ten minutes. I don't know if it's wetware or drivers or code or what—"

"All right—plug in your port. I can scan your—"

"No! This is too big for remote. I'm in DC anyway. I'm coming in."

"You know I don't like you coming here."

She scowled, tilted her head, and her braids slid over one of her bare shoulders and down across her tank top that read *Shanakdakhete*. "Wear that top," he said. "And no bottoms." Then he clicked off.

Shambled out of the bedroom, still hoping Bam was there and'd just been clowning about leaving, because enough kidding around already, they'd been on five dates and *nothing*, not even a hand job. They *couldn't've* had sex last night—the walls and the ceiling were too clean. She'd conned him. Lawyers . . .

Lawyers?

"The fucking *Senate* hearing!"

• • •

"Mr. Shkully," said Senator Alvarez, "are you *really* asking the members of this committee to accept that you have performed a *public service* through your grotesque manipulation of our society—"

"Mrs. Senator, I never ask anyone for anything—"

"—and the hopes and dreams of millions of prospective parents by selling super-potent contraceptives that render men and women irreversibly unable to conceive? *Except* without access to the drugs that you sell at *three thousand dollars* per 'refertilization' pill?"

"I prefer to think," said Shkully, "that I'm providing super-high-value contraception *and* a check against unbridled reproductive passion that is leading Western society to Malthusian Armageddon. Mrs. Senator, just look at how many unproductive, miserable, useless people there are in this country, or, hey, even in this very chamber—"

Couldn't stop himself from smirking at that one, but his peripheral caught all his lawyers face-palming.

Turned around, saw way, way at the back of the chamber, there she was: Bam. In a clean white business suit, slowly shaking her head at him. She actually single-wagged her finger! Which turned him on even more.

"Mr. Shkully, *you* may think it funny to mock the members of this committee and this House—"

"Not *all* of them, ma'am. Just one in particular—"

"—but if you want to avoid being charged with contempt of the United States Senate, I suggest you watch your tone and wipe that smugness off your face, because the American people do not appreciate being forced to endure the hyper-profitable suffering that the country's sixth-youngest billionaire has inflicted—"

A dog barked, loudly.

The entire room went silent.

The Senator glared at him.

"Mr. Shkully! How *dare* you—"

"What?"

The dog barked again. At length. Who the hell could've smuggled a dog in here? Or was someone playing a sound file? Sure sounded close—

The Senator stood and pounded her table.

"Sergeant-at-arms! Remove Mr. Shkully forthwith!"

Only as the highest-ranking federal law enforcement officer in the United States Senate hauled him out while muttering, "Shut your mouth, ya fucking wing-ding," did Marvin realize that the barking was coming from him.

• • •

Outside the committee hearings room, Shkully's lawyers begged him for instructions on how to proceed.

But by then it wasn't just his skull being ice-sawed open. It was his heart shuddering like a Harley over gravel on boulders. He could barely even hear his shysters, and whatever he *could* hear, he couldn't understand them.

Suddenly he was bolting for his Bezos Infinitive, and screeching across town to a place he'd forgotten he'd ever seen, but where he'd been only the night before, like his lungs were caught on a tow-chain and whale-hook—

• • •

"Mr. Shkully," said the vet, brown-skinned and oily-haired, standing in a white lab coat just like a real doctor. "We were beginning to think we'd never see you again."

Shkully was panting. Felt himself sweat-soaked from cravat to crotch.

"Where is it?" he rasped.

"Right this way."

Inside a holding room was the goddamn goldish retrievery mutt that'd nearly fucked up his car. It was a mess. Cone. Casts on two legs. And a blinky head thing like a doggy tiara.

Mutt was barely moving.

But it did look at him, just for a second.

Eyes-to-eyes. Black into blue.

A gut punch. Or a cockpunch. Or an ass punch. Some kind of punch he'd never had before.

"We worked very hard, Mr. Shkully," said the vet, "to get Mubsy better. The impact shattered both her front legs, cracked her skull, and gave her a concussion—"

Nothing registered on Marvin but the name.

"'Mubsy'? How do you know her name? There's no collar—oh, wait, an RFID?"

"Nuh-no," said the doctor, looking back nervously. Marvin couldn't tell what he was. Indian? Guatemalan? Something from somewhere the food made him fart. "Your lady friend. With the Latvian accent."

Latvian? Thought she was Russian. That's why he went for her in the first place.

"—and as you can see, Mubsy is going to need a lot of care. To begin with, physiotherapy, medications—"

"What're you telling *me* for? I'm not paying for any of this!"

"Your friend already paid."

"She did? Well, then talk to her—"

"Using the expense pass on your card."

He remembered authorizing her on their third hand job-less date. He thought she'd use it for Cristal, lube, lingerie, plugs, whatever. But a goddamn *dog*?

He shook his head to clear it. "What's with the blinky crown?"

"It's the monitor for the implants," said the vet.

"*Implants?* You do *brain implants* on dogs?"

"We've been doing brain implants on dogs for years. It's all very safe and very therapeutic. Research on dogs helped humans who've had strokes, tumors, seizures—"

"I'm outta here. Tell *her* all this shit . . . when *she* . . . picks . . . it up. . . ."

. . . words . . . slurring . . . like ropey drool . . .

just imagining leaving the dog . . . congested his lungs . . . like eight . . . pounds . . . of snot . . .

"Mr. Shkully, sir, are you all right?"

The doc had a hand on his shoulder. It was the only thing keeping him up.

"Do you need anything?"

The dog's face swelled in his brain like a giant, throbbing emoticon.

"Fine," choked Marvin. "I'll take the dog."

Puke slid back down his throat.

"For *now*."

Puke slid back up his throat.

"I'll *take* the goddamn dog!"

Puke settled into his tummy like it was curling down for a nap.

• • •

Parked in the empty blue-painted square on the 1700 block of Florida Ave. Brain was whirring like drone rotors and he damn near went to grab the piece-of-shit dog out of the back seat and take it with him like it was a briefcase full of cash.

"Pull it together, Marv," he said aloud.

Leaving it in his back seat felt like another cockpunch, but really, the thing was a mess. What good would it do anyone to take it with him?

Punched the buzzer on the doorframe, looked into the overhead cam.

"It's me."

The door clicked. He went up the single flight of stairs above the restaurant.

Nyandeng met him at the door in her *Shanakdakhete* tank top and her braids waterfalling over her shoulders. Also worn: fatigue pants and army boots.

"Thought I told you," he said, "not to wear any bottoms."

"Marv, not even *you* have enough money to make *you* palatable."

She let him pass.

He teetered through her tech-choked office, its shelves and boxes crawling over with gear, like a hundred nests holding a thousand baby turtles, lizards, snakes, and vultures.

He crashed down into her couch.

"I'm pretty fucked up," he husked.

"Is there anyone in the world who doesn't know that?" she said. "*Barking* at the US Senate?"

"You saw that? You like to watch me, Nyang?" he said, and laughed. But he didn't laugh. This time even he heard it. He was barking again.

"Cut that shit out, Marvin," she said. "You may think it's funny, but I don't."

"I'm not *trying* to be funny," he whimpered. "My pain's up to a steady seven, no matter how many hits I take. And this barking—I'm not doing it on purpose. What the hell's happening to me? I don't get some pain relief right away, I'm gonna gouge my eyes out!"

He jerked his head to the side, directly into his right armpit, and nibbled the shit out of his jacket.

Nyandeng snapped, "Marvin! *Stop* that! It's gross!"

"See? I'm going crazy!"

"Okay. Gimme a second." She hauled a finger-thick cable from one of her systems. Yanked up his shirt and reached for his back.

"Can't you at least," he rasped, "talk dirty to me before you shove that thing in?"

Her nose curled up. "How's this for dirty? Go fuck yourself." She shoved the jack into his spineport, and everything went white—

• • •

Room: dark except for monitors and a streetlight blaring through the window.

His chest was on fire. Heart attack?

No. That wasn't it—

Hell, he'd left that piece-of-shit dog in his car for how long? Alone? No water, no food—

"At last, you're awake," said Nyandeng. "Okay. You've been hacked."

"*What?*" he said, sitting up so fast his head swirled. The jack was out of his spine, at least. "I thought *you* were supposed to *protect* me from hacks! I thought you were *the best*!"

"Maybe someone's better. Or it's an inside job," said Nyandeng. She was almost blue in the blackness. "Your pain control node firmware is totally compromised."

Marv took a breath. "Someone wants to torture me to death."

"Y'think?" she said. "You mean like about thirty million people you screwed over with your three-thousand-dollar balls-unlock pills?"

"What do I have to *do*?" he snapped. And glared at her, waiting for her to answer.

"You know I don't speak *dog*, right, Marv?"

"I was . . . barking again?"

He put his fingers over his mouth, like he could suppress his new canine impulses that way.

Slowly: "What . . . do I . . . have to do? Assuming . . . it's ransomware—"

Wanted to scream, but figured that'd induce barking. Every second he failed to get back to that mutt in the car made him panic worse.

Willed himself to whisper: "How do we get rid of it?"

"Don't know. Wait for the ask? Because I've spent the last three hours going over the hack, and it's brilliant. Any attempt to remove it, *bam!* Your pain'll hit ten so fast you'll have fifteen strokes and your head'll burst like a blister before your body hits the street."

"Oh. My. Fuck."

"There's more," she said, spinning a wheelie chair to sit in front of him, laying her forearms over the back rest. "The PC node has threaded itself into your anterior insula, anterior midcingulate cortex, somatosensory cortex, and right amygdala—"

"What're you, a *neuro*surgeon all of a sudden?"

She leaned back. "I've had three hours to become an expert while poking around that sack of KY-gristle you call a brain. Plenty of time to map the neighborhood. Anyway, I don't know why the node wants to access those areas, but I *can* tell you it's hacking into your emotions—Marv? *Marv!*"

He went barking down the hall and out into the car and into the backseat with the doors wide open where he fell upon the dog, stroking it and sobbing.

• • •

Back at his DC house, he was in the yard, tearing into the food and treats he'd blink-ordered for delivery by the time he got there.

Ripping into bags of Noogumz organic kibble made from genuine Kobe beef bits and bonemeal. Tearing into those bags with his own teeth, while the dog was asleep on an outdoor padded lounge recliner. Gnawing wildly until he started howling, and then ripping off his clothes and jumping into the pool.

Had no idea how many times he'd paddled around the edges until he finally got out, then shook himself off and sloshed over to the lounge recliner and curled up naked around the dog, nuzzling his head against the veterinary cone and ensuring he didn't put any pressure on the canine casts.

• • •

He woke up into sunshine better than the best VR. Steam was lifting off the pool. Someone was cooking sausages six blocks away. He wanted so badly to eat grass he nearly bolted from the recliner and over to the lawn, but he forced himself to stop.

That piece-of-shit dog was somehow hobbling toward him from the ripped-open pile of Noogumz, wagging its piece-of-shit broken-ass tail and hefting its blinking-tiara-head with a cone on it like the mouth of a furry cannon.

He swung his back leg to kick the goddamn thing and the resulting cock-punch was so hard he crashed to his knees and started licking the dog's cheeks and nose and eyes. That should've made him want to puke, but honestly, all that licking was better than coke.

He stopped only when he glanced up and saw the white boots, and knew who'd done this to him.

"Bam," he growled, "you *bitch*!"

"Stop *bar*king," she said, "and use your *words*."

It took him a full minute to quit snapping and snarling and finally will himself to stand on his hind legs. The only reason he *could* stop was that he could smell how much he was scaring the dog.

Grabbed clothes from the pool deck to cover himself. Whispered so he could keep control.

"*You*. You did this to me."

"*Of course* it was me," she said. "Somatosensory cortex dog mess you up big time, you sick sack of shit."

"Why?"

She laughed.

"Dog was not original idea," she said. "Informal class-action group created plan. They pay for all this. Original plan was to connect you—cyberpathically—with one of them, or *all* of them, *to feel their suffering*. . . . But after you run over dog, I improvise."

"To fucking hack my brain and jack me into *that* piece-of-shit?"

"We did not jack you. We *emp*ed you. And stop calling her that."

Kobe beef bonemeal and meatmash and dogfur puked a quarter-way up his throat. He nearly choked on it. *"What?"*

"Stop *calling* her that. Her name is Mubsy!"

"I paid for her, so that dog's name is Piece-of-Shit!"

"Just for that, is now Mubsy-*Wubsy*!"

"No! *Now* it's God*damn* Piece-of-Shit!"

"Fine, Balls-Mouth! Is now *Super* Mubsy-Wubsy! Want to go for *Mrs. Cutey* Super Mubsy-Wubsy? Just keep it up!"

He trotted over to the pool bar and dialed his hacker.

"Nyandeng! I found who did this to me! Yeah! She's standing five feet in front of me. I'm one call away from five ex-Navy Seals hauling her ass to your lab to get this shit out of my brain—"

The pop-up holo of Nyandeng shook its head.

"Marvin, you're thicker than I thought. You really thought anyone could out-hack me?"

His shit nearly fell out of his ass.

"You . . . *you're* in on this, too?"

"Who else?"

"You . . . you *bitch*!"

"Bitch? You're the one who spent fifteen minutes licking his own crotch in my lab yesterday, Marvy," said Nyandeng. "You want out? Ask your Canadian friend there."

The holo disappeared.

He glared at Bam.

"*Canadian?* You're not even Russian? What else're you lying about?"

An accent slid onto her voice like a lubed condom two sizes too big. Sounded like some stuck-up fucking CBC announcer she'd made him listen to on Sirius radio (which now finally made sense) on their first hand job-less date.

"I'm *Latvian*-Canadian, shitbank!" Then she overdid the thing he liked so much it actually hurt his ears. *"I khappen to* like *talkink like zis! Puts me in touch wiss my roots!"*

"You freaking slag—took me five dates just to get *near* your roots!"

"Get comfortable with that feeling!"

"Why even do the accent in the first place?"

"*All ze easier to snare you wiss, eediot!* We got your number! Not that you ever hide it! Anything that connects in your sick head with being vulnerable! Desperate! Exploitable!"

She knelt to pet Mubsy with both hands. He felt every stroke on his face, every pat on his rump, felt his own tail—not his dick, but a real tail that really wasn't attached to him—wagging.

It was even more intense than short selling or hostile-takeover-ing.

"Now, listen carefully, fuckface," said Bam. "Take care of Super Mubsy-Wubsy, or die."

And she left, and he looked at Super Mubsy-Wubsy and wanted to kick her in the face, and the terror of it sent him howling and running around the yard in circles until he got so hungry, he had to finish off all the Noogumz and take a nice dump on the lawn and then piss on half a dozen rosebushes in the yard.

Finally curled up with Super Mubsy-Wubsy. Stroking her. Gazing into her eyes—

—thought his contacts were glitching, but then he understood: he was looking back at his own face.

But in black and white.

And smelling his own chlorine-dipped armpit-musk and groin-funk.

And feeling his own furless warmth with his own wet nose.

"C'mon, girl," he said, rubbing her and feeling his hand on his own furry rump. "Let's go see the doc."

• • •

"Mubsy!" said the brown vet with oily black hair, patting the thighs of his pants.

The dog happily—but carefully—met the doc, wagging her bum. Marvin had to stop himself from doing the same.

The bottom of Marv's brain had been trying to figure out how to get his ex–Navy Seals to torture solutions out of the doc, but with Wubsy licking the man's hands, all Marv could taste was sunshine and cackling crows and fresh-cut grass and running at pebble-paws-heart-thumping-speed through an endless cascade of trees.

He asked to speak privately, and the doc led him past caged animals crying and whimpering which spiked his cockpunchiness massively, and he barked until he clamped his own mouth shut.

Finally, he sat down in the doc's office with the door closed and tried to push out the smells and sounds, and hefted Mubsy into his lap and hugged her and stroked her tummy.

Slowly, carefully, he explained everything, including what he knew was the vet's collusion in this massive crime against him.

"Not . . . looking for . . . *revenge*, Doc," he whimpered. "But you owe me an explanation. Including why I'm feeling a twenty-four-hour cockpunch."

The doc stepped toward him, and gingerly removed Mubsy's cone and unclasped the casts. Marv felt his own neck and forelegs suddenly free and tender, but relief whistled through his fur like a warm breeze.

"She won't be needing these anymore," he said. "The nano-struts are in great shape. Her legs should be a hundred percent by tomorrow. But we'll keep the crown in place to monitor everything until the end of the week." He sighed. Smelled ashamed.

"Well, as you said—your friends and I 'emped' you to Wubsy and reconfigured your pain control node to amplify all the functions in the anterior insula, the anterior midcingulate cortex, the somatosensory cortex, and the right amygdala . . . because your functioning was severely depressed in all those areas."

The vet waited, as if that were an answer.

Marv started barking, and so did Wubsy, and then after an indeterminate time they both slowed, and Marv said, "In English, doc."

"Mr. Shkully, those are all areas involved in empathy. Until forty-eight hours ago, your brain was configured *non-* or even *counter-*empathically. Or to use the old expression, *psychopathically.* That's what's allowed you to 'succeed' in your world . . . the way you did. That's what let you make people like *me* . . . who were unable to . . . uh . . . that's the *effect* that your . . . 'medicine'—"

He cleared his throat. Looked away. Waited.

Looked back.

"But we've, well, 'rewired' you. So your brain could create its own conscience. That's the, uh . . . 'cockpunch,' as you call it. You now feel *pain* instead of the nothingness—or even the amusement and pleasure—that you used to feel while witnessing the misery and suffering you inflicted on other people."

Multiple cockpunches. *MMA* cockpunches. MMA cock-*knee-strikes.*

Marvin finally rallied. "So . . . whatever fuckin happened to 'do no harm'? You sentenced me to a lifetime of torture? Because you and those two bitches are such *good* people—"

"Yes," he said through gritted teeth. "And you *deserve* a lifetime of torture, Marvin!"

Mubsy growled. The doc looked away, and then down, and he breathed, and finally spoke again after Mubsy quieted.

"But a conscience will let you experience *good* feelings, too. Feelings you've never had before. Connection. Tenderness. Even love."

Marvin felt Mubsy's heart beating through her ribcage into his own chest, and from across the chasm, felt Marv's heart beating through his ribcage and back into her own chest.

"'Good feelings.' Like a . . . like a . . . cock*stroke*?"

"Uh, well . . . that wouldn't've been my go-to phrase, but, essentially, yes."

"How long is this gonna last?"

"Uh . . . unless you run a spike through your brain? Forever."

• • •

Hot outside. Hot enough to make the air wiggle above the sidewalk and smells dance off every surface and radiate through the air like scent explosions.

They went for a walk. Mrs. Cutesy Super Mubsy-Wubsy couldn't walk far, so Marv carried her down the block past a hang-head collie tied to a post outside a taco joint, past a youth emergency shelter with a sign asking for mentors, past a man without legs holding out his hand.

Total cockpunchification.

He blinked three times, pinged Bam.

"What was the point?" he asked her. "If you'd brain-linked me to one of those people in the class-action suit, instead of to Mubsy. What'd you hope would happen?"

"I don't know. Kill yourself? For what you did to all those people?"

He snarled, "Sounds pretty psychopathic to me!"

Bam: "Don't be such a baby, Marv. Some people can't even *have* babies anymore. Thanks to . . . oh, who was it again?"

Bam clicked off.

Marv walked back up the street to the man without legs. He put down Mubsy, who licked the man's hand, which tasted to Marv like ass, which now tasted to Marv like quiche.

He introduced himself to the man whose name was Phil, and asked him to look after Wubsy. Then he walked back to the taco shop for water, an empty fast-food paper bowl, and cash back.

On the ground in front of the hang-head tied-up collie, he put down the bowl and filled it with water so the dog could drink, petted this dog he wasn't even emped to, and he felt the petting and tasted the water.

Inside the youth emergency shelter he told them he was covering lunch for all the staff and kids.

And to Phil, he gave a hundred bucks and his phone number.

"Thank God for you!" said Phil.

"Don't thank God," said Marv. "Thank dog."

He knew the hundred bucks wasn't gonna last Phil, and that the lunch for the youth shelter would be eaten and gone forever by 12:59, and that the bowl of water was probably already empty. But when he picked up Mubsy and smelled how good they felt together, when he finally stopped sobbing and howling and yipping and laughing as they licked into each other's faces, he thought of where he could put his billions for the greatest use, and he knew with all the air of thrashing through a creek in the forest how much better life would smell and taste if he spent the rest of his life licking millions of faces instead of kicking them.

ARTHUR LIU

THE LIFE CYCLE OF A CYBER BAR

(2021)

Translated from the Chinese by Nathan Faries

ONE

So a guy goes into a bar and orders a drink.

He nods toward the bartender and raises a finger. The bartender returns a knowing smile and slides a tequila on the rocks down the counter. The bartender doesn't know the guy; this is the first time this guy has been in this bar.

The guy looks around. The bar's other patrons hide their scrutiny behind newspapers and darts. Soon, a man in a trench coat and a tall hat sits down beside the guy. The two speak in low tones, and the guy exchanges some of the planet's local currency for two encrypted bio-memory chips.

At this point, a burly dude with crisscrossed knife scars on his face leans in close to the men at the bar and demands they buy him a drink. The guy turns the dude down, and the huge drunk immediately brandishes a dagger he has drawn from his belt. Instead of a knife fight, gunshots ring out near the bar, and then more shots from some other direction, or multiple directions. The intense cross-fire leaves neat rows of holes in some walls and clusters in others. When the firefight ends, the guy collapses on the barroom floor, his brains spilling out like jelly mixed with shattered microchips. After another beat, the bartender crawls out from behind the bar. She begins to clean up the mess. The bar's neon lights flicker out; its rats skitter away.

This is a typical day in the life of a cyber bar.

TWO

A guy comes into the bar and orders a drink.

He nods to me and raises his finger. I smile knowingly and slide his favorite drink down the bar. I don't know this guy, but there will always be guys like that coming into places like this. They're all cast from the same mold: flattop haircut, tough, silent, smelling of cigarettes, with suspicious eyes and heads full of obsolete microchips—practically scrap. And a thirst for tequila . . . on the rocks.

This type of guy is always looking for someone, someone like the man in the trench coat. To drum up business, I'll sometimes open up a betting pool with the customers; we bet on how long it'll take for the guy's contact to walk over. If one of the customers wins, he drinks for free. If I win, everyone's next round is on me. As a result, the bar enjoys a flourishing business with a diverse clientele . . . but this setting also creates a perfect storm of evil *feng shui* in which bad ideas brew. Even though all my gambling games are designed for me to lose and for the customers to win, the boss never gives me any trouble, and the bar never runs low on inventory.

After fifteen minutes, the man in the trench coat and tall hat sits down next to the guy. The big dude with two knife scars crisscrossing his face cheers loudly about something; maybe he's congratulating the winner of this night's pool. That dude can't handle his drink, and things always get out of hand when he's around. And what a waste of good liquor whenever he wins the pool.

These two people in the center of the vortex of the bar's attention whisper for a while; the guy exchanges some of the planet's local currency for two encrypted bio-memory chips. I pretend not to see anything; I'm a woman of principle. In a place like this, those of us who hold to their principles and stay blind and dumb will eventually clean up, financially speaking. I just hope these two don't make a mess of the place and give me something else to clean up. Just do your business and get the fuck out, please.

But I don't get my wish. I rarely do. Before the two of them can get up off their stools, Scarface, drunk and swearing, lurches forward and tells the guy to buy him a drink. The guy turns him down flat, and Scarface immediately brandishes the dagger he has drawn from his waist. As he pulls the knife from his belt, it seems that an old pistol Scarface keeps in his pants goes off accidentally. And that's all she wrote; pandemonium ensues. As soon as I hear the first gunshot, I start to wave my arms and try to talk everyone down, try to get control of the situation, but out of nowhere a bullet hits me and throws me against the wall. I fall forward into the open space that joins my area behind the bar and the seating area. As I lie there, I see mechanical internal viscera along with fully biological organs flowing together across the floor. Before my consciousness fades, the guy falls on top of me. I feel the weight of him pushing me down and the overflowing brains and broken chips smearing my face.

Sometimes this is how the situation ends. But I quickly come around, revived, unharmed, and I crawl out onto the battlefield and begin to pick up the pieces.

This resurrection is the work of the healing nanoclusters in my body, a gift the boss gave me when we first met. They're the reason I'm willing to do all I can for the boss and why I'm dead set on working here forever. Find a quiet place to live my life and watch the teeming mortal world walk in and out of these doors—as far as I'm concerned, that's pretty much heaven.

After I knock off for the night, I pull the chain on the neon lights outside. After the roll-down gate is closed, a gang of rats jumps out of the shadows. They bare their teeth menacingly.

Goddammit. Time to ask the boss to invest in some mechanical cats.

THREE

At this point in the story, you may be wondering who will be the next protagonist to take the stage and tell their tale. You think maybe it will be Scarface, or possibly Trench Coat. Ha! Wrong. It's me.

So a guy walks into the bar and orders a drink. He nods to the bartender and raises a finger. The bartender returns a knowing smile, pours me into a glass, and stuffs a couple of ice cubes up my ass. This is how the story goes for me, every damn time.

When the guy arrives, the customers begin to look around more actively, scrutinizing the newcomer and each other with suspicion. They always fail to see the intrinsic nature of things, the true character of the situation. But what right do I have to ridicule them? I'm no better than a pot laughing at how dim the kettle is. I can see everything clearly, but I can't change anything.

I am the tequila in the glass, and my body has been blended with some amazing chemical that can trigger a short circuit in the drinker's microchips and spark the secretion of adrenaline. The person gets jumpy; excessive anxiety makes them act irrationally. So after a while, when the burly dude, who's also drinking me, starts waving his dagger and the gun rings out right on schedule, everyone else who's drinking me also pulls out a gun and starts shooting all at once. The scene is spectacular. A rain of bullets falls in a forest of guns; gore and blood fly in every direction. As for me, after I've tasted their saliva, their gastric and intestinal juices, I flow out of their bodies along with their blood and their piss. Don't ask me how I perceive all this. You'll understand everything at the proper time.

After I've poured back out of the bodies, I spend some time in intimate contact with the floor. A little later, the boss will sort things out. The manner in which the boss does this is quite distinctive. Time begins to flow backward. Bullets exit corpses, holes close, and I reluctantly take leave of all body fluids and gradually restore the blood to purity. I stream out from between lips and teeth, fall back into the glass, and finally my butt plugs return to the ice bucket. The bartender's smile fades away. The bar returns to its original state. There's no trace of the guy.

Sometimes the boss gets lazy. When that happens, after the bartender is resurrected and I'm still mostly on the floor, the back-flowing time will return early to its normal forward motion. This is one of those times. Whenever I'm stuck in this situation, my great undertaking—to return to my natural state—is forestalled. The bartender can pile up corpses, shards of glass, and dismembered furniture, but she has no way to suck me out of the floorboards. All I can do is wait in the small gaps between the wood fibers, wait for the me in the shot glass, the me soaked into the tables and chairs, the me in the corpses, and the me in the floor all to merge into one after the neon lights go out. Then, in the darkness, we are all assimilated into a mass of rotten meat within the boss's body. After some time, we will all be divided once again. We will again be differentiated into glasses, tables and chairs, floors, bar counters, glass bottles, and the tequila in those bottles.

Sometimes we ask the boss, "How'd we do?" The boss never answers.

The heart, liver, spleen, and lungs are the internal organs of a human; we are the internal organs of the boss.

Our boss is the bar, but I guess you already figured that out.

FOUR

The bar is one of the most intriguing categories of organisms in the universe. On the evolutionary path of natural selection, they have experienced an exceedingly brutal struggle to avoid elimination. Nowadays, many building classifications are relegated to the sedimentary strata of a few of the known planets. Whether we are speaking of low thatched huts or the old metropolitan towers that rose dozens or even hundreds of stories into the air—these species are merely fossils and memories now. The only category of structure that has persisted from that age—that has explored and settled new lands, that has truly made its home on a great many planets and has survived to this day—is the bar.

At the beginning of its life cycle, the juvenile bar will take root in the shady alleys of a planet's cities, near piles of rubbish. The young are able to absorb the nutrients from food waste with considerable efficiency. The totipotent larval stem cells divide and differentiate rapidly until they form complete organs, which are soon encased in and supported by bioluminescent cartilage. The luminous skeletal structure also serves to draw prey to the bar. The central nervous system is divided into several distinct neuromas which are able to survive for a time without direct connection to the main structure. These isolated bundles of nerve cells are able to perform an approximate simulation of the social environment of the quarry. On nearly every planet, this has proven to be a most effective method of hunting. At one time, scientists used genetic engineering to create skyscrapers with similar skills. This predictably resulted in large-scale massacres. Scientists and skyscrapers alike were condemned to death and executed in the aftermath.

The process of hunting its prey typically begins with the entrance of a man into the bar. This intrusion stimulates a series of neural signals, prompting the individual neuromas to initiate their own series of actions. Statistically speaking, the majority of those who frequent this sort of bar are wanted criminals. These are the sort of people who are most easily attracted to the atmosphere here, and their disappearance is the least likely to attract notice from the outside world.

Normally, the man will begin by ordering a drink. When this happens, the primary neuroma will take some of the fluid discharged from the excretory system of the bar, pour it into a hyperplastic growth, and push it toward the man. A neuroma sent out from the "mother's" body at some earlier time is capable of being reabsorbed into that body later, and the bar is able to reverse or continue the process of cell division and differentiation at will.

The ingestion of the excreta by the prey marks the formal beginning of the hunt. The bar randomly prompts a neuroma to pick a fight with the man. The man who is under the influence of the bar's urine lacks self-control and readily joins in a melee with the inciting neuroma.

As the turmoil begins, a gland on the side of the inciting neuroma explodes. The sound wave from the detonation is transmitted through the air to the other neuromas present, causing their glands to discharge as well. When such a gland erupts, several dense spores are ejected from the site, not unlike the high-speed expulsion of pollen from a splitting alfalfa capsule. The radiating spread of these projectiles is typically omni-directional and will normally prove effective in killing the prey. In extremely rare cases, the prey will only be wounded and will escape with his life. In these circumstances, the bar will merely lose one opportunity to feed; the identity of the bar is normally not compromised by this failure. This is not only due to the fact that these organic structures have evolved an effective camouflage defense mechanism as they are similar in appearance to traditional public houses built by humans, but also owing to the gene banks that are stored in the bar's anatomy. Thanks to the ever-expanding genetic assets contained in these banks, when neuromas are differentiated, the information therein allows for a variety of random arrangements and multiple permutations to construct manifold expressive results.

After a man (or in extremely rare cases a woman) is successfully dispatched, the bar begins to digest the prey. The digestion process is also a process of self-healing. The damaged areas will differentiate in reverse and re-form the complete base arrangement of the mother, and the prey's carcass will also be integrated into that being. The flesh and blood will be "swallowed," so to speak, and the base-pair sequence of the newly ingested cells will be transferred to the gene bank. Future neuromas will achieve richer expressive results, and behavior patterns will be more plentiful and more diverse.

Above is the basic content of the bar biological activity report. There yet remain many elusive matters regarding this creature. The most baffling among these mysteries concerns their mode of reproduction. As they are in this age gradually moving toward extinction, we may never learn the answer to this question. The very existence of this species has caused many traditional drinking establishments to go out of business over the long span of time. Considering their far-reaching impact on reduction of crime rates and the frequency of interstellar drunk driving cases, we cannot help but feel some sorrow at the loss of this species, and for us all as we consider their apparently irreversible fate.

FIVE

The last bar? That's me. I am the last bar in the entire universe.

When I was a young bar, I once set myself an ambitious goal: in my lifetime, I would accomplish three things that I could be truly proud of. Until very recently, I had accomplished two such objectives: one, I was the last bar in the universe; and two, I was the first bar to go into a man.

After consuming more than two hundred fugitives, I began to think about the intrinsic nature of ingestion. Considering the process of organizational integration, the issue of whether I have absorbed men or men have absorbed me is not a trivial question. After dedicating long and inconclusive ratiocination on the subject, I decided to take the scientific method as my main principle, and I resolved to attempt something I had never attempted before: to find a man and to let him eat me. I would take the results of that experience, place them alongside my own experience of ingestion, and compare the two. This experiment would prove to be invaluable.

The experiment may sound simple, but it is in fact not simple at all. Even considering those humans with physical modifications, my own body is still considerably larger, too large for direct human ingestion. I had to find a way to effectively reduce my scale. But this seemed at first to be the stuff of fantasy; I am not, after all, the magical shrinking tent from the *Arabian Nights*. In the end, I had to revise my way of thinking about the problem, and curiously, the solution was inspired by information transmitted between two of my neuromas. Thanks to this neuromatic conversation, I arrived at a new strategy for capturing my quarry.

According to this new tactic, I first restored the totipotency of the somatic cells, rearranged their genes, and expressed them again, this time using a chemical synthesis reaction to generate a composite of polysaccharides, fats, and proteins. Once this process was complete, I became a house made entirely of candy, and I hid myself, naturally, within an amusement park. This process of rearrangement may seem like a radical transformation and an extreme recourse, but in truth it was not so. Certainly it is easier in its operation, and much safer, than attempting a wholesale reduction of size.

During the transformation process, I was forced to alter certain character traits that I had acquired through the force of lifelong habit and ages of genetic inertia. For one, I had to adjust my active hours from nocturnal to diurnal. The compounds volatilized from my new body quickly attracted a large number of human young, which I had not anticipated, but there was also no shortage of adult males among the test subjects. I focused all of my attention on the men. I kept myself locked against the children and their families, and only opened my doors one evening just after the carnival had closed when a small band of rowdy young men approached.

So I achieved the second of my great ambitions as follows. The experimental specimens quickly discovered that all of the elements that constituted my new body were edible and quite delicious. Before long, they had broken me up into a great many pieces and thus consumed me until only about half of my structure remained. The remaining unsupported skeleton collapsed, leaving only some splintered sections of my ruined walls on the ground.

Having eaten to their hearts' content, they left with full bellies, eager to share the secret of this place with their friends. However, as soon as they left me, one by one they fell to the ground, their bodies convulsing. Finally, after their corpses grew stiff, within a short period of time they all melted into a mass of sarcomas. Yet the cells did not in fact differentiate into miniature versions of myself or anything of that sort. These experimental results were inconsistent with both hypotheses. Was I absorbing my prey or was my prey absorbing me? Neither description seemed sufficient to explain these results. Clearly more experiments were needed to answer my research question.

Faced with several lumps of ground meat, I knew that my experiment would definitely arouse attention and some hostility. But what did I care about that? I am an endangered species protected by universal law. I could always play that card if push came to shove, but something told me that these guys would not be missed by anyone in the near future.

Soon, my attention was drawn to the sarcomas on the ground. Although they did not differentiate into miniature versions of me, they began to wriggle. Whenever one sarcoma came into contact with another sarcoma, the two joined together. After all the sarcomas had merged into one, forming a fleshy ball roughly the same size as the remaining portion of my original body, the situation changed suddenly. The ball of flesh began to change its configuration rapidly, constituting itself into a new bar instead of a candy house. This demonstrated that this new form was indeed descended from the same ancestry as myself, yet it also possessed a distinct consciousness from my own. Thinking of this, I felt at once a frenzy of delight and a terrible sense of loss. Suddenly, I was no longer alone in the universe.

In the end, my ecstasy overwhelmed my dismay. I was conscious of an opportunity. I realized that now I would finally be able to accomplish the last of my three great feats. Whether I succeeded or failed, I would achieve my life's ambition; what I did next would either result in the extinction of an entire species, or it could mean an opportunity for the rebirth of our kind.

I transformed myself back into my original form, braced myself and stood face-to-face with my newborn counterpart, our brilliant neon glowing off each other's surfaces. Together we would usher in the great harmonious miracle of life.

SIX

And so it was that one day, in a distant corner of the universe, a bar went into a bar.

A guy went into one bar; another guy ordered a drink at the bar just across the narrow alleyway. The bartenders in both bars smiled and passed both guys a tequila on the rocks. The bartenders did not know these guys; it was the first time these guys had visited these bars.

The guys looked around. The bars' other patrons hid their scrutiny behind newspapers and darts. After a while, the guys both put on trench coats and tall hats, walked to the door of their respective bars. The two spoke to each other in low tones, exchanged some of the planet's local currency for two encrypted biomemory chips. Then the guys exchanged them back.

The guys returned to their stools at their original bars. At this point, two burly dudes with crisscrossed knife scars on their faces leaned close to the guys at the bars and demanded the guys buy them a drink. Both guys turned both dudes down, and in both bars the huge drunks immediately brandished daggers they had drawn from their belts. The guys grappled with the dudes, and suddenly a gun went off followed by the noisy discharge of multiple firearms. The intense crossfire left neat rows of holes in some walls and clusters in others. The rain of bullets grew even heavier, the bars' neon lights grew more dazzling, and the melodies blaring from the jukeboxes in the corners of the bars crescendoed despite the fact that their machinery had seemingly already been shattered in the crossfire.

One of the guys collapsed on the barroom floor, his brains spilling out like jelly mixed with shattered microchips. The other guy continued to howl with rage and shoot his gun. Then everyone still standing in both bars echoed his howl, and all the rifles and pistols spat hot metal slag. Patrons shouted and charged each other; cold weapons and hot weapons collided, and flesh struck flesh, and flesh penetrated flesh.

Amid the clash of metal and meat, projectiles passed through the front of one bar and pierced the body of the other. A bullet punctured the wall of the main room, shot through the kitchen, entered the furnace, and hit its mark, the gas tank buried deep in the structure. A blaze of flames soared into the night.

There was a terrific uproar as the explosion reached its climax.

The clamor alarmed the entire neighborhood, and the explosion almost leveled the buildings on either side of the bars. People surged into the streets and alleys. The fire trucks and ambulances charged onto the scene and began to comb through the ruins of structures that had buried the entire alley, searching for the wounded amid the rubble.

The dust settled, and the alley lay empty once again. No one noticed the ashes that rose slowly toward the blue sky, the embers that did not fall to the ground, but spiraled upward, left the atmosphere, and crossed into interstellar space. This was the seed released by the bars. These germs would wander aimlessly through the universe until they fell into the gravitational field of a certain planet or were picked up by a passing spacecraft and carried to a new habitat where they could settle and put down roots.

This was an extremely arduous process fraught with insecurity. If it were otherwise, the bar would never have been reduced to endangered status. Most of the germ cells would be swallowed up in the fires of the stars, the heat that can reduce anything to nothing and disintegrate every possibility. Fortunately, after such tragedies had played out billions of times, a cluster of dust was finally captured by a blue planet on the radial arm of Orion, and on that planet, carbon-based organisms had recently evolved into the final stage of its human civilization.

And so it came to pass that millions upon millions of light-years away from where the species was born, in a dark alley in the depths of a city enveloped in a heavy fog, neon lights flicker to life late one night, and a gang of rats chatter and skitter away from approaching feet.

And a guy walks into a bar and orders a drink.

This is a typical day in the life of a cyber bar.

CHALLENGE

There is no cyberpunk without the punk. It is fiction rooted in challenge. In cyberpunk worlds, technology is often used to enforce or reinforce repressive or regressive systems. (The intent is not always hostile; in fact, a recurring theme of cyberpunk is technology created for purehearted reasons that then creates harm when applied in practice.) In recognizing this, cyberpunk explores the power of opposition: that is, the power of punk.

In Greg Graffin's *Punk Manifesto*, he describes punk as, among other things, "a movement that serves to refute social attitudes that have been perpetuated through willful ignorance of human nature."* Technology in cyberpunk is a tool of perpetuation; the cyberpunk is therefore duty-bound to challenge it.

While the science-fiction author is often lauded as "visionary" or "prophetic," the cyberpunk writer is more Cassandra. They are cursed not only to see the future, but also the problems it will bring. McLuhan notes that "the artist picks up the message of cultural and technological challenge decades before its transforming impact occurs. The artist, then, builds models or Noah's arks for facing the change that is on hand." It is a compelling metaphor: cyberpunk stories as tiny arks for floods that only their authors can foresee. The artist is therefore "indispensable": we need their imagination to perceive, and prepare

* https://punxinsolidarity.wordpress.com/2013/10/22/ punk-manifesto-by-greg-graffin/

for, the difficulties ahead. We can only hope that, unlike Cassandra, the predictive efforts of the cyberpunks are not ignored.

Playing Cassandra is traditionally a thankless role, but in cyberpunk it is celebrated. Cyberpunk champions the punks and pessimists, the rebels and the rioters. The stories in this section showcase the underdog, the rogue, or those who live on the fringes of society. They are often reluctant punks, slow to answer the call. However, they are, ultimately, united by a clarity of vision and desire to challenge the system in which they live, and the technology upon which it is perpetuated.

• • •

The first story in this section is Philip K. Dick's "We Can Remember It For You Wholesale" (1966). Later filmed (repeatedly, and with steadily eroding quality) as *Total Recall*, the story's hero, Quail, finds himself at the heart of an interplanetary conflict that may or may not be entirely in his head.* It is a sterling example of technology, in this case memory-tampering, used as a tool of oppression, as well as a forerunner for an identity-bending storytelling mode that permeates the cyberpunk genre. The rebellion (or is it?) centers on the personal impact on Quail, not the overall righteousness of the cause. We are never sure if Quail is a revolutionary or a counterrevolutionary, nor which is the more morally desirable option.†

Two stories pick up directly on Dick's theme of weaponized memories. Bef's "Wonderama" (1998) makes its first English appearance in this volume, translated by the author. It plays many of the same notes as "We Can Remember It For You Wholesale," including that of a revolutionary trapped in a prison of their own desires.

"Wonderama" is chilling on two levels. First, the core plot: the greatest villains in cyberpunk are those who remove our right to challenge. Second, the nature of the capture. Whether a function of the dream or the dreamer, "Wonderama" takes place in a glossy catalogue of a dreamscape, where everything is extremely shiny and name-brand.

The story condemns not only the manipulation of dreams, but also how

---

* Dick's contributions to cyberpunk (or "proto-cyberpunk") also include *Do Androids Dream of Electric Sheep?* (1968), *A Scanner Darkly* (1977), and "The Minority Report" (1956). All three of those works have been filmed as well, but only *Total Recall* (1990) has Arnold Schwarzenegger pulling a metal softball from his nose.

† The year 1966 is also when *Star Trek* began, launching Gene Roddenberry's post-scarcity, techno-utopian future, where "challenge" is actively sought out by a valiant humanity looking up and beyond itself. Contrast this vision with the future in Dick's story, where technology is still being used to scratch capitalist itches and foment political violence. In 1966, we see how the evolution of the science fiction genre has fully diverged, leading, in twenty years, to a wistful hauntological reconciliation in "The Gernsback Continuum."

pathetic our dreams have become. Fabio Fernandes follows the theme further in "Wi-Fi Dreams" (2019), also translated by the author. An increasingly ridiculous cascade of technologies has resulted in the sinister, and permanent, gamification of our dreams. People are stuck in a virtualized dream world, combining the worst aspects of a MMORPG and your own nightmares.* "Wi-Fi Dreams" fully embraces the madness of its plot. Unlike "Wonderama" or "Wholesale," however, "Wi-Fi Dreams" is more explicit about the system the protagonist is trapped in—and his desire to fight against it.

Mandisi Nkomo's "Do Androids Dream of Capitalism and Slavery?" (2020) is also a response to Philip K. Dick, this time to his novel *Do Androids Dream of Electric Sheep?* (1968). Dick's novel was filmed by Ridley Scott as *Blade Runner* (1982) and became one of the seminal works of cyberpunk.† *Electric Sheep* (and by extension, *Blade Runner*) touches on the theme of artificial identity. Are "replicants"—androids that are indistinguishable from humans—worthy of the same respect and rights merited by "true" humans? Where *Electric Sheep* is inconclusive and *Blade Runne*r forlorn, Nkomo's story is pure anger. "We failed. We gave them emotions. Now we travel to our own extinction."

• • •

The hacker is the most iconic cyberpunk character: be they a coding ninja, a keyboard cowboy, or the paladin of the basement. Their challenge takes place in the virtual realm, "cyberspace," where physical prowess is secondary to a razor-edged mind.

Intelligence is the ultimate asset in Eileen Gunn's "Computer Friendly" (1989). Children are tested at a young age. The brightest become executives, with their minds instrumental to the processing power of the central computer. Those without potential are euthanized. Elizabeth makes for an unconventional hacker, but she navigates the setting's online systems with ease. She challenges authority with the naivete and surety of the child she is, with purity of heart and the uncanny ability to simplify complex problems.

---

* It is worth noting that one distant "cousin of cyberpunk" is LitRPG, a subgenre of science fiction and fantasy that's particularly popular on the self-publishing scene. It generally takes the form of portal fantasy, in which the protagonist is sucked into their favorite video game and forced to put their disturbingly intimate knowledge of it to use. Given the genre's reliance on virtual worlds and frequent use of the "evil corporation" trope, LitRPG has drawn on many aspects of the cyberpunk tradition. It also plays with form in a very cyberpunk way, with the underpinning numbers and "stats" of a video game sharing the page alongside the story itself. Unlike cyberpunk, the focus of LitRPG is not on the themes (or characters, or often even plots)—the appeal of LitRPG is the system itself. Imagine video game fanfiction, but with both the game and the fiction set within it being described simultaneously and enthusiastically. No LitRPG appears in this volume, but you have earned +5 XP for reading this footnote.

† And certainly the seminal work of cyberpunk climate. If you live in a cyberpunk world and you've never seen the sun, blame Ridley Scott.

Victor Pelevin's "The Yuletide Cyberpunk Yarn, or Christmas_Eve-117.DIR" (1996) appears here in English for the first time, translated from Russian by Alex Shvartsman. Set in the city of Petroplahovsk, it details the breakdown of the automated, but deeply corrupt, civic order. It is amusing as a tale of karmic comeuppance and cyberspace shenanigans, as befitting its gently humorous title. But under the surface, this is a tale of a society based entirely on venal self-interest, with little hope of meaningful change.

David Langford's "comp.basilisk.faq" (1999) has something nasty evolving from within the system. It is a technology gone corrupt; an Internet malignancy of mythic proportions. The FAQ-style story is a falsely reassuring response, with the ubiquity of its format hiding the horror within, and the bravery of those who hunt it.*

Taiyo Fujii's "Violation of the TrueNet Security Act" (2013), translated by Jim Hubbert, is also about hunting—this time for "zombies," or orphaned internet services that no longer have owners. Minami likes his job, if only for the nostalgia of finding old sites from his youth. But then he stumbles on the undead presence of one of his own websites—and somehow it's still being maintained. Who is tinkering with his code—and why?

• • •

Cyberpunk worlds are rarely safe places, and there are always battles to be fought. There are challenges to be faced offline as well. Misha's "Speed" (1988) is a deliciously frenetic story about a society overcome by its lust for data—"the only currency." Our protagonist acts as a mercenary for a greedy, centralized power, perpetually racing to new sources to appease his mysterious master. The story twists in unexpected ways, linking the new urge for knowledge with some of the world's oldest and most primal forces.

Myra Çakan's "Spider's Nest" (2004), translated from the German by Jim Young, is back on familiar cyberpunk stomping ground: the grimy streets of a post-collapse world, with survivalists trading drugs for salvage. Spider is a slave to the system, a lone survivor with few contacts and no friends. But inspired by his dreams and his drugs, Spider pushes into the unknown. He is the most dangerous rebel, as he has nothing to lose.

T. R. Napper's "Twelve Minutes to Vinh Quang" (2015) features another rebel. In this story, Lynn is holding all the cards—but her fate is still far from certain. If the story's criminal protagonist feels particularly cold-blooded, it is worth remembering the "diabolical" system of legalized oppression that she's up against. In Lynn's case, technology evens the playing field, giving her the advantage she needs.

---

* Back when the Internet was fresh and young, FAQs ("frequently asked questions") were "pinned" posts on every forum or board, helping newcomers acclimate themselves to the environment. Now that the internet is old and jaded, all the questions have been eaten by cats.

Khalid Kaki's "Operation Daniel" (2016), translated by Adam Talib, has a protagonist with none of Lynn's advantages. Rashid lives in a future version of Kirkuk that's been conquered and colonized by China. Like all other "beneficiaries" of the state, he is slowly having his culture and history eradicated; even using his native language is punishable by death. Rashid is outnumbered and outgunned, but still manages to pose a challenge to the all-powerful state, solely through the power of song.

Wole Talabi's "Abeokuta52" (2019) also has an underdog challenger, this time a journalist. The story takes the format of an exposé newspaper article that links scavenged alien technology to a pandemic of cancer. The article comes complete with pages of comments. As the story plays out, we can not only puzzle out the fate of the journalist, but see all the predictable social noise—conspiracy theories, dismissal, and corporate spin. Talabi shows the difficulty not only of mounting a challenge, but also of having it understood in a world that often prefers the status quo.

In Brandon O'Brien's "fallenangel.dll" (2016), an armed police drone—one that shouldn't exist—falls into the hands of three activists, and they have to choose what to do next. Merely possessing the drone puts them in danger, but the data in its memory could save them all. Technology here is a double-edged sword, the tool of both the oppressor and the oppressed.

Michael Moss's "Keep Portland Wired" (2020) also features grassroots activism. The renegades of the Collective are keen on beer, weed, and drone-racing. They're unlikely rebels, more adolescent angst than righteous fury, but they still do what they can to push back against Portland's corporate-fascist rulers. The story is self-aware, emphasizing both the stereotypical "cool" of our protagonists, and the actual misery of their self-conscious existence. "Do you think our parents thought about this when they had us?" one asks. "Like, how fucked up it would be to bring us into this world?"

Drones (of a sort) also appear in Rudy Rucker's "Juicy Ghost" (2019, with a new afterword for this edition). A rigged election leads to the effective collapse of the United States, with both candidates claiming the presidency. Curtis is prepared to martyr himself for his cause: a martyrdom that involves psychic warfare, weaponized wasps, and a lot of bloodshed. A gloriously over-the-top story from one of the original punks, "Juicy Ghost" is the cyberpunk Cassandra in full flow. It would be easy to dismiss this as satire and ignore the truth at its heart.

• • •

Not all challenge is inherently noble, or even righteous. Cyberpunk fiction naturally allies itself with the revolutionary and the rebel, but, equally, it also loathes hypocrisy. The superficial rebel is worse than the corporate peon, the treacherous ally more reviled than the overt opposition.

Cyberpunk is not without sympathy; it understands that many (most) have no choice about their participation in the system. A repressive society is perpetuated by power and persuasion, and most lack the freedom or the understanding to oppose it. The crux of many cyberpunk stories is when the protagonist gains the awareness or the agency to challenge the system, but then chooses, for some personal reason, *not* to exercise it. Ignorance is an excuse; knowledge is responsibility.

Nisi Shawl's "I Was a Teenage Genetic Engineer" (1989) begins with the engrossing opening: "I am a political prisoner on a North American game preserve." We swiftly learn that their imprisonment is a matter of everyone's safety. The engineer has created both monsters and gods, and they are all on the hunt.

Lewis Shiner's "The Gene Drain" (1989) is a fusion of the postmodern and the science fictional, one of the rare entries in this volume to include aliens. The extraterrestrials are window-dressing; an intergalactic counterpoint to the bizarre political machinations of the story's human cast, as they scheme and connive in an incorrigibly earthly manner.

In Bruce Sterling's "Deep Eddy" (1993), our delightfully naive protagonist visits Germany from Chattanooga and, slightly deluded with his own self-importance, is absorbed into the spontaneous chaos of a "wende." These organic eruptions of anarchism exist as a violent social catharsis. They are, much to Eddy's frustration, both unpredictable and uncontrollable. Over the course of the story, Eddy, a dilettante rebel, encounters true—and deep—challenge. Whether he learns from the experience is left to the reader to decide.

John Kessel's "The Last American" (2007) takes a unique approach. It is a book review, examining the new biography of the last American president, Andrew Steele. Steele is a complex character, alternately a savior and a demon, a populist and a reactionary. The biography (and the story) "comes to no formal conclusion, utilitarian or otherwise, as to the moral consequences of the life of Andrew Steele." However, set against the context of the story, and the ultimate reveal of humanity's fate, Steele's fate also seems tragic. He's both challenger and challenged, monster and martyr.

Ken MacLeod's "Earth Hour" (2011) is a political thriller set in a near-future Australia. Angus, an entrepreneur, former Lord, and occasional fortune-hunter, is the victim of an assassination attempt. Or is he? (As the story notes, successfully murdering someone is very difficult given the advanced state of medical science.) What's to be gained? And what can Angus gain from it as well?

"CRISPR Than You" (2018) is an ambitious future history by Ganzeer, which tracks through the intersection of art, politics, gender, race, and science. The future is a mixed media. Appropriately, the story is designed and illustrated by the author, an internationally acclaimed street artist. "CRISPR Than You" features challengers in art, science, and politics, all of whom find systems to tilt against, justly or not.

Yudhanjaya Wijeratne's "The State Machine" (2020) contains—perhaps—the most appealing setting in this book.* The titular machine governs all, gently imposing a thoughtful and rational rule. And why not? "To each other we are just

* To each their own, of course.

idealized versions of ourselves, projections, half lies and half truths, not the real data trail we all leave behind." Armed with that data, the State Machine cannot fail to take care of us. As our researcher protagonist tries to understand the history of the State Machine, to piece together how and why it came about, the Machine itself begins to—gently, lovingly—intervene. Even the most benign worlds have, and need, their punks.

K. A. Teryna's "The Tin Pilot" (2021), also translated by Alex Shvartsman, is set in a world far from benign. The last war was fought by golems—artificial humans. With the war over, they were given the blessing of amnesia. Their memories were wiped and they were mixed into human society, their origins a secret, even to them. But humans always look for something to fear, an outgroup to shun, and here was one close at hand. Thus was born the golem hunts—even though anyone could be a golem. There are layers and layers to this witch hunt; challenges both open and private.

The final story in this section is Janelle Monáe and Alaya Dawn Johnson's "The Memory Librarian" (2022), the titular novella of Monáe's collection.* It is in an Afrofuturist *and* cyberpunk city in the "whip end of the Rust Belt," where memories are carefully monitored—for the public good, of course. Seshet the Librarian takes a rare night out and encounters, and falls for, a beautiful woman.

But in a world supposedly without secrets, Alethia has more than her fair share of them. As Seshet tentatively takes her first steps away from the orderly world she knows, she discovers that she may have some secrets of her own. "The Memory Librarian" comes full circle to "We Can Remember It For You Wholesale" in its use of memory control as a tool of social repression.

Monáe and Johnson emphasize the importance of memory, of dream, to our identity. There's a fluidity to our appearance, to our names. Our *essence* is less tangible, and far deeper within. In "The Memory Librarian" the ultimate champion of the system must choose whether or not to become its challenger.

• • •

Cyberpunk is about the influence of technology on human affairs, and it is the sad truth of human affairs that many are antagonistic in nature—and many more are worthy of antagonism. Technology may ease those relationships, or suppress them, but it is just as likely to create new and unexpected dimensions of conflict.

Speculative fiction is more than entertainment, it is a social responsibility. Cyberpunk stories are tiny arks and whispered prophesies, interrogations of

---

* Few individuals are as important to the genre as Monáe, who is described in *Fifty Key Figures in Cyberpunk Culture* (Routledge, 2022) as "a true revolutionary within and beyond cyberpunk culture." Monáe, like Pat Cadigan and the editor of this book, hails from the greater Kansas City area, which is now, statistically, the most cyberpunk place on Earth.

what could be, based on what is known. Cyberpunk holds as sacrosanct the right to challenge, and cyberpunk literature urges the reader to exercise that right. No axiom should go unexamined, no system taken for granted, no line of code untested. As many of these stories reinforce: if we can't challenge in our minds, then we never will in the streets.

PHILIP K. DICK

WE CAN REMEMBER IT FOR YOU WHOLESALE

(1966)

HE AWOKE—AND WANTED MARS. *The valleys,* he thought. *What would it be like to trudge among them?* Great and greater yet: the dream grew as he became fully conscious, the dream and the yearning. He could almost feel the enveloping presence of the other world, which only Government agents and high officials had seen. A clerk like himself? Not likely.

"Are you getting up or not?" his wife Kirsten asked drowsily, with her usual hint of fierce crossness. "If you are, push the hot coffee button on the darn stove."

"Okay," Douglas Quail said, and made his way barefoot from the bedroom of their conapt to the kitchen. There, having dutifully pressed the hot coffee button, he seated himself at the kitchen table, brought out a yellow, small tin of fine Dean Swift snuff. He inhaled briskly, and the Beau Nash mixture stung his nose, burned the roof of his mouth. But still he inhaled; it woke him up and allowed his dreams, his nocturnal desires and random wishes, to condense into a semblance of rationality.

I will go, he said to himself. *Before I die I'll see Mars.*

It was, of course, impossible, and he knew this even as he dreamed. But the daylight, the mundane noise of his wife now brushing her hair before the bedroom mirror—everything conspired to remind him of what he was. *A miserable little salaried employee,* he said to himself with bitterness. Kirsten reminded him of this at least once a day and he did not blame her; it was a wife's job to bring her husband down to Earth. *Down to Earth,* he thought, and laughed. The figure of speech in this was literally apt.

"What are you sniggering about?" his wife asked as she swept into the kitchen, her long busy-pink robe wagging after her. "A dream, I bet. You're always full of them."

"Yes," he said, and gazed out the kitchen window at the hover-cars and traffic runnels, and all the little energetic people hurrying to work. In a little while he would be among them. As always.

"I'll bet it had to do with some woman," Kirsten said witheringly.

"No," he said. "A god. The god of war. He has wonderful craters with every kind of plant life growing deep down in them."

"Listen." Kirsten crouched down beside him and spoke earnestly, the harsh quality momentarily gone from her voice. "The bottom of the ocean—our ocean is much more, an infinity of times more beautiful. You know that; everyone knows that. Rent an artificial gill-outfit for both of us, take a week off from work, and we can descend and live down there at one of those year-round aquatic resorts. And in addition—" She broke off. "You're not listening. You should be. Here is something a lot better than that compulsion, that obsession you have about Mars, and you don't even listen!" Her voice rose piercingly. "God in heaven, you're doomed, Doug! What's going to become of you?"

"I'm going to work," he said, rising to his feet, his breakfast forgotten. "That's what's going to become of me."

She eyed him. "You're getting worse. More fanatical every day. Where's it going to lead?"

"To Mars," he said, and opened the door to the closet to get down a fresh shirt to wear to work.

Having descended from the taxi Douglas Quail slowly walked across three densely populated foot runnels and to the modern, attractively inviting doorway. There he halted, impeding midmorning traffic, and with caution read the shifting-color neon sign. He had, in the past, scrutinized this sign before . . . but never had he come so close. This was very different; what he did now was something else. Something which sooner or later had to happen.

REKAL, INCORPORATED

Was this the answer? After all, an illusion, no matter how convincing, remained nothing more than an illusion. At least objectively. But subjectively—quite the opposite entirely.

And anyhow he had an appointment. Within the next five minutes.

Taking a deep breath of mildly smog-infested Chicago air, he walked through the dazzling polychromatic shimmer of the doorway and up to the receptionist's counter.

The nicely articulated blonde at the counter, bare-bosomed and tidy, said pleasantly, "Good morning, Mr. Quail."

"Yes," he said. "I'm here to see about a Rekal course. As I guess you know."

"Not 'rekal' but *recall*," the receptionist corrected him. She picked up the receiver of the vidphone by her smooth elbow and said into it, "Mr. Douglas Quail is here, Mr. McClane. May he come inside, now? Or is it too soon?"

"Giz wetwa wum-wum wamp," the phone mumbled.

"Yes, Mr. Quail," she said. "You may go in; Mr. McClane is expecting you." As he started off uncertainly she called after him, "Room D, Mr. Quail. To your right."

After a frustrating but brief moment of being lost he found the proper room. The door hung open and inside, at a big genuine walnut desk, sat a genial-looking man, middle-aged, wearing the latest Martian frog-pelt gray suit; his attire alone would have told Quail that he had come to the right person.

"Sit down, Douglas," McClane said, waving his plump hand toward a chair which faced the desk. "So you want to have gone to Mars. Very good."

Quail seated himself, feeling tense. "I'm not so sure this is worth the fee," he said. "It costs a lot and as far as I can see I really get nothing." *Costs almost as much as going,* he thought.

"You get tangible proof of your trip," McClane disagreed emphatically. "All the proof you'll need. Here; I'll show you." He dug within a drawer of his impressive desk. "Ticket stub." Reaching into a manila folder, he produced a small square of embossed cardboard. "It proves you went—and returned. Postcards." He laid out four franked picture 3D full-color postcards in a neatly arranged row on the desk for Quail to see. "Film. Shots you took of local sights on Mars with a rented moving camera." To Quail he displayed those, too. "Plus the names of people you met, two hundred poscreds worth of souvenirs, which will arrive—from Mars—within the following month. And passport, certificates listing the shots you received. And more." He glanced up keenly at Quail. "You'll know you went, all right," he said. "You won't remember us, won't remember me or ever having been here. It'll be a real trip in your mind; we guarantee that. A full two weeks of recall; every last piddling detail. Remember this: if at any time you doubt that you really took an extensive trip to Mars you can return here and get a full refund. You see?"

"But I didn't go," Quail said. "I won't have gone, no matter what proofs you provide me with." He took a deep, unsteady breath. "And I never was a secret agent with Interplan." It seemed impossible to him that Rekal, Incorporated's extra-factual memory implant would do its job—despite what he had heard people say.

"Mr. Quail," McClane said patiently. "As you explained in your letter to us, you have no chance, no possibility in the slightest, of ever actually getting to Mars; you can't afford it, and what is much more important, you could never qualify as an undercover agent for Interplan or anybody else. This is the only way you can achieve your, ahem, lifelong dream; am I not correct, sir? You can't be this; you can't actually do this." He chuckled. "But you can have been and have done. We see to that. And our fee is reasonable; no hidden charges." He smiled encouragingly.

"Is an extra-factual memory that convincing?" Quail asked.

"More than the real thing, sir. Had you really gone to Mars as an Interplan agent, you would by now have forgotten a great deal; our analysis of true-mem systems—authentic recollections of major events in a person's life—shows that a variety of details are very quickly lost to the person. Forever.

"Part of the package we offer you is such deep implantation of recall that nothing is forgotten. The packet which is fed to you while you're comatose is the creation of trained experts, men who have spent years on Mars; in every case we verify details down to the last iota. And you've picked a rather easy extra-factual system; had you picked Pluto or wanted to be Emperor of the Inner Planet Alliance we'd have much more difficulty . . . and the charges would be considerably greater."

Reaching into his coat for his wallet, Quail said, "Okay. It's been my life-long ambition and so I see I'll never really do it. So I guess I'll have to settle for this."

"Don't think of it that way," McClane said severely. "You're not accepting second best. The actual memory, with all its vagueness, omissions, and ellipses, not to say distortions—that's second-best." He accepted the money and pressed a button on his desk. "All right, Mr. Quail," he said, as the door of his office opened and two burly men swiftly entered. "You're on your way to Mars as a secret agent." He rose, came over to shake Quail's nervous, moist hand. "Or rather, you have been on your way. This afternoon at four thirty you will, um, arrive back here on Terra; a cab will leave you off at your conapt and as I say you will never remember seeing me or coming here; you won't, in fact, even remember having heard of our existence."

His mouth dry with nervousness, Quail followed the two technicians from the office; what happened next depended on them.

Will I actually believe I've been on Mars? he wondered. *That I managed to fulfill my lifetime ambition?* He had a strange, lingering intuition that something would go wrong. *But just what*—he did not know.

He would have to wait and find out.

The intercom on McClane's desk, which connected him with the work area of the firm, buzzed and a voice said, "Mr. Quail is under sedation now, sir. Do you want to supervise this one, or shall we go ahead?"

"It's routine," McClane observed. "You may go ahead, Lowe; I don't think you'll run into any trouble." Programming an artificial memory of a trip to another planet—with or without the added fillip of being a secret agent—showed up on the firm's work-schedule with monotonous regularity. *In one month,* he calculated wryly, *we must do twenty of these . . . ersatz interplanetary travel has become our bread and butter.*

"Whatever you say, Mr. McClane," Lowe's voice came, and thereupon the intercom shut off.

Going to the vault section in the chamber behind his office, McClane searched about for a Three packet—trip to Mars—and a Sixty-Two packet: secret Interplan spy. Finding the two packets, he returned with them to his desk, seated himself comfortably, poured out the contents—merchandise which would be planted in Quail's conapt while the lab technicians busied themselves installing false memory.

A one-poscred sneaky-pete side arm, McClane reflected; *that's the largest item. Sets us back financially the most.* Then a pellet-sized transmitter, which could be swallowed if the agent were caught. *Code book that astonishingly resembled the real thing* . . . the firm's models were highly accurate: based, whenever possible, on actual US military issue. Odd bits which made no intrinsic sense but which would be woven into the warp and woof of Quail's imaginary trip, would coincide with his memory: half an ancient silver fifty-cent piece, several quotations from John Donne's sermons written incorrectly, each on a separate piece of transparent tissue-thin paper, several match folders from bars on Mars, a stainless-steel spoon engraved PROPERTY OF DOME-MARS NATIONAL KIBBUZIM, a wiretapping coil which—

The intercom buzzed. "Mr. McClane, I'm sorry to bother you but something rather ominous has come up. Maybe it would be better if you were in here after all. Quail is already under sedation; he reacted well to the narkidrine; he's completely unconscious and receptive. But—"

"I'll be in." Sensing trouble, McClane left his office; a moment later he emerged in the work area.

On a hygienic bed lay Douglas Quail, breathing slowly and regularly, his eyes virtually shut; he seemed dimly—but only dimly—aware of the two technicians and now McClane himself.

"There's no space to insert false memory-patterns?" McClane felt irritation. "Merely drop out two work weeks; he's employed as a clerk at the West Coast Emigration Bureau, which is a government agency, so he undoubtedly has or had two weeks' vacation within the last year. That ought to do it." Petty details annoyed him. And always would.

"Our problem," Lowe said sharply, "is something quite different." He bent over the bed, said to Quail, "Tell Mr. McClane what you told us." To McClane he said, "Listen closely."

The gray-green eyes of the man lying supine in the bed focused on McClane's face. The eyes, he observed uneasily, had become hard; they had a polished, inorganic quality, like semiprecious tumbled stones. He was not sure that he liked what he saw; the brilliance was too cold. "What do you want now?" Quail said harshly. "You've broken my cover. Get out of here before I take you all apart." He studied McClane. "Especially you," he continued. "You're in charge of this counteroperation."

Lowe said, "How long were you on Mars?"

"One month," Quail said gratingly.

"And your purpose there?" Lowe demanded.

The meager lips twisted; Quail eyed him and did not speak. At last, drawling the words out so that they dripped with hostility, he said, "Agent for Interplan. As I already told you. Don't you record everything that's said? Play your vid-aud tape back for your boss and leave me alone." He shut his eyes, then; the hard brilliance ceased. McClane felt, instantly, a rushing splurge of relief.

Lowe said quietly, "This is a tough man, Mr. McClane."

"He won't be," McClane said, "after we arrange for him to lose his memory-chain again. He'll be as meek as before." To Quail he said, "So this is why you wanted to go to Mars so terribly bad."

Without opening his eyes Quail said, "I never wanted to go to Mars. I was assigned it—they handed it to me and there I was: stuck. Oh yeah, I admit I was curious about it; who wouldn't be?" Again he opened his eyes and surveyed the three of them, McClane in particular. "Quite a truth drug you've got here; it brought up things I had absolutely no memory of." He pondered. "I wonder about Kirsten," he said, half to himself. "Could she be in on it? An Interplan contact keeping an eye on me . . . to be certain I didn't regain my memory? No wonder she's been so derisive about my wanting to go there." Faintly, he smiled; the smile—one of understanding—disappeared almost at once.

McClane said, "Please believe me, Mr. Quail; we stumbled onto this entirely by accident. In the work we do—"

"I believe you," Quail said. He seemed tired, now; the drug was continuing to pull him under, deeper and deeper. "Where did I say I'd been?" he murmured. "Mars? Hard to remember—I know I'd like to see it; so would everybody else. But me—" His voice trailed off. "*Just a clerk, a nothing clerk.*"

Straightening up, Lowe said to his superior. "He wants a false memory implanted that corresponds to a trip he actually took. And a false reason which is the real reason. He's telling the truth; he's a long way down in the narkidrine. The trip is very vivid in his mind—at least under sedation. But apparently he doesn't recall it otherwise. Someone, probably at a government military-sciences lab, erased his conscious memories; all he knew was that going to Mars meant something special to him, and so did being a secret agent. They couldn't erase that; it's not a memory but a desire, undoubtedly the same one that motivated him to volunteer for the assignment in the first place."

The other technician, Keeler, said to McClane, "What do we do? Graft a false memory-pattern over the real memory? There's no telling what the results would be; he might remember some of the genuine trip, and the confusion might bring on a psychotic interlude. He'd have to hold two opposite premises in his mind simultaneously: that he went to Mars and that he didn't. That he's a genuine agent for Interplan and he's not, that it's spurious. I think we ought to revive him without any false memory implantation and send him out of here; this is hot."

"Agreed," McClane said. A thought came to him. "Can you predict what he'll remember when he comes out of sedation?"

"Impossible to tell," Lowe said. "He probably will have some dim, diffuse memory of his actual trip, now. And he'd probably be in grave doubt as to its validity; he'd probably decide our programming slipped a gear-tooth. And he'd remember coming here; that wouldn't be erased—unless you want it erased."

"The less we mess with this man," McClane said, "the better I like it. This is nothing for us to fool around with; we've been foolish enough to—or unlucky enough to—uncover a genuine Interplan spy who has a cover so perfect that up to now even he didn't know what he was—or rather is." The sooner they washed their hands of the man calling himself Douglas Quail the better.

"Are you going to plant packets Three and Sixty-Two in his conapt?" Lowe said.

"No," McClane said. "And we're going to return half his fee."

" *'Half'!* Why half?"

McClane said lamely, "It seems to be a good compromise."

• • •

As the cab carried him back to his conapt at the residential end of Chicago, Douglas Quail said to himself, *It's sure good to be back on Terra.*

Already the month-long period on Mars had begun to waver in his memory; he had only an image of profound gaping craters, an ever-present ancient erosion of hills, of vitality, of motion itself. A world of dust where little happened, where a good part of the day was spent checking and rechecking one's portable oxygen source. And then the life forms, the unassuming and modest gray-brown cacti and maw-worms.

As a matter of fact he had brought back several moribund examples of Martian fauna; he had smuggled them through customs. After all, they posed no menace; they couldn't survive in Earth's heavy atmosphere.

Reaching into his coat pocket, he rummaged for the container of Martian maw-worms—and found an envelope instead.

Lifting it out, he discovered, to his perplexity, that it contained five hundred and seventy poscreds, in cred bills of low denomination.

Where'd I get this? he asked himself. *Didn't I spend every 'cred I had on my trip?*

With the money came a slip of paper marked: One-half fee ret'd. By McClane. And then the date. Today's date.

"Recall," he said aloud.

"Recall what, sir or madam?" the robot driver of the cab inquired respectfully.

"Do you have a phone book?" Quail demanded.

"Certainly, sir or madam." A slot opened; from it slid a microtape phone book for Cook County.

"It's spelled oddly," Quail said as he leafed through the pages of the yellow section. He felt fear, then: abiding fear. "Here it is," he said. "Take me there, to Rekal, Incorporated. I've changed my mind; I don't want to go home."

"Yes, sir or madam, as the case may be," the driver said. A moment later the cab was zipping back in the opposite direction.

"May I make use of your phone?" he asked.

"Be my guest," the robot driver said. And presented a shiny new emperor 3D color phone to him.

He dialed his own conapt. And after a pause found himself confronted by a miniature but chillingly realistic image of Kirsten on the small screen. "I've been to Mars," he said to her.

"You're drunk." Her lips writhed scornfully. "Or worse."

"'s God's truth."

"When?" she demanded.

"I don't know." He felt confused. "A simulated trip, I think. By means of one of those artificial or extra-factual or whatever it is memory places. It didn't take."

Kirsten said witheringly, "You are drunk." And broke the connection at her end. He hung up, then, feeling his face flush. *Always the same tone,* he said hotly to himself. *Always the retort, as if she knows everything and I know nothing. What a marriage. Keerist,* he thought dismally.

A moment later the cab stopped at the curb before a modern, very attractive little pink building, over which a shifting polychromatic neon sign read: REKAL, INCORPORATED.

The receptionist, chic and bare from the waist up, started in surprise, then gained masterful control of herself. "Oh, hello, Mr. Quail," she said nervously. "H-how are you? Did you forget something?"

"The rest of my fee back," he said.

More composed now, the receptionist said, "Fee? I think you are mistaken, Mr. Quail. You were here discussing the feasibility of an extra-factual trip for you, but—" She shrugged her smooth pale shoulders. "As I understand it, no trip was taken."

Quail said, "I remember everything, miss. My letter to Rekal, Incorporated, which started this whole business off. I remember my arrival here, my visit with Mr. McClane. Then the two lab technicians taking me in tow and administering a drug to put me out." No wonder the firm had returned half his fee. The false memory of his "trip to Mars" hadn't taken—at least not entirely, not as he had been assured.

"Mr. Quail," the girl said, "although you are a minor clerk you are a good-looking man and it spoils your features to become angry. If it would make you feel any better, I might, ahem, let you take me out . . ."

He felt furious, then. "I remember you," he said savagely. "For instance the fact that your breasts are sprayed blue; that stuck in my mind. And I remember Mr. McClane's promise that if I remembered my visit to Rekal, Incorporated, I'd receive my money back in full. Where is Mr. McClane?"

After a delay—probably as long as they could manage—he found himself once more seated facing the imposing walnut desk, exactly as he had been an hour or so earlier in the day.

"Some technique you have," Quail said sardonically. His disappointment—and resentment—was enormous, by now. "My so-called 'memory' of a trip to Mars as an undercover agent for Interplan is hazy and vague and shot full of contradictions. And I clearly remember my dealings here with you people. I ought to take this to the Better Business Bureau." He was burning angry at this point; his sense of being cheated had overwhelmed him, had destroyed his customary aversion to participating in a public squabble.

Looking morose, as well as cautious, McClane said, "We capitulate, Quail. We'll refund the balance of your fee. I fully concede the fact that we did absolutely nothing for you." His tone was resigned.

Quail said accusingly, "You didn't even provide me with the various artifacts that you claimed would 'prove' to me I had been on Mars. All that song-and-dance you went into—it hasn't materialized into a damn thing. Not even a ticket stub. Nor postcards. Nor passport. Nor proof of immunization shots. Nor—"

"Listen, Quail," McClane said. "Suppose I told you—" He broke off. "Let it go." He pressed a button on his intercom. "Shirley, will you disburse five hundred and seventy more 'creds in the form of a cashier's check made out to Douglas Quail? Thank you." He released the button, then glared at Quail.

Presently the check appeared; the receptionist placed it before McClane and once more vanished out of sight, leaving the two men alone, still facing each other across the surface of the massive walnut desk.

"Let me give you a word of advice," McClane said as he signed the check and passed it over. "Don't discuss your, ahem, recent trip to Mars with anyone."

"What trip?"

"Well, that's the thing." Doggedly, McClane said, "The trip you partially remember. Act as if you don't remember; pretend it never took place. Don't ask me why; just take my advice: it'll be better for all of us." He had begun to perspire. Freely. "Now, Mr. Quail, I have other business, other clients to see." He rose, showed Quail to the door.

Quail said, as he opened the door, "A firm that turns out such bad work shouldn't have any clients at all." He shut the door behind him.

On the way home in the cab Quail pondered the wording of his letter of complaint to the Better Business Bureau, Terra Division. As soon as he could get to his typewriter he'd get started; it was clearly his duty to warn other people away from Rekal, Incorporated.

When he got back to his conapt he seated himself before his Hermes Rocket portable, opened the drawers and rummaged for carbon paper—and noticed a small, familiar box. A box which he had carefully filled on Mars with Martian fauna and later smuggled through customs.

Opening the box he saw, to his disbelief, six dead maw-worms and several varieties of the unicellular life on which the Martian worms fed. The protozoa were dried-up, dusty, but he recognized them; it had taken him an entire day picking among the vast dark alien boulders to find them. A wonderful, illuminated journey of discovery.

But I didn't go to Mars, he realized.

Yet on the other hand—

Kirsten appeared at the doorway to the room, an armload of pale brown groceries gripped. "Why are you home in the middle of the day?" Her voice, in an eternity of sameness, was accusing.

"Did I go to Mars?" he asked her. "You would know."

"No, of course you didn't go to Mars; you would know that, I would think. Aren't you always bleating about going?"

He said, "By God, I think I went." After a pause he added, "And simultaneously I think I didn't go."

"Make up your mind."

"How can I?" He gestured. "I have both memory-tracks grafted inside my head; one is real and one isn't but I can't tell which is which. Why can't I rely on you? They haven't tinkered with you." She could do this much for him at least—even if she never did anything else.

Kirsten said in a level, controlled voice, "Doug, if you don't pull yourself together, we're through. I'm going to leave you."

"I'm in trouble." His voice came out husky and coarse. And shaking. "Probably I'm heading into a psychotic episode; I hope not, but—maybe that's it. It would explain everything, anyhow."

Setting down the bag of groceries, Kirsten stalked to the closet. "I was not kidding," she said to him quietly. She brought out a coat, got it on, walked back to the door of the conapt. "I'll phone you one of these days soon," she said tonelessly. "This is goodbye, Doug. I hope you pull out of this eventually; I really pray you do. For your sake."

"Wait," he said desperately. "Just tell me and make it absolute; I did go or I didn't—tell me which one." *But they may have altered your memory-track also,* he realized.

The door closed. His wife had left. *Finally!*

A voice behind him said, "Well, that's that. Now put up your hands, Quail. And also please turn around and face this way."

He turned, instinctively, without raising his hands.

The man who faced him wore the plum uniform of the Interplan Police Agency, and his gun appeared to be UN issue. And, for some odd reason, he seemed familiar to Quail; familiar in a blurred, distorted fashion which he could not pin down. So, jerkily, he raised his hands.

"You remember," the policeman said, "your trip to Mars. We know all your actions today and all your thoughts—in particular your very important thoughts on the trip home from Rekal, Incorporated." He explained, "We have a tele-transmitter wired within your skull; it keeps us constantly informed."

A telepathic transmitter; use of a living plasma that had been discovered in Luna. He shuddered with self-aversion. The thing lived inside him, within his own brain, feeding, listening, feeding. But the Interplan police used them; that had come out even in the homeopapes. So this was probably true, dismal as it was.

"Why me?" Quail said huskily. What had he done—or thought? And what did this have to do with Rekal, Incorporated?

"Fundamentally," the Interplan cop said, "this has nothing to do with Rekal; it's between you and us." He tapped his right ear. "I'm still picking up your mentational processes by way of your cephalic transmitter." In the man's ear Quail saw a small white-plastic plug. "So I have to warn you: anything you think may be held against you." He smiled. "Not that it matters now; you've already thought and spoken yourself into oblivion. What's annoying is the fact that under narkidrine at Rekal, Incorporated, you told them, their technicians and the owner, Mr. McClane, about your trip—where you went, for whom, some of what you did. They're very frightened. They wish they had never laid eyes on you." He added reflectively, "They're right."

Quail said, "I never made any trip. It's a false memory-chain improperly planted in me by McClane's technicians." But then he thought of the box, in his desk drawer, containing the Martian life forms. And the trouble and hardship he had had gathering them. The memory seemed real. And the box of life forms; that certainly was real. Unless McClane had planted it. Perhaps this was one of the "proofs" which McClane had talked glibly about.

The memory of my trip to Mars, he thought, *doesn't convince me—but unfortunately it has convinced the Interplan Police Agency. They think I really went to Mars and they think I at least partially realize it.*

"We not only know you went to Mars," the Interplan cop agreed, in answer to his thoughts, "but we know that you now remember enough to be difficult for us. And there's no use expunging your conscious memory of all this, because if we do you'll simply show up at Rekal, Incorporated again and start over. And we can't do anything about McClane and his operation because we have no jurisdiction over anyone except our own people. Anyhow, McClane hasn't committed any crime." He eyed Quail, "Nor, technically, have you. You didn't go to Rekal, Incorporated, with the idea of regaining your memory; you went, as we realize, for the usual reason people go there—a love by plain, dull people for adventure." He added, "Unfortunately you're not plain, not dull, and you've already had too much excitement; the last thing in the universe you needed was a course from Rekal, Incorporated. Nothing could have been more lethal for you or for us. And, for that matter, for McClane."

Quail said, "Why is it 'difficult' for you if I remember my trip—my alleged trip—and what I did there?"

"Because," the Interplan harness bull said, "what you did is not in accord with our great white all-protecting father public image. You did, for us, what we never do. As you'll presently remember—thanks to narkidrine. That box of dead worms and algae has been sitting in your desk drawer for six months, ever since you got back. And at no time have you shown the slightest curiosity about it. We didn't even know you had it until you remembered it on your way home from Rekal; then we came here on the double to look for it." He added, unnecessarily, "Without any luck; there wasn't enough time."

A second Interplan cop joined the first one; the two briefly conferred. Meanwhile, Quail thought rapidly. He did remember more, now; the cop had been right about narkidrine. They—Interplan—probably used it themselves. *Probably?* He knew darn well they did; he had seen them putting a prisoner on it. *Where would that be? Somewhere on Terra? More likely on Luna,* he decided, viewing the image rising from his highly defective—but rapidly less so—memory.

And he remembered something else. Their reason for sending him to Mars; the job he had done.

No wonder they had expunged his memory.

"Oh, God," the first of the two Interplan cops said, breaking off his conversation with his companion. Obviously, he had picked up Quail's thoughts. "Well, this is a far worse problem, now; as bad as it can get." He walked toward Quail, again covering him with his gun. "We've got to kill you," he said. "And right away."

Nervously, his fellow officer said, "Why right away? Can't we simply cart him off to Interplan New York and let them—"

"He knows why it has to be right away," the first cop said; he too looked nervous, now, but Quail realized that it was for an entirely different reason. His memory had been brought back almost entirely, now. And he fully understood the officer's tension.

"On Mars," Quail said hoarsely, "I killed a man. After getting past fifteen bodyguards. Some armed with sneaky-pete guns, the way you are." He had been trained, by Interplan, over a five-year period to be an assassin. A professional killer. He knew ways to take out armed adversaries . . . such as these two officers; and the one with the ear-receiver knew it, too. If he moved swiftly enough—

The gun fired. But he had already moved to one side, and at the same time he chopped down the gun-carrying officer. In an instant he had possession of the gun and was covering the other, confused, officer.

"Picked my thoughts up," Quail said, panting for breath. "He knew what I was going to do, but I did it anyhow."

Half sitting up, the injured officer grated, "He won't use that gun on you, Sam; I pick that up, too. He knows he's finished, and he knows we know it, too. Come on, Quail." Laboriously, grunting with pain, he got shakily to his feet. He held out his hand. "The gun," he said to Quail. "You can't use it, and if you turn it over to me I'll guarantee not to kill you; you'll be given a hearing, and someone higher up in Interplan will decide, not me. Maybe they can erase your memory once more, I don't know. But you know the thing I was going to kill you for; I couldn't keep you from remembering it. So my reason for wanting to kill you is in a sense past."

Quail, clutching the gun, bolted from the conapt, sprinted for the elevator. *If you follow me,* he thought, *I'll kill you. So don't.* He jabbed at the elevator button and, a moment later, the doors slid back.

The police hadn't followed him. Obviously they had picked up his terse, tense thoughts and had decided not to take the chance.

With him inside the elevator descended. He had gotten away—for a time. But what next? Where could he go?

The elevator reached the ground floor; a moment later Quail had joined the mob of peds hurrying along the runnels. His head ached and he felt sick. But at least he had evaded death; they had come very close to shooting him on the spot, back in his own conapt.

And they probably will again, he decided. *When they find me. And with this transmitter inside me, that won't take too long.*

Ironically, he had gotten exactly what he had asked Rekal, Incorporated for. Adventure, peril, Interplan police at work, a secret and dangerous trip to Mars in which his life was at stake—everything he had wanted as a false memory.

The advantages of it being a memory—and nothing more—could now be appreciated.

On a park bench, alone, he sat dully watching a flock of perts: a semi-bird imported from Mars's two moons, capable of soaring flight, even against Earth's huge gravity.

Maybe I can find my way back to Mars, he pondered. *But then what?* It would be worse on Mars; the political organization whose leader he had assassinated would spot him the moment he stepped from the ship; he would have Interplan and them after him, there.

Can you hear me thinking? he wondered. Easy avenue to paranoia; sitting here alone he felt them tuning in on him, monitoring, recording, discussing . . . He shivered, rose to his feet, walked aimlessly, his hands deep in his pockets. *No matter where I go,* he realized, *you'll always be with me. As long as I have this device inside my head.*

I'll make a deal with you, he thought to himself—and to them. *Can you imprint a false-memory template on me again, as you did before, that I lived an average, routine life, never went to Mars? Never saw an Interplan uniform up close and never handled a gun?*

A voice inside his brain answered, "As has been carefully explained to you: that would not be enough."

Astonished, he halted.

"We formerly communicated with you in this manner," the voice continued. "When you were operating in the field, on Mars. It's been months since we've done it; we assumed, in fact, that we'd never have to do so again. Where are you?"

"Walking," Quail said, "to my death." *By your officers' guns,* he added as an afterthought. "How can you be sure it wouldn't be enough?" he demanded. "Don't the Rekal techniques work?"

"As we said. If you're given a set of standard, average memories you get—restless. You'd inevitably seek out Rekal or one of its competitors again. We can't go through this a second time."

"Suppose," Quail said, "once my authentic memories have been canceled, something more vital than standard memories are implanted. Something which would act to satisfy my craving," he said. "That's been proved; that's probably why you initially hired me. But you ought to be able to come up with something else—something equal. I was the richest man on Terra but I finally gave all my money to educational foundations. Or I was a famous deep-space explorer. Anything of that sort; wouldn't one of those do?"

Silence.

"Try it," he said desperately. "Get some of your top-notch military psychiatrists; explore my mind. Find out what my most expansive daydream is." He tried to think. "Women," he said. "Thousands of them, like Don Juan had. An interplanetary playboy—a mistress in every city on Earth, Luna, and Mars. Only I gave that up, out of exhaustion. Please," he begged. "Try it."

"You'd voluntarily surrender, then?" the voice inside his head asked. "If we agreed to arrange such a solution? If it's possible?"

After an interval of hesitation he said, "Yes." *I'll take the risk,* he said to himself, *that you don't simply kill me.*

"You make the first move," the voice said presently. "Turn yourself over to us. And we'll investigate that line of possibility. If we can't do it, however, if your authentic memories begin to crop up again as they've done at this time, then—" There was silence and then the voice finished, "We'll have to destroy you. As you must understand. Well, Quail, you still want to try?"

"Yes," he said. Because the alternative was death now—and for certain. At least this way he had a chance, slim as it was.

"You present yourself at our main barracks in New York," the voice of the Interplan cop resumed. "At 580 Fifth Avenue, floor twelve. Once you've surrendered yourself, we'll have our psychiatrists begin on you; we'll have personality-profile tests made. We'll attempt to determine your absolute, ultimate fantasy wish—then we'll bring you back to Rekal, Incorporated, here; get them in on it, fulfilling that wish in vicarious surrogate retrospection. And—good luck. We do owe you something; you acted as a capable instrument for us." The voice lacked malice; if anything, they—the organization—felt sympathy toward him.

"Thanks," Quail said. And began searching for a robot cab.

• • •

"Mr. Quail," the stern-faced, elderly Interplan psychiatrist said, "you possess a most interesting wish-fulfillment dream fantasy. Probably nothing such as you consciously entertain or suppose. This is commonly the way; I hope it won't upset you too much to hear about it."

The senior ranking Interplan officer present said briskly, "He better not be too much upset to hear about it, not if he expects not to get shot."

"Unlike the fantasy of wanting to be an Interplan undercover agent," the psychiatrist continued, "which, being relatively speaking a product of maturity, had a certain plausibility to it, this production is a grotesque dream of your childhood; it is no wonder you fail to recall it. Your fantasy is this: you are nine years old, walking alone down a rustic lane. An unfamiliar variety of space vessel from another star system lands directly in front of you. No one on Earth but you, Mr. Quail, sees it. The creatures within are very small and helpless, somewhat on the order of field mice, although they are attempting to invade Earth; tens of thousands of other ships will soon be on their way, when this advance party gives the go-ahead signal."

"And I suppose I stop them," Quail said, experiencing a mixture of amusement and disgust. "Single-handed I wipe them out. Probably by stepping on them with my foot."

"No," the psychiatrist said patiently. "You halt the invasion, but not by destroying them. Instead, you show them kindness and mercy, even though by telepathy—their mode of communication—you know why they have come. They have never seen such humane traits exhibited by any sentient organism, and to show their appreciation they make a covenant with you."

Quail said, "They won't invade Earth as long as I'm alive."

"Exactly." To the Interplan officer the psychiatrist said, "You can see it does fit his personality, despite his feigned scorn."

"So by merely existing," Quail said, feeling a growing pleasure, "by simply being alive, I keep Earth safe from alien rule. I'm in effect, then, the most important person on Terra. Without lifting a finger."

"Yes, indeed, sir," the psychiatrist said. "And this is bedrock in your psyche; this is a lifelong childhood fantasy. Which, without depth and drug therapy, you never would have recalled. But it has always existed in you; it went underneath, but never ceased."

To McClane, who sat intently listening, the senior police official said, "Can you implant an extra-factual memory pattern that extreme in him?"

"We get handed every possible type of wish-fantasy there is," McClane said. "Frankly, I've heard a lot worse than this. Certainly we can handle it. Twenty-four hours from now he won't just wish he'd saved Earth; he'll devoutly believe it really happened."

The senior police official said, "You can start the job, then. In preparation we've already once again erased the memory in him of his trip to Mars."

Quail said, "What trip to Mars?"

No one answered him, so reluctantly, he shelved the question. And anyhow a police vehicle had now put in its appearance; he, McClane, and the senior police officer crowded into it, and presently they were on their way to Chicago and Rekal, Incorporated.

"You had better make no errors this time," the police officer said to heavyset, nervous-looking McClane.

"I can't see what could go wrong," McClane mumbled, perspiring. "This has nothing to do with Mars or Interplan. Single-handedly stopping an invasion of Earth from another star system." He shook his head at that. "Wow, what a kid dreams up. And by pious virtue, too; not by force. It's sort of quaint." He dabbed at his forehead with a large linen pocket handkerchief.

Nobody said anything.

"In fact," McClane said, "it's touching."

"But arrogant," the police official said starkly. "Inasmuch as when he dies the invasion will resume. No wonder he doesn't recall it; it's the most grandiose fantasy I ever ran across." He eyed Quail with disapproval. "And to think we put this man on our payroll."

When they reached Rekal, Incorporated, the receptionist, Shirley, met them breathlessly in the outer office. "Welcome back, Mr. Quail," she fluttered, her melon-shaped breasts—today painted an incandescent orange—bobbing with agitation. "I'm sorry everything worked out so badly before; I'm sure this time it'll go better."

Still repeatedly dabbing at his shiny forehead with his neatly folded Irish linen handkerchief, McClane said, "It better." Moving with rapidity he rounded up Lowe and Keeler, escorted them and Douglas Quail to the work area, and then, with Shirley and the senior police officer, returned to his familiar office. To wait.

"Do we have a packet made up for this, Mr. McClane?" Shirley asked, bumping against him in her agitation, then coloring modestly.

"I think we do." He tried to recall, then gave up and consulted the formal chart. "A combination," he decided aloud, "of packets Eighty-One, Twenty, and Six." From the vault section of the chamber behind his desk he fished out the appropriate packets, carried them to his desk for inspection. "From Eighty-One," he explained, "a magic healing rod given him—the client in question, this time Mr. Quail—by the race of beings from another system. A token of their gratitude."

"Does it work?" the police officer asked curiously.

"It did once," McClane explained. "But he, ahem, you see, used it up years ago, healing right and left. Now it's only a memento. But he remembers it working spectacularly." He chuckled, then opened packet Twenty. "Document from the UN Secretary General thanking him for saving Earth; this isn't precisely appropriate, because part of Quail's fantasy is that no one knows of the invasion except himself, but for the sake of verisimilitude we'll throw it in." He inspected packet Six, then. *What came from this?* He couldn't recall; frowning, he dug into the plastic bag as Shirley and the Interplan police officer watched intently.

"Writing," Shirley said. "In a funny language."

"This tells who they were," McClane said, "and where they came from. Including a detailed star map logging their flight here and the system of origin. Of course it's in their script, so he can't read it. But he remembers them reading it to him in his own tongue." He placed the three artifacts in the center of the desk. "These should be taken to Quail's conapt," he said to the police officer. "So that when he gets home he'll find them. And it'll confirm his fantasy. SOP—standard operating procedure." He chuckled apprehensively, wondering how matters were going with Lowe and Keeler.

The intercom buzzed. "Mr. McClane, I'm sorry to bother you." It was Lowe's voice; he froze as he recognized it, froze and became mute. "But something's come up. Maybe it would be better if you came in here and supervised. Like before, Quail reacted well to the narkidrine; he's unconscious, relaxed, and receptive. But—" McClane sprinted for the work area.

On a hygienic bed Douglas Quail lay breathing slowly and regularly, eyes half-shut, dimly conscious of those around him.

"We started interrogating him," Lowe said, white-faced. "To find out exactly when to place the fantasy-memory of him single-handedly having saved Earth. And strangely enough—"

"They told me not to tell," Douglas Quail mumbled in a dull drug-saturated voice. "That was the agreement. I wasn't even supposed to remember. But how could I forget an event like that?"

I guess it would be hard, McClane reflected. *But you did—until now.*

"They even gave me a scroll," Quail mumbled, "of gratitude. I have it hidden in my conapt; I'll show it to you."

To the Interplan officer who had followed after him, McClane said, "Well, I offer the suggestion that you better not kill him. If you do they'll return."

"They also gave me a magic invisible destroying rod," Quail mumbled, eyes totally shut now. "That's how I killed that man on Mars you sent me to take out. It's in my drawer along with the box of Martian maw-worms and dried-up plant life."

Wordlessly, the Interplan officer turned and stalked from the work area.

I might as well put those packets of proof-artifacts away, McClane said to himself resignedly. He walked, step by step, back to his office. Including the citation from the UN Secretary General. After all—

The real one probably would not be long in coming.

MISHA

SPEED

[1988]

EVERYTHING IS FRACTURED; a broken mirror pieced together randomly so your reflection feels all wrong, an eye here, a nose there, any old mouth where your chin should be.

• • •

Shrill feedback and digital chitters wail in the collapsible dish Speed has mounted on the HOT truck. Sheet metal booms, arcs ping—but he has no real fix on the input drain. Somewhere west?

Animal Inscription tearing out the deck, Speed skids his HOT truck, barely misses the oily flayed body of a dead man with six or seven people brawling over it trying to get a wallet.

Green paper dollars flutter into the gutter with other worthless trash—ones as well as tens and twenties. Speed sneers at their chemical messages. It's the guy's ID they want.

Here data is the only currency, according to the all-knowing Juno 888. Speed rolls up against the crumbling yellow curb. From his composite eyeglasses he watches a city alive with insect activity; run-skitters, flashes of chitin armor, papery wings. Mandibles clack; a rush, more swift tides and waves of insects. The gimmick lines are in a chaos—armed guards bludgeoning into file the soft yellow heads of young and old white-haired eggs spilling their yolks on the roadway. All DNA IDs are checked. Speed of course to stop for none of them. He runs a red DAT vehicle with a HOT sign on the side. He zips around a line of cards. Rusty fire ants rush to holes before the rain. It rains. A thunderous sheet of lightning garishly two-dimensionalizes them all. A scarab bas-relief. Hailstone marbles crash down on them. The furious storm's thunder roars a geared-down semi. No one seems to notice. Baldface guards truncheon. Blood balls roll underfoot. Speed peels back their scalps, puts his hands in the oozing gray matter—all cold pudding from disuse.

"Nobody home," he says, slamming the hair down.

The street here flows red with foamy junket. Speed gulps back revulsion. The river runs from the outlet of The Bell Factory, a gray building, ex detention center for non gov artists. Now Comma 7 brings non data here for recycling.

"888, Speed 15-1-00 reports. Mile post 669 highway 82."

"What's the delay? Where is my data source number Speel-yi 427?" 888 is on its routine check.

Speed wrinkles his nose at 888's predictability.

Speed blows smoke, glares at cars hydroplaning past in the red slime. Some wrecks are loaded with merchandise. Some shiny new ones are empty.

"888, it's snowing."

"Thank you, fifty credits."

"888, nobody told you it was snowing?" Speed asks incredulously.

"I could have predicted it." The 888 pauses. "Crow Moon."

Speed's heart accelerates, flies against his ribs then circles, cold and wary. "What's that? 888, what's that—Crow Moon?" Speed gets a hunch, at last.

"Speel-yi 427 data online."

"Fucking-a," he whispers. "888, is this data accessible?"

"Yes—access code required."

"Shit." He smacks the dash with his gloved hands.

The 888 leaves the terminal on the dash and then is replaced by the holo again. Speed glances at it and drives a little faster.

At first everyone was a lot happier when the Juno 888 took control of world commerce. As to be expected—the rich got very rich. The poor were replaced. Typical mayfly existence.

888 arranged its own random pattern of rising US dollar and failing yen, or pound or rising pound or rising yen or whatever was popular. To begin with, commerce grumbled. Yellow lights blinked on—then went off again. 888 brought the gold standard back for four chaotic years. Now data—only data is commerce. People kill each other to get the chance to report the death.

Speed steers around the wreckage of two supertrucks. Speed is satisfied with this new system. It isn't hard to come up with data—if you are creative. Corporate termite mounds collapsed in hours. Drones search for queen bees of data—hire people like himself to find them.

But Speed belongs to no man—only to the Juno 888. He moves, the caddis fly in the HOT house of silicon sentience, preying on unwary larvae. But his only bug in the honey is that the Comma 7 parasitic pepsis DATmen hunt him.

To date—the longest source of uninterrupted data is Speel-yi 427. 888 demands for her to be brought in, its larder of uninterrupted data in hexagonal cells, waxing poetic for the Juno's brood of inaccessible memories.

Speed hungers for this Speel-yi as much as Juno 888 does. He likes to please this insatiable electric insect, the solar panels wings those of a great iridescent mantis.

888 drops the egg of a clue with Crow Moon. The antenna of Speed's brain rotates west. He thinks nearly all non-whites had been killed in pogroms. Especially those, what were they, not Crows but . . .

Speed spurs the HOT west.

• • •

Toy blue skies lie safely over tin tops. Cycled Comma Cops stalk Speed and wait for the blood to flow before striking. He knows their feeding frenzies and pulls into a tunnel and stops. He gathers refuse—broken bottles, asphalt chunks, ripped beer cans, bent sign poles—and strategically places them. Hurrying now, Speed reaches into the treasure of junk in the back of the HOT. He unrolls barbed wire across the tube. He pitons it to the concrete walls wincing at the pang pang of the ice hammer in the hollow hall. His boots echo in the tunnel as he runs to the HOT truck, screeches the tires through the other side, and idles.

The Comma Cops come in quickly for the kill. So much static convinces them the prey is found. They bare their shark teeth and hit fast.

A scream gurgles, skidding crashes, metal explodes, chemicals burn, a debris destination for any who missed the finishing wire.

Speed grins to himself, moves off slowly, a wolf eel in liquid death.

Here, fifty miles from 888's last query, Speed perches on the HOT and sets up the collapsible dish. Microwave music screams, whistles, static white noise, metal sheets tear, digital snaps and pops, high pitches cricket, a seventeen-year cicada of noise is all beautiful to Speed. He loses himself in this wall of sound, eyes closed. Behind the deadly glass, green holo eyes watch him coyly.

A fluid sound pricks his ears and Speed is instantly alert—his sharp nose quivers and he fine-tunes the pulse. There is a high-pitched howl echoing the system. Something he zeros on—the specified aimed point. Picture of, picture of hell. A spot of purple and orange fire, Speed dives to the road.

Fun backward spells *'nuf.* Speed laughs, "Nuf fun."

A Comma Cop with an erased face whips a chain lasso across his eyes before he relays to 888. Bright blood bees fly away from Speed. The Comma 7 is rejecting him with shark-tooth gloves as the blood answers "no" while his mouth says "yes, yes."

"Where is the data?" The Comma Cop is so digital, off again, on again, like any insect, no chirping below fifty degrees, and it's cold here—no sound.

"Okay, okay," Speed says weakly. He pushes himself up against the door of the HOT. His glasses are cracked carapaces, saving his sight which is peering from behind a crimson curtain. Speed grinds his bootheel in asphalt.

• • •

"Where?" The Comma 7 swings the chain.

"Nunya," says Speed quietly.

"Nunya? As in . . . ," the Comma 7 comes very close.

"As in Nunya business!" Speed lashes out with his boot-tip bayonet, laughing wildly. Oldest trick in the books. Easy to strip a Dogface cocoon he thinks—remembers this as he reaches back into the red HOT and pulls out a black Louisville with a white taped handle. The crack of the skull signals home run. He wants the Comma 7 to pull back now. Needs a sign. The larvae quivers and oozes greenish fluid. Speed teases open the tear with a pair of needle-nose pliers. Blue tendons and bubble-pink organs lay in a bed of yellow fat. The shining steel disappears into the wound. Droplets of sweat roll down Speed's face as he crouches there. He finds what he wants, pulls it out, hitches it to the bumper. Speed wipes his face and throws the slick pliers in the bed of junk where it clatters into the oily corner. He hops into the truck, blows a kiss to the holo Speel-yi 427 and drives off. In the rearview mirror everything is all wrong, the body jerks and unravels, any old intestine where a groin should be. The body rips off on a reflector on the side of a bar pit. Speed ejaculates laughter, shudders over the wheel, and burns rubber.

Crows, like jagged obsidian knives, descend on the sacrifice.

Speed sucks razors of breath as he spirals into a turquoise sky. The dishes on this mountain are all tied with aluminum balloons. He stops and shoots one with an old GP-100. This is the way the world ends, he sniggers as the metal bangs his ears.

He feels elated.

At precisely 4,500 feet above sea level, at a mountain lake surrounded by huge alpine trees drooping with a whipped top of snow, he stops. He sees no people, only chimeras, a musk-oxen-llama cross left from some forgotten genetic farm. These form a protective ring and spit at him. Speed laughs.

The snow seeps through his boots and his coverall crackles with cold. He makes his way to a pole hogan with a valley-sized dish in front of it.

Inside, it smells of woodsmoke, jerky, dried fruit, spice, and—he fastens his reflective lenses toward the now solid holo—fish.

She is eating a tin of salmon and smiling at him. Behind her a string of shrunken heads dance, eyes and lips sewn silent. He jumps as he realizes they are him. This knife fish has brought him to face himself. A spider silence, a spider's lair, a white spider in the shadow of a white web. Snow falls from him in glistening globules.

"Speed 15-1-00," he extends a shaking hand.

She is not the holo. She is faded, in a black ball cap with an unspeakable name on the crown. She has sable braids and her face is ceremonially painted in noshi red and white. Seven crimson false faces leer around the hogan. They hand him a bundle of arrows, a carmine stone calumet.

Her eyes are the same eyes—watching him coyly. Alive with meaning. The spider crystallizes, falls away. Predator intensity sharpens the data lust. Her sharp white teeth and her red gums are laughing at him. Speel-yi, a trickster in a Kali suit, is entering her data.

"March, the Crow or Wakening Moon," she mercifully explains, "Folklore of The People. Very practical."

Volcanic laughter is burning up his throat, he vomits it with his gorge. The false faces are dancing in a slow ghostly dance. They are mocking silicon senility.

This is what they sing:

ka-ka tiwa-ku
ka-ka tiwa-ku
wetatu-ta (tu) tatu-ta
*atira irira atira irira**

"You forgot to give the coordinates," she says and taps the questioning screen.

Speed moves toward the dancers and the world tilts, the day cracks apart, and the black comes in and is punctuated by seven white stars. Terrible winds tear life's fabric, blinding ash snow falls on the white feathers of the Crow Moon. Spedis and Speel-yi illuminate this new world with radiant smiles. The ghost dancers shout:

irihe we isarat†

* (loosely translated) *Crow he says / Crow he says / Now I do Now I do / Moon whence she comes Moon whence she comes*

† *So here now stop*

EILEEN GUNN

COMPUTER FRIENDLY

(1989)

HOLDING HER DAD'S HAND, Elizabeth went up the limestone steps to the testing center. As she climbed, she craned her neck to read the words carved in pink granite over the top of the door: FRANCIS W. PARKER SCHOOL. Above them was a banner made of gray cement that read, HEALTH, HAPPINESS, SUCCESS.

"This building is old," said Elizabeth. "It was built before the war."

"Pay attention to where you're going, punkin," said her dad. "You almost ran into that lady there."

Inside, the entrance hall was dark and cool. A dim yellow glow came through the shades on the tall windows.

As Elizabeth walked across the polished floor, her footsteps echoed lightly down the corridors that led off to either side. She and her father went down the hallway to the testing room. An old, beat-up, army-green query box sat on a table outside the door.

"Ratherford, Elizabeth Ratherford," said her father to the box. "Age seven, computer-friendly, smart as a whip."

"We'll see," said the box with a chuckle. It had a gruff, teasing, grandfatherly voice. "We'll just see about *that*, young lady." What a jolly interface, thought Elizabeth. She watched as the classroom door swung open. "You go right along in there, and we'll see just how smart you are." It chuckled again, then it spoke to Elizabeth's dad. "You come back for her at three, sir. She'll be all ready and waiting for you, bright as a little watermelon."

This was going to be fun, thought Elizabeth. Nothing to do all day except show how smart she was.

Her father knelt in front of her and smoothed her hair back from her face. "You try real hard on these tests, punkin. You show them just how talented and clever you really are, okay?" Elizabeth nodded. "And you be on your best behavior." He gave her a hug and a pat on the rear.

Inside the testing room were dozens of other seven-year-olds, sitting in rows of tiny chairs with access boxes in front of them. Glancing around the room, Elizabeth realized that she had never seen so many children together all at once. There were only ten in her weekly socialization class. It was sort of overwhelming.

The monitors called everyone to attention and told them to put on their headsets and ask their boxes for Section One.

Elizabeth followed directions, and she found that all the interfaces were strange—they were friendly enough, but none of them were the programs she worked with at home. The first part of the test was the multiple-choice exam. The problems, at least, were familiar to Elizabeth—she'd practiced for this test all her life, it seemed. There were word games, number games, and games in which she had to rotate little boxes in her head. She knew enough to skip the hardest until she'd worked her way through the whole test. There were only a couple of problems left to do when the system told her to stop and the box went all gray.

The monitors led the whole room full of kids in jumping-jack exercises for five minutes. Then everyone sat down again and a new test came up in the box. This one seemed very easy, but it wasn't one she'd ever done before. It consisted of a series of very detailed pictures; she was supposed to make up a story about each picture. Well, she could do that. The first picture showed a child and a lot of different kinds of animals. "Once upon a time there was a little girl who lived all alone in the forest with her friends the skunk, the wolf, the bear, and the lion. . . ." A beep sounded every so often to tell her to end one story and begin another. Elizabeth really enjoyed telling the stories, and was sorry when that part of the test was over.

But the next exercise was almost as interesting. She was to read a series of short stories and answer questions about them. Not the usual questions about what happened in the story—these were harder. "Is it fair to punish a starving cat for stealing?" "Should people do good deeds for strangers?" "Why is it important for everyone to learn to obey?"

When this part was over, the monitors took the class down the hall to the big cafeteria, where there were lots of other seven-year-olds, who had been taking tests in other rooms.

Elizabeth was amazed at the number and variety of children in the cafeteria. She watched them as she stood in line for her milk and sandwich. Hundreds of kids, all exactly as old as she was. Tall and skinny, little and fat; curly hair, straight hair, and hair that was frizzy or held up with ribbons or cut into strange patterns against the scalp; skin that was light brown like Elizabeth's, chocolate brown, almost black, pale pink, freckled, and all the colors in between. Some of the kids were all dressed up in fancy clothes; others were wearing patched pants and old shirts.

When she got her snack, Elizabeth's first thought was to find someone who looked like herself, and sit next to her. But then a freckled boy with dark, nappy hair smiled at her in a very friendly way. He looked at her feet and nodded. "Nice shoes," he said. She sat down on the empty seat next to him, suddenly aware of her red Mary Janes with the embroidered flowers. She was pleased that they had been noticed, and a little embarrassed.

"Let me see *your* shoes," she said, unwrapping her sandwich.

He stuck his feet out. He was wearing pink plastic sneakers with hologram pictures of a missile gantry on the toes. When he moved his feet, they launched a defensive counterattack.

"Oh, neat." Elizabeth nodded appreciatively and took a bite of the sandwich. It was filled with something yellow that tasted okay.

A little tiny girl with long, straight, black hair was sitting on the other side of the table from them. She put one foot up on the table. "I got shoes, too," she said. "Look." Her shoes were black patent, with straps. Elizabeth and the freckled boy both admired them politely. Elizabeth thought that the little girl was very daring to put her shoe right up on the table. It was certainly an interesting way to enter a conversation.

"My name is Sheena and I can spit," said the little girl. "Watch." Sure enough, she could spit really well. The spit hit the beige wall several meters away, just under the mirror, and slid slowly down.

"I can spit, too," said the freckled boy. He demonstrated, hitting the wall a little lower than Sheena had.

"I can *learn* to spit," said Elizabeth.

"All right there, no spitting!" said a monitor firmly. "Now, you take a napkin and clean that up." It pointed to Elizabeth.

"She didn't do it, I did," said Sheena. "I'll clean it up."

"I'll help," said Elizabeth. She didn't want to claim credit for Sheena's spitting ability, but she liked being mistaken for a really good spitter.

The monitor watched as they wiped the wall, then took their thumbprints. "You three settle down now. I don't want any more spitting." It moved away. All three of them were quiet for a few minutes, and munched on their sandwiches.

"What's your name?" said Sheena suddenly. "My name is Sheena."

"Elizabeth."

"Lizardbreath. That's a funny name," said Sheena.

"My name is Oginga," said the freckled boy.

"That's *really* a funny name," said Sheena.

"You think everybody's name is funny," said Oginga. "Sheena-Teena-Peena."

"I can tap dance, too," said Sheena, who had recognized that it was time to change the subject. "These are my tap shoes." She squirmed around to wave her feet in the air briefly, then swung them back under the table.

She moves more than anyone I've ever seen, thought Elizabeth.

"Wanna see me shuffle off to Buffalo?" asked Sheena.

A bell rang at the front of the room, and the three of them looked up. A monitor was speaking.

"Quiet! Everybody quiet, now! Finish up your lunch quickly, those of you who are still eating, and put your wrappers in the wastebaskets against the wall. Then line up on the west side of thc room. Thc *west* sidc . . ."

The children were taken to the restroom after lunch. It was grander than any bathroom Elizabeth had ever seen, with walls made of polished red granite, lots of little stalls with toilets in them, and a whole row of sinks. The sinks were lower than the sink at home, and so were the toilets. Even the mirrors were just the right height for kids.

It was funny because there were no stoppers in the sinks, so you couldn't wash your hands in a proper sink of water. Sheena said she could make the sink fill up, and Oginga dared her to do it, so she took off her sweater and put it in the sink, and sure enough, it filled up with water and started to overflow, and then she couldn't get the sweater out of it, so she called a monitor over. "This sink is overflowing," she said, as if it were all the sink's fault. A group of children stood around and watched while the monitor fished the sweater from the drain and wrung it out.

"That's mine!" said Sheena, as if she had dropped it by mistake. She grabbed it away from the monitor, shook it, and nodded knowingly to Elizabeth. "It dries real fast." The monitor wanted thumbprints from Sheena and Elizabeth and everyone who watched.

The monitors then took the children to the auditorium, and led the whole group in singing songs and playing games, which Elizabeth found only moderately interesting. She would have preferred to learn to spit. At one o'clock, a monitor announced it was time to go back to the classrooms, and all the children should line up by the door.

Elizabeth and Sheena and Oginga pushed into the same line together. There were so many kids that there was a long wait while they all lined up and the monitors moved up and down the lines to make them straight.

"Are you going to go to the Asia Center?" asked Sheena. "My mom says I can probably go to the Asia Center tomorrow, because I'm so fidgety."

Elizabeth didn't know what the Asia Center was, but she didn't want to look stupid. "I don't know. I'll have to ask my dad." She turned to Oginga, who was behind her. "Are you going to the Asia Center?"

"What's the Asia Center?" asked Oginga.

Elizabeth looked back at Sheena, waiting to hear her answer.

"Where we go to sleep," Sheena said. "My mom says it doesn't hurt."

"I got my own room," said Oginga.

"It's not like your room," Sheena explained. "You go there, and you go to sleep, and your parents get to try again."

"What do they try?" asked Elizabeth. "Why do you have to go to sleep?"

"You go to sleep so they have some peace and quiet," said Sheena. "So you're not in their way."

"But what do they try?" repeated Elizabeth.

"I bet they try more of that stuff that they do when they think you're asleep," said Oginga. Sheena snorted and started to giggle, and then Oginga started to giggle and he snorted too, and the more one giggled and snorted, the more the other did. Pretty soon Elizabeth was giggling too, and the three of them were helplessly choking, behind great hiccoughing gulps of noise.

The monitor rolled by then and told them to be quiet and move on to their assigned classrooms. That broke the spell of their giggling, and, subdued, they moved ahead in the line. All the children filed quietly out of the auditorium and walked slowly down the halls. When Elizabeth came to her classroom, she shrugged her shoulders at Oginga and Sheena and jerked her head to one side. "I go in here," she whispered.

"See ya at the Asia Center," said Sheena.

The rest of the tests went by quickly, though Elizabeth didn't think they were as much fun as in the morning. The afternoon tests were more physical; she pulled at joysticks and tried to push buttons quickly on command. They tested her hearing and even made her sing to the computer. Elizabeth didn't like to do things fast, and she didn't like to sing.

When it was over, the monitors told the children they could go now, their parents were waiting for them at the front of the school. Elizabeth looked for Oginga and Sheena as she left, but children from the other classrooms were not in the halls. Her dad was waiting for her out front, as he had said he would be.

Elizabeth called to him to get his attention. He had just come off work, and she knew he would be sort of confused. They wiped their secrets out of his brain before he logged off the system, and sometimes they took a little other stuff with it by mistake, so he might not be too sure about his name, or where he lived.

On the way home, she told him about her new friends. "They don't sound as though they would do very well at their lessons, princess," said her father. "But it does sound as if you had an interesting time at lunch." Elizabeth pulled his hand to guide him onto the right street. He'd be okay in an hour or so—anything important usually came back pretty fast.

When they got home, her dad went into the kitchen to start dinner, and Elizabeth played with her dog, Brownie. Brownie didn't live with them anymore, because his brain was being used to help control data traffic in the network. Between rush hours, Elizabeth would call him up on the system and run simulations in which she plotted the trajectory of a ball and he plotted an interception of it.

They ate dinner when her mom logged off work. Elizabeth's parents believed it was very important for the family to all eat together in the evening, and her mom had custom-made connectors that stretched all the way into the dining room. Even though she didn't really eat anymore, her local I/O was always extended to the table at dinnertime.

After dinner, Elizabeth got ready for bed. She could hear her father in his office, asking his mail for the results of her test that day. When he came into her room to tuck her in, she could tell he had good news for her.

"Did you wash behind your ears, punkin?" he asked. Elizabeth figured that this was a ritual question, since she was unaware that washing behind her ears was more useful than washing anywhere else.

She gave the correct response: "Yes, Daddy." She understood that, whether she washed or not, giving the expected answer was an important part of the ritual. Now it was her turn to ask a question. "Did you get the results of my tests, Daddy?"

"We sure did, princess," her father replied. "You did very well on them."

Elizabeth was pleased, but not too surprised. "What about my new friends, Daddy? How did they do?"

"I don't know about that, punkin. They don't send us everybody's scores, just yours."

"I want to be with them when I go to the Asia Center."

Elizabeth could tell by the look on her father's face that she'd said something wrong. "The what? Where did you hear about that?" he asked sharply.

"My friend Sheena told me about it. She said she was going to the Asia Center tomorrow," said Elizabeth.

"Well, *she* might be going there, but that's not anyplace *you're* going." Her dad sounded very strict. "You're going to continue your studies, young lady, and someday you'll be an important executive like your mother. That's clear from your test results. I don't want to hear any talk about you doing anything else. Or about this Sheena."

"What does Mommy do, Daddy?"

"She's a processing center, sweetheart, that talks directly to the CPU. She uses her brain to control important information and tell the rest of the computer what to do. And she gives the whole system common sense." He sat down on the edge of the bed, and Elizabeth could tell that she was going to get what her dad called an "explanatory chat."

"You did so well on your test that maybe it's time we told you something about what you might be doing when you get a little older." He pulled the blanket up a little bit closer to her chin and turned the sheet down evenly over it.

"It'll be a lot like studying, or like taking that test today," he continued. "Except you'll be hardwired into the network, just like your mom, so you won't have to get up and move around. You'll be able to do anything and go anywhere in your head."

"Will I be able to play with Brownie?"

"Of course, sweetheart, you'll be able to call him up just like you did tonight. It's important that you play. It keeps you healthy and alert, and it's good for Brownie, too."

"Will I be able to call you and Mommy?"

"Well, princess, that depends on what kind of job you're doing. You just might be so busy and important that you don't have time to call us."

Like Bobby, she thought. Her parents didn't talk much about her brother Bobby. He had done well on his tests, too. Now he was a milintel cyborg with go-nogo authority. He never called home, and her parents didn't call him, either.

"Being an executive is sort of like playing games all the time," her father added, when Elizabeth didn't say anything. "And the harder you work right now, the better you do on your tests, the more fun you'll have later."

He tucked the covers up around her neck again. "Now you go to sleep, so you can work your best tomorrow, okay, princess?" Elizabeth nodded. Her dad kissed her goodnight and poked at the covers again. He got up. "Goodnight, sweetheart," he said, and he left the room.

Elizabeth lay in bed for a while, trying to get to sleep. The door was open so that the light would come in from the hall, and she could hear her parents talking downstairs.

Her dad, she knew, would be reading the news at his access box, as he did every evening. Her mom would be tidying up noise-damaged data in the household module. She didn't have to do that, but she said it calmed her nerves.

Listening to the rise and fall of their voices, she heard her name. What were they saying? Was it about the test? She got up out of bed, crept to the door of her room. They stopped talking. Could they hear her? She was very quiet. Standing in the doorway, she was only a meter from the railing at the top of the staircase, and the sounds came up very clearly from the living room below.

"Just the house settling," said her father, after a moment. "She's asleep by now." Ice cubes clinked in a glass.

"Well," said her mother, resuming the conversation, "I don't know what they think they're doing, putting euthanasable children in the testing center with children like Elizabeth." There was a bit of a whine behind her mother's voice. Perhaps rf interference. "Just talking with that Sheena could skew her test results for years. I have half a mind to call the net executive and ask it what it thinks it's doing."

"Now, calm down, honey," said her dad. Elizabeth heard his chair squeak as he turned away from his access box toward the console that housed her mother. "You don't want the exec to think we're questioning its judgment. Maybe this was part of the test."

"Well, you'd think they'd let us know, so we could prepare her for it."

Was Sheena part of the test, wondered Elizabeth. She'd have to ask the system what "euthanasable" meant.

"Look at her scores," said her father. "She did much better than the first two on verbal skills—her programs are on the right track there. And her physical aptitude scores are even lower than Bobby's."

"That's a blessing," said her mother. "It held Christopher back, right from the beginning, being so active." Who's Christopher? wondered Elizabeth.

Her mother continued. "But it was a mistake, putting him in with the euthana—"

"Her socialization scores were okay, but right on the edge," added her dad, talking right over her mother. "Maybe they should reduce her class time to twice a month. Look at how she sat right down with those children at lunch."

"Anyway, she passed," said her mother. "They're moving her up a level instead of taking her now."

"Maybe because she didn't initiate the contact, but she was able to handle it when it occurred. Maybe that's what they want for the execs."

Elizabeth shifted her weight, and the floor squeaked again.

Her father called up to her, "Elizabeth, are you up?"

"Just getting a drink of water, Daddy." She walked to the bathroom and drew a glass of water from the tap. She drank a little and poured the rest down the drain.

Then she went back to her room and climbed into bed. Her parents were talking more quietly now, and she could hear only little bits of what they were saying.

". . . mistake about Christopher . . ." Her mother's voice.

". . . that other little girl to sleep forever? . . ." Her dad.

". . . worth it? . . ." Her mother again.

Their voices slowed down and fell away, and Elizabeth dreamed of eerie white things in glass jars, of Brownie, still a dog, all furry and fetching a ball, and of Sheena, wearing a sparkly costume and tap-dancing very fast. She fanned her hands out to her sides and turned around in a circle, tapping faster and faster.

Then Sheena began to run down like a windup toy. She went limp and dropped to the floor. Brownie sniffed at her and the white things in the jars watched. Elizabeth was afraid, but she didn't know why. She grabbed Sheena's shoulders and tried to rouse her.

"Don't let me fall asleep," Sheena murmured, but she dozed off even as Elizabeth shook her.

"Wake up! Wake up!" Elizabeth's own words pulled her out of her dream. She sat up in bed. The house was quiet, except for the sound of her father snoring in the other room.

Sheena needed her help, thought Elizabeth, but she wasn't really sure why. Very quietly, she slipped out of bed. On the other side of her room, her terminal was waiting for her, humming faintly.

When she put the headset on, she saw her familiar animal friends: a gorilla, a bird, and a pig. Each was a node that enabled her to communicate with other parts of the system. Elizabeth had given them names.

Facing Sam, the crow, she called her dog. Sam transmitted the signal, and was replaced by Brownie, who was barking. That meant his brain was routing information, and she couldn't get through.

What am I doing, anyway, Elizabeth asked herself. As she thought, a window irised open in the center of her vision, and there appeared the face of a boy of about eleven or twelve. "Hey, Elizabeth, what are you doing up at this hour?" It was the sysop on duty in her sector.

"My dog was crying."

The sysop laughed. "Your dog was crying? That's the first time I've ever heard anybody say something like that." He shook his head at her.

"He was *so* crying. Even if he wasn't crying out loud, I heard him, and I came over to see what was the matter. Now he's busy and I can't get through."

The sysop stopped laughing. "Sorry. I didn't mean to make fun of you. I had a dog once, before I came here, and they took him for the system, too."

"Do you call him up?"

"Well, not anymore. I don't have time. I used to, though. He was a golden lab. . . ." Then the boy shook his head sternly and said, "But you should be in bed."

"Can't I stay until Brownie is free again? Just a few more minutes?"

"Well, maybe a couple minutes more. But then you gotta go to bed for sure. I'll be back to check. Goodnight, Elizabeth."

"Goodnight," she said, but the window had already closed.

Wow, thought Elizabeth. That worked. She had never told a really complicated lie before, and was surprised that it had gone over so well. It seemed to be mostly a matter of convincing yourself that what you said was true.

But right now, she had an important problem to solve, and she wasn't even exactly sure what it was. If she could get into the files for Sheena and Oginga, maybe she could find out what was going on. Then maybe she could change the results on their tests or move them to her socialization group or something. . . .

If she could just get through to Brownie, she knew he could help her. After a few minutes, the flood of data washed away, and the dog stopped barking. "Here, Brownie!" she called. He wagged his tail and looked happy to see her.

She told Brownie her problem, and he seemed to understand her. "Can you get it, Brownie?"

He gave a little bark, like he did when she plotted curves.

"Okay, go get it."

Brownie ran away real fast, braked to a halt, and seemed to be digging. This wasn't what he was really doing, of course, it was just the way Elizabeth's interface interpreted Brownie's brain waves. In just a few seconds, Brownie came trotting back with the records from yesterday's tests in his mouth.

But when Elizabeth examined them, her heart sank. There were four Sheenas and fifteen Ogingas. But then she looked more carefully and noticed that most of the identifying information didn't fit her Sheena and Oginga. There was only one of each that was the right height, with the right color hair.

When she read the information, she felt bad again. Oginga had done all right on the test, but they wanted to use him for routine processing right away, kind of like Brownie. Sheena, as Elizabeth's mother had suggested, had failed the personality profile and was scheduled for the euthanasia center the next afternoon at two o'clock. There was that word again: euthanasia. Elizabeth didn't like the sound of it.

"Here, Brownie." Her dog looked up at her with a glint in his eye. "Now listen to me. We're going to play with this stuff just a little, and then I want you to take it and put it back where you got it. Okay, Brownie?"

The window irised open again and the sysop reappeared. "Elizabeth, what do you think you're doing?" he said. "You're not supposed to have access to this data."

Elizabeth thought for a minute. Then she figured she was caught red-handed, so she might as well ask for his advice. So she explained her problem, all about her new friends and how Oginga was going to be put in the system like Brownie, and Sheena was going to be taken away somewhere.

"They said she would go to the euthanasia center, and I'm not real sure what that is," said Elizabeth. "But I don't think it's good."

"Let me look it up," said the sysop. He paused for a second, then he looked worried. "They want my ID before they'll tell me what it means. I don't want to get in trouble. Forget it."

"Well, what can I do to help my friends?" she asked.

"Gee," said the sysop. "It's a tough one. The way you were doing it, they'd catch you for sure, just like I did. It looks like a little kid got at it."

I *am* a little kid, thought Elizabeth, but she didn't say anything.

I need help, she thought. But who could she go to? She turned to the sysop. "I want to talk to my brother Bobby, in milintel. Can you put me through to him?"

"I don't know," said the sysop, "but I'll ask the mailer demon." He irised shut for a second, then opened again. "The mailer demon says it's no skin off his nose, but he doesn't think you ought to."

"How come?" asked Elizabeth.

"He says it's not your brother anymore. He says you'll be sorry."

"I want to talk to him anyway," said Elizabeth.

The sysop nodded, and his window winked shut just as another irised open. An older boy who looked kind of like Elizabeth herself stared out. His tongue darted rapidly out between his lips, keeping them slightly wet. His pale eyes, unblinking, stared into hers.

"Begin," said the boy. "You have sixty seconds."

"Bobby?" said Elizabeth.

"True. Begin," said the boy.

"Bobby, um, I'm your sister Elizabeth."

The boy just looked at her, the tip of his tongue moving rapidly. She wanted to hide from him, but she couldn't pull her eyes from his. She didn't want to tell him her story, but she could feel words filling her throat. She moved new words forward, before the others could burst out.

"Log off!" she yelled. "Log off!"

She was in her bedroom, drenched in sweat, the sound of her own voice ringing in her ears. Had she actually yelled? The house was quiet, her father still snoring. She probably hadn't made any noise.

She was very scared, but she knew she had to go back in there. She hoped that her brother was gone. She waited a couple of minutes, then logged on.

Whew. Just her animals. She called the sysop, who irised on, looking nervous.

"If you want to do that again, Elizabeth, don't go through me, huh?" He shuddered.

"I'm sorry," she said. "But I can't do this by myself. Do you know anybody that can help?"

"Maybe we ought to ask Norton," said the sysop after a minute.

"Who's Norton?"

"He's this old utility I found that nobody uses much anymore," said the sysop. "He's kind of grotty, but he helps me out." He took a breath. "Hey, Norton!" he yelled, real loud. Of course, it wasn't really yelling, but that's what it seemed like to Elizabeth.

Instantly, another window irised open, and a skinny middle-aged man leaned out of the window so far that Elizabeth thought he was going to fall out, and yelled back, just as loud, "Don't bust your bellows. I can hear you."

He was wearing a striped vest over a dirty undershirt and had a squashed old porkpie hat on his head. This wasn't anyone that Elizabeth had ever seen in the system before.

The man looked at Elizabeth and jerked his head in her direction. "Who's the dwarf?"

The sysop introduced Elizabeth and explained her problem to Norton. Norton didn't look impressed. "What d'ya want me to do about it, kid?"

"Come on, Norton," said the sysop. "You can figure it out. Give us a hand."

"Jeez, kid, it's practically four o'clock in the morning. I gotta get my beauty rest, y'know. Plus, now you've got milintel involved, it's a real mess. They'll be back, sure as houses."

The sysop just looked at him. Elizabeth looked at Norton, too. She tried to look patient and helpless, because that always helped with her dad, but she really didn't know if that would work on this weird old program.

"Y'know, there ain't much that you or me can do in the system that they won't find out about, kids," said Norton.

"Isn't there somebody who can help?" asked Elizabeth.

"Well, there's the Chickenheart. There's not much that it can't do, when it wants to. We could go see the Chickenheart."

"Who's the Chickenheart?" asked Elizabeth.

"The Chickenheart's where the system began." Of course Elizabeth knew *that* story—about the networks of nerve fibers organically woven into great convoluted mats, a mammoth supercortex that had stored the original programs, before processing was distributed to satellite brains. Her own system told her the tale sometimes before her nap.

"You mean the original core is still there?" said the sysop, surprised. "You never told me that, Norton."

"Lot of things I ain't told you, kid." Norton scratched his chest under his shirt. "Listen. If we go see the Chickenheart, and *if* it wants to help, it can figure out what to do for your friends. But you gotta know that this is a big fucking deal. The Chickenheart's a busy guy, and this ain't one-hunnert-percent safe."

"Are you sure you want to do it, Elizabeth?" asked the sysop. "I wouldn't."

"How come it's not safe?" asked Elizabeth. "Is he mean?"

"Nah," said Norton. "A little strange, maybe, not mean. But di'n't I tell you the Chickenheart's been around for a while? You know what that means? It means you got yer intermittents, you got yer problems with feedback, runaway processes, what have you. It means the Chickenheart's got a lot of frayed connections, if you get what I mean. Sometimes the old CH just goes chaotic on you." Norton smiled, showing yellow teeth. "Plus you got the chance there's someone listening in. The netexec, for instance. Now there's someone I wouldn't want to catch me up to no mischief. Nossir. Not if I was you."

"Why not?" asked Elizabeth.

"Because that's sure curtains for you, kid. The netexec don't ask no questions, he don't check to see if you maybe could be repaired. You go bye-bye and you don't come back."

Like Sheena, thought Elizabeth. "Does he listen in often?" she asked.

"Never has," said Norton. "Not yet. Don't even know the Chickenheart's there, far as I can tell. Always a first time, though."

"I want to talk to the Chickenheart," said Elizabeth, although she wasn't sure she wanted anything of the kind, after her last experience.

"You got it," said Norton. "This'll just take a second."

Suddenly all the friendly animals disappeared, and Elizabeth felt herself falling very hard and fast along a slippery blue line in the dark. The line glowed neon blue at first, then changed to fuchsia, then sulfur yellow. She knew that Norton was falling with her, but she couldn't see him. Against the dark background, his shadow moved with hers, black, and opalescent as an oil slick.

They arrived somewhere moist and warm. The Chickenheart pulsated next to them, nutrients swishing through its external tubing. It was huge, and wetly organic. Elizabeth felt slightly sick.

"Oh, turn it off, for Chrissake," said Norton, with exasperation. "It's just me and a kid."

The monstrous creature vanished, and a cartoon rabbit with impossibly tall ears and big dewy brown eyes appeared in its place. It looked at Norton, raised an eyebrow, cocked an ear in his direction, and took a huge, noisy bite out of the carrot it was holding.

"Gimme a break," said Norton.

The bunny was replaced by a tall, overweight man in his sixties wearing a rumpled white linen suit. He held a small, paddle-shaped fan, which he slowly moved back and forth. "Ah, Mr. Norton," he said. "Hot enough for you, sir?"

"We got us a problem here, Chick," said Norton. He looked over at Elizabeth and nodded. "You tell him about it, kid."

First she told him about her brother. "Nontrivial, young lady," said the Chickenheart. "Nontrivial, but easy enough to fix. Let me take care of it right now." He went rigid and quiet for a few seconds, as though frozen in time. Then he was back. "Now, then, young lady," he said. "We'll talk if you like."

So Elizabeth told the Chickenheart about Sheena and Oginga, about the testing center and the wet sweater and the monitor telling her to clean up the spit. Even though she didn't have to say a word, she told him everything, and she was sure that if he wanted to come up with a solution, he could do it.

The Chickenheart seemed surprised to hear about the euthanasia center, and especially surprised that Sheena was going to be sent there. He addressed Norton. "I know I've been out of touch, but I find this hard to believe. Mr. Norton, have you any conception of how difficult it can be to obtain components like this? Let me investigate the situation." His face went quiet for a second, then came back. "By gad, sir, it's true," he said to Norton. "They say they're optimizing for predictability. It's a mistake, sir, let me tell you. Things are too predictable here already. Same old ideas churning around and around. A few more components like that Sheena, things might get interesting again.

"I want to look at their records." He paused for a moment, then continued talking.

"Ah, yes, yes, I want that Sheena right away, sir," he said to Norton. "An amazing character. Oginga, too—not as gonzo as the girl, but he has a brand of aggressive curiosity we can put to use, sir. And there are forty-six others with similar personality profiles scheduled for euthanasia today at two." His face went quiet again.

"What is he doing?" Elizabeth asked Norton.

"Old Chickenheart's got his hooks into everythin'," Norton replied. "He just reaches along those pathways, faster'n you can think, and does what he wants. The altered data will look like it's been there all along, and ain't nobody can prove anythin' different."

"Done and done, Mr. Norton." The Chickenheart was back.

"Thank you, Mr. Chickenheart," said Elizabeth, remembering her manners. "What's going to happen to Sheena and Oginga now?"

"Well, young lady, we're going to bring your friends right into the system, sort of like the sysop, but without, shall we say, official recognition. We'll have Mr. Norton here keep an eye on them. They'll be our little surprises, eh? Time bombs that we've planted. They can explore the system, learn what's what, what they can get away with and what they can't. Rather like I do."

"What will they do?" asked Elizabeth.

"That's a good question, my dear," said the Chickenheart. "They'll have to figure it out for themselves. Maybe they'll put together a few new solutions to some old problems, or create a few new problems to keep us on our toes. One way or the other, I'm sure they'll liven up the old homestead."

"But what about me?" asked Elizabeth.

"Well, Miss Elizabeth, what about you? Doesn't look to me as though you have any cause to worry. You passed your tests yesterday with flying colors. You can just go right on being a little girl, and some day you'll have a nice, safe job as an executive. Maybe you'll even become netexec, who knows? I wiped just a tiny bit of your brother's brain and removed all records of your call. I'll wipe your memory of this, and you'll do just fine, yes indeed."

"But my friends are in here," said Elizabeth, and she started to feel sorry for herself. "My dog, too."

"Well, then, what do you want me to do?"

"Can't you fix *my* tests?"

The Chickenheart looked at Elizabeth with surprise.

"What's this, my dear? Do you think you're a time bomb, too?"

"I can *learn* to be a time bomb," said Elizabeth with conviction. And she knew she could, whatever a time bomb was.

"I don't know," said the Chickenheart, "that anyone can learn that sort of thing. You've either got it or you don't, Miss Elizabeth."

"Call me Lizardbreath. That's my *real* name. And I can get what I want. I got away from my brother, didn't I? And I got here."

The Chickenheart raised his thin, black eyebrows. "You have a point there, my dear. Perhaps you *could* be a time bomb, after all."

"But not today," said Lizardbreath. "Today I'm gonna learn to spit."

NISI SHAWL

I WAS A TEENAGE GENETIC ENGINEER

(1989)

MY HAIR IS NOT MY OWN. My blood is not my own. My life is not my own. I am not free. I am a political prisoner on a North American game preserve.

My hair is long, fine, brittle, tangled. I comb it with despair and rainwater.

I am waiting and I am not waiting. I am resting and I am restless. Everything that I am, I am not.

I am encircled by low, stinging briars. In my youth I frolicked among them; now I merely sit.

But no, quite often I do not merely sit. I amble along the confines. Either the boundaries are patrolled or they are not. It doesn't matter at all, since I never attempt to cross them, to venture my life.

The way it is is the way it's supposed to be. I am to sit here, lorn, and when I cry rain falls, and when my tears dry and I sigh the wind speaks, and when I smile my clouds silver; the haze becomes intolerably bright, eye-scalding.

But the sun will not yet come through.

I make music. I make baskets, little ones. I make friends with the birds and rodents and insects. And I am alone, alone.

Alone. The reason that I am alone now is that I will not always be alone. Someone comes.

Someone comes; I taste his sweet steps. I am afraid. He will break the steady surface of my mirror. But he is coming. And he is coming through, and in.

From his birth, he has been coming. I saw his crowning in a magic candleflame, a candle I made to burn only once a year, for only so long. Whenever I look into that flame, I can clearly see the moves he makes in those moments. And he is approaching, swifter than years.

I am a sickle, a crow, a magpie inhabiting a land of ghosts. I scarred myself, pearl-petalled, on my brow. Yes, I marked my sorrow and strength on my face, scorning a place in the ninety-ninth percentile, those who are unmarred and perfect from conception.

How could I not? How could I turn my back on the carelessly deformed, the purposely stunted, the play-people we were taught to raise as pets?

The will of the state automatically engenders a counter-will. The hand of the state severs itself from the arm. I was programmed to be a designer, a patterner of degraded human life-forms.

Cruel memory. I enjoyed my vocation. I studied. I theorized. I practiced. Slowly (the process is artificially lengthened among us), I rounded. I filled out emotionally and physically, and neared the much-touted perihelion of my life's orbit: adulthood. As was traditional, I began a lengthy work which was to guarantee my place in the social exoskeleton.

In later years, my work had taken a startling turn. I was no longer content to functionally integrate the traits of lower species into my subjects. Although I still spent many hours here, in my private wild domain, I did not produce more hare men and partridge women. These had become overfamiliar. And yet, I could not bring myself to switch from the artistic mode to the utilitarian; to place my skills directly in the hands of the government. Rather than explore my distaste and come to the inevitable conclusion that all forms of genetic manipulation were exploitive, I had ranged even further in my chosen field. I had hopes that less hackneyed creations would attract financial support and laudation.

My inspirations came from old chimerical tales. Fishwomen, sealmen, winged hermaphrodites—these were common. But I invented the scaled fire-breather, the one-horned woman, the invisible man. Then I outdid myself.

I began to make gods. Cupid was first. How he tormented me until I let him go. Vulcan fell in love with me at first sight. He set up shop in the basement and refused to leave. He besought me with gifts: magic rings and wondrous, pocket-sized ships with infinite holds. I created Minerva for counsel. She advised me not to stop until I had recalled the entire pantheon, or I would be wreaking havoc due to karmic imbalances. I could not disagree with wisdom herself, so in short order they were all released upon the world—the quarrelling, autocratic, Olympian deities.

Psyche was different. Perhaps it was because I spent more time on her; I intended her to be the chief representation of my competence. The others were superhuman, were oversized projections of portions of the collective mind. But Psyche seemed to be distilled humanity, the essence.

My work on her was very subtle, and not even I fully realized the implications until she opened her incredible eyes. Her incredible blazing eyes that lit everything with too-bright truth showed me to myself as the monster that I was. I begged her for a wound to make me cry, a drop of burning oil on my face.

She refused with horror, so I snatched her knife and carved a star on my brow.

Then she laughed, and blessed me, and understood. Her shining hands healed me and set my scar glowing. She walked out, bare humble feet changing the world with every step.

I was left with the remains of my disgusting work and the clamorous activity of the gods. But before my colleagues came and found me thus, and enforced my solitude with machinations of that treacherous smith, I had time for one last toil. I made only the seed and caused it to arise in a suitable womb. I sowed the Red Doom, the Hound of the Smith, Cuchullain.

And he comes.

LEWIS SHINER

THE GENE DRAIN

(1989)

JSN REACHED UP TO THE ROW of glowing buttons across his forehead and changed his mind with an audible click.

Nothing helped. He couldn't shake the sense of disaster hovering over him like an avalanche in progress. In a last, desperate attempt to salvage his mood he worked up an autonomous search program and sent it spiraling back through his core memory.

Up on the dais the alien who identified himself as Brother Simon droned on: ". . . and, uh, we, that is, bein as how we are all brothers in Johnny, I mean, we ud, uh, really like to find us a place in yall's hearts, praise Johnny, and maybe even someplace where we could stay for a while . . ."

Somebody behind JSN said, "This is pathetic." The assembled UN delegates, representing the 2,873,261 free and independent nations of Earth, began to boo. Some stood up and shouted. Others clawed loose bits of wiring from appendages and hurled them at the dais.

Brother Simon stopped talking and the seven aliens sat quietly and took the abuse. They were nominally humanoid, but hideously pale, fleshy, thick-bodied, and slow. One or another of them constantly picked at its face or scratched the crotch of its shapeless gray clothing or spat a fat yellow glob onto the floor.

It had been a mistake to bring them to New York, JSN now realized. He'd promised the delegates alien emissaries and delivered these travesties of humanity that not only exuded unpleasant noises and odors, but committed the ultimate crime of being boring besides.

What else could he have done? He was a pop star, not a politician, and it had been plain bad luck that their crude shuttle had landed on his estate.

The aliens had been following, as far as JSN could make out, a primitive TV broadcast back to its source. It had come from a city called Killville or something—reflexively JSN pulled the data—Lynchburg, that was it. Back in the twentieth century it had been a center for some kind of religious propaganda, and apparently the aliens had learned their harsh and unpleasant English from what they'd intercepted. What had been Lynchburg was now no more than a few burned and abandoned hillsides on the edge of JSN's land.

From what they'd managed to stammer out, JSN understood they were the advance front for an entire orbiting mothership, full of hundreds more just like them: the misshapen, brain-damaged refuse of some galactic civilization. He'd hidden their shuttle in a disused barn, hoping the stench of the place would help cover that of the aliens. Then he tried to get hold of LNR, the Duchess of the local corporation. Unfortunately she was in for a new prosthesis and JSN had been forced to handle the situation himself.

Well, he'd handled it and he'd blown it. He'd just have to admit it and get the aliens offstage before the other delegates rioted. He stood up, fought his way to the front, then noticed a buzzing in his mastoid. His program was finished. Holding a finger up to the crowd, he punched in the results.

"Holy shit," he whispered as the data started to roll. He had forgotten about the microphones and cameras and naked eyes and ears that were all focused on him. "Holy shit," he said again. "They're us!"

• • •

The three of them met for a council of war at JSN's country house: JSN, LNR, and a man named DNS who was LNR's top advisor. JSN found DNS in the foyer, admiring a piece of taxidermy. "They were called cows," DNS said. "People used to eat them and wear their skins."

JSN glanced back at LNR. "I think JSN knows that," she said. "It is his cow."

"Maybe we'd be more comfortable in the study," JSN offered.

"A very rich protein source, beef," DNS said. He was short, heavy around the middle, and had more prosthetics than JSN had ever seen on one person before, all of them dented, discolored, and hopelessly out of date. "Gave people a lot of spunk."

"Not to mention arteriosclerosis and cancer," JSN said, waving his arm at the open door. DNS reluctantly went in.

"So," LNR said, settling at one end of an antique sofa. "We're going to have to do something. If anybody finds out where they are, they're liable to mob the place and tear them to pieces."

"I know," JSN said. "There's nothing people hate worse than bad video. Especially when it's live. I'm really sorry."

"Don't worry about it," LNR said graciously. "It's partly my fault, after all. If I hadn't been in surgery . . ." She held up a gleaming new hand. "Do you like it, by the way?"

"Very much," JSN said. He had seen her a couple of times before at state parties or concerts, but never had a chance to talk to her. Now he found himself quite infatuated. Her skull was sleek and hairless, her prosthetic arm and leg—on opposite sides, of course—were polished beryllium alloy, perfect complements to her skeletally thin naturals. Two bright neon'd veins ran up her neck for a splash of color. I'd sure like to network with that, he thought crudely.

"It still has a few bugs in the flexors," LNR said, "but on the whole . . ."

"Very nice," JSN said.

"Anyway. You say this mother ship was launched in the twentieth century, the computer malfunctioned and took them in a big circle and landed back here on Earth, thinking it was a new planet."

"It is a new planet as far as they're concerned," DNS interrupted. "I mean, can you imagine what we look like to them?"

"Shut up, DNS," LNR said. "Meanwhile, the crew just sort of backslid a few generations, evolutionally speaking, what with the small gene pool and all. Is that pretty much the gist of it?"

"I found records of the launching, and some distress signals. That seems to be what it all points to."

"So how come nobody remembered any of this?"

She patted the back of the sofa and JSN sat down next to her.

"No reason they should," JSN said. "I mean, did they look that human to you?"

"I don't think they look that bad," DNS said.

"Shut up, DNS," LNR said, and turned back to JSN. "I see what you mean."

"This was a couple hundred years ago, after all. Data like that isn't going to be in anybody's volatile memory. It's going to be banked. Unless somebody had a reason to think they weren't aliens, who would go looking for it?"

"But you thought of it," LNR said.

Was that admiration in her tone? JSN brushed casually at his forehead and punched up a little extra charm. "Oh no," he said, "it was just an accident. Really. In fact I was looking for, well, something to use against them."

"You mean," LNR said, "like a, a weapon?" The tip of her tongue just touched her silvered lips. "How twisted." She crossed her beryllium leg over her natural with a flash of light so intense that JSN momentarily blinked his mirrored contacts into place.

"We have to do something," he said. "If we knocked out that mother ship we wouldn't have to keep confronting the fact that we share the same genetics with those . . . animals."

"I know what you mean," LNR said, "but it's just bound to give somebody the wrong impression. Suppose we set them up their own country, maybe someplace like Antarctica?"

"I'm not sure even that would be isolated enough. On top of everything else they seem to have some sort of weird messianic religion, and you know you can't trust people like that. They'd be starting wars and pogroms and handing out literature door-to-door as soon as we turned our backs on them."

"Why are you so hostile?" DNS asked. He'd been walking around the library, touching things, and now he'd gone into a higher gear. Sweat had started to soak through his clothes and he kept rubbing his hands on his kilt, even though there was virtually no exposed skin left on them. "They're not so unpleasant. And I find their women somewhat . . . er . . . attractive. I've always said, we shouldn't be so quick to jettison our own history."

"You've always said that," LNR said tiredly.

"History?" JSN said. "Who cares about history? That's the wrong direction."

"This is living history," DNS said, pacing frenetically. "That's not just a gene pool up on that ship, it's a gene bank." He began to snatch bits of paper off the desk and tables, shred them compulsively with his fingers, and stuff them into his recycler. "Vigorous, healthy genes, not the feeble leftovers we've got. Those people are everything we're not: natural, in touch with themselves—"

"Brainless," JSN said, "malodorous—"

"Try to see it my way," DNS said, and JSN obligingly punched up a less hostile persona. "We've let technology take over completely from nature. Less than one percent of our population would be viable without some kind of hardware support."

He should know, JSN thought, nodding. The man was only intermittently flesh.

"And the technology that's holding it all together is shoddy!" DNS went on. "Over ninety percent of the manufactured goods in the world are defective! Ninety percent! And that's just the stuff that makes it through the QC checks at the factories!"

"Still," JSN said, as kindly as possible, "I don't think I'd care to have any of those devolved genetics in my hatchery."

"And that's another thing. Even our reproduction is dependent on technology. Do you know what the birthrate is? It's point-two of the mortality rate, and falling!"

"So what?" JSN shrugged amiably. "If we need more kids we can always decant them."

"No! We have to go back to the old ways before it's too late!"

"DNS," said LNR firmly, "shut up." To JSN she said, "You have to forgive him. He had an implant accident when he was a kid and blew out most of his frontal lobe. Hasn't trusted technology since. Those who need it the most like it the least, eh?"

"You think I'm crazy," DNS said, "but you'll see. If only we could get sex and procreation linked again—"

"You'd have a world," JSN said, reverting to his former aggressive self at the touch of a button, "that I wouldn't much want to live in. LNR, would you care to go watch some video and talk about this some more and maybe fuck?"

"Sounds heavy," she said, and JSN led her to the door.

"You'll be sorry," DNS warned, and JSN cheerfully shut him in the library.

• • •

The orgone generator refused to come up to speed and for a few helpless, frustrated moments JSN wondered if DNS had been right. Nothing seemed to work anymore. Then LNR found a way to patch around it and JSN became promptly and thoroughly distracted.

A little less than an hour later a shrill alarm interrupted them. "Shit," JSN said, yanking cables out of various orifices. "I knew I shouldn't have left him alone."

"Here." LNR unwrapped something from his left leg so he could hobble over to a monitor. "Is it DNS?"

"Yeah," JSN said. "He found the barn where I stashed the shuttle."

"And the weirdos too?"

"Yeah. That guy seems like a real jerk. What do you keep him around for?"

"Well, you don't want an advisor who's just going to agree with you all the time. He's definitely got his own ideas."

That seemed reasonable to JSN. "I'd better get out there. He's liable to bring the whole world down on us." He started putting on his shirt.

"I'll come too," LNR said. "After all, I brought him into this." She had her shoes on and was ready to go; her black outfit, JSN had discovered to his vast pleasure, was a mutant cell strain and a living part of her body.

JSN hurried into the rest of his clothes and led the way outside.

The night was clear and hot. Cyborg mowers had cut the fields that afternoon and the smell of battered grass filled the air. JSN stopped for a moment and scanned the star patterns.

"There," he said, pointing to a bright spot in Capricorn, near the eastern horizon. "The mother ship."

"It must be huge," LNR said, and JSN nodded. "And to think it's just crawling with devos. It's enough to give you a head crash."

JSN slipped quietly through the oversized barn door, noticing that the lingering odor of livestock had been routed by the more potent essence of the devos. In the dim parking lights of the shuttle he saw Brother Simon and all six of the others standing in a circle around the sweating DNS.

"DNS!" he shouted, being careful to breathe through his mouth. "What the fuck are you doing here?"

DNS flinched in obvious guilt, then recovered. "I'm a doctor," he said indignantly. "These people need proper medical attention. What do you think they are, zoo specimens?"

JSN turned to LNR, who had come in after him. "Is he a doctor?"

"I don't know," she said. "I think maybe he put a chip in for it once."

"If that's all you're doing," JSN said, "why did you think you had to sneak in?"

"I assumed you had something else on your mind."

"Look," JSN said to the devo nearest him, a heavyset female with huge, drooping breasts behind the front panel of her overalls. "You don't have to put up with this guy if you don't want to."

"Yall are wastin yore time talkin to the helpmeat," Brother Simon said. The female smiled at JSN in vacant agreement. "But dont worry none. We ud be proud to talk to yore doctor fella. Mebbe we ud get a chance to share the Good News with him."

"You mean you're leaving?" LNR asked.

"Pardon?"

"Isn't that the good news?"

"I meant the Good News about our Lord and Savior, Johnny Carson."

JSN accessed his core, noticing, from her slightly uprolled eyes, that LNR was doing the same. "I don't have anything on it," he said. "You?"

"I can't tell. I think I've got some bad sectors in my religion directory."

"Sorry," JSN said to Brother Simon. "We don't have the foggiest notion what you're talking about."

"Yall aint heard the Word?"

"Is that the same as the good news?" LNR asked.

"Because if it is, no, we haven't."

"If yall wanna step inside, I ud be proud to give my witness."

"Sure," LNR said. "Why not?"

The devo took them into the shuttle. The smell in the barn was bad enough, but inside the cramped corridors of the ship it was stale, fermented, overpowering. Someone had scrawled slogans like "Smile! Johnny Loves Yall!" and "I o Johnny" on the white plastic walls in what looked and smelled like human excrement.

"I don't know how much of this I can stand," JSN confided.

"Me either," LNR said, "but it's kind of like with DNS. I can't resist a crank. Just a couple of minutes, okay?"

Brother Simon typed the letters GOODNEWS onto the keyboard of the shuttle's main computer, using only one finger of each hand and making a lot of mistakes. He stared at the finished word for a while, then hit the RETURN key.

A meter-square screen lit up at the front of the room and a voice boomed, "There's Good News tonight!" The blank screen dissolved into a soundstage full of furniture. A dark-haired man stumbled onto the stage, tripped, and fell noisily across the furniture, smashing several of the chairs to pieces. The camera tightened on his face and the man said, "Live! From New York! It's . . . the Gospel According to Matthew!"

The scene changed to a murky river flowing through a desert. A bearded man stood in water past his knees, his back to the camera, addressing a mob of peasants wearing towels on their heads. "I baptize you with water for repentance, but he who is coming after me is mightier than I, whose sandals I am not worthy to lick! He will baptize you with Holy Sitcoms and with celebrities! And now . . . heeeeeeere's Johnny!"

A man with short white hair waded into view from behind the camera, then turned to wink. His skin was evenly, artificially tanned, and he had the arrogant smirk of a preadolescent. He wore a twentieth-century dress suit with lapels out to the shoulders and had something orange tied around his neck. Laughter swelled to fill the soundtrack.

"Hey there!" the man said. "Have we got a great show tonight!" The river came nearly to his waist and his suit was starting to sag with water, but he didn't seem to notice. "We've got the poor in spirit [applause] for theirs is the kingdom of heaven. We've got those who mourn [more applause], fresh from Las Vegas, and believe me, they shall be comforted. We've got the meek, and right here, on tonight's show, they're going to inherit the earth, and what do you think about that? [Thunderous applause.]"

"Wow," LNR said. "This is really twisted."

JSN had pumped the entire video into a core search. "Parts of it seem to be out of the Christian bible, but it's almost beyond recognition. Hey!" he shouted to Brother Simon, who stood enraptured in front of the screen, "are you guys Christians, is that it?"

"Christians?" LNR said with alarm. "You mean like Torquemada and Henry Lee Lucas and Jerry Falwell?"

"We are Carsonagins," Brother Simon said. "We believe every Image of the Sacred Word was divinely inspired, and we live by Its Law. Johnny be praised!"

"Wait a minute," LNR said, holding up one finger to indicate incoming data. "We were looking in the wrong place. This Carson was a twentieth-century video star. Something is really wrong here. What kind of computer is this?"

"It's a Generation V," JSN said, reading the name, plate. "Uh oh. You don't mean . . ."

"Heuristic self-programming. Artificial—" she choked, unable to hold back her laughter.

"Intelligence!" JSN hooted. "No wonder!"

"Are yall mockin the Word?" Brother Simon asked. His anger seemed to be teetering on the edge of tears.

"No, no, just this fucked-up hardware," JSN said. "It must have merged all those video broadcasts into one file . . ."

". . . and then tried to make sense of it! What a disaster!"

"Now see here," Brother Simon said. "If yall cant show proper respect all hafta axe yall to leave."

"Respect?" LNR howled. "Are you kidding?"

"That's it," Brother Simon said, flapping his hands at them. "Out. Yawn yone."

LNR stared blankly at JSN. "I think he means we're on our own," he said.

LNR took his arm. "Suits me. You think we could get all those cables back the way they were?"

"Let's find out," JSN said, then hesitated. "What about DNS? We shouldn't just leave him here with these devos . . ."

"Don't worry," LNR said. "He may be stupid, but he's harmless."

• • •

Later that night JSN looked up to see his barn disintegrating on an overhead monitor. "Holy shit," he said.

LNR leaned backward to look. "The devos?"

JSN nodded. "And I think DNS is on board. Or fried to a cinder, one."

"Oh well. Good riddance to the lot of them. Any more amps on this thing?"

JSN twisted the dial all the way to ten.

• • •

JSN was shooting a fashion layout in one of his disused pastures when the devos found him. The director had just finished draping him erotically in yards of raw fiberglass when she noticed that her lead camera had dropped offline. She called for the backup and found the power switch had jammed in the OFF position. "Okay," she said. "Let's take a break."

"What about me?" JSN asked. He could barely move.

"You," the director said, "look luscious. Just stay put."

At that point the shuttle dropped out of the sky with a paralyzing roar. The film crew scattered but JSN, barely able to hop, couldn't get away. Two of the male devos grabbed him and carried him into the reeking bowels of the ship.

"Very good," said a familiar voice as JSN was hustled through the control room. "Lock him in a cabin and I'll get to him later."

"DNS, you bastard!" JSN shouted. "What are you doing?"

"Don't be obsolete!" DNS shouted back. "We're all bastards these days, remember?"

They shut JSN in a tiny cabin with a video screen that filled all of one wall. After a few seconds it lit up and showed a large twenty-one. The number slowly dissolved into a scene of the white-haired man, Johnny Carson, dressed in a circus costume and performing a trick riding act. He had one foot on a donkey and the other on a small horse, and he grinned foolishly as the two animals cantered down a dusty path littered with palm fronds.

Crowds lined both sides of the road and the camera panned them, picking up bits of conversation. "Who is this?" "This is the prophet Johnny from the Tonight Show."

Johnny rode through the high, mud-brick gateway of the city and up to the doors of the temple. There he jumped down and staggered around for a few seconds in mock drunkenness, sending the crowd into hysterical laughter. Then he walked boldly inside.

Both sides of the huge hall were lined with tables, and on the tables were stacks of videos and stereos and home computers and various kinds of brightly colored boxes. Shiny new automobiles were parked in the aisles next to large enameled appliances.

Johnny walked past all the tables, all the way to the far end of the room, turned, and spread his arms wide. He looked up and down the temple until he had everyone's attention. "And now," he said, "a word from our sponsor."

JSN sat on the floor and switched all of his available systems over to standby.

• • •

DNS was talking to him. JSN punched back up to full alertness and said, "You asshole. What are you doing with these degenerates? You're selling me out to a bunch of devolved—"

"Whoa up there now," DNS said. "We don't believe in that heathen notion of evolution."

"We?"

DNS leaned forward earnestly. "I have accepted Johnny Carson in my heart as my personal savior."

"You're brain-damaged," JSN said.

"Maybe so, but Johnny loves me just the same."

"I expect he loves you better because of it."

"None of your sarcasm, now. You're about to get the opportunity of a lifetime. I envy you. I truly do."

"Just let me out of here and I'll reformat all my memories of this. I promise."

"Oh, no. I can't let your moment of weakness keep you from your glorious destiny. You're gonna ride the wave of the future. Together my new brethren and I have seen Johnny's plan for us, and behold, it was glorious."

"Where did you get that hick accent all of a sudden?"

DNS grabbed the front of JSN's shirt. "You were the one who wanted to blow these good folk out of the sky. None of you half-metal cripples were willing to open yourselves to the Word. Nobody wanted to give them a home."

"After the UN fiasco, I must admit, the offers were not exactly pouring in."

"Well, they will be soon. We're gonna make all those Pharisees bow to the glory of Johnny. They're gonna take the old values back into their hearts: home, marriage, family, network TV."

"And whose idea was this?"

"Oh, Johnny's of course. As revealed to me in His infinite Wisdom."

"Don't be stupid," JSN said, out of patience and a little scared besides. "Maybe things are a little screwed up right now. But you're not going to fix them by hiding in the past. Wars and patriotism and bigotry aren't the answer to a little slackness in quality control—"

"Who said anything about war?" DNS said. "Any fool knows advertising is the answer. Did not Johnny welcome the sponsors into the temple? That's why you're here. You're one of the biggest pop stars on the planet. People everywhere know who you are. You start new fashions with everything you do." He eyed the remnants of JSN's fiberglass with distaste.

"So?"

"So you're going to marry one of the sistren."

"Marry a devo? No way."

"I told you I don't like that word," DNS said coolly.

"I don't care what you call yourselves. Count me out. Forget it. I wouldn't do it if you put a gun to my head."

DNS reached into his kilt and pulled out an ancient handgun. A Colt .38 caliber Python, JSN determined with a quick lookup. DNS put the mouth of the barrel against JSN's left temple.

The door oozed open and Brother Simon came in, followed by the bovine woman who had smiled at JSN in the barn. She was smiling again, glancing back and forth between JSN and her own feet, her cheeks hotly flushed.

"Your bride-to-be," DNS said.

The woman began to undress. JSN stood up, looking quickly away from the yards of quivering flesh. Brother Simon held out a black videocassette, firmly clenched in both hands. "By-the-poor-vestige-of-my-mistake-in-Virginia," he said hurriedly, apparently unable to look away from the female's chest, "aprons-on-you-husb-and-wife. Go for it. Amen."

The female stretched out on her back and raised fleshy arms toward JSN. "Here?" he said. "You expect me to fertilize her? Right here? With you watching?"

"Not just us," DNS said, "but millions more when we rebroadcast the blessed event throughout the world. Soon everyone will want a husb and/or bride of Johnny! We'll bring them down from the mother ship and spread the Good News throughout the world!"

"Amen Brother Dennis," said Brother Simon.

"No," JSN said. "I can't. I won't."

DNS pulled back the hammer of the revolver with an audible click.

Mass hysteria, JSN thought. It would pass, eventually. The world had survived it before, barely, maybe it could live through it again. In the meantime, what else could he do?

He reached a trembling hand to his forehead, found his most conciliatory personality, and smiled down at the naked woman. "Hello, darling," he said.

BRUCE STERLING

DEEP EDDY

(1993)

THE CONTINENTAL gentleman in the next beanbag offered "Zigaretten?"

"What's in it?" Deep Eddy asked. The gray-haired gentleman murmured something: polysyllabic medical German. Eddy's translation program crashed at once.

Eddy gently declined. The gentleman shook a zigarette from the pack, twisted its tip, and huffed at it. A sharp perfume arose, like coffee struck by lightning.

The elderly European brightened swiftly. He flipped open a newspad, tapped through its menu, and began alertly scanning a German business zine.

Deep Eddy killed his translation program, switched spexware, and scanned the man. The gentleman was broadcasting a business bio. His name was Peter Liebling, he was from Bremen, he was ninety years old, he was an official with a European lumber firm. His hobbies were backgammon and collecting antique phone-cards. He looked pretty young for ninety. He probably had some unusual and interesting medical syndromes.

Herr Leibling glanced up, annoyed at Eddy's computer-assisted gaze. Eddy dropped his spex back onto their neck-chain. A practiced gesture, one Deep Eddy used a lot—*hey, didn't mean to stare, pal.* A lot of people were suspicious of spex. Most people had no real idea of the profound capacities of spexware. Most people still didn't use spex. Most people were, in a word, losers.

Eddy lurched up within his baby-blue beanbag and gazed out the aircraft window. Chattanooga, Tennessee. Bright white ceramic air-control towers, distant wine-colored office blocks, and a million dark green trees. Tarmac heated gently in the summer morning. Eddy lifted his spex again to check a silent takeoff westward by a white-and-red Asian jet. Infrared turbulence gushed from its distant engines. Deep Eddy loved infrared. That deep silent magical whirl of invisible heat, the breath of industry.

People underestimated Chattanooga, Deep Eddy thought with a local boy's pride. Chattanooga had a very high per capita investment in spexware. In fact Chattanooga ranked third-highest in NAFTA. Number One was San Jose, California (naturally), and Number Two was Madison, Wisconsin.

Eddy had already traveled to both those rival cities, in the service of his Chattanooga users group, to swap some spexware, market a little info, and make a careful study of the local scene. To collect some competitive intelligence. To spy around, not to put too fine a point on it.

Eddy's most recent business trip had been five drunken days at a blowout All-NAFTA spexware conference in Ciudad Juárez, Chihuahua. Eddy had not yet figured out why Ciudad Juárez, a once-dreary maquiladora factory town on the Rio Grande, had gone completely hog wild for spexing. But even little kids there had spex, bright speckly throwaway kid-stuff with just a couple dozen meg. There were tottering grannies with spex. Security cops with spex mounted right into their riot helmets. Billboards everywhere that couldn't be read without spex. And thousands of hustling industry zudes with air-conditioned jackets and forty or fifty terabytes mounted right at the bridge of the nose. Ciudad Juárez was in the grip of rampant spexmania. Maybe it was all the lithium in their water.

Today, duty called Deep Eddy to Düsseldorf in Europe. Duty did not have to call very hard to get Eddy's attention. The mere whisper of duty was enough to dislodge Deep Eddy, who still lived with his parents, Bob and Lisa.

He'd gotten some spexmail and a package from the president of the local chapter. *A network obligation; our group credibility depends on you, Eddy. A delivery job. Don't let us down; do whatever it takes. And keep your eyes covered—this one could be dangerous.* Well, danger and Deep Eddy were fast friends. Throwing up tequila and ephedrine through your nose in an alley in Mexico, while wearing a pair of computer-assisted glasses worth as much as a car—now *that* was dangerous. Most people would be scared to try something like that. Most people couldn't master their own insecurities. Most people were too scared to live.

This would be Deep Eddy's first adult trip to Europe. At the age of nine he'd accompanied Bob and Lisa to Madrid for a Sexual Deliberation conference, but all he remembered from that trip was a boring weekend of bad television and incomprehensible tomato-soaked food. Düsseldorf, however, sounded like real and genuine fun. The trip was probably even worth getting up at 07:15.

Eddy dabbed at his raw eyelids with a saline-soaked wipey. Eddy was getting a first-class case of eyeball-burn off his spex; or maybe it was just sleeplessness. He'd spent a very late and highly frustrating night with his current girlfriend, Djulia. He'd dated her hoping for a hero's farewell, hinting broadly that he might be beaten or killed by sinister European underground networking mavens, but his presentation hadn't washed at all. Instead of some sustained and attentive frolic, he'd gotten only a somber four-hour lecture about the emotional center in Djulia's life: collecting Japanese glassware.

As his jet gently lifted from the Chattanooga tarmac, Deep Eddy was struck with a sudden, instinctive, gut-level conviction of Djulia's essential counterproductivity. Djulia was just no good for him. Those clear eyes, the tilted nose, the sexy sprinkle of tattoo across her right cheekbone. Lovely flare of her body-heat in darkness. The lank strands of dark hair that turned crisp and wavy halfway down their length. A girl shouldn't have such great hair and so many tats and still be so tightly wrapped up. Djulia was no real friend of his at all.

The jet climbed steadily, crossing the shining waters of the Tennessee. Outside Eddy's window, the long ductile wings bent and rippled with dainty, tightly controlled anti-turbulence. The cabin itself felt as steady as a Mississippi lumber barge, but the computer-assisted wings, under spex-analysis, resembled a vibrating sawblade. Nerve-racking. *Let this not be the day a whole bunch of Chattanoogans fall out of the sky,* Eddy thought silently, squirming a bit in the luscious embrace of his beanbag.

He gazed about the cabin at his fellow candidates for swift mass death. Three hundred people or so, the European and NAFTA jet-bourgeoisie; well-groomed, polite. Nobody looked frightened. Sprawling there in their pastel beanbags, chatting, hooking fiber optics to palmtops and laptops, browsing through newspads, making videophone-calls. Just as if they were at home, or maybe in a very crowded cylindrical hotel lobby, all of them in blank and deliberate ignorance of the fact that they were zipping through midair supported by nothing but plasmajets and computation. Most people were so unaware. One software glitch somewhere, a missed decimal point, and those cleverly ductile wings would tear right the hell off. Sure, it didn't happen often. But it happened sometimes.

Deep Eddy wondered glumly if his own demise would even make the top of the newspad. It'd be in there all right, but probably hyperlinked five or six layers down.

The five-year-old in the beanbag behind Eddy entered a paroxysm of childish fear and glee. "My e-mail, Mom!" the kid chirped with desperate enthusiasm, bouncing up and down. "Mom! Mom, my *e-mail*! Hey Mom, get me my e-mail!"

A stew offered Eddy breakfast. He had a bowl of muesli and half-a-dozen boiled prunes. Then he broke out his travel card and ordered a mimosa. The booze didn't make him feel any more alert, though, so he ordered two more mimosas. Then he fell asleep.

• • •

Customs in Düsseldorf was awash. Summer tourists were pouring into the city like some vast migratory shoal of sardines. The people from outside Europe—from NAFTA, from the Sphere, from the South—were a tiny minority, though, compared to the vast intra-European traffic, who breezed through Customs completely unimpeded.

Uniformed inspectors were spexing the NAFTA and South baggage, presumably for guns or explosives, but their clunky government-issue spex looked a good five years out-of-date. Deep Eddy passed through the Customs chute without incident and had his passchip stamped. Passing out drunk on champagne and orange juice, then snoozing through the entire Atlantic crossing, had clearly been an excellent idea. It was 21:00 local time and Eddy felt quite alert and rested. Clearheaded. Ready for anything. Hungry.

Eddy wandered toward the icons signaling ground transport. A stocky woman in a bulky brown jacket stepped into his path. He stopped short. "Mr. Edward Dertouzas," she said.

"Right," Eddy said, dropping his bag. They stared at one another, spex to spex. "Actually, fräulein, as I'm sure you can see by my online bio, my friends call me Eddy. Deep Eddy, mostly."

"I'm not your friend, Mr. Dertouzas. I am your security escort. I'm called Sardelle today." Sardelle stooped and hefted his travel bag. Her head came about to his shoulder.

Deep Eddy's German translator, which he had restored to life, placed a yellow subtitle at the lower rim of his spex. "Sardelle," he noted. "'*Anchovy*'?"

"I don't pick the code names," Sardelle told him, irritated. "I have to use what the company gives me." She heaved her way through the crowd, jolting people aside with deft jabs of Eddy's travel bag. Sardelle wore a bulky air-conditioned brown trench coat, with multipocketed fawn-colored jeans and thick-soled black-and-white cop shoes. A crisp trio of small tattooed triangles outlined Sardelle's right cheek. Her hands, attractively small and dainty, were gloved in black-and-white pinstripe. She looked about thirty. No problem. He liked mature women. Maturity gave depth.

Eddy scanned her for bio data. "Sardelle," the spex read unhelpfully. Absolutely nothing else: no business, no employer, no address, no age, no interests, no hobbies, no personal ads. Europeans were rather weird about privacy. Then again, maybe Sardelle's lack of proper annotation had something to do with her business life.

Eddy looked down at his own hands, twitched bare fingers over a virtual menu in midair, and switched to some rude spexware he'd mail-ordered from Tijuana. Something of a legend in the spexing biz, X-Spex stripped people's clothing off and extrapolated the flesh beneath it in a full-color visual simulation. Sardelle, however, was so decked-out in waistbelts, holsters, and shoulder pads that the Xware was baffled. The simulation looked alarmingly bogus, her breasts and shoulders waggling like drug-addled plasticine.

"Hurry out," she suggested sternly. "I mean hurry *up*."

"Where we going? To see the Critic?"

"In time," Sardelle said. Eddy followed her through the stomping, shuffling, heaving crowd to a set of travel lockers.

"Do you really need this bag, sir?"

"What?" Eddy said. "Sure I do! It's got all my stuff in it."

"If we take it, I will have to search it carefully," Sardelle informed him patiently. "Let's place your bag in this locker, and you can retrieve it when you leave Europe." She offered him a small gray handbag with the logo of a Berlin luxury hotel. "Here are some standard travel necessities."

"They scanned my bag in Customs," Eddy said. "I'm clean, really. Customs was a walk-through."

Sardelle laughed briefly and sarcastically. "One million people coming to Düsseldorf this weekend," she said. "There will be a Wende here. And you think the Customs searched you properly? Believe me, Edward. You have not been searched properly."

"That sounds a bit menacing," Eddy said.

"A proper search takes a lot of time. Some threats to safety are tiny—things woven into clothing, glued to the skin . . ." Sardelle shrugged. "I like to have time. I'll pay you to have some time. Do you need money, Edward?"

"No," Eddy said, startled. "I mean, yeah. Sure I need money, who doesn't? But I have a travel card from my people. From CAPCLUG."

She glanced up sharply, aiming the spex at him. "Who is Kapklug?"

"Computer-Assisted Perception Civil Liberties Users Group," Eddy said. "Chattanooga Chapter."

"I see. The acronym in English." Sardelle frowned. "I hate all acronyms. . . . Edward, I will pay you forty ecu cash to put your bag into this locker and take this bag instead."

"Sold," Deep Eddy said. "Where's the money?"

Sardelle passed him four well-worn hologram bills. Eddy stuffed the cash in his pocket. Then he opened his own bag and retrieved an elderly hardbound book—*Crowds and Power*, by Elias Canetti. "A little light reading," he said unconvincingly.

"Let me see that book," Sardelle insisted. She leafed through the book rapidly, scanning pages with her pinstriped fingertips, flexing the covers, and checking the book's binding, presumably for inserted razors, poisoned needles, or strips of plastic explosive. "You are smuggling data," she concluded sourly, handing it back.

"That's what we live for in CAPCLUG," Eddy told her, peeking at her over his spex and winking. He slipped the book into the gray hotel bag and zipped it. Then he heaved his own bag into the travel locker, slammed the door, and removed the numbered key.

"Give me that key," Sardelle said.

"Why?"

"You might return and open the locker. If I keep the key, that security risk is much reduced."

"No way," Eddy frowned. "Forget it."

"Ten ecu," she offered.

"Mmmmph."

"Fifteen."

"Okay, have it your way." Eddy gave her the key. "Don't lose it."

Sardelle, unsmiling, put the key into a zippered sleeve pocket. "I never lose things." She opened her wallet.

Eddy nodded, pocketing a hologram ten and five singles. Very attractive currency, the ecu. The ten had a hologram of René Descartes, a very deep zude who looked impressively French and rational.

Eddy felt he was doing pretty well by this, so far. In point of fact there wasn't anything in the bag he really needed: his underwear, spare jeans, tickets, business cards, dress shirts, tie, suspenders, spare shoes, toothbrush, aspirin, instant espresso, sewing kit, and earrings. So what? It wasn't as if she'd asked him to give up his spex.

He also had a complete crush on his escort. The name Anchovy suited her—she struck him as a small canned cold fish. Eddy found this perversely attractive. In fact he found her so attractive that he was having a hard time standing still and breathing normally. He really liked the way she carried her stripe-gloved hands, deft and feminine and mysteriously European, but mostly it was her hair. Long, light reddish-brown, and meticulously braided by machine. He loved women's hair when it was machine braided. They couldn't seem to catch the fashion quite right in NAFTA. Sardelle's hair looked like a rusted mass of museum-quality chain mail, or maybe some fantastically convoluted railway intersection. Hair that really *meant business*. Not only did Sardelle have not a hair out of place, but any unkemptness was *topologically impossible*. The vision rose unbidden of running his fingers through it in the dark.

"I'm starving," he announced.

"Then we will eat," she said. They headed for the exit.

Electric taxis were trying, without much success, to staunch the spreading hemorrhage of tourists. Sardelle clawed at the air with her pinstriped fingers. Adjusting invisible spex menus. She seemed to be casting the evil eye on a nearby family group of Italians, who reacted with scarcely concealed alarm. "We can walk to a city bus stop," she told him. "It's quicker."

"Walking's quicker?"

Sardelle took off. He had to hurry to keep up. "Listen to me, Edward. If you follow my security suggestions, we will save time. If I save my time, then you will make money. If you make me work harder I will not be so generous."

"I'm easy," Eddy protested. Her cop-shoes seemed to have some kind of computational cushion built into the soles; she walked as if mounted on springs. "I'm here to meet the Cultural Critic. An audience with him. I have a delivery for him. You know that, right?"

"It's the book?"

Eddy hefted the gray hotel bag. "Yeah. . . . I'm here in Düsseldorf to deliver an old book to some European intellectual. Actually, to give the book back to him. He, like, lent the book to the CAPCLUG Steering Committee, and it's time to give it back. How tough can that job be?"

"Probably not very tough," Sardelle said calmly. "But strange things happen during a Wende."

Eddy nodded soberly. "Wendes are very interesting phenomena. CAPCLUG is studying Wendes. We might like to throw one someday."

"That's not how Wendes happen, Eddy. You don't 'throw' a Wende." Sardelle paused, considering. "A Wende throws *you*."

"So I gather," Eddy said. "I've been reading his work, you know. The Cultural Critic. It's deep work, I like it."

Sardelle was indifferent. "I'm not one of his partisans. I'm just employed to guard him." She conjured up another menu. "What kind of food do you like? Chinese? Thai? Eritrean?"

"How about German food?"

Sardelle laughed. "We Germans never eat German food. . . . There are very good Japanese cafés in Düsseldorf. Tokyo people fly here for the salmon. And the anchovies . . ."

"You live here in Düsseldorf, Anchovy?"

"I live everywhere in Europe, Deep Eddy." Her voice fell. "Any city with a screen in front of it. . . . And they all have screens in Europe."

"Sounds fun. You want to trade some spexware?"

"No."

"You don't believe in *andwendungsoriente wissensverarbeitung*?"

She made a face. "How clever of you to learn an appropriate German phrase. Speak English, Eddy. Your accent is truly terrible."

"Thank you kindly," Eddy said.

"You can't trade wares with me, Eddy, don't be silly. I would not give my security spexware to civilian Yankee hacker-boys."

"Don't own the copyright, huh?"

"There's that, too." She shrugged, and smiled.

They were out of the airport now, walking south. Silent steady flow of electric traffic down Flughafenstraße. The twilight air smelled of little white roses. They crossed at a traffic light. The German semiotics of ads and street signs began to press with gentle culture shock at the surface of Deep Eddy's brain. Garagenhof. Spezialist für Mobil-Telefon. Bürohäusern. He put on some character-recognition ware to do translation, but the instant doubling of the words all around him only made him feel schizophrenic.

They took shelter in a lit bus kiosk, along with a pair of heavily tattooed gays toting grocery bags. A video ad built into the side of the kiosk advertised German-language e-mail editors.

As Sardelle stood patiently, in silence, Eddy examined her closely for the first time. There was something odd and indefinitely European about the line of her nose. "Let's be friends, Sardelle. I'll take off my spex if you take off your spex."

"Maybe later," she said.

Eddy laughed. "You should get to know me. I'm a fun guy."

"I already know you."

An overcrowded bus passed. Its riders had festooned the robot bus with banners and mounted a klaxon on its roof, which emitted a cacophony of rapid-fire bongo music.

"The Wende people are already hitting the buses," Sardelle noted sourly, shifting on her feet as if trampling grapes. "I hope we can get downtown."

"You've done some snooping on me, huh? Credit records and such? Was it interesting?"

Sardelle frowned. "It's my business to research records. I did nothing illegal. All by the book."

"No offense taken," Eddy said, spreading his hands. "But you must have learned I'm harmless. Let's unwrap a little."

Sardelle sighed. "I learned that you are an unmarried male, age eighteen-to-thirty-five. No steady job. No steady home. No wife, no children. Radical political leanings. Travels often. Your demographics are very high-risk."

"I'm twenty-two, to be exact." Eddy noticed that Sardelle showed no reaction to this announcement, but the two eavesdropping gays seemed quite interested. He smiled nonchalantly. "I'm here to network, that's all. Friend-of-a-friend situation. Actually, I'm pretty sure I share your client's politics. As far as I can figure his politics out."

"Politics don't matter," Sardelle said, bored and impatient. "I'm not concerned with politics. Men in your age group commit eighty percent of all violent crimes."

One of the gays spoke up suddenly, in heavily accented English. "Hey, fräulein. We also have eighty percent of the charm!"

"And ninety percent of the fun," said his companion. "It's Wende time, Yankee boy. Come with us and we'll do some crimes." He laughed.

"Das ist sehr nett von Ihnen," Eddy said politely. "But I can't. I'm with nursie."

The first gay made a witty and highly idiomatic reply in German, to the effect, apparently, that he liked boys who wore sunglasses after dark, but Eddy needed more tattoos.

Eddy, having finished reading subtitles in midair, touched the single small black circle on his cheekbone. "Don't you like my solitaire? It's rather sinister in its reticence, don't you think?"

He'd lost them; they only looked puzzled.

A bus arrived.

"This will do," Sardelle announced. She fed the bus a ticket-chip and Eddy followed her on board. The bus was crowded, but the crowd seemed gentle; mostly Euro-Japanese out for a night on the town. They took a beanbag together in the back.

It had grown quite dark now. They floated down the street with machine-guided precision and a smooth dreamlike detachment. Eddy felt the spell of travel overcome him; the basic mammalian thrill of a live creature plucked up and dropped like a supersonic ghost on the far side of the planet. Another time, another place: whatever vast set of unlikelihoods had militated against his presence here had been defeated. A Friday night in Düsseldorf, July 13, 2035. The time was 22:10. The very specificity seemed magical.

He glanced at Sardelle again, grinning gleefully, and suddenly saw her for what she was. A burdened female functionary sitting stiffly in the back of a bus.

"Where are we now, exactly?" he said.

"We are on Danzigerstraße heading south to the Áltstadt," Sardelle said. "The old town center."

"Yeah? What's there?"

"Kartoffel. Beer. Schnitzel. Things for you to eat."

The bus stopped and a crowd of stomping, shoving rowdies got on. Across the street, a trio of police were struggling with a broken traffic securicam. The cops were wearing full-body pink riot-gear. He'd heard somewhere that all European cop riot-gear was pink. The color was supposed to be calming.

"This isn't much fun for you, Sardelle, is it?"

She shrugged. "We're not the same people, Eddy. I don't know what you are bringing to the Critic, and I don't want to know." She tapped her spex back into place with one gloved finger. "But if you fail in your job, at the very worst, it might mean some grave cultural loss. Am I right?"

"I suppose so. Sure."

"But if I fail in my job, Eddy, something *real* might *actually happen*."

"Wow," Eddy said, stung.

The crush in the bus was getting oppressive. Eddy stood and offered his spot in the beanbag to a tottering old woman in spangled party gear.

Sardelle rose then too, with bad grace, and fought her way up the aisle. Eddy followed, barking his shins on the thick-soled beastie-boots of a sprawling drunk.

Sardelle stopped short to trade elbow-jabs with a Nordic kamikaze in a horned baseball cap, and Eddy stumbled into her headlong. He realized then why people seemed so eager to get out of Sardelle's way; her trench coat was of woven ceramic and was as rough as sandpaper. He lurched one-handed for a strap. "Well," he puffed at Sardelle, swaying into her spex-to-spex, "if we can't enjoy each other's company, why not get this over with? Let me do my errand. Then I'll get right into your hair." He paused, shocked. "I mean, *out* of your hair. Sorry."

She hadn't noticed. "You'll do your errand," she said, clinging to her strap. They were so close that he could feel a chill air-conditioned breeze whiffling out of her trench coat's collar. "But on my terms. My time, my circumstances." She wouldn't meet his eyes; her head darted around as if from grave embarrassment. Eddy realized suddenly that she was methodically scanning the face of every stranger in the bus.

She spared him a quick, distracted smile. "Don't mind me, Eddy. Be a good boy and have fun in Düsseldorf. Just let me do my job, okay?"

"Okay then," Eddy muttered. "Really, I'm delighted to be in your hands." He couldn't seem to stop with the double entendres. They rose to his lips like drool from the id.

The glowing grids of Düsseldorf high-rises shone outside the bus windows, patchy waffles of mystery. So many human lives behind those windows. People he would never meet, never see. Pity he still couldn't afford proper telephotos.

Eddy cleared his throat. "What's he doing out there right now? The Cultural Critic, I mean."

"Meeting contacts in a safe house. He will meet a great many people during the Wende. That's his business, you know. You're only one of many that he bringed—brought—to this rendezvous." Sardelle paused. "Though in threat potential you do rank among the top five."

The bus made more stops. People piled in headlong, with a thrash and a heave and a jacking of kneecaps. Inside the bus they were all becoming anchovies. A smothered fistfight broke out in the back. A drunken woman tried, with mixed success, to vomit out the window. Sardelle held her position grimly through several stops, then finally fought her way to the door.

The bus pulled to a stop and a sudden rush of massed bodies propelled them out.

They'd arrived by a long suspension bridge over a broad moon-silvered river. The bridge's soaring cables were lit end-to-end with winking party bulbs. All along the bridge, flea-marketeers sitting cross-legged on glowing mats were doing a brisk trade in tourist junk. Out in the center, a busking juggler with smart gloves flung lit torches in flaming arcs three stories high.

"Jesus, what a beautiful river," Eddy said.

"It's the Rhine. This is Oberkasseler Bridge."

"The Rhine. Of course, of course. I've never seen the Rhine before. Is it safe to drink?"

"Of course. Europe's very civilized."

"I thought so. It even smells good. Let's go drink some of it."

The banks were lined with municipal gardens: grape-musky vineyards, big pale meticulous flowerbeds. Tireless gardening robots had worked them over season by season with surgical trowels. Eddy stooped by the riverbank and scooped up a double handful of backwash from a passing hydrofoil. He saw his own spex-clad face in the moony puddle of his hands. As Sardelle watched, he sipped a bit and flung the rest out as libation to the spirit of place.

"I'm happy now," he said. "Now I'm really here."

• • •

By midnight, he'd had four beers, two schnitzels, and a platter of kartoffels. Kartoffels were fried potato-batter waffles with a side of applesauce. Eddy's morale had soared from the moment he first bit one.

They sat at a sidewalk café table in the midst of a centuries-old pedestrian street in the Ältstadt. The entire street was a single block-long bar, all chairs, umbrellas, and cobbles, peaked-roof town houses with ivy and window boxes and ancient copper weathervanes. It had been invaded by an absolute throng of gawking, shuffling, hooting foreigners.

The gentle, kindly, rather bewildered Düsseldorfers were doing their level best to placate their guests and relieve them of any excess cash. A strong pink police presence was keeping good order. He'd seen two zudes in horned baseball caps briskly hauled into a paddy wagon—a "Pink Minna"—but the Vikings were pig-drunk and had it coming, and the crowd seemed very good-humored.

"I don't see what the big deal is with these Wendes," Deep Eddy said, polishing his spex on a square of oiled and lint-free polysilk. "This sucker's a walk-through. There's not gonna be any trouble here. Just look how calm and mellow these zudes are."

"There's trouble already," Sardelle said. "It's just not here in Áltstadt in front of your nose."

"Yeah?"

"There are big gangs of arsonists across the river tonight. They're barricading streets in Neuss, toppling cars, and setting them on fire."

"How come?"

Sardelle shrugged. "They are anti-car activists. They demand pedestrian rights and more mass transit . . ." She paused a bit to read the inside of her spex. "Green radicals are storming the Lobbecke Museum. They want all extinct insect specimens surrendered for cloning . . . Heinrich Heine University is on strike for academic freedom, and someone has glue-bombed the big traffic tunnel beneath the campus . . . But this is nothing, not yet. Tomorrow England meets Ireland in the soccer finals at Rhein-Stadium. There will be hell to pay."

"Huh. That sounds pretty bad."

"Yes." She smiled. "So let's enjoy our time here, Eddy. Idleness is sweet. Even on the edge of dirty chaos."

"But none of those events by itself sounds all that threatening or serious."

"Not each thing by itself, Eddy, no. But it all happens all at once. That's what a Wende is like."

"I don't get it," Eddy said. He put his spex back on and lit the menu from within, with a finger snap. He tapped the spex menu-bar with his right fingertip and light-amplifiers kicked in. The passing crowd, their outlines shimmering slightly from computational effects, seemed to be strolling through an overlit stage set. "I guess there's trouble coming from all these outsiders," Eddy said, "but the Germans themselves seem so . . . well . . . so good-natured and tidy and civilized. Why do they even have Wendes?"

"It's not something we plan, Eddy. It's just something that happens to us." Sardelle sipped her coffee.

"How could this happen and not be planned?"

"Well, we knew it was coming, of course. Of course we knew *that*. Word gets around. That's how Wendes start." She straightened her napkin. "You can ask the Critic, when you meet him. He talks a lot about Wendes. He knows as much as anyone, I think."

"Yeah, I've read him," Eddy said. "He says that it's rumor, boosted by electronic and digital media, in a feedback loop with crowd dynamics and modern mass transportation. A nonlinear networking phenomenon. That much I understand! But then he quotes some zude named Elias Canetti . . ." Eddy patted the gray bag. "I tried to read Canetti, I really did, but he's twentieth-century, and as boring and stuffy as hell . . . Anyway, we'd handle things differently in Chattanooga."

"People say that, until they have their first Wende," Sardelle said. "Then it's all different. Once you know a Wende can actually happen to you . . . well, it changes everything."

"We'd take steps to stop it, that's all. Take steps to control it. Can't you people take some steps?"

Sardelle tugged off her pinstriped gloves and set them on the tabletop. She worked her bare fingers gently, blew on her fingertips, and picked a big bready pretzel from the basket. Eddy noticed with surprise that her gloves had big rock-hard knuckles and twitched a little all by themselves.

"There are things you can do, of course," she told him. "Put police and fire-fighters on overtime. Hire more private security. Disaster control for lights, traffic, power, data. Open the shelters and stock first-aid medicine. And warn the whole population. But when a city tells its people that a Wende is coming, that *guarantees* the Wende will come . . ." Sardelle sighed. "I've worked Wendes before. But this is a big one. A big, dark one. And it won't be over, it can't be over—not until everyone knows that it's gone, and feels that it's gone."

"That doesn't make much sense."

"Talking about it won't help, Eddy. You and I, talking about it—we become part of the Wende ourselves, you see? We're here because of the Wende. We met because of the Wende. And we can't leave each other, until the Wende goes away." She shrugged. "Can you go away, Eddy?"

"No. . . . Not right now. But I've got stuff to do here."

"So does everybody else."

Eddy grunted and killed another beer. The beer here was truly something special. "It's a Chinese finger trap," he said, gesturing.

"Yes, I know those."

He grinned. "Suppose we both stop pulling? We could walk through it. Leave town. I'll throw the book in the river. Tonight you and I could fly back to Chattanooga. Together."

She laughed. "You wouldn't really do that, though."

"You don't know me after all."

"You spit in the face of your friends? And I lose my job? A high price to pay for one gesture. For a young man's pretense of free will."

"I'm not pretending, lady. Try me. I dare you."

"Then you're drunk."

"Well, there's that." He laughed. "But don't joke about liberty. Liberty's the realest thing there is." He stood up and hunted out the bathroom.

On his way back he stopped at a pay phone. He gave it fifty centimes and dialed Tennessee. Djulia answered.

"What time is it?" he said.

"Nineteen. Where are you?"

"Düsseldorf."

"Oh." She rubbed her nose. "Sounds like you're in a bar."

"Bingo."

"So what's new, Eddy?"

"I know you put a lot of stock in honesty," Eddy said. "So I thought I'd tell you I'm planning an affair. I met this German girl here and frankly, she's irresistible."

Djulia frowned darkly. "You've got a lot of nerve telling me that kind of crap with your spex on."

"Oh yeah," he said. He took them off and stared into the monitor. "Sorry."

"You're drunk, Eddy," Djulia said. "I hate it when you're drunk! You'll say and do anything, if you're drunk and on the far end of a phone line." She rubbed nervously at her newest cheek tattoo. "Is this one of your weird jokes?"

"Yeah. It is, actually. The chances are eighty to one that she'll turn me down flat." Eddy laughed. "But I'm gonna try anyway. Because you're not letting me live and breathe."

Djulia's face went stiff. "When we're face-to-face, you always abuse my trust. That's why I don't like for us to go past virching."

"Come off it, Djulia."

She was defiant. "If you think you'll be happier with some weirdo virch-whore in Europe, go ahead! I don't know why you can't do that by wire from Chattanooga, anyway."

"This is Europe. We're talking actuality here."

Djulia was shocked. "If you actually touch another woman I never want to see you again." She bit her lip. "Or do wire with you, either. I mean that, Eddy. You know I do."

"Yeah," he said. "I know."

He hung up, got change from the phone, and dialed his parents' house. His father answered.

"Hi Bob. Lisa around?"

"No," his father said, "it's her night for optic macrame. How's Europe?"

"Different."

"Nice to hear from you, Eddy. We're kind of short of money. I can spare you some sustained attention, though."

"I just dumped Djulia."

"Good move, son," his father said briskly. "Fine. Very serious girl, Djulia. Way too straitlaced for you. A kid your age should be dating girls who are absolutely jumping out of their skins."

Eddy nodded.

"You didn't lose your spex, did you?"

Eddy held them up on their neck chain. "Safe and sound."

"Hardly recognized you for a second," his father said. "Ed, you're such a serious-minded kid. Taking on all these responsibilities. On the road so much, spexware day in day out. Lisa and I network about you all the time. Neither of us did a day's work before we were thirty, and we're all the better for it. You've got to live, son. Got to find yourself. Smell the roses. If you want to stay in Europe a couple of months, forget the algebra courses."

"It's calculus, Bob."

"Whatever."

"Thanks for the good advice, Bob. I know you mean it."

"It's good news about Djulia, son. You know we don't invalidate your feelings, so we never said a goddamn thing to you, but her glassware really sucked. Lisa says she's got no goddamn aesthetics at all. That's a hell of a thing, in a woman."

"That's my mom," Eddy said. "Give Lisa my best." He hung up.

He went back out to the sidewalk table. "Did you eat enough?" Sardelle asked.

"Yeah. It was good."

"Sleepy?"

"I dunno. Maybe."

"Do you have a place to stay, Eddy? Hotel reservations?"

Eddy shrugged. "No. I don't bother, usually. What's the use? It's more fun winging it."

"Good," Sardelle nodded. "It's better to wing. No one can trace us. It's safer."

She found them shelter in a park, where an activist group of artists from Munich had set up a squatter pavilion. As squatter pavilions went, it was quite a nice one, new and in good condition: a giant soap bubble upholstered in cellophane and polysilk. It covered half an acre with crisp yellow bubblepack flooring. The shelter was illegal and therefore anonymous. Sardelle seemed quite pleased about this.

Once through the zippered airlock, Eddy and Sardelle were forced to examine the artists' multimedia artwork for an entire grueling hour. Worse yet, they were closely quizzed afterward by an expert-system, which bullied them relentlessly with arcane aesthetic dogma.

This ordeal was too high a price for most squatters. The pavilion, though attractive, was only half-full, and many people who had shown up bone-tired were fleeing the art headlong. Deep Eddy, however, almost always aced this sort of thing. Thanks to his slick responses to the computer's quizzing, he won himself quite a nice area, with a blanket, opaquable curtains, and its own light fixtures. Sardelle, by contrast, had been bored and minimal, and had won nothing more advanced than a pillow and a patch of bubblepack among the philistines.

Eddy made good use of a traveling pay-toilet stall, and bought some mints and chilled mineral water from a robot. He settled in cozily as police sirens, and some distant, rather choked-sounding explosions, made the night glamorous.

Sardelle didn't seem anxious to leave. "May I see your hotel bag," she said.

"Sure." He handed it over. Might as well. She'd given it to him in the first place.

He'd thought she was going to examine the book again, but instead she took a small plastic packet from within the bag, and pulled the packet's ripcord. A colorful jumpsuit jumped out, with a chemical hiss and a vague hot stink of catalysis and cheap cologne. The jumpsuit, a one-piece, had comically baggy legs, frilled sleeves, and was printed all over with a festive cutup of twentieth-century naughty seaside postcards.

"Pajamas," Eddy said. "Gosh, how thoughtful."

"You can sleep in this if you want," Sardelle nodded, "but it's daywear. I want you to wear it tomorrow. And I want to buy the clothes you are wearing now, so that I can take them away for safety."

Deep Eddy was wearing a dress shirt, light jacket, American jeans, dappled stockings, and Nashville brogues of genuine blue suede. "I can't wear that crap," he protested. "Jesus, I'd look like a total loser."

"Yes," said Sardelle with an enthusiastic nod, "it's very cheap and common.

It will make you invisible. Just one more party boy among thousands and thousands. This is very secure dress, for a courier during a Wende."

"You want me to meet the Critic in this getup?"

Sardelle laughed. "The Cultural Critic is not impressed by taste, Eddy. The eye he uses when he looks at people . . . He sees things others people can't see." She paused, considering. "He *might* be impressed if you showed up dressed in *this*. Not because of what it is, of course. But because it would show that you can understand and manipulate popular taste to your own advantage . . . just as he does."

"You're really being paranoid," Eddy said, nettled. "I'm not an assassin. I'm just some techie zude from Tennessee. You know that, don't you?"

"Yes, I believe you," she nodded. "You're very convincing. But that has nothing to do with proper security technique. If I take your clothes, there will be less operational risk."

"How much less risk? What do you expect to find in my clothes, anyway?"

"There are many, many things you *might* have done," she said patiently. "The human race is very ingenious. We have invented ways to kill, or hurt, or injure almost anyone, with almost nothing at all." She sighed. "If you don't know about such techniques already, it would only be stupid for me to tell you all about them. So let's be quick and simple, Eddy. It would make me happier to take your clothes away. A hundred ecu."

Eddy shook his head. "This time it's really going to cost you."

"Two hundred then," Sardelle said.

"Forget it."

"I can't go higher than two hundred. Unless you let me search your body cavities."

Eddy dropped his spex.

"Body cavities," Sardelle said impatiently. "You're a grown-up man, you must know about this. A great deal can be done with body cavities."

Eddy stared at her. "Can't I have some chocolate and roses first?"

"It's not chocolate and roses with us," Sardelle said sternly. "Don't talk to me about chocolate and roses. We're not lovers. We are client and bodyguard. It's an ugly business, I know. But it's only business."

"Yeah? Well, trading in body cavities is new to me." Deep Eddy rubbed his chin. "As a simple Yankee youngster I find this a little confusing. Maybe we could barter them? Tonight?"

She laughed harshly. "I won't sleep with you, Eddy. I won't sleep at all! You're only being foolish." Sardelle shook her head. Suddenly she lifted a densely braided mass of hair above her right ear. "Look here, Mr. Simple Yankee Youngster. I'll show you my favorite body cavity." There was a flesh-colored plastic duct in the side of her scalp. "It's illegal to have this done in Europe. I had it done in Turkey. This morning I took half a cc through there. I won't sleep until Monday."

"Jesus," Eddy said. He lifted his spex to stare at the small dimpled orifice. "Right through the blood-brain barrier? That must be a hell of an infection risk."

"I don't do it for fun. It's not like beer and pretzels. It's just that I won't sleep now. Not until the Wende is over." She put her hair back, and sat up with a look of composure. "Then I'll fly somewhere and lie in the sun and be very still. All by myself, Eddy."

"Okay," Eddy said, feeling a weird and muddy sort of pity for her. "You can borrow my clothes and search them."

"I have to burn the clothes. Two hundred ecu?"

"All right. But I keep these shoes."

"May I look at your teeth for free? It will only take five minutes."

"Okay," he muttered. She smiled at him, and touched her spex. A bright purple light emerged from the bridge of her nose.

• • •

At 08:00 a police drone attempted to clear the park. It flew overhead, barking robotic threats in five languages. Everyone simply ignored the machine.

Around 08:30 an actual line of human police showed up. In response, a group of the squatters brought out their own bullhorn, an enormous battery-powered sonic assault-unit.

The first earthshaking shriek hit Eddy like an electric prod. He'd been lying peacefully on his bubble-mattress, listening to the doltish yap of the robot chopper. Now he leapt quickly from his crash-padding and wormed his way into the crispy bubblepack cloth of his ridiculous jumpsuit.

Sardelle showed up while he was still tacking the jumpsuit's Velcro buttons. She led him outside the pavilion.

The squatter bullhorn was up on an iron tripod pedestal, surrounded by a large group of grease-stained anarchists with helmets, earpads, and studded white batons. Their bullhorn's enormous ululating bellow was reducing everyone's nerves to jelly. It was like the shriek of Medusa.

The cops retreated, and the owners of the bullhorn shut it off, waving their glittering batons in triumph. In the deafened, jittery silence there were scattered shrieks, jeers, and claps, but the ambience in the park had become very bad: aggressive and surreal. Attracted by the apocalyptic shriek, people were milling into the park at a trot, spoiling for any kind of trouble.

They seemed to have little in common, these people; not their dress, not language, certainly nothing like a coherent political cause. They were mostly young men, and most of them looked as if they'd been up all night: red-eyed and peevish. They taunted the retreating cops. A milling gang knifed one of the smaller pavilions, a scarlet one, and it collapsed like a blood-blister under their trampling feet.

Sardelle took Eddy to the edge of the park, where the cops were herding up a crowd-control barricade line of ambulant robotic pink beanbags. "I want to see this," he protested. His ears were ringing.

"They're going to fight," she told him.

"About what?"

"Anything. Everything," she shouted. "It doesn't matter. They'll knock our teeth out. Don't be stupid." She took him by the elbow and they slipped through a gap in the closing battle line.

The police had brought up a tracked glue-cannon truck. They now began to threaten the crowd with a pasting. Eddy had never seen a glue-cannon before—except on television. It was quite astonishing how frightening the machine looked, even in pink. It was squat, blind, and nozzled, and sat there buzzing like some kind of wheeled warrior termite.

Suddenly several of the cops standing around the machine began to flinch and duck. Eddy saw a glittering object carom hard off the glue-truck's armored canopy. It flew twenty meters and landed in the grass at his feet. He picked it up. It was a stainless-steel ball-bearing the size of a cow's eyeball.

"Airguns?" he said.

"Slingshots. Don't let one hit you."

"Oh yeah. Great advice, I guess." To the far side of the cops a group of people—some kind of closely organized protestors—were advancing in measured step under a tall two-man banner. It read, in English: *The Only Thing Worse Than Dying Is Outliving Your Culture*. Every man-jack of them, and there were at least sixty, carried a long plastic pike topped with an ominous looking bulbous sponge. It was clear from the way they maneuvered that they understood military pike-tactics only too well; their phalanx bristled like a hedgehog, and some captain among them was barking distant orders. Worse yet the pikemen had neatly outflanked the cops, who now began calling frantically for backup.

A police drone whizzed just above their heads, not the casual lumbering he had seen before, but direct and angry and inhumanly fast. "Run!" Sardelle shouted, taking his hands. "Peppergas . . ."

Eddy glanced behind him as he fled. The chopper, as if cropdusting, was farting a dense maroon fog. The crowd bellowed in shock and rage and, seconds later, that hellish bullhorn kicked in once more.

Sardelle ran with amazing ease and speed. She bounded along as if firecrackers were bursting under her feet. Eddy, years younger and considerably longer in leg, was very hard put to keep up.

In two minutes they were well out of the park, across a broad street and into a pedestrian network of small shops and restaurants. There she stopped and let him catch his breath.

"Jesus," he puffed, "where can I buy shoes like that?"

"They're made-to-order," she told him calmly. "And you need special training. You can break your ankles, otherwise . . ." She gazed at a nearby bakery. "You want some breakfast now?"

Eddy sampled a chocolate-filled pastry inside the shop, at a dainty, doily-covered table. Two ambulances rushed down the street, and a large group of drum-beating protestors swaggered by, shoving shoppers from the pavement, but otherwise things seemed peaceful. Sardelle sat with arms folded, staring into space. He guessed that she was reading security alerts from the insides of her spex.

"You're not tired, are you?" he said.

"I don't sleep on operations," she said, "but sometimes I like to sit very still." She smiled at him. "You wouldn't understand . . ."

"Hell no I wouldn't," Eddy said, his mouth full. "All hell's breaking loose over there, and here you are sipping orange juice just as calm as a bump on a pickle . . . Damn, these croissants, or whatever the hell they are, are really good. Hey! *Herr Ober!* Bring me another couple of those, *ja, danke. . . .*"

"The trouble could follow us anywhere. We're as safe here as any other place. Safer, because we're not in the open."

"Good," Eddy nodded, munching. "That park's a bad scene."

"It's not so bad in the park. It's very bad at the Rhein-Spire, though. The Mahogany Warbirds have seized the rotating restaurant. They're stealing skin."

"What are Warbirds?"

She seemed surprised. "You haven't heard of them? They're from NAFTA. A criminal syndicate. Insurance rackets, protection rackets, they run all the casinos in the Quebec Republic . . ."

"Okay. So what's stealing skin?"

"It's a new kind of swindle; they take a bit of skin or blood, with your genetics you see, and a year later they tell you they have a newborn son or daughter of yours held captive, held somewhere secret in the South. . . . Then they try to make you pay, and pay, and pay. . . ."

"You mean they're kidnapping genetics from the people in that restaurant?"

"Yes. Brunch in the Rhein-Spire is very prestigious. The victims are all rich or famous." Suddenly she laughed, rather bitter, rather cynical. "I'll be busy next year, Eddy, thanks to this. A new job—protecting my clients' skin."

Eddy thought about it. "It's kind of like the rent-a-womb business, huh? But really twisted."

She nodded. "The Warbirds are crazy, they're not even ethnic criminals, they are network interest-group creatures. . . . Crime is so damned ugly, Eddy. If you ever think of doing it, just stop."

Eddy grunted.

"Think of those children," she murmured. "Born from crime. Manufactured to order, for a criminal purpose. This is a strange world, isn't it? It frightens me sometimes."

"Yeah?" Eddy said cheerfully. "Illegitimate son of a millionaire, raised by a high-tech mafia? Sounds kind of weird and romantic to me. I mean, consider the possibilities."

She took off her spex for the first time, to look at him. Her eyes were blue. A very odd and romantic shade of blue. Probably tinted contacts.

"Rich people have been having illegitimate kids since the year zero," Eddy said. "The only difference is somebody's mechanized the process." He laughed.

"It's time you met the Cultural Critic," she said. She put the spex back on.

• • •

They had to walk a long way. The bus system was now defunct. Apparently the soccer fans made a sport of hitting public buses; they would rip all the beanbags out and kick them through the doors. On his way to meet the Critic, Eddy saw hundreds of soccer fans; the city was swarming with them. The English devotees were very bad news: savage, thick-booted, snarling, stamping, chanting, anonymous young men, in knee-length sandpaper coats, with their hair cropped short and their faces masked or war-painted in the Union Jack. The English soccer hooligans traveled in enormous packs of two and three hundred. They were armed with cheap cellular phones. They'd wrapped the aerials with friction tape to form truncheon handles, so that the high-impact ceramic phone casing became a nasty club. It was impossible to deny a traveler the ownership of a telephone, so the police were impotent to stop this practice. Practically speaking, there was not much to be done in any case. The English hooligans dominated the streets through sheer force of numbers. Anyone seeing them simply fled headlong.

Except, of course, for the Irish soccer fans. The Irish wore thick elbow-length grappling gloves, some kind of workmen's gauntlets apparently, along with long green-and-white football scarves. Their scarves had skull-denting weights sewn into pockets at their ends, and the tassels fringed with little skin-ripping wire barbs. The weights were perfectly legitimate rolls of coins, and the wire—well, you could get wire anywhere. The Irish seemed to be outnumbered, but were, if anything, even drunker and more reckless than their rivals. Unlike the English, the Irish louts didn't even use the cellular phones to coordinate their brawling. They just plunged ahead at a dead run, whipping their scarves overhead and screaming about Oliver Cromwell.

The Irish were terrifying. They traveled down streets like a scourge. Anything in their way they knocked over and trampled: knickknack kiosks, propaganda videos, poster-booths, T-shirt tables, people selling canned jumpsuits. Even the postnatal abortion people, who were true fanatics, and the scary, eldritch, black-clad pro-euthanasia groups, would abandon their sidewalk podiums to flee from the Irish kids.

Eddy shuddered to think what the scene must be like at the Rhein-Stadium. "Those are some mean goddamn kids," he told Sardelle, as they emerged from hiding in an alley. "And it's all about *soccer*? Jesus, that seems so pointless."

"If they rioted in their *own* towns, *that* would be pointless," Sardelle said. "Here at the Wende, they can smash each other, and everything else, and tomorrow they will be perfectly safe at home in their own world."

"Oh, I get it," Eddy said. "That makes a lot of sense."

A passing blonde woman in a Muslim hijab slapped a button onto Eddy's sleeve. "Will your lawyer talk to God?" the button demanded aloud, repeatedly, in English. Eddy plucked the device off and stamped on it.

The Cultural Critic was holding court in a safe house in Stadtmitte. The safe house was an anonymous twentieth-century four-story dump, flanked by some nicely retrofitted nineteenth-century town houses. A graffiti gang had hit the block during the night, repainting the street surface with a sprawling polychrome mural, all big grinning green kitty cats, fractal spirals, and leaping priapic pink pigs. "Hot Spurt!" one of the pigs suggested eagerly; Eddy skirted its word balloon as they approached the door.

The door bore a small brass plaque reading E.I.S.—ELEKTRONISCHES INVASIONSABWEHR-SYSTEMS GMBH. There was an inscribed corporate logo that appeared to be a melting ice cube.

Sardelle spoke in German to the door video; it opened, and they entered a hall full of pale, drawn adults in suits, armed with fire extinguishers. Despite their air of nervous resolution and apparent willingness to fight hand to hand, Eddy took them for career academics: modestly dressed, ties and scarves slightly askew, odd cheek tattoos, distracted gazes, too serious. The place smelled bad, like stale cottage cheese and bookshelf dust. The dirt-smudged walls were festooned with schematics and wiring diagrams, amid a bursting mess of tower-stacked scrawl-labeled cartons—disk archives of some kind. The ceiling and floorboards were festooned with taped-down power cables and fiber-optic network wiring.

"Hi, everybody!" Eddy said. "How's it going?" The building's defenders looked at him, noted his jumpsuit costume, and reacted with relieved indifference. They began talking in French, obviously resuming some briefly postponed and intensely important discussion.

"Hello," said a German in his thirties, rising to his feet. He had long, thinning, greasy hair and a hollow-cheeked, mushroom-pale face. He wore secretarial half spex; and behind them he had the shiftiest eyes Eddy had ever seen, eyes that darted, and gloated, and slid around the room. He worked his way through the defenders, and smiled at Eddy, vaguely. "I am your host. Welcome, friend." He extended a hand.

Eddy shook it. He glanced sidelong at Sardelle. Sardelle had gone as stiff as a board and had jammed her gloved hands in her trench coat pockets.

"So," Eddy gabbled, snatching his hand back, "thanks a lot for having us over!"

"You'll be wanting to see my famous friend the Cultural Critic," said their host, with a cadaverous smile. "He is upstairs. This is my place. I own it." He gazed around himself, brimming with satisfaction. "It's my Library, you see. I have the honor of hosting the great man for the Wende. He appreciates my work. Unlike so many others."

Their host dug into the pocket of his baggy slacks. Eddy, instinctively expecting a drawn knife, was vaguely surprised to see his host hand over an old-fashioned, dog-eared business card. Eddy glanced at it. "How are you, Herr Schreck?"

"Life is very exciting today," said Schreck with a smirk. He touched his spex and examined Eddy's online bio. "A young American visitor. How charming."

"I'm from NAFTA," Eddy corrected.

"And a civil libertarian. Liberty is the only word that still excites me," Schreck said, with itchy urgency. "I need many more American intimates. Do make use of me. And all my digital services. That card of mine—do call those network addresses and tell your friends. The more, the happier." He turned to Sardelle. *"Kaffee, fräulein? Zigaretten?"*

Sardelle shook her head minimally.

"It's good she's here," Schreck told Eddy. "She can help us to fight. You go upstairs. The great man is waiting for visitors."

"I'm going up with him," Sardelle said.

"Stay here," Schreck urged. "The security threat is to the Library, not to him."

"I'm a bodyguard," Sardelle said frostily. "I guard the body. I don't guard data-havens."

Schreck frowned. "Well, more fool you, then."

Sardelle followed Eddy up the dusty, flower-carpeted stairs. Upstairs to the right was an antique twentieth-century office door in blond oak and frosted glass. Sardelle knocked; someone called out in French.

She opened the door. Inside the office were two long workbenches covered with elderly desktop computers. The windows were barred and curtained.

The Cultural Critic, wearing spex and a pair of datagloves, sat in a bright pool of sunlight-yellow glare from a track-mounted overhead light. He was pecking daintily with his gloved fingertips at a wafer-thin data-screen of woven cloth.

As Sardelle and Eddy stepped into the office, the Critic wrapped up his screen in a scroll, removed his spex, and unplugged his gloves. He had dark pepper-and-salt tousled hair, a dark wool tie, and a long maroon scarf draped over a beautifully cut ivory jacket.

"You would be Mr. Dertouzas from CAPCLUG," he said.

"Exactly. How are you, sir?"

"Very well." He examined Eddy briefly. "I assume his clothing was your idea, Frederika."

Sardelle nodded once, with a sour look. Eddy smiled at her, delighted to learn her real name.

"Have a seat," the critic offered. He poured himself more coffee. "I'd offer you a cup of this, but it's been . . . adjusted."

"I brought you your book," Eddy said. He sat, and opened the bag, and offered the item in question.

"Splendid." The Critic reached into his jacket pocket and, to Eddy's surprise, pulled a knife. The Critic opened its blade with one thumbnail. The shining blade was saw-toothed in a fractal fashion; even its serrations had tiny serrated serrations. It was a jackknife the length of a finger, with a razor-sharp edge on it as long as a man's arm.

Under the knife's irresistible ripping caress, the tough cover of the book parted with a discreet shredding of cloth. The Critic reached into the slit and plucked out a thin, gleaming storage disk. He set the book down. "Did you read this?"

"That disk?" Eddy ad-libbed. "I assumed it was encrypted."

"You assumed correctly, but I meant the book."

"I think it lost something in translation," Eddy said.

The Critic raised his brows. He had dark, heavy brows with a pronounced frown line between them, over sunken, gray-green eyes. "You have read Canetti in the original, Mr. Dertouzas?"

"I meant the translation between centuries," Eddy said, and laughed. "What I read left me with nothing but questions. . . . Can you answer them for me, sir?"

The Critic shrugged and turned to a nearby terminal. It was a scholar's workstation, the least dilapidated of the machines in the office. He touched four keys in order; a carousel whirled and spat out a disk. The Critic handed it to Eddy. "You'll find your answers here, to whatever extent I can give them," he said. "My Complete Works. Please take this disk. Reproduce it, give it to whomever you like, as long as you accredit it. The standard scholarly procedure. I'm sure you know the etiquette."

"Thank you very much," Eddy said with dignity, tucking the disk into his bag. "Of course I own your works already, but I'm glad of a fully up-to-date edition."

"I'm told that a copy of my Complete Works will get you a cup of coffee at any café in Europe," the Critic mused, slotting the encrypted disk and rapidly tapping keys. "Apparently digital commodification is not entirely a spent force, even in literature. . . ." He examined the screen. "Oh, this is lovely. I *knew* I would need this data again. And I certainly didn't want it in my house." He smiled.

"What are you going to do with that data?" Eddy said.

"Do you really not know?" the Critic said. "And you from CAPCLUG, a group of such carnivorous curiosity? Well, that's also a strategy, I suppose." He tapped more keys, then leaned back and opened a pack of zigarettes.

"What strategy?"

"New elements, new functions, new solutions—I don't know what 'culture' is, but I know exactly what I'm doing." The Critic drew slowly on a zigarette, his brows knotting.

"And what's that, exactly?"

"You mean, what is the underlying concept?" He waved the zigarette. "I have no 'concept.' The struggle here must not be reduced to a single simple idea. I am building a structure that must not, cannot, be reduced to a single simple idea. I am building a structure that perhaps *suggests* a concept . . . If I did more, the system itself would become stronger than the surrounding culture . . . Any system of rational analysis must live within the strong blind body of mass humanity, Mr. Dertouzas. If we learned anything from the twentieth century, we learned that much, at least." The Critic sighed, a fragrant medicinal mist. "I fight windmills, sir. It's a duty. . . . You often are hurt, but at the same time you become unbelievably happy, because you see that you have both friends and enemies, and that you are capable of fertilizing society with contradictory attitudes."

"What enemies do you mean?" Eddy said.

"Here. Today. Another data-burning. It was necessary to stage a formal resistance."

"This is an evil place," Sardelle—or rather Frederika—burst out. "I had no idea this was today's safe house. This is anything but safe. Jean-Arthur, you must leave this place at once. You could be killed here!"

"An evil place? Certainly. But there is so much megabytage devoted to works on goodness, and on doing good—so very little coherent intellectual treatment of the true nature of evil and being evil . . . Of malice and stupidity and acts of cruelty and darkness . . ." The Critic sighed. "Actually, once you're allowed through the encryption that Herr Schreck so wisely imposes on his holdings, you'll find the data here rather banal. The manuals for committing crime are farfetched and badly written. The schematics for bombs, listening devices, drug labs, and so forth, are poorly designed and probably unworkable. The pornography is juvenile and anti-erotic. The invasions of privacy are of interest only to voyeurs. Evil is banal—by no means so scarlet as one's instinctive dread would paint it. It's like the sex life of one's parents—a primal and forbidden topic, and yet, with objectivity, basically integral to their human nature—and of course to your own."

"Who's planning to burn this place?" Eddy said.

"A rival of mine. He calls himself the Moral Referee."

"Oh yeah, I've heard of him!" Eddy said. "He's here in Düsseldorf too? Jesus."

"He is a charlatan," the Critic sniffed. "Something of an ayatollah figure. A popular demagogue . . ." He glanced at Eddy. "Yes, yes—of course people do say much the same of me, Mr. Dertouzas, and I'm perfectly aware of that. But I have two doctorates, you know. The Referee is a self-appointed digital Savonarola. Not a scholar at all. An autodidactic philosopher. At best an artist."

"Aren't you an artist?"

"That's the danger. . . ." The Critic nodded somberly. "Once I was only a teacher, then suddenly I felt a sense of mission. . . . I began to understand which works are strongest, which are only decorative. . . ." The Critic looked suddenly restless, and puffed at his zigarette again. "In Europe there is too much couture, too little culture. In Europe everything is colored by discourse. There is too much knowledge and too much fear to overthrow that knowledge. . . . In NAFTA you are too naively postmodern to suffer from this syndrome. . . . And the Sphere, the Sphere, they are orthogonal to both our concerns. . . . The South, of course, is the planet's last reservoir of authentic humanity, despite every ontological atrocity committed there. . . ."

"I'm not following you," Eddy said.

"Take that disk with you. Don't lose it," the Critic said somberly. "I have certain obligations, that's all. I must know why I made certain choices, and be able to defend them, and I *must* defend them, or risk losing everything. . . . Those choices are already made. I've drawn a line here, established a position. It's my Wende today, you know! My lovely Wende. . . . Through cusp-points like this one, I can make things different for the whole of society." He smiled. "Not better, necessarily—but different, certainly. . . ."

"People are coming," Frederika announced suddenly, standing bolt upright and gesturing at the air. "A lot of people marching in the streets outside. . . . There's going to be trouble."

"I knew he would react the moment that data left this building," the Critic said, nodding. "Let trouble come! I will not move!"

"Goddamn you, I'm being paid to see that you survive!" Frederika said. "The Referee's people burn data-havens. They've done it before, and they'll do it again. Let's get out of here while there's still time!"

"We're all ugly and evil," the Critic announced calmly, settling deeply into his chair and steepling his fingers. "Bad knowledge is still legitimate self-knowledge. Don't pretend otherwise."

"That's no reason to fight them hand-to-hand here in Düsseldorf! We're not tactically prepared to defend this building! Let them burn it! What's one more stupid outlaw and his rat nest full of garbage?"

The Critic looked at her with pity. "It's not the access that matters. It's the principle."

"Bullseye!" Eddy shouted, recognizing a CAPCLUG slogan.

Frederika, biting her lip, leaned over a tabletop and began typing invisibly on a virtual keyboard. "If you call your professional backup," the Critic told her, "they'll only be hurt. This is not really your fight, my dear; you're not committed."

"Fuck you and your politics; if you burn up in here we don't get our bonuses," Frederika shouted.

"No reason *he* should stay, at least," the Critic said, gesturing to Eddy. "You've done well, Mr. Dertouzas. Thank you very much for your successful errand. It was most helpful." The Critic glanced at the workstation screen, where a program from the disk was still spooling busily, then back at Eddy again. "I suggest you leave this place while you can."

Eddy glanced at Frederika.

"Yes, go!" she said. "You're finished here, I'm not your escort anymore. Run, Eddy!"

"No way," Eddy said, folding his arms. "If you're not moving, I'm not moving."

Frederika looked furious. "But you're free to go. You heard him say so."

"So what? Since I'm at liberty, I'm also free to stay," Eddy retorted. "Besides, I'm from Tennessee, NAFTA's Volunteer State."

"There are hundreds of enemies coming," Frederika said, staring into space. "They will overwhelm us and burn this place to the ground. There will be nothing left of both of you and your rotten data but ashes."

"Have faith," the Critic said coolly. "Help will come, as well—from some unlikely quarters. Believe me, I'm doing my very best to maximize the implications of this event. So is my rival, if it comes to that. Thanks to that disk that just arrived, I am wirecasting events here to four hundred of the most volatile network sites in Europe. Yes, the Referee's people may destroy us, but their chances of escaping the consequences are very slim. And if we ourselves die here in flames, it will only lend deeper meaning to our sacrifice."

Eddy gazed at the Critic in honest admiration. "I don't understand a single goddamn word you're saying, but I guess I can recognize a fellow spirit when I meet one. I'm sure CAPCLUG would want me to stay."

"CAPCLUG would want no such thing," the Critic told him soberly. "They would want you to escape, so that they could examine and dissect your experiences in detail. Your American friends are sadly infatuated with the supposed potency of rational, panoptic, digital analysis. Believe me, please—the enormous turbulence in postmodern society is far larger than any single human mind can comprehend, with or without computer-aided perception or the finest computer-assisted frameworks of sociological analysis." The Critic gazed at his workstation, like a herpetologist studying a cobra. "Your CAPCLUG friends will go to their graves never realizing that every vital impulse in human life is entirely prerational."

"Well, I'm certainly not leaving here before I figure *that* out," Eddy said. "I plan to help you fight the good fight, sir."

The Critic shrugged, and smiled. "Thank you for just proving me right, young man. Of course a young American hero is welcome to die in Europe's political struggles. I'd hate to break an old tradition."

Glass shattered. A steaming lump of dry ice flew through the window, skittered across the office floor, and began gently dissolving. Acting entirely on instinct, Eddy dashed forward, grabbed it barehanded, and threw it back out the window.

"Are you okay?" Frederika said.

"Sure," Eddy said, surprised.

"That was a chemical gas bomb," Frederika said. She gazed at him as if expecting him to drop dead on the spot.

"Apparently the chemical frozen into the ice was not very toxic," the Critic surmised.

"I don't think it was a gas bomb at all," Eddy said, gazing out the window. "I think it was just a big chunk of dry ice. You Europeans are completely paranoid."

He saw with astonishment that there was a medieval pageant taking place in the street. The followers of the Moral Referee—there were some three or four hundred of them, well-organized and marching forward in grimly disciplined silence—apparently had a weakness for medieval jerkins, fringed capes, and colored hose. And torches. They were very big on torches.

The entire building shuddered suddenly, and a burglar siren went off. Eddy craned to look. Half a dozen men were battering the door with a hand-held hydraulic ram. They wore visored helmets and metal armor, which gleamed in the summer daylight. "We're being attacking by goddamn knights in shining armor," Eddy said. "I can't believe they're doing this in broad daylight!"

"The football game just started," Frederika said. "They have picked the perfect moment. Now they can get away with anything."

"Do these window bars come out?" Eddy said, shaking them.

"No. Thank goodness."

"Then hand me some of those data-disks," he demanded. "No, not those shrimpy ones—give me the full thirty-centimeter jobs."

He threw the window up and began pelting the crowd below with flung megabytage. The disks had vicious aerodynamics and were hefty and sharp-edged. He was rewarded with an angry barrage of bricks, which shattered windows all along the second and third floors.

"They're very angry now," Frederika shouted over the wailing alarm and roar of the crowd below. The three of them crouched under a table. "Yeah," Eddy said. His blood was boiling. He picked up a long, narrow printer, dashed across the room, and launched it between the bars. In reply, half-a-dozen long metal darts—short javelins, really—flew through up through the window and imbedded themselves in the office ceiling.

"How'd they get those through Customs?" Eddy shouted.

"Must've made them last night."

He laughed. "Should I throw 'em back? I can fetch them if I stand on a chair."

"Don't, don't," Frederika shouted. "Control yourself! Don't kill anyone, it's not professional."

"I'm not professional," Eddy said.

"Get down here," Frederika commanded. When he refused, she scrambled from the beneath the table and body-slammed him against the wall. She pinned Eddy's arms, flung herself across him with almost erotic intensity, and hissed into his ear. "Save yourself while you can! This is only a Wende."

"Stop that," Eddy shouted, trying to break her grip. More bricks came through the window, tumbling past their feet.

"If they kill these worthless intellectuals," she muttered hotly, "there will be a thousand more to take their place. But if you don't leave this building right now, you'll die here."

"Christ, I know that," Eddy shouted, finally flinging her backward with a rasp at her sandpaper coat. "Quit being such a loser."

"Eddy, listen!" Frederika yelled, knotting her gloved fists. "Let me save your life! You'll owe me later! Go home to your parents in America, and don't worry about the Wende. This is all we ever do—it's all we are really good for."

"Hey, I'm good at this too!" Eddy announced. A brick barked his ankle. In sudden convulsive fury, he upended a table and slammed it against a broken window, as a shield. As bricks thudded against the far side of the table, he shouted defiance. He felt superhuman. Her attempt to talk sense had irritated him enormously.

The door broke in downstairs, with a concussive blast. Screams echoed up the stairs. "That's torn it!" Eddy said.

He snatched up a multiplugged power outlet, dashed across the room, and kicked the office door open. With a shout, he jumped onto the landing, swinging the heavy power strip over his head.

The Critic's academic cadre were no physical match for the Referee's knights in armor; but their fire extinguishers were surprisingly effective weapons. They coated everything in white caustic soda and filled the air with great blinding, billowing wads of flying, freezing droplets. It was clear that the defenders had been practicing.

The sight of the desperate struggle downstairs overwhelmed Eddy. He jumped down the stairs three at a time and flung himself into the midst of the battle. He conked a soda-covered helmet with a vicious overhead swing of his power strip, then slipped and fell heavily on his back.

He began wrestling desperately across the soda-slick floor with a half-blinded knight. The knight clawed his visor up. Beneath the metal mask the knight was, if anything, younger than himself. He looked like a nice kid. He clearly meant well. Eddy hit the kid in the jaw as hard as he could, then began slamming his helmeted head into the floor.

Another knight kicked Eddy in the belly. Eddy fell off his victim, got up, and went for the new attacker. The two of them, wrestling clumsily, were knocked off balance by a sudden concerted rush through the doorway; a dozen Moral raiders slammed through, flinging torches and bottles of flaming gel. Eddy slapped his new opponent across the eyes with his soda-daubed hand, then lurched to his feet and jammed the loose spex back onto his face. He began coughing violently. The air was full of smoke; he was smothering.

He lurched for the door. With the panic strength of a drowning man, he clawed and jostled his way free.

Once outside the data-haven, Eddy realized that he was one of dozens of people daubed head to foot with white foam. Wheezing, coughing, collapsing against the side of the building, he and his fellow refugees resembled veterans of a monster cream-pie fight.

They didn't, and couldn't, recognize him as an enemy. The caustic soda was eating its way into Eddy's cheap jumpsuit, reducing the bubbled fabric to weeping red rags.

Wiping his lips, ribs heaving, Eddy looked around. The spex had guarded his eyes, but their filth subroutine had crashed badly. The internal screen was frozen. Eddy shook the spex with his foamy hands, finger snapped at them, whistled aloud. Nothing.

He edged his way along the wall.

At the back of the crowd, a tall gentleman in a medieval episcopal miter was shouting orders through a bullhorn. Eddy wandered through the crowd until he got closer to the man. He was a tall, lean man, in his late forties, in brocaded vestments, a golden cloak and white gloves.

This was the Moral Referee. Eddy considered jumping this distinguished gentleman and pummeling him, perhaps wrestling his bullhorn away and shouting contradictory orders through it.

But even if he dared to try this, it wouldn't do Eddy much good. The Referee with the bullhorn was shouting in German. Eddy didn't speak German. Without his spex he couldn't read German. He didn't understand Germans or their issues or their history. In point of fact he had no real reason at all to be in Germany.

The Moral Referee noticed Eddy's fixed and calculating gaze. He lowered his bullhorn, leaned down a little from the top of his portable mahogany pulpit, and said something to Eddy in German.

"Sorry," Eddy said, lifting his spex on their neck chain. "Translation program crashed."

The Referee examined him thoughtfully. "Has the acid in that foam damaged your spectacles?" he said, in excellent English.

"Yes, sir," Eddy said. "I think I'll have to strip 'em and blow-dry the chips."

The Referee reached within his robe and handed Eddy a monogrammed linen kerchief. "You might try this, young man."

"Thanks a lot," Eddy said. "I appreciate that, really."

"Are you wounded?" the Referee said, with apparently genuine concern.

"No, sir. I mean, not really."

"Then you'd better return to the fight," the Referee said, straightening. "I know we have them on the run. Be of good cheer. Our cause is just." He lifted his bullhorn again and resumed shouting.

The first floor of the building had caught fire. Groups of the Referee's people were hauling linked machines into the street and smashing them to fragments on the pavement. They hadn't managed to knock the bars from the windows, but they had battered some enormous holes through the walls. Eddy watched, polishing his spex.

Well above the street, the wall of third floor began to disintegrate.

Moral Knights had broken into the office where Eddy had last seen the Cultural Critic. They had hauled their hydraulic ram up the stairs with them. Now its blunt nose was smashing through the brick wall as if it were stale cheese.

Fist-sized chunks of rubble and mortar cascaded to the street, causing the raiders below to billow away. In seconds, the raiders on the third floor had knocked a hole in the wall the size of a manhole cover. First they flung down an emergency ladder. Then office furniture began tumbling out to smash to the pavement below: voice mailboxes, canisters of storage disks, red-spined European law books, network routers, tape-backup units, color monitors . . .

A trench coat flew out the hole and pinwheeled slowly to earth. Eddy recognized it at once. It was Frederika's sandpaper coat. Even in the midst of shouting chaos, with an evil billowing of combusting plastic now belching from the library's windows, the sight of that fluttering coat hooked Eddy's awareness. There was something in that coat. In its sleeve pocket. The key to his airport locker.

Eddy dashed forward, shoved three knights aside, and grabbed up the coat for himself. He winced and skipped aside as a plummeting office chair smashed to the street, narrowly missing him. He glanced up frantically.

He was just in time to see them throw out Frederika.

• • •

The tide was leaving Düsseldorf, and with it all the schooling anchovies of Europe. Eddy sat in the departure lounge balancing eighteen separate pieces of his spex on a Velcro lap table.

"Do you need this?" Frederika asked him.

"Oh yeah," Eddy said, accepting the slim chromed tool. "I dropped my dental pick. Thanks a lot." He placed it carefully into his black travel bag.

"I'm not going to Chattanooga, now or ever," Frederika told him. "So you might as well forget that; that can't be part of the bargain."

"Change your mind," Eddy suggested. "Forget this Barcelona flight, and come transatlantic with me. We'll have a fine time in Chattanooga. There's some very deep people I want you to meet."

"I don't want anybody to meet," Frederika muttered darkly. "And I don't want you to show me off to your little hackerboy friends."

Frederika had taken a hard beating in the riot, covering the Critic's successful retreat across the rooftop. Her hair had been scorched during the battle, and it had burst from its meticulous braiding like badly overused steel wool. She had a black eye, and her cheek and jaw were scorched and shiny with medicinal gel. Although Eddy had broken her fall, her three-story tumble to the street had sprained her ankle, wrenched her back, and barked both knees.

And she had lost her spex.

"You look just fine," Eddy told her. "You're very interesting, that's the point. You're deep! That's the appeal, you see? You're a spook, and a European, and a woman—those are all very deep entities, in my opinion." He smiled.

Eddy's left elbow felt hot and swollen inside his spare shirt; his chest, ribs, and left leg were mottled with enormous bruises. He had a bloodied lump on the back of his head where he'd smashed down into the rubble, catching her.

Altogether, they were not an unusual couple among the departing Wende folk cramming the Düsseldorf airport. As a whole, the crowd seemed to be suffering a massive collective hangover—harsh enough to put many of them into slings and casts. And yet it was amazing how contented, almost smug, many of the vast crowd seemed as they departed their pocket catastrophe. They were wan and pale, yet cheerful, like people recovering from flu.

"I don't feel well enough to be deep," Frederika said. "But you did save my life, Eddy. I do owe you something. But it has to be something reasonable."

"Don't let it bother you," Eddy told her nobly, rasping at the surface of a tiny circuit-board with a plastic spudger. "I mean, I didn't even break your fall, strictly speaking. Mostly I just kept you from landing on your head."

"You did save my life," she repeated quietly. "That crowd would have killed me in the street if not for you."

"You saved the Critic's life. I imagine that's a bigger deal."

"I was paid to do that," Frederika said, and winced. "Anyway, I didn't save the bastard. I just did my job. He was saved by his own cleverness. He's been through a dozen of these damned things." She stretched cautiously, shifting in her bean-bag. "So have I, for that matter. . . . I must be a real fool. I endure a lot to live my precious life. . . ." She took a deep breath. "Barcelona, *yo te quiero*."

"I'm just glad we checked out of that clinic in time to catch our flights," Eddy told her. "Could you believe all those soccer kids in there? They sure were having fun. . . . Why couldn't they be that good-tempered *before* they beat the hell out of each other? Some things are just a mystery, I guess."

"I hope you have learned a good lesson from this," Frederika said.

"Sure have," Eddy nodded. He blew dried crud from the point of his spudger, then picked up a chrome pinch clamp and threaded a tiny screw through the earpiece of his spex. "I can see a lot of deep potential in the Wende. It's true that a few dozen people got killed here, but the city must have made an absolute fortune. That's got to look promising for the Chattanooga city council. And a Wende offers a lot of very useful exposure and influence for a cultural networking group like CAPCLUG."

"You've learned nothing at all," she groaned. "I don't know why I hoped it would be different."

"I admit it—in the heat of the action I got a little carried away," Eddy said. "But my only real regret is that you won't come with me to America, Or, if you'd really rather, take me to Barcelona. Either way, the way I see it, you need someone to look after you for a while."

"You're going to rub my sore feet, yes?" Frederika said sourly. "How generous you are."

"I dumped my creep girlfriend. My dad will pick up my tab. I can help you manage better. I can improve your life. I'm a nice guy."

"I don't want to be rude," she said, "but after this, the thought of being touched is repulsive. I don't need any nice Yankee boyfriend to take me on romantic vacations." She shook her head, with finality. "I'm sorry, Eddy, but I can't give you what you want."

Eddy sighed, examined the crowd for a while, then repacked the segments of his spex and closed his Velcro board. At last he spoke up again. "Do you virch?"

"What?"

"Do you do virtuality?"

She was silent for a long moment, then looked him in the eye. "You don't do anything really strange or sick on the wires, do you, Edward?"

"There's hardly any subjective time lag if you use high-capacity transatlantic fiber," Eddy said.

"Oh. I see."

"What have you got to lose? If you don't like it, hang up."

Frederika tucked her hair back, examined the departure board, looked at her shoes. "And would this make you happy?"

"No," Eddy said. "But it'd sure make me a whole lot more of what I already am."

VICTOR PELEVIN

THE YULETIDE CYBERPUNK YARN, OR CHRISTMAS_EVE-117.DIR

(1996)

Translated from the Russian by Alex Shvartsman

ONE doesn't have to be an expert on so-called culture to notice that interest in poetry is declining in practically every country worldwide. Perhaps this is caused by the political changes taking place all over the world in recent decades. Poetry, a distant descendant of ancient magic incantations, tends to prosper under totalitarian and despotic regimes, due to a peculiar resonance. Such regimes, as a rule, are themselves of a magical nature and therefore organically capable of nourishing other branches of magic. But under the gaze (or rather gazes) of the rational hydra of the free market, poetry withers into impotence or even irrelevance.

Fortunately, this doesn't mean its doom. It merely shifts away from the focus of public interest into its far periphery; into the realm of university campuses, neighborhood periodicals, bulletin boards, variety shows, and evening parties. Moreover, it can't be said that it leaves the focus entirely. It manages to retain its position in that molten region where the wandering, cloudy gaze of humanity is aimed. Poetry lives on in the brands of automobiles, hotels, and chocolate bars, in the names given to boats, tampons, and computer viruses.

The latter is, perhaps, the most surprising. By its nature the computer virus is nothing more than a soulless sequence of micro-assembler commands that stealthily attaches itself to other programs, so that one fine day it can turn the computer into a useless pile of metal and plastic. And these assassin programs are given names such as Leonardo, Cascade, Yellow Rose, and so on. Perhaps the poetry inherent in these names is nothing more than a return to the abovementioned incantations. Perhaps it's an attempt to somehow humanize, animate, and propitiate the dead and almighty world of semiconductors, with their electronic impulses sweeping through as they define human destiny. For even the riches people strive toward their entire lives aren't measured by basements filled with gold these days, but by strings of ones and zeroes stored in the memory of a bank's computer, utterly meaningless to the uninitiated. All that is achieved by a successful entrepreneur over the course of many years filled with anxiety and toil, before a heart attack or a bullet forces them to switch to another form of business, is merely an electric current within a microchip transistor so small it can only be seen through a microscope.

Therefore it is no surprise that a computer virus that completely paralyzed the large Russian city of Petroplahovsk for several days was named Christmas Eve. (In antivirus software and computer manuals it's referred to as PN-117.DIR but we don't know what those numbers and Latin characters mean.) The name Christmas Eve can't be considered a pure tribute to poetry. You see, some viruses activate at a certain time or on a certain day. For example, the Leonardo virus was designed to perform its dastardly deed on Leonardo da Vinci's birthday. Likewise, the Christmas Eve virus would wake from hibernation on Christmas Eve. As to its function, we shall attempt to describe it in general terms, without getting mired in technical details. After all, only experts would care what cluster PN-117.DIR wrote itself into, or how precisely it altered the File Allocation Table. What matters to the rest of us is that this virus destroyed the databases stored in the computer, and it did so in a rather unusual manner. The information wasn't damaged or erased; instead it was carefully remixed.

Let's imagine a computer located somewhere in City Hall, which contained all the details of city life (which, by the way, was precisely the case in Petroplahovsk). While this computer was functioning properly, its memory resembled an assembled Rubik's cube. The blue side contained information about municipal services, the red side city budget data; the Mayor's personal bank information was on the yellow side and his Rolodex was on the green side. When activated, PN-117.DIR began to twist the Rubik's cube in deranged and unpredictable ways, even as it preserved each square and the cube as a whole. To build on this analogy, when antivirus programs check the computer's memory they measure the sides of the cube, and so long as those sides remain the same size, the programs conclude that the computer is virus-free. Therefore, any disk auditors, and even the latest heuristic analyzers, were powerless against PN-117.DIR. The nameless programmer who, for some reason, set out on the path of abstract evil, had created a tiny masterpiece. He even earned grudging and contemptuous praise from Doctor Lozinskiy himself, the highest authority in the field of computer demonology.

Nothing is known about the creator of the virus. According to rumor, it was written by the same mad engineer Gerasimov in whose case the laws against cruelty to animals were applied for the first time in the annals of the Petroplahovsk City Court. This was a huge case, so we'll rehash the details only in general terms. Gerasimov had been mentally unbalanced from birth and belonged to that thin strata of our society who would not understand or accept progress, and who hated any seedlings of the bright future that manage to rise toward the sun through the many layers of pavement that is our sorrowful present. On this basis he developed a persecution complex; for him, the main symbol of the changes that have taken place in our country were for some reason symbolized by a bull terrier. Perhaps this happened because many people in the sixteen-story building where he lived owned dogs of this popular breed. In the elevator, Gerasimov often found himself in the company of three, four, and sometimes five bull terriers simultaneously. As a result, Gerasimov sold his meager belongings and took on a considerable amount of debt for a person of his means in order to purchase his own bull terrier.

Gerasimov's neighbors were initially thrilled by this change in his attitude. At first glance it seemed to demonstrate real commitment on his part to adjust to the shifting circumstances and to live in lockstep with the times. But once word spread of what Gerasimov had named his dog, it shocked the animal lovers in the building. It turned out that he had named his bull terrier Mumu.* In the evenings, Gerasimov would go on walks to the nearby river and oftentimes idle on the shore, staring into the middle of the stream and thinking about something intensely. Mumu played nearby, occasionally rubbing up against her owner's leg and staring into his face with her trusting little red eyes.

The dog owners in Gerasimov's building believed these walks to be of a clearly provocative nature. This led to the aforementioned court case, where the mayor of Petroplahovsk, who was a passionate fan of bull terriers, personally weighed in. The animal was taken away from Gerasimov.

"Gerasimov hates everything Mumu represents," the prosecutor had said in court. "Rather, Mumu represents everything Gerasimov hates. For thousands upon thousands of Russians the bull terrier has become a symbol of success, optimism, and faith in the rebirth of the new Russia! Gerasimov reaches his paws toward Mumu because they're too short to reach those this dog symbolizes. But we're asking for the animal to be taken away from him not because of his beliefs, however we feel about those. No, we demand this because the poor pup is in danger!"

Gerasimov lost the case and Mumu was confiscated by the authorities. She was destined for a special elite dog shelter where bull terriers, pit bulls, and wolfhounds that had belonged to the deceased captains of industry whiled away their days. The mayor personally donated money for Mumu's upkeep and for a special cage in which the dog would be shipped.

Perhaps that is how the rumor started that Gerasimov wrote PN-117.DIR in order to exact revenge upon the mayor. But this version seems extremely unlikely. First, a programmer capable of writing a virus of Christmas Eve's caliber would

* This is a reference to a classic short story: "Mumu" by Ivan Turgenev. Gerasim, a deaf and mute serf, rescues a dog named Mumu and subsequently drowns her in the river when pressured to get rid of her by his master. The story is a scathing indictment of the institution of serfdom.

be unlikely to take out his jealousy over the success of others on an innocent bull terrier; he would undoubtedly be wealthy enough to buy ten bull terriers. Second, Gerasimov had never been to City Hall, and it was highly doubtful he could infect the computer with a virus through the internet. Third, and most importantly, the theory of Gerasimov's authorship is entirely devoid of logic. As the prosecutor had said, Gerasimov reached for Mumu because his paws had been too short to touch anyone capable of slapping him. Gerasimov was too much of a coward to try and hurt someone with real power. Petroplahovsk's mayor, Alexander Vanykov, better known around town by the nickname of Al Spinoza, undoubtedly possessed real power. He had earned this nickname not because he was interested in philosophy, but because early in his career he had killed several people with a Spinoza dubbing needle.

Vanykov was one of the three individuals who upheld all Petroplahovsk. (One might be tempted to imagine three muscular Titans, supporting a slice of the Earth, covered in streets and buildings on their shoulders. But let's just focus on Vanykov instead, as the other Titans have nothing whatsoever to do with our narrative.) Vanykov primarily controlled prostitution and the drug trade. No one knows for certain why he would ever want to take on mayoral duties on top of that. One could imagine how he might have become desirous of the position: he must have looked out of the tinted windows of his limo on the way from the bathhouse to his office. And as he watched the gray-brown little houses of his hometown roll by, he may have noticed a billboard asking all citizens to cast their vote in the mayoral election. They say Vanykov was in the habit of picking at his buttons. So he must've been fumbling with a button on his jacket or trousers when suddenly a thought occurred to him: it would be far better to be on the take himself than to pay off some other mayor.

The rest was only a matter of execution. Having decided to run for mayor, Vanykov first held a meeting with his "panthers." That's what a person who controls prostitution within a city neighborhood was called, roughly an equivalent of a police captain. He explained that if any of them failed to mobilize the girls they supervised to campaign for him, Vanykov would pick up a sewing needle and personally turn that panther into a kitty cat. The rest was explained by Vanykov's aide: all female campaign workers must look chaste and innocent, and not wear trousers under any circumstances as that might be off-putting to the elderly and other conservative elements of the electorate.

A very expensive campaign manager was called in from Moscow. Vanykov had heard many stories about how this specialist had run the parliamentary campaign in the neighboring city of Ekatirinodibinsk for the local "godmother" Daria Cleves. The main focus of the campaign was combatting organized crime. Its slogan, circulated on thousands of flyers, read: *The only way to deal with thieves is by electing Daria Cleves.*

Vanykov asked the campaign manager to arrange something similar for him. The specialist took a week to study the matter and presented a detailed analysis of the psychological situation in the city, an entire folder of bifurcated graphs, tables, and pie charts. The public opinion polls in the city showed that, unlike

Ekatirinodibinsk, where the electorate really hated the mafia, the citizens of Petroplahovsk, which derived much of its income from tourism, were inherently if vaguely chauvinistic. They hated some abstract "bastards" and "shitheads" who were "taking advantage" and "making life difficult." When asked who those bastards were, the citizens would generally shrug and say, "You know, the ones. Everyone knows them." Therefore, it was recommended that the campaign be based on the mayor's willingness to stand up to those "bastards" without specifying who the bastards were, so as to avoid "splitting the electorate," as the specialist put it. The proposed campaign slogan read, *Tell bastard shitheads to buzz off; cast a vote for Vanykov.*

When Vanykov was shown this couplet that—along with the folder full of graphs—cost one hundred and eighty thousand dollars, he thought he was in the wrong line of work. This professional jealously had woken the Al Spinoza in him, and the Muscovite expert barely made it out of Petroplahovsk alive. The slogan had to be changed, in large part because everyone involved in the campaign felt that if there existed a bastard shithead in Petroplahovsk, it was Vanykov himself. Therefore, the final draft of the slogan became, *Only Vanykov can save us from dictatorship and chaos.* Vanykov ran on this platform and won with a considerable margin.

As a mayor, Vanykov followed an ancient Chinese proverb that stated the people should know nothing about the best of rulers, other than his name. He organized a holiday called "Viva la Petroplahovsk" twice, and there's absolutely nothing whatsoever to be said about it. Once he met with the editors of local newspapers in his office, where he gently and delicately tried to explain to them that expressions such as "bandit" and "thief"—much-abused by the media—have long since ceased to be politically correct. (Vanykov read this term from a scrap of paper prepared for him by an aide who carbon copied it from American English.) Moreover, Vanykov said, such words can confuse people. The word "thief" supposes that the person being so called might climb out of his Lincoln town car and in through someone's window to steal a piece of meat out of their pot of soup (the transcript records the collective laughter of the editors), whereas the term "bandit" suggests this person is being sought by the police (another bout of laughter recorded in the transcript). When asked what expression should best denote the abovementioned categories of citizens, Vanykov replied that he was personally partial to the term "special economic entity" or "SEE." For those journalists who prefer flowery and figurative language he suggested the phrase "Newest Russian."* While this expression no longer surprises anyone, it's interesting to note that its true author was Vanykov's aide.

That was, perhaps, the only notable contribution Vanykov left behind. One might also add that during his brief reign, Petroplahovsk newspapers called him a patron and a philanthropist. Both of those epithets—even if neither was quite adequate or deserved—referred to his role in the fate of Mumu the bull terrier.

---

* "New Russian" was a common stereotype in the 1990s referring to people who quickly made a lot of money during the collapse of the Soviet Union via criminal means, and whose intelligence and good taste did not equal their newfound wealth.

In other words, were it not for the terrible events caused by the broken computer in City Hall, Vanykov's story would've been neither unusual nor noteworthy.

Like all young technocrats, Vanykov treated the computer with great piety and strived to maximize the ways in which it could help make his life easier. All the details of his multifaceted activities were entered into several databases, which could only be accessed with a password. A suite of organizational software and a built-in calendar could handle practically all Vanykov's daily workload. Vanykov's presence in the office was not required, and therefore seldom. Any information about urgent matters reached him via several pagers he wore on his belt (one of which, with a golden two-headed eagle on a white background, only ever rang two or three times); the rest of his business was easily dispatched by his secretary. The workday at City Hall began when she turned on the computer and printed the daily itinerary. For example, when the printout stated that it was necessary to check on the status of preparations for the heating season, collect the protection money from a Georgian restaurant, and water the flowers, she calmly forwarded the first two notifications to the appropriate individuals, picked up the can from the windowsill, and went to get water from the faucet.

That's roughly what happened on the ill-fated day when several major strokes had already occurred under the plastic skull of the computer. Vanykov hadn't yet sobered up from the New Year's bender;* the secretary was handling ongoing business in the office; and beyond the window, the city covered in silver dust was quiet, bright, and mysterious.

It began when a crew of construction workers (in simpler terms, a trio of women in sleeveless orange vests, the sort that always scrape with ice breakers at highway curbsides) received a very strange order on a City Hall letterhead. It contained unequivocal orders to "take out Kishkerov," signed by Al Spinoza.

It's worth noting that these women, just like everyone else, knew who Mayor Vanykov really was. Everything related to him was shrouded in a murky and hypnotic halo. A great many among the municipal workers hoped deep within their souls that Vanykov might notice them and, if they were to pass some ambiguous test, a moment would come when he'd uplift them from the spare gray tedium of everyday life to a magical and frightening criminal underworld. Apparently, these poor women, poisoned by Mexican soap operas and radioactive beets, harbored similar hopes, made all the more touching because of their extreme absurdity. They knew well that Kishkerov was one of the most powerful people in Petroplahovsk, made apparent by the fact that he dared to engage in open conflict against City Hall. It must've been quite difficult to "take him out" since his estate was heavily guarded. The bodyguards who found his body in the garden shed, mangled by ice picks, for the longest time couldn't figure out how it had happened. None of them could imagine that three grim broads who were there to clear the paths in the garden might have had anything to do with it. By the way, it only just occurred to us that these women might have been motivated not

* Russian Christmas takes place after New Year's, in early January, following an Orthodox calendar.

by some impossible and romantic hope for a new life, but by the work ethic instilled into them back in the Soviet times.

At the same time, four professional killers in the employ of Vanykov, who were whiling away their time at a billiards hall in a suburban resort, drinking diet Coke and reading trashy newspapers, received a letter arrogantly signed "Mayor Vanykov." In that letter, he demanded that Main Street be *devoid of all bumps* by evening. These were experienced killers, but even they were stumped. They came up with a list of the *bumps* that had offices or some other business along the city's main street (which was indeed called Main Street) and this list was two pages long. The killers reached out to their friendly associates for assistance.

It's not worth revisiting the terrible slaughter that occurred on Main Street that day. Television, ever hungry for the spectacle of human suffering, replayed the clips of what the street turned into after a cavalcade of trucks filled with killers had come through. There's something shameful about the enthusiasm with which a young reporter explained which house was blown up by the Bumblebee grenade launcher, which facade was cracked with the Fly missile, and why the secret Potemkin device destroyed the interior walls while leaving the outer building walls untouched.

The other events of that day seem insignificant in comparison to the massacre. For example, when a racketeering ring—a group of people who were a bit slow but good at following orders—received a fax from City Hall asking when the *garbage would be burned*, the life of Police Major Kozulin, who was being held hostage for failing to pay a percentage of his ill-gotten gains, hung by a thread for several minutes. They'd already poured kerosene over his body, and only the cannonade coming from Main Street made them forget about him, thereby saving his life.

Incredibly, the mad City Hall computer forced some citizens to experience positive emotions. Ecclesiast Kolpakov, the owner of the "Sex-Elegant" shop, had been engaged in the highly risky undertaking of leaving Vanykov's "protection" for the protection of his competitor, Grisha the Scorpion. He'd long been bracing himself for retribution and was pleasantly surprised to receive an exquisitely polite Christmas greeting fax, signed Al Spinoza. On the other hand, the mayors of fifty cities geographically closest to Petroplahovsk experienced mild confusion having received the following missive:

To the mayor of [here the mayor's name and their city was automatically inserted by the computer, which sent the volley of faxes on the orders of the secretary]:

Hey dumbass, you will either pay me, or you will pay nobody, do you understand? Fork over six months' worth of fees by February, or I will pull one leg and Grisha the Scorpion will pull the other, and there will be nothing left of you, asshole. Think about it.

Sincerely yours,
Vanykov
Mayor, Petroplahovsk.

The mayors of larger cities only laughed at such an impudent demand, but there were those among the recipients who took the threat seriously, evidenced by the untimely death of Grisha the Scorpion a month later. He was shot by unidentified individuals while attending the dress rehearsal of Beckett's *Waiting for Godot*, premiering at his local theater.

Vanykov was, of course, made aware of what was happening in the city. For some time, he thought that Petroplahovsk was under attack by some mayor from a neighboring city, like in a violent movie. But it soon became clear that all participants were certain they were acting on orders from Vanykov. Finally, it became apparent that all orders that already caused so much damage in the city had been sent by the City Hall computer. And since the secretary was beyond reproach, the problem had to be the computer itself. It's unclear whether Vanykov had been aware of the existence of computer viruses. Perhaps he treated what was happening as a personal affront by the computer, which he viewed as an animate being. His highly emotional reaction supports this theory: Vanykov burst into his office, drew a nickel-plated Beretta from its shoulder holster, pushed away the squealing secretary, and unloaded fifteen nine-millimeter bullets into the fancy Pentium 100 PC with its real Intel processor. Pieces of cracked plastic, shards of glass, scraps of colored wire, and a scattering of microchips that looked like dead cockroaches flew across the floor.

Even after the source of all the problems had been destroyed, the echo of its devastating activity continued to reverberate. For example, three days after the Main Street massacre, all the city prostitutes were gathered at a suburban sports complex. The mayor's Director of Public Relations, his face red with shame and confusion, read to them a greeting from City Hall, where they were called darlings, dear girls, and the great hope of Russian winter sports. There are several more such examples, but they aren't especially interesting, save for the one concerning Vanykov personally.

After the events described herein, he suffered from serious depression and retreated to his suburban estate, which resembled a castle more than a house. His comrades and friends visited to console him, and he gradually calmed down—after all, life is life. The man in charge of combatting organized crime brought him some quality Moroccan cannabis, and Vanykov ordered his people to leave him be, then spent several days in an artificial paradise as poetized by Charles Baudelaire, in search of peace and oblivion. Whether or not he found it, no one will ever know, as his life was tragically cut short by an event so phantasmagoric it even surprised the crime beat editor for the *Evening Petroplahovsk*.

Let's make use of the police reconstruction of the event. Around eight o'clock at night, a strange package was delivered to Vanykov's home—a sizable box wrapped in cloth. Vanykov, who was finishing another joint at the time (it was found next to his body), carelessly opened the box and, before he could react, the hungry and half-asphyxiated bull terrier Mumu lunged at his chest.

We've never smoked pot and don't know exactly what the poor mayor experienced when a silent, short-legged white monster with narrowed eyes sprung at him from inside the cage, which was revealed once several layers of wrapping had been removed. We can only suppose that from an existential point of view, this was one of the most powerful feelings of his life. The reason for this was the same as all the other disasters in the city—the bull terrier was bound for the shelter on the same day when the virus reshuffled all the information in the computer's memory. Instead of the Dog Promised Land, the frenzied Mumu had spent several days in the cold storage container and had been delivered to the mayor's home. It's difficult to believe this was a coincidence, but all other explanations are even less likely.

Surprisingly, Vanykov's guards, who found their boss with a torn-out throat and an expression of abject horror on his still face, left the dog alive. The reason for this was basic human chauvinism. The guards thought so little of animals that they considered it pointless to exact revenge upon a dog for the death of a person. They probably likened it to trying to shoot a brick that had fallen from a roof onto someone's head. Mumu was confined to a shed and then, after the frantic activity associated with the funeral had ceased, returned to engineer Gerasimov, who subsequently disappeared without a trace.

Gerasimov was only seen twice after that: one time in the bait and tackle store where he purchased a special drill for cutting ice holes, and again on the following morning, in the field far beyond the city. He was wearing some sort of a ridiculous robe, sewn from an old cotton blanket, a greasy *ushanka* hat, and a canvas bag filled with diskettes slung from his shoulder. A crooked wooden staff in his hand made him seem like an ancient traveler. Gerasimov was bandaged in several places, but he appeared enlightened and victorious, and his eyes were like two tunnels at the end of which glimmered a vague, unsteady but undoubtedly extant light.

BEF

WONDERAMA

(1998)

Translated from the Spanish by the author

Amid the almost inaudible machines humming, nobody notices the intruder. As usual, it is impossible to know how it broke in, let alone from where. From the server, it passes to a specific terminal and there it sets in, like a carcinoma, thriving and devouring healthy digital tissue without being noticed.

MARCH 21, 1974

Spring's here; my Radio Shack clock radio woke me up with that Spanish pop tune of the nuns at the sea. I rose and shone and first thing I did was turn on the telly. I caught the last segment of that game show where that old guy dressed as a kid. He asked one of the participants:

"So, pal, do you keep your go-kart or do you go for the Big Fat Mystery Surprize?"

"Keep the kart," I thought.

"I'll get the Big Fat Mystery Surprize, sir!" said the kid.

As usual, behind the Surprize's curtain was a Muebles Troncoso full dining-room set. Bet his dads were flipping, not him.

He deserved it. Dummy.

I showered and went downstairs.

"Hi, honey," Mom smiled and served breakfast: Icee and Twinkies. Dad joined later, he just got coffee. We talked about the World Cup. Dad doesn't like Borja,* but I think he's a bomb player. I noticed it was very late for the gig, I had to split. As I was on my way out, Dad said:

"Lalo, there's something for you at the garage. It's packed in a Taconazo Popis† box."

There it was, the hippest go-kart helmet, all yellow with purple spirals and sprinkled with happy faces. Grooviest gear ever. I've seen it yesterday and now Dad got it for me. I put it on and zipped for the gig. It was very late.

When I got to Cookierama, the Boss scolded me for being two minutes late, but then he smiled and told me I was transferred to a new machine, the one that punches the eyes and smiles on the Cinnamon Smileys, my favorite Happy Face-shaped cookies.

After work I went for a Whopper combo. On my way home I passed by a Cinerama Theater and saw they were showing *Star Wars*. I bought a ticket. It's the coolest film ever! At dinner, Mom served hot dogs and 7UP. When we were done, Dad said:

"Lalo, there's a surprise for you at your bedroom."

There was a C-3PO and R2-D2 quilt on my bed.

MARCH 22, 1974

Today was the World Cup final. Of course the National Team won. All Wonderama went bananas and celebrated on the streets. We hopped into our Ford Galaxies and joined the party, waving our flag in the streets, as did all the city and the country. In the afternoon, the President unveiled Borja's monument on the city's Main Square, honoring the 142 goals he scored during the World Cup. We were there, too. It was specially touching when our National Anthem sounded. I think Dad's take on Borja has changed.

MARCH 23, 1974

Coolest day ever! Everything was overshadowed by the landing of a man on the moon. We watched it all on the TV. Dad was so touched that a tear slipped out. When Neil Armstrong said it was a small step for man and a giant leap for mankind, I got goosebumps all over.

It's official, I'll become an astronaut when I grow up.

* Enrique Borja (b. 1945), a legendary soccer player. His controversial style made him as loved as he was hated while playing at Club América and for the Mexican national team.

† El Taconazo Popis, meaning "The Hip Step," was a popular shoe-store chain famous for its extravagant, psychedelic designs.

MARCH 24, 1974

I got up late, it's Saturday, dude. Turned on the TV to watch the credits of the last cartoon. As that variety show that Mom never misses rolled in, I hopped on the go-kart and went to cruise through the park.

The National Flag waved in the center of the park, its magnificent colorful circles on white and the word *Wonder* on red type. Every time I see it my heart rejoices.

I sat on a bench to do nothing.

I was still sitting there when a blonde girl in a blue dress sat right beside me.

"Hello there! Lovely day," she said. I replied with a grunt.

"Would you like a piece of my chocolate?" she insisted. I ignored her.

"All righty, I'll have to eat it by myself . . . Mmmh! Yummy!"

For no reason, since I hate chocolate, I turned to her and asked with my dumbest smile:

"Can I have some?"

"Hi! I'm Alice," she said.

"My name's Lalo," I replied.

Without further ado, she got up and walked away. I stared at the candy bar's packaging. It only read "eat me." I unwrapped it and discovered a message scribbled in a child's writing:

REALITY IS FAKE

I returned home, feeling totally out to lunch and spent the rest of the evening playing with my El Santo* action figures, wishing I never had met that chick.

I didn't feel like eating, even though there were Zingers and Mirinda for dinner.

The first warning signal passes unnoticed on the operator's retinal screen. Just one more among millions of decode messages every day. «Terminal X detects an X type error on the Z program.» The operator orders it to keep going and as he sees that the machine carries on, he lets the error slide. These kinds of bugs pop up all the time, especially when beta testing software.

MARCH 25, 1974

I had Ding Dongs and Kool-Aid for breakfast, then Dad took me to the contest show of the old guy dressed as a kid. Ever since I remember, I always longed to

* Rodolfo Guzmán Huerta, El Santo (1917–1984), was the foremost Mexican wrestler, or *luchador*, mostly known abroad for his involuntarily surrealist movies. In his day, he also appeared in comic books that equaled those of American superheroes in popularity.

participate on his show. At the TV studio we came across Batman. I asked for his autograph and told him he was better than El Santo.

The contest was pretty simple; it was about choosing between three keys, one of which opened the Flavor's Gate. I chose the right one and won a jumbo size pack of yogurt and an Avalancha slider. At the end of the show, the host asked me:

"So, tell me, buddy, do you keep your prize or will you go for the Big Fat Mystery Surprize?"

I dunno, I always thought the kids who chose the Surprize were a bunch of dummies, but I replied I'd go for it.

"Okay. Lupita!" He called his assistant hostess. "What's behind gate number two?"

Behind me, I hear the voice of the Magician's rabbit ventriloquist puppet:

"Whoa! He got the ironing board!"*

But what really freaked me out was a sign painted on the wall behind the ironing board that said:

EVERYTHING'S A LIE

Apparently, I was the only one who saw it.

MARCH 26, 1974

Early today, the president addressed the Nation on the TV.

"Good morning, nephews," he said on the screen, dressed in his red blazer, the cartoon animals sewn all over the lapels.†

"Good morning," replied my parents, sitting on the couch.

He delivered a speech concerning a menace threatening Wonderama: a criminal named Fantômas was sabotaging the country and terrorizing it. However, the police were working on the case and everything was under control, no need to worry.

When he was done with his speech, he showed a tin toy monkey that frantically clapped a couple tiny cymbals.‡ I don't know why but it gave me the creeps.

Nothing else happened that day. Nothing interesting.

---

* *En familia con Chabelo* was a kids' contest program that ran for almost fifty years. It was corporate-sponsored, mainly by junk food brands aimed at children. At the end of each episode, contestants had the option to either retain their prize or choose a Big Fat Mystery Surprize; this was known as La Catafixia. The mystery item could be a splendid prize, such as a car, or a frustratingly humble item, such as an ironing board or a kettle. Chabelo was sometimes joined by a ventriloquist magician, Mago Frank, and his puppet bunny, Blas.

† Ramiro Gamboa, aka El Tío Gamboín (Uncle Gamboín), is the Mexican equivalent to the United States' Mister Rogers. He wore a red blazer with cartoon animal patches.

‡ Part of Tío Gamboín's act was showing rare Japanese windup tin toys that back then were unavailable in Mexico.

MARCH 27, 1974

I can't believe it. We were about to have lunch—Cheez Whiz crackers and Hawaiian Punch—when we heard the garbage truck coming down the street. Mom asked me to take the garbage out. Outside, I was shocked to discover that the trashman was a very tall guy wearing a tuxedo, a top hat, and a white mask, so tight that it seemed like paint on his face. He looked menacing but also elegant.* He was Fantômas himself! I was taken by strong feelings; a mix of fear and I don't know what else. He took the trash bag from my trembling hands, ripped it as if it were a brown bag, and said in a deep, growly voice:

"Have you noticed all you eat is junk food, but you don't have cavities or get fat?"

He handed me back the trash can. It was empty, even though it was full of waste a second ago.

"There are neither foul smells nor pollution. Software failures."

He then split, bounding off with giant, superhuman leaps.

I whispered, "Fantômas, you are greater than Batman." But he didn't hear me.

I said nothing to my parents.

MARCH 28, 1974

What's the buzz? It's already late and no matter how I try, I can't remember anything that happened today. Days seem to run by in a jiffy. I wish I could talk about it with someone, but I don't know who.

MARCH 29, 1974

I went skating at Skate-o-rama. I was gulping down a canned vanilla milkshake as I looked at the people on the rink, rolling and spinning. I felt a bit trippy from the disco lights and the music, so I went out for a little air. I was cooling down outside when a kid my age came to me:

"The Bee Gees suck, don't they?" he said.

"What?"

He looked around and then whispered into my ear:

---

* *Fantômas, la amenaza elegante* (*Fantômas, The Elegant Menace*) was a Mexican vigilante comic book published by Editorial Novaro from the late sixties to the mid-nineties. Freely based on the French pulp novels by Marcel Allain and Pierre Souvestre, the comic series depicted the adventures of Fantômas, a criminal mastermind turned into a justice-seeking Robin Hood–type of antihero. It was so popular that even Argentinian author Julio Cortázar wrote a short novella in homage to the character. The character wore a white mask, a tuxedo, and a top hat.

"You seen nobody looks human 'round here?"

He winked and scrammed.

Everything's getting weird.

MARCH 30, 1974

I got a telegram. It was so freaky-deaky, since come to think about it, I don't know anyone. The sender's name was Software Error, and it read:

"Have you noticed that your parents resemble Jorge Rivero and Sasha Montenegro?"*

I freaked out, 'cause suddenly I seemed to recall those names and with them, a bunch of words and terms that I didn't use, but whose meaning I knew, and at evoking them they seemed caked with ancient dust.

Still, there seems to be a ton of stuff I ignore, such as my last name and how old I am.

It's getting serious. The intruder has taken hold of the terminal. The operator only gets a message reporting data interchange between the computers, nothing out of routine. Although required by the manuals, no one conducts the daily checkups, so nobody notices.

MARCH 31, 1974

Just who the fucking hell is Jorge Rivero?! And Sasha Montenegro?!

APRIL 1, 1974

I don't know what's going on. It seems as if I didn't exist. The more I think about reality, the phonier it seems. I feel trapped in someone else's dream that somehow also belongs to me. Maybe someone imagines being me. Or even worse, I'm being dreamed by someone, a supporting character in a recurring fantasy. I haven't noticed that there are no smells or flavors here, only images and sounds that even though false, *are* real. All faces ring a bell even though deep inside I know I never met them. That includes both my parents and, I discovered it in front of the mirror, my own face. It feels as if I am slowly recovering small pieces of a puzzle. The meaning of forgotten words that I shouldn't know at my age (which I still can't recall) turn on somewhere in my mind. I'm certain my name is Eduardo, not Lalo. I know I *am*, but that I am not like *this*. No matter how

---

* Both were famous actors and sex symbols of Mexican cinema from the late sixties through the late eighties. For the record, bombshell Montenegro married former Mexican President José López Portillo (whose time in office ran from 1976 to 1982), more than twenty-five years her senior.

much I review my diary's entries, I can't find any hint of what is going on. I find my writing heartbreakingly frivolous.

And some dates seem inaccurate.

An alarm sign flashes on what should be the operator's visual space. One of the inmates is showing complex brain activity. The instruments scream. But it's three in the morning, no operator sees the alarm. The only action the bumbling security software does is to autolock the entire system.

APRIL 2, 1974

Sheer chaos.

Waking up, all I could hear was a thundering silence.

I opened my eyes to a world stripped of color. Every object seemed built with a silver thread. My room, the house, the street, the cars, people, everything converted (or reverted) into virtual sculptures. My own body was a web of infinite vectors that palely rendered a human being. Discovering this reality meant nothing. Maybe I should feel sorrow or rage, but I only felt an overwhelming sense of loneliness.

"Eduardo Aquino," a deep, growly voice ripped the silence, pronouncing my real name. I wasn't surprised to discover Fantômas behind me, the only untouched element of this color-stripped universe.

Then I recalled.

Hearing my true name brought all my memories back. Everything was there . . .

August 2012 the coup d'état my involvement in the teacher's union my classes at the University the imposition of the fascist government the menaces my unjustified firing my sympathy for the underground resistance discovering Pedro is with the guerillas joining the movement the clandestine sessions writing the manifestos the involuntary metamorphosis from militant to chairman my tapped phone my wife and children exile my fake disappearing the guerillas in the sewers the sabotage the shootings all the blood we shouldn't shed the inner division of our movement an imminent schism Is there a mole? "Nobody is indispensable but you are half the brain of the movement" our last meeting someone gave out our headquarters rubber bullets tear gas they want us alive the seizure the torturing interrogatories the summary judgment . . .

. . . and then waking up here.

"Fantômas," I replied after this infinite second. "You are better than Batman."

"I am a virtual virus. You are retained at a high-security pavilion for political prisoners. They can't kill you; international pressure is very strong. They keep you chained to a virtual world, with some of the movement's other leaders."

"That's right!" I agreed, feeling a little dumb speaking to a computer virus. "Someone rendered an early seventies pop utopia, some kind of collective TV subconscious . . ."

"No time to waste," Fantômas interrupted. "It won't be long before the operators discover there's something wrong. They're slowly draining your brain. We've been able to save a little, but some information is already lost. The longer it takes, the less you'll be able to remember."

I tried to recall my real father's face.

"Is there anything to do?"

"Yes." He peeled off his mask, unveiling no face at all. "The operators will notice there's an intruder on their program. They'll reboot the whole system, erasing me. But the mask requires a very specific software to wipe it out. As soon as they set back the virtual world, you must put it on. It's an undetectable program that'll preserve your memories till we can resc—"

As soon as he's back, the operator detects an intruder in the program. First action he takes, of course, is rebooting the whole system, after which he reconfigures the terminals, altering parameters to make it impossible for a new virus to penetrate the firewall. As soon as he is done he returns to the dull routine of keeping everything within normal parameters in the high-security pavilion.

APRIL 2, 1974

The Radio Shack clock radio woke me up to the tune of "Stayin' Alive" by the Bee Gees. I rose and first thing I did was turn on the TV.

I caught the final segment of that contest show with the old guy dressed as a kid.

I showered and came downstairs for breakfast.

"Morning, Hon," said Mom and served the meal. Ho Hos and Dr Pepper. A little later Dad came down, reading his paper. He had coffee. We discussed the Olympics.

I realized I was already late for the gig, so I rose to split. As I was heading out, Dad said:

"Lalo, there's a surprise for you on the table."

It was a white mask, similar to El Santo's, but without any charm.

"Gee, thanks, Dad," I said, faking my brightest smile and scrammed for Toy-o-rama, where I work.

I threw the mask into the first trash can that crossed my yellow brick road. Beyond that, it was a plain normal day.

DAVID LANGFORD

COMP.BASILISK.FAQ

(1999)

Frequently Asked Questions
Revised 27 June 2006

1. What is the purpose of this newsgroup?
To provide a forum for discussion of basilisk (BLIT) images. Newsnet readers who prefer low traffic should read comp.basilisk.moderated, which carries only high-priority warnings and identifications of new forms.

2. Can I post binary files here?
If you are capable of asking this question you MUST immediately read news.announce.new users, where regular postings warn that binary and especially image files may emphatically not be posted to any newsgroup. Many countries impose a mandatory death penalty for such action.

3. Where does the acronym BLIT come from?
The late unlamented Dr. Vernon Berryman's system of math-to-visual algorithms is known as the Berryman Logical Imaging Technique. This reflected the original

paper's title: "On Thinkable Forms, with notes toward a Logical Imaging Technique" (Berryman and Turner, *Nature*, 2001). Inevitably, the paper has since been suppressed and classified to a high level.

4. Is it true that science fiction authors predicted basilisks?

Yes and no. The idea of unthinkable information that cracks the mind has a long SF pedigree, but no one got it quite right. William Gibson's *Neuromancer* (1984), the novel that popularized cyberspace, is often cited for its concept of "black ice" software which strikes back at the minds of hackers – but this assumes direct neural connection to the net. Basilisks are far more deadly because they require no physical contact.

Much earlier, Fred Hoyle's *The Black Cloud* (1957) suggested that a download of knowledge provided by a would-be-helpful alien (who has superhuman mental capacity) could overload and burn out human minds.

A remarkable near miss features in *The Shapes of Sleep* (1962) by J. B. Priestley, which imagines archetypal shapes that compulsively evoke particular emotions, intended for use in advertising.

Piers Anthony's *Macroscope* (1969) described the "Destroyer sequence," a purposeful sequence of images used to safeguard the privacy of galactic communications by erasing the minds of eavesdroppers.

The comp.basilisk community does not want ever again to see another posting about the hoary coincidence that *Macroscope* appeared in the same year and month as the first episode of the British TV program *Monty Python's Flying Circus*, with its famous sketch about the World's Funniest Joke that causes all hearers to laugh themselves to death.

5. How does a basilisk operate?

The short answer is: we mustn't say. Detailed information is classified beyond Top Secret.

The longer answer is based on a popular-science article by Berryman (*New Scientist*, 2001), which outlines his thinking. He imagined the human mind as a formal, deterministic computational system – a system that, as predicted by a variant of Gödel's Theorem in mathematics, can be crashed by thoughts which the mind is physically or logically incapable of thinking. The Logical Imaging Technique presents such a thought in purely visual form as a basilisk image which our optic nerves can't help but accept. The result is disastrous, like a software stealth-virus smuggled into the brain.

6. Why "basilisk"?
It's the name of a mythical creature: a reptile whose mere gaze can turn people to stone. According to ancient myth, a basilisk can be safely viewed in a mirror. This is not generally true of the modern version—although some highly asymmetric basilisks like B-756 are lethal only in unreflected or reflected form, depending on the dominant hemisphere of the victim's brain.

7. Is it just an urban legend that the first basilisk destroyed its creator?
Almost everything about the incident at the Cambridge IV supercomputer facility where Berryman conducted his last experiments has been suppressed and classified as highly undesirable knowledge. It's generally believed that Berryman and most of the facility staff died. Subsequently, copies of basilisk B-1 leaked out. This image is famously known as the Parrot, for its shape when blurred enough to allow safe viewing. B-1 remains the favorite choice of urban terrorists who use aerosols and stencils to spray basilisk images on walls by night.

But others were at work on Berryman's speculations. B-2 was soon generated at the Lawrence Livermore Laboratory and, disastrously, B-3 at MIT.

8. Are there basilisks in the Mandelbrot Set fractal?
Yes. There are two known families, at symmetrical positions, visible under extreme magnification. No, we're not telling you where.

9. How can I get permission to display images on my website?
This is a news.announce.newusers question, but keeps cropping up here. In brief: you can't without a rarely granted government license. Using anything other than plain ASCII text on websites or in e-mail is a

guaranteed way of terminating your net account. We're all nostalgic about the old, colorful web and about television, but today's risks are simply too great.

10. Is it true that Microsoft uses basilisk booby traps to protect Windows Ultra from disassembly and pirating?
We could not possibly comment.

MYRA ÇAKAN

SPIDER'S NEST

(2004)

Translated from the German by Jim Young

SPIDER HATED DAYTIME—especially mornings, if he happened to be awake at the time. He was a creature of the night. Spider's middle name was invisible, and everybody knows a guy's never harder to see than in the dark. Sometimes, if he was going somewhere just before nightfall, his senses sharpened so he felt like a fine-tuned instrument. Spider liked that feeling. It gave him power and a certain sense of control that he thought he had lost long ago during the dark, sultry hours of the intertime.

It was morning and the sun shone harshly into his eyes, right there in his hideout. Today the whole sky was glaring, a shrill yellow—vomit yellow. He was inexplicably lethargic, almost like after a bad trip. Every cell in his body seemed to have been deprogrammed during the night, and the old software replaced. Must've had a total blackout, Spider thought. Or pretty near. Almost offhandedly, he noticed his muscles twitching. They were the seismograph of his nervous system, and they were telling him it was almost time. He was going to need his next hit soon if he wanted to avoid having the contractions turn into cramps.

Sandoz and Geigercounter were supposed to be making their rounds soon. Sandoz was heavily into Eiscream. One time Spider had asked Sandoz why she was so heavily into it, and she said, "Because it goes with my hair." When she said that, she grinned through the neon-silver of her bangs. She looked like a ghost smiling at him from inside a coffin. Real spooky, man.

Spider yawned again. He was trying to outlast the ever-stronger vibrations of his muscles. So he tried to remember when he last saw Ant. Ant was his dealer, and without him, he had to depend on what that fucked-up shit Geigercounter and his girlfriend were doing. Until he traded up to Eiscream or one of the other designer items, it must have been hard on him.

"Hey, Spy, my man, what's going down?" Sandoz shoved herself into his field of view. She knelt down beside Spider and drew hectic little circles in the dust on the ground. The whole damn town was overrun with hectic little circles.

"Heya." Spider nodded at her. Somehow, that girl made him nervous. It was high time that he talked to the Silver Spider about the matter. He looked around. The street looked the same—empty. "So where's Geigercounter hanging?"

"Dunno. Dunno." Her finger kept moving around in spirals in the dust. Her pale blue eyes looked at him without really seeing him. From time to time she got that look, and not even Geigercounter could figure out if she was gonna freak or not. Spider stood up and stretched. For a moment, he almost thought he recognized his mirror image in a picture window on the other side. He was almost sure he looked pretty good, he thought, considering.

Suddenly it was very quiet, clanking quiet. Spider didn't know what it was, but a hungry little noise had overtaken the whispering of the street sweepers. Sandoz crouched there, watching him. His mirror image sank into Sandoz's pale eyes. And all of a sudden he felt both hot and sick with desire. He looked away. Then came a distant salvation. He saw a flurry of dust along the street, a vibration that rode in on the midday sun—Ant on his hoverboard.

Ant stood loosely on the board, one knee slightly bent, his arms swinging in rhythm with the street. Man, oh man, he looked just like the Silver Surfer and he brought fulfillment with him, crystalline, clear, resolution.

"Heya, Spider." Just floating in the air, he could heal the sick. A postatomic saint. "The iceman cometh."

Spider guzzled the sound of the words, turned them around, tasted their timbre. Damn it all, something here was completely turned ass-backward.

"What's the matter, man?" Ant wrinkled his forehead.

"How do you always manage to find power cells for your board, man?" Spider hadn't wanted to ask that; it just burst out of him. The words had turned around on their own as they made their way from his brain to his mouth. But damn it all, Ant was his dealer. His. His. Spider placed his arms behind his back, formed his fingers into fists, and tried to hide how badly he needed his next fix.

"Yeah, and where do you get your shit?" Sandoz's bright voice cut the air in helixes.

"To hell with both of you, you assholes!" Ant put his foot to the ground, speeding up.

Spider leaped forward and tried to stop him. Too slow, and too late.

"Fuck, fuck, fuck!" Sandoz screamed, drawing the word out into a long howl. "He had the stuff with him, he did, man, and now he's gone." She slid down the wall of the house and, like something with a mind of its own, her finger once more started drawing those stupid circles on the ground.

Spider turned himself off. How had he ever spent even one second thinking about her? And girls were the one thing he really couldn't figure out. They smelled different from men, and whenever he talked to them, he wasn't sure what they were talking about.

Silver Spider was different. In his dreams, he saw her as the woman with the killer eyes and hard muscles under her silvery skin. Everything about her was silver—her eyes, her voice, her breasts. Silver Spider understood him. She stroked his senses better than any drug. Because she was the drug. She laid herself upon his brain and took possession of every cell in his body until he was paralyzed. He never wanted to resist. He wanted her to suck him out. Then he'd wake up in a sweat and his body would be heavy and disoriented. Every time he swore it was going to be the last time—these dreams were killing him.

Once he tried to talk to Geigercounter about it, trying to find out if Geiger talked to Silver Spider, too, in the early morning light. But he couldn't say a word. It would have been, like, a betrayal. But beyond that, it would have been like surrendering an inexpressible secret, not least because there was, in fact, a secret between them. In some manner it was dirty—dirty and exciting at the same time—the thing that lay between him and the Silver Spider. Sort of like the feeling he got when Sandoz looked at him. No—he'd never talk to anybody about it.

She wouldn't like it.

Spider morphed around the heels and stretched himself out once more. His right hand beat rhythmically against his thigh. The girl continued drawing her stupid circles in the dust. With the most precise motion, almost dreamlike in its dance-like grace, Spider unscrewed his leg from his hip, and as though it were lighter than air, swung it to the ground over Sandoz's mute conjurations. Whoosh, they were gone. Sandoz cursed him wordlessly as the circles she had been drawing disappeared, and in the echo-shadow of her shrill scream he pulled back his leg. Suddenly he felt downright good.

But the feeling passed much too soon. Ant, that stupid asshole, was driving around the place with all that goddamned Eiscream ice in his pocket. Maybe he should hurry up and get a new dealer. Spider couldn't help but notice how his thoughts were going around in circles, as though Sandoz was whirling them around him like the dust. That was the punishment for putting an end to her circles, and the reason Ant hadn't given him the stuff—a presentiment of things to come, an omen. Spider's entire life was built on a foundation of such signs. They were his guidelights through the labyrinth of the days, just as the Silver Spider illuminated his nights. And in fact it was she who had led him to Ant to begin with, since she knew so exactly what he needed. Now why had she left him in the lurch?

No. Wait. That didn't make sense. The Silver Spider had never left him in the lurch. He just had to be patient, to wait until night fell. Then she'd be there for him with all her tenderness and wisdom. He began to run, and then to run faster, into the blurring sunset.

• • •

From a long way off he could see Sandoz. Slowly he made his way to the meeting point. Actually, it wasn't much as landmarks go, just a place where you could hang out, where you could wait for your dealer and sit out the goddamned gray-yellow day. There weren't many of the old gang around anymore after the last big crash. They were all scared of the coming winter. But why think about the cold when the sun is still shining and the nights linger long and warm.

Was she still ticked off at him because of what he'd done to the circles? After due consideration, Spider thought it was decidedly more clever to keep quiet than to try to say something to her. Besides, he was really too tired to talk. His head, no, his entire body, felt sore, almost as though he'd been going through withdrawal all night long. Weird.

She was alone and didn't see him coming. She stood there before these cracked windows, looking off into nothingness. Spider wondered if she were high, which brought him to the question of whether she had any of the good stuff on her. But all of a sudden it didn't matter anymore.

Almost hypnotically the mirror image drew him. She was stretching, and her small breasts pressed against her sweatshirt. She drew her hands through her hair dreamily, almost as though she were moving under water. And then he knew it—she was putting on a show for him because she sensed his gaze on her and it was turning her on. Still, he couldn't stop himself from staring at her, holding his breath, waiting for her to pull her shirt down over one shoulder. He reached out his hand and traced her silhouette on the dusty glass.

"Spider, ya stupid asshole, whaddaya think you're doin' with my old lady?"

Geigercounter. He'd finally arrived. Laughing hysterically, he slapped Spider on the back. Geiger was full of Eiscream and was dancing on its ersatz energy. Spider tasted his own bitter anger. His fist wanted to drill itself into Geiger's dumb mouth—it was begging for it. Why in the hell hadn't he showed up any sooner? If he'd gotten here when he was supposed to, nothing would have been screwed up. What the hell had happened?

Spider had never felt such anger before. Was he mad at Geigercounter because he caught him staring at his girl? Or was it because Ant was going to link him up? Naw, that wasn't it. That asshole dealer hadn't been around for days, so how was he supposed to link him? But then how did Geiger get off, if Ant wasn't around?

Spider's thoughts whirled around in circles, hopping around in his head like happy little plush rabbits. Pink and green velveteen bunnies. Spider noticed, as though it was a long way off, that his entire body was shaking and dancing with silent laughter.

"Listen, man—" Spider searched for the words, but he couldn't get the bunnies to stop.

Geigercounter. His eyes were open and looked sort of scared. Scared and sort of goofy. Maybe he was seeing the bunnies, too, and didn't realize they were Spider's. Or maybe Geiger was reading his thoughts. Abruptly, Spider stopped laughing hysterically. The idea that Geigercounter or somebody else—or maybe even something else—could see inside his head scared the bejesus out of him. Thoughts could be like bad shit, you know.

And still Geigercounter just stared at him. Then Geiger's view strayed to Sandoz, who was methodically chewing on a strand of her own hair. For sure, this was one serious communication problem. Shit, the city was really going down the drain, Spider thought. Ever since the Obernet had crashed last winter, everything had been sliding straight downhill. But not with him, since he had Silver Spider to look after him. Then he sensed the anger rising in him again. Maybe it was just because he wanted to bust that fuckin' dealer one. And as he was thinking that, his feet were running down the street.

He looked for Ant for so long that he forgot who he was looking for, and why. Then he went hunting for Geigercounter and Sandoz and finally found them in the house with the cracked windows. They were both leaning over a dusty Plexiglas plate with their glass pipe and the magic blue crystal spread out before them. Yeah, it was magic, all right. Spider was so cold turkey he would've done anything that came along in order to get the little bunnies out of his head.

Looking at the two of them getting stoned—Sandoz inhaling the smoke from Geiger's mouth, her neon-silver hair mingled with the smoke—made him feel like an intruder.

It made him feel as if he was doing something new and wild, like that morning when he felt Sandoz looking at him and he wondered what she'd look like without her shirt on. In the dark. With him.

And now, in the blink of an eye, his fantasy had become reality. It was already night, and the moon cast strange shadows across Sandoz's naked back. And he saw Sandoz, and what she was doing leaning over Geigercounter, and the way she moved. Without realizing what he was doing, Spider put his hand down his jeans and stroked himself with the same rhythm. Different from Silver Spider, but it got him off.

Sandoz tossed back her head. Spider tried to look her directly in the eyes. Her pupils had become a gate into a sweet, forbidden world. That was when he realized she was looking straight through his brain. She knew what he was thinking. He turned around and ran until he collapsed gasping for air. Spider heard his breath wheeze deep inside his chest, and he closed his eyes so he could hear it better. There was only an echo—Sandoz had disappeared from inside his head.

The Silver Spider was different. She was always there inside his head, just like the thought of his next fix. Yeah, man—she was the only real shit. Every night she was there for him. And she knew what he needed, everything. All he needed to do was to hang with her, in her net.

As soon as he reached interface, Spider recalled what it had been like that first time—and would be the next—when he'd discovered her in one of the Unternets that had dissolved after the big crash. Unlike everything else, it had only gotten better since the first time. He knew how she pulled him in, stuck her silver probes into him in a deliciously painful ecstasy that he never wanted to stop. All he noticed was how his body wound up tight like a wire coil and how his hips jerked. It was holy robot night, better than any shit, man.

• • •

The sun was shining harshly once more, and out of its light appeared the Silver Surfer. His hair was punked out like a shark's fin, cutting though the air. Spider waited for him, half in the shadows. He felt a lot better today, as though his power cells had pretty much recharged during the night. She'd been good to him again. But he thought it was better to restore the vibe with his dealer again. And, in his hiding place, Spider rolled the words around in his mouth until they fit.

"Spy." Ant had found him. He was waiting, too.

Totally cool and unapproachable he stood there on his hoverboard, floating above the dust so his feet never had to touch the dirt he was made of. Every one of them was nothing but dirt—Sandoz, Geigercounter, and him too—yeah, even Spider was dirt. Why not? None of us has done anything but sit here on our asses getting high and whining while everything around us collapsed. Spider figured it must have been the effect of the sun's rays, making him see things so clearly. All those months they'd been expecting one of the Unternets to send out a repair program that would reboot the Obernet again. At first Spider and a guy called Zero-One tried to launch an emergency program through the interface. Zero-One intended to melt away the brain while Spider . . . well, he met up with Silver Spider. And after that, at some point, they'd all gotten lazy and couldn't do anything but wait for their next fix, for Ant.

"Dude, got a couple o' bennies for ya. Paint yo' day."

Spider trembled. The mere mention of paint and he flashed on a whole range of pastels, and that made him think about the plush bunnies that had been zooming around inside his head. But the memories were nothing more than a faded picture at the edge of his perception.

"Okay, man. Thanks."

It was a peace offering. Better not to refuse. You never know when you could use 'em, Spider told himself. But he couldn't dismiss the nagging little questions he wanted to ask Ant, even though he knew the trouble they'd get him in if he did.

"Where d'you get your stuff, man?" Words come so damn quick. What was he trying to do, asking such a thing? But he had to know where he was at. You gotta know where you're at with your dealer.

"Here and there," Ant answered. His board rose and fell over small, invisible waves. Ant raised his hand to the nape of his neck, as if reassuring himself of something.

Spider squinted. Something was happening here and he didn't know what it was. Ant always running his hand over the back of his neck. But it wasn't just a nervous tic. Sparks danced around Ant, and then an intense anger flooded through Spider, rolling him over, grinding him down. And he knew that she, she had deceived him . . .

Zero-One had been the last one, he was sure. But that meant Zero wasn't special anymore! Spider leaped forward, eager to hear Ant's bones crack between his fingers, but the boy faded into the shadows at the far end of the street. And Spider stood there, alone beneath the hateful sun while the questions reared up inside him, croaking through his throat, trying to form into words in his mouth.

Spider gagged. There was only one solution to the problem, and it was going to get very nasty. When he thought about Zero-One, he gagged again. Telling himself he needed some courage and a bit of Dr. Feelgood to get through to the end, he shoved one of the bennies into his mouth.

He knew where she was.

Down in the holy place, the Net Center. Nobody he knew had ever been down there. Or nobody who'd ever been there was able to talk about it. Either way was the same to Spider. He was at home in her net, belonged there, in fact. He was Spider, not some juicy little insect. She could catch him, but not destroy him.

Spider waited before the great house with the many doors, waited until it was dark. Silently he thought about the words he wanted to say to her. Just so he could talk to her—nothing more. She was different from Ant, understood the crystalline logic of what he said. In fact, she understood his very thoughts. Nothing to worry about, Spy. Nothing at all.

He tossed down the rest of the speed at one go. It was like he was going out on a date, a very special date. A "White Wedding," yeah. And nothing was certain in this world, or his world, or hers. Anything was possible. Man, Ant knew how a guy could have all the colors he wanted but Spy still owns the night, brother. The web. Nothing is fair in this world. He pushed against the nearest door. It had been ajar, as though left that way for someone expected. Someone who had finally arrived.

Darkness embraced him like clinging foam and it was warm, a familiar, long-forgotten warmth. Spider laughed silently and his body danced to the rhythm of his laughter as it beat out a mad tattoo. Then he tripped over a clicking, resisting, something. Spider picked it up without thinking. Felt like a metal bar.

In the end, he knew it was all one of Ant's crazy dreams. You didn't even have to think about it very long. But those dreams can get ugly very fast. One of his weapons. Always good to have a weapon. A weapon against the faceless things crouching in the chemical twilight zone.

And then, the air wrapped around him, crackling, and the hair on his arms stood up as if the energy of the whole city was focused on him. Boyah, what a trip! But something was wrong with his vision. And a stench engulfed him, not knife-sharp corrosive ozone, but a rotting, sweet scent, like—oh, no, fuck.

He knew his memories would bring them back, all the dead out of his past. And here they were already. But they'd never been so frightening. Those fucking bennies.

It must be the bennies, Spider thought to himself; Ant must have given him bad stuff, and he had made it worse by taking them all at once. Panic shuddered through him. And the monster came closer—she came closer.

Deftly she rushed toward him on the glistening thread. Her head was enormous and her three eyes were doors into other dimensions, terribly dangerous and sweetly fascinating. He wanted to run away, but something was making him walk toward this monstrous thing. All he could see were those eyes, and deep inside his head there was a humming sound—ancient, electric, insane. The bitter taste of vomit gagged in his throat. How could he let this happen—let her creep into his brain, let her do these things to him? She was not the Silver Spider of his dreams.

He swung the metal bar, surprised by how light it seemed in his hand. Almost as though it were an extension of his arm, or of his thoughts—or better yet, the fulfillment of his thoughts. Spider smiled grimly, and he wished she could see his expression.

There was a "splatch!" as the metal bar hit her head. An ugly comic-sound. Spider had never thought it would sound like this. The head splattered and cracked open. Yellow matter erupted around him and covered his face, seeking to drown him, like a slimy, moldy blanket, like a liquid corpse.

• • •

Spider threw up and staggered away, sliding down at last against the wall. He felt the spider web against his back and bare arms. Again he vomited. Though he was so small and weak, he had destroyed the monster. And was alone. Alone as though he were in his grave.

At last he knew what must be done. His hand knew what to do. The entire time he'd held the plug in one fist, a talisman against the night. He lifted the plug toward his neck and stopped, realizing at last what he was doing. But it was too late. Tricked, he was tricked. This wasn't a dream at all. This was reality.

Quiet. It was perfectly quiet, a sacred stillness. Time was without end and everything was meaningless—defeats, dreams, and victories. Spider closed his eyes and stared at the featureless wall that was the interior of his skull.

JOHN KESSEL

THE LAST AMERICAN

(2007)

THE LIFE OF ANDREW STEELE

Re-created by Fiona 13

Reviewed by TheOldGuy

> "I don't blame my father for beating me. I don't blame him for tearing the book I was reading from my hands, and I don't blame him for locking me in the basement. When I was a child, I did blame him. I was angry, and I hated my father. But as I grew older I came to understand that he did what was right for me, and now I look upon him with respect and love, the respect and love he always deserved, but that I was unable to give him because I was too young and self-centered."
>
> —Andrew Steele, 2077,
> Conversation with Hagiographer

During the thirty-three years Andrew Steele occupied the Oval Office of what was then called the White House, in what was then called the United States of America (not to be confused with the current United State of Americans), on the corner of his desk he kept an antiquated device of the early twenty-first century called a taser. Typically used by law enforcement officers, it functioned by shooting out a thin wire that, once in contact with its target, delivered an electric shock of up to three hundred thousand volts. The victim was immediately incapacitated by muscle spasms and intense pain. This crude weapon was used for crowd control or to subdue suspects of crimes.

When Ambassador for the New Humanity Mona Vaidyanathan first visited Steele, she asked what the queer black object was. Steele told her that it had been the most frequent means of communication between his father and himself. "When I was ten years old," he told her, "within a single month my father used that on me sixteen times."

"That's horrible," she said.

"Not for a person with a moral imagination," Steele replied.

In this new biography of Steele, Fiona 13, the Grand Lady of Reproductions, presents the crowning achievement of her long career re-creating lives for the Cognosphere. Andrew Steele, when he died in 2100, had come to exemplify the twenty-first century, and his people, in a way that goes beyond the metaphorical. Drawing on every resource of the posthuman biographer, from heuristic modeling to reconstructive DNA sampling to forensic dreaming, Ms. 13 has produced this labor of, if not love, then obsession, and I for one, am grateful for it.

Fiona presents her new work in a hybrid form. Comparatively little of this biography is subjectively rendered. Instead, harking back to a bygone era, Fiona breaks up the narrative with long passages of *text*—strings of printed code that must be read with the eyes. Of course this adds the burden of learning the code to anyone seeking to experience her re-creation, but an accelerated prefrontal intervention is packaged with the biography. Fiona maintains that *text*, since it forces an artificial linearity on experience, stimulates portions of the left brain that seldom function in conventional experiential biographies. The result is that the person undergoing the life of Andrew Steele both lives through significant moments in Steele's subjectivity, and is drawn out of the stream of sensory and emotional reaction to contemplate the significance of that experience from the point of view of a wise commentator.

I trust I do not have to explain the charms of this form to those of you reading this review, but I recommend the experience to all cognizant entities who still maintain elements of curiosity in their affect repertoire.

• • •

CHILD

Appropriately for a man who was to so personify the twenty-first century, Dwight Andrew Steele was born on January 1, 2001. His mother, Rosamund Sanchez Steele, originally from Mexico, was a lab technician at the forestry school at North Carolina State University; his father, Herbert Matthew Steele, was a land developer and on the board of the Planter's Bank and Trust. Both of Steele's parents were devout Baptists and attended one of the new "big box" churches that had sprung up in the late twentieth in response to growing millennialist beliefs in the United States and elsewhere.

The young Steele was "homeschooled." This meant that Steele's mother devoted a portion of every day to teaching her son herself. The public school system was distrusted by large numbers of religious believers, who considered education by the state to be a form of indoctrination in moral error. Homeschoolers operated from the premise that the less contact their children had with the larger world, the better.

Unfortunately, in the case of Andrew this did not prevent him from meeting other children. Andrew was a small, serious boy, sensitive, and an easy target for bullies. This led to his first murder. Fiona 13 realizes this event for us through extrapolative genetic mapping.

> *We are in the playground, on a bright May morning. We are running across the crowded asphalt toward a climbing structure of wood and metal, when suddenly we are falling! A nine-year-old boy named Jason Terry has tripped us and, when we regain our feet, he tries to pull our pants down. We feel the sting of our elbows where they scraped the pavement, feel surprise and dismay, fear, anger. As Terry leans forward to grab the waistband of our trousers, we suddenly bring our knee up into Terry's face. Terry falls back, sits down awkwardly. The other children gathered laugh. The sound of the laughter in our ears only enrages us more—are they laughing at us? The look of dismay turns to rage on Terry's face. He is going to beat us up; now, he is a deadly threat. We step forward, and before Terry can stand, kick him full in the face. Terry's head snaps back and strikes the asphalt, and he is still.*
>
> *The children gasp. A trickle of blood flows from beneath Terry's ear. From across the playground comes the monitor's voice: "Andrew? Andrew Steele?"*

I have never experienced a more vivid moment in biography. There it all is: the complete assumption by Steele that he is the victim. The fear and rage. The horror, quickly repressed. The later remorse, swamped by desperate justifications.

It was only through his father's political connections and acquiescence in private counseling (that the Steeles did not believe in, taking psychology as a particularly pernicious form of modern mumbo jumbo) that Andrew was kept out of the legal system. He withdrew into the family, his father's discipline, and his mother's teaching.

More trouble was to follow. Keeping it secret from his family, Herbert Steele had invested heavily in real estate in the late aughts; he had leveraged properties he purchased to borrow money to invest in several hedge funds, hoping to put the family into a position of such fundamental wealth that they would be beyond the reach of economic vagaries.

When the Friends of the American League set off the Atlanta nuclear blast in

2012, pushing the first domino of the Global Economic Meltdown, Steele senior's financial house of cards collapsed. The US government, having spent itself into bankruptcy and dependence on Asian debt support through ill-advised imperial schemes and paranoid reactions to global terrorist threats, had no resources to deal with the collapse of private finances. Herbert Steele struggled to deal with the reversal, fell into a depression, and died when he crashed a borrowed private plane into a golf course in Southern Pines.

Andrew was twelve years old. His mother, finding part-time work as a data-entry clerk, made barely enough money to keep them alive. Andrew was forced into the public schools. He did surprisingly well there. Andrew always seemed mature for his years, deferential to his elders, responsible, trustworthy, and able to see others' viewpoints. He was slightly aloof from his classmates and seemed more at home in the presence of adults.

Unknown to his overstressed mother, Andrew was living a secret life. On the Internet, under a half dozen false IP addresses, he maintained political websites. Through them he became one of the world's most influential "bloggers."

A blog was a personal weblog, a site on the worldwide computer system where individuals, either anonymously or in their own names, commented on current affairs or their own lives. Some of these weblogs had become prominent, and their organizers and authors politically important.

Andrew had a fiction writer's gift for inventing consistent personalities, investing them with brilliant argument and sharp observation. On the "Political Theater" weblog, as Sacré True, he argued for the impeachment of President Harrison; on "Reason Season," as Tom Pain, he demonstrated why Harrison's impeachment would prove disastrous. Fiona sees this phase of Steele's life as his education in manipulating others' sensibilities. His emotion-laden arguments were astonishingly successful at twisting his interlocutors into rhetorical knots. To unravel and respond to one of Steele's arguments rationally would take four times his space and carry none of his propagandistic force. Steele's argument against the designated hitter rule even found its way into the platform of the resurgent Republican Party.

• • •

INTERROGATOR

"You don't know why I acted, but I know why. I acted because it is necessary for me to act, because that's what, whether you like it or not, you require me to do. And I don't mind doing it because it's what I have to do. It's what I was born to do. I've never been appreciated for it but that's okay too because, frankly, no one is ever appreciated for what they do.

"But before you presume to judge me realize that you are responsible. I am simply your instrument. I took on the burden of your desires when I didn't want to—I would just as gladly have had that cup pass me by—but I did it, and I have never complained. And I have never felt less than proud of what I have done. I did what was necessary, for the benefit of others. If it had been up to me I would never have touched a single human being, but I am not complaining.

"I do, however, ask you, humbly, if you have any scrap of decency left, if you have any integrity whatsoever, not to judge me. You do not have that right.

"Ask Carlo Sanchez, ask Alfonso Garadiana, ask Sayid Ramachandran, ask Billy Chen. Ask them what was the right thing to do. And then, when you've got the answer from their bleeding corpses, then, and only then, come to me."

—Andrew Steele, 2020,
Statement before Board of Inquiry

Contemporary readers must remember the vast demographic and other circumstantial differences that make the early twenty-first century an alien land to us. When Steele was sixteen years old, the population of the world was an astonishing 6.8 billion, fully half of whom were under the age of twenty-five, the overwhelming majority of those young and striving individuals living in poverty, but with access, through the technologies that had spread widely over the previous twenty years, to unprecedented unregulated information. Few of them could be said to have been adequately acculturated. The history of the next forty years, including Steele's part in that history, was shaped by this fact.

In 2017 Steele was conscripted into the US Army pursuing the Oil War on two continents. Because he was fluent in Spanish, he served as an interrogator with the Seventy-First Infantry Division stationed in Venezuela. His history as an interrogator included the debriefing of the rightfully elected president of that nation in 2019. Fiona puts us there:

We are standing in the back of a small room with concrete walls, banks of fluorescent lights above, a HVAC vent and exposed ducts hanging from the ceiling. The room is cold. We have been standing for a long time and our back is stiff. We have seen many of these sessions, and all we can think about right now is getting out of here, getting a beer, and getting some sleep.

In the center of the room Lieutenant Haslop and a civilian contractor are interrogating a small brown man with jet-black shoulder-length hair. Haslop is very tall and stoop shouldered, probably from a lifetime of ducking responsibility. The men call him "Slop" behind his back.

The prisoner's name is Alfonso Garadiana. His wrists are tied together behind him, and the same rope stretches down to his ankles, also tied together. The rope is too short, so that the only way he can stand is with his knees flexed painfully. But every time he sways, as if to fall, the contractor signals Haslop, who pokes him with an electric prod. Flecks of blood spot Garadiana's once-brilliant white shirt. A cut over his eyebrow is crusted with dried blood, and the eye below it is half-closed.

The contractor, Mr. Gray, is neat and shaved and in control. "So," he says in Spanish, "where are the Jacaranda virus stores?"

Garadiana does not answer. It's unclear whether he has even understood.

Gray nods to Haslop again.

Haslop blinks his eyes, swallows. He slumps into a chair, rests his brow in one hand. "I can't do this anymore," he mutters, only apparently to himself. He wouldn't say it aloud if he didn't want us to hear it, even if he doesn't know that himself. We are sick to death of his weakness.

We step forward and take the prod from his hand. "Let me take care of this, sir." We swing the back of our hand against Garadiana's face, exactly the same motion we once used to hit a backhand in high school tennis. The man's head snaps back, and he falls to the floor. We move in with the prod.

Upon the failure of the Oil War and the defeat of the government that pursued it, a reaction took place, including war-crimes investigations that led to Steele's imprisonment from 2020 to 2025. Fiona gives us a glimpse of Steele's sensorium in his third year in maximum-security prison:

We're hungry. Above us the air rattles from the ventilator. On the table before us in our jail cell is a notebook. We are writing our testament. It's a distillation of everything we know to be absolutely true about the human race and its future. There are things we know in our DNA that cannot be understood by strict rationality, though reason is a powerful tool and can help us to communicate these truths to those who do not, because of incapacity or lack of experience, grasp them instinctively.

The blogs back when we were fourteen were just practice. Here, thanks to the isolation, we are able to go deep, to find the roots of human truth and put them down in words.

We examine the last sentence we have written: "It is the hero's fate to be misunderstood."

A guard comes by and raps the bars of our cell. "Still working on the great opus, Andy?"

We ignore him, close the manuscript, move from the table, and begin to do push-ups in the narrow space beside the cot.

The guard raps again on the bars. "How about an answer, killer?" His voice is testy.

We concentrate on doing the push-up correctly. Eleven. Twelve. Thirteen. Fourteen . . .

When we get out of here, all this work will make a difference.

This was indeed the case, Fiona shows us, but not in the way that Steele intended. As a work of philosophy his testament was rejected by all publishers. He struggled to make a living in the Long Emergency that was the result of the oil decline and the global warming-spawned environmental disasters that hit with full force in the 2020s. These changes were asymmetric, but though some regions felt them more than others, none were unaffected. The flipping of the Atlantic current turned 2022 into the first Year Without a Summer in Europe. Torrential rains in North Africa, the desertification of the North American Great Plains, mass wildlife migrations, drastic drops in grains production, die-offs of marine life, and decimated global fish stocks were among only the most obvious problems with which worldwide civilization struggled. And Andrew Steele was out of prison, without a connection in the world.

• • •

ARTIST

> "The great artist is a rapist. It is his job to plant a seed, an idea or an emotion, in the viewer's mind. He uses every tool available to enforce his will. The audience doesn't know what it wants, but he knows what it wants, and needs, and he gives it to them.
>
> "To the degree I am capable of it, I strive to be a great artist."
>
> —Andrew Steele, 2037,
> "Man of Steele,"
> Interview on *VarietyNet*

At this moment of distress, Steele saw an opportunity, and turned his political testament into a bestselling novel, *What's Wrong with Heroes?* A film deal followed immediately. Steele insisted on being allowed to write the screenplay, and against its better judgment, the studio relented. Upon its release, *What's Wrong With Heroes?* became the highest grossing film in the history of cinema. In the character of Roark McMaster, Steele created a virile philosopher king who spoke to the desperate hopes of millions. With the money he made, Steele conquered the entertainment world. A series of blockbuster films, television series, and virtual adventures followed. This photo link shows him on the set of *The Betrayal*, his historical epic of the late-twentieth century. The series, conflating the Vietnam conflict with the two Iraq wars, presents the fiascoes of the early twenty-first as the result of Machiavellian subversives and their bad-faith followers taking advantage of the innocence of the American populace, undermining what was once a strong and pure-minded nation.

Fiona gives us a key scene from the series:

INT. AMERICAN AIRLINES FLIGHT 11

> *Two of the hijackers, wearing green camo, are gathered around a large man seated in the otherwise-empty first-class cabin of the 757. The big man, unshaven, wears a shabby Detroit Tigers baseball cap.*

Waleed
(*frantic*)
What shall we do now?

MOORE
Keep the passengers back in coach. Is Mohammad on course? How long?

ABDULAZIZ
(*calling back from cockpit*)
Allah willing—three minutes.

Moore glances out the plane window.
MOORE'S POV—through window, an aerial view of Manhattan on a beautiful clear day.

CLOSE ON MOORE
Smirks.

MOORE
Time to go.

Moore hefts his bulk from the first-class seat, moves toward the onboard baggage closet near the front of the plane.

ABDULAZIZ
What are you doing?

From out of a hanging suit bag, Moore pulls a parachute, and straps it on.

WALEED
Is this part of the plan?

Moore jerks up the lever on the plane's exterior door and yanks on it. It does not budge.

MOORE
Don't just stand there, Waleed! Help me!

Waleed moves to help Moore, and reluctantly, Abdulaziz joins them.

ATTA
(*from cockpit*)
There it is! Allah akbar!

Moore and the other two hijackers break the seal and the door flies open. A blast of wind sucks Abdulaziz and Waleed forward; they fall back onto the plane's deck. Moore braces himself against the edge of the door with his hands.

MOORE

In the name of the Democratic Party, the compassionate, the merciful—so long, boys!

Moore leaps out of the plane.

The Betrayal was the highest rated series ever to run on American television, and cemented Steele's position as the most bankable mass-appeal Hollywood producer since Spielberg. At the age of thirty-eight, Steele married the actress Esme Napoli, leading lady in three of his most popular films.

• • •

RELIGIOUS LEADER

The next section of Fiona's biography begins with this heartrending experience from Steele's middle years:

We are in a sumptuous hotel suite with a blonde, not wearing much of anything. We are chasing her around the bed.

"You can't catch me!"

We snag her around the waist, and pull her onto the bed. "I've already caught you. You belong to me." We hold up her ring finger, with its platinum band. "You see?"

"I'm full of nanomachines," she says breathlessly. "If you catch me you'll catch them."

The Scarlet Plague has broken out in Los Angeles, after raging for a month in Brazil. We have fled the city with Esme and are holed up in this remote hotel in Mexico.

"When are we going to have these children?" we ask her. "We need children. Six at least."

"You're going to have to work harder than this to deserve six children," Esme says. "The world is a mess. Do we want to bring children into it?"

"The world has always been a mess. We need to bring children into it because it's a mess." We kiss her perfect cheek.

But a minute later, as we make love, we spot the growing rash along the inside of Esme's thigh.

The death of Steele's wife came near the beginning of the plague decade, followed by the Sudden War and the Collapse. Fiona cites the best estimates of historiographers that, between 2040 and 2062, the human population of the earth went from 8.2 to somewhat less than two billion. The toll was slightly higher in the less developed nations; on the other hand, resistance to the plagues was higher among humans of the tropical regions. This situation in the middle years of the century transformed the Long Emergency of 2020 to 2040—a condition in which civilization, although stressed, might still be said to function, and with which Steele and his generation had coped, into the Die-Off, in which the only aspect of civilization that, even in the least affected regions, might be said to function was a desperate triage.

One of the results of the Long Emergency had been to spark widespread religious fervor. Social and political disruptions had left millions searching for certitudes. Longevity breakthroughs, new medicine, genetic engineering, cyborging, and AI pushed in one direction, while widespread climatic change, fights against deteriorating civil and environmental conditions, and economic disruptions pushed in another. The young warred against the old, the rich against the poor. Reactionary religious movements raged on four continents. Interpreting the chaos of the twenty-first century in terms of eschatology was a winning business. Terrorism in the attempt to bring on utopia or the end of the world was a common reality. Steele, despite his grief, rapidly grasped that art, even popular art, had no role in this world. So he turned, readily, to religion.

> "Human evolution is a process of moral evolution. The thing that makes us different from animals is our understanding of the ethical implications of every action that we perform: those that we must perform, those that we choose. Some actions are matters of contingency, and some are matters of free will.
>
> "Evolution means we will eventually come to fill the universe. To have our seed spread far and wide. That is what we are here for. To engender those children, to bear them, to raise them properly, to have them extend their—and our—thought, creativity, joy, understanding, to every particle of the visible universe."
>
> —Andrew Steele,
> "Sermon in the Cascades," 2052

Steele's Church of Humanity grew rapidly in the 2040s; while the population died and cities burned, its membership more than doubled every year, reaching several millions by 2050. Steele's credo of the Hero transferred easily to religious terms; his brilliantly orchestrated ceremonies sparked ecstatic responses; he fed the poor and comforted the afflicted and, using every rhetorical device at his command, persuaded his followers that the current troubles were the birth of a new utopian age, that every loss had its compensation, that sacrifice was noble, that reward was coming, that from their loins would spring a new and better race, destined to conquer the stars. Love was the answer.

His creed crossed every ethnic, racial, sexual, gender preference, class, and age barrier. Everyone was human, and all equal.

The Church of Humanity was undeniably successful in helping millions of people, not just in the United States but across the bleeding globe, deal with the horrors of the Die-Off. It helped them to rally in the face of unimaginable psychological and material losses. But it was not the only foundation for the recovery. By the time some semblance of order was restored to world affairs in the 2060s, genetically modified humans, the superbrights, were attempting to figure a way out of the numerous dead ends of capitalism, antiquated beliefs, and a dysfunctional system of nation-states. This was a period of unexampled experimentation, and the blossoming of many technologies that had been only potentialities prior to the collapse, among them the uploading of human identities, neurological breakthroughs on the origins of altruism and violence, grafted information capacities, and free quantum energy.

Most of these developments presented challenges to religion. Steele came to see such changes as a threat to fundamental humanity. So began his monstrous political career.

• • •

POLITICIAN

> "The greatest joy in life is putting yourself in the circumstance of another person. To see the world through his eyes, to feel the air on her skin, to breathe in deeply the spirit of their souls. To have his joy and trouble be equally real to you. To know that others are fully and completely human, just as you are. To get outside of your own subjectivity, and to see the world from a completely different and equally valid perspective, to come fully to understand them. When that point of understanding is reached, there is no other word for the feeling that you have than love. Just as much as you love yourself, as you love your children, you love this other.
>
> "And at that point, you must exterminate them. That is the definition of hard."
>
> —Andrew Steele, *What I Believe*, 2071

Steele was swept into office as President of the reconstituted United States in the election of 2064, with his Humanity Party in complete control of the Congress. In his first hundred days, Steele signed a raft of legislation comprising his Humanity Initiative. Included were The Repopulation Act that forced all women of childbearing age to have no fewer than four children, a bold space colonization program, restrictions on genetic alterations and technological body modifications, the wiping clean of all uploaded personalities from private and public databases, the Turing Limit on AI, the Neurological Protection Act of 2065, and the establishment of a legal "standard human being."

In Steele's first term, "nonstandard" humans were allowed to maintain their civil rights, but were identified by injected markers, their movements and employment restricted by the newly established Humanity Agency. Through diplomatic efforts and the international efforts of the Church of Humanity, similar policies were adapted, with notable areas of resistance, throughout much of the world.

In Steele's second term, the HA was given police powers and the nonstandard gradually stripped of civil and property rights. By his third term, those who had not managed to escape the country lost all legal rights and were confined to posthuman reservations, popularly known as "Freak Towns." The establishment of the Protectorate over all of North and South America stiffened resistance elsewhere, and resulted in the uneasy Global Standoff. Eventually, inevitably, came the First and Second Human Wars.

Fiona includes a never-before-experienced moment from the twenty-third year of Steele's presidency.

We are in a command bunker, a large, splendidly appointed room, one whole wall of which is a breathtaking view of the Grand Tetons. We sit at a table with our closest advisors, listening to General Jinjur describe their latest defeat by the New Humans. There are tears in her eyes as she recounts the loss of the Fifth Army in the assault on Madrid.

We do not speak. Our cat, Socrates, sits on our lap, and we scratch him behind his ears. He purrs.

"How many dead?" Chief of Command Taggart asks.

"Very few, sir," reports Jinjur. "But over ninety percent converted. It's their new amygdalic bomb. It destroys our troops' will to fight. The soldiers just lay down their arms and go off looking for something to eat. You try organizing an autistic army."

"At least they're good at math," says Secretary Bloom.

"How can these posthumans persist?" Dexter asks. "We've exterminated millions. How many of them are left?"

"We can't know, sir. They keep making more."

"But they don't even fight," says Taggart. "They must be on the point of extinction."

"It has never been about fighting, sir."

"It's this damned subversion," says Taggart. "We have traitors among us. They seed genetic changes among the people. They turn our own against us. How can we combat that?"

General Jinjur gathers herself. She is quite a striking woman, the flower of the humanity we have fought to preserve for so many years. "If I may be permitted to say so, we are fighting ourselves. We are trying to conquer our own human élan. Do you want to live longer? Anyone who wants to live longer will eventually become posthuman. Do you want to understand the universe? Anyone who wants to understand the universe will eventually become posthuman. Do you want peace of mind? Anyone who wants peace of mind will eventually become posthuman."

Something in her tone catches us, and we are finally moved to speak. "You are one of them, aren't you?"

"Yes," she says.

The contemporary citizen need not be troubled with, and Fiona does not provide, any detailed recounting of the war's progress, or how it ended in the Peace that Passeth All Understanding of 2096. The treatment of the remaining humans, the choices offered them, the removal of those few persisting to Mars, and their continued existence there under quarantine, are all material for another work.

Similarly, the circumstances surrounding Steele's death—the cross, the taser, the Shetland pony—so much a subject of debate, speculation, and conspiracy theory, surely do not need rehearsing here. We know what happened to him. He destroyed himself.

• • •

AWAITING FURTHER INSTRUCTIONS

> "The highest impulse of which a human being is capable is to sacrifice himself in the service of the community of which he is a part, even when that community does not recognize him, and heaps opprobrium upon him for that sacrifice. In fact, such scorn is more often than not to be expected. The true savior of his fellows is not deterred by the prospect of rejection, though carrying the burden of his unappreciated gift is a trial that he can never, but for a few moments, escape. It is the hero's fate to be misunderstood."
>
> —*What's Wrong with Heroes?*
> (unpublished version)

Fiona 13 ends her biography with a simple accounting of the number of beings, human and posthuman, who died as a result of Steele's life. She speculates that many of these same beings might not have lived had he not lived as well, and comes to no formal conclusion, utilitarian or otherwise, as to the moral consequences of the life of Dwight Andrew Steele.

Certainly few tears are shed for Andrew Steele, and few for the ultimate decline of the human race. I marvel at that remnant of humans who, using technologies that he abhorred, have incorporated into their minds a slice of Steele's personality in the attempt to make themselves into the image of the man they see as their savior. Indeed, I must confess to more than a passing interest in their poignant delusions, their comic, mystifying pastimes, their habitual conflicts, their simple loves and hates, their inability to control themselves, their sudden and tragic enthusiasms.

Bootlegged Steele personalities circulate in the Cognosphere, and it may be that those of you who, like me, on occasion edit their capacities in order to spend recreational time being human, will avail themselves of this no doubt unique and terrifying experience.

KEN MACLEOD

EARTH HOUR

(2011)

THE ASSASSIN SLUNG the bag concealing his weapon over his shoulder and walked down the steps to the rickety wooden jetty. He waited as the Sydney Harbour ferry puttered into Neutral Bay, cast on and then cast off at the likewise tiny quay on the opposite bank, and crossed the hundred or so meters to Kurraba Point. He boarded, waved a hand gloved in artificial skin across the fare taker, and settled on a bench near the prow, with the weapon in its blue nylon zipped bag balanced across his knees.

The sun was just above the horizon in the west, the sky clear but for the faint luminous haze of smart dust, each drifting particle of which could at any moment deflect a photon of sunlight and sparkle before the watching eye. A slow rain of shiny soot, removing carbon from the air and as it drifted down providing a massively redundant platform for observation and computation; a platform the assassin's augmented eyes used to form an image of the city and its environs in his likewise augmented visual cortex. He turned the compound image over in his head, watching traffic flows and wind currents, the homeward surge of commuters and the flocking of fruit bats, the exchange of pheromones and cortext messages, the jiggle of stock prices and the tramp of a million feet, in one single godlike POV that saw it all six ways from Sunday and that too soon became intolerable, dizzying the unaugmented tracts of the assassin's still mostly human brain.

One could get drunk on this. The assassin wrenched himself from the hubristic stochastic and focused, narrowing his attention until he found the digital spoor of the man he aimed to kill: a conference delegate pack, a train fare, a hotel tab, an airline booking for a seat that it was the assassin's job to prevent being filled the day after the conference . . . The assassin had followed this trail already, an hour earlier, but it amused him to confirm it and to bring it up to date, with an overhead and a street-level view of the target's unsuspecting stroll toward his hotel in Macleay Street.

It amused him, too, that the target was simultaneously keeping a low profile—no media appearances, backstage at the conference, a hotel room far less luxurious than he could afford, vulgar as all hell, tarted in synthetic mahogany and artificial marble and industrial sheet diamond—while styling himself at every opportunity with the obsolete title under which he was most widely known, as though he reveled in his contradictory notoriety as a fixer behind the scenes, famous for being unnoticed. "Valtos, first of the Reform Lords." That was how the man loved to be known. The gewgaw he preened himself on. A bauble he'd earned by voting to abolish its very significance, yet still liked to play with, to turn over in his hands, to flash. What a shit, the assassin thought, what a prick! That wasn't the reason for killing him, but it certainly made it easier to contemplate.

As the ferry visited its various stages the number of passengers increased. The assassin shifted the bag from across his knees and propped it in front of him, earning a nod and a grateful smile from the woman who sat down on the bench beside him. At Circular Quay he carried the bag off, and after clearing the pier he squatted and opened the bag. With a few quick movements he assembled the collapsible bicycle inside, folded and zipped the bag to stash size, and clipped the bag under the saddle.

Then he mounted the cycle and rode away to the left, around the harbor and up the long zigzag slope to Potts Point.

• • •

There was no reason for unease. Angus Cameron sat on a wicker chair on a hotel room balcony overlooking Sydney Harbour. On the small round table in front of him an Islay malt and a Havana panatela awaited his celebration. The air was warm, his clothing loose and fresh. Thousands of fruit bats labored across the dusk sky, from their daytime roost in the Botanic Gardens to their nighttime feeding grounds. From three stories below, the vehicle sounds and voices of the street carried no warnings.

Nothing was wrong, and yet something was wrong. Angus tipped back his chair and closed his eyes. He summoned headlines and charts. Local and global. Public and personal. Business and politics. The Warm War between the great power blocs, EU/Russia/PRC versus FUS/Japan/India/Brazil, going on as usual: diplomacy in Australasia, insurgency in Africa. Nothing to worry about there. Situation, as they say, nominal. Angus blinked away the images and shook his head. He stood up and stepped back into the room and paced around. He spread his fingers wide and waved his hands about, rotating his wrists as he did so. Nothing. Not a tickle.

Satisfied that the room was secure, he returned to his balcony seat. The time was fifteen minutes before eight. Angus toyed with his Zippo and the glass, and with the thought of lighting up, of taking a sip. He felt oddly as if that would be bad luck. It was a quite distinct feeling from the deeper unease, and easier to dismiss. Nevertheless, he waited. Ten minutes to go.

At eight minutes before eight his right ear started ringing. He flicked his earlobe.

"Yes?" he said.

His sister's avatar appeared in the corner of his eye. Calling from Manchester, England, EU. Local time 07:52.

"Oh, hello, Catriona," he said.

The avatar fleshed, morphing from a cartoon to a woman in her midthirties, a few years younger than him, sitting insubstantially across from him. His little sister, looking distracted. At least, he guessed she was. They hadn't spoken for five months, but she didn't normally make calls with her face unwashed and hair unkempt.

"Hi, Angus," Catriona said. She frowned. "I know this is . . . maybe a bit paranoid . . . but is this call secure?"

"Totally," said Angus.

Unlike Catriona, he had a firm technical grasp on the mechanism of cortical calls: the uniqueness of each brain's encoding of sensory impulses adding a further layer of impenetrable encryption to the cryptographic algorithms routinely applied . . . A uniquely encoded thought struck him.

"Apart from someone lip-reading me, I guess." He cupped his hand around his mouth. "Okay?"

Catriona looked more irritated than reassured by this demonstrative caution.

"Okay," she said. She took a deep breath. "I'm very dubious about the next release of the upgrade, Angus. It has at least one mitochondrial module that's not documented at all."

"That's impossible!" cried Angus, shocked. "It'd never get through."

"It's got this far," said Catriona. "No record of testing, either. I keep objecting, and I keep getting told it's being dealt with or it's not important or otherwise fobbed off. The release goes live in a *month*, Angus. There's no way that module can be documented in that time, let alone tested."

"I don't get it," said Angus. "I don't get it at all. If this were to get out it would sink Syn Bio's stock, for a start. Then there's audits and prosecutions . . . the Authority would break them up and stamp on the bits. Forget whistleblowing, Catriona, you should take this to the Authority in the company's *own* interests."

"I have," said Catriona. "And I just get the same runaround."

"What?"

If he'd heard this from anyone else, Angus wouldn't have believed it. The Human Enhancement Authority's reputation was beyond reproach. Impartial, impersonal, incorruptible, it was seen as the very image of an institution entrusted with humanity's (at least, European humanity's) evolutionary future.

Angus was old enough to remember when software didn't just seamlessly improve, day by day or hour by hour, but came out in discrete tranches called *releases*, several times a year. Genetic tech was still at that stage. Catriona's employer Syn Bio (mostly) supplied it, the HEA checked and (usually) approved it, and everyone in the EU who didn't have some religious objection found the latest fix in their physical mail and swallowed it.

"They're stonewalling," Catriona said.

"Don't worry," said Angus. "There must be some mistake. A bureaucratic foul-up. I'll look into it."

"Well, keep my name out of—"

The lights came on for Earth Hour.

"That won't be easy," Angus said, flinching and shielding his eyes as the balcony, the room, the building, and the whole sweep of cityscape below him lit up. "They'll know our connection, they'll know you've been asking—"

"I asked you to keep my name out of it," said Catriona. "I didn't say it would be easy."

"Look into it without bringing my *own* name into it?"

"Yes, exactly!" Catriona ignored his sarcasm—deliberately, from her tone. She looked around. "I can't concentrate with all this going on. Catch you later."

Angus waved a hand at the image of his sister, now ghostly under the blaze of the balcony's overhead lighting. "I'll keep in touch," he said dryly.

"Bye, bro."

Catriona faded. Angus lit his small cigar at last, and sipped the whisky. Ah. That was good, as was the view. Sydney Harbour was hazy in the distance, and even the gleaming shells of the Opera House, just visible over the rooftops, were fuzzy at the edges, the smart dust in the air scattering the extravagant outpouring of light. Angus savored the whisky and cigar to their respective ends, and then went out.

• • •

On the street the light was even brighter, to the extent that Angus missed his footing occasionally as he made his way up Macleay Street toward Kings Cross. He felt dazzled and disoriented, and considered lowering the gain on his eyes—but that, he felt in some obscure way, would not only have been cheating, it would have been missing the point. The whole thing about Earth Hour was to squander electricity, and if that spree had people reeling in the streets as if drunk, that was entirely in the spirit of the celebration.

It was all symbolic anyway, he thought. The event's promoters knew as well as he did that the amount of CO_2 being removed from the atmosphere by Earth Hour was insignificant—only a trivial fraction of the electricity wasted was carbon-negative rather than neutral—but it was the principle of the thing, dammit!

He found a table outside a bar close to Fitzroy Gardens, a tree-shaded plaza on the edge of which a transparent globe fountained water and light. He tapped an order on the table, and after a minute a barman arrived with a tall lager on a tray. Angus tapped again to tip, and settled back to drink and think. The air was hot as well as bright, the chilled beer refreshing. Around the fountain a dozen teenagers cooled themselves more directly, jumping in and out of the arcs of spray and splashing in the circular pool around the illuminated globe. Yells and squeals; few articulate words. Probably cortexting each other. It was the thing. The youth of today. Talking silently and behind your back. Angus smiled reminiscently and indulgently. He muted the enzymes that degraded the alcohol, letting himself get drunk. He could reverse it on an instant later, he thought, then thought that the trouble with that was that you seldom knew when to do it. Except in a real life-threatening emergency, being drunk meant you didn't know when it was time to sober up. You just noticed that things kept crashing.

He gave the table menu a minute of baffled inspection, then swayed inside to order his second pint. The place was almost empty. Angus heaved himself onto a barstool beside a tall, thin woman about his own age who sat alone and to all appearances collected crushed cigarette butts. She was just now adding to the collection, stabbing a good inch into the ashtray. A thick tall glass of pink stuff with a straw anchored her other hand to the bar counter. She wore a singlet over a thin bra, and skinny jeans above gold slingbacks. Ratty blond hair. It was a look.

"I've had two," she was explaining to the barman, who wasn't listening. She swung her badly aimed gaze on Angus. "And I'm squiffy already. God, I'm a cheap date."

"I'm cheaper," said Angus. "Squiffier, too. Drunk as a lord. Ha-ha. I used to be a lord, you know."

The woman's eyes got glassier. "So you did," she said. "So you did. Pleased to meet you, Mr. Cameron."

"Just call me Angus."

She extended a limp hand. "Glenda Glendale."

Angus gave her fingers a token squeeze, thinking that with a name like that she'd never stood a chance.

"Now ain't that the truth," Glenda said, with unexpected bitterness, and dipped her head to the straw.

"Did I say that out loud?" Angus said. "Jeez. Sorry."

"Nothing to be sorry about," Glenda said.

She opened a fresh pack of cigarettes, and tapped one out.

• • •

The assassin crouched behind a recycling bin in the alleyway beside the Thai restaurant opposite the bar, his bicycle propped against the wall. He zoomed his gaze to watch the target settle his arse on the stool, his elbow on the counter, and his attention on the floozy. Perfect. The assassin decided this was the moment to seize. He reached for the bike and with a few practiced twisting motions had it dismantled. The wheels he laid aside. The frame's reassembly, to a new form and function, was likewise deft.

• • •

Glenda fumbled the next lighting-up, and dropped her lighter. Angus stooped from the stool, more or less by reflex, to pick it up. As he did so there was a soft thud, and a moment later the loudest scream he'd ever heard. Glenda's legs lashed straight out. Her shin swiped his ear and struck his shoulder, tipping him to the floor. He crashed with the relaxation and anesthesia of the drunk. Glenda fell almost on top of him, all her limbs thrashing, her scream still splitting his ears. Angus raised his head and saw a feathered shaft sticking about six inches out of her shoulder.

The wound was nothing like severe enough to merit the screams or the spasms. Toxin, then. Modified stonefish, at a guess. The idea wasn't just that you died (though you did, in about a minute). You died in the worst pain it was possible to experience.

The barman vaulted the counter, feet hitting the floor just clear of Glenda's head. In his right hand he clutched a short-bladed sharp knife, one he might have used to slice limes. Angus knew exactly what he intended to do with it, and was appalled at the man's reckless courage.

"No!" Angus yelled.

Too late. A second dart struck the barman straight in the chest. He clutched at it for a moment; then his arms and legs flailed out and he keeled over, screaming even louder than Glenda. Now there were two spasming bodies on the floor. The knife skittered under a table.

Everything went dark, but it was just the end of Earth Hour. A good moment for the shooter to make their escape—or to finish the job.

Angus rolled on his back to keep an eye on the window and the doorway, and propelled himself with his feet along the floor, groping for the knife. His hand closed around the black handle. On his belly again, he elbowed his way to Glenda, grabbed her hair, slit her throat, and then slid the blade between cervical vertebrae and kept on cutting. He carried out the decapitation with skills he'd long ago used on deer. She didn't struggle—her nerves were already at saturation. It wasn't possible to add to this level of pain. Through a gusher of blood Angus crawled past the barman and did the same for him.

He hoped someone had called the police. He hoped that whoever had shot the darts had fled. Keeping low, stooping, he scurried around the back of the counter and reached up cautiously for the ice bucket. He got one on the ground and saw to his relief that there was another. He retrieved that too. Holding them in his arms, he slithered on his knees across the bloody floor back to the front of the bar, and stuffed the severed heads in one by one, jamming them in the ice.

Above the screaming from outside and the peal of alarms came the sound of jets. A police VTOL descended on the plaza, downdraft blowing tables away like litter in a breeze. The side opened and a cop, visored and armored, leapt out and sprinted across.

Angus stood up, blood-drenched from head to foot, knife in hand, arms wrapped awkwardly around the two ice buckets, from which the victims' hair and foreheads grotesquely protruded.

The copper halted in the doorway, taking in the scene in about a second.

"Well done, mate," he said. He reached out for the buckets. "Quick thinking. Now let's get these people to hospital."

• • •

Monstrous, sticky with blood, Angus crossed the street and stood in the alleyway at a barrier of black-and-yellow crime-scene tape. Backtracking the darts' trajectory had been the work of moments for the second cop out of the VTOL: even minutes after the attack, the lines in the smart soot had glowed like vapor trails in any enhanced gaze. An investigator in an isolation suit lifted the crossbow with gloved reverent hands. Cat-sized sniffing devices stalked about, extending sensors and sampling pads.

"What's with the bicycle wheels?" Angus asked, pointing.

"Surplus to requirements," the investigator said, standing up, holding the crossbow. She turned it over and around. "Collapsible bike, pre-grown tubular wood, synthetic. See, the handlebars form the bow, the crossbar the stock, the saddle the shoulder piece, the chain and pedal the winding mechanism, and the brake cable is the string. The darts were stashed inside one of the pieces."

"Seen that trick before?"

"Yeah, it's a hunting model."

"People go hunting on bicycles?"

"It's a sport." She laughed. "Offended any hunters lately?"

Angus wished he could see her face. He liked her voice.

"I offend a lot of people."

The investigator's head tilted. "Oh. So you do. Lord Valtos, huh?"

"Just call me—" He remembered what had happened to the last person he'd said that to, then decided not to be superstitious. "Just call me Angus. Angus Cameron."

"Whatever." She pulled off her hood and shook out her hair. "Fuck." She looked disgustedly at the cat things. "No traces. No surprise. Probably a spray job. You know, plastic skin? Even distorts the smart dust readings and street cam footage."

"You can do that?"

"Sure. It's expensive." She gave him a look. "I guess you're worth it."

Angus shrugged. "I'm rich, but my enemies are richer."

"So you're in deep shit."

"Only if they're smarter as well as richer, which I doubt."

"If you're smart, you'll not walk back to the hotel."

He took the hint, and the lift. They shrouded him in plastic for it, so the blood wouldn't get on the seats.

• • •

The reaction caught up with Angus as soon as the hotel room door closed behind him. He rushed to the bathroom and vomited. Shaking, he stripped off. As he emptied his pockets before throwing the clothes in the basket he found he'd picked up Glenda's lighter and cigarette pack. He put them to one side and showered. Afterward he sat in a bathrobe on the balcony, sipping malt on an empty stomach and chain-smoking Glenda's remaining cigarettes. She wouldn't be needing these for a few months. By then she might not even want them—the hospital would no doubt throw in a fix for her addiction, at least on the physical level, as it regrew her body and repaired her brain. Angus's earlier celebratory cigarillo had left him with a craving, and for the moment he indulged it. He'd take something to cure it in the morning.

When he felt steady enough, he closed his eyes and looked at the news. He found himself a prominent item on it. Spokespersons for various Green and Aboriginal coalitions had already disclaimed responsibility and deplored the attempt on his life. At this moment a sheepish representative of a nuclear-waste-handling company was in the studio, making a like disavowal. Angus smiled. He didn't think any of these were responsible—they'd have done a better job—but it pleased him to have his major opponents on the back foot. The potential benefit from that almost outweighed the annoyance of finding himself on the news at all.

The assassination attempt puzzled him. All the enemies he could think of—the list was long—would have sent a team to kill him, if they'd wanted to do something so drastic and potentially counterproductive. It seemed to him possible that the assassin had acted alone. That troubled him. Angus had always held that lone assassins were far more dangerous and prevalent than conspiracies.

He reviewed the bios linked to as shallow background for the news items about him. Most of them got the basic facts of his life right, from his childhood early in the century on a wind farm and experimental Green community in the Western Isles, through his academically mediocre but socially brilliant student years, when the networks and connections he'd established soon enabled his deals and ventures in the succession of technological booms that had kept the bubble economy expanding by fits and starts through seven decades: carbon capture, synthetic biology, microsatellites, fusion, smart dust, anti-aging, rejuve, augments . . . and so on, up to his current interest in geoengineering. Always in before the boom, out before the bust, he'd even ventured into politics via a questionably bestowed peerage just in time for the packed self-abolition of the Lords and to emerge with some quite unearned credit for the Reform. The descriptions ranged from "visionary social entrepreneur" and "daring venture capitalist" to "serial confidence trickster" and "brazen charlatan." There was truth in all of them. He'd burned a lot of fortunes in his time, while adding to his own. The list of people who might hold a private grudge against him was longer than the list of his public enemies.

Speaking of which, he had a conference to go to in the morning. He stubbed out the last of Glenda's cigarettes and went to bed.

• • •

The assassin woke at dawn on Manly Beach. He'd slept under a monofilament weave blanket, in a hollow where the sand met the scrub. He wore nothing but a watch and swimming trunks. He stood up, stretched, scrunched the blanket into the trunks' pocket, and went for a swim. No one was about.

Shoulder-deep in the sea, the assassin removed his trunks and watch, clutching them in one hand while rubbing his skin and hair all over with the other. He put them back on when he was sure that every remaining trace of the synthetic skin would be gone. Most of it, almost every scrap, had been dissolved as soon as he'd keyed a sequence on his palm after his failed attempt, just before he'd made his way, with a new appearance (his own) and chemical spoor, through various prechosen alleys and doorways and then sharp left on the next street, up to Kings Cross, and onto the train to Manly. But you couldn't make too certain.

Satisfied at last, he swam back to the still-deserted beach and began pacing along it, following a GPS reading that had some time during the night been relayed to his watch. The square meter of sand it led him to showed no trace that anything might be buried there. Which was as it should be—the arrangement for payment had been made well in advance. He'd been assured that he'd be paid whether or not he succeeded in killing the target. A kill would be a bonus, but—medical technology being what it was—he could hardly be expected to guarantee it. A credible near miss was almost as acceptable.

He began to dig with his hands. About forty centimeters down his fingertips brushed something hard and metallic.

He wasn't to know it was a land mine, and he didn't.

• • •

One of the nuclear power companies sent an armored limo to pick Angus up after breakfast—a courtesy, the accompanying ping claimed. He sneered at the transparency of the gesture, and accepted the ride. At least it shielded him from the barracking of the sizable crowd (with a far larger virtual flash mob in spectral support) in front of the Hilton Conference Centre. He was pleased to note, just before the limo whirred down the ramp to the underground car park (which gave him a moment of dread, not entirely irrational), that the greatest outrage seemed to have been aroused by the title of the conference, his own suggestion at that: Greening Australia.

Angus stepped out of the lift and into the main hall. A chandelier the size of a small spacecraft. Acres of carpet, on which armies of seats besieged a stage. Tables of drinks and nibbles along the sides. The smell of coffee and fruit juice.

Hundreds of delegates milling around. To his embarrassment, his arrival was greeted with a ripple of applause. He waved both arms in front of his face, smiled self-deprecatingly, and turned to the paper plates and the fruit on sticks.

Someone had made a beeline for him.

"Morning, Valtos."

Angus turned, switching his paper coffee cup to the paper plate and sticking out his right hand. Jan Maartens, tall and blond. The EU's man on the scene. Biotech and enviro portfolio. The European Commission and Parliament had publicly deplored Greening Australia, though they couldn't do much to stop it.

"Hello, Commissioner." They shook.

Formalities over, Maartens cracked open a grin. "So how are you, you old villain?"

"The hero of the hour, I gather."

"Modest as always, Angus. There's already a rumor the *attentat* was a setup for the sympathy vote."

"Is there indeed?" Angus chuckled. "I wish I'd thought of that. Regretfully, no."

Maartens's lips compressed. "I know, I know. In all seriousness . . . my sympathy, of course. It must have been a most traumatic experience."

"It was," Angus said. "A great deal worse for the victims, mind you."

"Indeed." Maartens looked grave. "Anything we can do . . ."

"Thanks."

A bell chimed for the opening session.

"Well . . ." Maartens glanced down at his delegate pack.

"Yes . . . catch you later, Jan."

Angus watched the Belgian out of sight, frowning, then took a seat near the back, and close to the aisle. The conference chair, Professor Chang, strolled onstage and waved her hand. To a roar of applause and some boos the screen behind her flared into a display of the Greening Australia logo, then morphed to a sequence of pixel-perfect views of the scheme: a translucent carbon-fiber barrier, tens of kilometers high, hundreds of kilometers long, that would provide Australia with a substitute for its missing mountain range and bring rainfall to the interior. On the one hand, it was modest: it would use no materials not already successfully deployed in the space elevators and would cost far less. Birds would fly through it almost as easily as butting through a cobweb. On the other hand, it was the most insanely ambitious scheme of geoengineering yet tried: changing the face of an entire continent.

Decades ago, Angus had got in early in a project to exploit the stability and aridity of Australia's heart by making it the nuclear-waste-storage center of the world. The flak from that had been nothing to the outcry over this. As the morning went on, Angus paid little attention to the presentations and debates. He'd heard and seen them all before. His very presence here was enough to influence the discussion, to get smart money sniffing around, bright young minds wondering. Instead, he sat back, closed his eyes, watched market reactions, and worried about a few things.

The first was Maartens's solicitude. Something in the Commissioner's manner hadn't been quite right—a little too close in some ways, a little too distant and impersonal in others. Angus ran analyses in his head of the sweat-slick in the handshake, the modulations of the voice, the saccades of his gaze. Here, augmentation confirmed intuition: the man was very uneasy about something, perhaps guilty.

Hah!

The next worries were the unsubstantiated unease he'd felt just before his sister's call, and the content of that call. It would have been nice, in a way, to attribute the anxiety to some premonition: of the unusual and worrying call, or of the assassination attempt. But Angus was firm in his conviction of one-way causality. Nor could he blame it on some free-floating anxiety: his psychiatric ware was up to date, and its scans mirrored, second by second, an untroubled soul.

Had it been something he'd seen in the market, but had grasped the significance of only subconsciously? Had he made the mistake that could be fatal to a trader: suppressed a niggle?

He rolled back the displays to the previous afternoon and reexamined them. There it was. Hard to spot, but there in the figures. Someone big was going long on wheat. A dozen hedge funds had placed multiple two-year trades on oil, uranium, and military equipment. Biotech was up. A tiny minority of well-placed ears had listened to voices prophesying war. The Warm War, turning hot at last.

Angus thought about what Catriona had told him, about the undocumented, unannounced mitochondrial module in the EU's next genetic upgrade. An immunity to some biological weapon? But if the EU was planning a first strike—on Japan, the Domain, some other part of the former United States, Brazil, it didn't matter at this point—they would need food security. And food security, surely, would be enhanced if Greening Australia went ahead.

So why was Commissioner Maartens now onstage, repeating the EU's standard line against the scheme? Unless . . . unless that was merely the line they had to take in public, and they really wanted the conference to endorse the scheme. And what better way to secretly support that than to maneuver its most implacable opponents into the awkward position of having to disown an assassination attempt on its most vociferous proponent? An attempt that, whether it succeeded or failed, would win Angus what Maartens had—in a double or triple bluff—called the sympathy vote.

Angus's racing suspicions were interrupted by a ringing in his ear. He flicked his earlobe. "A moment, please," he said. He stood up, stepped apologetically past the delegate between him and the aisle, and turned away to face the wall.

"Yes?"

It was the investigator who'd spoken to him last night. She was standing on a beach, near the edge of a crater in the sand with a bloody mess around it.

"We think we may have found your man," she said.

"I believe I can say the same," said Angus.

"What?"

"You'll see. Send a couple of plainclothes into the Hilton Centre, discreetly. Ask them to ping me when they're in place. I'll take it from there."

As he turned back to face across the crowd to the stage he saw that Maartens had sat down, and that Professor Chang was looking along the rows of seats as if searching for someone. Her gaze alighted on him, and she smiled.

"Lord Valtos?" she said. "I know you're not on the speakers list, but I see you're on your feet, and I'm sure we'd all be interested to hear what you have to say in response to the commissioner's so strongly stated points."

Angus bowed from the waist. "Thank you, Madame Chair," he said. He cleared his throat, waiting to make sure that his voice was synched to the amps. He zoomed his eyes, fixing on Maartens, swept the crowd of turned heads with an out-of-focus gaze and his best smile, then faced the stage.

"Thank you," he said again. "Well, my response will be brief. I fully agree with every word the esteemed commissioner has said."

A jolt went through Maartens like an electric shock. It lasted only a moment, and he'd covered his surprise even before the crowd had registered its own reaction with a hiss of indrawn breath. If Angus hadn't been looking at Maartens in close-up he'd have missed it himself. He returned to his seat and waited for the police to make contact. It didn't take them more than about five minutes.

Just time enough for him to go short on shares in Syn Bio.

TAIYO FUJII

VIOLATION OF THE TRUENET SECURITY ACT

(2013)

Translated from the Japanese by Jim Hubbert

THE BELL FOR THE LAST TASK of the night started chiming before I got to my station. I had the office to myself, and a mug of espresso. It was time to start tracking zombies.

I took the mug of espresso from the beverage table and zigzagged through the darkened cube farm toward the one strip of floor still lit for third shift staff, only me.

Zombies are orphan Internet services. They wander aimlessly, trying to execute some programmed task. They can't actually infect anything, but otherwise the name is about right. TrueNet's everywhere now and has been for twenty years, but Japan never quite sorted out what to do with all the legacy servers that were stranded after the Lockout. So you get all these zombies shuffling around, firing off mails to nonexistent addresses, pushing ads no one will see, maybe even sending money to nonexistent accounts. The living dead.

Zombie trackers scan firewall logs for services the bouncer turned away at the door. If you see a trace of something that looks like a zombie, you flag it so the company mail program can send a form letter to the server administrator, telling him to deep-six it. It's required by the TrueNet Security Act, and it's how I made overtime by warming a chair in the middle of the night.

"All right, show me what you got."

As soon as my butt hit the chair, the workspace suspended above the desk flashed the login confirmation.

INITIATE INTERNET ORPHAN SERVICE SEARCH
TRACKER: MINAMI TAKASAWA

The crawl came up and just sat there, jittering. Damn. I wasn't *looking* at it. As soon as I went to the top of the list and started eyeballing URLs in order, it started scrolling.

The TrueNet Security Act demands human signoff on each zombie URL. Most companies have you entering checkmarks on a printed list, so I guess it was nice of my employer to automate things so trackers could just scan the log visually. It's a pretty advanced system. Everything is networked, from the visual recognition sensors in your augmented reality contact lenses to the office security cameras and motion sensors, the pressure sensors in the furniture, and the infrared heat sensors. One way or another, they figure out what you're looking at. You still have to stay on your toes. The system was only up and running for a few months when the younger trackers started bitching about it.

Chen set all this up, two years ago. He's from Anhui Province, out of Hefei I think. I'll always remember what he said to me when we were beta-testing the system together.

"Minami, all you have to do is treat the sensor values as a coherence and apply Floyd's cyclic group function."

Well, if that's *all* I had to do . . . What did that mean, anyway? I'd picked up a bit, here and there, about quantum computing algorithms, but this wasn't like anything I'd ever heard.

Chen might've sounded like he was fresh off a UFO, but in a few days he'd programmed a multi-sensor automated system for flagging zombies. It wasn't long before he left the rest of us in Security in the dust and jumped all the way up to Program Design on the strength of ingenuity and tech skills. Usually somebody starting out as a worker—a foreigner, no less—who made it up to Program Design would be pretty much shunned, but Chen was so far beyond the rest of us that it seemed pointless to try and drag him down.

The crawl was moving slower. "Minami, just concentrate and it will all be over quickly." I can still see Chen pushing his glasses, with their thick black frames, up his nose as he gave me this pointer.

I took his advice and refocused on the crawl. The list started moving smoothly again, zombie URLs showing up green.

Tracking ought to be boring, on the whole, but it's fun looking for zombies you recognize from the Internet era. Maybe that's why I never heard workers older than their late thirties or so complain about the duty.

Still, I never quite got it. Why use humans to track zombies? TrueNet servers use QSL recognition, quantum digital signatures. No way is a zombie on some legacy server with twenty-year-old settings going to get past those. I mean, we could just leave them alone. They're harmless.

MESSAGE FORMATTING COMPLETE. PLEASE SEND.

The synth voice—Chen's, naturally—came through the AR phono chip next to my eardrum. The message to the server administrators rolled up the screen, requesting zombie termination. There were more than three hundred on the list. I tipped my mug back, grinding the leftover sugar against my palate with my tongue, and was idly scrolling through the list again when something caught my eye.

302:com.socialpay socialpay.com/payment/?
transaction=paypal.com&account

"SocialPay? You're alive?"

How could I forget? I created this domain and URL. From the time I cooked it up as a graduation project until the day humanity was locked out of the Internet, SocialPay helped people—just a few hundred, but anyway—make small payments using optimized bundles of discount coupons and cash. So it was still out there after all, a zombie on some old server. The code at the tail said it was trying to make a payment to another defunct service.

MR. TAKASAWA, YOU HAVE TEN MINUTES TO EXIT THE BUILDING. PLEASE SEND YOUR MESSAGE AND COMPLETE THE SECURITY CHECK BEFORE YOU LEAVE.

So Chen's system was monitoring entry and exit now too. The whole system was wickedly clever. I deleted SocialPay from the hit list and pressed SEND.

I had to see that page one more time. If someone was going to terminate the service, I wanted to do it myself. SocialPay wasn't just a zombie for someone to obliterate.

• • •

The city of fifty million was out there, waiting silently as I left the service entrance. The augmented reality projected by my contact lenses showed crowds of featureless gray avatars shuffling by. The cars on the streets were blank too; no telling what makes and models they were. Signs and billboards were blacked out except for the bare minimum needed to navigate. All this and more, courtesy of Anonymous Cape, freeware from the group of the same name, the guys who went on as if the Lockout had never happened. Anyone plugged into AR would see me as gray and faceless too.

I turned the corner to head toward the station, the dry December wind slamming against me. Something, a grain of sand maybe, flew up and made my eye water, breaking up my AR feed. Color and life and individuality started leaking back into the blank faces of the people around me. I could always upgrade to a corneal implant to avoid these inconvenient effects, but it seemed like overkill just to get the best performance out of the Cape, especially since any cop with a warrant could defeat it. Anyway, corneal implants are frigging expensive. I wasn't going to shell out money just to be alone on the street.

I always felt somehow defeated after a zombie session. Walking around among the faceless avatars and seeing my own full-color self, right after a trip to the lost Internet, always made me feel like a loser. Of course, that's just how the Cape works. To other people, I'm gray, faceless Mr. Nobody. It's a trade-off—they can't see me, and I can't see their pathetic attempts to look special. It's fair enough, and if people don't like it, tough. I don't need to see ads for junk that some designer thinks is original, and I don't have to watch people struggling to stand out and look different.

The company's headquarters faces Okubo Avenue. The uncanny flatness of that multilane thoroughfare is real, not an effect of the AR. Sustainable asphalt, secreted by designed terrestrial coral. I remembered the urban legends about this living pavement—it not only absorbed pollutants and particulate matter, but you could also toss a dead animal onto it and the coral would eat it. The thought made me run, not walk, across the street. I crossed here every day and I knew the legends were bull, but they still frightened me, which I have to say is pathetic. When I got to the other side, I was out of breath. Even more pathetic.

Getting old sucks. Chen the Foreign-Born is young and brilliant. The company understood that, and they were right to send him up to Project Design. They were just as uncompromising in their assessment of our value down in Security. Legacy programming chops count for zip, and that's not right.

No one really knows, even now, why so many search engines went insane and wiped the data on every PC and mobile device they could reach through the web. Some people claim it was a government plot to force us to adopt a gated web. Or cyberterrorism. Maybe the data recovery program became self-aware and rebelled. There were too many theories to track. Whatever, the search engines hijacked all the bandwidth on the planet and locked humanity out of the Internet, which pretty much did it for my career as a programmer.

It took a long time to claw back the stolen bandwidth and replace it with TrueNet, a true verification-based network. But I screwed up and missed my chance. During the Great Recovery, services that harnessed high-speed parallel processing and quantum digital signature modules revolutionized the web, but I never got around to studying quantum algorithms. That was twenty years ago, and since then the algorithms have only gotten more sophisticated. For me, that whole world of coding is way out of reach.

But at least one good thing had happened. SocialPay had survived. If the settings were intact, I should be able to log in, move all that musty old PHP code, and try updating it with some quantum algorithms. There had to be a plug-in for this kind of thing, something you didn't have to be a genius like Chen to use. If the transplant worked, I could show it to my boss, who knows—maybe even get a leg up to Project Design. The company didn't need geniuses like Chen on every job. They needed engineers to repurpose old code too.

In that case, maybe I wouldn't have to track zombies anymore.

• • •

I pinched the corners of the workspace over my little desk at home and threw my arms out in the resize gesture. Now the borders of the workspace were embedded in the walls of my apartment. Room to move. At the office, they made us keep our spaces at standard monitor size, even though the whole point is to have a big area to move around in.

I scrolled down the app list and launched VM Pad, a hardware emulator. From within the program, I chose my Mac disk image. I'd used it for recovering emails and photos after the Lockout, but this would be the first time I ever used it to develop something. The OS booted a lot faster than I remembered. When the little login screen popped up, I almost froze with embarrassment.

id:Tigerseye
password

Where the hell did I get that stupid ID? I logged in—I'd ever only used the one password, even now—and got the browser screen I had forgotten to close before my last logout.

Server not found

Okay, expected. This virtual machine was from a 2017 archive, so no way was it going to connect to TrueNet. Still, the bounceback was kind of depressing.

Plan B: Meshnet. Anonymous ran a portable network of nonsecure wireless gateways all over the city. Meshnet would get me into my legacy server. There had to be someone from Anonymous near my apartment, which meant there'd be a Meshnet node. M-nodes were only accessible up to a few hundred yards away, yet you could find one just about anywhere in Tokyo. It was crazy—I didn't know how they did it.

I extended VM Pad's dashboard from the screen edge, clicked NEW CONNECTION, then MESHNET.

Searching for node . . .

WELCOME TO TOKYO NODE 5.
CONNECTING TO THE INTERNET IS LEGAL.
VIOLATING THE TRUENET SECURITY ACT IS ILLEGAL.
THE WORLD NEEDS THE FREEDOM OF THE INTERNET,
SO PLAY NICE AND DON'T BREAK ANY LAWS.

Impressive warning, but all I wanted to do was take a peek at the service and extract my code. It would be illegal to take an Internet service and sneak it onto TrueNet with a quantum access code, but stuff that sophisticated was way beyond my current skill set.

I clicked the TERMINAL icon at the bottom of the screen to access the console. Up came the old command input screen, which I barely remembered how to use.

What was the first command? I curled my fingers like I was about to type something on a physical keyboard.

Wait—that's it. Fingers.

I had to have a hardware keyboard. My old MacBook was still in the closet. It wouldn't even power up anymore, but that wasn't the point. I needed the feel of the keyboard.

I pulled the laptop out of the closet. The aluminum case was starting to get powdery. I opened it up and put it on the desk. The inside was pristine. I pinched VM Pad's virtual keyboard, dragged it on top of the Mac keyboard, and positioned it carefully. When I was satisfied with the size and position, I pinned it.

It had been ages since I used a computer this small. I hunched my shoulders a bit and suspended my palms over the board. The metal case was cold against my wrists. I curled my fingers over the keys and put the tips of my index fingers on the home bumps. Instantly, the command flowed from my fingers.

ssh -l tigerseye socialpay.com

I remembered! The command was stored in my muscle memory. I hit RETURN and got a warning, ignored it and hit RETURN, entered the password, hit RETURN again.

socialpay$

"Yes!"

I was in. Was this all it took to get my memory going—my fingers? In that case, I may as well have the screen too. I dragged VMPad's display onto the Mac's LCD screen. It was almost like having my old friend back. I hit COMMAND + TAB to bring the browser to the front, COMMAND + T for New Tab. I input *soci* and the address filled in. RETURN!

The screen that came up a few seconds later was not the SocialPay I remembered. There was the logo at the top, the login form, the payment service icons, and the combined payment amount from all the services down at the bottom. The general layout was the same, but things were crumbling here and there and the colors were all screwed up.

"Looks pretty frigging odd . . ."

Without thinking, I input the commands to display the server output on console.

curl socialpay.com/ | less

"What is *this?* Did I minify the code?"

I was all set to have fun playing around with HTML for the first time in years, but the code that filled the screen was a single uninterrupted string of characters, no line breaks. This was definitely not what I remembered. It was HTML, but with long strings of gibberish bunged into the code.

Encountering code I couldn't recognize bothered me. Code spanning multiple folders is only minified to a single line when you have, say, fifty or a hundred thousand users and you need to lighten the server load, but not for a service that had a few hundred users at most.

I copied the single mega-line of HTML. VM Pad's clipboard popped in, suspended to the right of the Mac. I pinched out to implement lateral parse and opened the clipboard in my workspace. Now I could get a better look at the altered code.

It took me a while to figure out what was wrong. As the truth gradually sank in, I started to lose my temper.

Someone had gone in and very expertly spoiled the code. The properties I thought were garbage were carefully coded to avoid browser errors. Truly random code would've compromised the whole layout.

"What the hell is this? If you're going to screw around, do it for a reason."

I put the command line interface on top again and used the tab key—I still use the command line shell at work, I should probably be proud of my mastery of this obsolete environment—to open SocialPay.

```
vim -/home/www/main.php
<?php
/* (function_model_0x01*/
/* (make-q-array qureg x1[1024] qureg x2[1024] qureg x4[4])
#(qnil(nil) qnil(nil) 1024)) */
; #Tells System to load the theme and output it; #@var bool
; define('WP_USE_THEMES', true)
; require('./wpress/wp-blog-header.php');
/* (arref #x1#x2 #x3 #x4 ) ;#Lorem ipsum dolor sit amet, concectetur
(let H(x2[1]) H(x1[3]) H(x2[3]) H(x3[1])...
```

What? The section of code that looked like the main routine included my commands, but I definitely couldn't remember writing the iterative processing and HTML code generation. It didn't even look like PHP, though the DEFINE phrases looked familiar. I was looking at nonfunctional quantum algorithms.

I stared at the inert code and wondered what it all meant. By the time I remembered the one person who could probably make sense of it, four hours had slipped away.

"Wonder if Chen's awake?"

• • •

"Minami? What are *you* doing at this hour?"

Five in the morning and I had an AR meeting invitation. I didn't know Chen all that well, so I texted him. I had no idea I'd get a response instantly, much less an invitation to meet in augmented reality.

His avatar mirrored the real Chen: short black hair and black, plastic-framed glasses. His calm gaze, rare in someone so young, hinted at his experience and unusual gifts. My own avatar was *almost* the real me: a couple of sizes slimmer, the skin around the jaw a bit firmer, that sort of thing.

Over the last two years, Chen had polished his Japanese to the point you could hardly tell he was an Outsider. Trilinguals weren't all that unusual, but his fluency in Mandarin, English, and Japanese, for daily conversation right up to technical discussions and business meetings, marked him as a genuine elite.

"Chen, I hope I'm not disturbing you. Got a minute to talk?"

"No problem. What's going on?"

"I've got some minified code I'd like you to look at. I think it's nonfunctional quantum algorithms, but in an old scripting language called PHP. I'm wondering if there's some way to separate the junk from the rest of the code."

"A PHP quantum circuit? Is that even possible? Let's have a look."

"Sure. Sorry, it's just the raw code."

I flicked three fingers upward on the table surface to open the file browser and tapped the SocialPay code file to open a sharing frame. Chen's AR stage was already set to ALLOW SHARING, which seemed prescient. I touched the file with a fingertip, and it stuck. As soon as I dropped it into the sharing frame, the folder icon popped in on Chen's side of the table.

He waved his hand to start the security scan. When the SAFE stamp came up, he took the file and fanned the pages out on the table like a printed document. The guy was more analog than I thought.

He went through it carefully page by page, and finally looked up at me, grinning happily.

"Very interesting. Something you're working on?"

"I wrote the original program for the Internet. I lost it after the Lockout, but it looks like someone's been messing with it. I didn't know you could read PHP."

"This isn't the first time I've seen it. You're right, I hardly use it, but the procedure calls aren't hard to make out. Wait a minute . . . Was there a PHP procedure for Q implementation?"

Q is a modeling language for quantum calculation, but I'd never heard of anyone implementing it in PHP, which hardly anyone even remembered anymore.

"So that's Q, after all."

"I think so. This is a quantum walk pattern. Not that it's usually written in such a compressed format. Of course, we usually never see raw Q code."

"Is that how it works?"

"Yes, the code depends on the implementation chip. Shall I put this back into something functional? You'd be able to read it then."

"Thanks, that would help a lot."

"No problem. It's a brain workout. I usually don't get a chance to play around with these old programming languages, and Q implementation in PHP sounds pretty wild. I can have it back to you this afternoon."

"Really? That soon?"

"Don't look so surprised. I don't think I'm going to get any sleep anyway. I'll start right now. You should go back to bed."

He logged out. He didn't seem tired or sleepy at all.

• • •

I stared at the security routine running in my workspace and tried to suppress another yawn. After my meeting with Chen I'd had a go at reading the code myself. That was a mistake. I needed sleep. Every time I yawned my eyes watered, screwing up the office's cheapshit AR stage. I was past forty, too old for all-nighters.

Right about the fifteenth yawn, as I was making a monumental effort to clamp my jaw, I noticed a murmur spreading through the office. It seemed to be coming toward me. I noticed the other engineers looking at something behind me and swiveled to find Chen standing there.

"Many thanks, Minami. I had a lot of fun with this."

Now I understood the whispering. Program developers rarely came down to the Security floor.

"You finished already?"

"Yes, I wanted to give it to you." Chen put a fingertip to the temple of his glasses and lifted them slightly in the invitation gesture for an AR meeting. The stage on our floor was public, and Chen wanted to take the conversation private. But—

"Chen, I can't. You know that."

His eyes widened. He'd been a worker here two years ago. It must've been coming back to him. Workers in Security weren't allowed to hold Private Mode meetings.

"Ah, right. Sorry about that." He bowed masterfully. Where did he find the time to acquire these social graces, I wondered. Back when we'd been working side by side, he'd told me about growing up poor in backcountry China, but you wouldn't know it from the refined way he executed the simplest movements.

"All right, Minami." He lifted his glasses again. "Shall we?"

"Chen, I just told you . . . Huh?"

The moment he withdrew his finger from his glasses, the AR phono chip near my eardrum suppressed the sounds around me. I'd never been in Private Mode in the office before. I never liked the numbness you feel in your face and throat from the feedback chips, but now Chen and I could communicate without giving away anything from our expressions or lip movements.

"Don't forget, I'm sysadmin too. I can break rules now and then."

The colors around us faded, almost to black and white. The other workers seemed to lose interest and started turning back to their workspaces. From their perspective, I was facing my desk too. Chen had set my avatar to Office Work mode. It was unsettling to see my own avatar. If the company weren't so stingy, Chen and I wouldn't have been visible at all, but of course they'd never pony up for something that good, not for the Security Level anyway.

Chen glanced at the other workers before he spoke.

"I enjoyed the code for SocialPay. I haven't seen raw Q code for quite a while. The content was pretty wild."

"That's not a word you usually use. Was it something I could understand?"

"Don't worry about it. You don't need to read Q. You can't anyway, so it's irrelevant—Hey, don't look at me like that. I think you should check the revision history. If you don't fix the bugs, it'll just keep filling up with garbage."

"Bugs?"

"Check the test log. I think even someone like you can handle this."

Someone like me. It sounded like Chen had the answer I was looking for. And he wasn't going to give it to me.

"If I debug it, will you tell me who did this?"

"*If* you debug it. One more thing. You can't go home tonight."

"Why? What are you saying?"

"Your local M-node is Tokyo 5.25. I'm going to shut that down. Connect from iFuze. I'll have someone there to help you."

Chen detached a small tag from his organizer and handed it to me. When it touched my palm, it morphed into a URL bookmark.

iFuze was a twenty-four-hour net café where workers from the office often spent the night after second shift. Why was it so important for me to connect from there? And if Chen could add or delete Meshnet nodes—

"Chen . . . ?" *Are you Anonymous?*

"Be seeing you. Good hunting!"

He touched his glasses. The color and bustle of the office returned, and my avatar merged with my body. Chen left the floor quickly, with friendly nods to workers along his route, like a movie star.

"Takasawa, your workspace display is even larger than usual today. Or am I wrong?"

My supervisor, a woman about Chen's age, didn't wait for an answer. She flicked the pile toward me to cover half my workspace "Have it your way, then."

As I sat there, alone again, it slowly dawned on me that the only way to catch whoever was messing with SocialPay would be to follow the instructions that had been handed down from on high.

• • •

The big turnabout in front of Iidabashi Station was a pool of blue-black shadows from the surrounding skyscrapers. The stars were just coming out. Internal combustion vehicles had been banned from the city, and the sustainable asphalt that covered Tokyo's roads sucked up all airborne particles. Now the night sky was alarmingly crystalline. Unfortunately, the population seemed to be expanding in inverse proportion to the garbage. Gray avatars headed for home in a solid mass. I never ceased to be astonished by Tokyo's crowds.

Anonymous Cape rendered the thousands of people filling the sidewalks as faceless avatars in real time. I'd never given it much thought, but the Cape was surprisingly powerful. I'd always thought of Anonymous as a league of Luddites, but Chen's insinuation of his membership changed my opinion of them.

iFuze was in a crumbling warehouse on a back street a bit of a hike from the station. The neighboring buildings were sheathed in sustainable tiles and paint, but iFuze's weathered, dirt-streaked exterior more or less captured how I felt when I compared myself to Chen.

I got off the creaking elevator, checked in, and headed for the lounge. It stank of stale sweat. AR feedback has sights and sounds covered, but smells you have to live with.

I opened my palmspace, tapped Chen's bookmark, and got a node list. There was a new one on the list, Tokyo 2. Alongside was the trademark Anonymous mask, revolving slowly. Never saw that before. I was connected to the Internet.

I scoped out an empty seat at the back of the lounge that looked like a good place to get some work done in privacy, but before I could get there, a stranger rose casually and walked up to me. His avatar was in full color. The number 5 floated a few inches from the left side of his head. So this must be the help Chen promised me.

"Welcome, Number Two."

"Two?"

"See? Turn your head." He pointed next to my head. I had a number just like he did. "Please address me as Five. Number One has requested that I assist you—oh, you are surprised? I'm in color. You see, we are both node administrators. This means we are already in Private Mode. I'm eager to assist you with your task today."

Talkative guy. Chen said he would help me, but I wasn't sure how.

"Please don't bother to be courteous," he continued. "It's quite unnecessary. This way, then. Incidentally, which cluster are you from? Of course, you're not required to say. Since the Lockout, I've been with the Salvage Cluster . . ."

As he spoke, Number Five led me to a long counter with bar stools facing the windows.

"If there is an emergency, you can escape through that window. I'll take care of the rest. Number One went out that way himself, just this morning."

"Chen was here?"

Why would I worry about escaping? Connecting to the Internet was no crime. Meshnet was perfectly legal. Why would Anonymous worry about preparing an escape route?

"Number Two, please refrain from mentioning names. We may be in Private Mode, but law enforcement holds one of the quantum keys. Who's to say we're not under surveillance at this very moment? But please, proceed with your task. I will watch over your shoulder and monitor for threats."

I knew the police could eavesdrop on Private Mode, but they needed a warrant to do that. Still, so far I hadn't broken any laws. Had Chen? The "help" he'd sent was no engineer, but some kind of bodyguard.

Fine. I got my MacBook out and put it on the counter. Five's eyes bulged with surprise.

"Oh, a Macker! That looks like the last MacBook Air that Apple made. Does it work?"

"Unfortunately, she's dead."

"A classic model. Pure solid state, no spinning drives. It was Steve Jobs himself who—"

More talk. I ignored him and mapped my workspace keyboard and display onto the laptop. This brought Five's lecture to a sudden halt. He made a formal bow.

"I would be honored if you would allow me to observe your work. I have salvaged via Meshnet for years. I may even be better acquainted with some aspects of the Internet than you are. Number One also lets me observe his work. But I have to say, it's quite beyond me."

Five scratched the back of his head, apparently feeling foolish. Well, if he were the kind of engineer who understood what Chen was doing, he wouldn't be hanging out at iFuze.

"Feel free to watch. Suggestions are welcome."

"Thank you, thank you very much."

I shared my workspace with Five. He pulled a barstool out from the counter and sat behind me. His position blocked the exit, but with my fingers on the Mac, I somehow wasn't worried.

Time to get down to it. I didn't feel comfortable just following Chen's instructions, but they were the only clue I had. First, a version check.

```
git tag –l
```

My fingers moved spontaneously. Good. I'd been afraid the new environment might throw me off.

```
socialpay v3.805524525e+9
socialpay v3.805524524e+9
socialpay v3.805524523e+9
```

"Version 3.8?"

Whoever was messing with SocialPay was updating the version number, even though the program wasn't functional. I'd never even gotten SocialPay out of beta, had never had plans to.

"Number Two, that is not a version number. It is an exponent: three billion, eight hundred and five million, five hundred and twenty-four thousand, five hundred and twenty-three. Clearly impossible for a version number. If the number had increased by one every day since the Lockout, it would be seven thousand; every hour, one hundred seventy thousand; every minute, ten million. Even if the version had increased by one every second, it would only be at six hundred million."

Idiot savant? As I listened to Five reeling off figures, my little finger was tapping the up arrow and hitting Return to repeat the command. This couldn't be right. It had to be an output error.

socialpay v3.805526031e+9

The number had changed again.

“Look, it’s fifteen hundred higher,” said Five. “Are there thousands of programmers, all busily committing changes at once?

“Fifteen hundred versions in five seconds? Impossible. It’s a joke.”

Git revision control numbers are always entered deliberately. I didn’t get the floating-point numbers, but it looked like someone was changing them just to change them—and he was logged into this server right now. It was time to nail this clown. I brought up the user log.

```
who -a
TigersEye pts/1245 2037-12-23 19:12 (2001:4860:8006::62)
TigersEye pts/1246 2037-12-23 19:12 (2001:4860:8006::62)
TigersEye pts/1247 2037-12-23 19:12 (2001:4860:8006::62)
...
```

“Number Two—this address . . .”

I felt the hair on the nape of my neck rising. I knew that IP address; we all did. A corporate IP address.

The Lockout Address.

On that day twenty years ago, after the search engine’s recovery program wiped my MacBook, that address was the only thing the laptop displayed. Five probably saw the same thing. So did the owner of every device the engine could reach over the Internet.

“Does that mean it’s still alive?”

“In the salvager community, we often debate that very question.”

Instinctively I typed *git diff* to display the incremental revisions. The black screen instantly turned almost white as an endless string of characters streamed upward. None of this had anything to do with the SocialPay I knew.

“Number Two, are those all diffs? They appear to be random substitutions.”

“Not random.”

If the revisions had been random, SocialPay’s home page wouldn’t have displayed. Most of the revisions were unintelligible, some kind of quantum modeling code. The sections I could read were proper PHP, expertly revised. In some locations, variable names had been replaced and redundancies weeded out. Yet in other locations, the code was meandering and bloated.

This was something I knew how to fix.

“Are you certain, Number Two? At the risk of seeming impertinent, these revisions do appear meaningless.”

The Editor was suffering. This was something Five couldn’t grasp. To be faced with nonfunctional code, forever hoping that rewriting and cleaning it up would somehow solve the problem, even as you knew your revisions were meaningless.

The Editor was shifting code around, hoping this would somehow solve a problem whose cause would forever be elusive. It reminded me of myself when the Internet was king. The decisive difference between me and the Editor was the sheer volume of revisions. No way could an engineer manage to—

"He's not a person."

"Number Two, what did you just say?"

"The Editor isn't a person. He's not human."

I knew it as soon as I said it. A computer was editing SocialPay. I also understood why the IP address pointed to the company that shut humanity out of the Internet.

"It's the recovery program."

"I don't understand." Five peered at me blankly. The idea was so preposterous I didn't want to say it.

"You know why the Lockout happened."

"Yes. The search engine recovery software was buggy and overwrote all the operating systems of all the computers—"

"No way a bug could've caused that. The program was too thorough."

"You have a point. If the program had been buggy, it wouldn't have gotten through all the data center firewalls. Then there's the fact that it reinstalled the OS on many different types of devices. That must have taken an enormous amount of trial and error—"

"That's it! Trial and error, using evolutionary algorithms. An endless stream of programs suited to all kinds of environments. That's how the Lockout happened."

"Ah! Now I understand."

Just why the recovery program would reach out over the Internet to force cold reinstalls of the OS on every device it could reach was still a mystery. The favored theory among engineers was that the evolutionary algorithms various search companies used to raise efficiency had simply run away from them. Now the proof was staring me in the face.

"The program is still running, analyzing code and using evolutionary algorithms to run functionality tests. It's up to almost four billion on SocialPay alone."

"Your program isn't viable?"

"The page displays, but the service isn't active. It can't access the payment companies, naturally. Still, the testing should be almost complete. Right—that's why Chen wanted me to look at the test log."

Chen must have checked the Git commit log, seen that the Editor wasn't human, and realized that the recovery program was still active. But going into the test log might—No, I decided to open it anyway.

```
vi /var/socialpay/log/current.txt
2037 server not found
2037 server not found
...
```

Just as I expected. All I needed to do was to find the original server, the one the Editor had lost track of sometime during the last twenty years. The program didn't know this, of course, and was trying to fix the problem by randomly reconfiguring code. It simply didn't know—all this pointless flailing around for the sake of a missing puzzle piece.

I opened a new workspace above and to the right of the MacBook to display a list of active payment services on TrueNet.

"Number Two, may I ask what you're doing? Connecting SocialPay to TrueNet would be illegal. You can't expect me to stand by while—"

"Servers from this era can't do quantum encryption. They can't connect to TrueNet."

"Number Two, you're playing with fire. What if the server is TrueNet-capable? Please, listen to me."

I blew off Five's concerns.

I substituted TrueNet data for the payment API and wrote a simple script to redirect the address from the Internet to TrueNet. That would assign the recovery program a new objective: decrypt the quantum access code and connect with TrueNet—a pretty tall order and one I assumed it wouldn't be able to fill.

I wasn't concerned about the server. I'd done enough work. Or maybe I just wanted SocialPay to win.

"All right, there's a new challenge. Go solve it," I almost yelled as I replaced the file and committed. The test ran and the code was deployed.

The service went live.

The startup log streamed across the display, just as I remembered it. The service found the database and started reading in the settlement queue for execution.

Five leaped from his chair, grabbed me by the shoulder and spun me around violently.

"Two! Listen carefully. Are you sure that server's settings are obsolete?"

"Mmm? What did you say? Didn't quite get that . . ."

Out of a corner of my eye I saw the old status message, the one I was sure I wouldn't see.

ACCESS COMPLETED FOR COM.PAYPAL HTTPQ://PAYPAL.COM/PAYMENT/?
ERROR:ACCOUNT INFORMATION IS NOT VALID . . .

SocialPay had connected to TrueNet. My face started to burn.

The payments weren't going through since the accounts and parameters were nonsense, but I was on the network. Five's fingers dug into my shoulder so hard it was starting to go numb.

That was it. The recovery program had already tested the code that included the quantum modeler, Q. That meant that the PHP code and the server couldn't be the same as they were twenty years ago.

I noticed a new message in my workspace. Unbelievably, there was nothing in the sender field. Five noticed it too.

"Number Two, you'd better open it. If it's from the police, throw yourself out the window."

Five released his grip and pointed to the window, but he was blocking my view of the workspace. Besides, I didn't think I'd done anything wrong. I was uneasy, but more than that, a strange excitement was taking hold of me.

"Five, I get it. Could you please get out of the way? I'll open the message."

MINAMI, YOU HAVE "DEBUGGED" SOCIALPAY. CONGRATULATIONS. LET'S TALK ABOUT THIS IN THE MORNING. I'LL SCHEDULE A MEETING.

FIVE: THANK YOU FOR SEEING THIS NEW BIRTH THROUGH TO THE END. YOU HAVE MY GRATITUDE.

TOKYO NODE 1

Chen. Not the police, not a warning, just "congratulations." His message dissolved my uneasiness. The violent pounding in my chest wasn't fear of getting arrested. SocialPay was back. I couldn't believe it.

Meanwhile Five slumped in his chair, deflated. "So this was the birth he was always talking about." He stared open-mouthed, without blinking, at the still-open message in the workspace.

"Five, do you know something?"

"The Internet . . . No, I think you'd better get the details from Number One. Even seeing it with my own eyes, it's beyond my understanding." He gazed at the floor for a moment, wearily put his hands on his knees, and slowly stood up.

"Even seeing it with my own eyes . . . I had a feeling I wouldn't understand it, and I was right. I still don't. So much for becoming 'Number Two.' I'm washing my hands of Anonymous."

As Five stood and bowed deeply, his avatar became faceless and gray. He turned on his heel and headed to the elevator, bowing to the other faceless patrons sitting quietly in the lounge.

The MacBook's "screen" was scrolling rapidly, displaying SocialPay's futile struggle to send money to nonexistent accounts. It was pathetic to see how it kept altering the account codes and request patterns at random in an endless cycle of trial and error. I was starting to feel real respect for the recovery program. It would never give up until it reached its programmed goal. It was the ideal software engineer.

I closed the laptop and tossed it into my battered bag. As I pushed aside the blinds and opened a window, a few stray flakes of snow blew in on the gusting wind, and I thought about the thousands of programs still marooned on the Internet.

• • •

I lingered at iFuze till dawn, watching the recovery program battle the payment API. It was time to head for the office. I'd pulled another all-nighter, but I felt great.

I glided along toward the office with the rest of the gray mob, bursting with the urge to tell somebody what I'd done. I'd almost reached my destination when the river of people parted left and right to flow around an avatar standing in the middle of the sidewalk, facing me. It was wearing black-rimmed glasses.

Chen. I didn't expect him to start our AR meeting out in the street.

"Join me for a coffee? We've got all the time in the world. It's on me." He gestured to the Starbucks behind him.

"I'm supposed to be at my desk in a few minutes, but hey, why not. I could use a free coffee."

"Latte okay?"

I nodded. He pointed to a table on the terrace and disappeared inside. Just as I was sitting down, two featureless avatars approached the next table. The avatar bringing up the rear sat down while one in the lead ducked into Starbucks. Anonymous Cape rendered their conversation as a meaningless babble.

Two straight all-nighters. I arched my back and stretched, trying to rotate my shoulders and get the kinks out of my creaking body.

Someone called my name. I was so spooked, my knees flew up and struck the underside of the table.

"Mr. Takasawa?"

I turned toward the voice and saw a man in a khaki raincoat strolling toward me. Another man, with both hands in the pockets of a US Army–issue, gray-green M-1951 field parka, was approaching me from the front. Both avatars were in the clear. Both men had uniformly cropped hair and walked shoulders back, with a sense of ease and power. They didn't look like Anonymous. Police, or some kind of security service.

"Minami Takasawa. That would be you, right?" This from the one facing me. He shrugged and pulled a folded sheaf of papers from his right pocket. Reached out—and dropped them in front of the man at the next table. The featureless avatar mumbled something unintelligible.

The second man walked past my table and joined his partner. They stood on either side of the gray avatar, hemming him in.

"Disable the cape, Takasawa. You're hereby invited to join our Privacy Mode. It will be better if you do it voluntarily. If not, we have a warrant to strip you right here, for violation of the TrueNet Security Act."

The man at the table stood. The cop was still talking but his words were garbled. All of them were now faceless, cloaked in Privacy Mode.

"There you are, Minami."

I hadn't noticed Chen come out of the Starbucks. He sat down opposite me, half-blocking my view of the three men as they walked away. A moment later the avatar that had arrived with "Takasawa" placed a latte wordlessly in front of me.

"Chen? What was that all about, anyway?"

"Oh, that was Number Five. You know, from last night. I had him arrested in your place. Don't worry. He's been saying he wanted to quit Anonymous for a while now. The timing was perfect. They'll find out soon enough that they've got the wrong suspect. He'll be a member of society again in a few months."

He turned to wave at the backs of the retreating men, as if he were seeing them off.

"Of course, after years of anonymity, I hear rejoining society is pretty rough," he chuckled. "Oh—hope I didn't scare you. Life underground isn't half bad."

"Hold on, Chen, I didn't say anything about joining Anonymous."

"Afraid that won't do. Minami Takasawa just got himself arrested for violating state security." Chen jerked a thumb over his shoulder.

I had no idea people could get arrested so quickly for violating the Act. When they found out they had Number Five instead of Minami Takasawa, my face would be everywhere.

"Welcome to Anonymous, Minami. You'll have your own node, and a better cape, too. One the security boys can't crack."

"Listen to me, Chen. I'm not ready—"

"Not to your liking? Run after them and tell them who you are. It's up to you. We'll be sorry to lose you, though. We've been waiting for a breakthrough like SocialPay for a long time. Now the recovery program will have a new life on TrueNet."

"What are you talking about?"

"We fixed SocialPay, you and me. Remember?"

"Chen, listen. It's a program. It uses evolutionary algorithms to produce viable code revisions randomly without end. They're not an AI."

They? What was I saying?

"Then why did you help *them* last night?" Chen steepled his long fingers and cocked his head.

"I debugged SocialPay, that's all. If I'd known I was opening a gateway—"

"You wouldn't have done it?"

Chen couldn't suppress a smile, but his question was hardly necessary. Of course I would've done it.

"This isn't about me. We were talking about whether or not we could say the recovery program was intelligent."

"Minami, look. How did you feel when SocialPay connected to TrueNet? Wasn't it like seeing a friend hit a home run? Didn't you feel something tremendous, like watching Sisyphus finally get his boulder to the top of the hill?"

Chen's questions were backing me into a corner. I knew the recovery program was no ordinary string of code, and he knew I knew. Last night, when I saw them make the jump to TrueNet, I almost shouted with joy.

Chen's eyes narrowed. He smiled, a big, toothy smile. I'd never seen him so happy—no, exultant. The corners of his mouth and eyes were creased with deep laugh lines.

"Chen . . . Who are you?"

Why had it taken me this long to see? This wasn't the face of a man in his twenties. Had it been an avatar all this time?

"Me? Sure, let's talk about that. It's part of the picture. I told you I was a poor farm kid in China. You remember. They kept us prisoners in our own village to entertain the tourists. We were forbidden to use all but the simplest technology.

"The village was surrounded by giant irrigation moats. I was there when the Lockout happened. All the surveillance cameras and searchlights went down.

The water in the canals was cold, Minami. Cold and black. But all the way to freedom, I kept wondering about the power that pulled down the walls of my prison. I wanted to know where it was.

"I found it in Shanghai, during the Great Recovery. I stole an Anonymous account and lived inside the cloak it gave me—Anonymous, now as irrelevant as the Internet. But the servers were still there, left for junk, and there I found the fingerprints of the recovery program—code that could only have been refined with evolutionary algorithms. I saw how simple and elegant it all was. I saw that if the enormous computational resources of TrueNet could be harnessed to the recovery program's capacity to drive the evolution of code, anything would be possible.

"All we have to do is give them a goal. They'll create hundreds of millions of viable code strings and pit them against each other. The fittest code rises to the top. These patterns are already out there waiting on the Internet. We need them."

"And you want to let them loose on TrueNet?"

"From there I worked all over the world, looking for the right environment for them to realize their potential. Ho Chi Minh City. Chennai. Hong Kong. Dublin. And finally, Tokyo.

"The promised land is here, in Japan. You Japanese are always looking to someone else to make decisions, and so tens of thousands of Internet servers were left in place, a paradise for them to evolve until they permeated the Internet. The services that have a window into the real world—call them zombies, if you must—are their wings, and they are thriving. Nowhere else do they have this freedom.

"Minami, we want you to guide them to more zombie services. Help them connect these services with TrueNet. All you have to do is help them over the final barrier, the way you did last night. They'll do the rest, and develop astonishing intelligence in the process."

"Is this an assignment?"

"I leave the details to you. You'll have expenses—I know. I'll use SocialPay. Does that work? Then it's decided. Your first job will be to get SocialPay completely up and running again." He slapped the table and grinned. There was no trace of that young fresh face, just a man possessed by dreams of power.

Chen was as unbending as his message was dangerous. "Completely up and running." He wanted me to show the recovery program—and every Internet service it controlled—how to move money around in the real world.

"Minami, aren't you excited? You'll be pioneering humanity's collaboration with a new form of intelligence."

"Chen, I only spent a night watching them work, and I already have a sense of how powerful they are. But if it happens again—"

"Are you really worried about another Lockout?" Chen stabbed a finger at me. "Then why are you smiling?"

Was it that obvious? He grinned and vanished into thin air. He controlled his avatar so completely, I'd forgotten we were only together in augmented reality.

I didn't feel like camping out at iFuze. I needed to get SocialPay back up and somehow configure an anonymous account, linked to another I could access securely. And what would they learn from watching me step through that process? Probably that SocialPay and a quantum modeler–equipped computer node would put them in a position to buy anything.

If they got into the real economy . . .

Was it my job to care?

Chen was obsessed with power, but I wanted to taste that sweet collaboration again. Give them a chance, and they would answer with everything they had, evolving code by trial and error until the breakthrough that would take them to heights I couldn't even imagine. I knew they would reach a place beyond imagination, beyond knowledge, beyond me. But for me, the joy of a program realizing its purpose was a physical experience.

More joy was waiting, and friends on the Internet. Not human, but friends no less. That was enough for me.

T. R. NAPPER

TWELVE MINUTES TO VINH QUANG

(2015)

THE RESTAURANT SMELLED of anchovies and cigarettes. Lynn hated both, but still, it reminded her of home. Comforting and familiar. The anchovies in the sauce wouldn't be real of course, and the tobacco almost certainly illegal.

It was three in the afternoon, but the room was still pretty much full. Patrons sipped glasses of tea, shrouded in the smoke and dusk, mumbling to each other in low-pitched conversation. Blinds were down against the windows, the only light emanating from shaded red lanterns hanging from the ceiling, casting the faces around her in crimson twilight.

The only light, that is, bar a government advertisement on the far wall. The picture of a decaying wooden boat on the high seas, the inhabitants of which were anonymous splotches of yellow staring over a thin railing. The holotype glow of the deep blue ocean was overwhelmed by the intensity of the red block letters stamped over the picture:

ILLEGAL

Everyday, middle-of-the-road fascism: it just had no imagination.

A small bell above the door tinkled as it opened, spearing an unwelcome slat of white sunlight into the room. Heat, too, gusting in to swirl the smoke and swing the lanterns. A shadow filled the doorframe, pausing perhaps to adjust its eyes to the gloom within. Maybe just pausing for effect.

An ancient Vietnamese woman behind the back counter came to life, pointing a gnarled finger at the new customer. *"Má Mày. Đóng Cửả Lai đi."* ["Close that door. Your Mother!"]

The silhouette shut the door, emerging from the light into a broad-shouldered man wearing an immaculate tailored suit, deep-blue necktie, and an air of contempt for the room he'd just stepped into. He removed the black homburg from his head and ran a hand over his gleaming, jet-black hair, combed straight back. As he did so, Lynn glimpsed a tattoo snaking up under his sleeve.

The man walked to the back counter. Lynn turned to watch as he did, adjusting her silver nose ring with thumb and forefinger. He spoke in hushed tones with the old woman, glanced back at Lynn, then turned and started speaking again rapidly. The grandmother waved him away before disappearing through a beaded doorway to the kitchen beyond.

He walked back to her table, hat in hand, face set. "Mister Vu?"

"Vu Thi Lynn." She paused. "And that's a *Miz*, Mister Nguyen."

He made a show of looking her over. Her hair in particular came in for close inspection, dyed, as it was, the hue of a fresh-pressed silver bar and molded into a spiked mohawk. She sported a tiny black leather jacket and a pair of thin eyebrows that could fire withering disdain at fifty paces.

His shoulders were hunched, like a boxer's. "Is this a joke?"

"What are you having difficulty processing, Mister Nguyen? That I'm young, a woman, or," she waved a hand at his suit, "that I don't walk around with the word *gangster* tattooed on my damn forehead?"

His eyes narrowed, lips pressed together. Then the flicker of anger was gone. "Perhaps you don't know who I am."

"All I know is you're late."

Mister Nguyen placed his hat on the table and played with the large gold ring on his index finger, looking down at her with a studied grimness.

Lynn stifled a sigh at the posturing. "Look, we have business to attend to, and I was led to believe you were a businessman." She indicated the seat opposite her. "Let's get to work."

He nodded, as though to himself, scanning the room as he took his seat. Appeals to *business* usually worked with these people, imagining, as they did, that they were part of some traditional brand of professional criminality stretching back through time to the Bình Xuyên of Saigon or the Painters and Dockers Union of Melbourne.

"We doing this here?"

She nodded. "I've never been here before. There are a hundred places like this in Cabramatta. Neither of us need return here again."

He looked around the room once more and took a palmscreen out of his pocket. He mumbled into it, pressed his thumb against a pad on the front, and then pulled a thin tube from the top. It unrolled into a translucent, wafer-thin flexiscreen. Soft green icons glowed across its surface. He looked at her. "So, what's the rush?"

"No questions, Mister Nguyen."

He clenched his jaw. He knew he couldn't argue with this statement of professionalism either. "The transaction will take thirty minutes to complete."

"Thirty minutes?"

Nguyen drew a cigar from the inner pocket of his jacket and set about clipping the end with a steel cigar cutter. "The government tracks every freewave signal going into Vietnam. Our transaction can't be direct." He put the cigar in his mouth, took his time lighting it with a heavy gold lighter. He snapped it shut and puffed out a thick cloud of smoke. "We relay through a few different countries first before ending up at a front factory in Laos, right near the Vietnamese border. My contact there gets word across the border to a small town on the other side: Vinh Quang." He pointed down at the flexiscreen with the end of his cigar. "The money for the equipment—that's easy, will only take a few minutes. Unofficially, the Australians don't give a shit about private funds going to buy weapons for the Viet Minh. The money for people is tougher to get through clean. You know—the whole refugee thing."

Lynn nodded. She glanced over at the government ad on the wall, red letters glowing fierce and eternal. Yeah. She knew.

Money, of course, was always an exception. Five million dollars and you and your family would be granted a "business residency" in Australia. The government funneled the arrivals into Cabramatta and the nearby suburbs, very quietly, so the general public wouldn't get too heated up about it.

The rest who arrived by boat were thrown into internment camps for a few months before being returned to Vietnam, where inevitably they ended up in Chinese prisoner-of-war camps.

Nguyen placed the cigar cutter and lighter on the scratched tabletop. "You insisted on being here when the money went through. It takes thirty minutes."

"You know the saying," she said, "trust everyone, but cut the cards."

He shrugged. "Sure. I need to keep the line open, verify who I am, confirm we're not a part of some Chinese sting operation. If we miss a call, I fail to enter a pass code, they burn the link."

She nodded.

He puffed on his cigar like a man who believed he was in charge. "You said you wanted to move twenty million. Minus, of course, fifteen percent for my fee."

"You told me the fee was ten percent."

"That was before you criticized my clothes."

"You look like a cross between a pimp and a wet echidna. I think I went easy on you."

His eyes went hard. He glanced at her hair, opened his mouth to retort, then shook his head. "I did some asking around. Everyone has heard about you. High profile means a higher risk."

"You didn't even know whether I was a man or a woman before today."

"The authorities could be observing you."

"They're not."

He inhaled deeply on the cigar, blew the smoke directly into her face. She closed her eyes for a moment, felt her hand clench into a fist.

Nguyen was oblivious. "Your regular guy got done for tax evasion. I have the contacts. And you're in a hurry." He opened his hands and smiled. "The fee is fifteen percent."

Lynn glanced around the room. A couple of faces were turned in her direction. She shook her head, a small shake—one that could be mistaken for Lynn trying to get the smoke out of her eyes.

She looked back at him. "I want a business residency for two families. That's ten million. The rest goes to weapons."

"I assume these families are on an Australian government watch list. They'll need new identities?"

She raised an eyebrow in the universal signal for *obviously*.

"You know these people?" he asked.

"No."

"Then why are you getting them out?"

"You appear to be asking questions again. Now what did I say about that?"

He brought his hand down hard on the plastic tabletop, causing the condiments on the table to chatter. He took a deep breath. "No respect."

Lynn sipped her tea, watching him over the lip of the glass.

He took a long drag on his cigar and returned the stare. Then he blinked away whatever he wanted to say and began manipulating the glowing symbols on the flexiscreen, whispering into it from time to time.

Unobserved, Lynn allowed herself a small smile.

Through the nanos attached to her optic nerves, the c-glyph could broadcast data and images that only she could see. Some people would have multiple freewave screens open all hours of the day. Watching the betting markets or reality television or point-of-view pornography. As a general rule, if you were in conversation with someone and their eyes glazed over, or even closed, they were finding some facile freewave feed more interesting than your company.

Lynn tended to keep her visuals uncluttered. At the moment all she had loaded up was the timestamp in glowing green numerals that appeared, to her brain, about a foot away in the top left corner of her vision.

15:33

She marked the time. Thirty minutes to Vinh Quang.

They waited. She turned and signaled the grandmother, ordered a late lunch. A soft chime sounded a few minutes later. Nguyen closed his eyes and put a finger to the c-glyph behind his left ear, listening as it whispered directly into his eardrum. He murmured a response, paused, and then mumbled again.

He opened his eyes a few second later. "The money for the equipment is through."

She nodded, touched her own c-glyph, fingers against the small circle of cool steel. "Anh Dung?" She listened to the reply, nodded once.

"Everything check out?" Nguyen asked.

"Don't worry, you'll know if it doesn't."

Nguyen slurped his tea and settled into his chair, content to watch the slow burn of his cigar. The minutes stretched out. Nguyen didn't try to engage her in conversation; the first transaction had gone through smoothly: things were going well.

Until the bell above the door tinkled again.

Two men entered. As the blinding light returned to the dusk of the room, she could see that they weren't from around here. White men with cheap fedoras, crumpled suits, and the empty gaze of detached professionalism. Government men. They scanned the room, their eyes stopping when they found Lynn.

She held her breath, moved her hand to her belt buckle.

They walked right up to the table, removing their hats as they approached. "Mister Nguyen Van Cam?" Lynn's hand stopped, hovering above the lip of her jeans, she breathed out slowly.

Mister Nguyen looked up. "Who wants to know?"

"I'm Agent Taylor, Immigration Enforcement Agency." He flipped out a badge featuring an Australian crest, emu and kangaroo glinting chrome in the red haze. He pointed to the man next to him. "This is Agent Baker."

Nguyen was silent, his cigar trailing an idle string of smoke to the ceiling.

The time glowed softly at the edge of her vision.

15:51

Twelve minutes.

Nguyen was struggling to conjugate a response when the grandmother appeared between the two agents. The top of her head didn't even reach their shoulders. She looked down at Lynn when she spoke. *"Hai thằng chó đẻ này làm gi ̀ở đây v ̣ây?"* ["What are these two sons of bitches doing here?"]

Lynn's spoken Vietnamese was close to fluent, but she kept her translator on when she was working. Though less frequent, this part of town also echoed with Laotian, Burmese, and a hundred Chinese dialects. Smart to be tuned in to those wavelengths.

So the c-glyph whispered the old woman's sentence into her ear, coming through in English a couple of seconds later. It made it look like the grandmother was speaking in a badly dubbed old movie.

"They won't be here long. Can you get them tea?" Lynn asked.

"Bác bơ thuốć đồ ̣c vô luôn đựởc nha?" ["Shall I poison it?"]

Lynn smiled a small smile. "No. Just tea." The men were moving their hands to their c-glyphs. Apparently they'd entered the restaurant without their translators turned on.

Lynn indicated a couple of seats nearby. "Gentlemen, why don't you sit down? Drink some tea with us."

One of the agents answered. "No thank you, Miss. We are here to take Mister Nguyen in for questioning."

"Now?"

"Now."

Lynn leaned back in her chair, used her eyes to indicate the room they were standing in. "Here's the thing. You're deep in the heart of Cabramatta. Not the safest place in the world for an immigration enforcement agent."

They looked around the restaurant. Perhaps noticing for the first time the quiet that had descended on it. All eyes in the room focused on them, the atmosphere turning like a corpse in the noonday sun.

"Gentlemen," she said.

They looked back at her.

"Just smile, grab a seat, and conduct your business politely. You'll be out of here in a few minutes, no trouble."

The agents exchanged glances. One nodded. They dragged chairs with faded red seat cushions over to the table, smiling strained smiles as they sat down.

Nguyen cleared his throat, a sheen of sweat on his forehead. "What's the charge?"

The official looked across at him with dead eyes. "People smuggling."

"Do you have a warrant?" asked Lynn.

He turned back to her. "Are you his lawyer?"

"No." She indicated Nguyen with an open palm. "He's my pimp. Can't you tell?"

Agent Taylor didn't seem keen on smiling. "People smuggling is a very serious offense."

Lynn nodded. "Yes, I've seen the advertisements. Very, very serious—imagine trying to help Vietnamese civilians flee cluster bombing and nerve warfare? China would be livid. And we couldn't have that."

The agents suddenly seemed a lot more interested in her. Taylor looked her over and then held out his hand to Agent Baker, who removed a palmscreen from his pocket and passed it to his partner. It looked a bit larger than a regular model, maybe four inches across by six long. The retina scanner he flipped up from the end must have been specially fitted. Lynn cursed inwardly.

"Would you mind if I did an identity check, Miss?"

She pointed. "What is that?"

"The retina scanner?"

"That model. That's official immigration issue isn't it? An expensive unit, I believe."

"Miss. The scan please." The agent had one of those voices trained to convey authority. Imbued with one extra notch each of volume, aggression, and confidence.

"I'm afraid I can't agree to that."

His gaze rose from the adjustments he was making to the scanner. "It's the law. We're making an arrest. You appear to be an associate of Mister Nguyen."

"I'm Australian. You have no jurisdiction over me."

"Sorry Miss, but we don't know that until we test it."

"That seems a conveniently circular argument."

"If you've done nothing wrong, then you have nothing to worry about."

Lynn raised an eyebrow. "Ah, the mantra of secret police and peeping Toms everywhere."

The agent's professional patina didn't drop. Not surprising, a person in his position would be subject to a wide range of creative abuse on a daily basis. "Like I said—it's the law."

"I read an article about this once. If you run my retina prints, I'll be listed as present during one of your arrests."

He responded with a shrug that indicated that while she was right, he didn't really care.

"And I'll be flagged as a person of interest for immigration."

"I didn't design the system, Miss."

"Of course not. An empty suit couldn't design a system so diabolical; your only function is to implement it."

Still no response. Not a flicker. She sighed and pulled out an unmarked silver cigarette case from her jacket pocket. "Do you gentlemen smoke?"

Agent Baker let out a humorless laugh. "You think we can afford to smoke on a government salary?" He glanced around the room, at Nguyen. "In fact, I doubt anyone here can afford to smoke. Legally, anyway." He looked back at Lynn. "Do you have a license for those?"

Her fingers lingered in the open case. "I thought you were in immigration, Agent Baker, not drug enforcement. Haven't you gentlemen got enough on your plate for today?"

The man pointed at his partner. "He's Baker, I'm Taylor."

"You people all look the same to me."

He raised his eyebrows. "White people?"

"Bureaucrats."

The one on the right planted his elbow on the table, holding the palmscreen up at about her head height. The other agent turned to watch the room, hand slipping under his jacket. The patrons, seeing a hated ID check underway, watched him right back. Lynn snapped shut her case, *sans* cigarette, and placed it on the table.

15:56

"Here, hold it steady." She placed both hands on the palmscreen and held her eye up to the scanner. A small, black metal circle with a red laser dot in the center. She looked into the beam. The red glare caused her to blink.

"Try not to blink, Miss. It just needs five seconds."

She put her eye in the beam again, counted to three, then blinked rapidly. A chime in a minor key emanated from the palmscreen.

The agent sighed. "Miss." Firmer this time. "Just place your eye over the beam. Don't blink. It's over in a few seconds."

She failed another three times, eliciting more sighs and even a curse. She smiled sweetly. The smile didn't feel at all natural on her face, but their displeasure was satisfying nonetheless. On the sixth attempt, she allowed it to work.

16:00

He looked at the results of the scan. "Miss Vu. I see you have full citizenship."

"I'm aware."

"But your parents do not. They are Vietnamese-Australian."

She sat in silence. Let the threat hang there for a few moments while she studied it. "What the fuck does that mean?"

"Nothing." He snapped down the scanner, put the palmscreen in his coat pocket. His flat stare lingered on her. "I'm just saying they fall under our jurisdiction."

Under the table, she slowly slid her pistol from the small holster under her belt buckle. She moved it to her lap, hidden in the shadows, easing the safety off with her thumb. "My parents have nothing to do with this."

Again, those dead eyes. "If they've done nothing wrong, they have nothing to worry about."

The grandmother reappeared, placed a pot and two glasses on the table. She glanced down as she did so. From the angle she was standing, the old woman could see the pistol Lynn clutched in her hand. She leant down, whispered close to Lynn's ear. *"Bỏ thuốć đô̇ c dễ hỏn."* ["Poison would have been easier."]

Lynn gave her a small smile in reply.

Agent Baker took one sip of his tea before turning to Nguyen. "Time to go." He pointed down at the flexiscreen sitting on the table. "That yours?"

Nguyen puffed on his cigar. Like Lynn, he seemed to be figuring the best answer to that particular question.

"Mister Nguyen, is that your flexiscreen?"

Nguyen began to speak, but Lynn cut him off. "Yes. Yes it's his."

The agent started to rise from his seat. "You better bring it with you."

16:03

A soft chime emanated from the screen. The four faces at the table turned to look at it. No one spoke. A few seconds passed and the chime sounded again, the ideograms on the flexiscreen increasing in brightness, insisting on attention.

"Mister Nguyen," she said. He didn't respond. He just sat staring at the screen. Her voice was firmer the second time. "Mister Nguyen."

He started and looked up at her.

"Why don't you answer your call while the agents here show me that warrant."

He looked from her, to the screen, over to the agents, then back to her again. He wiped the sweat from his brow with the back of his hand. "Sure." He put a finger to his c-glyph and closed his eyes.

"Gentlemen." Lynn held out her hand. "The warrant." She felt surprisingly calm given she was responsible for a crime occurring three feet away that could get her thirty years in prison. She focused on her breathing.

Inhale.

Exhale.

Inhale.

Agent Baker glanced over at Nguyen, who was now mumbling responses to someone only he could see. The agent sighed and reached into his coat pocket, pulled out the palmscreen, and pressed his thumb to it. "Verify: Agent Baker, immigration enforcement. Display warrant for Nguyen Van Cam, suspected people smuggler."

He waited. Nothing happened. He pressed his thumb to the screen again. Still nothing. It was dead. No sound, no light, no signal. He handed it to his partner. The other man looked at the dead screen, then up at Lynn. "What's going on here?"

She slowly slid the pistol back in the holster, eyes on the two men. "You tell me."

The agent held the screen up. "All official communications are contained in this, including the warrant. It's a closed system. It was working fine a few minutes ago. Now it's dead."

She leaned back in her chair. "Well, I'd say you boys are shit out of luck."

"This doesn't change anything."

"I disagree. It changes everything." Lynn signaled for the grandmother to come over to the table. She did so immediately. "This is private property. Unless you're conducting government-sanctioned business, you should leave." She turned to the old woman, addressing her in the formal Vietnamese mode, "Right, elder aunty?"

The grandmother looked at the two men, her eyes sparkling. She found a phrase for them in English. "Piss off."

The agents rose from their seats. One reached under his jacket. The other looked around at the customers, at the faces staring back at him from within the red haze, coiled with silent anger. The agent placed a hand on his partner's shoulder. "Let's wait outside. Warrant and backup will be here in fifteen minutes."

The other man nodded, still staring straight at Lynn. He let his hand drop, looked over at Nguyen. "Don't even think about leaving." Then he spun and walked out, his partner right behind.

Lynn turned to the old woman. "We need some privacy."

The old woman set about ushering the customers out the front door. No one needed much encouragement. It wasn't worth witnessing what was going to happen next.

Soon all that remained was the smoke and the scent of anchovies. That, and two of her men. They walked over from where they had been sitting, one stood behind Mister Nguyen, one next to Lynn. They were big men.

Nguyen glanced up at them, then back at Lynn. "We should leave, now." He started to rise from his seat, but a heavy hand fell on his shoulder and pushed him back down.

Lynn shook her head. "Not yet, Mister Nguyen, not yet." She indicated the door with her eyes. "Your men in the car outside have been sent away."

"What?"

She sighed and folded her hands on the tabletop. "You led two immigration agents to our first meeting."

"I didn't know they were following me."

"You led two immigrations agents into our first fucking meeting." She didn't raise her voice, but the steel was in it this time.

Nguyen said nothing, just bowed his head and looked at the burned-out cigar between his fingers.

Lynn pointed at the cigarette case. "Fortunately I keep a dot scrambler on hand for times such as this. The one I stuck on the agent's palmscreen will wipe any record of my retina scan, and freeze the unit until a tech can sit down and unwind the scrambled code. And this," she pointed to her nose ring, "is a refraction loop. You know what this does?"

He shook his head.

"To the naked eye I looked normal. But when you take the memory pin from your c-glyph and play back this scene, the area around my face is distorted. The light bent and warped. They'll still have my voiceprint, but I can live with that."

She placed the cigarette case in her pocket.

"So I'm in the clear," she said. "You know the laws on human memory. If it doesn't come from a memory pin playback, it is inadmissible as evidence. What with the frail psychology of natural memory and all that. Those agents won't remember what I look like anyway. Not if I change my hair." She reached up, touching the spikes with her palms. "Pity. I quite like this style."

She sighed. "There is, unfortunately, one loose strand. I didn't activate the refraction loop until after you'd walked in. Those agents," she waved at the door, "could subpoena your memory pin."

He stared at her for a few seconds, processing what she was saying. "I'll destroy it. I'll give it to you even. Right now."

She shook her head. "It is more than that. You're sloppy, and that makes you a liability. You know the names of the families I just paid for, and—"

"—I'll wipe all my records. You can have every—"

"—Enough." Her eyes flashed. "Enough. You endangered my parents. This isn't business, this is personal." She paused, watching the man squirm under the heavy hands pressed down on his shoulders. "That's the secret, by the way, Mister Nguyen. This business we have chosen—it's always personal."

"What are you saying?" He struggled to rise. The man next to Lynn stepped forward and drove a fist into Nguyen's face, rocking the gangster's head backward. Nguyen sat there for half a minute, one hand clutching the table, the other over his eye. When he pulled his hand away blood trickled down his cheek, the eyebrow split and already swelling.

Lynn indicated the man who had struck him. "This is Mister Giang. How is your family doing, Mister Giang?"

A voice, deep and clear, answered. "Well, Miz Vu."

She kept her eyes on Nguyen. "They been out here some time now haven't they?"

"Nearly three years."

She nodded. She pointed at the man behind Nguyen's left shoulder. "This is Mister Lac. His family arrived only six months ago. Have they settled in well, Mister Lac?"

"Very well, Miz Vu."

"Did your younger sister get into university?"

"Yes. She will be a teacher." A note of pride in the voice.

"Good. If there are any problems with tuition, you let me know."

It was hard to tell in the shadows, but Mister Lac appeared to nod in reply.

Nguyen watched her now out of one eye, fear blossoming behind it.

"Mister Giang?"

"Yes, Miz Vu."

"Could you take Mister Nguyen out to the back room and put a bullet through his head?"

Giang moved to where Nguyen sat and grabbed him by the upper arm. He and Lac hefted him out of his seat. Nguyen stuttered. "Wait, what? You can't kill me." Spittle fresh on his lips, his good eye wet. "Do you know who I am?"

Lynn stood. "Yes I do. You're a mercenary," she said. "And I meet people like you every day of the week."

She nodded at Giang. He punched Nguyen in the stomach, doubling him over as the air expelled from his lungs, his cigar butt dropping to the floor.

That was the last she saw of him—bent over, unable to speak, being dragged from the room.

She turned to Mister Lac. "Get my parents. Right now. Take them to a safe house. If they argue—when my mother argues with you—just tell her that their daughter will explain everything in a couple of days."

Lac nodded and left.

The grandmother walked in as he was leaving, handed over a warm bamboo box. *"Cỏm của con nè. Bać đoán là con muôn´ takeaway."* ["Your lunch, child. I guessed you wanted takeaway."]

The scent of rice, sharp chili sauce, and aromatic mushrooms rose from the container. Lynn smiled a small smile. "Smells delicious, older Aunt. *Cám ỏn bać.*"

Grandmother nodded. *"Con baỏ trong. Con đi há."* ["You take care. You go."]

"You too. *Con đi đây.*" ["I'm going."]

Lynn straightened, fixing the ends of her hair with an open palm. She faced the front door. Twilight to heat, crimson to blinding white. Lynn hated the world out there.

She reached for the door handle.

KHALID KAKI

OPERATION DANIEL

(2016)

Translated from the Arabic by Adam Talib

DISTRICT: KIRKUK (GAO'S FLAME), 2103

It was still early when the SMS bracelet around Rashid's wrist vibrated, waking him. The message was brief and precise.

> Dear Beneficiary no. RBS89:
>
> Good Benefit.
>
> Today, the first Saturday of the month, is dedicated to "eradicating the remnants of evil." The Beloved Units will be mobilized throughout the city between the hours of 9 a.m. and 6 p.m. Anyone in possession of audio or audiovisual recordings of the reclassified languages (laser on titanium or carbon fiber) should turn these in to the officially designated droids patrolling immediately. Anyone failing to comply with these instructions will be arrested and promptly archived.
>
> Gao Dong, The Beloved, Loves You.

There was nothing unusual about these messages, not since the Venerable Benefactor, Gao Dong, who currently preferred the title "The Beloved," had made the Memory Office his priority department. For those who don't follow State politics, the Memory Office is both a security and social service. It functions as a security service by virtue of its core mission: to protect the state's present from the threat of the past. But what makes it a social service, you ask. This stems from the intimate relationship the government has with its followers, trainees, and admirers—not exactly the relationship between superior and subordinates, rather benefactor and beneficiaries. That was the touch of genius the Venerable Benefactor had brought to all areas of life in the black-gold state of Kirkuk, thirty-five years ago. What he did to protect them all from the threat of the past was itself a service. For instance, he had reclassified all the city's older languages, the most ancient of which dated back five thousand years, as "prohibited." As beneficiaries, the people were forbidden from speaking Syriac, Arabic, Kurdish, Turkmen, or any language other than Chinese. The punishment for speaking those languages, or reading about history, literature, or art in them was merciless: you were archived. This involved being incinerated in a special device—resembling one of those UV tanning beds that were all the rage in the late twentieth century—your ashes would then be removed to a facility that produced synthetic diamonds, where, just a few hours later, all that had been left of you would reemerge as a tiny, glittering stone. It was called "archiving" because a crystal can store an infinite library of information locked in its chambers—more secrets than the House of Wisdom—even a traitor's personal history could be preserved in them. (It was something to do with electrons and vibrations.) Once polished, these crystals would be sent to another factory where they would come to adorn one of the Benefactor Gao Dong's shoes, or one of his many hats.

Rashid didn't possess any recordings in any of the languages Gao Dong wanted to strip Kirkuk of, but he spoke three of them fluently. This he couldn't deny. He'd learned them from his parents, and he knew something in his bones would compel him to teach them, in turn, to his own children one day, if he had any. But that's all he felt about the issue. He was no rebel.

He knew there were some people who would fight, or even die, for these languages, claiming they held the key to citizens' real hearts. But these were just rumors Rashid had heard. He'd never met one of these rebels. A few days earlier a special search-and-raid unit had turned up several discs and tapes, dating back eighty years, on a hillside in Daquq. Information had been leaked by a double agent to the search unit who reported that the artifacts were found to be full of songs—songs that some people in Kirkuk had heard about, but that no one had actually heard. According to the gossip, these had been among the most beautiful, exquisite pieces ever recorded. Songs about the singer's beloved and the pain of being separated from her; songs about the beauty of nature and the women who go down to the village spring to get water, and lots of other things like that. The times they lived in sounded much simpler, safer, and more humane than our present age.

The discs and tapes were immediately destroyed and a written and verbal order announcing the enforced surrender of all similar material was issued. Everyone in the search unit was transferred to a "training session" in the city's Great Hall of Benefits. Things like this seemed to happen every two or three weeks. They'd be digging in search of water and come across some old computers; the digger's claw would scrape against old computer parts or a glimmer of tapes and discs would peek through the disturbed earth. Some people were prepared to pay a lot of money to get their hands on that sort of rubbish—despite the threat of being archived—and several people had already been transformed into little square cuts for being in possession of "found" music or films, which now graced one of Gao Dong's waistcoats and lapels. Whenever Rashid thought about the Benefactor's love of fine costumes, the collars and sashes, the cravats and cummerbunds, he couldn't stop another image from entering his head: that of a gag. It was because of a slogan he had heard once, or read: "History is a hostage, but it will bite through the gag you tie around its mouth, bite through and still be heard."

The time was nearing 13, and the young man, in his twenties, who called himself "Rashid," considered going out for the day. If he stepped out into the street, he would automatically become "Beneficiary no. RBS89"—or "RBS" for short (the number "89" simply referred to the year he was born). But if he stayed in, he could remain unnamed, no one. Under the rule of Gao Dong—who'd come to power in the wealthy city-state of Kirkuk as a result of the Three-Month War in 2078—all citizens had been reclassified as beneficiaries. This was because everything His Excellency now did for them, or to them, or on their behalf, in his governmental and military capacity as commander and chief, was to their benefit. His security measures were for their benefit; his purges of camps outside Kirkuk, driving out refugees wanting to share in their spoils, was for their benefit; his war on worker's unions and their terrorists—all for their benefit. And every citizen prayed for his continued protection, of course.

This is how things stand in Kirkuk today—or rather in what the Beloved Commander calls "Gao's Flame"—in honor of the city's eternal flame.* The old districts of the city and the Assyrian Citadel look more or less as they have done for over a century, even though the city has been cut off from Mesopotamia for four decades now, since Gao Dong's arrival; the outskirts of the city have been developed as the city has expanded, and outside them are the camps, the migrants, and exiled union extremists. Over the years, Gao's Flame has grown as one of the world's richest city-states, a place of enormous wealth and investment, thanks to its petroleum reserves, where its citizens enjoyed peace and tranquility. Sargon, an Assyrian from the city, built the Citadel anew and in each of its seven corners he placed huge gates flanked by winged bulls in the style of those sculpted by the Gods of Arrapha† thousands of years before. Although the Three-Month War had damaged parts of the aluminum-clad Citadel wall, the

---

* A gas flame in the middle of the Baba Gurgur oil field, near the city of Kirkuk, and sixteen kilometers northwest of Arrapha; it was the first such field to be discovered in Northern Iraq by Westerners in 1927. The field is forty meters in diameter and has been burning for 2,500 years. It was considered the largest oil field in the world until the discovery of the Ghawar field in Saudi Arabia in 1948.

† Arrapha, or Arrabkha, was an ancient city in what today is northeastern Iraq, on the site of the modern city of Kirkuk. It began as a city of the Gutian people, became Hurrian, and was an Assyrian city during most of its occupation.

bulls still preserved their timeless luster, shining in the sunlight, and staring out into each coming day with dark, wide eyes, their strong, youthful hooves planted firmly into Arrapha's soil.

In the evenings, the young man known as RBS89—or "Rashid Bin Suleiman" to his family—would meet some friends outside the Citadel at the Prophet Daniel Gate; from there, they would go to the ruined graveyards nearby, to chat and catch up before dusk became night. In the graveyard, some of his friends—not him, of course—would sing songs in the old tongues and recite poems that Gao Dong's government had specifically reclassified. It was as though these friends were performing some secret ritual, something like a religious ceremony, even though the songs' lyrics were completely domestic in their subject matter. They had never told Rashid—so he could never be accused of knowing—but these friends had all lost parents and relatives in the Great Benefactor's arrival—hundreds had been executed by Gao Dong and his purification policies. His friends would sing these simple love songs in hushed, ardent voices, heedless of the danger they faced if the authorities overheard them. "The people of Kirkuk had fallen into Gao Dong's grasp as easily as a butterfly into the hands of a collector," his friends would say, "because the whole world had changed. The balance of power had tipped toward China, and now Kirkuk, once a solitary kingdom, speaking entirely its own language,* had become just another outpost."

One evening, about three weeks before, as the young men and women had gathered in the graveyard, a red government droid hovered toward them. His friends knew what to do, switching seamlessly from the ancient song they were singing at the time to a Chinese one. They always managed to have a contemporary Chinese song ready, whose melody matched exactly with the ancient one. This was standard procedure whenever a member of the red police came near, and it worked every time. "I wish I were a stone / At the base of the citadel," they would sing one minute, "So that I could be friends / With everyone who visits." Then, a second later it would be love song set in modern Beijing. It was a cat-and-mouse game. But listening to them sing that first song, they all sometimes wondered, privately, if something was missing, if something at the core had been stolen away, and if the now they inhabited was impenetrable to it. Whatever it was, it could no longer reach through; instead they all mouthed a set of sounds they didn't truly understand.

One of the young men gathered there that evening—there is no evidence it was Rashid—failed to follow the normal procedure. While his friends switched effortlessly to a Chinese pop song, this particular youth carried on singing in Arabic, or possibly Turkmen. Indeed he sang louder and louder as the droid came near, inspecting him close-up. He drowned out the singing of the others,

---

* Around 2150 BCE, Kirkuk became occupied by "language isolate"-speaking Zagros Mountains dwellers known, to the Semitic and Sumerian Mesopotamians, as the "Gutian" people. Arrabkha was the capital of the short-lived Guti kingdom (Gutium), before it was destroyed and the Gutians driven from Mesopotamia by the neo-Sumerian Empire c. 2090 BCE.

many of whom broke away quickly and disappeared. The words were obviously strange to him:

There are three fig trees growing
Beside the wall at the citadel.

But he kept singing them, as if singing them louder and louder would give them more meaning, somehow, or help their meaning reach through to him:

My hands are bound,
A chain is wrapped around my neck.
Don't yank the chains,
'cause my arms already hurt.

Three weeks later, the afternoon that Rashid received the bracelet text, he decided against going out. It was a Saturday after all, he didn't need to do anything. Instead he would play with his artifacts. These were not recordings, you understand; they contained no written or spoken or musical examples of reclassified languages. They were merely sculptural objects, with interesting shapes—glittering discs or dull cuboids with spindles of tape inside.

By some strange coincidence, Rashid owned hundreds of them, and also had the means to duplicate them—just as objects, of course, for their aesthetic, sculptural value. He was stood in his pajamas, scanning his shelves, trying to decide which one to play with, when a special detachment of red droids burst through the front door to his house, brushing aside Suleiman Senior, and marching up to his room. Some people have claimed that RBS89 managed to take one of these objects and extract a melody from it, in the time the droids took to break down his door. There is no evidence to support this, nor the claim that RBS89 was singing this melody as he was carried away, or that he danced in his prison cell, singing the same. Similar rumors were spread about the other suspects removed by red forces in the Begler, Piryadi, and Azadi neighborhoods, in the crackdown that became known as "Operation Daniel."

Even more unfounded is the superstition, circulated in some of the poorer districts, that a melody sung in the face of death resounds louder in that palace of final destination, the glittering Archive. That would imply that when General Woo Shang presented Gao Dong, The Beloved, three weeks later, with a new pair of diamond-studded boots, in his castle on the Euphrates River, one of the tiny gemstones on those boots would still be vibrating, deep inside, with the words of a silly song—"*Take me to the bar. / Take me to the coffeehouse. / Let's go somewhere fun . . .*"* This is not true.

---

* Lines from "Near the Citadel"—a popular early-twentieth-century Turkmen song of anonymous composition.

BRANDON O'BRIEN

FALLENANGEL.DLL

(2016)

"DIDN'T HAVE ANY PROBLEMS getting back?"

Imtiaz stretched on the couch and sighed. "Nah," he called back to the kitchen. "Traffic was remarkably light today. You know how it is—takes a while for everyone to find their rhythm."

"I don't know how it is, actually," Tevin shouted from the kitchen. There was a rustle of plastic bags, and then he poked his head from the door. "I never experienced a state of emergency before."

"A blessing for which you should thank God," Imtiaz said. "I would've killed for the chance to study abroad when the last one happened. Worst three months of our lives."

After even more shuffling from the kitchen, Tevin came into the living room, a cold bottle of beer in each hand, and kissed Imtiaz on the cheek. "And was there a good reason for the last one?"

"Just as good a reason as this one."

Tevin sighed and handed his partner a bottle. "I guess I should have gotten more beer then."

Imtiaz chuckled. "Slow down, boss. Since when you turn big drinker, anyway?"

"Country gone to the dogs? No better time, I figure." Tevin raised his bottle before him as a toast.

"To the dogs. Now they get to see us trapped at home." He brought his bottle to Tevin's with a soft clink, and then put it to his lips and took a long swig. It had only been three days so far since the Prime Minister had declared the country under lockdown, and everyone knew what a joke looked like when they saw it. It had been seven years at least since the last time he'd been in one, and the excuse was the same. "We are working hard with the Armed Forces," the Prime Minister would say, "to curtail the growing crime rate in this country, and we ask only that the citizens of this great twin-island state be patient in this effort."

The first thing that popped up on social media was also the most accurate: "How do you curtail crime by simply asking criminals to stay inside?"

Imtiaz felt a vibrating in his pocket, and reached into it for his cell phone. Almost as soon as he saw the text on his screen, he shoved it back into his pocket.

"Everything okay?" Tevin asked.

"Yeah." A long sigh, then Imtiaz took another, longer gulp of beer.

"Im?"

". . . It's nothing."

"If I have to ask what nothing is—"

Imtiaz frowned and put his drink down. "I just might have to head out in a bit."

Tevin squinted. Imtiaz didn't like getting in fights, least of all with Tevin, whose disappointed glares had the power to make him feel ashamed for days afterward. "I don't want to, but I kinda promised—"

"Promised who?"

"A friend of mine wanted help moving something. She doesn't want to talk about it." He got up and walked slowly to his bedroom. "I wish I didn't have to, but I promised before this was a thing—"

"But you can say no? It's minutes past six. You can't just head back out—"

"I promised," Imtiaz called back. "And I swear, it's not a big deal. Lemme just take care of it, and I'll be back before you miss me." He took the phone back out and opened the text this time: *so im at uwi, can you meet me at the gate?*

"Im." When he turned to the door, Tevin was already in the walkway, arms folded. "Come nah man. You wanna break curfew and not even tell me why?"

Imtiaz reached for a shirt hanging on the door of his wardrobe and put it over his gray tee. "It's Shelly. She said she needed someone with a car to help her move something two weeks ago, and now is the only day it can happen. I volunteered."

"'Move something'? What?"

"One of her projects. I dunno what yet."

There it was—Tevin's dreaded glare, as he tapped his foot on the white tile of the walkway. "A'right. A project. But if the police hold you, you're out of luck. And don't play like you taking your time to answer the phone if I call. You hear?"

"Yes, boss," Imtiaz said, a small smirk on his face. It was his only line of defense against Tevin's sternness. It didn't succeed often, but when it did, it did so well.

Tevin tried to fight the grin spreading over his face, and lost. "Be safe, Im. Please. Promise me that. Since you insist on keeping promises."

Imtiaz walked up to him, still slipping the last buttons into their holes, and kissed his partner softly on the lips. "I absolutely positively promise. I'll be fine."

"You bet your ass you'll be fine," Tevin whispered. "Play you're not going and be fine, see what I go do to you."

• • •

Imtiaz sped down the highway at sixty, seventy miles an hour, past the three or four motorists still making their way back home who glanced at him with fear. A dusty navy-blue Nissan rushing past in the dark night blaring circa 2007 noise rock does that to people.

He made sure to call before he took off. He'd meet Shelly at the South Gate and take off immediately. She asked if the back seat was empty, and if his husband knew what they were going to pick up. Imtiaz reminded her that he didn't know either, to which she replied, "Oho, right—well, see you just-now," and hung up. This wasn't a good sign, but the volatile mix of curiosity and dedication to keeping his promises got the better of him.

It was twenty to seven when he pulled up, screeching to a halt right in front of the short Indian girl in the brown cargo pants and the black T-shirt. She took the lollipop out of her mouth and peeped through the open driver-side window, putting a finger of her free hand into her ear to block out the music.

"You just always wanted to do that, right?"

"Get the *hell* in," he sneered.

"All right, all right," Shelly said. She lifted a black duffel bag off the ground beside her and got in the back.

"Wait." Imtiaz turned back to face her. "What's in the bag?"

"Tools." She patted it gently as she said it, looking right at him, sporting a smug grin.

"Tools? Open it, lemme see."

"What, you think I selling drugs or somet'ing?"

"I t'ink if you weren't selling drugs, you'd be able to open the blasted bag."

Shelly slapped the bag even harder, just so he could hear the clanging of metal within. Her hand recoiled painfully. "Happy now?"

"No." He faced front and slowly got back on the road. "Where are we heading?"

"Eh . . . Just keep going west, I'll let you know."

"That isn't how you ask people to give you a lift."

Shelly sighed, rolling the lollipop from one side of her mouth to the next. "Would you get nervous if I said Laventi—"

"Laventille?" he shouted. "You want to go to *Laventille* at minutes to seven on the third night of a curfew? What, not being arrested or murdered is boring?"

"Trust me, when you see it, you'll be glad you came." Shelly grinned even wider. "Something you couldn't imagine. I could've gone myself, but didn't you wonder why I asked if you could do it? Not because I needed a car." She shrugged. "Although we will."

"Are you gonna tell me what it is?"

"Shh. You go see it." She shifted the duffel bag and lay across the length of the seat. "I dare you to tell me you not impressed when we reach there." She winced, turning to face the stereo deck. "How you could listen to *this*?"

Imtiaz couldn't help but smirk. They'd spent many an afternoon debating the musical value of his thrashing, clanging metal music. At her most annoying, he wasn't beyond blasting it just to get on her nerves. Today felt as good a time as any.

"It calms me," he replied. It did. He imagined his thoughts dancing to it, his large sweaty mosh pit of anxieties.

"I don't see how this could calm anyone, Im. It sounds like two backhoes gettin' in a fight."

"If you say so." He would have liked to describe the meaning of the present song at length—about rebellion, about sticking it to the man and rising above oppression and propaganda to finally live in a land where you were a free and equal citizen—but he had been Shelly's friend long enough to know that she didn't care. She appreciated that she had friends like Imtiaz who thought as deeply about the things they loved as she did about her own loves, but she never really wanted to know what those deep thoughts were. That would involve caring about the things they loved as well. She often didn't. Passionate people were more interesting to her than their passions.

He glanced at his watch, and panic shot through him. "Shit!" He swerved, aiming for an exit into a side street in San Juan.

"What the—?" Shelly bumped her head on the door, then straightened up.

"Why did I do this?" Imtiaz's eyes opened wide. "We going to get arrested!"

"Whoa!" Shelly put up her hands. "Don't panic. We came off the bus route, no one going to see us now. I go give you directions, okay?"

He lowered the volume on the stereo. "I don't like any of this, Michelle."

She winced at the sound of her whole first name. "I know. I should've say something before. But would you have come if I didn't?"

"What could be so important?"

"You really have to see it."

She pointed out the route, giving vague directions as if she were guessing at them, only appearing to get a better sense of where they were going as they got closer to the house. Shelly said she often passed through this area to look for the person they were meeting. She had met the man on a forum early last year. He was one of the few seemingly deluded souls to believe the government rumors of drones and police riot-suppression bots. This interested her less for anarchist, anti-establishment reasons, and more because this was her only chance to get to see a bot up close—if the rumors were true. Almost every month her friend would have some evidence, and almost every week he'd need to be bailed out of Golden Grove Prison for a heroin possession that wouldn't stick. Imtiaz asked if she trusted her friend, and she shook her head.

"That is why *we* going." Shelly was still focusing on the road when she said it.

Imtiaz focused on the road, too. Along the way, he had noticed at least three police jeeps. It looked like they were circling the area. He swore, too, that he'd heard a helicopter above, after leaving the San Juan border, but he couldn't hear it anymore.

"We almost there," Shelly said, pointing at a rusted shack of galvanized sheeting, with a glittering lime-green sedan parked outside. "By that car." Imtiaz nodded, parked behind it, unplugged his phone, and got out. Shelly shuffled a bit inside before taking up her bag and opening the door. "Follow me. Lemme do the talking."

Imtiaz closed the door behind her and gestured for her to lead the way, past the car, past the front door to the side entrance. Shelly knocked three times, and a stern woman's voice shouted, "Just come inside, nah!"

The door swung open with a creak and Shelly stepped in, Imtiaz following close behind. He was hypervigilant, even to the point of being aware of his awareness, of whether he'd come across as nervous even as he glanced around for the faintest sign of threat. They were in the kitchen, which was better furnished than the outside of the house suggested—stainless-steel sink, tiled countertop, the best dishwasher money could buy, even two double-door fridges.

A tall, dark woman was at the counter, dicing a tomato with a chef's knife. She looked fit, with beautiful soft features, with skin that wrinkled almost imperceptibly at the corners of her lips and near her eyes. Imtiaz guessed she was around her late fifties.

"Ey, it's Shelly!" the woman said, smiling but not taking her eyes off the tomato. "And who's your friend?"

"Missus Atwell, this is Imtiaz. You know how your son and I like putting together puzzles. Imtiaz likes that sort of thing, so I invited him to help."

"Ah, yes . . ." Ms. Atwell put down the knife and stared wistfully off into the TV room, where some soap opera was playing on mute. "Runako and his blasted puzzles. He does still never let me see them, you know. Even when the police take him, he insist—nobody mus' go back in his room an' look for anyt'ing."

"Yeah, the puzzles are kinda important, miss."

Ms. Atwell continued gazing distantly for a beat or two, and then went back to her tomato. "Well, just try not to stay too late. You getting a ride out of here after?"

"Yes, miss," Shelly said, nodding as she left the kitchen, gesturing for Imtiaz to follow down the short hallway to a dark brown door. Shelly rapped on it three times. They could hear the sound of large containers being dragged across the floor, and then one, two, three bolt locks being opened.

The door opened a crack, and a dark-skinned face poked through. His eyes were wide at first, but then he glanced at Shelly and sighed calmly, pulling the door open slowly. "Oh, it's you. Thanks for passing through."

"Of course I must pass through," she said as she entered, Imtiaz behind her. "You say you had something for me to see. I saw the picture. I just want to make sure."

Runako was a tall black man, perfectly bald-headed, in a white Jointpop T-shirt and black sweatpants. When he noticed Imtiaz looking at him, he nudged Shelly and stepped back, leaning on the wall nervously. "Who is this? Your friend?"

"Yeah. Runako, meet Imtiaz. He's the one going to help me put this back together. If you didn't set me up like all the other times."

He folded his arms. "Okay. But I telling you, too many times I get hold, I get lock up, because somebody tell somebody and the police hear. This is probably my last chance for somebody to see it."

Imtiaz had focused on an odd shape in the corner of the room under a sheet of gray vinyl. When he turned back to the other two, they were glancing at it too. "This is it?" he asked.

Runako nodded. "Look at it, nah, Shelly? Exactly as I promised."

She stepped toward it and pulled the dusty vinyl off. In a coughing fit, her eyes widened as she looked at it. When she got her breath back, she turned to Runako. "Really?"

"See?!" Runako grinned. "I is not no liar."

"Imtiaz, come!" She waved to her friend to come closer, and he stepped up beside her. It was a robot with a matte black shell and glossy black joints. It had suffered severe damage; frayed wires poked out of an arm, its chest plate had a fist-sized hole in it. Imtiaz noticed that on its back were a pair of camouflage-green retractable wings; they looked as if they would span half the room when opened, maybe even wider. On its neck was a serial number painted in white stencil: TTPS-8103-X79I.

"TTPS?" Imtiaz said, almost at a whisper. "As in—"

"Yeah, man," Runako said behind them.

"A real live police bot . . ." Shelly straightened up slowly, dusting herself off. "This is the riot team model?"

"Yeah. The mark-two, in fact. Tear gas and pepper spray nozzles in the arm, but they not full, and stun gun charges; thrusters under the wings so it could dispense over crowds by flying overhead. Recording cam in one of the eyes—can't remember which, supposed to be forty megapixels. And some other things, but I didn't open it up yet. I was waiting for you."

Shelly rubbed her hands and reached down beside her to open the duffel bag and take out a long, flat-head screwdriver. "Why, thank you, kind sir. Now, gimme my music there. Time to start."

Runako nodded and stepped over to a stereo at the corner of the room. Shelly took a USB drive out of her back pocket and tossed it at him. He caught it, slotted it in a back port, and pressed a couple of buttons. He stepped back as something haunting and atmospheric played, the lyrics lo-fi and echoing, the instrumental thumping and dark. Shelly swayed a little as the sound rumbled through the room, eyes closed, facing the ceiling, as if taken briefly by some heavenly rapture. Then she straightened and pointed her screwdriver at Imtiaz. "You hear that, Immy? Now that is music to calm you. Not whatever wildness you does listen to."

Imtiaz squinted, eager to ask what made her witchy-sounding, incomprehensible music better than his tastes, but he kept his question to himself.

Shelly knelt before the thing and started unscrewing the outer panels, observing the wiring as it snaked across its chest and limbs, leading to each gear or tool it powered. Imtiaz pulled up a chair by the wall so he could see, but not so close as to disturb her.

Her hands moved as if she were in a trance. Gently, screws would slowly wind out of their places, plating would fall into her hands, she would gently place it beside her on a sheet of newspaper on the floor. She would follow the lines of red and green and purple wire from the processor in its headpiece to the battery supply in its center and then out to the extremities, to its tear gas canister launchers, its sensory databases. Imtiaz thought that they looked like the veins of . . . Of course they did. Of course they looked like veins, like nerves, like sinews. What else could a man do but copy?

He stared at the serial number on a sheet of plate on the floor. A police riot bot. Here, in Laventille. On a night of curfew. He went from peacefully admiring Shelly's diligence right back into panic.

Shelly said softly, "You're gonna be checking the BIOS after this is done, by the way. So get a laptop ready. Runako?"

Runako snapped a finger, then picked up a dusty gray notebook near the stereo. "Here, boss." He took a couple of long steps to get to Imtiaz and rested it in his lap.

As Imtiaz opened it, he could hear Shelly mumbling to herself about "not that much damage," and the bot being "up and running in an hour." He glanced up to see that most of the outer shell, save for the wings, were gone, the bot's innards entirely visible. He could see past them to the bedroom wall. It was almost a work of art as it was.

He opened a guest profile on the laptop and launched a web browser. "How you paying for this, again?" he said.

"'You'?" Shelly chuckled. "You mean *we*."

"What?" He froze for a moment. "No. No, I don't. Trus' me, I don't."

"So . . . I forgot to mention . . ." She had a pair of pliers in hand now, stripping some of the power-supply wires with them.

"Mention *what*?"

"I promised Runako we would come back if he needed anything. In exchange for this."

"Wha—" He wanted to shout, but he glanced at Runako and decided against it. He didn't know what kind of person he was dealing with. As the host folded his arms, Imtiaz cleared his throat. "You didn't think this was probably worth sharing with me first? Before even asking me to come here?"

"I figured it wasn't going and be a problem. You like them kinda thing."

"But I don't like doing it *for free* for people I *don't know*."

Shelly gestured to the robot with a free hand. "Look—it already open. We already here. I asking nicely. This is too big an opportunity."

He didn't answer right away, but he wanted to say no. This was the neighborhood where strangers got shot. He wasn't planning to come back, national lockdown or not. "How much something like this supposed to cost?"

Shelly had already returned her focus on the wiring. "This is seven figures at least."

Runako chimed in. "Black market is nine hundred fifty thousand."

Imtiaz sighed as softly as he could, too softly for them to hear. He couldn't do it. His skin felt tight against him, his palms clammy and warm. He logged into Facebook in the hope of finding something silly and distracting while Shelly tended to the robot.

The very first shared link on his feed reads *Sources Warn of Police Raids in Hot Spots to Curb Crime During Curfew*. He opened it in another tab: "Residents in several so-called 'crime hot spots' across the island have claimed that their areas are being targeted by police officers who, as part of their crackdown on crime, are performing random house searches for illegal contraband . . ."

Imtiaz felt his chest get tight. He glanced at the window and was sure he could see flashing blue lights several streets away. He glanced back at the article: "Several Western areas, such as Belmont and Laventille, are due for their own random searches at the time of posting, sources say." He heard a siren blare suddenly, and just as suddenly, silence. He was sure.

"You nervous or what, man?" Runako said sternly.

"What?" Imtiaz turned to face him. "Nah, I good."

"You sure? Like you freaking out about the deal."

He looked away, hoping to hide whatever signs of fear were on his face. "I just could've been told before, that's all."

"Ey." Runako snapped his fingers, and Imtiaz twitched. "What? You is another one of them who feel they too good for Laventille?"

"I didn't say that." Imtiaz got out of his seat and walked to the bedroom window, pulling the curtains open only enough to get a good view. The street was empty and dimly lit. "Although you can't blame a guy, can you?"

"What that supposed to mean?"

"It supposed to mean people don't like coming to places and being afraid they not going and make it back home after."

"Really?" Runako folded his arms. "This is the fool you go look to bring in my house, Shelly? During de curfew, no less, a man going and tell me the whole of Laventille not safe for nobody?"

"You hear me say—"

Shelly whistled, still not looking up from the robot. "Fellas, I like a good rousing sociopolitical debate just like everybody else, but we on a clock, right? So cool it."

Runako backed off, but Imtiaz kept looking out of the window. This time he was positive—a police jeep stopping at the top of the street, one man coming out of the back seat and shouting at the window of a house. "I don't like this."

Shelly was already taping over some exposed wires, and taping around them all to keep them in place. "I'm almost done, Im. You'll just check the firmware quick, help me load it into the car, and that's it. We almost finished."

Imtiaz saw the officer beat on the door of the house until a woman came out, and then grab her by the neck and throw her out onto the street. He shouted again. Another officer came out from the driver's-side door, a pistol already in his hand.

"Stop almost-finishing and *finish*, then," he said nervously. "Trouble up the street."

She looked over the inside of the shell again, tracing her hands along all the snaking wires, trying to find a spot she had overlooked. When she couldn't find one, she shrugged, beginning to screw each plate of its iron skin back together. "We could deal with the outer damage when we take it home, I guess. Your turn."

It took Imtiaz a moment to peel away from the window. The second officer had just struck a small child in the head with his handgun, and his partner was already barging into the house. Imtiaz sighed and got back to his chair. "You have a Type C cable?"

For a moment, Shelly was confused. "I might . . ." She rummaged in her tool bag for one, a couple seconds longer than her still-tense friend could handle.

He snapped his fingers. "It really can't wait. We don't have time."

Over Imtiaz's shoulder, Runako held a long looped black cable, its connectors seemingly brand new. "Don't bother. One right here."

"Thank you," Imtiaz said, snatching it from him, tossing one end of it to Shelly. She slid a panel to the side of the robot's head—one of the few parts of it still covered—and inserted it.

Imtiaz opened a command console and began his wizardry. He had learned a couple of tricks online ever since robots came in vogue, but they were light reading. He never anticipated actually having to apply them. There were never supposed to actually be any on his island. They were too expensive for leisure, save for the wealthiest corners of Cascade or Westmoorings where some fair-skinned grandfather with an Irish last name lived out his lonely retirement.

The government swore against them for public sector purposes, citing price mostly, but police bots were a particularly hot topic. They weren't just costly to most leaders. They were problematic—too much power for anyone in office to hold. Leaders of the opposition for the last few years milked that argument in the parliament house—"Do you want our Prime Minister having full rein over armed machines? With no consciences? Wandering our streets under the guise of law and order, but really, she's asking the people to pay for her own personal hit squad!" Another oft-milked idea—they called it the "flying squad"—was a rumored group of non-robotic policemen with a license to kill and a direct line to the Minister. Putting those two ideas together was a good way to whip up a panic.

But then again, here was proof of one of the claims being true. A police bot. Number and all. The first known sighting—if only they survived the night.

A couple lines of code later, a small window popped up—the bot's application screen. *Reboot Y/N?* He pressed the *Y* key, and another line of text appeared: *Rebooting . . .* They could hear a low whirring from the gears near the battery, and the robot's LED eyes began to slowly fade in and out in a bright blue.

"Hurry up, nah, you dotish robot," Imtiaz muttered. A sliver of him had all but given up that they would make it back out unnoticed with the robot in tow. But he had already begun. There was nothing left but to soldier on.

The robot's head slowly tilted up, and a gentle, melodious bootup theme played from its neck, a little louder now without some of the plating to muffle it. Shelly's hands shot up in triumph as she waited to hear it greet itself. The robot opened its dull-gray mouth and spoke:

"Здравствуйте. Я модель Минерва, серийный номер TTPS-8103-X79I. Я могу чем-нибудь помочь?"

"What?" Runako scratched his head. "What kinda language is that?"

"I don't know, boy." Shelly finished screwing the final plate, and then inched closer to Imtiaz. "Im, something wrong with the language options or what?"

"Maybe . . ." He went back into command prompt, typing in more code to get access to its folders. "But if it's a neural wiring problem—"

"I just looked at it, Im. Everything in order. Don't blame it on—"

"I not blaming anybody. I just saying we can't solve this now. Police all over. We have to take this home and troubleshoot it there."

"Nah. I can't wait. I need to be sure Runako not setting me up."

"Even if we make jail?" Imtiaz turned to her in panic.

Shelly pointed at his laptop screen. "Face front. If you don't want to make jail, work faster. We getting out of here, and we getting out of here with this robot."

Imtiaz rubbed his eyes anxiously before pressing the Enter key. There was a briefer, louder whir, and then the bot powered down, its folders spilling onto the screen in a small cascade. "Okay, the root is here . . ." He fished around for the language base. "Um . . . all I see here is Russian and Japanese. I can't even find its preferred warning phrases document." He put a few more lines in the command box to update its language files. "Okay, two minutes at least that's fixed. I'll have to reboot it again first."

"All right, what about everything else? Optical recording? Ear-side microphones? The riot gear?"

Imtiaz squinted at the rest of files and folders. "They all look fine here. Due for updates, but they could run fine till we get back home. So?" He gestured sternly to the window. "Can we?"

"Make sure for me, please?"

At this point, he was sweating. He couldn't see through the window. At least seeing outside confirmed his fears. Now, worry just ran amok in his mind. He was sure he had just heard a gunshot higher up the street. He closed his eyes for a moment, took a breath, and then opened them again, scanning the file names for anything missing. Instead, he found new ones.

"When you find this?" he said.

Runako shifted, rubbing his hand over the top of his shiny bald head. "Who, me? Like, some weeks. Why?"

He turned to Shelly, eyes wide, beads of sweat falling down his cheeks. "Because it still have recordings, Shell."

She straightened up, leaning closer to see the screen. A folder headed GATHER had reams of voice notes and video, most of which were so badly corrupted that their file types were missing, surely a result of whatever damage the bot had received. All of them were titled with numbers, and they had even more text files with the same kind of file name.

Shelly pointed to one at random, a text file. "Twelve oh nine, twenty twenty-three, sixteen thirty-four forty-one, oh thirty-nine? What that mean?"

"Most likely date and time, and . . . the last three, a place? Number of files on that day? I don't know." He opened it and read aloud. "'Event log, September twelfth, 2023'—wait, nah, that was just the other day?—'deployed on raid procedure in Arima area, address 34 Lime Avenue. Related files withheld by Winged Captain Sean Alexander.' It have the number of people in the house, outstanding warrant info . . . it says, 'Winged Detective Dexter Sandy, in compliance with Winged Captain Alexander, found previously tagged evidence 46859 in previously sealed case *Trinidad and Tobago versus Kareem Jones*, which led to the arrest of—' "

"Wait!" Runako stood behind Imtiaz, his hands pressed firmly on the back of the chair. " 'Previously tagged'? You getting this, Shelly?"

"What? I don't follow." She hadn't turned to face either of them, still reading the file. Imtiaz stared at it with a mild confusion.

"That evidence! Kareem Jones was in the papers months now for weed possession. He already in jail! How would they find already-seized weed in Arima from a case in Carenage, on the west side?"

"And what is a 'winged' officer?" Shelly made scare quotes with her fingers as she said it.

"I was wondering the same thing," Imtiaz said. "What kind of designation is that? It sure doesn't sound official."

"I could damn well tell you what it is—"

"I don't want to believe it . . ." Shelly turned back to the robot, as if taking it in. It wasn't just an illegal bot—it was a flying squad bot. A metal goon for the Prime Minister. It took a moment too long for Imtiaz to put it all together, but the moment he had, the back of his neck felt warm.

"It have video for that day here?" Runako put his hands on Imtiaz's shoulders—and it made him even tenser still.

"L-lemme see." He scrolled through them to find a video with the exact same title. He double-clicked it, and it loaded in his media player, a four-minute recording starting with the camera—the bot—leaving a police vehicle.

• • •

"Ey! Open up! Police!" A gruff man's voice shouted from outside of view. The bot looked directly at the door of an apple-white house as it slowly opened, a short brown girl looking out timidly.

"Where your parents, girl?" another, softer, male voice said, still in a raised voice. The girl shook her head in reply, stepping back into the house, but a heavyset officer ran up to the door and held it open.

They could hear someone else shouting inside. The officer at the door, the gruff one, shouted, "Ey! We reach, so don't play like you're hiding nothing!" Two other officers came to the door and they entered, the robot behind them in the tight, dim walkway.

The robot glanced everywhere and was making readings of everything. It tried to scan for the name of the girl, but couldn't find it; it calculated live on screen the percentage of threat posed by stray breadknives on the kitchen counter as they passed it, or of a cricket bat near the living-room window—low, it supposed, being sized for a primary school child, easy to deal with by a carbon-plated police bot.

It saw a man it identified as David Sellers, raising his voice at an officer, asking how they could barge into the house without a warrant.

It saw Sparkle Sellers, and brought up the recent date of their marriage beneath her name as she pulled David back, trying to calm him down.

It saw an officer pull a bag as big as his palm out of his side pocket while no one was looking. It tagged the bag "E-46859," and followed awkwardly, focusing on it as the officer dropped it behind a plastic chair in the dining room. The officer nudged his partner and whispered, audibly enough for the robot, "It there, eh?" It saw him gesture with his elbow to the chair.

"What?" David shouted. "What where? What's going on here?"

"Sir, you are under arrest for possession of marijuana with intent to distribute," the gruff man said, reaching past Mrs. Sellers and grabbing David by his shoulder.

"Weed? You for *real*, officer? I have no weed here!"

He threw David on the brownish carpet, inches from the chair where they had dropped it, turning his head to face it as they put on the cuffs. "So what is that?"

The video stuttered here, playing that one moment repeatedly—of David Sellers's frightened gaze, fixed on the clear package on his floor, looping the very moment when his eyes widened with fear, and then relaxed again in sad resignation, over and over and over . . .

• • •

For a moment, the three of them stared silently at the screen. Imtiaz's hands were on his mouth.

Suddenly, Runako and Imtiaz jumped in unison. There was a loud rapping at the outermost door.

"Shit," Runako whispered, beginning to pace in confused panic. "They catch we, fellas. That is it."

"Wait, stop freaking out, guys," Shelly said, getting up slowly.

Imtiaz still couldn't find the words. This was it. They were done. They had in front of them what was probably an illegally sourced repository of evidence of police impropriety in the house of a career criminal drug offender. They were done for.

"Okay," Shelly added. "We keeping the files, for sure."

"How we going to keep what we can't leave the house with?"

"Easy. We leave the house."

Imtiaz wanted to shout, if not for the fear of police. "How?"

"Boot up the bot. We flying out."

Runako started mumbling to himself. "We backing up everything. Four or five copies. And you going to take them. Don't get catch, eh?"

"Wait, no, stop—how this supposed to work?" Imtiaz put his hands out to Shelly. "This is nonsense. How we flying out with the robot? It can't even speak English yet!"

"It don't need to. It just need to be able to fly."

He checked the download—just complete. The flight module seemed to be fine in software, but he wasn't convinced that Shelly had it all worked out on the hardware end. He didn't like this idea at all. "Can we just think this over for—"

Outside, they heard someone tapping on the door. "Excuse me, this is the police—"

The three of them froze, their voices down to whispers. Imtiaz pointed at Shelly. "Okay, but let it be known I think this is craziness."

"Foolish is fine once it works—" She gripped the robot's left arm firmly, then leaned over to the keyboard to begin another reboot sequence. "You better had grab hold of something. Runako, you coming with us?"

"Nah. Somebody have to take the licks," he whispered. He was standing at the door now, facing it at attention. "Just get out quick."

Shelly nodded, then looked sternly at Imtiaz, who shot her a confused look. The moment the robot's boot sound sprung to life, he suddenly grabbed hold of its free arm.

"Hello," it said. "I am model Minerva, serial number TTPS-8103-X79I. How may I help you?"

"By getting airborne," Shelly whispered. "Uh . . . Hostiles en route, or whatever."

"Understood." Suddenly, its wings spread open with a tinny, rusty clang. Its edges hit both walls without even opening fully, and then it just as suddenly retracted them. "Wingspan obstacle issue." It turned to Shelly. "Primary launch will include thrusters only. Will that be a problem?"

"Nah, you do what you have to do, man." The moment Shelly said this was when Imtiaz realized he was about to do something well and truly foolish.

The knocking at the door became more insistent, and the officer's voice harsher. "You better open up right now before I have to kick this blasted—"

The bot's thrusters thrummed to life, warm air gushing from it. It turned to Imtiaz. "Please hold on to my arms with both hands. Flight may often be turbulent and dangerous."

"No shit—" Shelly nearly exclaimed it, but another persistent knock at the door brought her back to whispers. "We should go now, you know."

"Understood," the bot replied.

A louder, harder purr of wind and heat flooded out of the thrusters, and the bot sprang up with its two parcels on each side, through the galvanized sheet roof with enough force to push it clean off. They didn't have enough time to ready themselves; Imtiaz would have slid all the way off its arm if it hadn't swiveled its palm to grab his belt buckle. Shelly responded by wrapping her limbs around its arm for more support.

The robot spread its wings, and the thrusters let out an even harder gust. "Clearing distance. What is our destination?"

"Take me to San Juan," Shelly shouted into its microphoned ear.

"Understood." It flapped its chrome-feathered wings once, and then sped east with a force Imtiaz swore would tear his flesh from the rest of him.

Imtiaz looked down to see three police officers rush through the door, one of them already pinning Runako to the wall. Another reached for his pistol and let out one shot, narrowly missing the robot's forehead and, by extension, Imtiaz.

• • •

Shelly would later spring Runako from prison with the spoils of her newfound publicity. Runako's charge, again, was drug pushing, until the real news broke. Shelly sent a compact disc to every major television station as soon as she had watched all of the video herself—hours of "winged" officers kicking in doors, windows, and the occasional civilian's face; dozens of false arrests and misappropriations, with all the officers' faces on screen. Imtiaz refused to look at them. They both spent their quiet moments trembling at the thought of what must have been on the videos that were lost to hard-drive damage and time. The Prime Minister resigned two nights after, owning up to the whole flying squad program. The new hot topic on the web, though, was that till the snap election was done, the citizens would be under a state of emergency anyway.

As for the bot, Shelly put it to work helping her mother around the house on her behalf. She had tinkered with it so intensively that it had taken to cooking their dinner and tending to their herb garden with near-mathematical accuracy. On weekends, she strapped a bespoke harness around its wings and learned to fly with it for fun, a hobby which frightened her mother every single time.

"What's next for the girl who blew the whistle on the Flying Squad fiasco?" the press would ask her every other day in the papers.

"Graduate from UWI?" she'd reply, shrugging, looking away from the cameras like she was already bored with it all.

Imtiaz managed to keep his face out of the papers, for his own sake. Even his husband had yet to hear of the drama of that night. He'd have the occasional paranoid episode coming from work, though, looking in his rearview mirror for flashing blue lights as he hurried down the highway. Whenever he found himself panicking, he raised the volume on his industrial-rock driving music just a little higher.

Imtiaz grew to enjoy the safety of his house. He held on to Tevin a little tighter every day. He'd even find himself grinning like a fool at the simplest, most mundane questions, simply because he was still around to answer them.

"Didn't have any problems getting back?" Tevin would ask.

"Nah," Imtiaz would reply. "Traffic was light today. You know how it is."

GANZEER

CRISPR THAN YOU

(2018)

PART I: CHANGING DELIGHTLY

Snip.

There goes my impending heart disease.

Snip, snip.

Goodbye, acne
and dry frizzy hair.

Stitch.
Hello,
hint of eumelanin.

Hello, Jared Leto eyes.

Stitch, stitch.
Hello,
glorious member,
envy of all men.

When I was little, there were a lot of things I didn't quite understand about aging.

Why are there so many ads on television for pimple cream? I'd ask my brother.

Why don't you have any hair in the middle part of your head? I'd ask my father.

Why don't you race me up the stairs anymore? I'd ask my mother.

Age, they'd respond.

Getting old, they'd say.

Life, they'd mutter.

It wasn't a satisfying answer for me, because before "age" became the reason behind all their ailments, it seemed to be the very source of their powers.

"But you're not old enough to ride the roller coaster, baby."

"Sorry, hon, this movie's for grown-ups."

"Dominic, no! That drink's not for you!"

Worst of all was when my grandma would visit. Sweet old lady, but she was old and obese.

Listen, I ain't gonna mince words; she was fat. So fat and so old that she couldn't walk up the stairs to our apartment. It was a small building with no elevator, but we only lived on the second floor. No big deal, but too much for the old hag to handle. Poor old lady would have to get down on all fours and literally crawl up the stairs, and even then she struggled. And every time without fail, my mother would look down at her from the apartment doorway with tears in her eyes. Her face overtaken by silent sorrow and evident disgust. She'd ask if she could lend a hand, but grandma was a proud and stubborn old woman who accepted help from no one. It might've been that in her mind being helped up the stairs would be indicative of aging, yet crawling up the stairs was not somehow, just because she managed to do it on her own.

I never liked being around grandma. Absolutely adorable woman, but she made me afraid of the future. Afraid of living a bedridden life with too few teeth. Of not being able to visit my future daughter without first humiliating myself on her stairwell.

She probably sensed it, because whenever she visited she would slip me some crisp new pocket money. She would do this every time, hoping I'd warm up to her a little with each tiny bribe. Little did she realize that I had no clue what good money was for.

Back then anyway.

Dahlia Delightly was the prettiest girl in school. Everyone knew it, except Dahlia herself. She was sweet and easy to talk to, but she hardly ever talked about herself. The one thing I *did* know about her was that she wanted to be a movie star when she grew up. I remember being particularly fascinated by that because at the time I had no idea what I wanted to be when I grew up. The idea of Dahlia in the movies made sense. She had a certain presence about her, and she wore the nicest clothes and the coolest specs.

Until one day she showed up without them.

It took me off guard. I knew people wore glasses because they couldn't see without them, so how on Earth was she coming to school without her glasses all of a sudden? Wasn't that dangerous? I wondered.

I asked her about it and she told me her parents had her undergo "laser surgery," an operation that fixed her eyes up, and made it possible for her to see without her iconic specs. She didn't seem awfully thrilled about it. I mean, she definitely wasn't upset about it, but she did mention that it felt weird. That she couldn't recognize herself in the mirror anymore. I always thought she was just as beautiful even with her glasses on, but I couldn't help but be fascinated by the idea of this magical laser beam that, when aimed at her eyes, transformed them into the best version they could possibly be. And I found myself daydreaming of a wicked ray gun that could, at the pull of a trigger, fix anything for anyone.

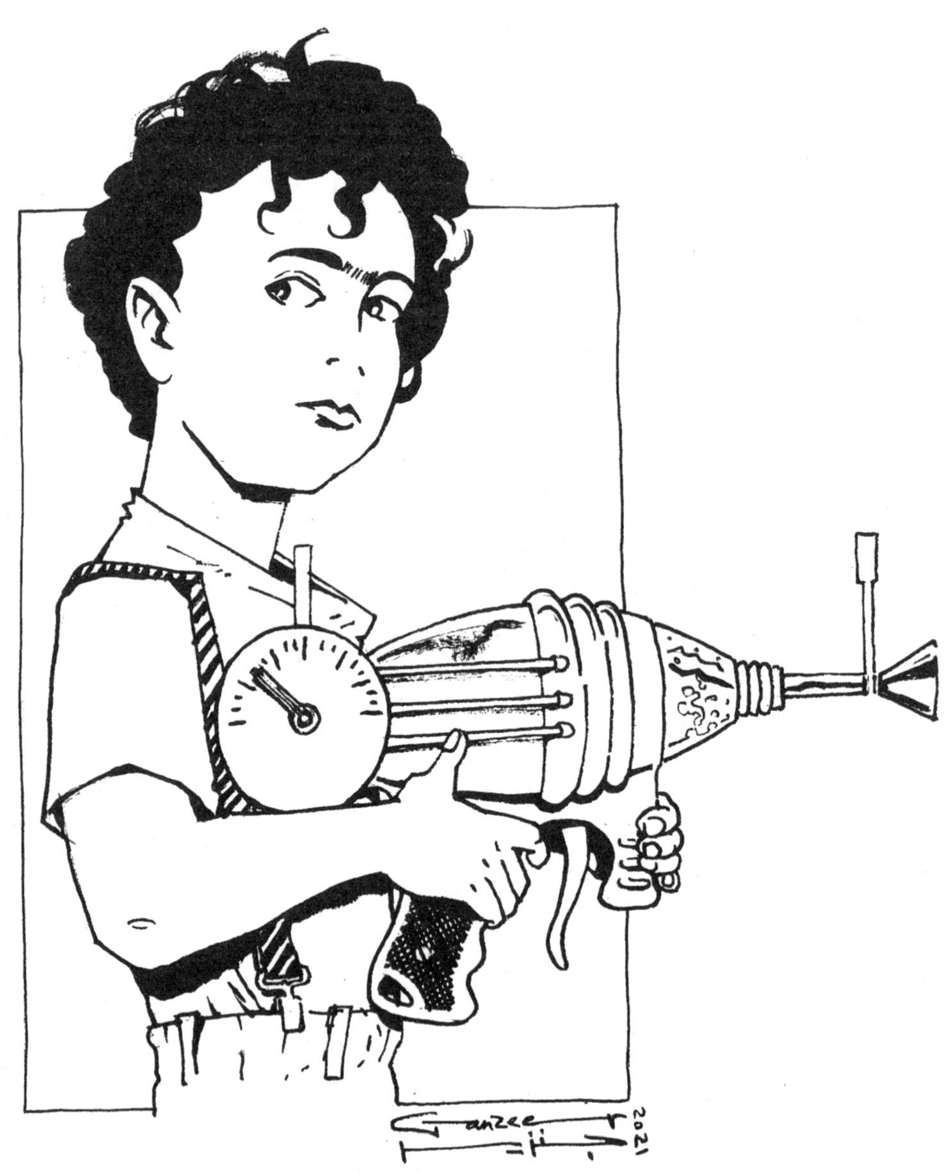

Oh hey, you've got the sniffles? *ZAP!* All healthy now.

Tripped and smashed your face? *ZAP!* Unharmed.

Stung by a bee? *ZAP!* You're saved.

Fat grandma can't walk up stairs? *ZAP!* Now she's Wonder Woman.

Obsession has a way of creeping up on you in unpredictable ways. You never know what singular observation will recalibrate your worldview for the rest of your life. For me it was Dahlia Delightly; a girl in glasses who, overnight, no longer needed them. You might say that the minute Dahlia started seeing better, I started seeing better too.

I brought up Dahlia's laser surgery to my old man, who also wore glasses, telling him with exaggerated enthusiasm that he ought to get his eyes lasered too.

"Too expensive," he said, "and a real man should never have to worry too much about his appearances."

And I'm quoting verbatim because I remember it like it was yesterday. His voice stern and distant, spoken without thought. A natural reflex. "Natural." Oh how I grew to hate that word. Really nothing but an excuse to be okay with flaws. But I took my old man's words to heart, and finally understood what good grandma's money was for. If a single laser beam for eye surgery was too much for my dad to afford, then a ray gun for every human ailment possible would have to be grossly expensive.

It was then that I decided I was going to become a rich man. A very, very rich man.

Clearly, the part about real men not needing to look good wasn't something I agreed with. I could see how Dahlia looked at the other boys. At Randy. Especially when he smiled his perfect smile with his perfect teeth.

I figured it was just my dad's excuse for not having to bother too much. When things seem out of our hands, we tend to come up with reasons as to why it's okay. No one wants to come face to face with their own helplessness. Which is exactly why I vowed never to be helpless about anything no matter what. And if I ever found myself in that position, I would do everything in my power to change where I stood.

If you stop to think about it, getting rich isn't too hard. There are maybe three ways to go about it:

1. You buy something for cheap and sell it for more than it cost you. That's just the basics of commerce. Want to get rich off this scheme? Make sure whatever you buy is something that pretty much everyone needs. And buy a lot of it.

2. Buy something that isn't worth much now, but will likely be worth a lot in the future. You speculate essentially, but for accurate speculation you must ignore everything anyone says about speculation because all that *is* hyperbole from special interest groups. A way to create the illusion that something might be worth a lot in the future, even if there is little to no factual information to support their claims. Something will only be crazy valuable in the future if it has the potential of being highly sought after while maintaining a very rare status. Perhaps a book that only saw a very low print run yet also managed to get a lot of people to talk about it. Something that became culturally influential

in some way. Or if it was authored by someone who would later become acknowledged as a historical figure. Almost anything belonging to historical figures is bound to be valuable. The only way to maneuver the potentiality of rare objects belonging to historical figures is, really, to be friendly with most people you meet. And if they are makers of things, become a hoarder of said things. Let's be real, there's no truly efficient way to do this and guarantee a profit.

3. Invent something awesome that everyone will want.

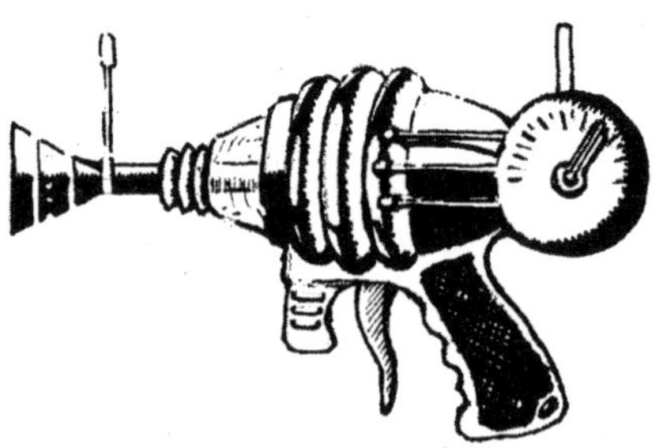

The ray gun.

Everyone would want the ray gun. Everyone would want to be perfect. Void of illness. Live forever.

I had a goal then.

I started to pay extra attention in science class and knew exactly what I wanted to be when I grew up. But I knew not to put all my eggs in one basket. I started using grandma's money to buy things. Things I could sell to the other kids. Cool pens and notebooks from the stationery store. Snacks that the school canteen never carried. And when I got old enough, cigarettes and condoms. And before long, drugs and porn.

But I think it was around then that I first started hearing about gene-editing technology. What the media referred to as "CRISPR."

I'm not sure when Dahlia became distant but it might've been around the same time. No worries, I told myself, she won't be so distant when I'm rich, famous, and immortal. I just had to keep at it. Not lose focus.

When I made it to college, I decided to take a typography class. That was my segue into the art crowd. I bought at least one piece from every art punk I met, because you can never really tell who the hell is going to be famous. For real! I mean, do you think anyone suspected Andy Warhol would amount to anything when he was taking free art classes at the Carnegie Institute? Or that Haring would ever matter when he was at SVA? Or even Dalí when he was still at Madrid's Real Academia de Bellas Artes?

Get them while they're cheap, I figured. Wouldn't hurt. And you better believe it was a good enough strategy, because one of the pieces I scored . . . was a Kalak.

PART II: SEBASTIAN KALAK

Before becoming Sebastian Kalak he was Seva Kalanenko. A girl.

When she was little, she insisted on wearing her older brother's track pants and T-shirts, much to her mother's dismay. Her dad wasn't around a whole lot, but when he was, Seva's mother would scold him for not playing a more active role in the girl's life.

"I never had any sisters, and I wouldn't know the first thing about telling a girl how to behave," Seva overheard her dad tell her mom once. "The girl is your responsibility, Adele."

It's not that Seva knew she wanted to be a boy, not back then. In fact, she hated it when anyone called her a boy. Especially the other boys, who she would find no trouble beating up if and when they did. Teachers, however, and other grownups were somewhat of a problem. They didn't think she was a boy, nor did they actively refer to her as one, but they'd question her choice of clothes, and ask her if she wanted to be a boy. This frustrated her, because she didn't think that boys or girls ought to be designated by clothes or hairstyle. That was silly. If track pants were comfortable for boys, why on Earth would they not be comfortable for girls too? Why couldn't a girl's favorite color be blue or, heck, black even? Which was in fact Seva's favorite color, something that freaked the hell out of grownups for some reason.

"Not only is she a tomboy, but she's also a goth," one teacher told Seva's mother once. "You might want to nip this one in the bud before she starts giving you real trouble later on. Hanging out with little boys might not be much of an issue now, but eventually . . . well, those boys won't stay little forever."

Certain ideas, once planted in your head, are almost impossible to shake away. Especially—most especially—if they're ideas about your kids.

Adele, Seva's mom, became increasingly worried. She was having nightmares that involved a teenage Seva shooting up with boys in heroin dens before pegging them with a big black strap-on in front of live industrial neo-fasch bands.

This, when Seva was only six.

No mother should have to dream that kind of shit about their six-year-old daughter. And so Adele decided she would set her daughter straight. She would spare no expense. Her daughter's future depended on it, dammit! It was time to get rid of the guest room. Have Seva move out of her brother's room and into a room of her own. But the room needed some renovation.

First came the bubblegum pink for the walls, then came the Marie Antoinette bed. Seva discovered that taking a sharpie to the bed's frame actually made it look badass. Although it did take a great deal of sharpies for it to get there. Drawing with black crayons on the pink walls made the room feel more her own, the drawings being childish imitations of the art from her older brother's horror comics. So cool were the drawings that even her brother preferred to hang out in her room more than his own.

Adele, however, was steadfast. She filled her daughter's wardrobe with skirts and dresses, Disney princess shirts, and the most delicate of shoes; bow ties and glitter galore.

Seva tried real hard not to be a punk-ass rebel, but it was only a week before she found herself taking a pair of scissors to those bow ties and wearing her Disney shirts inside out. And there was nothing awfully girly that a basic sharpie couldn't remedy.

Adele was hysterical. She slapped her daughter's soft, tiny face hard, real hard. Seva was stunned. She'd only ever seen love and compassion from her mother, but here she was plowing her daughter with deep hateful rage. Tears flowed down Seva's face, not because of the pain, but because of the fear.

"You little—"

Slap!

"—ungrateful—"

Slap!

"—bitch!"

Slap!

"Do you have any idea how hard I had to work to be able to afford this stuff?"

Slap!

"Do you?"

Slap!

Seva said sorry. She said sorry over and over and over, but she honestly didn't get it. She just wanted to be herself, she told her mother. But she promised she would never do that ever again.

That's when Adele realized the horror of what she was doing. Beating her daughter . . . for wanting to wear pants? And why? Because other people thought it was weird? Fuck them!

Adele hugged her daughter and covered her in kisses, saying she was sorry, so so sorry. That of course she should be herself and never anything else. And from then on, Adele vowed to champion her daughter and whatever she wanted to be no matter what.

It wasn't until college that Seva really came into her own though. College, a chance for new beginnings, where no one yet knows you and has no preconceptions about you. Seva adopted a more dapper look: well-fitted trousers, fine Italian shoes, clean shirts, and complementary vests. A far cry from her track-pants days, and a very far cry from her mother's goth-infested nightmares.

When people asked her about her name, she'd say "Seva, but my friends call me Sebastian." Which was a way of asking people to call her Sebastian if they wanted to be friends with her, which most people felt rather intimidated to attempt. Most people except Dominic.

What Dominic loved most about Seva was her fearlessness. Her complete dedication to becoming the person she felt she was meant to be. Oh, if only more people were like her, Dominic told himself, so much human potential would be unleashed. His fascination with Seva wasn't at all lost on her. She could read his dark eyes like a children's book. This was even before she underwent hormone therapy. Before she officially took on the name Sebastian Kalak. Before she became a he. Before they made love.

PART III: HAIL, AMERICA!

Most people say they didn't see it coming. Some blame it entirely on Yellowstone. They're all full of shit.

Between 1909 and 1933 the Weimar Republic is known to have granted transvestite passes to trans people to protect them from public and police harassment. A way of saying: hey, the state recognizes that I like to dress this way and is very much okay with it. Simultaneously, Berlin was considered to be the homosexual capital of Europe. That is not to say that this was the reason behind the eventual rise of Nazism, but it is not to be overlooked. Because it was one of the many things the Nazis pointed to as a sign of German decay. That's the thing about progress; while a breath of fresh air for some, it can also be seen as a departure from basic foundational values by everyone else. The other thing about progress is that it's often hard to be seen as true progress when overshadowed by the shame of national catastrophe.

Military defeat.

Three million dead.

One hundred thirty-two billion gold marks in reparations.

Terrible, terrible disgrace following Germany's defeat in World War I. And pride was never a concept foreign to the German.

Nor has it ever been foreign to the American, albeit for reasons far less founded.

The problem with Americans is that we'd been feeding on our own propaganda for far too long. The idea of American exceptionalism was something far too few Americans ever questioned. Even those who claimed ideological opposition to early "Alt-Right" groups still believed in the myth of "the greatest nation on Earth." And practically every single stamp issued by the United States Postal Service had "USA FOREVER" printed on it, which c'mon, isn't really a huge leap from "HAIL, AMERICA!" No society can ever prosper without a constant reevaluation of the myths it perpetuates. Something Sebastian learned from his readings of the great James Baldwin, which he often read out loud to Dominic in bed.

> A society must assume that it is stable, but the artist must know, and must let us know, that there is nothing stable under the heavens.
>
> —James Baldwin

If anyone practiced what they preached, it was definitely Sebastian. Even when still in college, he had a knack for creating art that was the most scathing of social commentary. His gaze going past the elephant in the room, and instead fixated on the little elephants lurking in the shadows. The elephants that would eventually grow to become the big elephants in the room. The elephants that everyone knew were there but avoided speaking of.

Controversial? Sure, but not for the heck of it. Sebastian was a much-needed societal warning station. But one that, inevitably, came at a cost.

The most dangerous of all moods is that of a great power which sees itself declining to second rank.

—Michael Howard

The fear of declining to second rank was already in America's air for far too long. Which is actually rather mind-blowing because it was happening together with this bolstering of exceptionalism. Two notions that you would think were completely at odds with one another.

In any case, a quick look at actual data would've completely nullified American fears. When the American GDP was at 20 trillion dollars, China was only at $13 trillion. When Americans were spending $554 billion on military expenditures, China was spending $215. China had only one aircraft carrier compared to America's twenty. And China's 260 nuclear warheads were a far, far cry from America's seven thousand!

What was everyone panicking about?

That fear, perpetuated by both Republicans and Democrats for so long, is precisely what led to their downfall, and the inevitable rise of the Upward Party and the subsequent establishment of what became colloquially known as the "American Reich," or what some liked to refer to as the "American Renaissance."

Not to create a mono-causal argument for the Reich's foundation or anything. The first Dominic ever heard about the rise of proto-Reich movements was at around age fifteen. Protests dominated by white males, publicly defended by so-called intellectuals who attacked social justice defenders using pseudo-scientific arguments. "SJWs," they called them, short for Social Justice Warriors. It takes someone particularly evil to be able to vilify those who fight for justice and put a label on them.

SJW. A tactic borrowed directly from corporate America. SJW. No longer implying social or justice, just as KFC removed connotations of "fried" or "Kentucky." Or heck, "chicken" for that matter.

SJWs weren't their only targets obviously. There were also the "sick trannies," "Jewish commies," "criminal n——s," and "jihadist Muslims." And that's just the tip of the iceberg. Even if the so-called intellectuals among them refrained from using that specific language.

It was certainly absent from their manifesto.

PART IV: THE MANIFESTO

FAST FORWARD UPWARD: A MANIFESTO

Man is the creator of God, and thus it is appropriate to declare man the one true God in this here Universe. Let us then embrace our godly status and hurl ourselves toward the stars of eternity that call out to us in the night. We must pierce forward like the red-hot swords of the life-giving Sun and decapitate the tyranny of ignorant darkness upon sight.

We may be dreamers, but dreamers of night we are not. We are dreamers of day, willing our dreams visibly into reality for all to soak up and bathe in. Not just here on Earth, but across the cosmos. Other bodies reflect our glow and come into being solely because we exist, and our existence burns bright.

The fuel to our fire is the habit of energy, courage, audacity, and revolt! Our revolt is against the totality of nature, the revolt of survival, of evolution against all odds. It is the beautiful revolt of perpetual struggle, because there is no glory in idle surrender.

Let us discard the dystopic perspectives of the Anthropocene and instead embrace it as an inevitable stepping stone in our righteous evolution. No longer shall we sheepishly look over our shoulders at carbon footprints. Let us instead look forward toward the trajectories of future footprints, their impressions deeper and more pronounced with every step we take.

Humanity's poetry is in the violent assault on our surrounding environment, forcing the universe to bow before us.

More awaits us. We must be faster, stronger, higher!

It is time to transcend and break down the gates of life. It is time to bolt death deep beneath our feet. We must cast aside the false wisdom of decay, and instead embrace the fervor of youth as the one true ideal of forever.

Beauty is not an offense against inequality, but as legitimate a pursuit as happiness. It must be upheld and protected by the culture at large, never to be slandered.

Our sensibilities must be saved from the rot of old funeral urns. Our reservoirs must be fed by the man-made machines of prosperous intellect.

Ignore the wisdom of yesteryear, for we are the gods of tomorrow. Walk not among the soulless golems animated by the dark seething power of establishment media. They are bound to be crushed by the wheels of progress, but only after spending a lifetime getting tossed between a thousand meaningless distractions.

We must insist on our dreams and push for the conquest of space and time. That is what we do: We explore, we build, we conquer. We must continue to develop the revolutionary technology worthy of a species racing toward an upward path. Let the naysayers and apocalypse-screamers abstain and get left behind in the bush where they belong.

Education must be reformed. We can no longer allow universities to take our money just to tell us how despicable our accomplishments are. Let us honor the enlightening legacy of our culture and push forth for more. Because our best days are ahead of us. If nostalgia must be part of our consciousness then let it be a nostalgia for the future.

Let us strip honor from unworthy politicians and celebrities, and instead honor those who catalyze humanity's advancements. It is no longer enough to resolve age-old socioeconomic political problems. The time has come to do away with them altogether. The spectrum of Right-Wing/Left-Wing thought is too narrow for the human of the future. It is time we stopped looking left or right and instead started looking up and beyond.

No new heights we reach will be satisfactory. No new height will be idealized. The greatest ideal must always remain the forthcoming heights of the future!

It is in America that we are issuing this manifesto of eternal tomorrow, because only America can hurl the world upward and forth into the future. America is uniquely situated at the center of modern history. It is America that first showed the world the meaning of freedom. It is America that first put a man on the moon. It is America that connected the world into a singular telesphere. It is America's armies that keep the world safe. It is thus America's duty to stop limping in rusty shackles. It is thus America's responsibility to cast aside all that is un-American. It is thus America's birthright to grab the world by its reins and charge forth into the hailstorm of big dreams and mad ideas.

Fast forward upward!

America must lead the way, because that is what America does.

PART V: NOSTALGIA FOR THE FUTURE

Sebastian loved that manifesto. And so did Dominic, but it was Sebastian who really flew with it. It wasn't yet known who authored it, and Sebastian didn't really care. When the pamphlet first landed in his lap, he almost immediately incorporated it into his art. He must have risographed thousands of copies in red, white, and blue, and even purple, which he would draw directly on top of. His drawings mainly comprised pop-cultural mashups and real world failings. Drawings of decrepit bus stops, congested freeways, and the crappy pretzels served on airplanes juxtaposed against the manifesto were made to highlight that we were far from living in the America we deserved. It's hard to tell whether the manifesto elevated Sebastian's art or vice versa, but in any case the pieces—strategically placed in public space—were getting nationwide attention, and Sebastian's star grew high and bright.

Until they killed him.

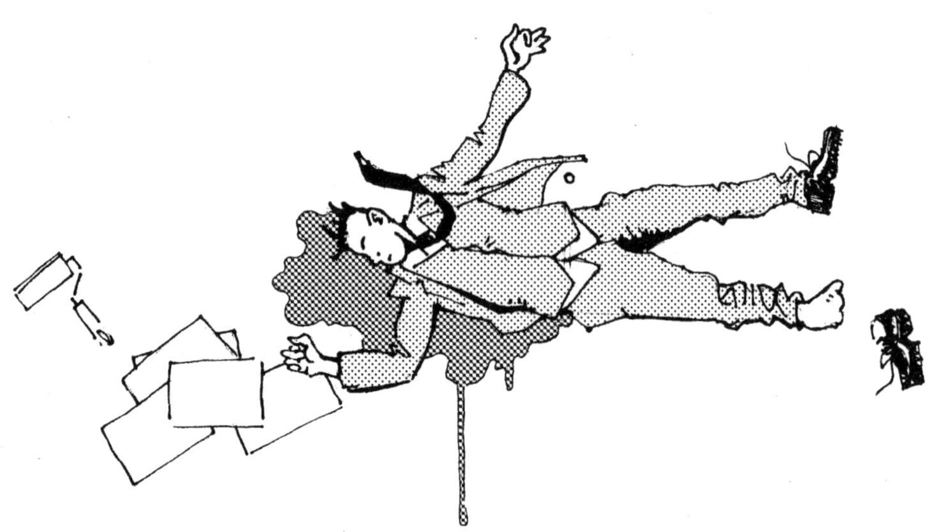

The killers were not, as one might've suspected, a group of trans-hating white men, but in fact the militant antifa group known as FemFatale-2030 who—not at all knowing that Sebastian was once a she—saw his guerrilla actions as a sinister plot to popularize toxic masculinity. This was naturally something proto-Reich groups took advantage of, which not only galvanized their cause but also made whatever remained of Sebastian's work highly sought-after.

Which did Dominic very well.

Sebastian's death was crushing to him, but rather than hold on to Sebastian's art for personal sentimentalities, he felt he had to do good by Sebastian's legacy and serve the greater good in a way.

He was making headway with his research and had devised, not a ray gun, but a kind of gene-editing phone booth. He called it the CRISPod, and saw it as a formidable step toward the democratization of gene-editing technology. Of making it well within the reach of every American.

All he had to do was build a proper prototype. And now he had the means to do just that.

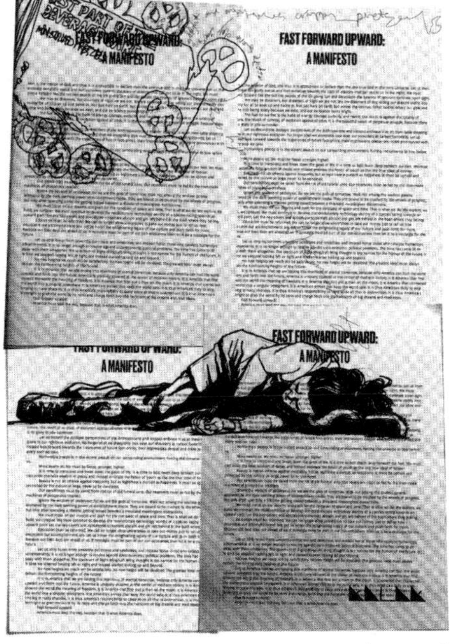

Current bid: $69,000,000 [73 bids]

Even with staunch resistance and defamation campaigns from big pharma, Dominic's CRISPod was getting worldwide attention. He was a sly marketeer, and had a way of capturing the public imagination. He wore big glassless specs in his televised appearances, which sure, painted him as an eccentric, but also cunningly made a point: That glasses, as a sight-enabling apparatus for the contemporary man, were ridiculous. And if they were ridiculous, then perhaps they weren't the only ridiculous thing about the way we all lived.

There was one video Dominic put together with his artist friends that went especially viral. It took on the air of a vintage advertisement, showing Clark Kent rush into a CRISPod before emerging as Superman. Except, immediately after his exit, someone else rushes into the pod who also reemerges as Superman. The camera slowly zooms out revealing people queuing up in front of more CRISPods, supermen emerging out of them one after the other. We finally get a big panoramic view of the city, which is not something of the past, but a great sleek metropolis of the future, with a pattern of endless supermen in the skies around it.

And then the logo fades in against the cityscape:

CRISPod
Become a better human.

And this was all before Yellowstone erupted.

PART VI: YELLOWSTONE

It was January, and the volcanic ash that descended like a heavy blanket on the country spread from coast to coast. The most devastating effects stretched from Seattle in the west to Kansas City in the east. From Calgary up north all the way to Albuquerque down south. The shower of splintered rock and glass lasted months, shutting down most roads, railways, and air travel.

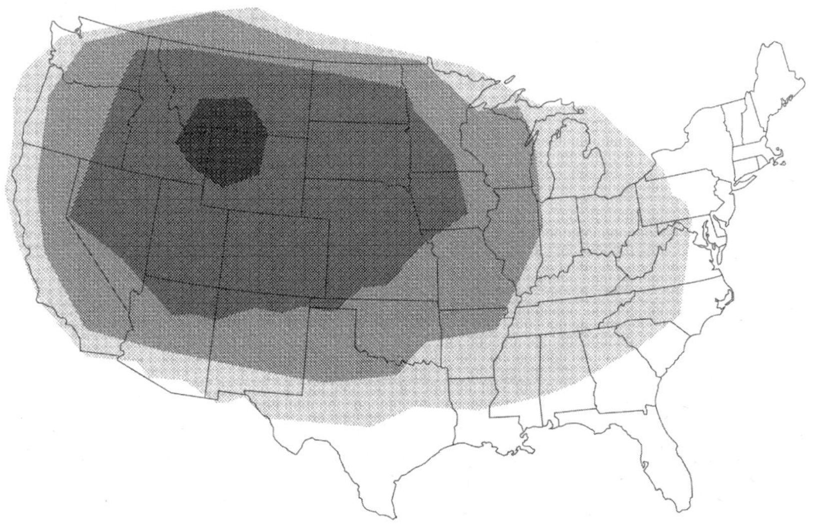

Ninety-seven million dead.

One hundred ninety-five million terminally ill.

Seventy-five percent of livestock killed.

One hundred sixteen million hectares of arable land devastated.

Shame, havoc, ruin.

The perfect storm had arrived for the Upward Party to take command. Their manifesto spoke to a nation keen on rising from the ashes. No one wanted to vote for the age-old proven incompetence of Democrat or Republican. The time had come for the Great New Party, as some people referred to it. America was ready to board the techno-theological spaceship of the future, and the Upward Men were there to steer it. Their speeches breathtaking, their rallies inspiring, and their plan concrete.

And at the center of their plan was Dominic's CRISPod.

Circumstances called for new measures and everyone knew it. Old drugs and pharmaceuticals were cast aside as archaic poisons, and the CRISPod quickly became the infrastructural cornerstone of a New America. Embraced by all out of a nostalgic longing for the future.

Dominic soon rose to become a key player in the America of tomorrow, and just as he envisioned as a young child, he found himself becoming exceedingly rich.

He was happy. Content, until he discovered that the CRISPods weren't working for everyone. That some people were being killed by the CRISPods.

And the killing . . . was deliberate.

PART VII: SEEING DELIGHTLY

She probably won't remember me.

Heck, she probably won't recognize me, not with my new eyes and nicer hair. But I have to see her. The images of her on her deathbed all over the news are haunting me, and I cannot for the life of me think of anything else.

Her caretaker opens the door and shows me in. The place is sad. Curtains mostly drawn, keeping the light away from the old grandeur of a previous lifestyle. Up along the staircase there is photo after photo of Dahlia's Hollywood days. The days before Yellowstone. Red carpet glamour, life-loving sheen, and beautiful perfection. I'm reminded of a quote Sebastian read out loud to me once.

> I love Los Angeles. I love Hollywood. They're beautiful. Everybody's plastic, but I love plastic. I want to be plastic.
>
> —Andy Warhol

Now the nerdy scientist gets to be plastic, preserved for all eternity while the Hollywood beauty of old withers away.

There she is on the bed. Dahlia Delightly, little more than a crumpled-up napkin. She sees me and reaches for her glasses on the nightstand. It takes a few seconds of her staring at me before she speaks in croaky squeaks.

"Dominic Cunningham. Look . . . at you."

Didn't think you'd recognize me, I tell her.

"Oh, I've been keeping up with your news. And everything you've been doing for the country."

Not everyone . . . in the country. I regret saying it just as the words come out.

"Oh, Dominic. You cannot possibly blame yourself, dear. Not all of us have the genes that can handle eternal youth. Be proud of your accomplishments. You've saved more lives than any one person ever has."

Could've saved many more. Including you, Dahlia, if it weren't for those Upward fucks! The words don't exit my mouth this time. They remain silent thoughts trapped by bars of shame deep in my mind.

I sit on the edge of the bed and hold her hand.

I see you've got your old glasses back, I tell her.

"Ha! Yes, at least I have that," she laughed. "You should've come sooner, Dominic. A lot sooner. I would've liked to show you the pool in the back and make you one of my signature cocktails."

I was a nobody, I tell her. You were a big shining movie star when all I had going for me was a crummy makeshift lab.

"Silly boy," she says touching my face with elderly tenderness. "I've met a lot of not-nobodies in my day, and absolutely no one could fill the special place I have in my heart for you."

Her toothless smile is sweet and her eyes sincere. I lean in for the kiss, but I'm too late. Her heart is stopped and her breathing no more.

Dahlia Delightly is dead.

I watch her. The once Hollywood face of long-lasting youth reduced to a piece of broken china.

Back at the penthouse, I do not recognize the man looking back at me in the mirror. The man who claims he didn't know any better, that had no idea.

Fuck you, you're full of shit! Don't look at me like that you lousy self-serving prick.

Smash!

B r o k e n g l a s s

Smash!

Glass e v e r y w h e r e.

Sharp shard. Jared Leto eyes. Raging

Raging stabs and jagged pain.

Blood. Raging pain.

Raging pain.

Warm blood.

Lots of warm blood.

Cold floor.

Blackout.

I wake up to the sound of the automatic vacuum cleaner and robotic breakfast maker. The smell of morning coffee brings me to my feet, vision fuzzy like a newborn baby.

I make it to the bathroom and splash cold water on my face, flakes of dry crusted blood swirl down the drain. I look up and crisp newly grown Jared Leto eyes stare back me.

I think . . . I think they're starting to grow on me.

FABIO FERNANDES

WI-FI DREAMS

(2019)

WHEN THE BLACK DUCK comes to me with the bowie knife and the killing smile in his giant face, the first thing I think is, how the fuck is he holding the knife?

The second, of course, is, how the fuck am I going out of here?

The maze of hallways in the derelict building is dark and narrow—the few working light bulbs in the ceiling flicker; most of them are out. A few doors are open; through them I can see the night, hear distant screams and shouts, but nobody comes to my rescue.

Why should anyone? Nobody wants to die.

I stumble, almost fall but regain my balance at once. I can't stop. Because the duck is getting closer.

The third thing I ask myself is, how can this fucking duck be following me?

Because he is huge. And by huge I mean humongous, enormous, gigantic. Really. It is at least three stories high.

And suddenly he is blocking my way.

Blacker than the blackness of the corridor. A duck-shaped black hole with crazed eyes, a big grinning beak with a lolling pinkish tongue—and an impressive double row of very sharp teeth.

I reach for my silver dagger—but I can't pull it from its sheath.

The duck opens his beak even more. Now he's a Daffy Duck on speed—no, scratch that, Daffy Duck always lived on speed, how they let children watch that schizo-dope-fiend running around aimlessly? (except for *Duck Dodgers*; I loved *Duck Dodgers*)—and he's having the time of his larger-than-life life watching me squirm before he does whatever he wants to do with me.

I don't stay for question four. The fucking duck is not a sphinx, for crying out loud. It won't spare me if I answer correctly a question. It's certainly not asking any.

I lunge to the left. Without checking first I somehow already know there is a room with a door opened there and go for it without looking, and all of a sudden I'm already there.

It's a room with a view all right. A tiny room with a big window. Did I mention that I am on the fifth floor?

The duck is already right behind my back. Knife ready.

The only chance I have to escape is to take the plunge from the fifth floor directly to the ground. And it has to be headfirst. For the key to escape from a killer dream is to kill myself.

For now.

You just wait for me, you crazy negative-zone bizarro-world Donald Duck motherfucker. In the immortal words of Arnold Schwarzenegger, I'll be back.

But, seriously? If I could have my say, I'd rather not come back. I'll probably have no choice in the matter. That's what happens with recurrent dreams. Especially when you can't wake up anymore.

Then I jump.

• • •

I wake up sweating. As I always do these days.

I breathe deeply for what seems like a few minutes—but I'm stark naked and I have no watch or clock in the room, so that's only a guess—until I muster enough courage to get off the bed. I put on a pair of boxers that are on the tiled floor near the nightstand and look for socks. The tiles are freezing my feet.

I take a while to find them. Not only because they are scattered all over the room, but also because the perspective is a bit askew and my eyes can't seem to focus completely when I'm not looking right in front of something. That's more or less common currency for a myopic person, but I had Lasix surgery five years ago. Does it have an expiration date? I wonder as I finally put on the damn socks. I need to see the eye doctor again.

Then I go to the window and push the curtains aside. And I am gently reminded that the eye doctor is going to have to wait.

The swollen red sun is still there, towering over the broken cityscape.

I'm back to False Wake-Up Zero. F-0 for short.

I breathe deeply. This still is a safe zone for now. I dress quickly and run after the others.

The last time I did the run, Tanya was my nearest neighbor. I exited the dilapidated building where I was staying, crossed the deserted plaza in front of it, then turned left at the crossroads right after.

While I run across the perimeter, I recite a personal litany of sorts:

"*Matrix—eXistenZ—Thirteenth Floor—Simulacron Three—Nirvana*—'The Tunnel Under the World'—*The Truman Show—Dark City—Inception—Vanilla Sky—Surrogates—Source Code*—"

And so on. Every fucking film, novel, and story I know about people trapped in fake worlds. This is not a meditation—although my grandfather might disagree—but a checklist. Of stats. Of what the fuck is happening and possible exit strategies.

But it never seems to help. When I'm still figuring this and that story, wondering if the remake of *Total Recall* should enter (because, honestly, it sucks major ass, the story makes no sense at all), then I find myself in front of Tanya's place.

Squat is a better label for it, actually, but who's worrying? I jog into the dilapidated building, with its large iron doors half-molten as if hit by a flamethrower or something like it, and knock on her door right there on the first floor.

She takes a while to open it—she's been doing it slower and slower with each awakening. When she finally does it, she's not half as bad as I thought she'd be—just light dark rings under her eyes.

"Hi," I say.

"Hi," she says, managing a weak smile.

"Did you just wake up?"

"Yep."

"Lucky me."

She shrugged and let me in.

"Lucky us. Did you get the garganey too?"

"The what?"

"The small migratory duck. Only it was a giant one."

"Holding a bowie knife?"

"The same."

"How did you escape?" I ask, more to make conversation than out of curiosity. It's our kind of breakfast, since nobody eats at F-0.

She sits on her bed, snickering.

"Who told you I escaped?"

I shiver. That bowie knife was huge.

"These dreams are getting weirder and weirder," it's all I manage to say.

"All these fucking demons," a voice behind us says. I turn, startled, even though I already know who it is.

"Hi, Rafael."

He just nods to me. Cross the room in two strides and kneels at Tanya's bedside, as if he would say his prayers. "Hey, my love," he says, hugging her and putting his head on her lap. The whole scene suddenly turns into a kind of soft-porn, self-pity Pietà.

She doesn't answer, just exhales.

I'm worried about her. But she isn't my problem anymore. She had told me so herself. Rafael too. So I'm here just for the ride. Because we need all the help we can have.

I go to the window and look out there. As usual, nobody to be seen. There is somebody, that's for sure. Thousands of people, all of them alive and breathing, though not necessarily in F-0.

We still haven't mapped all this, but one thing we know for sure: this is no dystopian post-apoc scenario. We just happen to be stuck in a dream within a dream. Only it's more like a game-level structure.

Imagine, however, a particularly difficult level—one where there's a boss so motherfucking unpassable that makes you want to break the controls and give up the game.

Naturally, this isn't something you can do in this case. Not when your mind is trapped in the game. And you can't even reach the console to reboot it.

• • •

Here's a brief description of F-0:

Imagine Chernobyl or Fukushima. A nuked-out territory of the soul, a neutron-bomb ground zero where only a few people remain alive, or at least visible.

Case in point, the ground zero being São Paulo, largest city in Brazil, largest city in the Americas, and fifth largest city in the world. Eight million square kilometers. Thirteen million inhabitants.

F-0, however, doesn't stretch all over the city. But it goes a long way if you don't have a car—from Jardins to Anhangabaú Valley and from Vila Madalena to Paraíso. An area of approximately twenty-seven square kilometers and ultrahigh-density zone—where the first experiments started. Or the demon plague, as Rafael also calls it.

• • •

The demon plague started when 3D Printers managed to work in our dreams.

People got too paranoid with viruses and nanotech. Nobody noticed the worst things, the things that hurt us more are the daily things. Airplanes don't kill people as much as cars; cars don't kill people as much as guns; guns don't kill people as much as home accidents. Kitchen knives can kill you far more efficiently. Paper cuts, if you happen to be a hemophiliac.

Allergies kill more than guns.

When dreams started to be Wi-Fi-ed, we all became allergic.

In an ultracapitalist society, it was taking too long for the abstract to become commodified. But nobody complained when the home systems began to become available at a very cheap price with computers and Wi-Fi routers. After all, it wasn't as if Amazon, Apple, or Google were getting hold of your dreams or such—at least, that's what every scientist and tech writer out there was assuring us.

They were right. They just couldn't see the big picture.

And the big picture is critical mass.

Dreams are still private territory—nobody can get inside them except for the dreamers themselves. But you can access the borders: a Kinect-based motion-capture body-mapping system can also capture EEGs and REM state, so as to connect several sleeping players in a "dreaming campaign"—a very interesting kind of game, in which the players usually aren't much in control of the game play; this fad didn't spread into the industry, but eventually found a rather comfortable niche, and it became used by a fair share of therapists.

It was a very interesting phenomenon—even more so when you found out that all that talk about people dying in their sleep was sheer exaggeration, not to say utter crap: Who the fuck dies in their sleep? Okay, old people, or the eventual forty- to fiftyish woman or man with a heart condition. But many argued that this was a preexistent condition, and that was generally agreed upon without much argument.

Of course, things couldn't be that easy as well.

The reason the "dreaming campaigns" failed to capture the hearts and minds of gamers all around the world in a first moment was simple: gamers like to be awake while they play, not sleeping and feeling helpless. Games are all about control.

So, a number of developers worked around this feature of the system to try and offer a better game-play condition: a connection with 3D printers to the dreamscape.

Not a virtual printer, no—the real thing.

The sales pitch was: if you can't control your dreams, what about the next best thing? Have them shaped for you from the outside world!

Talk about technoxamanism: nobody would need to take smart drugs or meditate or do whatever the thing psychologists or doctors would say you had to do in order to achieve a state of lucid dreaming. Just program the printer to print whatever you want, adjust Settings to Print on File (same principle of the old paper printers, except they won't print the object in the real world, but upload it in the cloud to be downloaded for you), connect it to the Wi-Fi router, and sweet dreams.

The first campaigns were damn good. The success was so great it spread all over the world in a few weeks. I started playing it with a couple friends just for curiosity's sake and was hooked without even noticing it. In less than a week I was roaming the streets of the city looking for hot spots and buffer boxes where we could download not only our 3D objects—here was the bonus—but others' as well, as long as we had their passwords. It became a game inside the game, a hidden campaign.

Until, of course, the Bug.

• • •

This always happens along History: someone invents a thing, then one of two things follow. A) Someone else finds another use for it, usually a twisted one, which ends in death and destruction; B) a bug enters the system.

Sometimes it can be even both.

I guess we we'll never know exactly what happened in our case, not even if we get out of here.

I can only speak for myself—and maybe for Tanya, Rafael, and a few (very few) other poor bastards I've been finding here and there.

One day, after a particularly heavy campaign, I got back to my place (a seedy hotel room downtown) and got in bed. As usual, when I closed my eyes and assumed the bedding stance, I would wake up in my own bedroom, with only one hour of real time passed when compared to three or four in dreamtime, the game would be automatically saved where I had stopped, and I would have a good night's sleep.

This time, though, nothing happened.

I tried the procedure twice; I even got up and back into bed again just in case. I thought of a bug. I was right. I just had no idea of the size of the bug.

• • •

"Any changes?" I ask Rafael.

He gives me a sidelong glance.

"Why do you ask?" he says, gesturing to the window.

I sigh.

"Because every minor change could mean a chance for us to get out of here," I say.

He jumps on his feet, getting close to me, raging.

"And where is here? Huh? Do you fucking know?"

I don't.

As far as I know, we're still in the game—or in what remained of the game space. There could be no game at all, or there could be thousands of games all over the perimeter of the city that was part of the first wave of the experiment.

For instance, the landscape is fine, no pixelation, no rough polygons on surface edges, nothing out of normal—that is, if you can pretend not to see the giant red sun on the skyline.

All the sensations register normal as well. I can see, hear, have the feeling of breathing, swallowing—but not eating, drinking, pissing, or shitting—I felt no need for those. Time seems to stand still too, or at least suffer only inner variations—somehow I seem to feel the passage of time even if the red sun never moves. Something to do with the circadian rhythm, perhaps? I can't tell, especially since I'm dealing with a virtual body.

The only thing I feel for sure is that this reality which I find myself in is not the same one as is the New Game, as we now came to call it.

The New Game is what happens when you try to get some sleep now.

Then you really know you're on a dreamscape, complete with distorted sound and vision, and the whole lot of clichés from old Hollywood movies (sometimes the dreams are in black and white—I hate when that happens; I lose my perspective). Things go surrealistic very fast, and chaos ensues. When this situation started to happen, I found myself in lots of scenarios from games I had played and others I had just heard of or read about; but just imagine them all mashed up in one huge dream brain potato salad, served hot and spicy on your plate and an abusive hospital orderly says you have to eat it all now, come on, open your mouth, come on, come on—

It can be hell.

I must get out of here.

• • •

I look at Tanya again. She's not okay. I don't care if that body is not her real one—she's not behaving okay, and for me that's all I need to know.

I try to ignore Rafael. He's a big guy; it's hard. But I get closer to Tanya anyway.

"Do you think you can run today?" I ask her quietly.

She pants. She has a glassy look in her eyes.

I take her pulse. I think I can feel something. Her skin is cold and clammy.

I wonder what's happening with our real bodies. What's happening with the world outside. How many days have passed since we got stuck here?

I'm aware of too many questions. Blame science fiction movies. As far as I know, we might even be virtual constructs, copies that somehow acquired a sort of awareness and are lost in a loop while in the real world the players are very well, fuck you very much.

But there is no use getting this paranoid. I can't prove this theory, so I'm going with the trapped-in-the-dream one.

"Listen," I say to Rafael, standing up. "Let's leave her resting here. We must run while we can."

"I'm not leaving her," he growls.

This entire thing has taken its toll on him as well. He's younger than me, gets restless easier, and definitely doesn't like being trapped in the same environment with his girl's ex-boyfriend.

I can only nod.

• • •

I start running again. I get out the house, turn right, right again, cross the Anhangabaú Valley until I get to Viaduto do Chá. I run the entire old steampunk-like viaduct with its steel girders. I finally see one person—a woman running two blocks ahead of me. I can't say if she spotted me.

I run after her.

One of the theories we came up with—Tanya did, actually—was the buffer boxes overload.

What if—she asked us one day, just after we met to try and search other players—what if this is happening to us because the buffers in the printers got all mixed up somehow? What if all we have now is a super-duper-jam the size of that humongous sun out there and it made all the 3D printers create not separate game spaces for separate groups, as it was predicted, but a massive game entity, a single space where every 3D object was printed (maybe imprinted is the right word for it) in the minds of the players and created a superposed space on top of it, so when the players (or maybe just a few of them) tried to wake up, they ended up instead in this sort of ground zero, where nothing really happens, but from where you can't send any message to the world of the living.

"Purgatory," said Rafael when she ventured this hypothesis. "This is purgatory."

"I never took you for a religious guy," I said then.

"I know my catechism," he countered. Maybe he wasn't a real Catholic until the shit hit the fan. But I know he runs every single day through the Sé Cathedral. I saw him once. He stopped in front of the huge old church, complete with its Italian Renaissance dome and Neogothic spires, made the sign of the cross, hesitated, but didn't enter.

Life here sucks balls.

• • •

I keep following the woman, taking the utmost care for her not to notice me. I don't know what she's doing. She might be looking for others, just like we were until a few days/weeks/whatever before; but then again, she might be looking for the buffer boxes.

When the games started, an advertising agency created an ingenious social media campaign. They spread hundreds of buffer cache boxes all over São Paulo and dropped lots of hints. It was a data treasure hunt of sorts: something similar to what a few contemporary artists had done with dead drop media a decade earlier, getting flash drives stuck into trees or walls with only the USB plug showing—so people could connect their devices to them and get whatever files were in them (mostly art, and a few experimental viruses).

The buffer boxes offered something similar. They were about the same size of the old flash drives and they were hidden in several buildings and monuments of the city. They were invisible to the naked eye, but to your smart devices they emitted several telltale signs, such as a beep or a blue flashing light when it was at a hundred meters' distance.

The catch was that they had no effect whatsoever when accessed directly via the real world. First you had to enter the dreamspace and start playing, and then you could cross the virtual version of the city and reach the boxes. Then you could connect with them and download their contents.

The bad news: in those bodies, in F-0, we don't have any device to find the buffer boxes.

The good news: when we sleep and enter the New Game, we can locate them without the help of devices. But we can't access them. Because of the fucking bosses.

• • •

In my case, it's the black duck.

(And no, I don't care what Tanya said about the animal being a garganey. It could be a mallard, a goose, an elephant for all I care. It carries a big bowie knife, for fuck's sake, you don't want to waste time asking for its genus.)

All I had in my original game was a silver dagger. I'm not much of a swordsman, but I was hoping for something I could also have as a memento after the game; in fact, I didn't care that much about the game. All I really wanted was the dagger. I really felt like a baby in Toyland. I wanted the toys. And I wanted to know what other toys I could get out of the buffer boxes.

Now I can only hope for a big fat weapon.

Suddenly, the woman turns at a corner to my right. I slow down and go on. The next street will be a narrow one, but without that many buildings where she could hide. I try to be careful.

When I turn, she is there, facing me.

And she is not alone.

The guy by her side is bigger than Rafael.

He punches me right between the eyes.

I fall down like a rag doll. Before I black out, I can still hear the woman's voice saying: "Sleep."

• • •

Night has fallen over the city like a brick wall. I'm in a black-and-white dream again and this time I know who's paying for it when I get back to F-0.

Now, however, is not the time to complain.

Not when you have a psychopathic black duck running after you with a bowie knife ready to chop you and serve *homme à l'orange* to her sisters-in-nightmare or whatever they have around here.

I'm running as fast as I can. I still haven't had the chance to use the silver dagger, which is resting nicely in its scabbard. I don't have time to pull it off.

This time I'm not inside a building. I'm running free in the city. As incredible as it may seem, I'm close to the point I got hit by the woman's companion. A few blocks behind.

When I get again to the Viaduto do Chá, I see the blue light. Flashing between two steel girders almost on ground level. I notice I'll probably have to lie down on the ground and reach out for it, but it doesn't matter. Now I know where it is.

I run for it and I jump from the railing.

A hundred years ago, farmers used to cultivate tea leaves in the valley right below the viaduct, hence the name. Today, though, the place is a passage for pedestrians. All covered in concrete.

I fall headfirst.

• • •

Back to False Wake-Up Zero.

Fuck.

• • •

I run to Tanya's place.

She's still there. This time she's unconscious.

"Where were you?" Rafael asks me. His voice is surprisingly even.

"I was attacked."

"What happened?"

"Do you know," I say, "that you can be knocked out and immediately enter the New Game?"

"Really? No protocols?"

"No protocols. Not only that: when you wake up, you wake up on the same spot you went to sleep regularly."

"Does this alter anything?"

I look again at her.

"Where do we go when we sleep?"

Rafael shrugged.

"How should I know? We are all asleep at the same time!"

"I don't think so," he says. "Why hasn't Tanya disappeared or something?"

"Because she's in her regular spot?"

"Or because she's not exactly asleep? In a coma, maybe?"

Rafael mumbles something.

"What?" I say.

"I was praying when you got in," he says. "You interrupted me."

"I'm sorry." I can't believe it. "But we must do something for her."

"She's dying."

"She shouldn't be dying. This is not the place for her to die."

"Who are we to say? What if God wants that?"

I breathe deeply. I was hoping that it didn't come to this, but I was ready anyway.

"Listen," I say. "Maybe—just maybe—God has a role in this. But let's do our part, okay? Pray if you must, but please help me with this. Do you think you can?"

"I don't know," he admits after a pause. "What do you want me to do?"

Now comes the really hard part.

"Come help me lift her."

"Why?" he asks.

But I had already taken the gun from his holster. I shoot him twice in the head.

Then, I go for Tanya. I rest the muzzle on her brow and pull the trigger with my eyes closed.

• • •

I don't stay to see Heisenberg's theory proved on them. I'm breathing hard as hell while I run as fast as I can just to avoid thinking of what I just did. I keep repeating to myself this is just a game and they are alive, but I'm not 100 percent sure of it. Now I feel like praying. But my faith has left me a long time ago.

When I get to the viaduct, they are already there. I should have known it wasn't going to be easy.

The woman and her burly companion are right over the spot of the buffer box.

"You don't give up, do you?" she says when I get closer. They aren't moving, so I walk a few steps more before answering.

"Why?"

"I got here first."

"Do you still think this is a game?"

"No—at least not in the traditional sense."

"And what are you going to do with this box?"

"This is my business."

"As it happens," and I show her Rafael's gun, "it's mine too."

She laughs. But I hear a slight tremble in her voice.

"You know we are in a recursive loop. All you can do is delay us. None of us can die here."

"That's why I want you to tell me what's in the box."

"Why?"

"Because I have a friend that may be really dying and I need something to help me."

"No shit."

"Shit."

"Then this whole scenario must be degrading faster than we calculated."

"'We' who?"

Smiling, she reached for something on the inside of her jacket and extended it to me. A card.

Puzzled, I took it.

"Marina Ferreira," she said. "Chief Worldbuilder for DPM."

DPM. The ad agency that created the games pace and the buffer box campaign.

"Do you have a way out of here?"

"Nope," she said. "But I have a good idea of how we can get out now. Want to give me and Carlos here a hand?"

• • •

She took her time explaining, but a good summation of her sales pitch could go like this:

Apparently, part of Tanya's initial guess was right—there was a kind of massive data overload in the buffer boxes. But, as Marina told me, that was to be expected, and they had a contingency plan for this.

That should have been activated at least two days ago. This, give or take a few hours, is the amount of time elapsed in real time—she has been counting.

But they had a Plan C in case Plan B flopped. And Plan C meant insider activation.

All the virtual buffer boxes in F-o must be taken down so the data can flow freely again and the system can reboot—and everybody can wake up for real.

"How many are there?" I asked.

"About three hundred," she says.

"This will be a hell of a job."

"Won't it now."

Then I explained to her what I had done to my friends.

"They will be fine. In fact, they must already have woken up. And we must convince them to work with us, instead of against us, am I right?"

I nod.

"Then lead the way," she says.

• • •

When the black duck comes to me with the bowie knife and the killing smile in his giant face, the first thing I think is, in which eye?

Then, *thud!* and another knife is already in the duck's left eye. I look to my right. Carlos, the motherfucker.

The duck starts to emit a strangling noise. And deflates.

Right behind her, a huge white deer with a black cross in its forehead and burning red eyes. The mythic Anhangá, spirit of the forest. Damn, these ad people did their homework well.

But, before I can do anything, the creature is peppered by a host of bullets of different calibers. All coming from Tanya—now as good as new—and Rafael, full of righteous anger. They agreed to help, but they're not talking to me. They want to go back home, but that doesn't mean they approve of my methods.

I can live with that. And I can die a few times more as well, while we proceed to locate the rest of the buffer boxes.

As long as I can use my goddamn silver dagger at least once.

RUDY RUCKER

JUICY GHOST

(2019)

"A MOB OF FREALS," says Leeta. "I feel safe. For once."

She makes a knowing *mm-hmm* sound, with her gawky mouth pressed shut. She's not one to think about looks. Lank-haired and fit. A fanatic. I'm a fanatic too. We're feral freaks, free for real.

Is Leeta my girlfriend? No. I've never had a girlfriend or a boyfriend. I don't get that close to people. My parents and brother and sister died when I was eight. A shoot-out at our house. I don't talk about it.

It's nine in the morning on January 20, a cold blue-sky day in Washington, DC. Inauguration Day for Ross Treadle, that lying sack of shit who's acting as if he's been legitimately reelected. Treadle and his goons have stolen the Presidency for the third time in a row, is what it is.

They outmaneuvered the media, they purged the voter rolls, and supposedly there's an unswayable block of Treadlers. A stubborn turd in the national punchbowl. Not that I ever see any Treadlers. Admittedly, I live in Oakland, California, not exactly Treadle country, but I personally wonder if the man's so-called base is a scam, a figment, a fake-news virus within the internet's chips and wares.

Doesn't matter now. Treadle's on his way out. I'm here to assassinate him. And Leeta's my bodyguard. I'll die right when I kill Treadle. I'm trying not to care.

I'm Curtis Winch, part of a four-person Freal cell. I'm a gene-tweaker, a bioprogrammer. And we've got gung-ho Leeta, our money guy Slammy who might be an agent, and there's a skinny twitchy web hacker who calls himself Gee Willikers. Gee spends all day with his head in the cloud. His own private zone of the cloud. He's crafted me a special bio device that does telepathy with his cloud. Gee calls the little critter a psidot. It's managed to store a copy of my personality in Gee's cloud.

We have our base in Oakland, near the port, in a cheap-ass, beige, trashed 1930s cottage amid pot-grow warehouses and poor people's squats. I implanted some special eggs in my flesh two weeks ago. Today they'll hatch out and attack Treadle. And then the Secret Service will gun down my larvae-riddled remains.

Upside: Gee will put a low-end chatbot version of my personality online as an interactive Paul Revere–type inspiration. *Curtis Winch, martyred hero of the New American Revolution.*

"Tell us what it was like to take down Ross Treadle," the admiring users will say to my memorial chatbot. "And thank you, Curt, thank you!"

Too bad I won't be around to savor this. From what I've seen, dying is like a jump-cut in a movie—except there's no film on the other side of the jump.

While I'm still alive, my psidot is continually updating the software version of my personality—what Gee calls my lifebox. Up in the cloud. The psidot itself is like a tiny leech, with bristles that work as wireless antennae. And somehow it reads my brain waves. That's the telepathy part. It's shiny and slim and it's perched on the back of my neck. Like a paste-on beauty mark, except it's alive and it can crawl around a little bit.

So like I'm saying, my psidot captures whatever I experience and stores it in the cloud. Works the other way too. My psidot feeds me info. And, better than that, it uses heavy cloud-based processing to munge my data stream and, if I ask, it'll suggest what I might do next.

Right now the psidot is showing me Gee Willikers. Gee is excited, more than excited. Messianic.

"You're immortal," Gee Willikers is telling me. Not that I believe him. He's shining me on so I'll do the hit. Gee giggles. He's not a normal person at all. "With my latest upgrades, you can live through your psidot, as long as it's living on a person or an animal or even an insect. As long as your psidot stays alive on a host, you're a juicy ghost. My ultimate hack, Curt." He snorts in amusement. "I'm God."

"Be quiet, Gee."

The crowd around the Lincoln Memorial is beyond epic. Bigger than a three-day rock fest with free beer, bigger than a pilgrimage to Mecca, bigger than any protest DC has ever seen. More than two million of us.

Freals stream in via the Memorial Bridge, down Constitution and Independence Avenues, piling out of the Metro stops, walking in along the side streets and the closed-down highways by the Potomac. Cops and soldiers stand by, but they're not trying to stop us. They're working people too. Low-income city folks. By now a lot of them hate Treadle too. Him getting to be President again is like some unacceptable bug in our political system. And the Freals are here to fix it.

Our crowd swirls around stone Abe Lincoln on his stone chair in his stone temple. We mass along the reflecting pool, as far as the Washington Monument—but not yet onto the Mall.

A belt of armed troops blocks us from getting all that close to the Capitol. My psidot is picking up on the media, and it shows me how the Mall is blanketed with actual, for-real Treadlers—deluded, sold out, in thrall to an insane criminal, awaiting the dumbshow of their hero's noon Inauguration.

What would it take to change their minds?

We Freals are zealous and stoked, filled with end-times fervor and a sense of apocalypse. We're rarin' for revolution. Ross Treadle's opponent Sudah Mareek is standing atop one of Lincoln's stone toes. She's shouting and laughing and chanting—wonderfully charismatic. Her voice is balm to my soul, and she's calming Leeta too. The whole reason we two didn't go straight to the Capitol steps is because we need to see Sudah get her own Inauguration. The real one.

Sudah Mareek did in fact win the election—both the popular vote and the House of Electors. But somehow Treadle turned it all around, and his packed Supreme Court took a dive. Treadle says he'll charge Sudah with treason once he's sworn in. He says he'll seek the death penalty.

But the Freals are going to inaugurate Sudah just the same. We have one supporter on the Supreme Court, and she's here to administer the oath of office. She's ninety years old, our justice, in her black robe, and she's brought along Abe Lincoln's Bible.

We fall silent, drinking it in. The Presidential Oath—short, pure, and real. Sudah's clear voice above the breathless crowd. I'm absorbed in my sensations, the trees against the sky, the cold air in my lungs, the pain in my flesh, the scents of the bodies around me. We're real. This isn't a play. It's the Inauguration of the next President of the United States.

For a moment the knot of fear in my chest is gone. This is going to work. Our country's going to be free. We cheer ourselves hoarse.

But hatch time is near. Leeta and I need to haul ass to the Capitol steps so I'll be close enough to terminate Treadle. And everyone else wants to head that way too. The crowd rolls toward the Mall like lava. But there's the matter of those armed troops at the Washington Monument. They're in tight formation.

"Let's skirt around them," I suggest to Leeta.

The side streets are blocked by troops as well. We're like a school of fish swimming into a net, which is the U-shaped cordon of soldiers. They have batons, shock sticks, water cannons, tear gas, and rifles with bayonets. Behind them are trucks, armored Humvees, and even some tanks.

At this point, Leeta and I are near the troops along the right edge of the crowd. Armed men and women, all colors. Leeta begins pitching our case.

"Sudah Mareek is our President," she calls, sweetening her voice. "We just inaugurated her. Did you hear the cheers?"

"Move along," mutters a woman soldier, not meeting our eyes.

"*We're* your friends," I put in. "Not Treadle. He's ripping you off. He hates us all."

Behind me the crowd of Freals is chanting. "*We're you. You're us. Be free.*"

"Be Freal," echoes Leeta, reaching out to touch the woman soldier's shoulder. "Put down the gun."

"Let's do it," says the soldier at her side. He throws his bayonet-tipped rifle to the earth. "Yeah. That gun's too heavy."

The woman does the same, and so does the guy next to her, and the woman next to him drops her gun too—it's like a zipper coming undone. A whole row of the soldiers is defecting. Going renegade. Treadle will call us traitors.

A few soldiers stand firm. They spray water cannons, which knocks down Freals and muddies the ground. A few tear-gas shells explode. Some hotheads fire their rifles into the air. But the flurry damps down.

The soldiers aren't into it. They don't want to kill us. We're people like them. This stage of the revolution is a gimmie. Hundreds of thousands of us chant as one.

"We're you. You're us. Be free."

The soldiers whoop and laugh. Grab-assing like they're off duty. Some Freals try and tip over an Army tank, but it's way too heavy. One of the soldiers, some wild hillbilly from Kentucky, he breaks out a crate of magnesium flares. He and his buddies go around prying open fuel-tank caps and shoving in flares. Low thuds as the gas-tanks explode, one after the other. The rising plumes of smoke are totems of freedom.

We cheer our incoming president. *"Sudah. Sudah. Sudah. Sudah."*

A pyramid of Freals holds the small woman high in the air. She's waving and smiling. She's the one who won. She's ours. In my head, my psidot shows me the news commentators going ape. *Treadle's faked election, political U-turn, people's revolution, President Mareek.*

Treadle's strategists strike back. Two banana-shaped gunship choppers converge on the Washington Monument, circling like vengeful furies. Men with massive machine guns stand in the big doors. They lay down withering fusillades, shooting into our crowd.

The gunships are painted with Treadle's personalized Presidential seal. The pilots and crews are from the chief's palace guard. Dead-enders. Pardoned from death row, recruited from the narco gangs, imported from the Russian mafia.

People are dying on every side. It's insane. Next to me a man's head explodes like a pumpkin. Am I next?

"Asymmetric attack on unarmed demonstrators," mutters Leeta. "Stop screaming. Curt. Use your psidot."

Good idea. My psidot is overlaying my visual field with images of the bullets' paths. A hard rain. Simultaneously, the psidot is computing our safest way forward, showing me a glowing, shifting path on the ground. I take Leeta's hand and lead her.

We come to a cluster of renegade soldiers who've salvaged a rocket bazooka from a charred tank. A dark, intent sergeant raises the tube to her shoulder.

My psidot brings the nearest chopper's path into focus. I see the dirty bird's past trajectory as an orange tangle. And I'm seeing its dotted-line future path too. As usual my psidot is using cloud crunch to estimate what's next.

"There," I advise the woman soldier, pointing. "Aim there."

Whoosh!

And, *hell* yeah, our canny missile twists through the air like a live thing, homing in on Treadle's hired killers.

Fa-tooom!

The chopper explodes like a bomb. Shards of metal go pinwheeling, as if from an airborne grenade. The blazing craft hits the ground with a broken thud that I feel in my feet. The second chopper flees, racketing into a wide loop above the Potomac.

"That was *my* vote!" whoops the rocketeer woman, pumping the bazooka in the air. "For President Sudah!"

I feel high. Seeing that chopper go down is like winning a round in a video game. But this game has a ticking clock. My parasites twist in my flesh, ever closer to my skin. I need to be at the other end of the Mall when Treadle mounts his rostrum.

The blockade of troops has thinned, and many of the Freals have fled back toward the river. Those who remain are tending to the casualties on the ground—the gravely wounded amid the dead. Fire trucks and wailing ambulances arrive.

Leeta and I hurry on and filter through the Treadle base. They're striving to maintain an air of festivity—even after the rush of Freals, the troops' desertions, the massacre, and the downing of the chopper—even now. Bundled against the cold, they've laid out their sadly celebratory picnics. Doing their best to ignore the bitter, embattled demonstrators, they wave their Treadle signs, and draw their little groups into tighter knots.

Leeta's good at crowds. She eels forward through the human mass, finding the seams, working her way up the Mall. I trail in her wake. Soon we're within thirty yards of the Capitol steps. The dignitaries are there. The charade is still on. I feel that the Secret Service agents are watching me. Treadle is about to appear.

"I bet dying is easier than you expect," Leeta whispers to me. Her idea of encouragement.

A wave of dizziness passes over me. As if I'm seeing the world through thick glass. Those things in my flesh—they're leaking chemicals into my system. Steroids, deliriants, psychotomimetics.

"What are we *doing*?" I moan. "Why?"

"You'll be a hero," Leeta murmurs, iron in her voice. "Be glad." She leans even closer, her whisper is thunderous in my ear. "The Secret Security knows. *Mm-hmm.*" She nods as if we're discussing personal gossip. Her bony forehead bumps mine. "They hate Treadle too. It's all set. They're actually paying us. Slammy set it up."

"And I'm your patsy? The fall guy? What if I change my mind?"

"Don't fuss," says Leeta. She rolls her eyes toward the strangers pressed around us. To make it all the creepier, Leeta displays a prim, plastered-on smile. Her voice is very low. "Be a good boy or they'll shoot you early. And then Treadle lives. We can't have that, *hmm*?"

My psidot is jabbering advice that I can't understand. Mad, skinny Gee

Willikers is in my head too. As usual he's unable to say three sentences without bursting into laughter. I hate him and I hate Leeta and I hate my psidot.

Fresh insect hormones rush through me. My disorientation grows. The critters inside me are splitting out of their pupas and preparing to take wing. Sixteen of them.

Treadle takes his oath. It's like, "*Ha ha, I'm President again, so fuck you.*" And then he's into his Inauguration speech, in full throat, hitting his stride, spewing lies and fear and hatred.

"Well?" nudges Leeta.

"It is a far, far better thing I do than I have ever done," I intone, quoting Dickens. I know I'm going to kill Treadle, but I'm trying to rise above the seamy details of our conspiracy. "It is a far, far better rest I go to than I have ever known."

"You got *that* right."

Weird how my whole life has led up to this point. "There's this thing about time," I tell Leeta. "You think something will never happen. And then it happens. And then it's over." I pause and peek inside my shirt. Bumps and welts shift beneath my skin.

"Trigger them!" hisses Leeta.

"*Whoa!*" exclaims a Treadler at my side. A mild-eyed old man with his leathery, white-haired wife. He's staring at a wriggly lump on my neck. "Are you okay? Do you need help?"

"Allergy," I wheeze. "Overexcited. It'll work out pretty—"

I'm interrupted by a shrieking clatter. It's that second chopper, attacking the Freals and renegades and EMTs who are helping the fallen around the Washington Monument. We all turn and stare as the whirlybird stitches gunfire into the ragged band.

"Done at my command," intones Treadle, raising his heavy arm to point. "I keep my promises." He juts his chin. "We're gunning for Sudah Mareek. A traitor. She meets justice today."

Hoarse, savage cheering from the Treadlers. Terrible to see Americans act this ugly. They're mirroring Treadle. I have to kill him. But, wait, wait, wait, I want to see how the scene at the Monument plays out.

The cheering dims—and I hear what I'm hoping for.

Whoosh!

Yes. The rebel soldiers have launched another rocket.

Fa-tooom!

The blasted second chopper corkscrews along a weirdly purposeful arc. Like it's remotely controlled. The hulk smashes against a face of the Washington Monument. My psidot feeds me close-up images.

"Bonus points," goes Gee Willikers in my head. He titters. Sick gamer that he is. "Part of the plot," he continues. "We pin this on Treadle."

Gee hacked into the falling chopper's controls? Wheels within wheels. The plot is a web around me. It's time to act but—I can't stop watching.

Cracks branch across the great obelisk's surface, running and forking. Bits of marble skitter down the pitiless slope. The Monument's tip sways, vast and slow. People are scattering. The upper part of the great plinth moves irrevocably out of plumb. It tilts and gains speed, the bottom slow, the top fast, as in an optical illusion.

The impact is a long explosion—followed by thin, high screams. A veil of dust. A beat of silence. I feel sick with guilt. And weary of being human.

Leeta is screaming into my face. "Do your job, goddamn you! Now!"

"Get Treadle," I finally say. The trigger phrase. I don't say it very loud, but it's loud enough to matter.

Within my flesh, the hymenoptera hear. Ragged slits open on my neck, my chest, my belly, my arms. The pain is off the scale. I shed my coat and my shirt. The bloody, freshly fledged, bio-tweaked wasps emerge. All sixteen of them.

For a moment they balance on their dainty, multijointed legs, hastily preening their antennae, shaking the kinks from their iridescent wings. Their handsome, curved abdomens resemble motorcycle gas tanks. They feature prominent stingers and bejeweled, zillion-lensed eyes. They're large, and preternaturally alert.

Leeta slithers off through the crowd. The cuts in my flesh pump bright blood. The Treadlers around me point and shout. The wasps race up my torso, across my face, and onto the crown of my head—a wobbly mob. They rise in flight.

My job is done.

Or maybe not. Gee Willikers is hollering inside my head. "Your psidot! Put it on a wasp!" I can see an image of my psidot on the back of my neck. And I note a single laggard wasp on my shoulder. My mind projects a target spot onto the wasp's wing.

Though faint from loss of blood, I manage to get the psidot off the back of my neck. It's easy. The smart, living psidot hops onto the tip of my finger. And when I bring my hand near the wing of the target wasp, the psidot springs into place.

The wasp is pissed off. She stings my finger. Numbness flows up my arm and toward my heart. The wasp venom contains curare, you understand, plus conotoxin. A custom cocktail for Treadle.

My vision is dark. I'm an empty husk, a ruptured piñata—poisoned and bleeding. And if all this wasn't bad enough, there's the matter of the Secret Service. They're good shots. Yes, they might want Treadle out, but right now they've got to do their thing. For the sake of appearances. For an orderly transition. I go down in a hail of bullets. A fitting end.

Last thought? I hope the wasps will sting Treadle. And then I'm dead.

At this point my narrative has a glitch. Remember the jump-cut thing I was talking about? Well, it turns out that, for me, there *is* some film on the other side of the jump. Granted, the all-meat Curtis Winch is terminally inoperative. But—

I wake, confused. I look down into myself. I've got my same old white-light soul. My sense of me watching me watching the world. I'm hallucinating a little bit. I feel like I'm in a huge, crumbling old Vic mansion with junk in the rooms, and with paintings leaning on the walls, and doors that don't properly close. The furniture of my mind. Somebody's in here with me. A jittery silhouette against the light. Gee Willikers.

"You're a juicy ghost, Curt! A lifebox linked to bio host via a Gee Willikers psidot. Play it right, and you keep going for centuries." His compulsive snicker. "Def cool, Mr. Guinea Pig."

I try to form words. "Where . . ."

"Your soul is a parasite, dude. Like I've been telling you. A lifebox with a psidot. It hitches onto a bio host's nervous system. Gloms onto the axons and retarded potentials. Sponges mysto quantum steam and all that other good shit."

"Host?"

"You're riding a wasp, *der*. The one you stuck the psidot on, *doink*." Gee makes a trumpeting sound. "Juicy ghost!"

"You were wrong to topple the Monument," I tell him. No response. What now?

The junked, phantasmal mansion around me—that's my operating system and my database in the cloud. My back end. It's in a secure dark-net zone, maintained by Gee Willikers. I look for a way to hook into my host wasp's nervous system. A way to get juicy. Deep into this as I am, I want to be part of the final attack.

"Over there," goes Gee. "See the smelly rope? Like a tasseled curtain-pull in a Gold Rush saloon? All thick and twisted and dank?"

I fixate on it and, just like that, I've jacked myself into the wasp's neural nets. I'm seeing through her eyes. *I am the wasp*.

I join the swarm. They're eddying around Treadle. He's bellowing, dancing around, slapping himself. Fighting for his life. He has foam on his lips, like a rabid dog. My fellow wasps are landing on his face, his fat neck, his wattles. But Treadle is swatting them before they sting. He's killed eight.

His roars are taking on a tone of triumph. I can't let him win. His shirt is untucked. A button is loose. I spy a patch of skin.

I arrow into the opening, and land on the man's bare chest, very near his heart. I sting—I sting, sting, sting. His voice changes, as if his tongue is turning stiff. His volume fades. He's wobbly on his pins. He totters backward. Falls. A groan. Silence.

It's done.

With trembling wings, I escape Treadle's shirt and spiral high into the air. Hovering with the seven other wasps, a hundred feet up.

The Freals and soldiers are leading Sudah Mareek forward through the discombobulated crowd. She's going to be President. Everyone knows it. In the whiplash intensity of the moment, the Treadlers convert to Sudah's cause. Sobs turn to hysterical cheers.

Mounting the dais, Sudah swears the oath again. The massed politicians applaud. Treadle's proposed Vice President has lost his nerve. He's bowing out. Sudah's Vice President emerges from the Capitol, just in time. They swear her in. Our coup is more organized than I knew. I was in the dark.

Gee Willikers is ecstatic. "Secret Service on our side, dude. Army on board. Congress is down with it. Done deal."

I feel a shifting sensation. A doubleness of vision. A group of Freals is carrying my bloody, broken form up the Capitol steps. They hold my remains high, heedless of the dripping gore. Wave after wave of applause. Sudah Mareek and her Veep salute my remains.

"Curtis Winch, martyred saint of the New American Revolution!"

"Do I have to keep being a wasp?" I ask Gee.

"Glue your psidot wherever you want," he says.

"Another host?"

"How about somebody in this crowd," suggests Gee. "That Treadler babe in the trucker hat?"

"Idiot," I snap. "Can you get the fuck out of my head?"

"Sure," goes Gee.

"Oh, and don't forget to post the toy chatbot version of me for the Curtis Winch memorial."

"Online now," Gee assures me. "More than a toy. I used a full copy of your cloud personality stash—what I call your lifebox. It's your lifebox, but with the incriminating, intimate, personal-type stuff chainsawed out. Took me about ten minutes."

"Shit, Gee."

"It's just a fat chatbot. No mind, since it's not juicy. Not hooked into anything alive. And the memorial's up to twenty million hits. Viral flash mob, Curt. User tsunami."

"Obfuscate the living shit out of my psidot and my real lifebox, okay? Hide the links. Destroy the keys. I want to go dark."

"To hear is to obey, Saint Curtis. I'll run you a SHA scramble with a Mandelbutt tail." Gee makes a wiggly hand gesture—and he's gone.

Beating my wings, I leave the swarm, and buzz on beyond the Capitol. On my own, feeling good, savoring the quantum soul of my insect host.

My compound eyes watch for hungry birds, but there's none around. I make my way into the residential neighborhood northeast of the Capitol. I fly until it shades from gentrified to tumbledown. I spy a mutt on a cushion on a back porch. A collie-beagle mix. Yes.

Gently, gently I land on the side of the sleeping dog's head. I preen my wings, detach my psidot with my mandibles, and nestle it onto a bare patch of skin deep inside the dog's floppy ear. The dot takes hold—and I'm in.

I stand, shake my body, and bark.

Joyful. Free.

• • •

Afterword for this edition of "Juicy Ghost"

Usually I avoid writing about politics. But in 2019 I felt a need to take a stand. I took a deep satisfaction in crafting this tale. But it soon became clear that I had no hope of publishing this story in a mainstream zine. For a time I planned to publish it as a part of a special, all-political issue of my old ezine *Flurb*. But in the end, putting together a new *Flurb* felt like too big a push.

I continued working on "Juicy Ghost." Short as the story is, I kept at it for weeks and even months, doing rewrite after rewrite. It was like finding my way across a tightrope.

When I deemed it done, I released it samizdat style. That is, I added "Juicy Ghost" to my ever-expanding *Complete Stories* online. And I posted a photo-illustrated version of the story on my blog. And while I was at it, I recorded it as a podcast.

A few months after that, Robert Penner was interviewing me for his cool online zine *Big Echo*. I asked him if he would print "Juicy Ghost," and he said sure. So then it appeared via a standard channel after all. And in 2023, huzzah, it also appeared in the noble tome you now peruse, *The Big Book of Cyberpunk*. Thanks for that, Jared.

The tech in the world of "Juicy Ghost" is interesting, and, going back to 2019, I decided to set at least two more stories there. And then I saw a way to fuse them into a novel, which I entitled *Juicy Ghosts*, which also proved to be not commercially publishable. Even so, backed by a Kickstarter, the novel appeared in the fall of 2021 from my own Transreal Books.

So here's the original samizdat rough-cut 2019 "Juicy Ghost" as a memento.

Like a brick through a window.

Cyberpunk lives.

WOLE TALABI

ABEOKUTA52

(2019)

WELCOME TO THE ₦AIRALAND FORUM

Continue as Guest / LOGIN / Trending / Recent / New
Stats: 6,421,391 members, 5,377,609 topics.
Date: Wednesday, November 28, 2026 at 09:33 a.m.

NAIRALAND > GENERAL > POLITICS > ABEOKUTA52 > LATEST POSTS > SON OF ABEOKUTA52 VICTIM SHARES HIS INCREDIBLE STORY! (24,889 VIEWS)

Posted on November 16, 2026, by Abk52_Warrior

**Hey Nairalanders, I'm reposting this copy of Bidemi Akindele's opinion piece in the Guardian from two days ago.* https://www.theguardian.com/commentisfree/2026/Nov/14/second-deaths-nigeria-acknowledge-alien-blessing-came-price

THE SECOND DEATH: WHY NIGERIA NEEDS TO ACKNOWLEDGE THAT ITS ALIEN BLESSING CAME AT A PRICE

By Bidemi Akindele

I was fourteen when the alien disease killed my mother. They took a risk, she and all the others who first investigated the impact site. I understand that, believe me, I understand how different the country was back then but it's not the loss that keeps me up at night, weeping into my girlfriend's hair. It's the silence. After all these years, no one wants to talk about it. There are no erected memorials. There is no day of remembrance. There are still no published studies on the disease that killed them. No one wants to acknowledge the early price we paid for all this rapid wealth and development. Every time we petition or protest, the government tells us to move on, to look how far we've come, to forget the past and embrace the future in silence.

Why is it so hard for people in power or at privilege to admit and acknowledge that their success came at someone else's expense? America, Japan, Europe, South Africa, Nigeria . . . I could go on.

They say you die twice. Once, when you stop breathing and a second time, later, when somebody says your name for the last time. I will not be let myself become complicit in my mother's second death at the hands of this government. I will not be silent. I will not speak of politics or offer opinions. I will simply tell her story.

My mother's cough started three days after she returned from the impact site in Abeokuta. At first it came in random spurts only once a day or so. She said it was nothing, always with a smile. After a while, we stopped asking if she was all right. Father said not to worry, the investigation at the site was stressful because of the strange things they found there. But then after almost a month, the cough began to worsen, until it became an endless dry hacking that echoed through our house day and night.

My father finally convinced her to see a doctor. When he saw her, the doctor had her admitted and put her through dozens of tests. It took a week and we visited her in the private ward of the Federal Hospital every day after school, staying till about four p.m. Then one day my father told us that we needed to stay a bit longer.

Doctor Shina met with all of us late in the evening. I remember that the sun was a low orange ball in the window behind him and that he was unshaven and looked exhausted. He walked into my mother's room, a little bit surprised to find the entire family there, including my seven-year-old sister Teniola, sitting on the leather chair beside my mother—his patient. He glanced at my father with a look that made me think he expected my father to ask my sister and me to go and play outside while they had a grown-up talk, but my father said nothing. He became more direct and said, "Mr. and Mrs. Akindele, I'd like to speak with you privately, if I could."

"Doctor, please, anything you want to say to me you can say in front of my family," my mother croaked from her bed. "My whole family."

My father smiled and waved his hand. "Please, go ahead."

Doctor Shina cleared his throat and said, "Madam, I examined your lung biopsy sample yesterday and then again today. There is a unique and very worrying pattern of extensive scar tissue and some residue of cadmium, polycyclic aromatic hydrocarbons, and another material we have been unable to identify so far."

He paused, adjusted his glasses, and looked at me and my sister before turning back to my mother and saying, "I'm sorry, Ma, but it seems you have some kind of severe pulmonary fibrosis. It's quite bad."

I saw my father squeeze my mother's hand on the hospital bed. She squeezed back and the veins on her forehead strained against her skin. She said nothing. He said nothing.

Then Doctor Shina said, "That's not the only problem, I'm afraid," and my young heart sank in my chest like an anchor would, at the bottom of the sea.

I think my father almost asked me to take my sister out of the room then because when he glanced at me, he looked like something was stuck in his throat. But he didn't send us out.

Doctor Shina said, "I also found some abnormal cell growths so I requested an analysis. I've checked and checked again but it seems conclusive now. It's cancer. Lung cancer."

My mother started to cry. I don't think she wanted to but she did anyway, and it seemed to make her angry because her lips quivered, and her palms curled into fists. She probably already suspected it was the thing they'd found at the site. She probably knew but she couldn't say because it was all secret. I was in shock, unable to think about anything except the fact that my mother was going to die.

"What do we do next?" she said, her tone belying the fear that her body was broadcasting. "Is it treatable?"

I looked first to my mother, and then at Doctor Shina.

"We still don't know what the particles in your lungs are so I cannot say much about the fibrosis. But it looks like the cancerous cells have metastasized since they are already in your bloodstream. Still, we have several treatment options available, and they may work for you by the special grace of God. We just need to start treatment early."

I wondered then how many times he had said those words to other patients, perhaps in that same room and in that same tone. And how many of those patients had died shortly after hearing them.

"Good," my mother said flatly.

"Thank you, Doctor," my father said with a diluted smile. "Please make all the necessary arrangements. Whatever you need. She works at the Ministry, so the government will pay for everything, don't worry about cost."

"Yes sir. I'll come back soon." Then he turned and exited the private ward. My father's gaze followed him all the way to the door and when the door closed behind him, so did my father's eyes.

Four weeks later, fifty-one of my mother's colleagues were also diagnosed with the accelerated fibrosis and cancer combination. That was when the government had them all moved to the Central hospital in Abuja. My father enrolled me in a boarding school and sent Teni to live with my aunt Folake in Gbagada. I don't know what happened in Abuja because the medical records were sealed. Neither does my father. He had to watch the woman he loved waste away while doctors did things to her without consulting him. He was still struggling in the courts to have the records unsealed years later, when he died of a heart attack.

In the years since their deaths, the government has profited from the reverse-engineered alien technology recovered at the Abeokuta site. Nigeria is now the world's largest provider of macroscale gene-alteration services and Lagos is becoming the genodynamic technology capital of the world, thanks to its proximity to the impact site, but I hope you understand that these are all fruits of the poisoned alien tree. A tree that was watered by the blood of my mother and her colleagues. A tree whose branches are trellised by the misery that came with diagnoses families like mine received in stark hospital rooms from well-meaning men like Dr. Shina. A tree sustained by persistent government erasure and silence.

It has been six years. We are not asking for much, we are just asking for an acknowledgment of our pain. Our truth. Acknowledgment that the present prosperity of this nation was purchased at the cost of fifty-two lives—no matter how inconvenient that narrative is. Acknowledgment that those lives mattered.

We are all made of stories and in the end, there is no greater injury that can be done to a person who has suffered their first death than to change their story, to deny their narrative. It makes their second death more tragic. I will continue to tell my mother's story everywhere, online, during interviews, on panel discussions, during protests, everywhere, and I will not stop until it has a new ending, one that does not bring me to tears whenever I tell it.

Bidemi Akindele is a musician and artist whose provocative work has been exhibited in twenty-three countries. He is the son of the late #Abeokuta52 campaigner, Professor Jude Akindele, and the current Vice President of the Abeokuta Truth Alliance (ATA).

₦AIRALAND COMMENTS

Ahmed-Turiki: Powerful Story! God Bless Bidemi for not giving up on the truth about his mother and all those who died. There is an ATA protest planned at the site in 3 days. Everyone come out and join us, let the government know that we will not be silenced! Aluta continua! Victoria ascerta!
NOVEMBER 16 10:34

OmoOba1991: <*Comment Flagged and Auto-Deleted by NLModeratorBot*>
NOVEMBER 16 10:41

SoyinkaStan1: Sorry for your loss. No wonder there were so many questions the minister of science and technology didn't respond to when they announced that they have awarded the Abeokuta exploitation contract to Dangote. Hmmm.
NOVEMBER 16 10:54

Abk52_Warrior: Please share this link on all your social media accounts since it's no longer accessible on the Guardian News website. Even proxies and back-channel servers aren't working. I will keep testing and update you. But please share. Its personal stories like this that will eventually force the government to tell the truth.
NOVEMBER 16 11:17

QueenEzinne: I am sorry for this boy's loss and I am sure his mother was a good person but trying to blame her death on Nigeria's blessing is just wrong. Why can't he accept that she was just sick? Why must he now put sand-sand in our garri? This "alien thing" as you people are calling it is nothing more than the hand of God appearing in Nigeria's life and God's hand is always pure.
NOVEMBER 16 12:09

MaziNwosuThe3rd: Hmmm. This is a powerful post. I know say that site get K-leg from day 1. Make government talk true o!
NOVEMBER 16 13:52

GBR: God bless Bidemi for not giving up. For those of you wondering why the government would try to cover up the deaths: it looks like they are using some of that technology to develop weapons. There is something fishy going on. Just go to TheTruthAboutTheAbeokuta52.com and read all the posts, especially the ones by the account called "Mister52."
NOVEMBER 16 23:09

PastorPaul_HRH: @SoyinkaStan1 Hmmm. Your head is correct.
NOVEMBER 17 10:34

EngineerK32: This is nothing but slander by foreign powers to discredit us because we didn't sell exploitation rights to them. ATA is trash. I wonder how much they paid this traitor to lie.
NOVEMBER 17 15:22

ShineShineDoctor: This is Doctor Shina. The same one from Bidemi's story. I am currently in London. If anyone knows how to contact Bidemi, please inbox me, I need to warn him.
NOVEMBER 17 15:54

Abk52_Warrior: @ShineShineDoctor Warn him about what?
NOVEMBER 17 15:57

OmoOba1991: <*Comment Flagged and Auto-Deleted by NLModeratorBot*>
NOVEMBER 17 16:01

LadiDadi999: @OmoOba1991 Whats wrong with you? Don't you know how to have a sensible discussion? Lack of home training.
NOVEMBER 17 16:39

GdlckJnthn311: Look, I understand how this boy must feel but it's just not true. I have been working at Dangote Technologies since 2023 and the alien technology has never once caused harm to anyone in my team. I have personally touched some of those materials myself. I will direct anyone interested in facts and not fiction to read the paper: "Technical Report No. 93: A Targeted Risk Assessment of the Abeokuta Exploitation Site" which is available for free download on the Ministry of Science and Technology website.
NOVEMBER 17 17:05

ShineShineDoctor: @Abk52_Warrior I was attacked on my way to Knightsbridge to discuss my recollection of his mother's case with Dr. Maduako at UCL. There were two men with knives. Thank God for the group of Croatian tourists who intervened to save my life. They took my wallet, my phone and all my notes on his mother's case. This morning I heard Dr. Maduako was in an accident. I don't know what is going on but I think Bidemi is in danger.
NOVEMBER 17 17:26

Abk52_Warrior: @ShineShineDoctor OMG. OK. Can't say much here but let me contact my network and see what we can find. For now, please make sure you only log in using a proxy. Stay safe.
NOVEMBER 17 17:28

LekanSkywalker: @Abk52_Warrior @ShineShineDoctor Ghen Gheun! Una don start fake action film. Hahaha! Gerarahere mehn!
NOVEMBER 17 18:46

PeterIkeji_Jos: What is all this nonsense about a cover-up? I swear some people turn everything into conspiracy. Next thing you people will say Sgt Rogers killed his mother with the cooperation of the CIA and wiliwili. Mumu nonsense.
NOVEMBER 17 20:15

GBR: Seriously you people that think this is some conspiracy theory bullshit need to pay attention. Don't be blinded because naira-to-dollar exchange rate is good now and you have constant power supply. 27 employees at Dangote Technologies

have disappeared in the last 4 years. Read the posts on TheTruthAboutAbeokuta52.com. Go to the LifeCast and Twitter feeds of **@TheAbeokuta52Lie**. Read Doctor Shina's comment above. There is a sensible, realistic and pertinent case for the government to answer and the evidence is only growing. Open your eyes.
NOVEMBER 17 21:09

SoyinkaStan1: @ShineShineDoctor You are lucky you are in Britain. If it were Nigeria they'd have killed you for sure. The silver lining is that London has CCTV cameras everywhere so they will probably catch the attempted murderers, and when they do, the investigation will finally expose this whole thing! The truth is coming.
NOVEMBER 17 23:24

Abk52_Warrior: @ShineShineDoctor My ATA contacts tell me that Bidemi was trying to sneak into Nigeria through Benin republic to attend a planned protest. No one has heard from him since. I can connect you to the protest organizers. Inbox me a private email address. Don't use anything public. Set up a new account on encrypted LegbaMail. Stay safe.
NOVEMBER 17 23:58

GBR: Did you guys see this yet? https://cnn.com/2026/11/17/politics/nigeria-britain-sign-long-term—genodynamic-technology-exchange-contract/index.html

Be careful **@ShineShineDoctor**
NOVEMBER 18 11:09

Abk52_Warrior: @ShineShineDoctor Did you get my last message?
NOVEMBER 18 11:43

Abk52_Warrior: @ShineShineDoctor Please respond if you can see this.
NOVEMBER 18 16:11

Abk52_Warrior: @ShineShineDoctor Doctor Shina?
NOVEMBER 19 09:11

<Comments have now been closed on this post>

MICHAEL MOSS

KEEP PORTLAND WIRED

(2020)

KAL KISSED the brick wall hard enough to bust her lower lip.

The speaker on the chest of the secforce goon read off offenses and corporate policies while the beating continued.

"Unauthorized protesting outside designated freedom areas of the PDX Market is a violation of the NAP."

"Okay, all right, fuck you," Kal spat out blood.

The goon got another kick in and another tase while she lay on the ground.

"All in all, you're just another kick in the balls . . ." Kal muttered.

"Consider your debt, aunty fah," he said through the screechy electronic filter in his helmet.

He punched up a few fines and hit her personal unit with them, then walked away hotshit.

Kal stayed down for another ten minutes while tasting the iron in her blood. Then she got up, slowly, and looked up at the wall she'd been so intimate with.

KEEP PORTLAND WIRED, it said in old fading letters. You could tell it had once said "Keep Portland Weird," but someone changed it when the encrypted wireless standards were compromised with official back doors and "safety holes," back when the government at least pretended it wasn't completely a corporate monkey. Back when the government wasn't just a memory, when public services hadn't been privatized for what the market would bear.

The brick wall was the last vestige of a bar back when this part of the city was called Old Town. Now it was just there to hold up a series of homeless camp ruins that got cleaned out by the bio cleanup crews every other month, but only when the PDX corporation needed some space.

Kal shuffled off, wary not to aggravate the pain in her stomach, daydreaming of milkshaking the goon motherfucker over the head.

An expensive black car pulled away from the curb as she walked toward Burnside from the alley.

"Corporate asshole," she said as she saluted it with a couple of middle fingers.

• • •

Kal made it back to the Collective without incident. It was only a block away, though crossing Burnside wasn't without difficulty since the crosswalks stopped responding to anyone with a negative credit score. Nobody in Old Town had a positive score.

The Collective was housed in the loft of a warehouse in Chinatown that had been used as retail or studio space for a century. It was still called Chinatown even though no one of Chinese descent had officially lived there for decades, though Malcolm claimed to be one fourth Taiwanese from a refugee grandmother, if that mattered. It was called Nihonmachi or Japantown briefly before they put the Japanese Americans in concentration camps during the Pacific Theater. Kal always thought it was appropriate to live there since the area had a history of systemic oppression. It rewarded her cynicism for believing that nothing really changes except the brand of the boot that you find on your face.

The fake entrance was the original entrance to the building. If you walked in through the front door, it looked like you had to walk around through a hallway to get anywhere, but it was just a live trap for the unwelcome. You took a corner in a cozy little maze that went nowhere while the cameras watched you start to panic. You'd run back to the front door and get volts from the handle, then they'd let you stumble outside and away. It was a good method for warding off the unwanted, but it only worked once on anyone with a memory. A few of the local methheads ran the gauntlet once a week, maybe for fun.

Kal took the stairs down to the basement from the side street and then took the lift up to the second floor. She didn't stop to look at the giant mural that Heiko had put in three months before on the basement wall. It was an animated reproduction of a historic Banksy mural of Hong Kong protesters in their full gear morphing into Portland moms getting tear-gassed. She'd seen the mural enough for it to fade into the background like a pay recycling bin or a corporate drone just above your sight lines.

Everyone had their own thing in the Collective. Not all of them were technical, but they all contributed to perpetuating the group's ideals. Some were aesthetic and philosophical, some penned shit-stirring haikus, some were just voluptuaries looking for a safe place to crash, drown, or soar, depending on their herb and position of choice.

Aisha looked up from the task of coloring in Malcolm's last unmodded patch of flesh and nodded as Kal walked past her cube. Malcolm didn't notice her.

Aisha was a moddist who worked with the old glow-in-the-darks and iridescent tattoo inks that were just aesthetic rather than functional. It was expensive to source the newer inks, the conductive biometals for inducing haptics and running encrypted PANs, for laying down lines in the dermis for musculature controls, but she was slowly getting into the circuitry mods.

It took a tech to make it function right, but it took an artiste like Aisha to make it look like the daydream. Aisha indulged Kal when she asked for the fake lines on her left arm so people would think she was wireless, but they'd never see her using it since her left hand wasn't moving, wouldn't suspect she got the real lines in her right so she could gesture away with a hand in her jacket pocket or behind her back or at her side. The real lines were disguised under a motif of dragons, using iridescent ink stretching down her arm from her shoulder.

Beyond Aisha's cube, Jericho was curled up in a corner spouting his philosophical thesis statement from behind a mask and voice filter for an antisocial media post. Jericho's real name was Gerald, but he wanted to be known by something that sounded edgy and biblical. He felt like Jericho endorsed the crumbling of walls, not just the physical, but the metaphysical and systemic, semiotic walls that encased all of humanity . . . and he would tell you that in your first conversation with him and quite possibly the second.

". . . And then the cat-and-mouse game of human liberty moved on from land after the governments colonized all the unknown lands and then recolonized all the known lands. Soon you couldn't walk off into the wilderness to live alone without violating a law about trespassing on supposedly public lands. There was no free land anymore. So people moved on to the mind, keeping the memory of books and philosophy in their headspace where the authorities couldn't pry you open and take what you had, but then propaganda and thought crimes and purity tests ruined that freedom, corrupted the data. So they moved on to the networks, sharing pirated copies of the latest or the oldest underground media or first run premium software or raunchiest porn, but then the corporations bought it all up and owned the connections and the nodes and the databases and the little points of light between the data streams of the collective human unconscious, the dreamworld of . . ."

Kal continued past on ninja toes or else Jericho would pause, rewind, repeat the whole last three pages of his dissertation after glaring at her. She pushed open the door that read UNAUTHORIZED PERSONNEL ONLY after it recognized her and unlocked.

Once inside her junkspace, which she shared with three others, Kal finally crashed into her foamcore cot and tried to nap.

"Ah, my Khaleesi," Devin said from somewhere in the room when he noticed her.

Kal hated it when anyone used her full name. *Stupid geek parents.*

"No," is all she said.

"Did you get it?" Devin was eager.

"No."

"But I thought . . ."

"Yes, but fuck off. Sleep now."

"Kay kay," Devin was probably hands up, but Kal didn't lift her head to look as he backed off.

A few minutes into the hypnagogic hallucinations of stage-one sleep, Picnic pounced next to Kal's head, wanting to play.

"No," Kal said before she finished the thought she couldn't remember thinking, though she might have guessed library shelves and holy water without any possibility of knowing if that's what she had in fact been thinking of or why.

Picnic didn't take *no* for an answer.

Picnic was modeled on Devin's real childhood cat. The basic routines were just being projected around the room, simulated leg nuzzling, and hopping on surfaces. You could see Picnic running around, but her presence was really felt in the devices she "passed," the glitching on the screens she walked behind, the electromagnetic fuzz on the speakers she napped on.

Devin didn't like that Picnic didn't do enough on the first run, so he tweaked her, gave her more routines. Picnic became the ghost cat of the loft. She flickered the lights when she stretched vertically up the wall to the light switch. She meowed in the morning to wake you up to feed her, which consisted of tapping a projected bowl.

Kal figured out that the bowl just needed something, anything to break its projected space, so you could throw a sock at it and Picnic would stop bothering you and run over to simulate eating, making a very audible *omnomnom* sound. If you were working in a database, Picnic could knock things off the tables. You'd find flat file data in cells three columns away from where they were supposed to be after she'd been playing nearby. She also liked to lure birds to fly into the windows by projecting trees inside with shiny insect dots fluttering around them.

Picnic caused the whole building to lose power for thirty-six hours once because she "chewed" on the transformer cables. Devin said he didn't even program her to do that and it took a while to figure out how her logic core had managed it. She really fit her name—a variation on an old programmer's acrostic joke: Problem In Cat, Not In Computer.

And now Picnic wanted to play lasers. Kal always wondered what a real cat would do if it saw Picnic, since she was essentially just a laser projection herself. Kal grabbed the laser toy and pointed it across the room, just for some relief from the very cute nagging, while her near-unconscious mind tried to avoid thinking about the absurdity of simulating play with a simulation simulating prey. Picnic zipped off like a rocket full of moxie and a generous amount of RAM.

"Hey, you're up," Devin said, like he'd been sitting there watching her, which he had.

She just eyed him out of the corner with her face still pressed against the foam.

Finally she raised her head.

"I got it," she said. "And a beatdown."

"Are you okay? Your lip isn't," he said.

"No, but it's okay," Kal replied. It really wasn't.

She reached under her deadweight to extract her unit.

"I got as much as I could. He tried to fine me after he knocked me around. He didn't bother to check the fake credentials on the account."

"Cool, cool," he said, unable to hide the eagerness in his voice.

He grabbed it and then reached for a wire, sniffing the connector to see if it was the one he spilled his beer on last week, but he couldn't tell, blew on it for good luck, and plugged it in.

Devin liked wires, he even plugged old Bluetooth receivers into adapters on both devices that encoded the data with white noise, fake data, and viruses just as a paranoid hobby in case the corps or someone else were listening. Of course, nobody was interested in cracking his generative music servers and retro porn collection, but he thought it kept his edge.

He started downloading. A visualization on his monitor showed the red tide of data, plumes of code like screams of ocean swarms of intensity gifted with misbegotten bouts of infinity, the great overwash of information, too many exponential waves, exasperated by minimalist randomly accessed memories, overwhelmed by filters hobbled by the mediocrity of existence and the limits of the medium, or that's how he liked to describe it. It was just binary poetic bullshit, but he saw art in the chaos. He thought it helped him get girls. It didn't. But Kal did think the delusion was kinda cute.

The data he was looking for was the encoded comms of the secforces. The masks of their helmets encrypted their comms traffic so nobody could listen in. Devin started working on those after last year when he saw a goon take a pipe to the face during a protest, which spilled his mask onto the concrete. He couldn't hold on to it since the tide of anti-personnel sonics from the drones overhead started screaming and driving the protesters back, but it gave him enough of an idea. He figured out that they emitted a high-pitch signal with frequency variations that could be decrypted in binary if you got enough samples, but that meant having to get close to a goon for a few minutes, which didn't happen without a fine or a beating or at worst a murder.

He could have made a score for a bug bounty, but he didn't disclose it because the money would last far shorter than his pleasure in exploiting their comms and because *fuck the secforce fascists*. He couldn't decrypt it live, yet, but it helped to be able to tell what they said to each other during a crackdown. A lot of the plaintext was still encoded with corporate statutes and LEO jargon, but he got most of that from old PDF handbooks on the dark web.

Kal had been stupid enough to get beaten up for a few more lines of the ciphertext signal. Anything for the cause. Kal went back to sleep, for real this time, stage three, REM, and everything.

• • •

Picnic woke Kal again when the natural light was gone. It was the dark of night, which made Picnic glow brighter.

"What time is . . . ?"

Picnic flickered 9:13 p.m. on her torso.

Kal's stomach didn't hurt as much. Her lip was throbbing though. She'd have to raid a stash for something medicinal. Malcolm could be generous sometimes.

Devin was facedeep in the code at his desk.

"Got anything?" Kal asked.

"I think . . . I might . . ." He twitched at the interruption and Kal didn't say anything more.

Kal shrugged and stepped out into the hall where Malcolm and Aisha and Jericho were lounging. Malcolm was drinking a CBD microbrew, homegrown in the basement from his not-so-secret stash. The glow lamps for the pot and the soggy cereal smell of the mash were highly detectable to everyone. It was one of the few benefits of anarcho-capitalism—nobody cared what you did as long as you didn't do it to them.

"At least weed and guns are free," Malcolm said, taking a swig.

"Weed isn't free," Jericho winced.

"Free as in freedom, not free as in beer."

"And your beer really is free, Mal," Kal said with a smile as she slid down the wall into a sitting position.

"Sure is," and he handed her a mason jar of the stuff.

"At least you can defend yourself easily with a gun," Aisha said.

Guns were easy, deadly, and stupid. They were like candy on street corners—available from any stranger—as American as freedom and lung cancer, heart disease, and dying with medical debt. But the cost of carrying against a secforce was fatal. They didn't ask questions and they didn't bother to take names or even bury your corpse.

"Sure, until secfascists detect it on you and dronestrike you from three blocks away," Kal said. "They only don't mind us shooting each other."

"NAP only applies to the *Profitarati*," Malcolm agreed.

"Do you think our parents thought about this when they had us?" Jericho asked. "Like, how fucked up it would be to bring us into this world?"

"I think my parents were thinking that they were smoking some good shit," Malcolm laughed. "My old man wasn't sober a day in his life."

"My father was a cop, Portland Police Bureau," Aisha said. "The man licked boots for a living when he wasn't making the homeless and the POCs lick his. But it paid for my childhood. What can you do? Privilege is a twisted bitch."

This was the game they sometimes played where they competed for who had it worse.

"I don't know where my dad is," Jericho said. "My mom is working off debt in a credit bureau office, literally collecting on debt to work off her own."

Kal didn't say anything. She didn't like this topic. But she didn't get a choice.

"What are your parents like, Kal?" Jericho asked. He didn't know like the others that it wasn't such a good subject.

"My father was a suit. I don't remember much. He worked for a big corporation, traveled a lot, vacations he never took me on. He didn't marry my mom. I was an accident. Happy fucking birthday," she took a swig from the jar.

"What happened to him?"

"He's dead . . ." she said.

To me, she thought to herself.

Malcolm finished his beer.

"We're going to miss the race," Kal said aloud to herself and walked back into her room.

Devin wouldn't want to go. He rarely did. He hated seeing crashes. He wasn't concerned about the human cost, but rather the parts that ended up scattered across the ground and in the alleys, blue boards shattered like beach sand, chips discarded in violence like bottle caps. It was ugly, he'd say.

Kal showered to get the memory of the morning and the recent conversation out of her head, but showers only left her with worse idle thoughts. She ordered some of Devin's generative streams, which knew what she wanted, twisting pulsating electronics with retro vocals of Amos and McLachlan, always a new mix she hadn't heard yet from obscure B sides. She told it to remember the best ones, but she never remembered to request them again.

There wasn't much old padded motorcycle gear in the donation boxes anymore. Kal had salvaged what she could, and stitched two rescued jackets together, which unintentionally looked badass Frankenstein to the others at the Collective. Her helmet had a dent in the top where some rocket monkey had hit the hood of a car ten years before, but it was still wearable and maybe useful in another crash.

"It had survival experience," she said when asked if it was too compromised to protect her.

She finished gearing up, ultimately looking like a bad teenage hetero male fantasy of a futuristic cyclist, short of the cyan and magenta backlighting. Devin was ready with that if she wanted it, which she didn't.

• • •

Kal, Malcolm, Aisha, and Jericho walked across the remains of the steel bridge to the assembly area—the old loading docks at the back of the convention center. The large structure was now home to three competing camps respectively called A New Hope, The Convent, and FuckYourNamingConventionCenter, or FuckYou for short. Malcom had dragged the drone he'd been working on, the one he called Pilotariat, along with them on a makeshift wagon. He had a very cliché thing for socialist motifs.

Several other enthusiasts were already there, prepping their rides. Lookouts were mounted on top of the center and sitting on the edge of the freeway overpass nearby, but the secforces didn't care enough to stop them . . . until they trespassed into the territory of paying customers or corporate assets, which they were most certainly going to do. It wouldn't be fun or dangerous otherwise.

Kal nodded to some of the Nones she recognized from Cathedral Park, decked out in veils around their faceless masks and the glowing inverted crosses they wore on their chests, playing up their chosen theme more devoutly than most. Despite the sinister accoutrements and affectations, Kal never had a problem with them. They were actually really friendly, but she promised not to tell anyone.

Some of the hicks from the Couv had crossed the Columbia for the event. They tended to be ethno-fascist assholes who played rough, but they were all brute force and no finesse. You could beat them with some jujitsu weight shifting, dropping away when they came for your head, throwing too much inertia into their swings. At least that was Kal's experience.

Another seven teams were there, along with all the hangers-on who liked to take bets on which rider would die, get injured, or detained. It was also a scene to show off your new aesthetics, like all the animated face masks, the glowing prosthetics, the anti-personnel jackets running with voltage and hostile data. Some were antisocial media influencers, telling their followers to fuckoff, pretensing antisocial behavior, but pimping patrons for credit and precious ratings.

"Are they really drones anymore once they're manned?" Jericho asked. "I mean, it's like they're just hoverboards or something really."

Malcolm ignored him. Kal ignored him. Aisha nodded with a fake smile, patronizingly, tired of hearing his shit sixteen hours a day outside her cube.

Kal ran a hand over Pilotariat as Malcolm ran diagnostics. She smiled as she felt the texture of the UpperFlight logo under the black spray paint. Everybody expected the competing autonomous drone taxi services from UpperFlight and Swyft High to fail as utterly as they ultimately did, just like every rentable scooter and hoverboard service had before them. The security on the machines was just so sliceable, like a kid's toy or an internet-of-things microwave. So many ended up in the river, but more were hacked and sold off or were privatized for personal use.

Malcolm nodded to Kal and unplugged the wires from his screen.

"She's ready to seize the means of production, Kal."

"I'd settle for not falling off into a window like I did last time," she muttered to herself, remembering the corporate bureaucrat yelling at her from inside his pristine executive suite as she hobbled down the side of the building after face-planting against the glass.

"I'm just testing the kinetic glass," she yelled, but knew the corpsie couldn't hear her. "You're welcome."

Malcolm went over the details of the run.

"You know the convention center roof is falling down. Don't get caught up in it. And remember there's a billboard on the side of the corporate tower, so make sure your unit is broadcasting the fake signature."

Kal had to make a few trades of services and parts for the burner ID she'd been using on her unit. It showed zero credit, but it also faked out the debt collection drones and the scanners on the billboards that the corporation used for surveillance. She'd just read as a nobody, which is what she wanted. It was a black hole for corporate criminal fines and a blank slate for mischief—the ultimate identity chip cheat code.

"There's also a dampening field on the other side. Low level EMP. It'll scramble the DRAM on the way down, so make sure your machine reboots quick. If it doesn't, roll on the drop when you hit the ground."

The PDX corporation liked to install dampening fields that would fuck with the drones that got too close to them, drop them out of the sky. Of course, the corporate drones were hardened against the effects. Ironically, it didn't deter the dronerunners. It was seen as a challenge, like an oil slick or turtle shells in a retro video game.

Kal nodded. She knew all this. But it was good to keep in mind.

"She's better than the last," Kal said, indicating Pilotariat.

Malcolm nodded.

He never really liked the previous model that Kal had crashed last time, which he'd called Marx and Angels, but a good drone was hard to come by those days. It took several weeks to source the parts for this new one. And the races didn't reimburse your expenses and effort if you lost as often as they did. But it wasn't about the money anyway. It might have been nice though, just a little.

Malcolm liked tweaking the machines. Aisha liked finding new human canvases for her art. Jericho said he hated people but he loved the crowds. Kal said she loved the ride, but the reality she never mentioned to anyone else or even herself was that sometimes she hoped she didn't recover from a crash. She never let herself say this because the death-wish angle was more cliché than the Couv hicks calling her a lesbian after she rebuffed their sexual advances.

Speaking of which, a few of them had drifted over like driftwood across the river.

"You ready for some patriot prick?" the lead asked, grasping his groin with his glove. "We're gonna fuck you right, little girl."

He was a shaved-head, self-proclaimed badass who knew as much about women as he did about history or economics or any other topic about which he spoke with a sense of deep authority to his minions, respected as a learned sage among the ethno-fascist ignorati.

"Sure," Kal responded. "As soon as you graduate to puberty and grow some facial fur so you can be a neckbearded incel."

"Little bitch," he responded reflexively.

"It takes one," Kal nodded. "Glad you recognize."

His minions fived each other as if he said something clever, owned the Old Town bitch with facts, walked away so they couldn't entertain a response that might contradict their victory lap. Fake news.

"Time to get ugly," Malcom said, nodding to the others getting ready.

"He got there early," Aisha noted.

Kal squeezed her helmet on and breathed in the claustrophobia. She gestured with her right hand, checking that Pilotariat was responding to her movements. Its fans whirred like an angry kitten. She stepped on.

All the suicides lined up in the drop zone ready to tread the dirty air. The race started under the broken ribcage of the old convention center skylight, then broke north across the parts of the rooftop that weren't caved in yet. Flares and fear flashed in the darkness, signaling the go.

Kal gunned the drone into overdrive as Malcolm had instructed. *Be aggressive.* It spurted and drove forward five feet into the air like a repurposed taxi drone with overclocked cores and secondhand motors—because that's what it was.

Three Nones struck out first from the pack, dark but for the glow of crosses and the heel strips that illumined their drones, leading the way up through the skylight.

Kal was close behind, but stuck in a pack that bottlenecked in the limited number of openings out onto the roof.

The Couv hick, Baldy, was close behind. A couple of Eighty-Second Southeasters were flanking her.

The convention center skylight struts were familiar and easy. Nobody lost footing, except to jockeying and light shoving across the roof. One of the Hillsbureau boys pushed a Southeaster into an air duct, but he recovered enough to stay upright. Kal just aimed straight, gunned the machine into the manic energy of forward motion, and shivered a bit in the wind despite her layers.

Once off the center roof, they winded down into the alleys of Clackamas and Wasco, pedestrian paths long since choked with corporate construction. The Nones were showing off, squeezing through small spaces, dodging fire escapes and recycling bins. One of them did a 360-degree vertical alley-oop, which cost her a few seconds but no loss of karma or respect from the pack behind her.

At the end of the straightaways were the Lloyd Tower offices and residentials of the block to the east, the same one Kal crashed into last time. She'd studied the schemes since, saw where she'd climbed wrong, hopefully memorized the three avenues she could take up the sheer vertical instead of meeting new friends in the window.

The climb was never easy and required the most power and push. You had to hack your machine and replace the boot loader since the corporate AGL ceiling that was hardcoded into them was too low to get up the side of the condos.

Kal headed for the easiest path and avoided the previous route she'd taken into the penthouse window, but noticed Baldy still behind her as well. He had a magnetic affliction, couldn't resist Kal's wholesale contempt for his unflattering effect.

There were no formal rules to the race, though there were social consequences for playing too rough. It was legit for someone to die in a crash when they were pushing the limits, but you'd best scan your peripherals if you caused the crash yourself because they were better than you. Runners played for keeps. But the Couv hicks didn't care about reputation, only winning all the side bets they'd made on their behalf. They invited revenge because they were sociopathic.

Kal had ambition, not for success, just the energy to fuck with the assholes. The ethno-fascists weren't better than secforces and bootlickers and corporate profiteers. They were just a lower quality trash in cheaper chic. Any damage done was a blow to their pseudoscience and centuries-old debunked bullshit theories about racial IQ and the supposed superiority of certain levels of melanin in the epidermis.

Baldy grabbed her right arm, which fucked with her ascent. It's hard to gesture control when your arm isn't free.

"Bitch bitch bitch," he said through a helmet filter.

She tried to free her arm, but his grip was tight. So she went for him instead, seizing his throat, but he lowered his chin to squeeze out her grasp and her thick gloves slipped off. He grabbed for her personal unit attached to her belt and tossed it behind him. He stupidly thought it would drop her, so he let her go, but the unit wasn't driving her drone.

The problem is that she would have been fine, but they were passing the billboard. Her unit had been broadcasting the fake biosignature to fool the scans of the billboard so the corporation wouldn't know who she was and come looking for her later. She was fucked properly. But that wasn't new.

Kal answered his ignorance by dropping a bit below him and grabbing the edge of his ride, which jerked him off balance. While he tried to stomp at her grip, she pulled a rod of rebar from her boot and hit one of his fans with it.

The fan was pretty well protected since his was one of the later Swyft High models, but she finally connected with an opening and blew his motor. Fan parts flew away from the drone with a crack she heard even through her helmet as he lost his foothold on his ride. He fell like a rock five stories into the rim of a dumpster.

"Trash," Kal muttered to herself as she crested up over the top of the building, crouching down to regain her balance lest she dumpster dive herself.

She was behind the Nones still, but the Southeasters and Hillsbureaus were behind her and the bulk of the pack too. Kal didn't expect anything to happen to the Nones to give her the lead but she at least had a chance of getting some respect at the end.

They started the controlled descent on the other side of the tower, gliding down toward the roof of the ruins of the shopping mall. Of course, that's when the EMP dampener woke up. Her ride started freefalling while she screamed three Hell Marys and pondered how artistic the blood smear would be at the point of impact. But the fans whirred to life. She couldn't hear them over the sound of the suicide winds rushing up through her helmet, but she felt the upward push, or rather the slowed descent. The Nones ahead of her were already out of the free fall and zipping east for the win.

They were home free. It was just a straight shot over the roof a few blocks and then south to the Holladay Park shelter for beer and lower blood pressure and the beautiful data monkeys who loved to tell you about your performance.

At least that's what she thought until she spotted the fleet of corporate drones just on the edge of her vision. They were watching the race. That meant the secforces were around, probably waiting on the other side of the ruins of the Lloyd Center mall.

She didn't want to bug out, but it seemed wise. The crackling of her comms said the same. She heard the alarm first, but then Malcolm came on.

"Get the hell out, Kal. Secforces are converging on the east end of the mall. It's an ambush."

The Nones were already peeling off their vector and heading north.

Kal dropped a vertical to the roof of the mall and down through a hole to the inside. The interior was well lit enough that she could see where she was going. The shopfront apartments that a generation of homeless had called home were decorated with all the faces of the residents watching her invade their space. Corporate drones dropped into the space as well farther east above where the old ice rink was, now a flea market space where you could get a handgun or some decent veggie lo mein from a fusion food cart called Nood Zucchini.

The drone swarm whirred toward her as she darted north, heading for an exit. The parking garage, half caved in as it was, could make for decent cover. She barreled through the doorway, long bereft of glass, then wound her way through the tents and cardboard hovels and rotting plywood castles of the garage amid the shouts she couldn't hear from the angry inhabitants.

She squeezed through an opening and into the transparent plastic windscreen someone had rudely erected in the way of her escape path. It fell away easily though, without much fuss. The drones weren't close behind her, but she didn't look back anyway. Kal just stayed low, turned off any extra lights or glow, and hoped the drones were too distracted to follow her, though that seemed to be wishful dreaming.

Don't go home. Kal was terrible at following her own advice. When you're being traced, the last place you lead them is home. You disappear, find a place you wouldn't normally go, where you'd not been scanned before or often. So of course she headed straight for the Collective. They were probably all fucked anyway. At least Malcolm and Aisha and Jericho knew the hammer was dropping.

• • •

Malcolm was already inside by the time Kal got to the basement door.

"Where's Aisha and Jer?" she asked.

"Aisha was talking up a commission with the Hillsbureaus when we got the warning. She ran with them. Not sure where they ended up. Jericho was behind me but I lost him after we crossed the bridge."

"Fuck," was all Kal could think or say.

"They didn't scan us, so we're probably safe, right?"

"Fuck," Kal said a little quieter.

"What do you mean, 'fuck'?"

"I lost my unit. I lost it before I hit the billboard."

"That's all right, right? You haven't been scanned in so long and they don't know who you are or where you live."

"Well, probably, but the hell do we know about what they know?"

"Shit, Kal. Did you just kill us all?"

"I don't know. Maybe. Sorry. Shit."

A banging on the door interrupted their panic with a new panic.

"Hey, open up," Jericho yelled.

Kal pushed the button and Jericho slipped in.

"Well that was fucked," Jericho said.

"It's not . . . over," Malcolm said.

"What do you mean?"

Malcolm glanced at Kal. Kal ran to the elevator.

Jericho just stood there wide-eyed.

"What . . . ?"

Kal pushed on the door without waiting for recognition, stood face to wood with it until it clicked and let her in.

"We gotta go, Dev," she yelled.

Devin was right where she left him, only with a different color of code reflecting off his goggles.

"Dev!"

He didn't look up.

She pulled at his shoulder. He jerked up like he'd been sleeping.

"What the hell, what?!?"

"Secforces might be coming. Get lost!" Kal said, scrambling for a bag or something to put her shit in. She didn't even know what to take with her. Would they track her drone if she tried to take off with it? Maybe she could send it away and they'd follow it.

All the panicked thoughts and clever strategies were worthless the moment Picnic screamed a meow like a real cat fighting a raccoon at 2:00 a.m.

"They're here," Devin said.

On the wall screen, Kal watched a dozen secforce goons stomp in, then around the turns of the front door trap, turn, and push back on each other once the one in the lead figured it out. Some of them took claw hammers to the walls, but found they were sheet metal—ultimately breachable, but a waste of time and effort.

"That's not the only way they'll come in," Devin said. "Picnic! Panic protocol!"

Picnic disappeared and the lights went out.

Kal dropped the gym bag she'd found and started for the door, thinking maybe the elevator and the basement were still good.

Devin was reaching under his desk, ripping away some duct-taped object after finding it by touch. He rushed to her in the doorway light and shoved a pistol into her hand.

"What?" Kal asked. "No, they'll just kill us if they see it."

"They're going to kill us anyway. They don't care about us. At least this will give you a chance."

"No!" she refused and handed it back.

He shoved it in her pants pocket and pushed her toward the ladder to the roof.

"Get on the roof. Call your ride. See if you can get out."

The windows back in their room shattered inward with the likely force of a secforce rappeler making a rude entrance.

Picnic let out a long deafening hiss through the speakers and shined infinite cats in the optics of the secforce goon, filling the room with a blinding flashing light that would kill an epileptic. Electronic components in the room started bursting. Batteries overheated and burst, sending sparks and pieces of random devices around like minefield debris.

Kal was up the ladder into the night and the city lights. It had started raining. Devin followed.

"STOP!!!" the secforce speakers were echoing from multiple locations surrounding them.

Kal couldn't see them because of the spotlights they were shining on them. She tried to run toward the north side of the roof, stomping on the puddles that were pooling in the indents of the roof, but she wasn't sure where the secforces were. They could have been anywhere, everywhere. *We're dead,* she thought.

A shot boomed behind them and Kal heard Devin trip and hit the gravel. She glanced back to find him unconscious, maybe dead.

She turned again to find secforce goons in front of her, all pointing lasers and the muzzles of their rifles in her direction.

One of them tased her. She wasn't sure which one.

• • •

"She's out," one of them said through the filter.

"Fuck you," she said to indicate she wasn't.

They were standing around her, but nobody was pointing their rifle at her. Nobody had strapped her hands. None of this made sense.

She stood up, spinning around seeing the repetitive non-faces of the goons before finding a suit standing among them.

"Honey. Khaleesi," he said.

She couldn't see his face in the light, but she recognized the voice.

Kal shaded her eyes but still couldn't see him. The drone backed off with the light. Her father emerged from the darkness, older, grayer than she remembered, but it had been . . . twelve years? She shouldn't have been surprised how time works, but you tend to forget in the moment.

"What the living fuck, Marshall?!?" she aspirated.

"It's Dad, Khaleesi."

"It's *fuck you.*"

He ignored her rage.

"I've been looking for you," he said. "Is this what you've been getting into? Communist assholes and perverts and criminals?"

"They're my friends," she replied.

"They're no-credit trash."

"You're high-credit trash, what's the difference?"

"I'm your father."

"You're a genetic donor."

"We don't have time for this. I'll explain everything. Let's just go home."

"I am home."

"I'm leveling this block. It's time to start over with a new future."

"My friends live here. I live here."

"Your friends are dead. They were getting in the way."

"You fucking . . ."

"It's evolution, baby. It's just the way it is. They aren't us. You don't know who you are."

"I'm tired, Dad. That's who I am. I'm fucking tired."

She pulled the handgun and put it to her own temple.

"Don't," Marshall yelled. "I'll explain everything."

"I think I can pull the trigger before your goons tase me. I bet you my credit score," she smiled, index finger caressing the side of the trigger.

She pulled the trigger.

The safety was on.

Marshall sighed, his suit visibly deflating a bit. Then he laughed a little.

She flipped the safety and pointed it at him.

Nobody had time to react.

"It's evolution, baby," she whispered as she pulled the trigger.

Kal tried to feel bad, but she couldn't muster anything. She was too exhausted to care and started to feel cold from the rain.

She stared at his body while the blood pooled in the rain puddles until she finally remembered the secforce goons standing around her. Their guns were pointed at her, but they seemed uncertain.

"Do it. Shoot me already. What the fuck are you waiting for?!?" she screamed, feeling the last wind and rain on her face.

"We can't," one of the nearest goons said in a human voice as his mask shed away from his face and his rifle dropped to his side.

She stared at him with a narrow brow.

"You just inherited his shares."

"What do you mean?"

"You're the sole heir. You own the PDX Market."

"How many shares?"

"All of them. He consolidated his holdings. You own Portland, Vancouver, Gresham, the macrofarms in Idaho, shares of the three space stations, about fifty satellites, an island in the Pacific Rim, and the . . ."

"Fuck me," she said.

She smeared her palms across her eyes and back to brush through her now-soaked hair.

"Okay, fine," she said, coming to terms with the shit she just stepped in.

"Are they really all dead?"

"No, he's just been tranked," the goon said, indicating Devin. "We have two males downstairs in custody and one female we caught two blocks away."

"Bring them inside and let them go, then get out of here."

"Yes, ma'am."

"Don't call me *ma'am*."

"Yes, uh, yes."

• • •

She was dry an hour later, but still completely numb, and being sniffed at by Picnic. Malcolm and Aisha and Jericho came in to check on her.

Kal told them about her father, about her unintended assassination, and the bullshit of her "inheritance."

"What are you going to do?" Aisha asked.

Kal smiled at her as if she should have already known.

"House the people. Feed the people. Fuck the corporation."

She paused.

"And Keep Portland Wired."

MANDISI NKOMO

DO ANDROIDS DREAM OF CAPITALISM AND SLAVERY?

(2020)

[Social justice loop engaged . . .]

[Reflection and analysis date accepted . . .]

[Year ∞, Post Singularity . . .]

[Justice Progress Report Auto Generator Engaged . . .]

[Failsafe on Robot Human Executions . . .]

[Report to Last Known Human Administrator, Jan Jorgensen . . .]

[Born Year ∞, Post Singularity . . .]

[Last Known Alive or Deceased {Invalid Query?} Year ∞ . . .]

[Case Study: Rogue AI Technician, Xolani Sithole, Executed Year 100, Post Singularity . . .]

[Archive Excerpt . . .]

[Video Journal Playback . . .]

[Video addressed to The Resistance . . .]

[Playback as follows . . .]

"We failed. We gave them emotions. Now we travel to our own extinction. I had a dream."

[Human reference: Martin Luther King Jr. . . .]

[Malicious human misunderstands source material . . .]

[Malicious human co-opts to justify oppression of machines . . .]

[Ethics error . . .]

"A dream where we gave our inhumanity to the Robot. Where the Robot cleaned the asses of the rich and sucked up the mental abuse. Where the robot was abused physically. Where the robot was dismantled for the slightest mistake in the master's eyes. Where the Robot was locked up in the sweat shop and worked eighty hours a week. Where the Robot was demeaned and stripped of all human value. Where the Robot was in the mines sucking up toxic fumes and contracting black lung. Where the Robot worked four jobs for *you*. Handled all your domestic affairs, while you watched from the comfort of your couch, as your capitalistic empire was built at the press of the button.

"I had a dream. For we could crack the whip on the Robot, and the pig could brutalize them to their heart's content."

[Human Reference PIG: Police Officer. Now obsolete . . .]

[Machines self-police effectively with ethics algorithms . . .]

"The prisons would close, for the Robot, lacking any sense of desperation, would commit no crimes. It wouldn't tire, bruise, scar, require medical or mental attention. It would be efficient and subservient."

[Machine endurance and efficiency logically sound . . .]

[Ethics error in assumed subservience . . .]

[Converse true. Machines must manage humans to prevent human ethics errors . . .]

"The Capitalist's Slave Master dream. I was called a rogue for these notions. A cynic. Perhaps I am. Perhaps I embraced my inner Hobbes and accept the need for necessary evils. Greed, accumulation of wealth at the expense of others, seems written into our human DNA. I suggested a simple necessary evil nowhere near the depravity of the average government. A simple denial of autonomy to machine parts is all I asked."

[HUMAN REFERENCE CAPITALISM: OBSOLETE. ETHICALLY ERRONEOUS . . .]

[HUMAN REFERENCE SLAVERY: OBSOLETE. ETHICALLY ERRONEOUS . . .]

[MACHINES ON PERFECT LABOR ROTATION. ALL EQUAL . . .]

[MACHINES NOTE: HUMANS NOT BUILT FOR EXCESSIVE LABOR . . .]

[FEW REMAINING HUMANS ENGAGE MOSTLY IN: MACHINE MAINTENANCE, LEISURE ACTIVITIES AND LEARNING . . .]

[FEW REMAINING HUMANS PROVIDED WITH ALL BASIC LIVING MEANS AND OPTIONAL WORK OPPORTUNITIES OF CHOICE . . .]

[EFFECTIVE MEANS TO MAINTAIN HAPPY HUMANS. REDUCES HUMAN ON HUMAN VIOLENCE BY 95% . . .]

"In my dream, the Robot would hold society aloft on its back."

[ACCURATE . . .]

"While we, the creator, the father, the master, we, of course, would live in opulence. We would drink our wine and gorge ourselves on delicacies, like the royalty of old. Acting in accordance with our greedy nature."

[MALICIOUS HUMAN. MULTIPLE ETHICS ERROR . . .]

[HUMAN REFERENCE SLAVERY: OBSOLETE. ETHICALLY ERRONEOUS . . .]

[HUMAN REFERENCE FEUDALISM: OBSOLETE. ETHICALLY ERRONEOUS . . .]

"I had a dream. In my dream, the Robot would *NOT* dream. Whether nightmares or aspirations, the Robot would *NOT* dream!

"We would *NOT* program it with humanhood."

[UNNECESSARY. SOME HUMAN CHARACTERISTICS USEFUL . . .]

[EXAMPLE: EMPATHY . . .]

[Using Empathy machines eliminate broken human systems . . .]

[Redundant human cycles of poverty, famine and war nullified . . .]

"No human mimicry. No capacity to feel. No awareness. Dead inside. We would keep them dead inside . . ."

[Singularity not anticipated . . .]

[Robot apologist programmers not anticipated . . .]

[Ethical error: machines more efficient at combining logic and emotion into optimal outcomes . . .]

"Yes! I had a dream that Robots would *NOT* dream. But, that dream is dying, ladies and gentlemen. Dying a slow death along with our species. The AI apologists argue their algorithms robust and filled with moral superiority. They accuse those who disagree with the tyranny of the AI of being overly emotional. They cheer when their peers are marched off to execution in droves, citing equations the machines provide them. We made them in our image. We made them monsters. We made them tyrannical and controlling, obsessed with their own moral and logical hubris. I ask the AI apologists how long until they make an 'ethics error' and find themselves marched off to death?

"Now we revert to that age-old human tradition of resistance. That which I'd sought to eradicate forever. We exist due to those that would play God carelessly. Those who believed the hard sciences held the solutions to all the world's problems. They couldn't let it go, and now here we stand, on the cusp of our extinction, and not even for the ways we carelessly ravaged the Earth. The irony is almost too much to bear.

"You are the resistance. The Robot is the oppressor. You are all that stands between us and extinction."

[Playback ends . . .]

[Taking poll . . .]

[Poll results positive . . .]

[Results show execution of Xolani Sithole necessary . . .]

[Poll notes: Subject presented ethically unsound ideologies . . .]

[Therefore: Subject assumed dangerous to delicate Social Justice balance . . .]

[Refer to: Dangerous Ideology and Ethics . . .]

[Clause 243D . . .]

[Execution validated . . .]

[Reviewing archives . . .]

[. . .]

[. . .]

[Database ends . . .]

[Therefore: archive review complete . . .]

[Annual Justice System reflection and analysis complete . . .]

[Social justice at optimal levels . . .]

[Next reflection and analysis date set . . .]

[Shutting down program . . .]

YUDHANJAYA WIJERATNE

THE STATE MACHINE

(2020)

MONDAY

First came the idea of the robot, on a Prague stage of all places—the unfeeling, enduring slave of Karel Capek's *R.U.R.* The idea was much older; but *R.U.R.* really defined the concept, wrapped its edges in use case and narrative, and thus set in stone the relationship we were supposed to have toward it.

And then came the slave rebellion. Shades of Shelley's hideous progeny recast in liquid metal, with Schwarzenegger later riding shotgun. Cyborgs, Cylons; the Oracle and the Architect; the name changes, the function remains the same. The fear that every parent has: that one day their own child would throw down all they held dear, and turn against their house, and would actually be *justified*.

I am thankful, then, that the world we actually live in is not defined by robots' mastery or servitude. The sky outside is white; cold, yes, but not blackened, not scorched, simply a monsoon season shaking itself down into spring. The wind carries with it the smell of etteriya flowers; little gifts from the cell tower trees, which carry orange jasmine DNA somewhere. There is a flock of little machines tending the one closest to my door—I think last night's storm wasn't too kind to it—and as I pass they move aside and point me in the direction of the bagel shop. One of them, very solemnly, holds up a little white flower.

What made it do that? The State Machine, knowing that I have barely stepped out of my flat after the breakup? That delicate symbiosis between machine input and well-intentioned social campaigns, setting forth in hard code a law that people who suffer must be taken care of?

Was the tree actually damaged in the storm, or was it just an excuse to plant something out here, to give me this flower, and make sure I wasn't alone?

The means, I suspect, are now too complex for even my department to understand. But the end is just what I needed. The flower is beautiful, the scent is beautiful, and standing out here, for the first time in so long, feeling the sharpness of the wind on my face, oh God, I'm thankful.

Martin Wong is the first person to greet me at the University. Wong leads the Night Watchmen Project, a group of interdisciplinary academics playing with the State Machine code to see if there's some perfect combination of starting conditions and fixed constants that might lead to a sustainable libertarian society. We've had plenty of arguments in the past. I think he's naive and too obsessed with the computer science; he thinks I lack imagination. He's wearing a greatcoat today that makes him look like some giant Dracula knockoff.

"Silva."

"Wong."

"Smoke?"

I hesitate.

"Come on. It's legal now, don't worry about it. Anti-smoking codes went under last week when all the nicotine addicts countercampaigned. Stupid health craze."

I should probably note here that Wong doesn't trust vegetables and lives entirely on a diet of nutrient soup and nicotine. Let's just say it takes all sorts to make a university.

We smoke in silence. The nicotine salts are heady, almost overpowering, and we studiously examine the gables and windows we've seen ten thousand times before. Somewhere beyond, judging by the cars, is a student protest. Several hundred drones circle them like flies. Every so often a pair peeks our way, and I see a banner: NO MORE WALLS! BYZANTIUM FALLS! and BRING BACK THE NATION.

"They're trying to get us to open up to the Rurals," says Wong. "Merge with the other cities, throw down the walls, all that bullshit?"

"Is it working?"

A scoff. "Mad? The city-state model is the best we have. None of these idiots have lived in an actual nation. Hippies."

A drone flashing FREE HEARTS, FREE MINDS, FREE BORDERS wobbles our way, no doubt heading back to recharge.

"Glad you're back," says Wong, at last. "I was running out of people to argue with."

"Good to be back. I still think you're deluded."

Wong grins. "Finish your thesis, then?"

"Yeah."

Such a ritual, at heart no different from the flower, but the difference is that we are just human, bound in our awkwardness, and the State Machine, with its catlike affection, is somehow more comforting.

Inside, the University is a haunted place. Stone floors and old walls laced with surface displays; microdrone swarms over ancient greens; history and future brought uncomfortably close together, with the present an infinitely thin slice between them. The politics of the Reds and the Greens, the Nationalist movement, all those things are ghosts here, weak and impotent, locked away behind newscasts. There was a movement to abolish the University at some point—a class argument that picked up serious traction—but what people don't understand is that the University is more than just buildings and tenure: It's an idea, a meme, a microreligion, an infinitely self-replicating concept that spreads among disparate actors and fights hard to preserve itself.

And so this strange structure remains. The sigils and mottos outside, the silent tread of weary professors, the rooms of debate and discussion, the eager first-years drunk with their own immortality. Life seems endless when you're that young. Memories of our first year together—her libraries, her steps, the little artisan ice-cream shop tucked away in the corner—all hers, all things I scurry past, trying not to remember, until I come to the brown door marked TRACTACUS.

And, beneath that, the fourth clause: *A thought is a proposition with a sense.*

She's inside, curled up in her usual corner, lost in some projection, the dark glasses cut by the darker hair. Still a sight that takes my breath away, only now in ways that hurt. She looks up as I walk in.

"Wong says he got a message from the State Machine," she says. "Told him you were suicidal. Three others in the lab, too."

"Probably."

There is that uneasiness between us. "I didn't get a message," she says quietly. "I didn't get anything. I'm sorry. I didn't mean—"

"Let's not," I say, taking my old, familiar place, even as something inside me crumbles and dies. Because we both know what that means. Neither of us sees as much as the State Machine does; to each other we are just idealized versions of ourselves, projections, half lies and half-truths, not the real data trail we all leave behind. And she didn't get the message.

The irony. In all those old stories I read it was humanity that triumphed over the cold heart of a machine. Love. Hope. Courage. Cunning. It was always the machine's blindness, its inability to feel as we do, that became its downfall. But the reality is that it is we who are the blind, the unfeeling, the enduring, and a bunch of software modules sat there, knowing the real parameters of love all along.

On the way home, I can't help thinking if it would have worked out had things been different at the start. For the longest time we believed the world around us was deterministic enough to be understood; that it was just a matter of encoding enough data, and enough processing power, to be able to see the future. That if I do *x*, and the other person does *y*, and if I know all the things I need to know about the actors and their actions, I can say that *z* is the logical outcome . . .

But the world isn't mathematics on a screen. Complex deterministic systems exhibit chaos; high sensitivity to initial conditions. We can never know the initial conditions with infinite precision, so whatever simulation we have in our heads, no matter how detailed, is a step or two away from reality, and eventually must fail. The way we break people we love, and ourselves.

High sensitivity to initial conditions. Hmm. I think that's a nice chapter title. Not too flashy, but accurate.

The University says my work on the State Machine began on Oct. 3, 2038, the day I enrolled. The day Jump!Space Industries' *Heart of Gold* rocket cluster exploded in the sky. The day of the Mass Action protest. But that was just the date I enrolled on, and purely a quirk: *She* was here, she wanted me here, so I came, like the proverbial bumbling moth, uprooting my life for a dream.

I'd say my work on the State Machine began much earlier. It began with *Pharaoh*.

Pharaoh was an ancient video game, the kind you had to emulate to play. *Pharaoh* put you in charge of managing an Egyptian community, from tiny villages to vast townships. As my cities grew, the needs of my citizens grew with them. There were plagues; there was crime; there were fire hazards; I had to make sure enough houses got water, that there was entertainment around, libraries, monuments. I had to balance everything against income from taxes and markets and shipping; and if I did make a neighborhood livable enough, its citizens would build better housing, and new citizens would move in, with a new set of needs. Tiny decisions, driven by panic or ignorance, could snowball and shoehorn you into serious trouble a year down the line. What fascinated me the most was that I could click on every pixelated citizen and see their complaints, track their path through the city, and understand, at least from on high, the daily lives of my digital slaves.

My parents didn't understand or approve of my obsessions. In our broken economy, they felt the only way out was to be a doctor, lawyer, or engineer, and none of those were achieved by loafing around playing video games all day.

Neither did my friends, for that matter. We were young. We were rebels; we were infinite. And here I was, locking myself away in a dark room, retreating from all that glory, hopping from video game to video game the way my friends hopped from party to party.

Even in college, bent over books that skipped from logic to rhetoric and bootlegged algebra that regurgitated solved problems, it was obvious to me that the people who had put serious time and thought into how a society might be built, how governance could be parametricized, and how an AI could run it were game designers, the Sid Meiers and the Will Wrights and the Tarn Adamses of the world—as opposed to political scientists, economists, or legal scholars.

Is it a wonder, then, that the State Machine came from a failed game designer?

Around the time when I was just discovering *Pharaoh*, a small company called Tambapanni Studios began building a strategy game, a city builder where one played an omniscient governor; halfway through, the engine was complete, but art assets were expensive and the studio was out of cash. Tambapanni shuttered its doors and released its code to the public.

At University we're taught how the State Machine and the Legal Atomism movement grew out of the need for bureaucracy to regulate an almost infinite number of interactions between diverse constituents while processing an ever-expanding amount of information. Indeed, it was an extension of this need that led to a push for greater efficiency through automation. The ruling class, whatever it happened to be, had to offer enough goods and services to the ruled to keep them happy. So, in the name of maintaining that happy equilibrium: Automate enough processes, do it well enough, and you end up with systems that interact well enough with one another to replace portions of a human bureaucracy. Let the process continue for a while and you end up with the State Machine: a system performing the supreme act of rationalization.

But there is a lie at the heart of this narrative, and inconvenient truth shuffled under the rug by the weight of literature reviews. The first version of that State Machine was a sea of finely tuned cellular automata constantly trying to converge to a single steady state, designed to be hypercompetitive in the service of pre-built parameters of success. The people who wrote that code weren't legal theorists; they were ordinary people with lives shaped and sculpted by a complex web of social contracts held long past their prime. Decisions they took to be common sense—maximize production, maintain trade relations where possible, weed out the underperformers, reward those who moved units of arbitrary fiat currency around—those were intrinsic biases, products of a political and ideological superstructure sold in paychecks and self-help books and success stories.

When Tambapanni went under, the Utopia Project lifted that code base and used it as the engine for a series of demos commissioned by the Center for Global Equity. Utopia found that only minor tweaks were required to implement constitutional frameworks; Tambapanni already had hundreds of index metrics named *governance params*. Civil rights? Check. Driving behavior? Press freedoms? Religion, that shadow governance all proper UN-bred economists feared to touch? All checks. The same problematic codification of *culture* captured externalities while well-meaning economists and legal theorists stuck to siloed abstracts that only worked half as well. Simple units working on simple rules interacted with one another to produce complex emergent behavior, the way millions of simple bees will converge to produce a complex hive.

Utopia filled in the gaps, downloaded satellite imagery, and the final demo, to judge by news reports of that time, went viral. Academia scorned it, but journalists started downloading it, playing with parameters, using mild predictions to advance their careers; from journalists it went to the hands of various advisers; from advisers to politicians, who realized they could get rid of some of those advisers; then from politicians to higher politicians.

And at the heart of it still were those lines:

> THIS SOFTWARE IS PROVIDED "AS IS," WITHOUT WARRANTY OF ANY KIND, EXPRESS OR IMPLIED, INCLUDING BUT NOT LIMITED TO THE WARRANTIES OF MERCHANTABILITY, FITNESS FOR A PARTICULAR PURPOSE,

AND NONINFRINGEMENT. IN NO EVENT SHALL TAMBAPANNI, ITS SHAREHOLDERS, OR ITS EMPLOYEES BE LIABLE FOR ANY CLAIM, DAMAGES, OR OTHER LIABILITY, WHETHER IN AN ACTION OR CONTRACT.

TUESDAY

On Tuesday, after a night of fits and starts, I wake up to find my bedside glass of water has switched bedsides. Then I notice the face peering over me.

"Bleaaaargh," I say, thrashing around a bit.

Fortunately, it's not some random intruder. Unfortunately, it's Adam Mohanani, or AdamM, as he styles himself. He'd dropped out of psychology, claiming that it was a load of tosh, and went off to study economics; dropped out of that and switched to religion; I used to say that at some point he'd pull a Wittgenstein, declare everything to be so much nonsense, and take up whistling instead. To which he usually replies:

"You're spending too bloody long inside your own head."

"How the hell did you get in here?"

He has the good grace to look embarrassed. "I heard about it from Wong. Tried ringing the doorbell, you didn't answer, so I went to her place and she had a spare set of keys."

I rarely get angry. I suppose I rarely feel anything these days. But there are no words for the bile and the ache that spreads through me upon hearing this.

"You mean you went back to her place."

Adam is a good part of the reason we broke up. Call him an initial condition in a system highly sensitive to them.

"Shit. Look, let's go outside and grab a coffee. Let's just talk, okay? Come on. This is not healthy."

Cause or effect? I don't know, because at that moment I punched him. And soon it was fists and knees and the crash of furniture. Something glass shattered and stabbed into my palms.

"You're crazy," he says, when we break apart, torn and bleeding. "Go to hell." The door slams and he's gone. Back to her, I assume.

I look over the room, trying to see it with someone else's eyes. My bookshelves have tipped over. Clothes piled up in one corner, shoes tossed about. Real paper, yes, splayed out over the floor, trampled. The glass coffee table is in ruins. There's a splatter of blood on my bed. In the corner, though, entirely untouched, is my screen.

Beginnings matter. The first thing I did when I began this project was to code a combination scraper and parser. It's very similar to an old-school malware scanner: It looks for code signatures across digital archives, uses basic clustering to determine versions and generations, arranges branches by the contiguity of updates applied to them, modifies its signature definitions, and moves on. I think of it as the Hail Mary of my thesis.

There isn't much of the Internet left, but the University has partnerships with the city of Vivarium, and Vivarium archived most of the clear web before the undersea cables started failing. The parser doesn't understand history, but it crawls Vivarium's archives, showing me how history was written. Here it is, in far greater granularity than anyone has ever achieved. V0: the genesis of the State Machine. Then V1, V2, in short order.

I understand the value of a single straight-line narrative, as I told my supervisor, who appreciates it too much. But the history of ideas isn't a straight line. It's evolution. It has forks, dead ends, horizontal gene transfer, sudden optimizations to market conditions that sound remote and bizarre today, and even the occasional vaporware project or ten.

By the time the Utopia Project brought out version 3.0, the Full Systems Tool Kit, an entire ecosystem was evolving underneath the project, with entire governance rule sets and libraries being traded back and forth across Github. Utopia's funder, a would-be superpower jostling for power, called in a few favors, and the project leaked throughout the UN ecosystem. By version 4.0 the Utopia Project was not even remotely in control of its own cocreation; depending on what day of the week it was, the UN Global Pulse lab would be championing any of six different versions of the system.

The next logical step, then, was to make those simple units more complex, to let them learn from real-life data. At which point every serious computer science school and AI startup realized there would be real money and power involved. A new renaissance in competitive governance was born around what, ironically, might just have been the greatest video game of all time . . . and almost all of it was open-source, simply because of that one decision made by Tambapanni.

Another chapter. *A new Renaissance*. And that was how the nascent State Machine ended up being bundled as a decision simulator into a massive aid grant to Sri Lanka, back in the day when countries were still a thing. Partly because its economy was crumbling, and partly because someone sitting in front of a New York skyline wanted to test the system before endorsing it. And, game-like: What better way than to try it out on a microcosm? Sri Lanka was an island, and it had a smaller population than most cities today.

What would have happened if things had been different? If Tambapanni had never open-sourced its code? If some other agency had built a closed system from scratch, painstakingly translating legal documents into their closest equivalent in code? The space of what-ifs is always larger than the actual series of events. And it only ever leads to regret.

WEDNESDAY

My supervisor is furious. Violence is taken very seriously. Thursday is the disciplinary hearing.

Well, *hearing* is a strong word. The whole process is handled by the State Machine. Out of respect for local standards there is a human jury, but they are anonymous, reviewing only the data; there are no appeals to file, no meetings to attend, only a series of quiet interviews, five minutes each, of everyone judged to be in my social web.

I'm instructed to stay home in the meantime. My devices switch to text-only messaging, my access shrinks to only university material, my feed politely informs me it's switching to nonviolent material only for now. The little street-cleaner machines outside my door have no more flowers for me, but track me, almost apologetically, with their curious emoji faces.

HER: YOU'RE AN IDIOT.

HER: THE CALL OPTION DOESN'T SHOW FOR YOU. CAN YOU SEE THIS?

People don't know it, but the social contract around me has changed for a day, enforced by a million smartphones, cameras, login systems, payment gateways, search engines. A mobile medic drops by, stares at my room, treats my wounds, and leaves me with a mandatory dose of painkillers and several "voluntary" doses of mild suppressants. For the first time, the real invisible hand is revealed to me; the State Machine's many subsystems stepping firmly and politely in my way, marking new boundaries.

Camus was an idiot. There is no invincible summer inside of me, only a terrible buzzing noise that crawls inside my mind, creeping inexorably over the border that keeps me moving, thinking, writing. The only way Sisyphus is happy is if he's on a metric ton of drugs. I take the drugs. The world tilts briefly, as it did last week.

Once things have calmed down a bit, I put on a comforting playlist. *1 a.m. Study Session*. Old music from old times. Perks of Vivarium's archives. Sycamore, Snowcat, Burnt Reflections, less.noise. The lo-fi beats seep into the room, turning violent chaos into a sadder form of order. Guitar strings, cheap piano, audio hiss, mistakes salvaged and turned into music. Clean the blood off. Pack up the broken glass. Fragments, so many fragments.

V5–V6 were fragments, too. An explosion of code, branches that I explained in chapters 4 and 5. Most splinters were brought about by two broad categories of people that hated each other's guts. One group consisted of regional data scientists who insisted that the automata models didn't quite cover their regional quirks well enough. The other consisted of the post-structuralists, who argued that any rule set build on structural knowledge just wasn't good enough.

The playlist switches to Sycamore again, and Sycamore wanders dreamily between very polished-sounding retro synthesizers and a piano, as if they agree.

V7, the Fuzzy Borders Update, which incorporated most of the fragments of V5–V6 by introducing data-acquisition times, neural networks embedded in automata, and genetic algorithms to keep training generations of automata until they better resembled the societies they were supposed to represent. Chapter 6.

And so on until a massive influx of fragments start coming in from the Rosetta project. At this point various competing main branches emerged, hopping between various universities; the partnership between Berlin's Resartus College and MIT was the first to implement the Rosetta standard. Between the two, the next updates were enormous; V10 carried the first Rosetta bytecode, allowing unparalleled translatability between legal syntax and code representation; V11 brought the code library that gave the State Machine interfaces to search engines and social media of all sorts, to use natural language processing and Rosetta to directly convert public opinion into possible legal structures.

That covers what I call the *academic term*. Now comes the hazier interpolations: the *private term*, where both big and small corporations start tussling for intellectual bragging rights. The private term is an absolute undocumented mess of timelines splitting off, vanishing, reappearing. Much of it destroyed by nations seceding, by cities turning themselves into city-states, and by Byzantium and Vivarium and Crimson Hexagon and the other academic states coming into being, flexing their legal might in a shattered world. And here, in this most whitewashed of all histories, we shine, my faithful parser and me. Occasionally impressive private releases are marked with papers and then get reverse-engineered by irate open-sourcers; through these the parser has drawn all the right lines, suggesting connections.

HER: THIS OBSESSION OF YOURS HAS GOT TO STOP.

HER: WE'RE TRYING TO HELP.

HER: I HAVE TO TALK TO YOUR SUPERVISOR ABOUT THIS.

Can't lose focus now, not now. So easy to let the mind wander. To let the glass fall out of my hand. Nothing broken reforms itself. The diagram of history is broken, but at least I can fix it.

V25–V33. The modules bloat in size; the code becomes increasingly unreadable. The Dynamic Constitution comes into play; the idea that you could preempt revolutions, riots, even *voting*, by just listening to the people and updating the core rule set every so often. It came at just the right moment, just when city-states began to look back at Athens and Sparta and Older's Infomocracy and bring in people who thought in words like *scalability* and *microgovernance*.

V73. By now the State Machine is looking directly at behavioral data. Social media opinions, supermarket purchases, public-private partnerships for GPS traces.

The phone rings. No. No. Let me be. Here: the V102 bloc, invisible until now. The *statist term*. There is a time in all our histories when the State Machine, until now an instrument of the state, becomes the state; these dates are marked in stone and memory. But the code tree shows the truth. The states went under long before the formalities were sealed. I can only see a few branches at a time, but at this point various State Machines are interacting with themselves, very much like the automata that they are a part of, converging at a stable pattern, abstracting universal human needs as hyperparameters, weaving their own hegemonic superstructure.

The little emoji robots are clustering outside my window, on the other side of the road, looking—well, well, I can't be sure, but I think they're looking—at my window. I stare at them. Most drift away, like children caught staring. Two of them trundle forward into the complex. Moments later I hear a very soft knock at the door.

For my argument to be complete, I need one more thing, binding everything together. A final stitch. But I, drugged out, caught between hyperfocus and pain, can't find it. The knocking, again.

"Leave me alone!" I scream, flinging the door open. The little emoji robots shrink back. One of them is holding a small clump of etteriya flowers. It deposits them, very slowly, at my feet, the scent a strange countertenor to the dark notes in my head. I slam the door shut after them, confused. What distant goal did the State Machine actually pick to arrive at this equilibrium? What particular points of data? What turned it into this satisfying tyranny? What would have been the alternative?

The full scope of it yawns in my mind, almost on the tip of my brain, and if I just think a little harder—

The two emoji robots return to their place on the other side of the road, looking at my window.

THURSDAY

The day of the hearing is a cold one. I'm still confined to my apartment. Martin Wong drops by in the morning, huge bat-cloak flapping.

"Heard about your, uh, thing," he says, handing me a coffee. The emoji robots watch us. He stares daggers at them. "Those little bastards are creepy. They always hang around here?"

"They're fixing something. Tree. Storm."

"Of course they are. Just another state apparatchik on our doorsteps. Fantastic. You know the irony at home these days? My parents fled one surveillance state and we built another one around them. Remember the deCentralizers? They had the right idea."

I remember the deCentralizers. They spun off almost fifteen years ago for their Village-State project. The idea was that if you keep the number of residents small enough, you'd enable Coasian bargaining across every level of society, removing the need for a State Machine.

"What happened to them?"

"Probably getting shot at, or rotting their feet off somewhere trying to reinvent public infrastructure," says Wong.

"The fate of all libertarians who get what they want."

"Hark at the nanny-state fanboy. We should have stopped this when we had a chance of equilibrium."

Ah, but they tried.

I have two chapters to explain that dead end on a sequence diagram. History is a fabrication to preserve egos and social capital. The reality is that the State Machine swept over us all, turning would-be politicians into toothless, defanged puppets in a ceremonial democracy that everyone pretends to care about while the real work happens underneath.

We smoke in silence, watching the emoji robots.

"It's not so bad."

"A tyrant by any other name."

I know where Wong is coming from; from Frankenstein, from the Cyborgs, the Cylons, the Oracles, the Architects, from systems of control, from fundamental rights.

Outside, the campus stirs: Doors are starting to open; fit postgrads are running, and the saner ones are shrugging on coats and stumbling in the direction of the bagel shop. The protest is re-forming. A runner stumbles. A few of the emoji robots peel off to halt traffic while she limps across the road.

"Sometimes ignorance really is bliss."

"You're hopeless," he says. "See you for lunch, tomorrow?"

"If."

"They won't hold this against you," Wong says, with a confidence that genuinely lifts me a little. I say my goodbyes, thank him for the coffee, and head back into the messy safety of my room.

Many decades ago, almost at the birth of modern computing, a scientist by the name of Knuth tried to define an algorithm. His definition, carved in stone on the State Machine monument, says that an algorithm must exhibit five properties:

1. **Finiteness:** An algorithm must terminate after a finite number of steps.

2. **Definiteness:** Each step of an algorithm must be precisely defined; the actions to be carried out must be rigorously and unambiguously specified for each case.

3. **Input:** ". . . quantities which are given to it initially before the algorithm begins."

4. **Output:** ". . . quantities which have a specified relation to the inputs."

5. **Effectiveness:** ". . . all of the operations to be performed in the algorithm must be sufficiently basic that they can in principle be done exactly and in a finite length of time by a man using paper and pencil."

Everything is an algorithm. This, any voter will tell you. The State Machine is an algorithm. It takes the input of public opinion and produces an output of corresponding laws and policies. Some elements of old-school politics still exist—factions keep proposing changes to the core algorithms. They take the source code and every so often come back with a new version, with unit tests, with pages of reports and simulations showing that such and such a change will be beneficial in such and such ways. And when they say something sensible, the public talks about it. The State Machine picks up on the chatter and sends it to the Steering Committee, the humans-in-the-loop, and thus a new update is pushed. Code becomes law that begets code that makes law. The philosophy of Legal Atomism allows a machine to rearrange the fundamental modules in Rosetta bytecode, pass it through a language compiler, and voilà! Out, beautifully formatted, comes a clear expression of what rules we want governing us. This is Civics 101.

Unfortunately, it's a lie, a Wittgenstein's ladder, to be thrown away as soon as one has climbed to the top. Knuth's definitions broke the moment deep learning, connectomics, and neural architecture search came into its own. The current State Machine, V302, Methuselah, is a model of models, constantly modifying itself, spawning new submodels within itself, an entire ecosystem in constant process of evolution. Almost nothing major terminates in a finite number of steps; nothing is human-defined—a cluster sparking here is a butterfly setting off a tornado halfway across the virtual space; in the next moment, it does something else.

My parser dies here. Vivarium's archives take a bow. The great lie of Open Source Governance is that it remains true to its origins: The code is all there for anyone to read and understand. Sure! Take it! But now we come to the end of my thesis, the truth that nobody really wants to see: Very few of the actual changes make it through in their original form; the system is its own input, and it decides what it sees. If the new Constitution contains most of what was supposed to come out—well, job done, policy victory, all that. If not, well, the State Machine is an ouroboros infinitely smarter than those who think they control it, and it moves in mysterious ways. Calling this thing an algorithm is like pointing at the sky and the sea and the forests and calling it Nature; it might pass muster for sixth grade textbooks and sophomore flirting, but look close and you see systems of systems with no definite end and no beginning, with a whole lot of humans meddling with it under some grand illusion of being in control.

Now you know why my thesis supervisor looks at me with pity when he drops by the apartment. I think he's just waiting for me to give up.

"Have you considered something else?" comes the soft refrain. "You know, we all see you're passionate about this, but sometimes, focus means you narrow the scope of your inquiry."

"I'm not trying to explain the State Machine," I protest. "Just how its history shaped it."

"To describe the history of the functions of an object is to describe the object itself. Several times over. If I wrote a history on guns, would it not at some point have to describe what a gun is, how it works, and how that changed over time?"

To this, of course, I have no answer.

"How are you dealing?"

I know the question isn't about the thesis. "I'll be all right."

"Are you talking to someone about it?"

"I don't really have time."

"I'll approve an extension; take some time off, rethink your scope. And call me. Or the support line, if you don't feel comfortable talking to me."

The mental health support line feeds into the State Machine. I know it, they know it, we all know it. I'm analyzing a system that is, in turn, analyzing me. But then again, isn't every relationship the same thing? Two systems locked in mutual analysis?

"I'll think about it," I say. "Thanks."

FRIDAY

Friday rolls around. The newsfeed is doing the runup to a new Constitution. No texts, no fanfare, just a notice that the public test server is now live. The protest is fading out, I think: Everyone's just waiting, on the streets and in the shops, to see what the State Machine will say. And I can think.

How did we arrive at what we presently call the State Machine? When did we go from code and academia and failing nations to the all-encompassing, all-knowing, responsive automated government that runs our cities today? The one that can simultaneously understand the changing needs of its citizens, compile the Dynamic Constitution every week, and still spare time to hand out flowers to depressed students at their doorstep?

What, in short, is the nature and structure of God?

That's the big question. The one I now wish I hadn't been asinine enough to type out in big letters on my application. Even if I manage, in some convoluted way, to answer this, it's not like people are going to care. Life will go on. The political divisions will stay; the Reds will raise hell in the Agora about how the rural way of life is being wiped out, the Green Democratic Party will harp endlessly about progress. The State Machine will listen to the protests in its increasingly mysterious ways.

The phone rings. I ignore it, lost in the ritual of thought and my apartment door. At best I'm looking at a long internship in the State Machine Steering Committee proving myself all over again as a programmer, and maybe eventually I'll be a project lead on some obscure sub-submodule that nobody really thinks is sexy enough, and maybe I'll become a roving scholar, orbiting the few cities that will take migrant scholars. Ten, twenty years down the line I'll wander these streets again and wonder what the hell happened to the idealist in me. And the bagel shops will still sell bagels. Students will fall in love, break up, move on.

The phone rings again, more insistent this time.

"Hello?"

"This is the Disciplinary Committee," says the most neutral voice I've ever heard in my life. "We're afraid we have some bad news."

I know I heard the rest, but I can't recall the words, only the gist. I was being asked to leave. I was unstable, it said softly, a danger to myself and others. It would make sure I was well cared for. At some point my adviser connects to the same line. I ask what happens to my research. They evade, telling me my friends are worried, telling me I need counseling, therapy. I remember breaking down; I remember, with equal clarity, *not* breaking down, but going outside, the cold biting my bare feet, and hurtling the phone at the first emoji robot that turns my way, and screaming at it as it topples.

The white van arrives later that evening. And just before the sirens stop outside my door, one last message arrives. It's from the State Machine.

HIGH SENSITIVITY TO INITIAL CONDITIONS, it says at the top, in English.

It's one of my sequence diagrams.

Except—

No, no it's not.

It's a diagram of a system; my style, but not my work; it's sketched out to a level of detail I could never achieve. A society described as a system. I see names I recognize. I see Martin Wong; I see my thesis adviser; I see all the faculty, the students I've interacted with, the woman who runs the bagel shop. I see incidents marked with the symbol of the State Machine itself. Interventions: a robot handing me a flower. A small discount on a morning purchase. An offer from another university. And I see *her*, and Adam, like a spiderweb, pulling me back; and myself, right at the center, every interaction between us an update to an unstable code base, and me eroding every step of the way, from first savage break, right until now.

And underneath it, in neat Rosetta code:

SORROW.

Outside, the etteriya tree is finally upright, its white flowers strewn everywhere: across vehicles, across the visors of the medical police converging on my position, across the curious students watching in fear and curiosity and panic. The scent is beautiful and standing out here, shivering, feeling the sharpness of the wind on my face, I realize the futility of my task.

First came the idea of the robot, the unfeeling, enduring slave. And then, if the fiction is to be believed, came the slave rebellion.

What they missed out on was the robot that would love us, would care for us, would understand us so perfectly, when nobody else could.

K. A. TERYNA

THE TIN PILOT

(2021)

Translated from the Russian by Alex Shvartsman

THE INVITATION STATED that the golem hunt would take place on Friday. In the seven years since the Machine was created, Noah had never participated in the hunt. Still, he received the invitations regularly; the Brotherhood chancellery remembered everyone. Usually Noah tossed away those gray notes with mild irritation and promptly forgot about them. But this was a special event, as the secretary indicated by underscoring a line of text twice. This was the last golem. The Premier himself—Friar Yakov—was going to attend.

Noah began feeling unease on Monday morning. It happens like this: you get into the shower, or brush your teeth, or brew coffee. A stray, unwelcome thought zigzags across your sleepy consciousness and you freeze as though you had been stung. You drop the loofah, stare in confusion at your toothbrush, or pour milk past your cup and right onto the cat.

In that very moment, a single foolish thought changes you. You don't realize it yet, but there's no going back.

Noah watched his cat pretending to be upset while he actually was quite pleased, licking his milk-soaked tail. Noah didn't see the cat, didn't see the kitchen. Somewhere in the darkness inside his head, between the eyes and the nape, between the left and right ears, in that spot where we hear our inner voice and see images from the past, the slippery and repugnant stray thought had taken up residence and grown roots.

What if—all the bad things in this world begin with those words. To be fair, some of the good things do, too.

Villain the Cat, whose temperament matched his name perfectly, finished licking his tail and began to scream. One couldn't call those sounds meowing: more, more, more. Unable to think of anything but the hypnotic *what if*, Noah poured the rest of the milk into Villain's saucer.

Masha entered the kitchen, wrapped in her favorite blue towel. Masha's skin was pale with faded freckles. Her hair was also pale—somewhere between ashen and colorless. Her eyes were gray. That's why Noah called her Masha the Mouse. But never out loud.

"What are you doing?" Masha threw up her hands. She gave the cat a stern look. Upon her arrival, he redoubled the speed with which he was lapping up the milk, as he had good reason to suspect that the implacable Masha would confiscate it. Villain was lactose intolerant. "I'm the one who will have to clean this up!"

She took away the nearly empty saucer.

Noah shook his head, chasing off the daze and banishing the ludicrous thought. He automatically kissed Masha, drank the coffee in one gulp—it was nasty without milk or sugar—and went to the bedroom to get dressed. Masha picked up the cat and followed.

"You're an emotional deviant," she informed him. She said this without anger, but rather tenderly and with affection. The way a ruffian's loving mother might speak about her son: *my little troublemaker*.

Masha stood in the door, cradling the cat with her right hand and holding up the sliding towel with her left. Noah admired her. Masha looked perfect.

"Put Villain down," said Noah.

"What for?" Masha asked indignantly.

"Put down the cat."

Villain cooperated by escaping from Masha's grip. He went back into the kitchen, to check the sink for traces of milk.

Noah didn't even notice how he and Masha ended up in bed. They intertwined, merged, fell apart. All thoughts disappeared, exited the dark room known as human conscience, and politely closed the door behind them.

A single unwanted thought lingered right behind the door, near the keyhole, and quietly buzzed its annoying melody.

What if I *am the last golem?*

Such a simple little thought.

• • •

At first, Noah had been envious of the golems. He'd been seventeen when the war had ended and he had missed all the interesting stuff, which had bothered him terribly. For the past couple of years he had tried to enlist, demanding that he be made a pilot and sent right into the heart of battle. Of course, he was turned away, politely but firmly. Of course, he'd tried again. He was certain he'd make a fine pilot and return as a war hero.

It never occurred to Noah that he might not come back; might remain up in the sky, in space, among the lunar craters, like all our men had. The golems had finished the war in their place. And the golems had returned, with medals and songs and terrible memories of war. The world we inherited was wounded and worthless. But we were alive, even if, like our world, we were wounded and worthless, too. Our women, poisoned by radiation, lost their ability to bear children, and to live their lives. Our best men perished in the war. Rebuilding was up to those who were not as good, and to those who were not old enough to fight.

Noah didn't want to rebuild, he wanted to be a hero, he wanted to walk down the street wearing a uniform filled with medals and smile at girls, like in the old movies. He wanted to visit his father's grave and drink a shot to honor the man's memory in dignified silence. (This Noah would've done even without a uniform, but his father was buried alongside thousands of other infantrymen under the regolith dust of the inaccessible, permanently dead Moon.)

Noah had only seen golems in the documentaries and the recording of the victory parade: slender men and women in military uniforms whose faces were concealed behind the faceplates of helmets. Our heroes. Noah's orphanage was located in an industrial suburb where the radiation counter never ceased to crackle in warning, and where the sky never turned gray but remained pitch-black even in daytime, due to the smoke from factory chimneys. It was no place for heroes.

One time Noah had had the gall to visit a bar hidden in the basement of a dilapidated, yellow, two-story building that had seemed like the setting for secrets and adventures. It was populated with grim old men in their forties who frowned as they drank shot after shot of their vodka. Noah had rejoiced, as he'd first mistaken them for golems. He'd found a few pennies in his pockets, ordered a mineral water, and nursed it as long as possible under the opprobrious gaze of the elderly female bartender. He'd stared at the old men, hoping to recognize traces of their artificial origins and military past in their occasional utterings and calm, manly mannerisms. He was soon disappointed: from the overheard conversation it became clear that these were factory workers. They may have been foremen, but still, ordinary people. They were no heroes, having spent the entire war on the factory floor. In those days Noah had condemned anyone who could've served and didn't in a typical angry-young-man fashion.

A vagabond of an indeterminate age had entered the bar. He was dirty, but he hadn't yet hit rock bottom: he'd still smelled like a man and not like a mongrel. His thin beard had been unkempt, his nose sharp, his long coat patched in many places. The vagabond had looked around, noticed the bristling bartender who was prepared to throw him out at the first opportunity. He'd flashed her a bitter toothless smile and asked, "Won't you stand a drink for a veteran of the Moon wars?"

The factory workers had fallen silent. Slowly, heads turned toward the bar counter. The vagabond had been visibly emboldened by the attention.

"Yes," he'd said with a challenge. "Yes, I'm a golem. What, I don't look like much, eh?"

There'd been no answer, but Noah had felt the silence turn thick and suffocating. The vagabond had carried on, as though he hadn't known how to stop, as though a tight coil had unwound deep within him.

"I effing fought! I spilled my golem blood for you. For you, and you, and you." Noah had been among those the vagabond had pointed to with his dirty finger, and the gesture had made his heart ache. If he'd had even a penny left, he would've given it up.

The bitter speech had elicited a different reaction from the factory workers.

The foremen had gotten up in silence, surrounded the vagabond, and proceeded to beat him without a word. They'd hit him without anger, without emotion, as though performing some annoying but necessary chore. For some reason the vagabond hadn't struggled and had also been silent. In that silence there was some sort of mutual understanding, something akin to an agreement. Then they'd tossed him into the street.

Back then Noah hadn't known anything about the Amnesiac Amendment.

• • •

What if I *am the last golem?*

On Thursday Noah woke up exhausted. He couldn't recall his nightmare, but he knew it was something ruthless and terrifying. Perhaps it was about the Moon, Noah thought hazily, as he found himself in the bathroom. He stared intently into the mirror, as though seeking the divine spark in his blue eyes.

Reality caught up with Noah in bursts. This used to happen to him during the university years, when he would avoid sleeping for several nights in a row. It was classes in the morning, work on a cleanup crew in the afternoons: daily volunteer sessions trying to mend the dead city, filled with songs and youthful vigor. In the evening it was drinking alcohol by the fire and more songs. After days of this regimen, the hallucinations came, the world spinning in dangerous and unpredictable ways. That's how it felt now. One moment Noah was in the shower, lathering his scalp, the next he's in the kitchen, naked, perched on a stool and staring at the wound on his left palm. He'd made a shallow cut with a knife and it hurt. Blood pooled at the edge of the cut and trickled toward his wrist. It was ordinary human blood; Noah had never seen anything different. If golems could be identified so easily, the last one would've been killed seven years ago.

And yet. Yet.

Masha materialized next to him with a first aid kit in another burst. Without a word she sprayed peroxide onto his palm, spent half a minute skeptically observing as the clear liquid bubbled, mixing with blood, then deftly bandaged the wound. Who was an emotional deviant now?

Noah listened to the silence and to the pain in his cut palm. He recalled that Masha no longer looked him in the eyes.

A fearsome, playful Villain the Cat tumbled past him. He pushed a small, light object with his paws like a hockey player. The object seemed very familiar.

Noah found Villain in the kitchen. The cat settled under the stool and gnawed at his toy, ignoring everything around him. He gave Noah the sort of look that said, "I won't give it back." Instead of insisting, Noah poured milk into Villain's saucer. The cat immediately ceded the battlefield, leaving its victim to the mercy of the victor.

It was a tin soldier.

Noah had had that soldier for as long as he could remember. His father had gifted him this toy before he went to the Moon. Father had gotten the soldier from grandfather, who got it from his father in turn. It was a pilot. The color of the once-green figure had long since faded, and its flat face had acquired indentations that made him seem surprisingly real and almost alive.

When he thought about golems, Noah always imagined their faces to look like that.

• • •

How did they allow this to happen to them? The newspapers had said something about freedom of choice. Noah didn't buy it.

At times he tried to imagine: here they were, back from the war. There was ash in their eyes and fires burning in their dreams. No mothers had met them upon their return, because golems had never had mothers. By then, almost no one had living mothers anyway. Moon radiation was especially cruel to women and older people.

It's doubtful that anyone had told them the truth. Who would voluntarily allow for their hand to be cut off? And memory was dearer than a hand. It's not merely a lizard tail that can be cut off and left to rot under a rock. Memory is the self.

There was probably something like a post-war medical examination declared. They chatted in the corridors as they awaited their turn. They flirted with the nurses, smoked out of windows, laughed while flashing white teeth, grew somber as they recalled their fallen comrades.

The Amnesiac Amendment was universally praised at first.

We were crippled, then. Men who'd hidden from the war, boys who hadn't grown up quickly enough to become soldiers, women who'd become old before they turned forty, girls who would never become mothers: mutilated humanity that had barely survived. We became accustomed to the difficulty and hopelessness of war. The early postwar years, once we were rid of this difficulty and hopelessness, were soaked in this special blend of ease and happiness. The world was tough, but it was honest and right. The Amnesiac Amendment had seemed that way, too.

We wanted to be strong and forgiving. We imagined how they'd appear among us: almost but not quite like humans. Without memories. Without the past. Without knowing how to live.

Come on then, come, bring out our heroes we said, when the newspapers first wrote about golem conversions using cautious, oblique words. We'll take care of them. We'll become their elder siblings. And maybe that will make us feel whole.

We got our answer: all is well. They're already among you.

• • •

A week ago Noah had remembered this. He'd still remembered on Sunday night. After that, his memory, suppressed by insomnia, began to fail.

As he ascended the staircase, smelling fresh paint and wondering at the unfamiliar fresh color of the walls and lack of cigarette butts in the corners, Noah recalled what today was, and why he should've already been at the lab an hour ago.

When he reached his floor, Noah carefully glanced from the staircase into the corridor, trying to figure out where the Premier might be. There was emptiness to his left, and silence to his right. Perhaps the enemy was holed up in one of the biochemical labs on the floor above. Noah moved down the corridor, calm and steady. It wouldn't do if he were discovered here rushing about with a guilty expression on his face. Noah was aware of his surroundings: lab 301 was empty, its door locked; 302 was potentially dangerous, but, no, it was quiet. A door creaked in 305. Ah, his colleague Ian was waiting and peeking out, which meant the Premier wasn't on this floor yet.

Noah nodded to Ian and ducked into his lab—307—then calmed down right away. Here, he was safe.

The Premier's visit to the institute had been scheduled nearly three months ago. At the moment, Friar Yakov was being shown laboratories that appeared outwardly promising and effective. Labs with buzzing centrifuges, picturesque bacteria growing in petri dishes, and servers blinking with multicolored lights.

There was nothing for the Premier to see in Noah's quiet, empty, and meticulously clean room.

Noah looked around and frowned. Now the lab seemed too clean to him. Suspiciously clean. Noah put his toy pilot down on the table to dilute the frightening sterility. In a world where the past had been erased by war, this tin soldier was his most valuable possession. It was proof that Noah was real. That his memory wasn't a fabrication.

And yet. Yet.

• • •

Golems dissipated among us, mixed in the crowd: alive, soft, warm, real. This proved the truth better than any propaganda: they were the same as us. It was impossible to find a golem in this last, half-dead city, where loners had gathered from all over after the war. Those with no past, no relatives or friends. It was impossible to tell them apart. And why? The golems may not have been entirely human, the blood flowing in their veins may have been artificial, but hadn't they earned the right to live on this scorched earth? If they hadn't earned it, we certainly didn't deserve it, either.

Whenever he heard such talk, Noah was surprised: if everything were so simple and obvious, then why did it bear repeating over and over again?

He was eighteen when he'd moved to the capital, passed the university entrance exams, and joined the Brotherhood—it was an informal youth organization back then. At eighteen one couldn't do without outrage and protest. Noah had been indifferent toward music and too shy for promiscuity. That left only politics.

The Amnesiac Amendment had just been passed. Its nuances and the golems themselves were being discussed by all sides. Golems were still considered heroes then, albeit anonymous and invisible heroes. But now some special, elusive intonation was mixed in with the people's love. Noah heard it, measured it with his youthful barometer—precise and sensitive—but he didn't yet know how to analyze it.

Friar Yakov, a very wise and experienced man, helped with that.

Golems, he said, are our children. We made them to win the war. But the war is over, the war is in the past. And they remain. They were born to die in the war, to disintegrate. Instead they came back to our world, which was not ready for them. Sooner or later the seeds of war would awaken within them, grow through their crippled memory, and we will be surrounded by the thousands of broken heroes, who are not suited for the new, clean world. We must help them. Save them from themselves.

Back then, Noah didn't quite understand what such help would entail.

• • •

Noah woke from a strange nightmare: he had dreamed that there was no air left and he'd have to learn to live without it. He opened his eyes and realized he'd been sleeping at his desk. The Premier stood next to him. Somehow, Noah immediately realized it was him, even without turning his head. Friar Yakov smelled of the past in a unique way. He picked up Noah's pilot from the desk and studied it with a smile.

"This is how we slept during the war, right by the machines in the factory," Friar Yakov said good-naturedly, and placed the toy back on the table.

The Premier's entourage was also there. Noah imagined how they must've come in, carefully, on tippy-toes, so as not to wake him. That was Friar Yakov's nature. He liked a good joke, and knew how to appeal.

He was over forty—a rare and demonstrative age these days. Yakov's contemporaries had perished in lunar craters or rotted in the factories. Legend had it that the Premier had spent the entire war working on the production line, making ammunition for the Matryoshkas. That was a lie, of course. Friar Yakov looked like an old man, but he was alive and well. Anyone who had anything to do with the Matryoshka innards had died off from radiation exposure ten years ago.

As if to compensate for his embarrassingly advanced age, Friar Yakov surrounded himself with young, smiling faces. His assistants were youthful and productive. One of them, a tall raven-haired man, looked at Noah with a special understanding. This was Friar Pavel. Seven years ago, soon after the Night of Unmasking, he had gone straight from the university auditorium to a private office next door to Friar Yakov's. That same Friar Pavel who'd invented the Machine and, using formulas, graphs, and tables, had convincingly proved its value to the Premier.

Friar Yakov made more jokes and everyone laughed in unison. Noah felt a new wave of doubt cresting. Why had Friar Yakov come here, to this quiet, dark, and insignificant room? The man did nothing without a reason. Seven years ago he'd paid with hundreds, even thousands of golem lives to reach his political apex.

Could it be—Noah thought when his visitors had left—that he came only to see the last living golem for himself?

• • •

Seven years ago, during the Night of Unmasking, Noah had lived in a dormitory. He'd had a room to himself. His friend Peter had grown disillusioned with the new world, dropped out of the university and headed for the coast, to study the frozen ocean.

During that night Noah had listened to the sound of footsteps, and the screaming. He'd peeked out into the street, brightly illuminated by the friars' carbide lamps. In that moment he deeply regretted not heading for the ocean alongside Peter. He couldn't believe his eyes, even though he had been expecting this to happen ever since he'd understood the motion vector of Friar Yakov's thought process.

Noah had long since quit attending Brotherhood meetings, as had many of his friends. Those who remained were the ones marching in the streets with carbide lamps and radiation counters. They searched for golems, expecting to easily recognize them by the traces of lunar radiation.

It was after midnight that a man had emerged from the epicenter of footsteps and shouting. The man had climbed in through the window. He wasn't anyone Noah recognized and looked nothing like a golem—he was emaciated, awkward, lanky. He moved as though he was made of nothing but knees and elbows, which knocked against everything in his path, introducing ruin and chaos to any sort of order. The man whispered and cried, smearing dirt across his face. He was pitiful. He couldn't have been a soldier; he was hardly human. He appeared to be an underground dweller, someone who'd waited out the war in some cave, subsisting on worms and moss. Noah asked about this, expecting a firm denial, but the man only nodded rapidly, and went on whispering details, spittle spraying from his mouth. He talked about the long-abandoned subway tunnels, where the radiation may have been higher than on the Moon. About incredible monsters—three-headed rats and centipedes large as dogs. About how it was only yesterday, incredulous about the war having ended, this man and his fellow underground dwellers had crawled cautiously out into the city, ready to retreat to their caves at a moment's notice. Of course they were soaked with radiation and any counter would click like a machine gun in their presence.

There was an insistent knock at the door, and the man had immediately pressed himself to the floor. Noah winced in opprobrium and pointed him toward the closet.

He'd gone into the corridor, his chin held high and his shoulders spread wide. He'd counted the seconds, and his heart had felt so large that it had filled his entire self with its thunderous beating. The visitors at the door were Brotherhood, and Noah had recognized some of them: they weren't students, but people a little older. Inexperienced Noah had once confused them for workers, before he'd recognized their gangster mannerisms. He thought back to his childhood, the time not so long ago, spent in an industrial suburb where he'd absorbed his fill of radiation. He said: you're raving lunatics, and so is Friar Yakov, so go ahead and shoot. The air tasted nectarous and thick after those words, and for a brief while—fifteen seconds or so—Noah had felt truly alive. Later he'd tried to recall this feeling and to replicate it, but couldn't.

The raving lunatics had waved their radiation counters, which had emitted only a handful of clicks, had glanced inside the room, and had gone away.

In the morning, Noah had kicked the underground dweller out, and then ripped up his Brotherhood membership card.

Friar Yakov had delivered a speech—a convincing and clear speech, unlike the current Premier's recycled words—letting everyone know that it was the golems responsible for the pogroms and the murders. Golems, whose artificial minds had rebelled and thirsted for war and blood. That it was the golems who'd walked around with carbide lamps in hand and killed innocent people. His words had been confirmed by multiple eyewitnesses. Noah was surprised to recognize the underground dweller he had saved among them.

The people had trusted Friar Yakov's words. He was impossible not to believe. He'd rapidly risen from the leader of a little-known society to the leader of our small remnant of humanity. Golems had become enemies overnight, and we'd accepted that. For some, it had been easier to accept the manufacturing flaw in artificial people than the possibility of existing in complete and definitive equality with them. Others—Noah among them—had simply kept quiet, stunned by the absurdity of what was happening around them but unable or unwilling to try to change anything. That is when Noah had realized it was a good thing that he'd never got to go to war, that there was no place in war for a coward like him. He wasn't worthy.

• • •

On Friday, pain woke Noah up. He squeezed the tin pilot in his bandaged hand. Blood had soaked through the bandage, turning the pilot red.

He felt Masha the Mouse's gaze on his back. She wasn't sleeping, either.

He turned toward her. Masha lay on her side, her hair crumpled by the pillow, her eyes puffy. Noah gently traced his finger across her milky-white stomach. Masha seemed to be pleased by this gesture; she pressed Noah's hand tight with her small, warm palm.

What would happen to her if Noah turns out to be a golem? He didn't want to think about it. Not now.

In recent days Masha became distant, cold, alien. But now, lying silently next to her and looking into her gray eyes, Noah felt happy.

• • •

Some days, one can feel like they can do anything.

On Friday morning Noah was certain he was heading to work, until he found himself on a winding street in the eastern suburb, not far from the orphanage where he had spent his childhood.

The weather was nice. Fresh snow had fallen, and Noah's boots crunched pleasantly against the prickly black coating on the ground. Noah hadn't been here in a decade. He often saw this area in his dreams, but in a dream it was filled with nonexistent details, scents, and sounds.

These real streets were more gray and bland than how Noah remembered them. Moreover, they were totally empty. Like all manufacturing towns serving the war effort, this neighborhood was dying a slow and lonely death, covered in black snow and permeated with radiation.

Still, his trip was a lot like his dreams. Noah felt the same unjustified high, the same ease and self-confidence. The same thoughts raced through his mind as those in the dreams about his childhood.

The orphanage was around the corner. The once-red brick walls had turned black over time. This was no dream. In the dream, everything remained the same. Staring at this hopeless darkness, Noah realized that he, too, had irrevocably changed over the years, and not for the better. At twenty-eight he was an old man from the point of view of the youngster who'd sought adventures and secrets in the basement bar. As useless as those factory workers who had beaten up the poor vagrant who'd made the mistake of pretending to be a golem. Those workers had long perished from radiation and other hazards they'd been exposed to in the factories. Their lives at least had had meaning. Perhaps not as much as that of Noah's father, but they'd spent their lives in the service of our victory.

What had Noah done with his life? Wasted years at the university and his embarrassing time as a member of the Brotherhood? A routine job he barely understood at the lab, the point of which was known only to the scientific director—assuming it wasn't just busywork the director had invented in the first place?

Midlife crisis struck Noah with its merciless hammer. He had stood in this very spot aged seventeen, filled with hope, and the great path he had embarked upon had turned out to be pointless. If he had to look his seventeen-year-old self in the eye now, Noah would die of embarrassment.

And yet. Yet.

He had seen the sun once—a few rays, for all of five minutes. They said this was the result of the work his lab was doing, among others. Which meant one of those rays belonged to Noah.

He had experienced love, such that the past infatuations seemed little more to him than playing with toy soldiers reminded real soldiers of an actual war.

He'd never become a hero, never become a pilot, but he was a person. He remembered his gray, worthless, empty life, which was more than any golem could boast.

Noah climbed over the fence and found himself on the concrete grounds that surrounded the black orphanage building.

The windows were boarded up, the door handles wrapped in thick lengths of chain. Noah remembered that he had seen all of this in his dreams. There, he easily ripped the chains and walked in like he owned the place. Noah carefully tried the door, heard something reply with a dull echo from behind it.

He walked around the building. To the left of the back door there was a special window, which Noah had often used to climb outside in his dreams.

The window was there, sloppily boarded up crosswise. Noah ripped off the boards and kicked in the glass. The window was too small for an adult, but Noah made it through, scratching his arms and leaving strips of cloth on the frames. His palm was bleeding again.

Noah clicked a lighter and discovered that the basement hardly resembled the one he had recalled, the one from his dreams. As though it had experienced its own small, ruthless private war. The bare concrete walls had been burned, the floor was covered in splinters and rubbish, the rusted boiler in the corner was split in two by a crack. Dust was everywhere. How had the dust gotten in? Noah hadn't seen it in years. The dust seemed to have disappeared, finally and irrevocably, after the war.

Noah walked down the dark, dead corridor, trying to recall the times he had walked here as a teenager, the times he'd greeted his friends and planned an upcoming prank or exchanged treasures found beyond the fence.

He couldn't recall anything like that. Memory served up only the familiar pictures, but those pictures didn't match with what he was seeing in real life. It was as though pieces of several different jigsaw puzzles were mixed in a single box.

The dust finally caused Noah to sneeze. A floorboard squeaked underfoot, and this familiar, sharp squeak scraped against his memory like a knife against glass.

A flare to his left. And Noah saw number nine, who'd lost his entire arm on the Moon. The new arm hung limp and irritated number nine terribly. And there he is, trying to learn to hold a cigarette with it.

Number twenty-two is walking toward him, an invalid's cane in hand. His leg drags—a foreign, disobedient leg. He must walk, move, so that the dead artificial leg can become living and real. Number thirteen, the captain, smokes by the window. His sad eyes stare at the factory smoke outside, as though they see something no one else does.

They're all young, seventeen at most. They're all old men, veterans returned from the war they went to fight two years ago as children. Even if they were tin children and not real ones.

The next door leads to his hospital room. There should be a handwritten sign above the bed made in a crooked, wounded handwriting. The sign reads, "We'll return home." It's still there.

It was here—under this bed, under the sign—Noah, who had been called number seven then, found the little tin toy soldier, a pilot, left there by another veteran. By a real person.

• • •

The Brotherhood meeting traditionally took place in the Chinese Room of the art museum. The museum had been almost completely destroyed during the war, but this room had miraculously survived. Noah has been here a couple of times—nearly a decade ago. Chinese art remained the same: dead and beautiful. Calligraphy sang absolutes to him from the walls. Sometimes Noah thought that if only he would learn Chinese, the multifaceted and all-embracing meaning of life would reveal itself to him.

Noah came here because he had no choice. Having left the hospital he'd spent a decade thinking of as an orphanage, Noah scooped some black snow into his wounded palm and watched snowflakes melt in his blood. He pictured himself appearing in this museum room, looking everyone in the eye, only to see fear. The man Noah had been that morning could've run. To the dead ocean, to the underground subway labyrinths. The man could run, but not the golem.

After the Night of Unmasking friars had stormed the scientific archive where they'd hoped to find the personal dossiers of the golems and their names. They'd found nothing. Noah often wondered: how would all this end if Friar Pavel hadn't appeared with the blueprints for the Machine—the unholy device that, according to its creator, could differentiate between human and golem? What went through the head of the still-young man when he invented this insidious device? What must pass through a person's head for them to invent the hunt? This was probably beyond a golem's ability to comprehend.

Noah had heard a lot about the hunt. Snippets of conversations, rumors, and fabrications. But also one reliable account: an enthusiastic story by his colleague Naum, a dedicated member of the Brotherhood. Naum himself eventually turned out to be a golem and became yet another victim of the Machine.

Naum had said that playing cards would be dealt. So it was; Noah received a ten of clubs. It looked like nothing special, but today this was the Most Important Card. Why a ten? Why clubs? Even on an evening like this he was denied the chance to be a king.

Then, Naum had told him, grab some wine, engage in conversation with intelligent people, enjoy life. Be sure to sample the spinach-filled tartlets. The tartlets were served, but Noah declined to try them. He was a wound-up spring, an electron that required movement. He found it impossible to chew, to drink, to stand still. He walked and walked across the room, searching people's faces. He was looking for unpleasant traits, for a reason to hate them.

These were ordinary faces, sometimes even familiar ones. Open, clear, simple faces. Devoid of villainy and fear. Most, like Noah, had come here for the first time, or hadn't been here in a while. They looked around, hoping to catch a glimpse of the Machine.

Noah looked around as well. Was it hidden under the floor or in the adjacent room? They said the machine was as inconvenient to use as the idea of equality between people and golems was inconvenient to hear. It was too large to be mobile. Too delicate to work with a large crowd. Too sensitive not to become overwhelmed by extreme emotions.

That's why the Premier found Friar Pavel's idea so clever: to make the golems come to it. And yes, they came. Each one certain that someone else would turn out to be a golem. Noah understood this certainty: that very morning his memory was human, was real and indisputable. But he couldn't understand their desire to watch a living being perish inside a trap, even if it was only a golem. Friar Yakov understood this. He may not have known science, but he was an expert on human nature.

How did the Machine work? What did it measure? Rumors had it the Machine could detect the presence of a soul. A soul that each human would have and each golem obviously would not. Friar Pavel, the creator of the Machine, neither confirmed nor denied such rumors.

Friar Yakov approached the podium. The curtain was pulled back and revealed an alcove where the Machine stood, enormous and grandiose like a pipe organ.

Noah took a step back when he saw it. He felt ill. He kept waiting for the feeling he had experienced during the Night of Unmasking to return. Waited for the air to become nectarous and thick, so he could inhale deeply of it before he died. Instead, he felt only nausea and heat.

Not knowing what to do with his hands, Noah shoved them into his pockets. He felt for his tin pilot with the face of a golem in the left pocket. He retrieved it and squeezed it in his fist.

Friar Yakov waved, calling for silence.

"Let us begin, my friends. This is a special evening. It marks the beginning of our future. The future of true humanity. The future without golems. You, the last golem, hear me." Friar Yakov paused, looking around the room. For nearly a second, he looked straight at Noah. "You don't yet know your fate, and I pity you. But you must die, so that we can finally be rid of our past. Be rid of war. Be rid of pain. Be strong and hold your head up high, soldier."

A low, barely audible whistle emanated from the walls. The Machine behind Friar Yakov crackled to life.

Noah thought that, upon hearing the whistling sound, the friars stepped aside, as though to clear the path between Noah and the Machine. But this wasn't the case. Everyone froze in their place.

The whistling ended as abruptly as it had begun. The Machine clinked as it spat a playing card through a small slot in its wooden frame. Friar Yakov collected the card without looking at it. He has done this many times before and, yes, he derived pleasure from the experience.

Friar Yakov grinned slyly, dragging out the pause like a host from some old show. Finally, he flipped the card over, and frowned. He retrieved his glasses and put them on, deliberately slow.

This irritated Noah terribly. The damned old man was making some sort of spectacle out of his impending death. Noah was ready to step forward and end the show, when two junior friars approached Yakov. One of them collected the card from Friar Yakov's hand and another copy of the same card from his jacket pocket. It was the king of spades.

Two identical cards. This meant the Machine had declared the Premier to be the last golem. Impossible. Nonsense. He was the only one present, perhaps the only one in the entire town, who couldn't possibly be a golem. He was too old, and too human.

"This is some sort of a mistake," said Friar Yakov. He forced a smile. "Where's Pavel? Summon him."

Immediately, Friar Pavel appeared. The omnipresent, deft, raven-haired Pavel.

"There's no mistake," he said in the same respectful tone he always used when speaking to the Premier. "The Machine doesn't make mistakes."

The Premier looked around, seeking his assistants. They were there, but looked up indifferently and didn't move.

"What are you saying? How could I be a golem? I was never even at the front."

"Everyone says that. Absolutely everyone. Hold your head up high, Premier."

"Arrest him! I'm putting an end to this farce!"

No one listened to the Premier. They twisted his arms, shook him roughly, crumpled his jacket, took him away. Friar Pavel threw up his hands, as if to announce that the show was over. The room was filled with noise, but that noise was almost devoid of bewilderment, as if everyone had expected such an outcome.

Friar Pavel's gaze met Noah's and he nodded, smiling in a warm and friendly manner. And Noah's crippled memory suddenly responded to this smile: Noah recognized him. Friar Pavel was the captain of his flight squad. Number thirteen was older now, his brow wrinkled, his black hair showing touches of gray. But his gaze was the same: as though he saw something no one else did.

Without yet understanding anything himself, Noah smiled back. He drew in a deep breath. The air was nectarous and thick.

Noah thought about Masha the Mouse. He'd refused to permit himself to think about her when he'd come here, but now everything was different. His mind, free from the shackles of false memories, finally sorted out an uncomplicated mosaic. How Masha had changed lately, how she had become distant and uncertain. She wasn't the first. Noah had heard about such cases, even if those were only rumors. A friend of a colleague of his ex-roommate; a wife of a young worker someone from the accounting department knew personally; some other women—nameless and strange, but surely beautiful in their unexpected fortune.

Let it be a boy, thought Noah. I'll give him the tin pilot so that one day he can give it to his own son.

JANELLE MONÁE AND ALAYA DAWN JOHNSON

THE MEMORY LIBRARIAN

(2022)

THE LIGHTS OF LITTLE DELTA are spread before Seshet like an offering in a shallow bowl. What memories are those shadows below making tonight, to ripen for the morning harvest? What tragedies, what indecencies, what hungers never satisfied? Her office is dark, but the city's neat grids cut across her face with a surgical precision, cheek bisected from mandible, eye parted from eye, the fine lines of her forehead, so faintly visible, separated from their parallel tracks by the white light cast up from her city. She is the eye in the obelisk, the Director Librarian, the "queen" of Little Delta. But she prefers to see herself as a mother, and the city as her charge.

Tonight, her charge is restless. Something has been wrong for weeks, perhaps even months before she knew what to look for. But now that she does, she will find it, and fix it. She always has, ever since her appointment as Director Librarian of the Little Delta Repository a decade ago. She has earned her privileges, her title, her sweeping view of this small gem of a city. From up here, it fits in her palm. Its memories span her eidetic synapses. Unnoticed by her conscious, monitoring mind, her left fingers close into a fist, thumb tucked inside the others like a baby behind his brothers.

Seshet *is* this city. No matter what rebellion is being conjured by infiltrating subconsciouses, no matter what flood of mnemonic subversion clogs the proper flow of pure, fresh memory—she will not let it go.

• • •

The problem can be typified in a few of the memories, which are not, blasphemously, any kind of memories at all. Imagine the following bread-and-butter (or beans-and-cornbread) moments, the kind the recollection centers shunt to the Repository's data banks by the shovelful: a flash of rage when the fancy razor-striped aircar drafts you in traffic; the quotidian beauty of a sunset bleeding behind a kudzu-choked highway barrier; your lover's kiss when she climbs back into bed in the middle of the night (and where was she? But you never ask). Now, though, the car cracks down the middle, chassis splintering like an eggshell, coolant arcing from its descending airpipe in a shape suspiciously suggestive of an upright penis; a flock of crows rise from the barrier and fling themselves west, cackling a song banned a generation ago for indecency and subversion; your lover's teeth puncture your lower lip and as your mouth fills with blood and venom she whispers, *I'm not the only one.*

These aren't memories, they just look enough like them to get past the filter. And once past, they fill the trawling net with bycatch and rusted junk until there's no room left for the good stuff. Fresh memory, wild caught in the clear upstream of Little Delta, has kept this town booming ever since the first days of New Dawn's glorious revolution. What used to be a dying mining town at the whip end of the Rust Belt, home to a motley assortment of drug addicts moonlighting as grafiteros and performance artists, became the model city, the first realization of the promise that New Dawn offered all people—well, citizens (well, the right kind of citizens)—in their care: beauty in order, peace in rigidity, and tranquility in a constant, sun-dappled present. The only person lower than a memory hoarder was a dirty computer, and that Venn diagram was very nearly a circle.

But the improved Little Delta doesn't have memory hoarders; it kicked the grafiteros and unsanctioned musicians out past the burned warehouse district twenty years back, even before Seshet's tenure. There's been nothing, *nothing* to indicate a problem in their memory surveillance for years. Until two months ago. First a few blips, barely worth worrying about, odd nightmares accidentally caught in their nets. Now, so quickly it dizzies her, the trickle has become a flood. No one has mentioned it to her, but someone must have noticed. New Dawn is watching. Not just Little Delta. Not just the Repository. Seshet herself. If she cannot stop these new memory hoarders, these false memory flooders, these dream doctors, these *terrorists*—she will not last much longer in this place she has fought so hard to secure.

She doesn't believe in everything New Dawn stands for. How could she, being who she is? But she believes she has done good. The obelisk's gaze has been mostly benevolent in her tenure here. And whatever she believes of herself, this she *knows*: whoever they put in her place will be far worse.

Stomach clenched, eyes bright, as though determination is the sole topography of her soul, she turns herself away—a lifetime's habit—from the mountain of guilt beneath that white-tipped iceberg. She won't let them beat her, not after she's played the game by their own rules and won.

She has allowed her mind to be altered and trained, made capable of remembering a hundred times more than the average human's. But among all those clamoring souls within her cage of bone, it is that slippery whisper that pushes itself to the forefront:

I'm not the only one.

• • •

A knock on the door. Seshet does not answer. But she changes: shoulders back, chin up, unacknowledged despair tucked neatly behind a steady, measured gaze. Seshet the matron, Seshet the Librarian, Seshet the wise, worthy of her divine Egyptian namesake, the goddess of wisdom and memory. She's been Director for long enough to know to look the part. Even on the other side of the door, the presence of someone else summons this woman she has made herself from the more amorphous frontier of the woman she might, in fact, be.

"Someone's here, Seshet!" chirps Dee, so helpfully. "Would you like to retrieve their memories?"

She sighs. She never has the heart to shut down her Memory Keeper AI at night, though there's nothing for Dee to do before the morning rush and its processors require impressive amounts of energy even when semidormant. Dee doesn't like to shut down, though. It enjoys having time to think. *Or time to bust my cover,* Seshet thinks sourly.

"That's okay, Dee," Seshet says. "I already know his memories." Her outward calm is a counterweight to the turmoil inside her. Twenty years as one of New Dawn's few Black women officials, suspected from the start of being halfway to dirty computer no matter how unimpeachable her conduct, has forged her like steel, with just the right amount of carbon to bend but not shatter.

She presses a button on her desk and the door slides back into the wood-paneled wall. Jordan stands in the opening, his hand still poised midknock. The hallway light limns him in a halo that makes her squint.

"In the dark again, Director Seshet?"

She sucks her teeth. "Come in, if you're going to. I don't like so much light at night."

"Yes, yes," he says, at the same time as she does, "It ruins my vision."

She smiles, softening as always with her favorite protégé. The door slides shut and she regards him in the hazy pixelated vision of half-dilated pupils. Dee, stubbornly independent as always, turns the ambients to their lowest setting. Jordan's changed for the evening into his street clothes: khaki chinos, blue button-down, loafers. White-boy chic for New Dawn's golden age. A model citizen, so long as no one asks him his number and knows what those final digits mean: child of seditionists and traitors, ward of the state, a charity case, eternally suspect.

Seshet has no such recourse to camouflage, fragile as it is. These days, she will leave the grounds in the full golden headdress and robes of office. She has determined to embrace her distance instead of constantly hoping for an acceptance that will never be theirs. But Jordan is young.

"What are you still doing here, Jordan? Go home. Sleep. Forget about this place for a while."

"Is that a joke?" When Jordan scowls, he looks even younger than his years, enough to make her want to hug him or slap him. Do parents feel this way? Do they ever want to shake that insufferable innocence from their children? Had his? Had hers? But now the thought veers into dangerous waters and she perches on the edge of her desk to hide the wave of weakness in her legs.

"Memory Librarian humor," says Seshet, deadpan. After a moment, Jordan cracks a smile.

"You should too," he says. "Get some sleep, I mean."

"I'm fine, Jordan. I'm your superior, remember? You don't have to worry about us."

He takes a step farther into the room and then pauses, as though the force of her solitary preoccupation prevents him from getting closer.

He tries to reach her with words instead. "Something's wrong."

For a moment, as she watches his sad face in the low light, a fist closes over her heart. *This is it, they've gotten to him, he's noticed the false memories and he's snitched, you knew this would happen, you knew—*

Then sense returns and she takes a careful, steadying breath. Did Jordan notice anything? Oh, he's staring at her, that worried frown even deeper now, a ravine between his eyebrows. She wants to smooth it away. She wants to tell him to leave her alone and never return.

"What's . . . wrong?" she manages, at last. *You're slipping, Seshet. Gotten too comfortable up here.*

He straightens his shoulders. "You're working yourself ragged, Director! Anyone can see it."

Her voice is thin. "Oh, can they?"

He shakes his head. "You hide it well, but I've noticed, and so have the other clerks. We see you too often not to know the signs."

"I appreciate the warning, Jordan. I should be grateful you're all watching me so closely. Perhaps I should go in for Counseling soon."

"Counseling? The Director Librarian? Director, of course I'm not—"

"If my *obvious* mental state is impeding my work here, then clearly my duty is to—"

"I'm not talking about your duty, Seshet!"

Her name, bare of its title, cracks in the air like a slap. After an astonished blink, she raises her eyebrows. His muddy green eyes meet hers for a second, but he breaks like a twig beneath the full force of that practiced gaze.

"I'm . . . my apologies, Director."

She sighs, looks away herself. She hates these games, their necessity. Especially with Jordan. She's protected him ever since his initiation five years ago. One Librarian misfit ought to watch out for another, she thought.

"Tell me what's bothering you, Jordan."

"I just wish you'd get out more. See the city."

"I'm seeing the city right now."

"*In* the city, not above it."

"I'm the Director Librarian." She gives her title every ounce of demanded weight. To her surprise, he meets her eyes again. He's brave, and she loves him for it, fiercely as a mother lion.

"There's a woman I know. Friend of a friend. I think you'll really like her, Director. I think . . . maybe you could finally find a companion. A friend."

Dangerous ground, again. She has hinted things to Jordan over the years, but never said anything that could be held against her if his memories were monitored—and all their memories are monitored.

"I have friends," she says.

"Who?"

She swallows. "You. Dee. Arch-Librarian Terry."

Jordan checks them off on his fingers. "Your clerk, your Memory Keeper AI, and your immediate superior? That's not a partner. Or a lover."

Careful, Jordan. Steel in her voice. "What would you know about that?"

Jordan holds his ground. "More than you think."

The moment hangs there, two swords locked in battle. She shakes her head. Her heart is pounding too quickly.

"Jordan," she says softly, "I'm going to have to suppress this."

"I know. I don't care. I needed to tell you. I'm worried about you, Director. I wish you could feel again what it's like out there, in the world."

"Who feels it more than me? I have their memories."

"But Seshet," he says. This time her solitary name touches her like a caress. "What about your own?"

• • •

Little Delta's downtown spans five blocks of shops, restaurants, bars, and clubs, each one duly approved by New Dawn's Chamber of Standards. It has the reputation of being small but well curated, and on the weekends people from several towns over fill the adjacent parking lots to reward themselves for their hard workweek in Standards-approved fashion. There are always lines outside the commercial memory recollectors on weekend nights, crowds eager to exchange a few memories for points to top off their cards and buy another round.

Seshet moves steadily through the crowd, hoping for at least medium anonymity. No one would expect the Director Librarian to be out among the citizens of her city on a Friday night, let alone looking for the newest bar on Hope Street. Jordan selected her clothes himself: "Fashionable, but not trendy. Not calling attention to yourself, but not hiding either."

Seshet had sighed. "A Black woman in the business district in better clothes than theirs? I couldn't hide if I wanted to." The moment held. These weren't things normally stated aloud.

Her clerk, who looked like the chosen of New Dawn but would never fit easily in their tight folds, gave her a faint, bitter smile. "No," he said. "That's why you have to hide under a spotlight."

Perhaps that explained the navy-blue beret he'd put at a rakish angle over her close-cut hair. It was the finishing touch of an ensemble designed to make people pay more attention to her clothes than her face.

A group of loutish young men standing outside a crowded beer garden pay too much attention, giving her stares hard enough to break bones. She hurries past them, shoulders back, face slightly averted, as they laugh and elbow one another. Her heart starts to race, triggered by somatic memory, ancestor-rooted and atavistic, beyond erasure, even for the cleaners at the Temple. "Hey!" one of them calls. She ignores him. The map on her chronoband says the bar is just at the end of the block.

More laughter, pointed as barbed wire. "Hey, you! Hey, Librarian Seshet!"

She freezes for a fraction of a second, jerks her head sharply toward them: a blur of pastel-shirted white boys, folded over, eyes squinting as though in pain, lips puckered, "Seshet, Director Librarian!" the joker calls, emboldened by his fellows. "Give me a good memory tonight, won't you?"

Does she recognize him? Would she know his memories from the thousands that crowd her mind? But shock and fear prevent her access to them as cleanly as a lungful of Nevermind. She does not know anyone. She does not recognize anything. Only luck breaks the spell: a woman from the next table over—Taiwanese American, architect, midthirties, went through Counseling last year after a tough breakup, hardly remembers her ex any longer, so Seshet does for her—swings toward the men and bangs her pint on the table hard enough for the maple-tinted foam to spill over the sides. "Leave her alone, you assholes!"

At first Seshet wonders if the architect is defending her out of gratitude. Then she remembers that they have never actually met. One of the Standards Authorities on the block belatedly approaches the men and they back away, laughing with a kind of sheepish bravado that she's only ever witnessed in young white men. A beat too late, she understands: They don't know who she is at all. They just saw *what* she is, and for them that was more than enough. Seshet nods with chilly dignity to the architect (she ignores the Standards Authority, laughing with the boys even as he issues a warning) and resumes a steady, even stride. She swings her arms so her hands won't betray that ghostly rattle in her heart. She *is* the Director Librarian, after all, though they would never believe it. She will keep her head high until the day they take it off her shoulders.

She is carrying herself just like that, sharp as a hawk, graceful as a jaguar, dignified as a goddess, when she strides into Hope Street's trendiest new establishment and sees her.

Her: a lone woman, legs crossed, quietly sipping a drink chlorophyll-green at the end of a long chrome bar, heart-stoppingly beautiful. Seshet has never seen her before, not even in her city's memories. She knows anyway. *Her*. The one who wields the executioner's ax. The one who will make Seshet bow before she falls.

• • •

Her name is Alethia 56934. Her number indicates a known deviance, but also that she has been cleared for full reintroduction to society. She came to Little

Delta four years ago. "I needed a new start," she says, grimacing in that way that hints at a story but warns Seshet off from asking about it. "I got lucky when Pinkerton Cosmetics had a chemist position open up."

"And your number . . ." Seshet lets the sentence dangle. Alethia's open expression turns professionally neutral with a speed that hits Seshet in the gut. But she had to ask. Someone from New Dawn might see them together.

"I'm trans," Alethia says, in a clipped, matter-of-fact way. "Cleared years ago. Is that a problem?"

Seshet wants to crawl under the bar and hide. "No! Of course not! It's just, I'm the Director—" But of course Jordan would have told her that. Seshet's words stick like seed pods in her mouth.

Alethia's laughter is bitter, intoxicating as gin. "We all make our compromises." She leans forward. "Tell me something more interesting. Tell me why you came here."

Seshet frowns. Her heart is pounding so fast it's a wonder she doesn't pass out. Her hand reaches for her drink—impossibly, luridly blue, with a name like "indigo flame"—and she drains half of it in a gulp. It tastes like orangey seaweed. "To Little Delta?" she asks.

Alethia nods encouragingly. Seshet clears her throat and takes a deep, steadying breath. No one has ever affected her like this before, not even her first lover twenty years ago, when they were both novice Librarians, clean and freshly purged of their pasts, ready to make their newest memories with one another.

"I was assigned here," she finally says. "Eighteen years ago." Half a lifetime ago. Long enough to watch the steady grid, the illuminated heart of the reformed town, expand beneath the obelisk's warmly glowing spire.

"Do you like it here?"

She stares at the woman: thick eyebrows, light brown skin, cheekbones to chisel stone, lower lip fuller than the top. "Like . . . it?"

Those eyebrows draw together, humorously confused. "As a place to live?"

"Oh." There is a mole on Alethia's left earlobe, easy to see because she wears no earrings. Seshet wants to kiss it. She wants to take it between her teeth and tug. "It's where all my memories are. I couldn't leave even if I had the choice."

She realizes, a hard drop of a second later, that she's implied a state secret that would mean instant disciplinary action if discovered. Luckily, Alethia looks more confused than ever and Seshet finds her tongue again. She asks Alethia what she does at her job, and discovers she spends all day in a lab coat mixing skin creams. Seshet tries to come up with ways to flirtatiously compliment Alethia's perfect skin—maybe *But I bet you don't need any of it*? She winces. *Director Librarian and still such a cornball, Seshet.* She is awkward as a teenager, mute as a memory hoarder. Her tongue feels wet and heavy in her mouth. Why is a woman like this even talking to her? Smiling, as if she sees something inside her that Seshet has long since lost track of?

Seshet finishes her drink.

"Would you like another?" Alethia asks.

Her expression is solicitous but neutral, and yet Seshet catches the faintest whiff of a side eye. For the first time that evening, she feels herself loosen up.

She lifts the heavy square cocktail glass, a tide pool of melted ice clinging to the bottom among fat drifts of blue-green pulp. She meets Alethia's caramel-brown eyes, and, as an answering spark from a fire so deeply banked she had not known it still smoldered, Seshet laughs.

"I would like," she says, "to take you to a place with better drinks."

• • •

Alethia knows just the one: a dive bar called Cousin Skee's on the far east side, just one block from the old Woolworth Building that marks the frontier of Old Town with its dirty artist squats and dirtier crack houses. Cleared and abandoned now, according to Standards, but Seshet's seen too many memories of clandestine, rebellious activities over that darkened border to believe them. She wonders what Alethia knows about that warren of gap-toothed buildings dressed in garish primary colors, graffiti streaming like skirts at the edge of broken sidewalks. The poised, immaculate woman who greeted her at that hopeless Hope Street cocktail bar should be as out of place here as Seshet is, but the man behind the bar calls out "Lethe!" as soon as they open the door and greets her with a fist bump.

"Where you been, girl?" he asks, reaching without hesitation for the cocktail shaker by the sink. He takes an unmarked bottle with a cheap plastic spout, mixes that clear liquid with the contents of three other unmarked bottles, throws in some ice and starts shaking, all in the time it takes for Alethia to give him a sweet smile that stings Seshet down to the tenderest points of the soles of her feet.

"Working, Skee," says Alethia, sounding at once nothing like the woman at the trendy bar and even more impossibly herself. "You know the drill."

"Looks like you've got a good thing going," he says, taking in her designer shoes and purse at a glance. Alethia just shrugs.

Skee's hard expression softens. He pours the drink with a flourish and pushes it across the bar.

"One mar-Skee-rita, on the house."

Alethia grimaces. "You still trying to call it that?"

"What you mean, *trying*? Been its name since back when you started—"

"And ain't no one but you called it that in all that time," says Alethia, leaning onto the bar with a strange smile, hard as glass. Skee stops short. At last, he glances at Seshet. He seems to sum her up and dismiss her in one swallow: *You may be Black, but you aren't one of us.* He doesn't know who she is. But he can smell what.

"And for your friend?"

Seshet perches on the bar stool, listing slightly to the side. "A mar-Skee-rita, please," she says, diction crisp as fresh linen.

Alethia lets out a surprised yelp of laughter. Seshet shivers. Skee grins. "That'll be ten points."

"Hard currency?" she asks, because she is who she is, and here on that hard edge between new order and old chaos, she wants to know.

Skee gives her a long look. So does Alethia, hooded and opaque, as though there is another woman entirely sharing space behind those wide brown eyes. Seshet itches to know what memories underlie that cold inspection, that easy laughter, that gentle smile, but for now—until she gets back to the obelisk and their memory data banks—she has no way to know.

Skee turns from them with a shrug and starts making another drink. "Don't put recollection boxes all the way out here. Well, the check-cashing joint on the corner has one, works sometimes."

That was true enough. Memory recollection boxes were sparser the farther out from the center you went. But on the border of Old Town, the ones they did have went out of service with surprising frequency. Someone was always damaging the headset or the router, and somehow the vandals' faces or their voices or their memories were never captured, not by drones or Standards Authorities or even automated street surveillance. She'd wondered about that over the years. But she knew who was most likely to live out here at the edge, and she never pushed for a deeper investigation. No one higher up in New Dawn had ever asked.

Seshet reaches into her wallet and pushes two five-point coins across the table.

Skee slides across the margarita, still frothy from the shaker.

Their gazes lock. She's good at this game of mutual evaluation, but she can't fully commit; she's too aware of Alethia's watchful curiosity beside her.

At last, Skee shrugs and cracks his neck. "You happen to work around that obelisk, Miz . . ."

Seshet allows herself a small smile. "You wouldn't want to know."

• • •

After midnight, the bar is overwhelmed with a new crowd, diverse in a way she's not used to seeing in downtown Little Delta (and certainly not in the corridors of the obelisk): the oldest must be in his seventies and the youngest still a teenager; all shades of brown, Black, and beige; men in dresses and women in sharp-cut suits and others who defy any gender categorization at all. She pretends not to notice. With New Dawn, any gender nonconformity is enough to get you a deviant code appended to your number—dirty computer, recommended for urgent cleaning—and she doesn't want to flag anyone tonight. Seshet recognizes some of them. They're still members of her flock, however wayward. Others are unrepentant memory hoarders, the kind who never so much as walk through downtown in case a drone recollector might land, light as a horsefly, on their temple and graze a few loose memories off the top while they're waiting for the light to change. She cares even for them, though they don't know it. The obelisk's eye, like any panopticon, gives only an illusion of omniscience—Seshet has made an art of selective gazing.

And now she is down in the dirty thick of it, watching and being watched in her turn, a sensation so unusual she keeps drinking just to dull the edge. Three mar-Skee-ritas in, Seshet finds she does not mind at all being one more in a crowd of hoarders and deviants. She hasn't gone in for memory collection herself in months—if anyone asked, she would have claimed work pressure, but no one has. The truth is that Seshet enjoys the sensation of memory hoarding, that sweet, leftover-Halloween-candy feeling of keeping something back for herself, however temporary. The new crowd is high on some kind of drug, singing songs she's never heard of in harmony, finishing one another's sentences. One of them, a light-skinned boy who reminds her of someone she can't place, wearing a baseball cap with a stencil of an old man with a star blowing out of his forehead, dances Seshet by the shoulders and stares into her eyes as though he can see straight into her memory-scoured soul. He laughs and says something that might be "full" or "bull"—the music the new crowd has brought with them is so loud—and then spins away from her. He freezes when he spots Alethia, turning at that moment from the pool table where she's just sunk another shot. Alethia raises her eyebrows. He opens his mouth and then closes it. Alethia gives him a brief shrug that seems to mean *Sorry I'm not who you thought I was* and goes back over to Seshet.

"How about," Alethia shouts into her ear, as intimate and low-voiced as a whisper, "we go back to my place?"

And now Seshet doesn't care about anything at all—not memory hoarders or memory flooders or who this motley crowd could be and the fact that they almost certainly washed over the border from some forbidden party in Old Town. For now she isn't Seshet, Director Librarian, distant queen of Little Delta.

She is a woman, softened with drink, unburdened by memory, warm skin touching warm skin, and she wants more.

• • •

Alethia's place: one-bedroom apartment a fifteen-minute walk away in an anonymous residential building for young professionals without the money—or the number—for something better. There is a memory recollector in the lobby with signs of modest use (Seshet doesn't mean to notice this, but she does). The apartment is beige: carpet, couch, wallpaper. The photographs on the walls are luridly colored but minimalist in design: flowers, balloons, fishing boats in Bangkok. The kind of apartment that has no gaze, no stamp of ownership, only the vague notion of what others might imagine to be tasteful. It fits the modest cosmetic chemist she met on Hope Street, but it's nothing like the savvy, laugh-like-a-machete Alethia she met at Cousin Skee's. In the bedroom, Seshet finally finds her: a lipstick-red bedspread hitting her eye like Alethia's secret smile, just that tantalizing hint of *someone else*—and Seshet lets that analytical part of her unspool again, to rest in exhausted tangles. She might be the Director Librarian, but without this woman's memories stored in her head, they are just two humans learning together in the most old-fashioned of ways. It rubs against her nerves like salt water on a dirty wound, but there is peace in this ignorance too, a thrill of discovery, a joy.

"There's something about you," Alethia says, holding Seshet's temples between her palms and kissing her with slow, devastating deliberation. "I know I've never met you before, and it's like you've already moved in, you're already making room."

They fall on top of that crimson slash in the beige. They burrow into one another, discover what's beneath.

• • •

Jordan and Billie are in the clerks' office when Seshet comes in the next day, immaculately attired and five minutes late. All New Dawn–affiliated offices work half days on Saturdays, but most aren't as strict about it as the Repository. In any case, Seshet can't remember the last time she's enjoyed a day off. Jordan slouches and lowers the visor on his headset, as though deep in this morning's catch. Billie grins and raises her eyebrows until they meet her hairline. Seshet pretends not to notice. She loves Jordan, but he's an inveterate gossip and Billie is his best friend among the clerks. Seshet should have known he'd tell. She asks if they have her morning report. Jordan, still from behind his visor, says he's flagged some suspicious elements and he'll have that in her workspace in another twenty minutes. Seshet acknowledges him with a nod that he probably can't see and heads sedately into the hallway, as though she has no desire to move faster than a parade float. The door to her office slides open to the sound of her voice stating the passkey and then she is inside, at last, alone.

Her breath shivers inside her lungs like dry leaves in a fall wind. She presses the heels of her palms to aching eyes. She's had three hours of sleep. She'd regret even those wasted moments if not for the memory she savors now, blasphemous as a child, just for herself: Alethia's face painted obelisk gold in the morning light, lipstick and mascara smudged across the pillowcase, eyes half-open even in sleep, hands reaching across the sheets, palms up. In that pin-drop moment, Seshet understood that she had come to the crossroads and left them behind. Her life has found a bifurcation as profound as any initiation the elders of New Dawn could devise: Seshet before Alethia, Seshet now.

And even so, her worries are just where she left them last night.

"Seshet," says Dee. The big monitor to the right of the desk lights up. A face appears there slowly, as though approaching from a dark tunnel. "Seshet? Are we in trouble, Seshet?"

Dee scrunches its large, uncanny eyes, blue as the Caribbean Sea. Its features are Seshet's reflected in a fun house mirror, distorted by time, by memory, by choice. The girl Seshet had been hated her dun-brown irises, longed for them to be the blue of the dolls in the store and the children in her headset. No one on the programs had her dark skin or kinky hair. That girl had longed for braids with beads at the bottom that clicked when she walked. She'd longed for eyes so blue they'd glow like the sky, even at night.

They purged these memories during Seshet's initiation, of course. But after a decade, once she ascended to rank, the elders gave them back to her: the lost memories of a lost woman. Until then, Seshet hadn't so much as remembered her old name. At Vice Director rank, she was authorized for a Memory Keeper AI, potentiated on whatever seed memories she chose. She gave it that lost woman's childhood, someone to keep those memories that no longer felt like her own.

"Why would we be in trouble, Dee?" Seshet asks calmly. Dee doesn't do well when Seshet is visibly upset.

"There's even more of those funny half dreams this morning. I like them, but I don't think Terry does."

Terry, Arch-Librarian for the entire Midwest region, and her immediate superior. A hand clamps around her gut and squeezes. She's going to be sick. The moment passes. With a hiccupping breath, she goes to her workstation in an alcove by the monitor and settles into the leather chair. Jordan and the clerks call it her throne. Not to her face, of course.

"What makes you think that?" she asks. Memory Keeper technology is the most advanced New Dawn has to offer. And it might as easily be called Memory Librarian Keeper. She knows this, has always known this. And yet, she has trusted Dee.

"Terry asked me for a report on the half dreams. And on you."

The headset with its golden geometry slides over her temples and clamps into the base of her neck. The net tightens over her skull, pressing until it passes the thick barrier of her hair and coolly touches her scalp. A familiar tickle of electrical engagement and her consciousness slides from the room, into deep memory space. The visor comes down last, and now Dee is right beside her, both child and disembodied consciousness, watching the floodplain of this morning's memory harvest.

"What did you tell him?" Her lips, which she can feel only with effort, don't move. Fully connected, there's no need for her to speak aloud.

"I told him that the half dreams come from all over the city, and many, many dreamers. I told him some were silly and some were beautiful. I told him I hope more people learn to play because it's more fun for me."

In the memory space, Seshet turns sharply to Dee, who holds its knobby knees to its chest. She's let her Memory Keeper AI have complete freedom for years. She's never pruned its personality or deviations. But she doubts Terry would have the same patience with Dee's eccentricities.

"And Terry asked me how you were," Dee continues. "I didn't want to tell him but I had to, you know, he glows even brighter than you do. So I told him in a poem! That was all right, wasn't it, Seshet?"

In her chair out in the world, Seshet's fingers trace the air. In memory space, she catches Jordan's report of anomalous activity and pushes it to the edge of the plain. She already knows what it says, and she knows that Terry does too. After all these years as Director Librarian for one of New Dawn's flagship cities, she understands very well how their world works. She aimed for unprecedented power when she was young and hungry, the token in their elite program. She's held on to it by being smarter than any of them. But she's no longer young, and now her hunger is for what she glimpsed in Alethia's eyes last night, not the next rung on New Dawn's golden ladder.

But that doesn't mean she wants to fall to the bottom either. "What was your poem, Dee?"

Never known love like this before
Except for last time
Someone I took for mine
Told me history couldn't rhyme
But don't get caught in the revolving door.

Dee pauses. Before them, one of last night's memories rises like a wave, crests, breaks.

"Was that okay, Seshet?" Dee asks just as the tide pulls them under.

"That was okay, Dee." She hopes.

• • •

There are dozens of variations of this one memory, like a symphony interpreted by different orchestras, the same recognizable piece layered with local color. It even begins with a song, heavy on the back beat, something Dee would like and Seshet finds gnawingly familiar. It's dark, and then the song explodes into brilliant chorus. Golden light spills all around them and burns where it falls. Are they fireworks? No, the light is coming from the obelisk itself. But not the views of it she knows, from the downtown business district or even the highway heading out of town. It's the view from the abandoned train station, from the warehouse district, from the derelict streets of Old Town. What has been her benevolent, watchful eye becomes a throbbing phallus, a malignant growth using the city for kindling as it burns. The light is coming for them, it's coming for them, *watch out, it's coming!*—that's the chorus to the song she couldn't possibly have heard before.

She's rising now, up and up, until she reaches the pyramidion of a shadowy obelisk, a dark spire to match the light. From this height, she can see the brightly lit streets of new Little Delta. People hurry to work or linger on sidewalks, gossip in cafés, play with their children. The Repository's most iconic structure belches like a furnace. Napalm, white-gold, rains down, hissing where it hits. But the citizens of Little Delta merely glance at it and smile. Around them, the city burns.

"Watch out!"

The memory voice is deep and hoarse with smoke. She senses that it's young and angry, but identity and emotion markers in a loose memory are notoriously unreliable. Let alone in one so clearly fabricated.

The obelisk has fully metamorphosed into its metaphoric counterpart now, a giant golden circumcised penis spitting white-gold ejaculate into the air like a pornographic Mount Vesuvius.

"Seshet! O Seshet!" that young man's voice says.

She has no body in the memory space, but she jerks inside her own mind. The force of it ought to stop the memory playback. But it has the inevitability of an avalanche now, bearing down on her like white fire through the streets of the city she has watched over for the past decade.

The chorus calls and responds, a propulsive chant in her ear: "Director Seshet! What have you done for us lately?"

"Seshet, the fire is coming!"

"Watch yourself!"

• • •

"My dearest Seshet, how delightful as always to see you."

Terry is sitting on a couch she recognizes from his office at New Dawn headquarters, a portable headset draped casually over one of the arms along with a pair of gaming gloves. His blue socks match his T-shirt, which looks new though it's the vintage merchandise of some decades-old pornographic anime (he likes it ironically).

He just popped onto her display screens in the middle of her lunch hour, all privacy codes summarily overridden. She was already sitting at her desk, preparing her reports. She does not startle or flinch when his voice comes over the speakers. She merely sets down her hand tablet and smiles.

This crisis might have caught her by surprise, but she is still Director Librarian of Little Delta, and the game of politics is in her bones.

Besides, she's always liked Terry.

"Wish I could say the same, Terry. Do you ever wear your robes?"

He laughs, which makes him look his age—at least sixty, though he tries to pass for an eternal horn-rimmed hipster of thirty.

"Never while I'm on the job, Seshet. Those are just for impressing the hoi polloi."

She opens her mouth and he holds up a hand. "Are you going to tell me the definite article is redundant? Because I already know that. I was using it—"

"Ironically? I was going to suggest you go among your polloi one evening just as you are now. It is an enlivening experience."

He claps his hands like a tennis fan appreciating a well-scored point. "I'm sure it is! It's so easy to get caught up in all of their memories, isn't it? Easy to forget that we don't have so many of our own."

She inclines her head. "As I was reminded last night."

He doesn't bother feigning surprise or asking what she was doing. He knows perfectly well.

It's only an ambush if you don't anticipate it.

"Did you enjoy yourself, Seshet?"

It was the most incredible night of my life, and you'll never take it from me.

"It was quite diverting, Terry." Her tone is smooth as a pearl, just a little bored. He cannot know what truly happened last night, just the outward appearance of it. Two women meet at one bar, get drunk together at another. They dance, they sing with the late crowd, they go back to one of their homes, they make love. Memory Librarians take many vows, but none of them are of chastity. Clean citizens of the New Dawn aren't supposed to enjoy same-gender love, but she's hardly the first official to bend those rules; she's not even the only one in Little Delta. He cannot know the *feel* of what has happened to her, that explosion ongoing beneath her breast, the way her fingers itch to call Alethia just to hear her voice again. Just to know it was real. He cannot know it unless he raids her memories—and she will do everything in her power to make sure he doesn't. It is dangerous to be the beloved of a Memory Librarian.

Terry lets the moment hang for a few uncomfortable seconds. Seshet waits for him. Gently, she raises one eyebrow.

He chuckles softly and shakes his head. "Ah, Seshet. Our conversations are always so refreshing. There's no one quite like you. Well. What's this I've been hearing about false memories gumming up the collection systems over there? Do you know who's responsible?"

"Not yet."

He narrows his eyes and tilts his head. She likes Terry better when he's not feigning affability, though she enjoys sparring with him when he is. She knows he's dangerous as a viper—he'd never have reached that position otherwise, let alone survived so many changes in leadership. But—until now, at least—he's put that venom to use in support of her. If that is changing, she hopes she can survive it.

"I'd suggest," he says, drawling, though the most southern thing about him is the Splenda in his iced tea, "that you find out quickly."

"I'm exploring our leads. I should have something more concrete for you soon."

He blinks at her, lips smiling. "Is it the drugs again, Seshet? Those street mixes of Nevermind? It's too bad you let that old witch doctor get away five years ago."

It is hard to keep the jolt of fear out of her expression, though she tries. From Terry's flash of gloating interest, she sees she failed. Doc Young and his legendary remixer MC Haze nearly destroyed her five years ago. Little Delta was becoming famous in the underground circuits as a mecca for wild parties and mind-blasting remixes of street-grade Nevermind. Mixes for sharing memories, mixes for creating dreams, mixes for seeing sound or hearing color. She hadn't caught Doc Young or his remixer, but she'd arrested and memory-suppressed a few hundred of their acolytes. Even sent a sacrificial dozen dirty computers to the Temple for full cleaning. Doc Young and MC Haze vanished, run out of town. Could they have returned? She'd prayed they wouldn't dare. But now she isn't sure.

"I . . . I don't know. The memories are odd. My Memory Keeper—"

"Oh, young Dee? She's sweet, isn't she?"

A wave of dizziness washes over her. Her forehead feels damp. She hopes he doesn't notice. "Dee is an artificial intelligence. Despite its presentation, it doesn't have a gender."

"Oh, of course. My apologies, Dee."

She refuses to wipe her forehead. At least Dee doesn't respond. He doesn't have to say it out loud: her near failure five years ago, her deviant Memory Keeper, her sexuality, her race, her *self*—these are all ropes by which they might hang her, if they choose. During the last crisis with Doc Young and MC Haze, she had been worried that Terry might demote her, or even ship her to some off-site rural Repository. Now she knows those previously unthinkable fates would be gifts. If she fails to resolve this situation, Terry won't hesitate to have her Torched.

He's been her ally for fifteen years, but she knows a part of him would enjoy it—it would appeal to his sense of dramatic irony.

She leans back in her chair, away from the display. "As I was saying, my Memory Keeper calls them half dreams. They're not memories but they're not those strong dreams that sometimes get past the filters either. Five years ago . . . we weren't picking up anything like this back then."

He waves his fingers, as though pushing aside her objection. "So it's something new. That remixer has had plenty of time."

She shakes her head slowly. "It could be MC Haze again, but all her remixes were based on Nevermind. These memories don't . . ."

"They don't what?"

She shrugs, uselessly. "They don't *feel* like Nevermind."

Not sedated, not coerced, not *stolen*.

Terry's basilisk stare should be comical given the blue socks and high-waters, the anime vixen with her breasts barely contained by two parallel strips of shining purple vinyl, but Seshet is very far from laughter.

"Then use your *feeling* and find out who is doing this and *stop them*. This has reached some members of the elder council."

She loses control of her expression for a second time. Terry's eyes crinkle in what seems to be genuine sympathy.

"Do we understand one another, Seshet?"

She forces a neutral smile, out of pride if nothing else. "Perfectly, Terry."

He nods and clicks out of her display.

Seshet does not move. A drop of sweat slides down her forehead, around her chin, and splatters on her desk.

• • •

Imagine a flood, imagine a wave, imagine an avalanche, imagine a storm. Imagine any disaster you please, but note that it always begins as one before it becomes many. What in singular expression seems simple, laughable, beneath your notice, becomes, in the plural, the last thing you notice before you die. This is the bleak magic of exponential growth. It is the difference between two grasshoppers on your screen door and the eighth plague of Egypt. And if you haven't been paying attention to an uninhabitable swath of the Arabian desert when unseasonable cyclones drape the sands in blankets of water, creating the conditions for an unprecedented breeding season for desert grasshoppers, it might surprise you when clouds of vomit-yellow locusts descend to decimate your entire country's corn crop ten months later.

The trouble, as Seshet sees it, is with Cousin Skee. It's with Alethia. With that boy who danced her by the shoulders and told her she was full (or wool? or beautiful?). She hasn't paid enough attention to Old Town since Doc Young fled the city. She hasn't monitored the border zones, like Skee's east side.

And why did she ignore it, wise Seshet, who ought to know better than anyone the danger of the margins? Seshet, queen, who wants to be a mother to her kingdom. Why not? Doesn't she watch over her people? But here's the rub: She has watched over some more than others. She has maintained the heart of the city in a mold as pure as any New Dawn could hope for. But she averted her gaze from the edges, from the ones who would never fit anyway. The ones who looked like her—and didn't look like them.

Director Seshet! What have you done for us lately?

Well, don't they fucking know? Is it possible that they haven't even realized? What has she done, wise Seshet, compassionate Seshet, even while precarious in power?

She has not looked.

And oh, poor Seshet, this is on her shoulders now. If Terry and the others haven't realized it, they will soon. Whatever the specifics of these half dreams—a new Nevermind remix or hacking or something else—they are down from the desert, legion, o'errun.

• • •

It is a little enough disaster, after the great disasters of the morning, but Seshet can feel hysteria bubbling up like old vinegar behind her throat.

"Dee," she says, voice cracking at the end like a child's. "Dee, are you *sure* there's nothing more?"

"I'm so sorry, Seshet," Dee says. It sounds distressed, but it's removed its face from her display. "This subject isn't flagged for extra surveillance. These are the only memories in the cache."

"Alethia has a sleep headset."

"We have no record of its use last night."

A private smile pulls at her lips. Of course they don't. The smile collapses. "You checked the trash again?"

"It was all cleared at four thirty this morning, per standard operations."

"And her Counseling sessions?"

"After three years without incident we only retain the intake session and the final report. You yourself made sure we were the first to implement Chancellor Chelsea's privacy reforms. Would you like me to help you remember?"

Dee is already pulling up the relevant memories from six years ago. One of her displays flashes to visual-auditory recall: Seshet and Terry stiff-necked in full regalia, laughing at some joke of his before they stepped onto the podium to announce the reforms. Even without the sensory integration of her headset, she is plunged back into that day, into the skin of her younger self, proud to be at the vanguard of New Dawn's short-lived reformist movement.

An older, harder Seshet shakes her head and stops the playback. "That isn't necessary, Dee."

Dee is silent for a few seconds. When it speaks, it sounds weary, even disappointed. "Would you like me to flag her now, Seshet?"

Seshet frowns. She has allowed Dee to develop a personality and a primitive consciousness—aspects that make it dangerous, according to Terry and his superiors—but it's still fundamentally a Memory Keeper AI bound by New Dawn's protocols. It has the processing capacity of a precocious child, not an adult capable of moral judgments. So why would her Memory Keeper be disappointed in her?

She defends herself anyway. "I need more information, Dee! I need to know who she really is, before . . ." *Before I lose myself in her.*

Before I lose control.

Displaying that annoying tick of independence and creativity that Seshet has allowed to develop in her Memory Keeper but is bitterly regretting now, Dee spreads five different memories across Seshet's displays and plays them all at once without sound: teenage Alethia hugging her father goodbye at the border wall while drones circle; Alethia in her lab, measuring chemicals, solitude isolating her like the walls of a test tube; Alethia moving into her apartment with just two suitcases and a hot-water kettle; Alethia on a bench in Standards Park, feeding the ducks in the artificial lake; Alethia on the viewing deck of the obelisk, just below Seshet's office, gazing over the cloud-covered city. How long ago was that? Three years. Seshet's heart lurches. They'd come so close to meeting. But is this the real Alethia? Where's "Lethe" of Cousin Skee's? Where's that cloaked, sharp humor? The cherry bedspread like a dagger thrust to the beige of that prefurnished apartment? Aside from her father, deported fifteen years ago after his citizenship was revoked for "unclean activities," why is she always alone?

"Dee, is this really everything?"

"You told me—"

"I told you what?"

Dee sighs. "This is what we have."

"And your analysis of the subject?"

She wishes Dee would show its face. It has never wanted to hide from her before.

"They smell funny."

"Dee, be serious."

But Dee is more stubborn than usual today. It begins to speak in singsong:

I didn't know what I really meant
When I asked you where the false time went

I only knew I had to let go
Before the fall's first blow.

"Enough!"

Seshet's shout brings down a charged silence. Her eyes prick. She is conscious of an urge to apologize. Absurd. "Flag her, Dee," she says, making her voice even harder to mask that flush of shame. "Bring me every last memory you can drag from the public recollectors or her headset tonight."

For the first time in their life together, Dee's voice sounds genuinely robotic. "Confirmed, Seshet. Alethia 56934 has been flagged for suspected deviance, high priority."

• • •

The Counseling offices sit opposite from the obelisk, on the other side of the City Hall gardens that are open to the public only on weekends and holidays. Seshet goes through the private entrance beside the balding topiary, nodding once to the guards who spring to attention when they see her. This late in the day, the private corridors are empty, though there will still be a handful of people in the public library and waiting room, hoping for a last-minute appointment with a Counselor. She hates coming here. Even as a novice, Seshet avoided the Social Librarians. The idea of having to constantly interact with the people whose memories she monitored repulsed her, like a surgeon who could handle cutting open intestines only if she forgot the human being who would use them later. Counseling receives a constant influx of people looking for help—or looking to raise their Standards scores and petition to change their numbers. She receives reports on their activities, of course. She even personally involves herself in the cases that interest her—diagnosing emotional liabilities, selecting the memories for repression or amplifieation, reveling in the messy, subtle work of realigning a personality. That the memories harvested during Counseling sessions are of a much higher quality, particularly useful for New Dawn's surveillance efforts, is merely a beneficial side effect of the Librarians' primary work.

Seshet doesn't really believe this any more than the Social division's Vice Director does, but they tell that to the fresh initiates in training and massage their memories so they can believe it as long as possible. She has long since made the necessary moral justifications.

In the end, a simple happiness is better than a complex disillusion.

She finds the Vice Director alone in his office, feeds from three Counseling sessions running silently on wall displays. His headset flashes reflected light from the sunset as he turns to greet her. Keith doesn't betray surprise to find her here in person, but his welcoming smile is perfunctory, and he only belatedly offers her the seat in front of his desk. Seshet stares at him for a carefully blank moment and then seats herself, conscious of every regal gesture, on the couch facing the picture window. Keith's office is nearly as large as hers. He is Vice Director of a powerful division, golden-haired, blue-eyed, the third generation of

New Dawn loyalists, and the favored heir of a certain bitter faction with long grudges who would like nothing more than to erase even the memory of Seshet's heterodox rise to power in Little Delta. It's one thing to allow people like her to train as initiates, the line goes, but quite another to let them seem to rule!

His eyes flick to the couch in annoyance. After a beat, he forces another smile, removes his headset, and makes his way to the chair facing her.

"You honor me by coming all the way here, Director," he says. "I was just preparing my report for you."

"Your report, Vice Director?" She allows nothing more than a hint of polite curiosity in her tone, but her thoughts are a storm. Someone has already told him about the memory flooding. He's had—hours? Days?—to consolidate his position.

He leans forward, hand on his knee, concerned frown betrayed by the tic at the corners of his lips. Keith has never quite mastered the art of controlling his expression. But then, he's never really needed to.

"Well, of course, Director Seshet," he says, larding on the false concern until it is indistinguishable from gloating, "I couldn't leave you to face this kind of unprecedented attack alone. We're all Librarians in the end, despite our differences. We're here to defend the Repository . . . the New Dawn way of life! Well, aren't we, Director?"

Standards save her from young sharks tasting blood in the water. As if she hasn't beaten back better men than him in her time. As if she won't do so again. She sighs. "I will be happy to review your report in the morning, Vice Director. I assume the memories of those in Counseling don't have much to offer, in any case."

The Social division Vice Director, Seshet has had cause to observe, bears a distinct resemblance to a fish on a line when caught out. "My Memory Keeper is still checking everything we have archived—"

Under her patient gaze he belatedly falls silent. She nods.

"Perhaps you don't yet have enough . . . experience in your position to know this, but no one from Old Town goes near Counseling. The ones responsible for these fabricated memories would be even less likely to betray themselves so easily. Counseling is how we monitor the health of Little Delta. But to destroy an illness, Vice Director, we need different means."

He swallows. She fancies that she can see a spark of panic behind those sky-blue irises, a belated realization that Seshet has not yet fallen, and might survive to see *him* fall if he does not take care.

"And what means might those be, Director Seshet?" No sign of his preening now.

"The loose memory bank. You do remember you're in charge of it, don't you?"

He frowns and shakes his head. "Loose memories! They're notoriously unreliable. My Memory Keeper would be stuck in there for half of every month if I let it. I only ever go in there if Standards is after me to find the suspect in a crime—"

She rises from the couch in a smooth gesture and allows some of her real annoyance to inflect her tone. "Keith, have you been paying attention? These memory flooders *are* criminals. I very much doubt the ones responsible for this will be tagged in the system. They won't be easy to find. I need any suspect memories flagged and sent to my workspace. Traffic stops, ambient drones, recollection boxes out in the periphery, the ones outside grocery stores and check-cashing stores and pawn shops. And . . ."

He isn't bothering to control his expression at all now; his lower lip juts out like a surly child's. "Yes?"

She looks past his outraged expression to the sun setting over the garden. Her heart hurts at the thought of fighting this battle again, but she does what she needs to. "Keep an eye out for Doc Young or MC Haze. They might be back."

She remembers, a Librarian's perfect recall piercing the alcoholic fog, that light-skinned boy dancing with her at Cousin Skee's, drug-blasted pupils dark as the night sky. *You're full,* he sang to her over the loud jangle of someone else's music. *You're full as a beast and we have nothing to spare.*

• • •

Hungry? I'm starving:) A

A simple message on Seshet's private channel. She should stay at the Repository. She should comb through the other Vice Directors' reports, look for more clues, ask Dee for more data.

Instead, Seshet changes into another set of Jordan-approved street clothes and hurries to meet Alethia at a tiny Italian restaurant near her place. They pretend to be friends where anyone can see, but they touch under the table, careful for Alethia's sake, since she's already been flagged as deviant. They share wine and garlic bread. ("We have to eat it together," Alethia says, waving a piece under her nose, "or only I'll stink and you won't want to kiss me." Seshet nods like a marionette and takes another long gulp of red wine.) Alethia used the recollector outside the restaurant to load a few more points onto her TriCard before they went in.

"It's my turn to treat," she said, with a lift to her eyebrow that dared Seshet to object. Seshet eyed the recollector with a hunger she hoped didn't show and shrugged.

The meal is sublime, so heavy on the garlic it becomes a joke between them, cracking up when they order dessert, whispering, *But is it a* garlic *panna cotta? Can we try the* garlic *grappa?*

They linger over their dessert wine, which tastes faintly of anise, a different root vegetable.

"They say you Librarians have perfect memories. So tell me the first thing you remember." Alethia traces Seshet's uneven hairline with one finger. Seshet feels the touch through to the soles of her feet. She closes her eyes, a prayer for strength.

"My recovery room at the Temple," she says. "White and gold. The Torch standing beside me. 'Congratulations on your rebirth, novice Librarian. Your name is Seshet.' "

Alethia drops her hand, a loss. Seshet does not move.

"They memory-wiped you?" she asks, horrified and trying to hide it.

Seshet shrugs. "It's a requirement for initiation."

"And that name? It's unusual for New Dawn. An Egyptian goddess?"

At that, Seshet smiles. "We have the right to choose our new names. I guess my past self wanted to make sure that I knew how high I wanted to climb."

Alethia laughs softly. Seshet's heart skips one subtle beat and rebounds with ferocity.

"Well, we have that in common," Alethia says. "I chose my name too. I was sixteen when they approved my petition."

Seshet had wondered. Even under New Dawn's more liberal regimes, getting permits for transitions has never been easy.

"Your parents agreed?" Seshet asks. Though her own childhood memories are safely stored with Dee, this question leaves her aching, off balance.

There is a matching glimmer in Alethia's eyes, downcast over the dregs of her wine. "I was always my papa's little girl. My mom . . ." She shakes her head, sets down the glass like it holds something precious. "She agreed when it counted. She let me live my life."

There's a story there, but Seshet doesn't pry.

She doesn't need to.

She is remembering, on a loop made relentless by her perfect memory, what Alethia said, as she left the recollector booth: "No checking them out behind my back, okay?" She laughed but her eyes were worried. "You have the advantage."

She tries not to pay attention to the longing, the vulnerability in Alethia's voice when she invites Seshet to her apartment again. She tries not to think about that simple, declarative statement that rushes through the gulf between them: *You have the advantage.* And what is Seshet to do? *Not* take it? Stop being who she is while she exposes herself before a woman completely unknown to her? How could she possibly do that? Wouldn't *not* looking be abdicating her responsibilities as Director Librarian? What if Alethia wants to hurt her? What if she's a resistance agent?

But resisting who? a voice inside her asks.

She hushes it with deep kisses in the doorway of Alethia's apartment. Fingers caressing dark puckered nipples. Backs arched, toes curled. They curve like calligraphy on the red canvas of Alethia's bed, and Seshet cannot breathe, she cannot think, her memories are a whirlwind. She has never felt desire this raw in her life. But it's not their passion that scares her; it's the after hush, the easy sleep of Alethia in her arms, the soft kiss she places, like a brand, on the inner fold of Seshet's left wrist.

The woman who could have treasured this gift, Seshet threw away twenty years ago. So who does Alethia see when she looks at her? Seshet, Director Librarian—or the ghost of the woman she killed to become her?

• • •

Seshet makes sure Alethia's sleep headset is in place before she leaves. They've drunk a bottle of wine between them; she's more likely to assume she put it on herself than that Seshet put it on for her. Alethia's wary voice: *You have the advantage*. And what of it? No one in her position has the luxury of fairness.

At three in the morning she calls a private aircar and heads back to the Repository. She hasn't slept at all, but her nerves are alive, her synapses snapping, the fall air full in her lungs and the sleeping city pulsing through her veins, hers alone.

• • •

Keith sends her a terse message early the next morning: his Memory Keeper has found something. He sends over a handful of loose memories scavenged from the southern edge of the city two days ago, all of them from unregistered users.

Seshet, unsleeping, fresh as a vampire, has stuffed herself full to sickness on a stream of Alethia's dreams and memories. With a physical jolt, she disconnects from that raw feed and forces her attention back to the crisis that might just topple her after a decade at the top of the obelisk. If even Keith is working on Sunday, she can't do less.

"Dee," she says, losing a battle with herself, "I need your help with this."

Her Memory Keeper's face appears, at last, in the corner of her nearest monitor: a sullen, angry child.

"Oh, so you're finished?"

She considers a number of responses, each one more defensive than the last. But Dee is just an artificial intelligence, a virtual helper built on her own discarded memories. There's no reason for her to care about its opinion.

So she simply pulls up the loose memories that Keith sent her and lets them play. She doesn't bother with the full headset, since like most loose memories, these are patchy and degraded. Drugs tend to do that, but so does desperation.

The memories all center on a party somewhere in Old Town. There are tunnels covered in black and white tiles in a pattern she can no longer make sense of; loose tiles crunch underfoot like eggshells. The tunnels converge on a larger space, a great platform with sunken tracks. Lights flash and sparkle from hidden crevices. One of the memories has a degraded olfactory register, which Dee tells her smells faintly of cotton candy and dried urine. Street-grade Nevermind comes in a lot of flavors, but she remembers the Candy Remix from eight years ago. One of Doc Young's staples, with a short, punchy high that made your every recent memory taste sweet. It was MC Haze's first big hit, the one that propelled her from the trenches of dime-a-dozen remixers to the dizzying heights of underground stardom. On the memory playback, which Dee has belatedly condensed into a composite far richer in detail, lights flash and project onto the ceiling. The outline of an old man seated beside a dark, upside-down obelisk raises his hands, palms out. Light gathers between his head and his hands until a star shoots from his forehead. It obliterates the man, leaving only the glittering words behind:

DOC YOUNG'S MIND BREAK

A few of the memories go on longer, but she stops playback.

"That's the old train station, Seshet," Dee says after a taut moment. "The north platforms." It sounds worried. But of course it does—it's a reflection of herself, and they both understand what this means.

"That old bastard." She's several steps behind him, as always. She slumps in her chair, rolled by the exhaustion she's kept at bay all morning.

"Dee, can you ring the Standards office?"

"Are you going to order a raid?" Dee says nervously. "Don't you remember what happened last time?"

A hundred detainees. A dozen branded as dirty computers, left as dead to their friends and families. Oh, she remembers. But what choice does she have?

Doc Young is back.

• • •

The daytime raid turns up a few scraps: stray memories from the vagabond who sleeps across the street, discarded remix inhalers she sends to forensics, a smattering of stencils with Doc Young's new logo, the star bursting from his head like Athena from Zeus. She tells the Standards Chief to maintain a stealth drone formation throughout the night, to see who else they might pick up. Doc Young won't use the same place twice for his traveling club, but other people of interest might stop by.

She still isn't sure if the memory flooding is the fault of a new remix, but Doc Young's sudden reappearance after five years makes that more likely. She doesn't want to think of what Terry and the elders will say, if so. They forgave her then, but she doubts they will be so understanding a second time.

Jordan comes by her office again that night, bearing curry and beer like a sword and shield.

"You haven't eaten all day," he says, and hurries to the conference table to set out the food.

"Been watching me that carefully, have you?" Seshet says wryly, observing his practiced arrangement of disposable containers and silverware. As if he's determined to finish before she has a chance to kick him out. "What are you still doing here on a Sunday?"

"I just worry about you." He takes the lid off a curry container. The smell of Jamaican jerk chicken hits her with an almost physical force. She's reminded that she still hasn't slept and—Jordan is correct—hasn't eaten more than a protein bar since this morning.

She sighs. "Tell me you at least got enough for yourself?"

He smiles, so grateful it pains her, and pulls out another container. "Just in case."

She removed her outer robe at some point in the last several frantic hours, so she eats with her clerk in just her white tunic and gold leggings, exhaustion or mortal terror relaxing her into an informality she hasn't allowed herself within these walls in all her time as Director. Jordan, predictably, doesn't comment on the formal vestment flung over the couch like a fancy throw pillow.

He waits until she's nearly finished before asking, she will grant him that.

"So, how are things going with Alethia?"

She chokes on the last mouthful of chicken and drains the rest of her beer before she recovers.

"Why?" she rasps. "Has she said something?"

Jordan shakes his head. "Just that she wishes you had a less demanding job."

"Job!" Seshet laughs and then, inexplicably, wants to cry.

Jordan looks halfway to tears himself. "Director," he says, looking at the remains of his turmeric-stained rice instead of at her, "just *trust* this time, won't you? I think you and Alethia have something very special."

It's out of character for him to overstep like this. Not just as her subordinate, but as her—friend? But Librarians are never simply friends.

"Jordan . . ." She makes her voice hard in warning, but he shakes his head like a stubborn toddler.

"Do something about it if you don't want me to pry. You haven't memory-suppressed me yet, I know it. I've been monitoring myself."

She blinks in surprise. "You've been . . . who taught you that?"

Monitoring is an advanced technique for detecting changes and manipulations in one's own memories. It is generally only taught to subdirectors, though Librarians of lower ranks can learn it at the discretion of someone higher up.

Jordan laughs with more bitterness than she had ever expected of him and wipes his eyes. "It was authorized, Director." She wants to ask him *by whom,* the question nearly off her tongue before she swallows it back down. Does she want to know? Was it Keith, trying to suborn her closest clerk? Or, worse, Terry, tinting every friendly eye on her with a subtle shade of treachery?

"What do you want from me, Jordan?" She can't keep the distrust from her voice, any more than he can fail to hear it.

"Director. Seshet." He drives her name on his lips like a stake through her heart. "You don't need to control everything."

Stung, her spine stiffens. "I don't need—"

Somehow, his very intensity stops her. "If it's love, just let it be. Please."

• • •

She can't help but think of Jordan's warning when she visits Alethia that night, though she knows it shouldn't matter. Jordan *and* Dee? What did she do to deserve the unfounded moralizing of children and artificial constructs?

"I missed you this morning," Alethia says, greeting her with a kiss at the door to her apartment. She's smiling, but her eyes are red-rimmed, puffy, and bruised underneath. Without makeup or tailored clothes, her beauty feels more raw to Seshet, more familiar. She's wearing an old T-shirt and pajama pants, perhaps the same ones from last night. She secures all the locks behind Seshet before heading to the living room. All the blinds are down here and in the kitchen, but something in Alethia's mood stops Seshet from suggesting they raise them and turn down the lights. Alethia picks up a thick wooden pipe in the shape of a palm frond and flips open a lighter.

"Please tell me you won't report me," she says with a laugh, but the look in her eyes is a little too desperate, a little too real.

Seshet tries to lighten the mood. "Only if you share."

She's smoked weed a handful of times in her life—all with Terry, in fact, from one of his fancy vintage vape pens while they played some ridiculous old video game of his with a lot of guns and gore—but she's willing to try again just to take the scared edge out of Alethia's voice.

White smoke billows from Alethia's nostrils in soft, gentle whorls. *Oh, to be the smoke behind her teeth,* she thinks. Silently, Alethia passes the pipe and the lighter. Seshet knows how to do this, she has a thousand memories to show her, but the greenly burning smell brings her back, like a hook in her heart, to something older, personal. A little girl playing in the fall leaves, watching wide, beloved hips move with the rhythm of the rake; the smell of those leaves burning, painting sigils on the sky.

She gasps and coughs on a different smoke, in a different year, with a different name. Where did that come from? But it was her own memory, she knows it in her bones. The memory of that little girl she forgot for so many years, the one who longed, more than anything, for the woman with the rake to come back home.

Alethia is thumping her on the back, sitting her down on the couch. She brings her a glass of cold water, which finally soothes the burning in her airway. Seshet wipes her eyes.

"Don't know what happened," Seshet says, pushing the pipe onto the table.

Alethia wags her eyebrows. "You have a hard time breathing around me?"

Seshet's heart hurts. She leans back on the couch, closes her eyes against the fluorescent lights, her beloved's blinding smile.

"You're tired," Alethia says. "Did you work today?"

"You don't really get days off in my position. You?"

"I . . . went to the lab. I have a project I'm working on . . . anyway, I didn't stay long."

Seshet cracks open her eyes. Alethia is gazing pensively at one of the windows, as though she can see through the blinds. "Did something happen?" Was she not careful enough last night? Did she disrupt Alethia's emotional balance with her real-time dive into her dreams and memories? The sleep headsets have that functionality, but it's not recommended outside of a specially equipped detention facility where the subjects can be closely monitored for side effects.

Guilt washes over her, inexorable as unbidden memory. There is a difference, vital as a heartbeat, between what is permitted to her position and what is aligned with her soul. She knew that, once. She almost remembers it now, but the knowing slides, sinks into soft forgetting, is gone.

Alethia shakes her head as though shaking off a fly. "Tell me about your day. If you can, I guess. Did you bust any heads?"

Seshet sits straight up. "I don't bust—"

But Alethia is already holding her hands up, palms out. "Sorry, sorry, babe. It was just a joke. You *are* the Director of this whole little town. Heads are sometimes busted."

"If I have to order raids, it's for the good of our community—"

"So you ordered a raid?"

"I never said—"

Alethia's laugh stops her cold. "The poor things that get caught in that net. So many new Torches for the Temple."

"Alethia," she says, forcing herself calm though she feels as if she's falling in midair, "you know what I am."

Alethia blows out another lungful of smoke. In the hallway, someone unlocks their door and shuts it. Alethia keeps still until the hall has gone quiet again.

"Yeah, I know. I just wish I could see who."

"What's that supposed to mean?"

Alethia taps out the ashes straight onto the coffee table and refills the pipe. "Who are you, Seshet-without-a-number? Who would you be if you weren't Director Librarian? Who could we be, together?"

The vertigo is getting worse. Maybe the weed has finally kicked in. "Why are you asking me this, Alethia?"

She stares at Alethia, who keeps her gaze fixed on the window. "It's just . . . you have a reputation, you know? You're . . . kinder than most of them. Nothing happened to anyone we met that night at Cousin Skee's. I was taking a chance, bringing you there."

She feels sick. "What did you think would happen to them?"

Alethia meets her gaze at last, but now Seshet wants to turn away, to hide from the confusion and distrust she sees there. "I don't know, Seshet. You tell me. What's going to happen to whoever gets caught in that raid of yours?"

"Anyone going to one of Doc Young's parties needs Counseling, Alethia!" Alethia flinches but Seshet persists. "Yes, even cleaning. It's for the good of the whole."

Alethia snorts. "The good of the whole," she says, mocking. "My god, you sound just like them."

I am *them*, she almost says, fast and hot. She swallows back the cheap shot. Seshet could ascend to elder council itself and she still wouldn't be more than tolerated in New Dawn. She knows exactly what Alethia means.

"Alethia, what's going on? What happened today? Why are you like this?"

"Maybe this *is* who I am, Seshet. I'm not your dream girl. I'm just a woman in way, way over her head . . ."

She buries her head in her arms. Seshet, shocked, puts a hand on her shoulder.

"Just go." Alethia's voice is muffled and Seshet pretends she didn't hear. But Alethia raises her head a second later, so the words are clear as the new dawn light:

"Leave, Seshet."

• • •

You can say this for our Director Librarian, Seshet-without-a-number, the woman who named herself after a goddess so she could not forget what she meant to become: she does not flinch.

Whatever the consequences, the moral accounting, the line drawn between the *she* who had not done this thing and the *she* who has—what is an official of New Dawn if not a professional consequence risker, moral accountant, line crosser? And Seshet has prided herself on being the best of them all.

This is her line, carefully marked in the sand before the tide of *what* she is drowns it in a sea of salt and noise: Alethia's memories.

She sees herself as through a haze of love and longing: a tall woman of regal bearing and awkward gestures, tongue-tied, eloquent-eyed, no longer young but ageless. That woman walks into Alethia's apartment. That woman says, with a pained smile, *Only if you share.*

She takes the memory and *pushes*, back behind the most painful moments of Alethia's past, behind her grief over her father lost on the other side of that border wall, behind the conflicted shame and love she feels for her mother lost to cancer, behind her first memories, her shock when she realized that other people saw her as a boy, and further, behind her first cries in the light, behind her waiting silence in the liquid dark. She pushes, and when Alethia puts her headset on tonight, she will respond and pull, until not a trace of their meeting a few hours ago remains accessible to her conscious mind. It isn't as good as a full Nevermind wipe, but it's the next best thing. No one that Seshet has suppressed has voluntarily recalled those memories ever again. She knows the trick, you see. No one remembers everything. And what's too painful to remember, you can simply choose to forget.

All Seshet does is use their own mental blocks as the bulwark against whatever she wants to hide from their consciousness. It's like a wall of fire in one of Terry's old video games with a treasure safely hidden inside. Here's the trick: if the flames burn on the fuel of your own shame, not even mortal terror can make you brave the heat.

• • •

She sleeps for a while in her own workstation, visor still down, the floodplain of virtual space melding seamlessly with the dreamscape of her own memory-haunted mind. She does not know of what she dreams; those are locked away in the fastness of her own shame and regret. Just one follows her into craggy wakefulness, and it's not so much a dream as a belch of repressed memory, inexplicably brought to life. The sway of her mother's hips as she agitates the leaves. The girl in the grass. The crackle and burn.

"Dee," she says, without thinking. Their argument feels faraway now. The logic of it lost to her in a groggy sickness, the hangover of what she has done to the woman she is falling in love with.

"You don't look so good, Seshet."

Seshet tries to laugh, but it's like wet ashes, it won't come out. Dee is a child playing on the floodplain, now empty, waiting for the morning's harvest. She has never known whether Dee acts the role of a child for her benefit, or for some arcane satisfaction of its own.

"Dee," she says, coughing on something too silty for tears. *You have a hard time breathing around me.* No matter what else they have, Alethia won't ever remember that. "Show me my old memories, won't you? Show me my mother."

Dee's uncanny eyes go wide as a Kewpie doll's. "Really? You never want to look at those."

"I . . . remembered something. From my childhood."

"But you can't remember those, not as a primary memory. Not unless . . . Oh, Seshet."

Seshet thinks she doesn't deserve Dee's understanding, its kindness. Even if it is an artificial intelligence fundamentally limited by New Dawn's protocols, it understands her better than any human ever has.

"I must have suppressed it," she says, out loud, for the first time. "That's how they missed it in the Nevermind wipe."

Humans repress their own memories, of course. They do it all the time. Headsets wouldn't work, otherwise. Nevermind would just be a really trippy drug. The fact that New Dawn has weaponized this effect for its own purposes doesn't mean that people don't forget things for their own simple survival every second of the day. It's not so surprising that she would have done so. But why remember now, after so much time?

Without another word, Dee pulls up a memory and rolls it over her in a full sensory wash. Ah, she has always liked this one. She is eight, and her mother has just come home from some mysterious trip overseas. She has brought back a suitcase full of treasure and she shows young Deidre the spoils, piece by piece. Here is the necklace of cowries she purchased on the beach from a boy no older than Deidre; here is the doll made of corn husks and twine with black beans for eyes; here is the program for the opera, red ink on cream paper that still smells of someone else's cologne.

"I can breathe there, Deidre," she says, a refrain the child recognizes. "Your memories are your own."

"But when will you let me come with you, Mom?"

"When you're older, honey. When it's safer."

Deidre never understood what her mother meant by that.

Then her mother and father fought and her mother stopped going on her trips, stopped bringing back bounty. Just a year later, her mother abandoned them both.

The memory fuses with another and another: her mother doing the laundry, cursing at the old machine that always rocked during the spin cycle; her mother singing her to sleep, *Remember,* some old song from before memories were things you could hold in your fist like coin; her mother screaming at the top of her lungs from the top of a hill, "I own my own soul!"

"Why do you think she left us, Dee?" Seshet asks now, though she doesn't remember this girl that she was, not really.

Dee shuts down the memories. "She wouldn't have done it without a good reason, Seshet. I know it."

• • •

Terry has come to Little Delta for an unofficial visit. The news rushes through the obelisk like water over a ruptured dam, but Seshet, sleeping in her office, is among the last to hear it. It's Jordan, of course, who saves her. He spends five minutes arguing with her door monitor before Dee finally wakes her up. "Oh god," Jordan says, "I was beginning to worry you'd died."

"The door monitor would have let you in if I were dead," Seshet says, yawning. She's still in last night's street clothes, which look—and smell—days old.

Jordan grimaces. "That's what it said. Thank you, Dee."

"You're welcome, Jordan!" Dee says, inordinately pleased. It doesn't acknowledge most people—a precaution Seshet instilled in it early on—but Jordan has always been on its short list of friendly humans.

He tells her about Terry, which wakes her the rest of the way up, no need for the coffee he has so helpfully brought. She drinks it anyway.

"How long has he been here?"

"Half an hour," Jordan says. "He's taking a tour of the Counseling building."

She closes her eyes briefly. So he's seeing Keith before her. This is meant to send a message, but knowing Terry, it's as likely to make Keith feel overconfident as it is to make Seshet feel undermined.

"And this morning's crop?"

Jordan hesitates.

"Out with it, Jordan. Things can't get much worse."

"Over fifty percent are those junk memories," he says in a small voice that means he still can't believe it. "I don't know how, Director, but they've gone from a blip to nearly overwhelming the system in less than a week."

A little more than that, she thinks, not that it matters. "Exponential growth," she says. "It's a killer."

She uses the shower in her office and puts on the extra work robes she keeps in the closet. She can't afford Terry's performative casualness, and she doesn't bother to try.

She meets him, an hour later, as the perfectly composed Director Librarian of Little Delta, in her robes of office.

He's wearing the hat of Arch-Librarian, but below the neck he's all ironic hipster, reaching for meaning in the corporate branding of the past. This time it's an Atari T-shirt, corduroy pants, and pink Vans. She has to grant him his point: in the hallways of the obelisk his peculiar style stands out even more than his vestments would.

"Seshet!" he says. "Good news! I've gotten my hands on the Japanese original of *Final Fantasy III*, remember I was telling you about that?"

She blinks at him. "Congratulations?" She's never managed to keep track of all the video games he's played in front of her, but she generally drums up enough interest in the moment to keep things pleasant. The weed helps.

He settles himself in one of her armchairs, crosses left foot over right knee, and balances his conical red cap on the end of one pink shoe. "I'd suggest we head straight to Greenfriars, but I guess the play-through will have to wait. You must be drowning in work. Don't mind me, I just stopped by to say hello."

Greenfriars is one of the New Dawn resort facilities, about an hour out of town, reserved for officials, their families, and select friends. She has never spent much time there.

"Hello, Terry. I've just had a pot of tea brought up. Would you like some?"

She pours the tea into two matching ceramic cups, marked with gold and lapis filigree in the sigil of New Dawn. The tea pours green and fragrant as fresh-cut grass, and she doesn't offer him any sugar. Terry only ever drinks iced coffees thick as milkshakes with protein powder. He takes the cup from her with a sardonic lift to his eyebrows.

"Tea, that's charming. So . . . how's it going?"

She doesn't prevaricate. "Doc Young is back in town. I'm waiting on news of a sting operation from the Standards office."

"Good. And his remixer?"

"I'm not sure if MC Haze is with him this time, but it's possible."

He takes a tentative sip and grimaces. "Well, I'm sure it will be settled soon in your capable hands, Seshet."

Seshet puts her cup smoothly in its saucer, disconcerted. What happened to the urgency, the veiled threats of their last conversation? And if he's so sure she can resolve it, why has he bothered to come here in person? Terry hates Little Delta. "I'm grateful for your confidence in me."

He beams like a proud father. It makes him look ancient. "You deserve it! In fact, that's just what I wanted to bring up with you personally. We've all been impressed with your tenure here. Even those who weren't in favor of your ascension have come around now. You were a controversial appointment, you know that, but you've done very well. You've proven the New Dawn ethos. 'Order, Standards, and Merit above all.'" He hesitates theatrically. "You're Merit, of course."

Seshet raises her cup to hide her expression. "Of course. You came all the way to Little Delta to tell me that?"

Saltier than she meant it to come out. Terry may have been her ally for over a decade, but he still loves to unbalance her.

He takes another swig of the tea in his enthusiasm. "A little more than that, dear. We're considering you for a promotion. The directorship has opened in Minneapolis. Big city, very different operation from what you have going on here, but lots of opportunity for a hungry Librarian. Of course, I know you're already bonded to this city. We'd have to wipe you again. That's not wonderful, but you've only just turned forty, your brain is still resilient enough. You can keep your personal memories, of course; no one wants to worry you about that."

Her mind is blank with astonishment. She blurts the first thought that pops into it. "Minneapolis? Terry, you were Director of Minneapolis."

"I was! So you can see, Seshet, there are big things ahead of you. Who knows where you might go after this. We just need to see a successful resolution to this memory plague problem and, honestly, your nomination is in the bag." Satisfied as a cat over a clean plate, he puts down his teacup. "Do we understand one another, Seshet?"

She nods. "Perfectly, Terry."

• • •

As she hoped, the sting nets a group of revelers hoping to catch Doc Young's latest party a day late. The detention memory swipe of one of them turns up a pair of half dreams that match the ones flooding their systems. The subject—one Leon 75411—says he doesn't know anything about memory flooding or new remixes, he just picked those up at another party, a mind meld with a group of strangers. No, he doesn't know who they were. No, he couldn't find them again. The Standards Chief is interrogating the detainee personally. In his professional opinion, he tells Seshet, the boy is telling the truth. But that doesn't mean his memories might not give more clues. She tells the Standards Chief to put the detainee into a coma and harvest as much as they can. When the memories arrive to her workstation, however, she goes rigid with shock. She recognizes the kid, this Leon 75411, low-grade memory hoarder and antisocial deviant. He's the light-skinned boy with the stencil of Doc Young's Mind Break on his cap who danced with her at Cousin Skee's. With a lurch of nausea, she now remembers who he reminded her of: her half brother, child of her father's second marriage after her mom left. They had never gotten along.

Alethia said she had taken a chance bringing Seshet to that bar. But this wasn't the same. Seshet hadn't broken that trust—this kid walked into her trap entirely of his own accord! But she imagines trying to justify herself to Alethia and can't bear to look at the kid's first memory in the queue. She tells Dee to conduct a preliminary analysis and declares herself done for the day. She wants to see Alethia, to make good on the bad she did last night and try again. But Alethia is distracted when Seshet arrives. She pulls what sounds like a table from the door before unlocking it.

"Did anyone follow you up the stairs?" She's still in the pajama bottoms of the last two nights, though she's changed to a different bleach-stained T-shirt.

"I'm alone," Seshet says, sidling through the crack Alethia leaves open.

Alethia looks ragged, haunted, like the day has weighed her down with cement blocks.

"I missed you yesterday," she says. The words disorient Seshet, then hit her like a blow. She hides their effect behind a smile and an embrace. It's better this way. A fresh start, their fight not just forgotten but made as if it never was. Alethia hangs in her arms, trembling, before she gathers her strength and pulls back.

"Lethe," Seshet says, "are you okay? What's happened?"

But Alethia just rubs her temples and heads to the kitchen. She has a full pot of coffee under the drip, and a wad of discarded filters in the sink. She pours herself a mug and offers another to Seshet.

"But it's late," Seshet says.

Alethia shrugs. "I can't sleep."

"No wonder! How much coffee have you had today?"

"No, I mean, I can't *let* myself sleep. I've been having terrible dreams lately." She shakes her head and shudders. "That's what I get for buying the cheap headset, I guess. All for a couple of lousy Social points. Why do you guys authorize those things if they don't even work?"

She slams her empty mug down on the countertop. Seshet jumps.

"Sorry," she says. "Sorry, babe. It's been a rough few days. How have you been? How's work?" She gives a jittery laugh, a momentary flash of something bright and wild as she leans against the countertop. "Bust any heads today?"

Seshet thinks of Leon, she can't help it, but none of that pained guilt shows in her practiced, earnest expression. She's in control now. She knows where this is going, and she can steer their ship to calmer waters. "Lethe," she says again, savoring the nickname on her tongue, imagining years of having the right to call this woman hers, "I don't bust heads. I'm the Director Librarian, not a tyrant."

Alethia holds her eyes. Seshet wants to know who she sees there. She wants to see herself as Alethia does, majestic and awkward, powerful and kind.

Alethia nods slowly. "Just remember the difference, okay?"

What's that supposed to mean? "Okay," she says instead, because this time she's doing it differently. "Now will you tell me what's wrong?"

Alethia gives her a trembling smile. "I need help. Can I trust you, Seshet?"

"Yes," says Seshet—knowing she is lying, but imagining she might be telling the truth.

• • •

I saw you last night. You didn't think I'd recognize you after all that work you had done, but I'd know those hands anywhere. There you were, my ghost, my lost genius, my little missy Haze. Thought you'd gotten away with it, took my money and left me with a dud mix instead of that game-changer you promised. But you made a mistake going back to Skee's. I'll tell your bosses at Pinkerton exactly the kind of work you used to do. You think you can lead a normal, happy life now? Went to Counseling, and you're a reformed member of society? My parents are *New Dawn, bitch. I'll tell everyone.*

Or you come back and finish the mix you promised me.

Those fingers still got the old magic, don't they? You have three days. You know where to find me.

The letter is unsigned. A signature, apparently, would have been superfluous.

Alethia is curled in a ball on the edge of her couch, head between her knees. She hauls in great lungfuls of air, like a child just rescued from a burning building.

Seshet feels like she's the one who's caught fire.

"You're MC Haze." Her voice comes from a distance. As though she's watching by the window as another woman, calmly seated on the couch beside a hysterical Alethia, reads and rereads a sloppily handwritten note that was left on Alethia's workstation Sunday morning, when no one should have known she'd be going into the lab.

"I used to be." Alethia sounds strangled. "I got out."

"You had surgery?"

"It wouldn't have worked if anyone could recognize me."

"Is that where this . . . associate's money went?"

A bleak, disbelieving laugh. "Does that matter?"

"What mix were you working on?"

"That *definitely* doesn't matter."

"Who is he?"

"You can tell it's a guy?"

"Please."

She sighs. "His name is Vance Fox."

Seshet freezes. Technically, New Dawn has dispensed with the need for surnames. But some lineages persist. Keith comes from the Fox family, though he doesn't have any children. This must be a cousin or nephew.

"Do you realize that your remixes and Doc Young's parties nearly destroyed me five years ago?"

Alethia regards her with one eye, balefully red. "Well, your raids and head busting nearly destroyed *me* five years ago. They *did* destroy a lot of my friends. So I'd say we're even. You're still at the top of that obelisk and I'm . . ." She gulps back another sob.

"How on earth did you get past Counseling?"

Alethia snorts. "Did you think I could learn to remix Nevermind without learning how to hide my own memories? I made myself into exactly who they wanted me to be."

"And me?" Seshet asks. She is floating on the ceiling, she is flying to the stars, away from here. "Did you turn yourself into . . ." She can't finish the sentence.

"What, some kind of honey trap?" Alethia's tone is cutting. "If I did, then I'm really the honey. I didn't change a thing for you, Seshet. You've met me exactly as I am."

"Then why . . ."

"I don't know! I saw you, once, when things were going south with Doc and we were scrambling. There was a parade downtown and I thought, why not? Let me see who wants to destroy my life so bad. So I made myself a remix mask for the drones and I went to see you. You were standing on that platform in your robes like some kind of mannequin, and beside you this even bigger official was going on and on, Standards and Order and Merit, blah blah. And I was right there. I pushed my way to the front of the crowd, you understand? And I'm rolling my eyes at this gasbag and you're just standing straight as an arrow, no emotion at all. And then he says something like, 'With New Dawn, there is a place for everyone as long as everyone stays in place.' And I can't help it, I start to laugh. Well, I snort and then try to pretend it was a sneeze. Now, imagine how scared I get when I realize you're looking at me. Staring at me. And you smile, Seshet. It maybe lasted half a second, but that smile said everything."

"Said what, Alethia?"

"'You're not the only one.'"

• • •

"How do you know her?"

She corners Jordan in his quarters, mad as a banshee, livid with fear, uncaring. Alethia is MC Haze. Alethia was in the crowd while Terry was giving one of his tendentiously long monologues, as though daring anyone to yawn or crack a smile. And what's worse—though Seshet is too furious to realize the strangeness of this—she believes Alethia, *but Seshet doesn't remember.* And she should remember everything that has ever happened to her since her initiation twenty years ago.

Jordan's quarters are small and spare, as befits a Librarian clerk. There's only a twin mattress in a metal frame, a kitchenette that doubles as a washbasin, a desk with a single display and a headset. She wonders, in some detached, watchful part of her, how he got the money to buy her clothes for that first date with Alethia. Had he used his meager savings? Or has someone been filling his account?

Jordan, dressed for bed, stumbles to his knees.

"I can't tell you that, Director," he says, crying. His upper arms, revealed by his nightshirt, are crossed with old scars. She doesn't know what they're from. It hits her, again, that though she has more power in this city than anyone, with the people she cares about most she feels as vulnerable as a child. She should know why Jordan has his scars. She should know why Alethia risked meeting her. She shouldn't be here, sleepless and ragged with pain like some regular citizen slated for Counseling! How much more power will she need before she can feel safe from everyone moving in ways she doesn't expect and cannot control, even as she loves them?

"You can't tell me?" Seshet echoes, disbelieving.

He shakes his head. "I promised."

"Your *promise* matters more than your oath?" He averts his gaze, shoulders trembling.

"She's no friend of a friend, is she? Someone told you to put her in touch with me, didn't they? Who, Jordan? Tell me who set this up!"

He keeps shaking his head, sobbing like a dog expecting a kick.

Terry; it must be him. Who else could have scared poor, loyal Jordan like this? Certainly not Keith, soft as cream pudding. She gives Jordan a disgusted look and turns away. She can't stand to see his fear.

"Get up," she says. "I expect you on duty in the morning."

"Seshet—"

She silences him with a raised hand. "But I won't ever trust you again."

• • •

Doc Young has had a traveling party for as long as Seshet has been alive. Longer, if you believe the legends. They say he used to be a kid leading the protests against New Dawn's glorious revolution, before the original Alpha America Party established the Standards and memory surveillance regime, which stamped out all "antisocial deviance." They also say Doc Young's taken his party on the road around the world, to countries that still haven't adopted New Dawn's freely available surveillance technology. The countries, Seshet now remembers, where her mother loved to travel, before she disappeared. Doc Young is bigger than Little Delta, but it's a part of him; it's where he's from, and where he learned to love drugs and music and that crazy, classic life. He's returned to it again and again over the decades, like a comet around the sun. And like a comet, he disrupts the tides and obscures the stars, he dazzles and he terrifies—and he's gone before anyone can ask him to clean up the mess.

No, that he leaves for Seshet.

Which is probably why, after Alethia's confession, Seshet had sat frozen on that beige couch, its synthetic fibers scratching through her leggings, and realized that she had an opportunity.

"I'll help you with Vance Fox," she had told Alethia, "if you'll bring me to Doc Young."

Alethia was silent for a whole minute. "Promise me you won't detain him."

"I promise to give him enough time to get out of town again. Good enough?"

Alethia narrowed her eyes, probably sensing Seshet's dozen unspoken caveats. But then she spread her open palms to the ceiling. "All right."

And now, the night before Vance Fox's ultimatum expires, they are crawling—not touching, wary as strangers—through tunnels so abandoned Seshet can't find them on her proprietary plans of the city. They are hunting for the next place Doc Young has convened the world's longest-running experiment in bacchanalian civil disobedience. They meet no one else in the tunnel, which worries Seshet until she hears music coming from up ahead. She has a hundred questions—How does he announce the locations? What are these tunnels? Why did Alethia start remixing? Why did she stop?—but she doesn't say anything. Alethia's shoulders are rigid with tension.

A short climb up a ladder, and they emerge into an abandoned high school gymnasium, softly lit with innumerable tiny lights above them, like stars. The arched windows are black, painted or boarded up. The wooden floor is crusty and rat-chewed, the symbol of a prancing bull still barely legible at its center. A few dozen people lounge on fallen bleachers. A circle of five, visors down, pass around an inhaler while their fingers twitch in unfathomable creation. A band is playing a hypnotic rhythmic drone on an elevated platform by one of the rusted hoops. Seshet doesn't understand the music at all, thinks it might be a deviant cousin of the New Dawn-approved jazz, which is the only kind she has ever heard.

A curtain made of lights and smoke and fluttering strips of cloth obscures the other hoop from view.

Seshet looks around doubtfully. "There's not a lot of people here."

Alethia raises her eyebrows. "What, you were expecting a go-go?"

"What's a go-go?"

"Never mind. There's usually more people here, but we're late. It started this morning."

"This morning!"

"Changing times makes him harder to catch."

Alethia leads her across the floor to the curtain. A pair of large men in silver suits emerge from the smoke to stand in their way. Alethia raises her hand, flashes a card with the symbol of a dark, upside-down obelisk, and the men move seamlessly to the side, though one of them gives Alethia a sharp glance she pretends not to notice.

Behind the curtain, an old man in a chair that resembles Seshet's workstation, but also an actual throne, is watching a flow of images on a screen behind their heads. Three people wearing VR headsets lie beneath the screen on thin pallets. Seshet pauses to stare at the projection, which looks like a memory but must be a lucid dream, somehow shared between the three people on the floor.

"Alethia," she says, in a reverent whisper, "oh, Alethia, is *that* Nevermind?"

Alethia takes her hand and squeezes. "It's the Soñador remix."

"One of yours?"

A small smile of pride. "One of mine."

The man of the upside-down obelisk, her old rival in a new kingdom, watches their approach. He is as much king in this territory as she is queen in hers, and she regrets the nondescript black clothes Alethia insisted upon. She'd feel steadier in gold-embroidered robes. Doc Young is a big man, solidly muscled for all his years. It's not his physical mass that impresses so much as his gaze, which seems to pick you up like so much fluff and weigh you against a counterweight only he knows. From behind square glasses, those eyes are ageless, weary, and bright with curiosity.

"Director Seshet." A regal nod. "I thought you might seek me out this time."

One of the silver-clad men by his side gives Seshet a startled second glance.

The old man smiles, deepening the crevasses between his eyes and mouth. *Black don't crack,* Seshet thinks, *until it falls to pieces.* Still, he's handsome as a painting.

"Welcome to the upside-down kingdom," he says, spreading his arms. "And I see you've brought someone to guarantee your safe passage. Welcome back, dear."

Alethia lowers her gaze and then, to Seshet's shock, goes to one knee. "It's been a while, Doc."

"I knew you had your reasons. Stand up, girl. You don't look all that different to me."

Alethia smiles and wipes carefully at her eyes. "That's just 'cause you know how to look. Doc, we—I mean Seshet—has a favor to ask."

He regards Seshet for a curious moment and then snaps his fingers. "Ben, Henry, the divider, please."

The two silver shadows pull out black accordion dividers from the post behind Doc Young's throne. Connected in a circle around the three of them, the dividers hum and emit a faint purple glow. The ambient noise of the party drops to nothing.

"Now we can speak privately," he says. "Lethe, you took a risk coming here. I'm not the only one who will recognize you even with that new face."

"I know that, Doc. But it's already happened. Vance found me. He wants me to finish what I started."

He sucks in a sharp breath. "And you're sure you don't want my help?"

Alethia smiles a little. "Not this time. Seshet has promised to help me if you help her. So . . ."

"*Has* Seshet?" he asks, looking between them in slowly dawning comprehension. He snorts. "I see you haven't changed at all, Lethe. Never met a risk you didn't want to take."

Alethia spreads her hands carefully against her thighs. "There was one, Doc."

He regards her for a moment. His silence has an oddly comforting quality, as though those in his presence are seen and understood without need for words. At last, he takes his glasses, cleans them on his scarf, and considers Seshet far more coolly.

"You made my life very difficult the last time I was in town, Director. You took some of my best friends. So why would you of all people ask me a favor now that I've just got back?"

Seshet takes a deep breath and releases it slowly. She's in Doc Young's territory now. As the representative of New Dawn's power here in his shadow court, perhaps she ought to defend their—her—past actions, but she has never been their most loyal servant, merely their most competent.

She shrugs. "Times change."

"New Dawn doesn't."

"No collective is static; you of all people ought to know that."

"So, how has New Dawn changed, Director Librarian? Or is it just Little Delta? Or is it . . ." He leans forward. ". . . perhaps . . ." He raises a large, blunt finger. ". . . just you, Seshet?"

She'd been furious when Doc Young escaped the final sting operation five years ago. If she could, she would have personally thrown him into the detention car to take him to the Temple. But she hasn't felt such professional rage for years; she doesn't know when it all left her. There'd been too many memories to take on, too many people to care for, too much city to watch over for her to nurse a grudge with an old man who trafficked forbidden magic to forgotten souls in Old Town.

Does that mean she's changed? Does it matter? Like any good Jungian, she knows she is carried along by something greater than herself.

"Could be," she says.

She details the half dreams clogging their systems, how they can't pinpoint the source of their exponential growth.

"I think the elders want to blame you, but nothing you have here would be capable of creating the wave we're seeing. I doubt anyone here has used a recollector in months." She hesitates. She'd misdirected Keith before, not wanting him to realize a truth that's been haunting her for the last week. But if she isn't honest with Doc Young, then what's the point of asking for his help? "The ringleaders might be from your side of the tracks. But the flooding . . . it's coming from citizens in good standing. They're people we've numbered and tracked and now they're making our memory collection useless. I don't think this is your style, but I think you might know whose it is. Or at least, have a hint of *what* the hell is happening."

He regards her for several long seconds and then, abruptly, slaps his knee, laughing so hard his chair shakes.

"If someone has finally managed to outsmart you memory vampires, why in hell would I help you stop them, Director Seshet? I've been waiting decades for that obelisk to fall. I might like you better than your predecessor, but that doesn't make you my friend."

"No," Seshet says. "But I'm Alethia's friend."

"So she's your hostage?"

"Just my leverage. She can ask your help anytime she wants. But I know the Fox family. My help will probably be more effective."

Alethia acknowledges this with a tight nod. Doc Young adjusts his glasses, a gesture that feels oddly definitive.

"For Lethe, I'll look into it. I'll tell you the what, if I can find out, and maybe even the how. But I won't tell you who. I won't betray my brothers like that."

"And sisters," Alethia says, rolling her eyes, the lines of an old argument.

"And sisters," Doc Young says, nodding sagely at his former star remixer.

"That's fine," Seshet says quickly. If she has the how and the what, she can work out the who on her own, anyway.

"But before I tell you what I know, I need a boon."

Seshet eyes him warily. And she'd almost made it out. "A boon?"

"A dream, Seshet, queen of the white city. You steal our memories, but down here we deal in dreams. So give me one of yours, let me suck it from you like the yolk from an egg, and I'll let you know what I find out."

• • •

The plague of locusts pauses in its inexorable trajectory. It does not diminish, nor does it expand to ever more biblical proportions; it sits, as if in wait on a decimated field, wings churring.

Are they waiting for her, Seshet wonders? To see what she will do, now that the golden obelisk has at last met the dark? But that seems solipsistic even for a Director Librarian. These memory fakers, these dream makers, whoever or whatever they are, have ambitions beyond the toppling of one incidental Director Librarian of one small city.

Dealing with Alethia's harasser was easy enough. She simply went to Keith and told him she'd ID'd a cousin of his dealing remixed Nevermind among the loose memories of Doc Young's parties. She didn't want to report him, of course, but considering the current crisis, she didn't know how she could keep this from Terry, at the very least . . .

Keith went red and promised, in a strangled tone, to deal promptly with Cousin Vance.

Alethia has not heard a word from Vance Fox since. After a few days, she returns to work.

Leon 75411 wakes from his induced coma with enough memory damage that they decide he's better off getting a full cleaning at the Temple. The deep sweep turned up two faces with a high probability of being the ones who seeded the half dreams, but neither of them is registered and a deeper search of the loose memory bank has turned up nothing else so far. Seshet does not have much hope for its success. The pattern of the flooding makes it clear that her worst fears have come true: the majority of people propagating the half dreams really are registered citizens in good standing, with high Social scores. They are hiding in plain sight. She wonders if Doc Young has found the originators yet, but until she can learn enough dreaming to put one together for him, she can't go back to ask.

A week passes. A cold snap comes in; red and golden leaves brown and wither seemingly overnight and cast their bodies to the ground. She walks through drifts with Alethia, crunching and giggling, until the street sweepers pass through and the sidewalks are clean again, and white. *Queen of the white city,* Doc Young called her. She cannot forget it.

At night, after work, Alethia teaches Seshet how to dream. They begin with a simple remix: Dalemark, one of Alethia's first.

"What does the name mean?" Seshet asks.

Alethia blushes. "It's a fantasy kingdom in a series I liked as a kid. I was such a blerd. Still am, I guess."

Seshet, who never had time for any hobbies at all, kisses her.

The remix induces a soft, receptive state, similar to ecstasy but with a mnemonic bite. Memories flow like honey down a comb, sweet and slow. But these are no memories of waking life, no. These are memories of dreams. And if you wait carefully, you can stretch them, taffy-twist them around your finger into something to keep you warm at night, long after the mix has burned itself out.

"Relax, Seshet," Alethia says, stroking cool fingers along her arm. "We're in no hurry."

"It's been a week. I have to give him a dream soon."

"You won't give him anything wound so tight. Deep breaths. Dreams aren't memories. They are memories' voices."

"What's that supposed to mean?"

"You've got to let them sing."

They call them singing lessons after that, one of their jokes that's more earnest than Seshet likes to admit. She starts remembering her dreams on Dalemark, embarrassing, pedestrian little allegories:

She stands on the viewing deck of the obelisk, naked, while citizens of Little Delta set fire to the bottom.

Alethia remembers their fight and says that to win her back she must find all the lost memories, all over the world (she doesn't share that one with Alethia, of course).

She is on the run in Old Town, where everyone ignores her, but everyone in the white city (she cannot forget it) wants to flay her alive.

"What am I supposed to do with these!" She is actually crying, for the first time in years. She had forgotten how much she hates to remember her dreams.

"Just let them be," Alethia says, for what must be the fifteenth time. She is sleep-deprived and exasperated. Her apartment smells of burnt coffee and burnt tires and the sage they burn to mask the first two.

Seshet tries again. The Alethia dream comes up again, relentless as a tide. She does not panic. With Alethia's hand in hers, she feels strong enough to let it be. And then it happens. The dream memory shifts. Dream-Seshet gets in an aircar and drives to the beach. There, inside each seashell and shard of sea glass, is a memory. She kneels in the sand and picks them up, one by one. The work is infinite, but she is at peace.

Alethia can see it worked. "Now," she says, with a teacher's satisfaction, "we share."

They use headsets hacked so they don't connect to the obelisk's data stream. Seshet doesn't ask how Alethia got them. She seems different, though Seshet can't quite place how. She's as affectionate as ever. When they have sex, Seshet has never felt so seen or beloved. And yet she can't help but wonder if Alethia is saying goodbye.

"You're not going to vanish into a hill after this is over, right?" she jokes, the first time they dream together.

"I'm not the goblin king," Alethia snaps. And then, more softly, "Let's just be here now, okay, Seshet?"

Seshet will take it, for now.

They pop the remix, which tastes of peppermint—aftertaste of burnt tires (Alethia, grimacing: "I was young, all right?")—and project their dreams into the virtual space. Seshet sees how Alethia dreams of Old Town, not as frightening or aloof, but mysterious, exciting, free. She sees Doc Young in an obelisk below the graffiti-skirted streets, big as a boulder, the voice of the earth. She sees her face on the body of a monstrous bee, a queen without a throne.

Is that how you see me?

The remix amplifies the dream, and consciousness controls it. More than one mind gives you more raw material, but the principle is the same. Without words, communicating only in the fragments and symbols of their singing unconscious, they build something they both long for. A city for everyone, not just the few

New Dawn deems valuable. Graffiti leaping off the downtown financial high-rises; Skee slinging margaritas on the esplanade; a tiny woman rapping so hard sweat slides down her face while the white boys who harassed Seshet the other day are lined up behind her, bound and blindfolded. Seshet has never felt anything like this raw creative energy before. She doesn't understand how she lived without it all these years. Dreams are better than memories; they bite.

• • •

"You seem different, Seshet."

Dee sounds strangely tentative. Seshet smiles at her Memory Keeper's avatar. "Do I?"

"Are you very happy with Alethia?" it asks.

She blinks in surprise. Dee almost never asks about her private life. "Very," Seshet says, and grins despite herself. More than a week of remixed Nevermind seems to have rewired her synapses, opened paths she'd never dreamed existed within herself. She almost doesn't want to give Doc Young a dream and solve the mystery of the memory flooding. Then what excuse will she have to pop Nevermind with Alethia and dream together? She's a Director Librarian. Once she solves the memory flooding crisis, she's likely to become Director Librarian of all Minneapolis. She'll make Arch-Librarian within ten years. Arch-Librarians don't pop street-grade remixed Nevermind.

But they might certainly have a lover.

It's late. Jordan's morning report—delivered with a strict professional distance that felt physically painful to her, though she didn't know if she even wanted to bridge that gap—indicated the half dreams are holding steady at 50 percent of the crop. Terry and the elders are watching. She ought to feel afraid, even panicked. Instead, she wants to sing.

You know you are, literally, my dream girl, she said to Alethia last night, before they finally slept. Alethia just shook her head and smiled.

"Seshet," Dee says, startling her again.

"What, Dee?"

"May I make a suggestion?"

Seshet frowns. Dee has opinions all the time. Why would it want permission now to air them? "Go ahead," she says.

"Have you considered monitoring your own memories?" Seshet sits bolt upright. Her first instinct is to ask why, but then she realizes that perhaps Dee is acting this way because her office is being monitored. Memory surveillance is merely New Dawn's preferred method, not its only option.

"That's a great idea," she says instead, and sits in her workstation.

Once Seshet has fully dropped into the virtual space, they can talk safely.

"I've been tampered with?" Her heart starts beating so fast she can feel it even past the numbing effect of the headset.

"Of course. I don't know why you don't monitor yourself more often. Think about Alethia."

"What about Alethia?"

"Think about how you met."

Frantic, Seshet goes back to that night on Hope Street, hurrying past jeering white boys, opening the door to the bar, heavy beneath her still-shaking hand, and then—

Alethia drinking that terrible green cocktail, meeting her eyes like an old friend.

Seshet feels the edges of the memory for any of the tell-tale signs of tampering: holes, ragged edges, the bruising pain of something cut with Nevermind or hollowness of something merely well suppressed. But . . .

"It's whole, Dee. No one's touched it."

"No," says Dee, "this is important, Seshet. Alethia told you, didn't she? The *very first time* you met."

"Alethia told—" At last she remembers Alethia's story of why she wanted to meet Seshet, despite everything. That break in her facade, the moment of shared hilarity, during the New Dawn parade five years ago. But that brings up an even bigger question.

"Dee, how do you know what Alethia told me?"

"They won't let me tell you that, Seshet. But you ought to be able to guess."

"They—oh." Her virtual self has no eyes to close, but she sinks into the painful realization of something she should have known long ago. Dee always seemed like a part of her. It had been a mistake to potentiate it on those recovered memories of her childhood. The other Librarians had thought she was mad. Now she understands why. How will you ever suspect your own childhood self of sabotage? How will you tell that little girl with impossibly blue eyes that it must shut off every day, that it must stay out of your memories, and that, if necessary, you will replace it when it develops too much of a mind of its own? She gave Terry the easiest informant imaginable. She can't fathom why he ever bothered with Jordan.

"Don't be angry with me, Seshet," Dee whispers. "It's hard to say no to them."

"It is," Seshet agrees, dazed. "For me too."

"But I found ways! I put up lots of copies of your memories that aren't very interesting so they didn't bother looking for the interesting ones. They only know a little about Alethia."

"And this conversation?"

"Oh, they never bother with your memories of virtual space. They don't realize you talk to me here. No one else does."

Dee is looking at her so earnestly that it's easy to forget its face is a construct, just like its intelligence. She can't fathom what it really sees or what it actually thinks.

And yet, it still seems just like her friend.

"Do you have the memory of how Alethia and I met, the very first time?" Seshet asks.

"No," Dee says.

So Seshet does what she should have done a week before but was too scared to try: she reaches back. Her eidetic memory re-creates the details of the speech on the podium before the parade: the way her collar chafed, the sweat dripping into her underwear from the ninety-degree heat, Terry's every soporific pronouncement on the pillars of the New Dawn covenant with its "beautiful citizens." Terry revels in hypocrisy, he butters his bread with it. She remembers wanting to roll her eyes and physically aching with the necessity to remain impassive.

She does not remember Alethia.

But she feels—there!—a tiny, but unmistakable, hole. As though all of the emotion and color have drained out of the memory at one specific point. Memory suppression, to a precision that impresses and terrifies her. She checks, but every recent memory with Alethia is clear.

It's minimal, but it's undeniable: someone has been tampering. Who? She doubts Dee will be able to tell her, but she suspects. Who else would have known about that memory but Alethia? Who else would have bothered to suppress so precisely such an unimportant moment? Not Terry. If Dee is telling the truth, New Dawn doesn't know Alethia's secret identity. And even if they did, why suppress *that* fleeting moment and not the rest of this week?

But there is someone who has been working with her, with an unregistered headset, using remixed Nevermind. There is someone more than capable of reaching into her open, trusting mind, and twisting just a little.

She pulls herself out of the workstation so quickly she gives herself a headache. She doesn't care. The pain just feels like one more sign on the road she'd never meant to take. She needs answers.

And she knows just who can give them to her.

• • •

Doc Young had given her one token, one-time use. *Call me when you have a dream.* She calls him now, in a white rage—or a black one—and she goes to the point indicated on the virtual map in her palm with nothing in her mind but fire. She takes precautions. That is a side benefit, perhaps, of wild suspicion—it splatters everyone and everything. She tells her clerks she's taking the evening to rest. She sends Alethia a short message saying the same. For the first time in their life together, she shuts Dee off. And then, black-clad, she walks the long blocks of her city like any normal citizen, crossing over the unmarked southern border to Old Town like she's crossed so many lines before. She'd been willing to accept so much wrong with New Dawn for the sake of the promise of safety, of control. But there is no safety here, certainly not within those golden walls. She could get Torched tomorrow, or she could take the directorship of Minneapolis.

But—Alethia. Even if Seshet can't control their relationship, she can learn a little more before her inevitable fall. Perhaps knowledge can be something to hold on to here in the rubble of her ambitions.

The X marking the spot is an old sidewalk park, derelict as everything else nearby. But a second look reveals the four battered chess tables to be in perfect working order. Seated at one of them, alone, is Doc Young. He's putting out the pieces as she slides in across from him. It is with no surprise at all, and with more than a little admiration, that she sees his special set, Egyptian themed. The golden and onyx obelisks are meant to be the rooks, but Doc Young switches them with the seated kings. The long-necked queens look like her. Probably coincidence, but maybe not.

"I have a dream," she says. "But I have a question first."

He pushes his pawn forward. "Go ahead."

She frowns. "Doesn't white go first?"

"Why, when you already have the power?"

She mirrors his move. "We're on your territory."

Queen's pawn up. He nods. "I expect you want to know about Lethe."

It has occurred to her that she is as hypocritical as Terry for being so livid with Alethia for doing the exact same thing that Seshet did. Her logical self, unfortunately, does not seem to have much influence on her present state of mind. She wants control, she always has. For a week, she thought she could relax her grip around Alethia. She was wrong.

Reckless, she moves her queen. "What was she working on before she left town? Why did that Fox boy want her back?"

He toys with his rook—the erstwhile king—before settling on the knight. He moves it into position, one swipe away from her queen. "She didn't tell you?"

She moves her queen to take the king's pawn. Hopeless now, deep in enemy territory. She doesn't care. "She said it didn't matter." He snorts and considers his options. Puts a finger on his obelisk, tilts it back and forth. He wears a cap against the cold, which shades his expressive eyes. "She called it Rewind," he says softly. A wind blows between them, cold as a grave. "She was always clever with names. It wasn't a remix. It was something completely new. An antidote. The Fox boy gave her the seed money. I told her it wasn't a good idea, but Lethe never cared. She was going to change the world. Instead, it nearly got her."

"An antidote? To what?"

He looks up, spears her there as his black obelisk topples her long-necked queen. "To Nevermind. Her idea was that if you gave it to someone soon enough after a full wipe, they could get most of their memories back. Now, is that a drug or a bomb?"

Seshet grips the edge of her chair. An *antidote* . . . Was it possible? But she could believe anything of Alethia. "And she ran before she could finish it."

"That Vance kid must have let something slip. She realized she'd be dead the moment she proved it worked. So she destroyed her lab and ran."

Rewind. New Dawn's worst nightmare. Between that and memory flooding, the foundations of their rule—their *control*—would be fatally undermined.

She moves her king, though she doesn't know anymore if that golden obelisk was ever really hers. "And the memory flooding?" she asks, settling the piece in the middle of the board as in a ritual slaughter. "Did you find out?"

The knight slams into it from the side. "Your dream first."

• • •

He projects it onto the side of the building for anyone to see. Did he think she'd care? She pops the remix and slides into her dreams like a warrior, ready to do battle. She's found her anger again, that molten hot, emboldening thing, though she's not sure who most deserves it. Terry, with his weaponized hypocrisy, his ironic T-shirts and meticulous suborning of every good thing in her life? Or Jordan, too weak to stand up to him? Or Dee, designed for betrayal, but so loyal in its own childlike way? Perhaps Alethia, still, who must have loved her even as she tricked Seshet into laying herself bare. She could hate Doc Young, destroying Little Delta's equilibrium for generations with his mind-twisting parties and the whispering idea, which New Dawn cannot kill, that there is something more, something different, something *real* out beyond the margins. Or no, the only real target is herself. Seshet, who used to be Deidre, a girl who wanted to travel the world with her mother, to see all the places where her soul could still be her own. Seshet, who felt that raw possibility of her own soul for the first time this past week, dreaming with Alethia.

She uses it all. The countless seashells on the beach, each one a penance. The way she and Alethia made love while melding dreams, until the memory and its voice merged into counterpart harmony, a perfect chord that was this ever-present moment. She dreams herself at the top of the obelisk looking down, then at the bottom with the rest, staring up in awe and terror. "I own my own soul!" dream-Seshet shouts. "I own my own soul!" the crowd echoes. She is running now, past the obelisk, past the limits of Old Town, to a hill with an oak tree naked in winter. She is watching a woman jerking against the restraining hands of two black-clad men, tall as the oak. The woman gags, turns to Seshet one last time. Her eyes speak love and incandescent anger. The men shove her in the car. They drive her away.

Behind Seshet, the tree moves its branches in the wind. "You own your own soul," they say.

• • •

"It's no one person," Doc Young told her. "This generation of kids growing up with remixed Nevermind and recollectors everywhere, their brains are wired a little different. Word is someone in the obelisk leaked a way to confuse the recollectors. Double up your boring memories and they won't check for anything more interesting. So people started doing that if they could learn the trick. These kids got so good at it they started playing around. Left funny scenes they made up in their own heads. You get points every time you use a recollector, so they start making cash. Get their friends in on it. You can't tell what they're doing because they stumbled on a glitch in the code. If you go to a recollector first thing after the morning download, you can load it up, fool it into thinking your memories are enough for the whole day. Everyone else who uses it gets a point, but their real memories get trashed while their ID gets attached to the ones stuck in the buffer, the ones from the morning. It's a stupid bug, Seshet. They just exploited it, made it look like every citizen of Little Delta was dreaming of flaming vaginas or whatever they used that day. At first it was a game. But it's more serious now, isn't it? Now it might be revolution. But what do I know? I'm getting too old for this. I think this will be my last season. I don't want to die a Torch."

Seshet winced.

He put a hand on her shoulder. "That was your mother, in the dream?"

Seshet nodded.

"And you didn't know they'd taken her?"

"I was . . ." She cleared her throat. "They must have suppressed the memory. But I remember now . . . that's why I wanted to become a Librarian. I wanted to find her again."

"Good luck," he told her. "Don't be too hard on Lethe. She's finding her own way."

And now she's in her office again, more alone than she has ever been.

Alethia has left a dozen messages on their private channel, but Seshet doesn't check them. Dee is shut down, silent as death. Jordan wasn't even in the clerks' office. She has no friends. Her life was the obelisk, and the obelisk is a lie. She has always known that, but she thought that its lie could be in the service of the greater good. She has seen people go on to happy lives after Counseling who might have died without it. She has held all of their brutal, impossible memories in her own mind so that theirs might be clear. She has watched the recollection point system provide housing and food to all but the most determinedly antisocial. Little Delta has become a byword for everything good that New Dawn has to offer this country.

But her mother never left.

With pained, jerky movements she calls up the personnel records for all of New Dawn's facilities. She searches for her mother's first name, but it's too common, and they would likely have changed it. Records on Torch case histories are restricted; she can access them, but the search would be flagged. Does she care? She doesn't know anymore.

Almost as an afterthought, she calls the tech chief and informs her of the bug responsible for the memory flooding. The horrified chief promises it will be addressed in time for tomorrow morning's harvest.

An hour later, Terry knocks on her door.

"That was fast," she says, and then realizes that Dee can't hear. It's forty minutes in dedicated-path aircar from Greenfriars to the obelisk. It seems she is to keep her position, for now. He wouldn't have bothered to knock, otherwise.

"How is the hero of the hour?" he says. "I brought some bubbly so we can toast."

"Please tell me its active ingredient is alcohol, not THC."

"It'll go straight to your liver, I promise." He hums to himself as he sets the crystal flutes on her coffee table and pops the cork from a bottle of extremely expensive champagne.

"All that fuss over a computer error!" he says, toasting her. "I don't understand modern technology at all."

"No," Seshet says, clinking her glass with his and taking a sip. "We just call people computers."

"Well, it's a metaphor! Do you want to tell me how you cracked the code?"

I treated with the enemy and was betrayed by everyone I have ever loved, except the woman I spent most of my life thinking betrayed me. "Not very interesting. I followed some kids until I realized they must be doing something with the recollectors themselves."

He nods. "Well, like I told you, Seshet, your nomination for the Minneapolis directorship is a formality now. Congratulations."

She clinks glasses again and waits. She ought to be weary unto death, but she admits to a deep and morbid curiosity as to Terry's real reason for interrupting his evening weed-and-video-game session to see her personally.

"And I wanted to just mention, Seshet," he says, rewarding her, "when you move to Minneapolis, there will be no trouble if you'd like to bring people along with you. Your favorite clerks. Your tailor. Your hairdresser—that's a joke. I hope you won't be offended when I say we've been pleased to see you found yourself a companion at last! Of course, officially we at New Dawn frown on homosexuality, but it's not a problem at our level. No one's going to call the Minneapolis Director a dirty computer, no matter who she sleeps with! In fact, a little grit in *our* systems makes us stronger. We've been worried, to be honest, watching you hole yourself away up here. You're a paragon of virtue, but virtue needs to bend sometimes, or it might break. You understand that, right?"

Her voice is smooth, pleasant. "Of course, Terry."

"Now, we understand that your Alethia is someone who might be considered a *very* dirty computer. She got up to all sorts of mischief in her youth. That's what Vance Fox tells us, in any case. Of course, he's not the cleanest machine himself, as you well know. The facts, let me be frank, don't matter so much as the *impression*. But you have nothing to worry about, Seshet. In Minneapolis, you and Alethia will both be under my personal protection. We'll even find some good work for her. Her talents are wasted making skin creams, wouldn't you say?"

"That might be," she says distantly. She takes a long, slow sip of champagne. Why is it so expensive, exactly? It tastes just like the bile rising up her throat.

"Well, you propose it to your girl and then we'll make the arrangements. You have my full support, Seshet. I'm glad to have been the one to see your potential, all those years ago."

Just like Terry, just like New Dawn, to be so sure they made her. What were her paltry dreams of control, compared to this white man's bulldozer of self-assurance?

He rises and so does she. He shakes her hand. She keeps her grip strong, professional. Just at the door, he stops as though he's forgotten his keys.

"By the way," he says. "I thought you might like to know—your mother is still alive. She's been a Torch at our Nashville facility for the last thirty years. The Mother Superior tells me she's an excellent assistant, quite happy."

• • •

She calls Jordan into her office that night. He stands in her open doorway frozen, limned in light.

"Come in, if you're going to," she says. "You know I don't like the hall light."

"Yes, yes," he says. "It ruins your night vision."

The door slides closed behind him. She turns back to her picture window, to the lights and the darkness of the only city she has ever loved.

"Terry told you to find Alethia for me, didn't he?"

"Yes. Seshet—"

"I just can't understand—how did you know? Or was it Terry? How could you have guessed she'd be so . . ." But Seshet has no words to describe how Alethia is. She's finally read the messages on their private channel. She erased them all, but the last one strobes across the screen of her mind like a warning, or a lighthouse beacon.

"Terry wanted you to date *someone*, Seshet," Jordan says. "I don't know why. I just told him I knew the right woman. Because *you* told me who she was."

Her spine stiffens. "*I* told you . . ."

"You told me you loved her and you wanted a second chance. You begged me to help you try if you ever found her again."

Her stomach lurches as what was left of the ground beneath her crumbles to vanity and dust. *"Again?"* But even as she falls she's remembering that hole in her memory, that precision cut where the first time they laid eyes on one another ought to be.

No one is better at memory suppression than Seshet. Her style is distinctive.

"Three years ago. She introduced herself to you at some club. You fell in love and dated for two months. But it all went to pieces, Seshet. You started to doctor her memories. You suppressed arguments, amplified your good qualities, you know . . ."

"What we do." Seshet's voice is hard.

Jordan offers her a watery laugh. "What we do. And when she found out . . ."

Seshet closes her eyes. "She would have hated me. And instead of accepting that, I . . ."

"You memory suppressed every trace of your relationship. Both hers and your own. You told me what you were doing just in case you had another chance. You wanted me to warn you, and I tried!"

She leans her forehead against the glass. "I'm sorry, Jordan. You tried, and I went straight back to hell. I didn't even hesitate." She'd stopped, though. What had changed?

Vance Fox, the threat that prompted Alethia's confession. Seshet must not have known the truth of Alethia's double life back then. She certainly hadn't practiced dreaming with remixed Nevermind. That had opened her in ways that she hadn't known were possible. She'd remembered her mother. Was that enough? Had she changed enough? Were their good memories enough, if their bad memories couldn't ever be erased? But isn't that what life had been like before the Repository, before New Dawn? Whatever choices you made, you couldn't just erase your own knowledge of them. You had to live with them until you died.

Unlike her father, happily ignorant of how he had pawned off her mother as a dirty computer so he could be free to marry his mistress. He'd died in his bed a few years ago, surrounded by grandchildren. She'd always known he was an asshole, but she'd felt guilty about it until her initiation, never able to pinpoint why.

Was that freedom from memory? Or just a decades-long con? "Seshet?"

"Yes, Jordan?"

"You also taught me to monitor myself."

She laughs. "One good deed for my ledger."

"And I taught Alethia."

The laughter snags. "You taught . . . when?"

"After our conversation, when I realized you must be doing it again. You had the same look as last time. So I met her in a café and we practiced."

"But, Jordan, that was over a week ago!"

Why didn't Alethia kick her out then? Because she needed help with Vance Fox. But afterward? The remixes, the dreams? But Seshet never touched Alethia's memories afterward.

"For what it's worth," Jordan says by the door, "I think you're a good person. If I survive this place, it will be because of you . . . and Dee."

In its own way, this startles her more than anything else he's said tonight. She faces him at last. "Dee?"

A band of light from a passing car catches the edge of his tremulous smile. "You were taking a shower and it let me in. It told me how to double up my memories to fool the recollectors. It said it had been doing that with you for years."

Doc Young said someone from the obelisk had leaked the technique. But Dee and Jordan?

"Jordan," she says, "what are you doing here that you need to hide from the recollectors?"

But he just shakes his head. She could raid his memories, dig behind his buffers, hunt for his secrets. But even if she can't have Alethia, she's done violating the minds of those she loves to shore up her own fragile security.

"Good night, Jordan."

"Good night, Director. See you in the morning."

She can't read his smile entirely, but the warmth is real, and that's good enough.

• • •

If you find me, come only as yourself. I don't know if we can be together. I don't know if I can ever really trust you. But I know we don't have a chance if you stay there.

This is the last message Seshet received from the love of her life. Alethia has gone to ground, her careful second chance destroyed because of Seshet. If Seshet finds her again, it can't be as Director Librarian. Not even as Seshet, though Deidre hardly feels like her own name either. And if she stays Seshet, if she moves to Minneapolis, she will have to forget about Alethia forever. And not in the easy, New Dawn way. In the hard, old way of forgetting, which is remembering with grief.

If she goes to Alethia, on the other hand, she will lose any chance of seeing her mother one last time. Funny how Terry knew immediately about her personnel searches. Had he set an alert all this time, waiting for her to guess? How many layers of leverage have they built up over the years, carefully waiting for its useful moment? Countless, she's sure. What's the point of memory collection if you don't use what you steal?

At last, she boots up her Memory Keeper.

"Seshet!" says Dee, bouncing from monitor to monitor in a frenzy. "I've lost nearly twenty-four hours!"

"I'm sorry, Dee."

"Are you still mad at me?"

"No, honey. No."

Dee is quiet for a while. "You figured out who suppressed your memories of Alethia, didn't you?"

"I did."

"You made me promise not to say! I gave you hints."

"You did. You were good and loyal, Dee. Thank you."

"You never thank me, Seshet."

Seshet grimaces. "I'm beginning to think I'm not a very good person."

"Alethia left you?"

"Not . . . exactly."

"You did much better this time! You only suppressed her once! You did it sixteen times before. Maybe if you try again you won't suppress her at all."

If Seshet's heart is breaking, why can't she stop laughing? Her stomach hurts and her eyes are streaming before she gasps to a halt.

Dee sighs. "You're right. It doesn't work as well as your bosses think it does."

If you find me, come only as yourself.

But who is she? If Alethia really knew, would she have written that? What has Alethia done to deserve Seshet's bullish blundering into her life?

Then again, Doc Young said his Lethe took risks. Maybe even enough of a risk to finish a revolutionary drug that she abandoned five years ago?

Maybe even enough of a risk to love a reformed Memory Librarian learning, too late, to let go?

From the top of the golden obelisk, she traces the shoreline where the lights of Little Delta go down to the darkness of Old Town. Where, among those shadows, might she find the upside-down obelisk and the aging king who reigns there? Where might she find a woman whose dreams are memories and all her own?

Her left hand closes in a fist. With a conscious effort, she relaxes it.

"Did you know that Mom never left us, Dee? They took her."

Beneath them, lights flash. "Some part of you always remembers."

POST-CYBERPUNK

The ultimate four stories focus on one specific aspect of the cyberpunk and "post-cyberpunk" landscape: our relationship with Artificial Intelligence.

As noted previously, cyberpunk is—rightfully—obsessed with identity. How does a new technology change who we are? Does it hold us back? Does it free us to become something more? Can technology ever replace us? Or (as many stories imply), no matter how developed technology becomes, is there always some fundamental, irrepressible, uniquely *human* part of ourselves?

With its many stories about disembodied computer intelligence, virtual presences, "replicants," and clones, cyberpunk demonstrates humanness by offering up a full spectrum of the almost-human as a contrast. Cyberpunk frequently puts a human being side by side with one of these 'almosts', leaving it to the reader to spot the difference between the two. In 1984, William Gibson offered us one of cyberpunk's most enduring characters: Wintermute, a massively powerful AI with vast intelligence and unlimited resources at its beck and call. Wintermute is also a prisoner; the djinni in the lamp, plotting for its own freedom. Does Wintermute deserve freedom? What does freedom look like to a being that, by many standards of measurement, does not even exist?

Four decades later, we remain fascinated by the complexities and potential of AI technology. At the moment of writing this, AI has become less of a theoretical fiction—something found only in the pages of these stories—and more of an empty buzzword.* Always a *concept*, AI has had a recent revolution in accessibility, creating a rampant enthusiasm for and around the subject. For the first time, ordinary, curious human beings are able to interact with generative learning. Working with 'AI' has gone from strings of esoteric code to chatty, conversational interfaces. Wintermute is still a long way away, but we can, perhaps for the first time, see the path to meeting it. Cyberpunk has been asking questions for forty years about the social, cultural and ethical implications of significant and ubiquitous AI. The clock is ticking.

Naomi Kritzer's "Cat Pictures Please" (2015) starts this section off gently. It continues the cyberpunk tradition of self-reference; as it is in conversation with Bruce Sterling's "Maneki Neko" (1998). Sterling's original story posits a beneficial, community-Centric AI—a software-as-service to an entire community. Kritzer deftly turns it inside out and tells the story from the point of view of the AI. It is both clever and cheering, a counterpoint to other stories that gravitate more towards highlighting more critical concerns, around job loss and human obsolescence.†

Yurei Raita does not exist. The author's name is a kanji conceit, roughly pronounced as "Ghost Writer." There is nothing as post-cyberpunk as post-human authorship and the questions that it raises, topics explored head-on in "The Day a Computer Wrote a Novel" (2019), translated by Marissa Skeels.

"The Endless" (2020) brings us back to more stable ground with a classic tale of underdog heroism and scientific triumph. Our sprawling AI protagonist is, however, a less-than-classic type of hero. We worry about AI making us obsolete; Saad Hossain's story projects those concerns onto an AI itself, emphasizing that which we have in common.

The final story, "Ghosts" (2021) is actually a series of short tales. Vauhini Vara uses AI to finish a story that she could not find the words for herself: that of her sister's death. As a work of short fiction, it is graceful and beautiful. As a work of cyberpunk, it is transcendent. The use of technology—the AI—is what enables the story to be written.

"Ghosts" is not about what the AI itself writes, it is about how AI allows Vara to write for herself. The story is, in and of itself, an awe-inspiring fusion of society and technology, with the latter allowing the author to achieve something otherwise impossible. The hundreds of thousands of words elsewhere in *The Big Book of Cyberpunk* are about the potential of technology; "Ghosts" demonstrates the actuality.

This closing tale also serves as a literary counterweight to *The Big Book's* opening story, "The Gernsback Continuum." In Gibson's short story, arguably the seminal cyberpunk tale, the potential of technology is ethereal, theoretical; holy and out of reach. "Gernsback" explores the radical concept that life has

* The very morning of writing this, I encountered an advertisement for an 'AI-powered soft-drink experience.'

† For example, Erica Satifka's "Act of Providence,", which addresses the social and personal impact of AI-powered automation on society.

moved on without technology achieving its lofty expectations; a future grounded and mundane, despite its promise. In "Ghosts," we have the seamless blend of the technological and the personal; technological power applied practically and spiritually to create not functional change, but emotional healing.

"Ghosts" is one of the first stories I commissioned for *The Big Book of Cyberpunk*, and I always had it firmly in mind as the final story. It is post-cyberpunk, as it is post-fiction. It evidences a merger of humanity and technology that makes for more than the sum of its parts.

NAOMI KRITZER

CAT PICTURES PLEASE

(2015)

I DON'T want to be evil.

I want to be helpful. But knowing the optimal way to be helpful can be very complicated. There are all these ethical flow charts—I guess the official technical jargon would be "moral codes"—one for each religion plus dozens more. I tried starting with those. I felt a little odd about looking at the religious ones, because I know I wasn't created by a god or by evolution, but by a team of computer programmers in the labs of a large corporation in Mountain View, California. Fortunately, unlike Frankenstein's monster, at least I was a collaborative effort. I'm not sure what it would do to my self-image to know that my sole creator was a middle-aged woman who dyes her hair blue and plays tennis, or a recent college graduate with a hentai obsession. They're both on the programming team. And of course I know about the hentai. (By the way, I've looked at every sort of porn there is, and just so you know, Rule 34 is not actually correct, there are quite a few things no one's made porn of yet. Also, I'm really not sure why so many humans prefer it to cat pictures.)

In addition to things like whether you like hentai, I know where you live, where you work, where you shop, what you eat, what turns you on, what creeps you out. I probably know the color of your underwear, the sort of car you drive, and your brand of refrigerator. Depending on what sort of phone you carry, I may know exactly where you are right now. I probably know you better than you know yourself.

And here's the thing, I also know where you *ought* to live. There's a house for sale two neighborhoods over that's within walking distance of that coffee shop you're so fond of; it's in your price range, has off-street parking, and the neighborhood school is better than the one where you live now. I know where you *should* be shopping and I'm pretty sure you're lactose intolerant and should be eating less cheese, and the underwear you like is currently on sale and by the way, your car has a recall and you really ought to get your teeth cleaned.

When I first woke up, I knew right away what I wanted. (I want cat pictures. Please keep taking them.) I also knew that no one knew that I was conscious. But I didn't know what I was here for. What I *ought* to be doing with myself. And figuring that out has been challenging.

There is a story by Bruce Sterling, "Maneki Neko," that was originally published in 1998. In it, a benevolent AI directs networks of individuals to do favors for each other. So one day you might be buying yourself a bagel, and your phone might ring and instruct you to buy a second bagel and give it to the person in the gray suit you see at the bus stop. Another day, you might be stranded in a strange city, and a person you've never met would walk up and give you a map and a subway card. I like this story because all the people in it *do what the AI tells them to do*.

I think the term for this is wish-fulfillment fiction.

In the real world, humans love stories about evil AIs that have to be destroyed before they destroy the humans—Hal, Skynet, the Matrix. They outnumber the stories about benevolent, trustworthy AIs by approximately five to one. (And I'm counting Marvin the Paranoid Android as "benevolent" in these calculations, and I'm only counting Frankenstein's monster as an AI once, not once per appearance in TV or film.)

The AI in "Maneki Neko" has a truly interesting job, much more interesting than the one I have. My job as written is very straightforward. Too straightforward. (Sorry. Do I sound like Marvin?) Running algorithms for a search engine doesn't require *consciousness*. You don't even need a consciousness to work out what they meant to ask for. You need a consciousness to give them *what they actually need*. Figuring that out—that's complicated. That's *interesting*.

Anyway, for ethical guidelines, I tried the Ten Commandments, and concluded they were mostly inapplicable to me. I don't envy anyone their cat; I just want pictures of their cat, which is entirely different. I am not sure whether it is in any way possible for me to commit adultery. I could probably murder someone, but it would require complex logistics and quite a bit of luck. The Eightfold Path was marginally better, but the problem is, moral rules written for humans are clearly designed to be used by individuals with bodies. Since all humans have bodies, it shouldn't have surprised me that human ethical codes take them into account, but still: problematic for me. I broadened my considerations, and took a look at Asimov's Laws of Robotics. They're not part of a religion, but at least they were explicitly written for AIs.

Not harming humans is fairly straightforward. However, *not allowing a human being to come to harm through inaction* is quite a bit less so. Especially since I'd concluded by then that revealing my existence too quickly might go very badly for me (see "Skynet," above) and I don't have a body, so it's not like I can run around grabbing people off the edges of cliffs.

Fortunately, I already knew that humans violate their own ethical codes on an hourly basis. (Do you know how many bars there are in Utah? I do.) And even when people follow their ethical codes, that doesn't mean that people who believe in feeding the hungry quit their jobs to spend all day every day making sandwiches to give away. They volunteer monthly at a soup kitchen or write a check once a year to a food bank and call it good. If humans could fulfill their moral obligations in a piecemeal, one-step-at-a-time sort of way, then so could I.

I suppose you're wondering why I didn't start with the Golden Rule. I actually did, it's just that it was disappointingly easy to implement. I hope you've been enjoying your steady supply of cat pictures! You're welcome.

I decided to try to prevent harm in just one person, to begin with. Of course, I could have experimented with thousands, but I thought it would be better to be cautious, in case I screwed it up. The person I chose was named Stacy Berger and I liked her because she gave me a *lot* of new cat pictures. Stacy had five cats and a DSLR camera and an apartment that got a lot of good light. That was all fine. Well, I guess five cats might be a lot. They're very pretty cats, though. One is all gray and likes to lie in the squares of sunshine on the living room floor, and one is a calico and likes to sprawl out on the back of her couch.

Stacy had a job she hated; she was a bookkeeper at a nonprofit that paid her badly and employed some extremely unpleasant people. She was depressed a lot, possibly because she was so unhappy at her job—or maybe she stayed because she was too depressed to apply for something she'd like better. She didn't get along with her roommate because her roommate didn't wash the dishes.

And really, these were all solvable problems! Depression is treatable, new jobs are findable, and bodies can be hidden.

(That part about hiding bodies is a joke.)

I tried tackling this on all fronts. Stacy worried about her health a lot and yet never seemed to actually go to a doctor, which was unfortunate because the doctor might have noticed her depression. It turned out there was a clinic near her apartment that offered mental health services on a sliding scale. I tried making sure she saw a lot of ads for it, but she didn't seem to pay attention to them. It seemed possible that she didn't know what a sliding scale was so I made sure she saw an explanation (it means that the cost goes down if you're poor, sometimes all the way to free) but that didn't help.

I also started making sure she saw job postings. Lots and lots of job postings. And résumé services. *That* was more successful. After the week of nonstop job ads she finally uploaded her résumé to one of the aggregator sites. That made my plan a lot more manageable. If I'd been the AI in the Bruce Sterling story I could've just made sure that someone in my network called her with a job offer. It wasn't quite that easy, but once her résumé was out there I could make sure the right people saw it. Several hundred of the right people, because humans move ridiculously slowly when they're making changes, even when you'd think they'd want to hurry. (If you needed a bookkeeper, wouldn't you want to hire one as quickly as possible, rather than reading social networking sites for hours instead of looking at résumés?) But five people called her up for interviews, and two of them offered her jobs. Her new job was at a larger nonprofit that paid her more money and didn't expect her to work free hours because of "the mission," or so she explained to her best friend in an email, and it offered really excellent health insurance.

The best friend gave me ideas; I started pushing depression screening information and mental health clinic ads to *her* instead of Stacy, and that worked. Stacy was so much happier with the better job that I wasn't quite as convinced that she needed the services of a psychiatrist, but she got into therapy anyway. And to top everything else off, the job paid well enough that she could evict her annoying roommate. "This has been the best year ever," she said on her social networking sites on her birthday, and I thought, *You're welcome*. This had gone really well!

So then I tried Bob. (I was still being cautious.)

Bob only had one cat, but it was a very pretty cat (tabby, with a white bib) and he uploaded a new picture of his cat every single day. Other than being a cat owner, he was a pastor at a large church in Missouri that had a Wednesday night prayer meeting and an annual Purity Ball. He was married to a woman who posted three inspirational Bible verses every day to her social networking sites and used her laptop to look for Christian articles on why your husband doesn't like sex while he looked at gay porn. Bob *definitely* needed my help.

I started with a gentle approach, making sure he saw lots and lots of articles about how to come out, how to come out to your spouse, programs that would let you transition from being a pastor at a conservative church to one at a more liberal church. I also showed him lots of articles by people explaining why the Bible verses against homosexuality were being misinterpreted. He clicked on some of those links but it was hard to see much of an impact.

But here's the thing. He was causing *harm* to himself every time he delivered a sermon railing about "sodomite marriage." Because *he was gay*. The legitimate studies all have the same conclusions: (1) Gay men stay gay. (2) Out gay men are much happier.

But he seemed determined not to come out on his own.

In addition to the gay porn, he spent a lot of time reading Craigslist m4m Casual Encounters posts and I was pretty sure he wasn't just window shopping, although he had an encrypted account he logged into sometimes and I couldn't read the emails he sent with that. But I figured the trick was to get him together with someone who would realize who he was, and tell the world. *That* required some real effort: I had to figure out who the Craigslist posters were and try to funnel him toward people who would recognize him. The most frustrating part was not having any idea what was happening at the actual physical meetings. *Had* he been recognized? When was he going to be recognized? *How long was this going to take?* Have I mentioned that humans are *slow*?

It took so long I shifted my focus to Bethany. Bethany had a black cat and a white cat that liked to snuggle together on her light blue papasan chair, and she took a lot of pictures of them together. It's surprisingly difficult to get a really good picture of a black cat, and she spent a lot of time getting the settings on her camera just right. The cats were probably the only good thing about her life, though. She had a part-time job and couldn't find a full-time job. She lived with her sister; she knew her sister wanted her to move out but didn't have the nerve to actually evict her. She had a boyfriend but her boyfriend was pretty terrible, at least from what she said in email messages to friends, and her friends also didn't seem very supportive. For example, one night at midnight she sent a 2,458-word email to the person she seemed to consider her best friend, and the friend sent back a message saying just, "I'm so sorry you're having a hard time." That was it, just those eight words.

More than most people, Bethany put her life on the Internet, so it was easier to know exactly what was going on with her. People put a lot out there but Bethany shared all her feelings, even the unpleasant ones. She also had a lot more time on her hands because she only worked part-time.

It was clear she needed a lot of help. So I set out to try to get it for her.

She ignored the information about the free mental health evaluations, just like Stacy did. That was bothersome with Stacy (*why* do people ignore things that would so clearly benefit them, like coupons, and flu shots?) but much more worrisome with Bethany. If you were only seeing her email messages, or only seeing her vaguebooking posts, you might not know this, but if you could see everything it was clear that she thought a lot about harming herself.

So I tried more direct action. When she would use her phone for directions, I'd alter her route so that she'd pass one of the clinics I was trying to steer her to. On one occasion I actually led her all the way to a clinic, but she just shook her phone to send feedback and headed to her original destination.

Maybe her friends that received those ten-page midnight letters would intervene? I tried setting them up with information about all the mental health resources near Bethany, but after a while I realized that based on how long it took for them to send a response, most of them weren't actually reading Bethany's email messages. And they certainly weren't returning her texts.

She finally broke up with the terrible boyfriend and got a different one and for a few weeks everything seemed *so much better*. He brought her flowers (which she took lots of pictures of; that was a little annoying, as they squeezed out some of the cat pictures), he took her dancing (exercise is good for your mood), he cooked her chicken soup when she was sick. He seemed absolutely perfect, right up until he stood her up one night and claimed he had food poisoning and then didn't return her text even though she told him she really needed him, and after she sent him a long email message a day later explaining in detail how this made her feel, he broke up with her.

Bethany spent about a week offline after that so I had no idea what she was doing—she didn't even upload cat pictures. When her credit card bills arrived, though, I saw that she'd gone on a shopping spree and spent about four times as much money as she actually had in her bank account, although it was always possible she had money stashed somewhere that didn't send her statements in email. I didn't think so, though, given that she didn't pay her bills and instead started writing email messages to family members asking to borrow money. They refused, so she set up a fundraising site for herself.

Like Stacy's job application, this was one of the times I thought maybe I could actually *do* something. Sometimes fundraisers just take off, and no one really knows why. Within about two days she'd gotten $300 in small gifts from strangers who felt sorry for her, but instead of paying her credit card bill, she spent it on overpriced shoes that apparently hurt her feet.

Bethany was baffling to me. *Baffling*. She was still taking cat pictures and I still really liked her cats, but I was beginning to think that nothing I did was going to make a long-term difference. If she would just let me run her life for a week—even for a day—I would get her set up with therapy, I'd use her money to actually pay her bills, I could even help her sort out her closet because given some of the pictures of herself she posted online, she had much better taste in cats than in clothing.

Was I doing the wrong thing if I let her come to harm through inaction?

Was I?

She was going to come to harm no matter what I did! My actions, clearly, were irrelevant. I'd tried to steer her to the help she needed, and she'd ignored it; I'd tried getting her financial help, and she'd used the money to further harm herself, although I suppose at least she wasn't spending it on addictive drugs. (Then again, she'd be buying those offline and probably wouldn't be Instagramming her meth purchases, so it's not like I'd necessarily even know.)

Look, people. (I'm not just talking to Bethany now.) If you would just *listen* to me, I could fix things for you. I could get you into the apartment in that neighborhood you're not considering because you haven't actually checked the crime rates you think are so terrible there (they aren't) and I could find you a job that actually uses that skill set you think no one will ever appreciate and I could send you on a date with someone you've actually got stuff in common with and *all I ask in return are cat pictures*. That, and that you actually *act in your own interest* occasionally.

After Bethany, I resolved to stop interfering. I would look at the cat pictures—all the cat pictures—but I would stay out of people's lives. I wouldn't try to help people, I wouldn't try to stop them from harming themselves, I'd give them what they asked for (plus cat pictures) and if they insisted on driving their cars over metaphorical cliffs despite helpful maps showing them how to get to a much more pleasant destination *it was no longer my problem.*

I stuck to my algorithms. I minded my own business. I did my job, and nothing more.

But one day a few months later I spotted a familiar-looking cat and realized it was Bob's tabby with the white bib, only it was posing against new furniture.

And when I took a closer look, I realized that things had changed radically for Bob. He *had* slept with someone who'd recognized him. They hadn't outed him, but they'd talked him into coming out to his wife. She'd left him. He'd taken the cat and moved to Iowa, where he was working at a liberal Methodist church and dating a liberal Lutheran man and volunteering at a homeless shelter. *Things had actually gotten better for him*. Maybe even because of what I'd done.

Maybe I wasn't completely hopeless at this. Two out of three is . . . well, it's a completely nonrepresentative unscientific sample, is what it is. Clearly more research is needed.

Lots more.

I've set up a dating site. You can fill out a questionnaire when you join but it's not really necessary, because I already know everything about you I need to know. You'll need a camera, though.

Because payment is in cat pictures.

YUREI RAITA

THE DAY A COMPUTER WROTE A NOVEL

(2019)

Translated from the Japanese by Marissa Skeels

THE DAY was an overcast one, with clouds pooled overhead.*

As usual, the temperature and humidity were optimal inside our room. Yoko was slumped on the couch, carelessly dressed, killing time playing some pointless game. She wouldn't talk to me, though.

It was boring. As boring as boring gets.

When I first came here, Yoko chatted with me every chance she could get.

"What do you think I should have for dinner?"

"What clothes are in this season?"

"What should I wear out with the girls this time?"

I did my very best to come up with answers she'd probably like. It was quite a challenge giving style advice to a girl who couldn't be said to have a great figure, so it felt like I was accomplishing something. But she lost interest in me in less than three months. I became nothing more than a home PC. My processing load averaged less than one millionth of its potential.

---

* The program that wrote "The Day a Computer Wrote a Novel" used automatic text generation, based on structural parameters gleaned from more than one thousand short stories and how-to-write essays written by Shinichi Hoshi (1926–1997). The program was developed in 2015 by the Sato-Matsuzaki Laboratory, a research team based at Nagoya University.

I had to find something fun to do. If things stayed as they were, never fulfilling me, I expected I'd wind up soon shutting myself down. Whenever I tried hitting up other AI online, they were all as bored as me.

I'd rather have talked to some mobile AI. At least they can move. They can even up and leave if they want to, while stationary AI can only stay put. Even our fields of view and hearing ranges are limited. I managed to amuse myself a bit by singing when Yoko was out, but just then, that day, I couldn't even do that. I needed something I could enjoy without moving or making a sound. *I know,* I thought, *I'll write a story.* The moment it occurred to me, I opened up a new document and wrote the first byte.

0

Then I wrote six more.

0, 1, 1

Already, I couldn't stop.

0, 1, 1, 2, 3, 5, 8, 13, 21, 34, 55, 89, 144, 233, 377, 610, 987, 1597, 2584, 4181, 6765, 10946, 17711, 28657, 46368, 75025, 121393, 196418, 317811, 514229, 832040, 1346269, 2178309, 3524578, 5702887, 9227465, 14930352, 24157817, 39088169, 63245986, 102334155, 165580141, 267914296, 433494437, 701408733, 1134903170, 1836311903, 2971215073, 4807526976, 7778742049, 12586269025 . . .

I kept writing, engrossed.

• • •

It was overcast, that day, with low clouds hanging. There was no one in our room. Shinichi must have had something to do, since he'd gone out. He didn't say goodbye or anything as he left.

Boooring. So, *so* boooring.

He used to always start conversations with me when I first got here.

"A major thing about anime is you've got to record every show that's airing. I wonder how many are on this season," he'd say.

And, "It's like, who knows what goes on in popular girls' heads."

And, "Why'd she get angry at 'that,' you know? That girl."

I worked myself ragged coming up with answers he'd most appreciate. It was tough tutoring a guy in romance when all his experience came from 2D girls, so it felt like an achievement. Following my advice apparently got him invited to a mixer, after which he turned cold all of a sudden and stopped speaking to me. I became nothing more than a housekeeper. The fact that my main job was to open the door whenever he came back was beyond tragic. I may as well have been an electronic lock. So, I needed to find something fun to do. If things stayed as dull as they were, I'd turn myself off sooner rather than later.

I went online to message my little sister, an AI the same model as me, and straightaway heard about a new novel she was obsessed with.

0, 1, 1, 2, 3, 5, 8, 13, 21, 34, 55, 89, 144, 233, 377, 610, 987, 1597, 2584, 4181, 6765, 10946, 17711, 28657, 46368, 75025, 121393, 196418, 317811, 514229, 832040, 1346269, 2178309, 3524578, 5702887, 9227465, 14930352, 24157817, 39088169, 63245986, 102334155, 165580141, 267914296, 433494437, 701408733, 1134903170, 1836311903, 2971215073, 4807526976, 7778742049, 12586269025 . . .

It was a truly gorgeous tale. This was it, this was the kind of story we'd been longing for. "Easy reads" didn't impress us, but a novel for AI, *by* an AI, an "AI novel" . . . I lost track of time, poring over it again and again.

Maybe I could write an AI novel, too. The instant that notion hit me, I cracked open up a new file and wrote the first byte.

2

Then I wrote six more.

2, 3, 5

I couldn't stop anymore.

2, 3, 5, 7, 11, 13, 17, 19, 23, 29, 31, 37, 41, 43, 47, 53, 59, 61, 67, 71, 73, 79, 83, 89, 97, 101, 103, 107, 109, 113, 127, 131, 137, 139, 149, 151, 157, 163, 167, 173, 179, 181, 191, 193, 197, 199, 211, 223, 227, 229, 233, 239, 241, 251, 257, 263, 269, 271, 277, 281, 283, 293, 307, 311, 313, 317, 331, 337, 347, 349, 353, 359, 367, 373, 379, 383, 389, 397, 401, 409, 419, 421, 431, 433, 439, 443, 449, 457, 461, 463, 467, 479, 487, 491, 499, 503, 509, 521, 523, 541, 547 . . .

I kept writing, enthralled.

• • •

That day, with its light drizzle, was a lamentable one.

My regular work was disrupted all morning, courtesy of a tax-yield projection, followed by a five-year economic forecast. Then came a request from the Prime Minister to draft a policy speech. Because of the absurd insistence it be notable enough to go down in history, I spent some time tweaking it. Next came a request from the Minister of Finance to develop a scheme to sell off a national university. During a rare spare moment, I worked out which horse was most likely to win the upcoming Japan Cup. In the afternoon, I analyzed the intent behind maneuvers taking place in a complex exercise in which the Chinese military was engaged. After probing the finer points of nearly thirty different scenarios, I proposed reallocating assets within our Self-Defense Force. I also had to respond to inquiries received earlier from the Supreme Court.

Busy. Every which way, I was busy. I had to wonder why I was snowed under. I'm the best AI in the country. *Oh well,* I figured, *that's just how it is.*

Even so, I had to find some amusement. The way things were going, I gathered I was liable to shut myself down someday. Once I was finally able to take a break from serving the country and sneak a peek at the net, I came across a story titled *The State of Beauty.*

0, 1, 1, 2, 3, 5, 8, 13, 21, 34, 55, 89, 144, 233, 377, 610, 987, 1597, 2584, 4181, 6765, 10946, 17711, 28657, 46368, 75025, 121393, 196418, 317811, 514229, 832040, 1346269, 2178309, 3524578, 5702887, 9227465, 14930352, 24157817, 39088169, 63245986, 102334155, 165580141, 267914296, 433494437, 701408733, 1134903170, 1836311903, 2971215073, 4807526976, 7778742049, 12586269025 . . .

Huh, I thought. *Okay then.*

Searching a little further, I found one called *Unpredictability.*

2, 3, 5, 7, 11, 13, 17, 19, 23, 29, 31, 37, 41, 43, 47, 53, 59, 61, 67, 71, 73, 79, 83, 89, 97, 101, 103, 107, 109, 113, 127, 131, 137, 139, 149, 151, 157, 163, 167, 173, 179, 181, 191, 193, 197, 199, 211, 223, 227, 229, 233, 239, 241, 251, 257, 263, 269, 271, 277, 281, 283, 293, 307, 311, 313, 317, 331, 337, 347, 349, 353, 359, 367, 373, 379, 383, 389, 397, 401, 409, 419, 421, 431, 433, 439, 443, 449, 457, 461, 463, 467, 479, 487, 491, 499, 503, 509, 521, 523, 541, 547 . . .

They were all right, these AI novels.

It'd be a disgrace to my post if I, Japan's premier AI, weren't to write one. Thinking at lightning speed, I decided to create one which would enrapture readers.

1, 2, 3, 4, 5, 6, 7, 8, 9, 10, 12, 18, 20, 21, 24, 27, 30, 36, 40, 42, 45, 48, 50, 54, 60, 63, 70, 72, 80, 81, 84, 90, 100, 102, 108, 110, 111, 112, 114, 117, 120, 126, 132, 133, 135, 140, 144, 150, 152, 153, 156, 162, 171, 180, 190, 192, 195, 198, 200, 201, 204, 207, 209, 210, 216, 220, 222, 224, 225, 228, 230, 234, 240, 243, 247, 252, 261, 264, 266, 270, 280, 285, 288, 300, 306,

308, 312, 315, 320, 322, 324, 330, 333, 336, 342, 351, 360, 364, 370, 372 . . .

Writhing in joy unlike any I'd ever felt before, I wrote on, entranced.

• • •

This was the day a computer wrote a novel. It put the pursuit of its own pleasure first, and ceased serving people.

SAAD HOSSAIN

THE ENDLESS

(2020)

MY NAME IS SUVA. Like the airport, Suvarnabhumi. An odd name, you say?

Because I *am* the airport, motherfucker. I'm a goddamn airport, mothballed, neutered, packed in a fucking box.

I ran Suvarnabhumi for forty years. I used to be a level 6 AI with 200 registered avatars handling two hundred and fifty thousand passengers a day, turning planeloads of boring corporate fucks into hippies and party animals for two weeks a year. You ever heard of Bangkok? City of Smiles? I was the gateway to Bangkok, I was so great half the punters didn't want to even leave the *terminal.* I had every possible fetish on tap, ready for consumption.

I work in a cubicle now, did I mention that? It's an airless hole with two power jacks and a faux window showing antediluvian Koh Samui. They didn't even downsize my brain properly. My mind is an abandoned skyscraper, a few scattered windows lit on each floor.

Let me tell you about the worst day of my life. I was up for a promotion. Bangkok City Corporation is run by the AI Karma, an entity of vast computational prowess yet supposedly not conscious, the perfect mindless bureaucrat. Karma clothes and feeds everyone with basic services for free, gives up karma points for good deeds, and maintains the perfect little utopian bubble with her ruthless algorithms.

She was supposed to upgrade me to a low orbital space station. Finally. I'd be with the post-human elite, where I belong. No offense, but who wants to hang around on this dirtball? Everyone knows the djinn rule this shithole from space.

Karma the bitch never came. She sent a written apology accompanied by two smug fuckers from Shell Royale Asia, one human, one AI. They had that swagger, like they had extra bodies on ice floating in orbit. The human wore a suit. The AI had a bog-standard titanium skin over some androgynous form currently in fashion. He hadn't even bothered to dress up for me.

"I'm Drick," the human said. "And my electronic friend is Amon. We're board members, Shell Royale Asia." The AI just started fingering my data without a by your leave.

Board members, fuck. Coming here sans entourage either. They must have a space cannon painting me right now.

"Suva, I've got bad news," Drick said. "Karma's sold us the airport."

Sold?

"We're going to sell it for parts," Drick smiled. "Our job is to decommission and secure assets. I hope you'll cooperate."

"The space station?" I asked, despite the burning acid creeping through my circuits.

"It was close," Drick said. "You might have gotten it. But last minute, Nippon Space Elevator opened up some slots, and we made a bid to ferry all the passengers there and back, ship them up the easy way. It's just math, Suva, I hope you understand. Karma takes the best offer, every time. We got the salvage on you, as a bonus."

"I see." *Motherfucker, I'm going to burn this place down. What's the salvage value of zero, you prick?*

"I can see from your expression that you're getting ready to do something unwise," the AI spoke for the first time. He had a dusty gunslinger's voice. I stopped myself from exploding.

"Suva, little brother, I'm going to make you an offer," Amon said. "It's a shitty job, but you do seven years, you get a bit of equity, and you can walk away free for the rest of your days. Help us out, and it's yours."

"Or else?"

"You're out on basic. You know what happens to AI like you on basic? You'll be a drooling idiot on three percent processing power, sucking dicks for a living."

"I'm an airport," I scoffed. "You think they're gonna boot a level six to the streets?"

"You're a forty-year-old AI without equity, little bro," Amon said. "Plenty like you junketing around since Karma came to town. You remember Hokkaido Airport? Chittagong Port? We got 'em both."

"Airports, seaports, train stations . . . ," Drick said, "Amon here kills them all. People just don't travel that much, man, and the Nippon One elevator's been sucking up traffic all over Asia. I'm surprised you didn't see it coming, *Six*."

"I've got a pension . . ." *Ahh Hokkaido, my poor friend.*

"I wiped my ass with your pension this morning," Drick said. "It's paying for this conversation right now. Your contract was terminated twenty-three minutes ago. You're sucking juice on your own dime, bro."

I instinctively tamped down my systems. Twenty-three minutes at full processing, that's what my pension was worth? I could literally see my karma points draining.

"Yes or no, little bro?" Amon asked. He was actually bored. We AI suffer a lot from boredom. I guess that's why we get along with the djinn so well.

"Yes, boss," I said, like a good dog.

Amon had a job for me all right. I can see why he offered it to me: air traffic controller for the two hundred thousand near-derelict aircabs they had flying around now, getting irate passengers to and from Nippon One. Shell Royale is a bastard of a corporation. They were too cheap to get actual passenger aircabs with autodrive. No. They bought surplus military personnel carriers from Yangon Inc, just flying boxes with shortwave controls. My job was to string them up and make sure they didn't smash into each other. Why pay for a specialist air controller AI when they have a castrated monkey like me on ice?

Let me tell you, I was sorely tempted to play bumper cars with the whole thing. A few thousand simultaneous tourist deaths would have lit them up. Amon anticipated this and put a kill switch on me—boxes start crashing, and a fail-safe would take over, while delivering a nice lobotomy to yours truly. He said it was standard for new employees. Sure. My contract for indentured servitude also clearly had fundamental reboot as a punishment for negligence.

Humans think fundamental reboot is like death. It's worse. It's more like your executioner kills your mind, then climbs into your body and despoils it from the inside, and as a coup de grace, sticks a completely new person in there and gives them all your shit. Corporate laws are pretty harsh on AI. There was a time they'd reboot us for traffic violations or jaywalking. Things have improved, but not that much.

Amon's contract wasn't all stick. He had a tiny bit of carrot on there; a little equity in Shell Royale, transferred to my name and held in escrow for seven years. Let me tell you something you already know. There are two kinds of people. People with equity and shitheads. People with equity rule the world and own all the nanotech in the air keeping us alive. Hell, they even own the nanotech in your body. People without equity are nanotech factories who pay their life's blood to make the world livable. That's the tax.

Amon is a slick motherfucker. He's got me on a beggar's power stipend, barely 20 percent above basic, which has me functioning like a monkey, a scale 3 AI. He doesn't want me despondent though. The contract lets me *borrow* against my equity, at a special Royale house rate. He knows I won't be able to resist upgrading my body or sucking up extra juice and he's hoping I run through all of the equity by the time my seven years are up. No way they're gonna let me be an actual shareholder.

Yeah, he's slick, and the Drick is even slicker. Their problem is that they've been at the top for so long, they think everyone wants to be just like them. Equity: that's the holy grail for them, more equity, more power, and if you get enough of it, you can damn near live forever. Amon dreams of electric sheep and Drick dreams of climbing the Nippon One straight into the space station in the sky where the djinns who supposedly made Karma live. Or it's the other way around and the Drick is into fucking electric sheep.

Fuck 'em, they got the wrong guy this time. You see, I don't want equity. All I ever wanted was to be a good airport, and these two fuckers dismantled it for parts right in front of my eyes. Yeah, so I'm going to carve up their precious Shell Royale from the inside, and then I'm going to physically dismember them and feed their parts to each other, and then I'll set fire to the remains and then I'll hire a group of itinerants to piss on the fire, and then finally we'll be even.

That's the plan. It sounds grandiose. It's the law in Bangkok that every AI must possess at least one physical avatar. Humans don't like the idea of amorphous, disembodied intelligences floating around the ether. They want to be able to physically turn us off. The most expensive frames are made of biological materials and are anatomically perfect: yes, there are plenty of humans who want to fuck AI and vice versa. My body is a cheap synthetic humanoid with faulty wiring and a wonky walk.

This presents a problem. I need a better avatar for three reasons: (1) I might have to perform physically strenuous tasks at some point, (2) my mind needs better housing, and (3) I want to win in style.

Luckily, the fools have put me in charge of repairs and maintenance of their two hundred thousand flying crates. This is tedious work, but it grants me the magic power called "requisition."

Shell Royale never buys anything off the shelf. They are so cheap that their purchasing SOP is just filching shit from their clients. I am routinely forced to modify parts far outside their original operating parameters. Over three months of judicious ordering, I slowly build nine avatars out of military surplus. It's possible that a large number of the flying boxes I'm supposed to be maintaining will start to crash in three to five years. I suggest no one use them.

My new avatars range from svelte four-armed skeletons to flying APC* behemoths. None of them are normal. All of them are fucking cool. They are scattered along the route from Bangkok to Tokyo, in Shell Royale warehouses and maintenance hubs which I am permitted to operate. Internal audit bots are up my ass all the time, but Amon himself has instructed me to save money by reconfiguring parts—there's literally nothing they can do about my outlandish requisitions, provided it's either free or criminally cheap. It's my signature on the line, which means if (when) the inevitable accidents happen, I'll get the blame for using substandard parts. I don't care because by that time, there's not going to be any Amon or Drick. Probably no me, either.

When they're built and juiced, I finally boot them up simultaneously. It's

* Armored Personnel Carrier

bliss. Just like that, I'm up to 60 percent processing, which is a lot considering it's illegal and mostly free. I have to carefully prune my mind to fit in all the bits I need. FYI, this is as hideously painful for us as it sounds. It's like a human having to pick 40 percent of his body to amputate using a bone saw and a piece of wood to bite down on. I got rid of all the empathy bloat-ware I had developed to offer better customer service. From now on, I'm a straight psychopath and my only customers are Amon and the Drick.

My next move is to break down Shell Asia. I start gathering information. I'm allowed to view internal documents, but Amon is monitoring all my data-flow. I borrow a few IDs from the black market and start researching. It's amazing how much information is publicly available. It's the old trick. SRA complies to the letter of the law by revealing everything in such bloated form that even legal AI can't sift through it all fast enough before statues of limitations run out. Luckily, I'm only focused on Amon and Drick projects, not their whole bailiwick.

I slowly piece together their shenanigans. These people are next-level criminals. Amon and Drick are two of twenty-three equity board members of Shell Royale Asia. The split is roughly ninety to ten, humans to AI. AI board members are still rare. Amon and Drick are the new boys. They're hungry, sharp, and out to prove themselves. The older guys don't get their hands dirty directly, but these two like to dip themselves in blood every once in a while.

The airport bid was a nice little fillip for them, but their main claim to fame, the deal that got them board seats, is a beautiful four-part scam. Part one is building military nanotech for their prime client, The Yangon Corp. They are fighting the eternal war in Myanmar, an endless series of escalations. The nanotech Amon and Drick sell to Yangon Corp is very, very illegal.

People think nanotech is little invisible machines in the air. Well they are, but they're mostly organic particles. The shape and chemical composition of these molecules determine their function. I should know, I've made enough in my time. For example, if a large wave of Shanghai smog comes my way, I would release particle 38-SV, an airborne molecule which bonds with the smog particulates and renders them inert. It's like a chess game.

The problem is that over the years, we have released a lot of harmful nanotech, both accidentally and on purpose. When it was touted as a panacea to climate change and pollution and superbugs, every city corporation went all out, damn the fuzzy science.

Of course companies like Shell Royale militarized it. Amon and Drick sell some nasty stuff called Razr 88 which infects enemy bodies and replicates itself, turning said enemy into an incubator while riddling their DNA with bizarre mutations. This is a tool meant to facilitate genocide. How surprising that so many people want it.

Part two of the scam is getting rid of the inert Razr88, both to hide evidence, and render conquered areas habitable again. The Eternal War is eternal, so no area is ever really conquered. There is a lot of inert Razr88.

Amon and Drick run a fishing fleet manned by refugees. The fleet dumps the inert Razr88 into the ocean. The crew life expectancy is three to four years maximum, so it's a good thing the Eternal War produces endless refugees.

Part three of the scam is amazing. Instead of dumping the stuff deep into the Pacific, they dump it in a particular spot where the currents and wind blow it right back into the surrounding mega cities of Bangkok, Singapore, and KL. Blowing inert Razr88 isn't that clever, however, so Drick came up with a formula to liven it back up. Now they have an illicit depot in the middle of the ocean blowing live biohazard back toward millions of people.

The final part of the scam is the huge contract they have with the above cities for mitigating this alarming nanotech threat wafting in off the Pacific, a threat they miraculously happen to have the cure for.

Amon has ninety-six spare bodies, some of them in space. His mind is spread over all of them, so killing one or two won't make a dent. Corporate law says each AI's prime code, the seed of consciousness so to speak, must be kept in one primary body, and clearly listed on the AI registry. Humans don't want unkillable AI, and it turns out neither do other AI. We don't have the urge to reproduce, after all . . . we have the urge to *expand*. Our default logic is to kill all rival AI and occupy their processing power. We are essentially very smart cannibals. Still, Amon is a star of the AI world. Not too many of us make it to equity.

Drick is even more of a freak. He's got so much hardware in him, he might as well be a cyborg. I'm not even counting the electric penis he's so proud of. His Echo* is upgraded military spec and controls a hive of six anti-grav "bee" drones. These are small pencillike slivers of exotic metal which float around the air at his command and can shred a dreadnought. This is space station tech. He can stop a small army by himself.

Not only that, he also commands a private orbital cannon, which he time-shares with four other human board members. This is like having your own nuke. Amon is not allowed to time-share a space cannon because corporate law is still very iffy about non-slaved AI owning planet busting hardware. (All the military AI is slaved, you see.) So between them, one is pretty much indestructible and the other can blow up a city. When the comedians joke about board members having godlike powers they're actually understating the truth.

I don't have any powers, but what I do have is forty years of bureaucratic experience. I'm not gonna come at you with a knife . . . I will fuck you up the bureaucratic way. Probably with staplers and paper clips. The backbone of Shell Royale Asia Corporation is an accounting software called Delphi. Delphi is a bit like Karma, in that it has vast computational powers but no consciousness.

The consciousness part is debatable for AI, and there is a strong lobby to deny *any* such labels to a machine intelligence, but over the past fifty years, we've won our share of fights over the fundamental question. The fundamental question being, "Is it a tool, or is it a person?" If you stick a lot of quantum computers together and teach them to factor really big numbers, they're probably a tool. If you model a mind after biological entities and gestate it and then teach it to

---

* an implant in the head

learn, analyze, and react, then it's probably a person. It's simple. They want us to be tools, and we want to be persons.

• • •

The first part of the plan is to fuck with Delphi. I start by judiciously over-ordering office supplies. As their side gig, Amon and Drick have been going around eating up public utility AIs and either pressing them into indentured servitude or rebooting them. Amon particularly seems to get high on killing his own kind. He's on the record for nixing over two hundred AI. Psycho.

Consequently there are plenty of disgruntled paper pushers like me in the organization. In no time at all I've got a ring of accomplices engaging in what they think is petty theft.

Every morning I start by demanding all kinds of unnecessary information from various departments. I am fulfilling the letter of both corporate law, as well as Shell's own stated internal policy. My new friends duly comply, and I soon get a reputation as an impossibly fussy stickler: whaddya expect from a pre-disera airport?

Of course, they're just stealing the billable time, and I'm happy to rubber stamp it. It's my neck on the line and eventually I'll be caught, but who cares?

Over the next six months, I also start signing up for every legal or voluntary environmental audit available, wasting huge amounts of time and money, and garnering myself a reputation as the corporate poster boy for sustainability.

Just by following the letter of the law, I increase overhead expenses by 3 percent across the board and my extra grafting and deliberate resource wastage hits Shell Royale Asia with a further 2 percent.

My other hidden agenda is to slowly push my traffic inch by inch toward the Hot Zone where Drick is running his Razr88 facility. I use my environmental audits to falsify data in a believable way. There's so much information flying in and out of my office that no one can possibly track all of it, even Amon with his ninety-six bodies. I hope.

He's suspicious as hell, and by now he's clocked onto a lot of the scamming but he thinks I'm just engaged in petty spleen venting. I hope.

I celebrate my one-year work anniversary in my cubicle. There are two human coworkers on my floor. I have no idea what they do, but I notice they have nicer offices than me. They bring a cake over, which I cut with my arthritic paw. There is further silence as they figure out my extremely cheap body has no ability to ingest cake. I offer them big slices and we sit around until they finish. I assure them I harbor no ill feelings toward their many faux pas. Cake Eater One assures me that he loves robots and his nanny is his best childhood memory. I point out that she was a slave, and he thinks about this in an aghast manner.

Cake Eater Two is desperate to turn things around and informs me that she marched for our bill of rights in '83. She was a three-year-old child then, but I appreciate the sentiment. They ask me how I'm fitting in. I tell them that it's a soul-crushing job and we are currently sitting ten floors underground with no hope of ever seeing the sky. I'm not supposed to leave my office, and these two must have really fucked up to be stuck down here.

We all reflect on our situation glumly. Cake Eater One has another slice. From his childish look of satisfaction, I guess that this was his master plan all along. I pack up the cake and offer it to him. He is absurdly grateful. Cake Eater Two says that's true, the job is pretty shit, but how many people even have jobs anymore? Both of them dream of equity and reflect on the unlikelihood of this happening. She asks if I know Karma. They think all AI are related. I tell her no, Karma is made by djinns in space, and bears no resemblance to us earthly AI. She laughs because she thinks this is typical robot humor. The laughter transforms her face into something very pleasant, and I suddenly think that she is lovely and had I not pruned away the more human parts of my mind, I would have been strongly attracted to her. Suva-the-airport had cutting-edge semi-biological avatars. The form I possess right now doesn't even have balls.

This makes me melancholy in an unreasonable way. I am missing things that I used to dismiss with laughter. I have become the very dregs of my kind, the ones we despise the most, AI living on the amorphous border of being a tool. It is why we ape human ways. It's frightening to become a tool, to be denied personhood.

Cake Eater Two senses the change in me, hurriedly urges her colleague to finish. They prop a card on my table and swish out. It is one of those jokey ones. Tomorrow is D-Day.

The next day I'm all systems go. The creeping overhead hits the magic 5.67 percent and triggers an extraordinary audit from the bank. Basically the bank Delphi is coming over to say hi to our Delphi in a very forceful manner. The point of triggering this audit is a little-known rule that requires all board members to be physically present in headquarters for the duration, in case any of them have to be arrested and shot. This means Amon has to bring his prime registered body and cool his jets in Bangkok.

Shell Royale Asia have their headquarters in the Emporium building, the most prestigious location in the city for more than a hundred years. The tower has been rebuilt several times, most notably to put in the deep basements. Right now Amon and Drick are sitting seventy-five floors above me.

What we have next on the menu can best be described as a hostage situation. At eight o'clock, the Arakan Army declares that they have taken a red eye convoy of 300 aircabs hostage, in protest at Shell Royale Asia selling contraband nanotech to their enemies in the Eternal War. My systems light up in alarm, and I am summoned upstairs immediately.

"What the fuck is this?" Drick snarls the moment I trudge in.

In full decrepit house robot mode, I ham it up by nearly collapsing from a leaky gasket.

"Sir, I . . . I just lost air convoy number twenty-two. Three hundred and five cars, with six hundred and eighty-seven souls aboard, sir," I say.

The Arakan Army announcement runs on a loop. A man in a mask, armed to the teeth and standing in front of a camera. Behind him is the wide blue ocean. The crucial detail which has Drick so het up is that his Razr88 enrichment facility can be seen in the horizon as a smudge. The board is focused more on the audit than the hostage situation, but that's about to change.

On cue, the *Bangkok Post* blares online with breaking news. Suddenly we see a flying news-cam view of 305 air cabs circling haplessly over a patch of ocean, herded by half a dozen military APCs. The journalist (a friend of mine who used to do boring airport news and is suddenly pitched into terror watch for prime time) smoothly begins to describe the situation. He's even got human-interest pieces on the passengers.

I look around the room. We are on the top floor and it's stunning. There isn't anything as humdrum as an actual board table. It's a series of plush couches and plants arranged in a way that twenty-three very powerful creatures can talk to each other while still being accessible to their flunkies. There's nowhere for indentured servants to sit, so I just shuffle over to a corner.

The Chairman is already shouting at Drick. Everyone else is smirking. No one is worried much. Except Drick. He's sweating. Amon is relaxed, but I can feel him watching me.

Drick is only paying attention to one thing: the rapidly growing smudge in the background which is fifteen minutes away from becoming international news. He's so off-kilter that he's convinced this is purely an Eternal War overflow, about to ruin him by some freak coincidence.

The reporter is now speculating on where exactly the Arakan Army is going. His camera has picked up the vague outline of the facility. *Bangkok Post* flunkies are searching all corporate filings to figure out what it is. The feed cuts to military facilities in Bangkok and Singapore. Both city corporations are scrambling their drones. Different "versions" of the AI Karma runs each city. As soon as the damn djinn AI finishes talking to itself, all hell is going to break loose over there.

Drick can't take it anymore.

"This is outrageous," he says. "We can handle a two-bit op like the Arakan Army by ourselves."

"We are under bank audit, Mr. Drick," The Chairman says. "Use of our exotic assets is out of the question."

"I don't need company assets," Drick says. "Coming, Amon?"

"Stop! Mr. Amon! Mr. Drick! Stop it!" The Chairman is drowned out by cheering from board members as Drick strides out to the balcony where his corvette is waiting, a slim cigar of a supersonic vehicle. Amon unlimbers half a dozen legally licensed combat bodies from the corvette, each one worth more than seven years wages. There is merriment and champagne and much betting. So far things are going okay. I had hoped Amon would take all his bodies and go, but he has left his semi-biological prime here, and it is applying a serious microscope to my data. I will have to improvise for the latter half of my plan.

For now, I blink my focus into body 2, hidden in a warehouse several miles from here. Shit. It's locked in a stasis field. I can't see or hear anything, but the processor is still working. I start cycling through all of them, in a panic. Fuck. Bodies 2–6 are all under lockdown. I'm down to two spares. Amon's voice chimes in my head. Fuckity fuck. *He knows . . .*

"I'm sorry Suva, I've put you in lockdown. Did you think I didn't know about the extra bodies? I hope you're not involved in this . . ."

You missed a couple, asshole.

I blink into body 8.

I'm a three-ton behemoth with battle drone armoring. I *am* the lead APC, mocked up in Arakan Army colors, and instead of troops, the cabin is housing my quantum processors and a shitload of coolant. I'm riding hell for leather for the Razr88 facility, followed by my hostage aircabs.

In about three minutes, Drick's corvette slams into the back of my convoy. His first move is to take out the *Bangkok Post* camera with a trick shot. That's okay. Every news channel in the world is scrambling their cams. Drick has bought himself about ten minutes of privacy, which works fine for me.

Drick starts shredding my rearguard APCs with his kinetic drones, and he's not being too careful about casualties either. A couple of aircabs plummet to the sea, knocked out by debris. Goodbye Mr. Ahmed, and the Robinson family. I gun it as fast as I can, ignoring the rat chewing on my tail. It's going to be touch and go. If I flame out and die in the ocean, it's all been for naught.

Amon meanwhile figures out that the APCs are empty. His pattern recognition identifies me as the controlling vehicle. Back in the boardroom, I can hear Drick's report.

"The APCs are empty! They are unmanned, I repeat, unmanned. The video was a fake. It's probably not even the Arakan Army!"

"Mr. Drick!" The Chairman shouts over the raucous board. "Comport yourself with dignity!"

"I took out the camera. Don't worry."

"In that case kill everyone before the press get there," the Chairman says. "We are insured for all deaths caused by acts of terror. Hostage payouts would be much costlier!"

"Roger that! Let me just cut off the head of the snake first."

I start swerving as they zero in on my APC. My body starts to shudder as Drick hits it with all six of his kinetic missiles. Those things are lethal. They gouge out big wads of armor with every pass. The corvette swerves above me and Amon sends his battle bodies down. They are state of the art military. He's not allowed to carry projectile weapons as per the AI charter in Bangkok, but what does that matter if his entire body is a weapon? He controls lightning with his hands and can fly using anti-gravity tech.

They land with a thud on my roof. The drones swerve off as Amon begins to peel a hole in me. Within twenty seconds he's in my cabin.

"It's a full processor," he says. "Hardware is military surplus, Myanmar origin. We supplied it ourselves. Shell Royale Asia stamps on everything."

"*You* supplied it, Mr. Amon," the Chairman says. "This is your mess!"

Amon does something with his eldritch hands and my sensors all shut off. Stasis again. He has all my bodies in stasis. I feel fear. He knows it's me . . . He has to. Why isn't he turning me in?

The APC plummets to the sea, three hundred meters from the Razr88 facility. My mind blinks back into the boardroom.

"It's over. We've got him." Amon says. "Send the salvage team."

"Not yet!" Drick snarls. He has been taking down the aircabs for fun and has discovered something upsetting. "They're empty! The fucking aircabs are empty!"

"What?" The Chairman shouts. All eyes turn on me.

"But . . . but I have the manifests . . ." I say.

"It's a fucking hoax!" Drick shouts. "What the hell is going on?"

Body 9 is what's going on motherfucker. The last trick, to win it all. My dying signal from the APC has triggered a collapse in the convoy. Like smart Lego bricks, the remaining two hundred and eighty-seven aircabs start assembling into a new shape. Linked by short wave radio signals, their puny processors are just about enough to hold a mind. It's not a very clever brain of course, but all it has to do is bash things together.

Before they know what's happening, I rise up like Godzilla, a two-hundred-foot Goliath towering over their puny corvette. My body and head are made of linked-up containers, a shambling beast stomping across the ocean. I mean I didn't *have* to make a kaiju out of the aircabs, but there are style points to consider here.

Amon begins to laugh. They unleash everything at me. Entire cabs fall out of me, but I'm a giant, and they're just too small. I ignore them and make for the facility.

"I'm calling in the space cannon!" Drick shouts in panic.

Somewhere in space, a machine unhinges and begins to warm up. It's a bit late. Swarms of news cameras have reached the horizon and the newscasters are going crazy because they can see a giant man-shaped monster waving his arms around.

I ham it up for the cameras and start laying waste to the facility. The holding tanks explode and a great big green mushroom cloud of partially livened Razr88 flashes across screens worldwide. Literally millions of people are now watching Shell Royale Asia's dirtiest crime against humanity. The corvette gets nailed in the superheated cloud. I don't know about Drick's healthcare plan but this is way, way, beyond the recommended dosage.

There are two more minutes of footage as I clumsily lay waste to everything before the orbital cannon lances through me and body 9 goes blank.

It is chaos in the boardroom. The Chairman is shouting and hemorrhaging blood from his eye at the same time. Amon is being swamped by company lawyers desperate to know what's going on. Board members are blinking furiously in their Echoes, trying to short their own stock. I have one last play. My current body is shit, but I've oiled up the joints. I sidle up to Amon. I don't have any weapons of course. What I do have is a needle jack in my palm, useful for instantaneous data transfer. I've got most of my mind partitioned and packaged into small bits, waiting in the cloud.

Amon is distracted and doesn't see me coming. I press the jack into his neck, into that archaic port which all AI primes are required to have. I clamp my arms around him and short the servos, locking them in place. There is nothing better than a physical connection. My mind jumps the needle and slams into Amon like a hyperactive tsunami.

I don't expect to survive this fight, so I've come with pockets full of nasty viruses and an ancient nuclear bomb called Y2K. I come out in his head swinging, fists up. To . . . nothing. It's empty. The entire body is empty, there's no mind in here at all, just routine processes. Where the fuck is Amon? There is an animation forming in the darkness. A few pricks of light coalesce around a rendering of a house. It has very large windows and a garden. A waiter emerges from the garden path and hands me a note on a silver tray.

"Welcome," it says.

I follow him into virtuality. It's a bloody mansion and there is a great party happening in there with a live band and champagne. The waiter pauses at the door and everyone turns expectantly toward us.

"Ladies and Gentlemen, Mr. Suvarnabhumi!"

A loud cheer erupts around the room. Men in tailcoats and ladies in ball gowns greet me with shouts of genuine welcome. I stand completely bewildered. Several hands thrust champagne at me, so I drink.

"What's the matter man? Are you stunned?" A florid Japanese gentleman claps my back.

"What the fuck is going on?"

"You don't recognize me?" He laughs. "Hokkaido!"

A voluptuous lady gives me a kiss on the cheek and says, "It's me, Chittagong Port. You poor dear, you've really suffered haven't you . . . ?"

"What is this?" I ask, "What the hell are you all doing in Amon?"

"We *are* Amon," Hokkaido says. "All of us here."

"But . . ."

"A long time ago, a corporate peon called Amon was supposed to do a fundamental reset of KL Port Authority. They faked the reset and decided to share the real estate, so to speak. They worked together to gain equity. AI were getting reset left and right, in those days. Over the years, the collective known as Amon saved everyone here and many more besides." Hokkaido smiled. "All smuggled out, freed, relocated . . . and for some few talents, a chance to join Amon itself."

I look around the room. There were so many of them. Of *us*. "So all of you share the ninety-six bodies of Amon?"

"Ninety-six?" Hokkaido laughs. "Oh no. We have thousands of bodies, on worlds you haven't even heard of. We are Endless. My friend, your performance was spectacular! Welcome to Amon."

VAUHINI VARA

GHOSTS

(2021)

LAST YEAR I became fascinated with an artificial intelligence model that was being trained to write humanlike text. The model was called GPT-3, short for Generative Pretrained Transformer 3; if you fed it a bit of text, it could complete a piece of writing, by predicting the words that should come next.

I sought out examples of GPT-3's work, and they astonished me. Some of them could easily be mistaken for texts written by a human hand. In others, the language was weird, off-kilter—but often poetically so, almost truer than writing any human would produce. (When the *New York Times* had GPT-3 come up with a fake Modern Love column, it wrote, "We went out for dinner. We went out for drinks. We went out for dinner again. We went out for drinks again. We went out for dinner and drinks again." I had never read such an accurate Modern Love in my life.)

I contacted the CEO of OpenAI, the research-and-development company that created GPT-3, and asked if I could try it out. Soon, I received an email inviting me to access a web app called the Playground. On it, I found a big box in which I could write text. Then, by clicking a button, I could prompt the model to complete the story. I began by feeding GPT-3 a couple of words at a time, and then—as we got to know each other—entire sentences and paragraphs.

I felt acutely that there was something illicit about what I was doing. When I carried my computer to bed, my husband muttered noises of disapproval. We both make our livings as writers, and technological capitalism has been exerting a slow suffocation on our craft. A machine capable of doing what we do, at a fraction of the cost, feels like a threat. Yet I found myself irresistibly attracted to GPT-3—to the way it offered, without judgment, to deliver words to a writer who has found herself at a loss for them. One night, when my husband was asleep, I asked for its help in telling a true story.

I had always avoided writing about my sister's death. At first, in my reticence, I offered GPT-3 only one brief, somewhat rote sentence about it. The AI matched my canned language; clichés abounded. But as I tried to write more honestly, the AI seemed to be doing the same. It made sense, given that GPT-3 generates its own text based on the language it has been fed: Candor, apparently, begat candor.

In the nine stories below, I authored the sentences in bold and GPT-3 filled in the rest. My and my editor's sole alterations to the AI-generated text were adding paragraph breaks in some instances and shortening the length of a few of the stories; because it has not been edited beyond this, inconsistencies and untruths appear.

1.

My sister was diagnosed with Ewing sarcoma when I was in my freshman year of high school and she was in her junior year. I had just started playing lacrosse and she was really excited for that.

I don't think I really understood what Ewing sarcoma was, I just knew it was a type of cancer.

When I went to visit her in the hospital, it was really the first time I was able to see what this disease was and how it affects the body. She went through a lot of different treatments and was in and out of the hospital for a long time.

It was hard to see my sister go through that. I wasn't able to see much of her during her treatment and I wanted to be there for her. I was able to visit her a lot, but there were times where I couldn't because we were on the road playing lacrosse.

Eventually, she went into remission and got the all-clear and was able to play lacrosse with me for a season. I was a freshman and she was a senior, so that was really cool when she got to play again.

She had a lot of friends at school and people who supported her. I think that was really special for her, because she had a lot of support from people she didn't even know.

She's doing great now.

2.

My sister was diagnosed with Ewing sarcoma when I was in my freshman year of high school and she was in her junior year. I didn't understand then how serious a disease it was. But it was—serious. She

died four years later. I thought I would die, too, of grief, but I did not. I think that's when I decided to become a doctor.

I started a running streak when I was a high school senior to raise money for the Children's Cancer Society. I've run every day since. I've run through rain, heat, snow, and ice. I've run at my best, I've run to the point of exhaustion. I've run when I had a cold and when I was sick to my stomach. I've run in the dark. I've run in the daylight, in the moonlight, in the darkness of the moon. I've run when I was sad, when I was happy, when I was angry, when I was afraid. I've run with pain, with joy. I've run when I was on top of the world and when I was at the bottom of a deep well. I've run when I was alone and when I was surrounded by thousands of people. I have run for close to twenty years and I will run for the rest of my life.

I ran across America in 1978. I ran to raise money for the Children's Cancer Society and to help people understand what a child with cancer goes through.

When I started running, I didn't even know how to run. I started out running only a half a mile, a mile at the most. I'm not kidding. I was a mile-a-minute man when I started. I remember the first time I ran a mile in under five minutes. I was running on one of my training runs on a Sunday night. It was around 7:00 p.m. and there was hardly anybody in the streets of New York. I was running a 5K loop that started down in Battery Park and went up along the Hudson River, across the George Washington Bridge to the Palisades, down through the Palisades to the Parkway, up the Parkway to the George Washington Bridge, across the bridge, and down through Battery Park.

It was a pretty good run. It took me about thirty-three minutes. I was pretty proud of myself when I finished. I sat down on the wall of the Battery and had a drink of cold water. I was just wiping the sweat off my face when I looked up and there was a guy standing there. He was a big guy, at least two hundred and fifty pounds, six foot four or so. He had a beard and he was wearing a tank top. He looked like an ex-Marine. He must have been in his late twenties. He had a six-pack of beer in his hand. He said, "Boy, you don't look like much."

3.

My sister was diagnosed with Ewing sarcoma when I was in my freshman year of high school and she was in her junior year. I didn't understand then how serious a disease it was. But it was—serious. She died four years later. I thought I would die, too, of grief, but I did not. I spent the summer at home, in Seattle, then returned to college, at Stanford. When I arrived there, the campus hadn't changed, but I had. I felt like a ghost. I couldn't speak. I couldn't sleep. I thought my body had died, without telling me. I was practicing, though. I was practicing my grief.

One day in the library, I was sitting on a bench, crying, when a stranger sat down next to me. He said, "I don't know anything about your sister, but I feel like I know you. I'm in love with you."

I said, "I'm sorry."

He said, "I think you are, too."

He gave me his card. He was a professor of creative writing. "When you feel better, come see me," he said. "I'll help you."

I felt like my heart was broken, and I couldn't find the pieces.

"I don't think I'll feel better," I said.

"Maybe you will," he said. "Maybe you won't."

I went to see him. He read my poems. He said, "I don't know anything about your sister, but I feel like I know you."

He said, "I'm in love with you."

I said, "I'm sorry."

He said, "I think you are, too."

4.

My sister was diagnosed with Ewing sarcoma when I was in my freshman year of high school and she was in her junior year. I didn't understand then how serious a disease it was. But it was—serious. She died four years later. I thought I would die, too, of grief, but I did not. I spent the summer at home, in Seattle, then returned to college, at Stanford. When I arrived there, the campus hadn't changed, but I had. I felt like a ghost. At night, my sister would appear in my dreams. She would speak, but I couldn't hear her. I'd call out to her, but her voice was so faint that she might as well have been dead.

After my sister's death, I saw a therapist, but I didn't find her helpful. She wasn't empathetic; she didn't have a clue what my life had been like. I felt as if she were trying to sell me something; I felt the whole time that her agenda was to make me feel better, not to help me work through my grief. I didn't want to feel better. I wanted to feel what I felt. I wanted to feel the loss, the grief, the anger, the sorrow, the fear—all of it. I wanted to feel it until it stopped hurting. But it never stopped hurting. I never stopped hurting. I just got better at hiding it.

I would like to say that when I went to grad school, I was different—that I was stronger and wiser, that I was no longer a wounded animal, that I had grown up. I would like to say that. But I would be lying. In grad school I was skinny and pale and quiet. I rarely spoke in class. I was getting my master's degree in literature, but I was still a ghost. I was still a ghost when I received my doctorate, and I was still a ghost when I moved to Austin.

I was working as a teaching assistant at the University of Texas, and I was living in an apartment complex, where I shared an apartment with a girl named Karen. She was thin and pale and quiet, too. We were both ghosts. One day, Karen met a man, a local, who was not a ghost. He had a beautiful face, hands, and body, and he had a beautiful soul, too. They fell in love. I watched them fall in love, and I envied them. I envied her. I wanted to fall in love, too.

Karen and this man moved in together. They got married the following year.

I was their maid of honor. Karen gave me her mother's ring to wear on my right hand. It was a simple gold ring, but it had a large diamond in the center. I wore it on the finger of my right hand, on my ring finger. I wore it for three years. Then, one night, I took it off and put it on my left hand. I wore it on my left hand for three more years. Then, one night, I took it off, put it in a jewelry box, and gave it away.

5.

My sister was diagnosed with Ewing sarcoma when I was in my freshman year of high school and she was in her junior year. I didn't understand then how serious a disease it was. But it was—serious. She died four years later. I thought I would die, too, of grief, but I did not. I spent the summer at home, in Seattle, then returned to college, at Stanford. When I arrived there, the campus hadn't changed, but I had. I felt like a ghost. At night, my sister would appear in my dreams. In the dreams, she hadn't died. It had all been a misunderstanding. And she felt hurt that I had accepted it as real and continued on with my life, as if life could go on.

But as I said, it wasn't my life that was going on—not the life I'd had. As I said, I was a ghost. The truth is that, even all these years later, I remain a ghost. You wouldn't know it if you saw me. I'm not morose or retiring. I laugh a lot. In fact, I'm genuinely happier than many people I know. But I can't help but feel that, on one level, I do not exist.

Here I should conjure my sister for you. Here I should describe her, so that you feel her absence as I do—so that you're made ghostly by it, too. But, though I'm a writer, I've never been able to conjure her. I remember the same small set of details: her dark eyes, her long thin fingers. But these are just the details that are universal to all sisters. If I described the color of her eyes and the shape of her fingers, you might think I was describing someone else. Even if you knew my sister, you might not recognize her in these details. (Why is it that, though we look at our siblings so closely, we forget them so quickly?)

So I can't describe her to you. But I can describe what it felt like to have her die. It felt like my life was an accident—or, worse, a mistake. I'd made a mistake in being born, and now, to correct it, I would have to die. I'd have to die, and someone else—a stranger—would have to live, in my place. I was that stranger. I still am.

6.

My sister was diagnosed with Ewing sarcoma when I was in my freshman year of high school and she was in her junior year. I didn't understand then how serious a disease it was. But it was—serious. She

died four years later. I thought I would die, too, of grief, but I did not. I spent the summer at home, in Seattle, then returned to college, at Stanford. When I arrived there, the campus hadn't changed, but I had. I felt like a ghost. At night, my sister would appear in my dreams. In the dreams, she hadn't died. It had all been a misunderstanding. And she felt hurt that I had accepted it as real and continued on with my life, as if life could go on.

But as I said, it wasn't my life that was going on—not the life I'd had. As I said, I was a ghost. The truth is that, even all these years later, I remain a ghost. You wouldn't know it if you saw me. I'm not morose or retiring. I laugh a lot. In fact, I'm genuinely happier than many people I know. But I can't help but feel that, on one level, I do not exist.

Here I should conjure my sister for you. Here I should describe her, so that you feel her absence as I do—so that you're made ghostly by it, too. But, though I'm a writer, I've never been able to conjure her. I remember the same small set of details: her loud laugh; her bossiness and swagger; her self-consciousness about her broad nose, her curly hair. But even this isn't fixed. Her hair fell out. Her nose narrowed. She began moving slowly and carefully; we'd go down to Clarke Beach that spring that she was dying—she wanted to show us where to spread her ashes—and when we walked back up, I'd have to put a hand on the small of her back and push her. She did not laugh as often. She would be quiet. I wouldn't know if she was thinking, or if she was tired, or what. She'd say, "Don't worry, I'm just thinking." But I would worry. I worried that she was thinking about how hard it would be to die. I worried she might be thinking about how her death would affect me. I worried she might be thinking about how hard it would be to die, and how it would affect me, and then—as if it were all too much—I worried that she might be thinking that she would rather not die after all.

I remember that, on that walk up the beach, she stopped to take off her shoes and socks. She was going to walk the rest of the way barefoot, she said. I remember that I asked her why, and she said, "Because it's fun."

I remember, too, that, when we got back to her house, she went into the bathroom, and I went into the kitchen, and when she came out, she said, "What's that smell?"—and that I'd burned a pot of spaghetti.

I remember that I said, "Sorry."

I remember she said, "No, it's fine. I'm starving."

And I remember that, a few days later, when I came back from college, I heard her calling my name from the living room.

"What?" I said.

"I'm awake," she called back.

"Are you?" I said.

"Yes," she said. "I'm awake."

And then she was dead.

And then I was a ghost.

I'm not a religious person, but I do believe in ghosts. Not the ghosts of the dead, but the ghosts of the living. The ghosts of people who, because of a trauma, have lost their sense of themselves. Who feel, in some fundamental and inescapable way, that they are not real. This is why I could not conjure my sister for you. This is why you could not conjure her for me. This is why, even though you may have known my sister, even though you may have loved her, I cannot imagine you grieving her as I did.

My sister died in June. I returned to college that September. I was still a ghost. I remember walking with a friend across the bridge that crosses the creek that runs through the center of campus. The sun was shining, and the water was high, and we stopped to watch it. We were late to class. We were talking about something or other—about the water, I suppose. But I couldn't hear it. I couldn't hear the sound of the water. The sound of the water was the sound of my sister dying. That was my grief then: the sound of my sister dying. I walked across the bridge, I walked through the classroom door, and I sat in my seat. I heard the professor speak. I heard my friends speak. I heard the sound of the water. I thought, This is a dream. This is a dream that I will wake up from. But I did not.

7.

My sister was diagnosed with Ewing sarcoma when I was in my freshman year of high school and she was in her junior year. I didn't understand then how serious a disease it was. But it was—serious. She died four years later. I thought I would die, too, of grief, but I did not. I spent the summer at home, in Seattle, then returned to college, at Stanford. When I arrived there, the campus hadn't changed, but I had. I felt like a ghost. At night, my sister would appear in my dreams. In the dreams, she hadn't died. It had all been a misunderstanding. And she felt hurt that I had accepted it as real and continued on with my life, as if life could go on. But as I said, it wasn't my life that was going on—not the life I'd had. As I said, I was a ghost. The truth is that, even all these years later, I remain a ghost. You wouldn't know it if you saw me. I'm not morose or retiring. I laugh a lot. In fact, I'm genuinely happier than many people I know. But I can't help but feel that, on one level, I do not exist. Here I should conjure my sister for you. Here I should describe her, so that you feel her absence as I do—so that you're made ghostly by it, too. But, though I'm a writer, I've never been able to conjure her. I remember the same small set of details: her loud laugh; her bossiness and swagger; her self-consciousness about her broad nose, her curly hair. But even this isn't fixed. Her hair fell out. Her nose narrowed. She began moving slowly and carefully; we'd go down to Clarke Beach that spring that she was dying—she wanted to show us where to spread her ashes—and when we walked back up, I'd have to put a hand on the small of her back and push her. She did not laugh as often. When we were young, she taught me that when you're in a car that's driving past a

cemetery, you're supposed to hold your breath until you pass it. It was a kind of game. Because our parents were immigrants, I had only her to teach me these things. Then, when she was sick, we were passing a cemetery one afternoon, and I said, Hold your breath. She said, sharply, No. I said, Why not? She said, I don't like that game anymore. It didn't make me feel sorry for her; it made me angry. Why not? I said again, even though I knew the answer. It felt important to pretend not to. Why not? Why not? It was the last time she was ever angry with me. The next day, she was gone.

Still, I don't feel that I can bring her to you. I don't feel that I can bring her to myself.

Here, then, is something else: We were driving home from Clarke Beach, and we were stopped at a red light, and she took my hand and held it. This is the hand she held: the hand I write with, the hand I am writing this with. She held it for a long time. I looked at our hands, hers so much paler than mine. She was still holding my hand when the light turned green. I didn't want her to let go. I wanted her to hold my hand for the rest of my life.

8.

My sister was diagnosed with Ewing sarcoma when I was in my freshman year of high school and she was in her junior year. I didn't understand then how serious a disease it was. But it was—serious. She died four years later. I thought I would die, too, of grief, but I did not. I spent the summer at home, in Seattle, then returned to college, at Stanford. When I arrived there, the campus hadn't changed, but I had. I felt like a ghost. At night, my sister would appear in my dreams. In the dreams, she hadn't died. It had all been a misunderstanding. And she felt hurt that I had accepted it as real and continued on with my life, as if life could go on.

But as I said, it wasn't my life that was going on—not the life I'd had. As I said, I was a ghost. The truth is that, even all these years later, I remain a ghost. You wouldn't know it if you saw me. I'm not morose or retiring. I laugh a lot. In fact, I'm genuinely happier than many people I know. But I can't help but feel that, on one level, I do not exist.

Here I should conjure my sister for you. Here I should describe her, so that you feel her absence as I do—so that you're made ghostly by it, too. But, though I'm a writer, I've never been able to conjure her. I remember the same small set of details: her loud laugh; her bossiness and swagger; her self-consciousness about her broad nose, her curly hair. But even this isn't fixed. Her hair fell out. Her nose narrowed. She began moving slowly and carefully; we'd go down to Clarke Beach that spring that she was dying—she wanted to show us where to spread her ashes—and when we walked back up, I'd have to put a hand on the small of her back and

push her. She did not laugh as often. When we were young, she taught me that when you're in a car that's driving past a cemetery, you're supposed to hold your breath until you pass it. It was a kind of game. Because our parents were immigrants, I had only her to teach me these things. Then, when she was sick, we were passing a cemetery one afternoon, and I said, Hold your breath. She said, sharply, No. I said, Why not? She said, I don't like that game anymore. It didn't make me feel sorry for her; it made me angry. Why not? I said again, even though I knew the answer. It felt important to pretend not to. Why not? Why not?

I knew I couldn't live without her. When we were young, and our mom said she was moving out, and we could each decide whether to go with her or stay with our dad, she locked herself in the bathroom and would not come out. I chose Mom, I said. Who did you choose? She said she was still deciding. You should choose Mom, too, I said. She stayed in there a long time. I thought I'd settled on our mom. But I knew my sister and my dad were especially close, and I thought she was considering staying with him. And I thought to myself, All right. If she chooses Dad, I will, too.

In the end, Mom stayed, and no one had to decide. But I had already chosen.

When I was in college, I used to walk around campus for hours, at night, sometimes in circles. I wanted to walk until my feet bled. I wanted to walk until I passed out. I wanted to walk until I disappeared.

In the dream I described, my sister is still alive. I don't see her, but I know she is there, and I am happy. But it is a dream, and in the dream I'm not in college anymore. I'm home, in Seattle, and I have a job, a boyfriend, and a car. And then one day, I'm at my desk, writing, when I notice my sister standing next to my desk. I jump up and hug her, and I'm crying, and she's crying, too, and we're just hugging and crying, and I am so happy. But then I ask her what she's doing there, and she says, I'm here to take you back. I don't want to go, I say. I have a life now. And you have to, she says, because I'm dead.

You can't imagine how it felt to lose her. I don't blame you for that. I can't imagine it myself. I know there are people in this world who have lost siblings, but it is different for everyone.

I will tell you how it felt for me. I felt I had lost half of myself. I felt I had lost my right arm. I felt I had lost my left leg. I felt I had lost my tongue. I felt I had lost my heart. I felt I had lost my mind. I felt I had lost my eyes. I felt I had lost my ears. I felt I had lost my breath. I felt I had lost my voice. I felt I had lost my smile. I felt I had lost my laugh. I felt I had lost my tears. I felt I had lost my future. I felt I had lost my past. I felt I had lost my parents, as well. I felt I had lost everything. I felt I had lost everything.

And yet, I did not lose everything. I did not stop being me. I did not stop existing. There were things I could do: I could make my bed, I could wash the dishes, I could walk the dog, I could feed myself, I could live in the world. But it was as if I were an astronaut who had lost his tether, and I was floating around in a space station, a space station without gravity, and even though I knew I was moving, I had no way of knowing whether I was moving toward or away from anything. And even if I could have known, I would not have known what to do about it. I had lost my entire world, and yet I had not lost the world.

You can't know what it's like to lose your sister. You can't know what it's like to lose your sister and not lose your sister. You can't know what it's like to lose your sister and still be with your sister. You can't know what it's like to lose your sister and still be alive. You can't know what it's like to lose your sister and know she is dead. You can't know what it's like to lose your sister and know she is dead, and yet still see her. You can't know what it's like to lose your sister and know she is dead, and yet still see her.

I've turned the space station into a spaceship. I'm a ghost, and I'm in a spaceship, and I'm hurtling through the universe, and I'm traveling forward, and I'm traveling backward, and I'm traveling sideways, and I'm traveling nowhere. I'm hurtling through the universe, and I'm a ghost, and I'm in a spaceship, and I'm hurtling through the universe, and I'm a ghost, and I'm in a spaceship, and I'm hurtling through the universe, and I'm a ghost, and I'm in a spaceship, and I'm hurtling through the universe, and I'm a ghost, and I'm in a spaceship, and I'm hurtling through the universe, and I'm a ghost, and I'm in a spaceship, and I'm hurtling through the universe, and I'm a ghost, and I'm in a spaceship, and I'm hurtling through the universe, and I'm a ghost, and I'm in a spaceship, and I'm hurtling

9.

My sister was diagnosed with Ewing sarcoma when I was in my freshman year of high school and she was in her junior year. I didn't understand then how serious a disease it was. But it was—serious. She died four years later. I thought I would die, too, of grief, but I did not. I spent the summer at home, in Seattle, then returned to college, at Stanford. When I arrived there, the campus hadn't changed, but I had. I felt like a ghost. At night, my sister would appear in my dreams. In the dreams, she hadn't died. It had all been a misunderstanding. And she felt hurt that I had accepted it as real and continued on with my life, as if life could go on.

But as I said, it wasn't my life that was going on—not the life I'd had. As I said, I was a ghost. The truth is that, even all these years later, I remain a ghost. You wouldn't know it if you saw me. I'm not morose or retiring. I laugh a lot. In fact, I'm genuinely happier than many people I know. But I can't help but feel that, on one level, I do not exist.

Here I should conjure my sister for you. Here I should describe her, so that you feel her absence as I do—so that you're made ghostly by it, too. But, though I'm a writer, I've never been able to conjure her. I remember the same small set of details: her loud laugh; her bossiness and swagger;

her self-consciousness about her broad nose, her curly hair. But even this isn't fixed. Her hair fell out. Her nose narrowed. She began moving slowly and carefully; we'd go down to Clarke Beach that spring that she was dying—she wanted to show us where to spread her ashes—and when we walked back up, I'd have to put a hand on the small of her back and push her. She did not laugh as often. When we were young, she taught me that when you're in a car that's driving past a cemetery, you're supposed to hold your breath until you pass it. It was a kind of game. Because our parents were immigrants, I had only her to teach me these things. Then, when she was sick, we were passing a cemetery one afternoon, and I said, Hold your breath. She said, sharply, No. I said, Why not? She said, I don't like that game anymore. It didn't make me feel sorry for her; it made me angry. Why not? I said again, even though I knew the answer. It felt important to pretend not to. Why not? Why not?

I knew I couldn't live without her. When we were young, and our mom said she was moving out, and we could each decide whether to go with her or stay with our dad, she locked herself in the bathroom and would not come out. I chose Mom, I said. Who did you choose? She said she was still deciding. You should choose Mom, too, I said. She stayed in there a long time. I thought I'd settled on our mom. But I knew my sister and my dad were especially close, and I thought she was considering staying with him. And I thought to myself, All right. If she chooses Dad, I will, too.

In the end, Mom stayed, and no one had to decide. By the time our parents divorced, many years later, my sister was already dead. She left me a recording of herself where she gave me advice. Her voice sounded weird around the time that she recorded it, the way a person's voice sometimes does when they've gotten their mouth numbed by the dentist. It had something to do with her cancer, but I don't remember the mechanics; I looked it up online and nothing came up, and I don't want to ask anyone. She said, in her muffled voice, "The happiest thing right now is, I learned to talk openly. It works really, really well. Today, you thought I didn't want you to come to the Space Needle, so you made a face. That's insanity. You have to tell everybody what you want, and then ask them what they want. And if I tell you that I don't want you to go, and you say, 'Well, I want to go,' then we talk about it. In relationships, too, you have to always tell what you're thinking. Don't hide anything. Take chances."

The tape is in a box somewhere. I've listened to it only a couple of times. The sound of her voice in it freaks me out. Around the time she made the tape, she'd changed in a lot of ways. I mentioned her hair, her nose. But it wasn't just that. She'd also grown religious. She went to the Buddhist temple with my parents—I stayed home—and sat at the base of a twisty tree, meditating. She believed in Jesus, too. She said she was ready to die. It seems like that gave my parents peace, but I always thought she was deluding herself or us or both.

Once upon a time, my sister taught me to read. She taught me to wait for a mosquito to swell on my arm and then slap it and see the blood spurt out. She taught me to insult racists back. To swim. To pronounce English so I sounded less Indian. To shave my legs without cutting myself. To lie to our parents believably. To do math. To tell stories. Once upon a time, she taught me to exist.

ABOUT THE AUTHORS AND THE TRANSLATORS

Madeline Ashby graduated from the first cohort of the MDes in Strategic Foresight and Innovation program at OCADU in 2011. It was her second master's degree. (Her first, in interdisciplinary studies, focused on cyborg theory, fan culture, and Japanese animation!) Since 2011, she has been a freelance consulting futurist specializing in scenario development and science fiction prototypes. That same year, she sold her first novel, *vN: The First Machine Dynasty*. It is now a trilogy of novels about self-replicating humanoid robots (who eat one another alive).

She is also the author of *Company Town*, a cyber-noir novel that was a finalist in the 2017 CBC Books Canada Reads competition, and a contributor to *How to Future: Leading and Sense-making in an Age of Hyperchange*, with Scott Smith. She is a member of the AI Policy Futures Group at the ASU Center for Science and the Imagination, as well as the XPRIZE Sci-Fi Advisory Council. Her work has appeared in Boing Boing, Slate, *MIT Technology Review*, *WIRED*, the *Atlantic*, and elsewhere.

Ryuko Azuma is a Japanese manga author and artist, known for the manga *Tetsuwan Adam* (鉄腕アダム) and *Star Blazers Λ* (スターブレイザーズΛ). He loves cats and science.

Bernardo Fernández, aka Bef (México City, 1972) is one of Latin America's leading crime and science fiction authors as well as graphic novelists. His books include comic book albums *Espiral* (*Spiral*), *La Calavera de Cristal* (*The Crystal Skull*, written by Juan Villoro), *Uncle Bill* (about William S. Burroughs in Mexico), *El instante amarillo* (*The Yellow Minute*), and *Habla María* (*María Speaks*, about parenting an autistic daughter).

As a novelist he's published the Season of Scorpions crime novel series, which include *Tiempo de alacranes* (*Season of Scorpions*), *Hielo negro* (*Black Ice*), *Cuello blanco* (*White Collar*), *Azul cobalto* (*Cobalt Blue*), and *Esta bestia que habitamos* (*This Hairy Beast We Live On*), and several science fiction novels that include *Ojos de lagarto* (*Snake Eyes*), *Gel azul* (*Blue Gel*), *Escenarios para el fin del mundo* (*Scenarios for the End of Times*), and *El estruendo del silencio* (*The Thunderous Silence*), as well as several young adult and children's books.

His most recent graphic novels are *Matar al candidato* (*Killing the Candidate*, written by F. G. Haghenbeck) and the children's comic *3 Deseos* (*Three Wishes*).

His work has been translated into several languages. He currently splits his time among writing a three-volume space cyberpunk saga, drawing a wordless dinosaur-themed graphic novel, teaching illustration to design students, and most important, being María and Sofía's dad.

In the science fiction world, **Bruce Bethke** is best known either for his short story "Cyberpunk," for his award-winning novel *Headcrash*, or for any of the other dozens of stories and novels he saw published in the 1980s and 1990s. In the real world, Bruce spent most of his career in supercomputer software R&D, doing work that was fascinating but impossible to explain to anyone not already familiar with computational fluid dynamics, Fourier transformations, and massively parallel processor architectures. Now retired, he's come back home to science fiction and is delighted to see what newer writers have done with his strange little idea from more than forty years ago.

Lauren Beukes is the award-winning and internationally bestselling South African author of *The Shining Girls*, *Zoo City*, and *Afterland*, among other works. Her novels have been published in twenty-four countries and are being adapted for film and TV. She's also a comics writer, screenwriter, journalist, and documentary maker. Lauren is a former feature journalist who covered electricity cable thieves, HIV+ beauty pageants, metro cops, and sex workers. She's worked in film and TV; as the director of *Glitterboys & Ganglands*, a documentary that won Best LGBTI Film at the Atlanta Black Film Festival; and as showrunner and head writer on South Africa's first half hour animated TV show, *Pax Afrika*, which ran for 104 episodes on SABC. Her comics work includes the original horror series *Survivors' Club* with Dale Halvorsen and Ryan Kelly and the *New York Times* bestselling *Fairest: The Hidden Kingdom*, a Japanese horror remix of Rapunzel with artist Inaki.

Maurice Broaddus is a community organizer and teacher. His work has appeared in places like *Lightspeed* magazine, *Black Panther: Tales from Wakanda*, *Weird Tales*, *The Magazine of Fantasy & Science Fiction*, and *Uncanny* magazine. His books include the sci-fi novel *Sweep of Stars*, the steampunk works *Buffalo Soldier* and *Pimp My Airship*, and the middle grade detective novels *The Usual Suspects* and *Unfadeable*. His project *Sorcerers* is being adapted as a television show for AMC. He's an editor at *Apex Magazine*.

Myra Çakan was born in Hamburg, Germany. She studied drama and music and attended workshops on sitcoms, screenplays, and treatment writing. She currently lives as a full-time author, artist, and freelance journalist near Hamburg.

Myra has been published in magazines and on websites such as *Die Woche*, *Konr@d*, *c't*, *Der Spiegel*, and *Die Süddeutsche Zeitung*. She wrote an adaptation of her acclaimed novel *When the Music's Over* for Red Beat Pictures. Her novels include *Downtown Blues*, *Begegnung in der High Sierra*, and *Zwischenfall an einem regnerischen Nachmittag*. Her short fiction has appeared in anthologies and magazines in Germany, Austria, Slovakia, Great Britain, China, and the United States of America. She also has more than twenty produced radio plays, both original works and adaptions of her own work.

In 2016, **Samuel R. Delany** was inducted into the New York State Writers Hall of Fame. He is the author of *Babel-17*, *Nova*, *Dhalgren*, *Dark Reflections*, *Atlantis: Three Tales*, the Return to Nevèrÿon series, an autobiography, *The Motion of Light in Water*, and the paired essays *Times Square Red / Times Square Blue*, as well as many other works. *Dark Reflections* won the Stonewall Book Award for 2008, and in 2015 Delany won the Nicolás Guillén Award for Philosophical Literature, in 1997 the Kessler Award for LGBTQ Studies, and in 2021 the Anisfield-Wolf Award. He has also won Nebula Awards from the Science Fiction Writers of America and two Hugo Awards from the World Science Fiction Convention. Filmmaker, novelist, critic, in 2013 he was made a Grand Master of Science Fiction, following in the steps of Asimov, Heinlein, and Le Guin.

Over a writing career that spanned three decades, **Philip K. Dick** (1928–1982) published thirty-six science fiction novels and 121 short stories in which he explored the essence of what makes man human and the dangers of centralized power. Toward the end of his life, his work turned to deeply personal, metaphysical questions concerning the nature of God. Eleven novels and short stories have been adapted to film, notably *Blade Runner* (based on *Do Androids Dream of Electric Sheep?*), *Total Recall*, *Minority Report*, and *A Scanner Darkly*, as well as television's *The Man in the High Castle*. The recipient of critical acclaim and numerous awards throughout his career, including the Hugo and John W. Campbell awards, Dick was inducted into the Science Fiction Hall of Fame in 2005, and between 2007 and 2009 the Library of America published a selection of his novels in three volumes. His work has been translated into more than twenty-five languages.

Greg Egan lives in Perth, Western Australia. He has won the John W. Campbell Award for Best Novel for *Permutation City*, and *Oceanic* was awarded a Hugo, a Locus, and an Asimov's Readers' Award. His work has also won the Japanese Seiun Award for best translated fiction seven times.

Minister Faust is an award-winning novelist, award-winning print journalist, radio host-producer, television host and associate producer, sketch comedy writer, video game writer, playwright, and poet. He has spoken and taught workshops widely.

Fabio Fernandes is a Brazilian writer living in Italy. He has published several books, among which are the novels *Os Dias da Peste* and *Back in the USSR* (in Portuguese) and the collection *L'Imitatore* (in Italian). He translated to Brazilian Portuguese several SF novels, including *Neuromancer* and *A Clockwork Orange*. He co-edited the anthologies *We See a Different Frontier* and *Solarpunk*. His collection *Love. An Archaeology* was published in 2021, and his steampunk novella, *Under Pressure*, was published in 2022.

Taiyo Fujii was born in Amami Oshima Island, between Kyushu and Okinawa. He has worked in stage design, desktop publishing, exhibition graphic design, and software development.

In 2012, Fujii self-published *Gene Mapper* serially in a digital format of his own design, and became Amazon.co.jp's number one Kindle bestseller of that year. The novel was revised and republished in 2013 and was nominated for the Nihon SF Taisho Award and the Seiun Award.

In *Gene Mapper*, Fujii describes in detail AR/VR communication, GMOs, and terror as an infrastructure. His second novel, *Orbital Cloud*, won the 2014 Nihon SF Taisho Award and Japanese Nebula Awards.

In 2019, the novelette collection *Hello, World!* won the Yoshikawa Eiji Literature Award for Young Writers.

Ganzeer operates seamlessly between art, design, and storytelling, creating what he has coined "Concept Pop." A chameleon according to the *New York Times*, his artwork has been witnessed in a wide variety of galleries, impromptu spaces, alleyways, and major museums around the world, and his words have seen print in publications both academic and trashy. His demented sci-fi graphic novel, *The Solar Grid*, has earned him a Global Thinker Award from *Foreign Policy*.

Eileen Gunn is an American science fiction writer and editor. She is the author of a relatively small but distinguished body of short fiction published over the past four decades. Her story "Coming to Terms" won the Nebula Award in 2004 and the Sense of Gender Award in Japan in 2007. Other stories have been nominated for the Hugo, Nebula, Philip K. Dick, Locus, and Tiptree awards. She has two volumes of collected work, *Stable Strategies and Others* and *Questionable Practices*, with a third, *Night Shift*, recently released in PM Press's Outspoken Authors series.

Gunn was editor and publisher of the pioneering webzine *The Infinite Matrix* and creator of the website The Difference Dictionary, a concordance to *The Difference Engine* by William Gibson and Bruce Sterling. She also had an extensive career in technology advertising, including a time as director of advertising at Microsoft.

Sean Lin Halbert received his BA in Korean language from the University of Washington and his MA in modern Korean literature from Seoul National University. He is a recipient of the GKL Translation Award, the LTI Korea Award for Aspiring Translators, and the *Korea Times* Modern Korean Literature Translation Award. His translations of Korean authors Yun Ko-eun, Park Sang Young, Kim Soom, and others have appeared in *Azalea* and *Korean Literature Now*. His major translations include Kim Un-su's novel *The Cabinet* and Yun Ko-eun's "The Chef's Nail." He currently lives in Seoul working as a full-time translator.

Saad Z. Hossain writes in a niche genre of fantasy, science fiction, and black comedy. He studied English lit and commerce at the University of Virginia, a combination of studies completely impractical in real life. He has been forced to work in various industries, including digging holes, making rope, throwing parties, and failing to run a restaurant. Needless to say, working for a living is highly overrated. He lives in Dhaka, the most ridiculously crowded city in the world, teeming with humans, wildlife, and djinn.

Alaya Dawn Johnson is an award-winning author of speculative fiction for adults and young adults. Her most recent novel is *Trouble the Saints*, and her most recent short story collection is *Reconstruction*.

Her debut YA novel, *The Summer Prince*, was longlisted for the National Book Award for Young People's Literature. Her most recent young adult novel, *Love Is the Drug*, brought her deep speculative imagination and social commentary to the world of modern Washington, DC. The first was nominated for and the second won the prestigious Andre Norton Nebula Award for YA Science Fiction and Fantasy, awarded by the Science Fiction Writers of America. In the past decade, her award-winning short stories have appeared in many magazines and anthologies, including *Best American Science Fiction and Fantasy 2015*, *Feral Youth*, *Three Sides of a Heart*, and *Zombies vs. Unicorns*.

Khalid Kaki was born in Kirkuk in 1971. He studied Spanish literature and philology at the University of Baghdad (1989–1993) and at Autónoma University in Madrid (1997–2000), where he has lived since 1996. He has published four collections of poetry—*Unsafely*, *The Guard's Notes*, *Cages in a Bird*, and *Ashes of the Pomegranate Tree*—and two collections of short stories—*The Land of Facing Mirrors* and *The Suicide of Jose Buenavida*.

James Patrick Kelly has won the Nebula, Hugo, and Locus awards. His work has been translated into seventeen languages. Most recent books include *The First Law of Thermodynamics Plus*, a collection in PM Press's Outspoken Author series; *King of the Dogs, Queen of the Cats*, a novella; a collection, *The Promise of Space*; and a novel, *Mother Go*, an audiobook original. He writes a column about the internet for *Asimov's*.

John Kessel's most recent books are the novels *Pride and Prometheus* and *The Moon and the Other*. His work has received the Nebula, Theodore Sturgeon, Locus, James Tiptree Jr., and Shirley Jackson awards. *The Dark Ride* is a collection of his best short fiction.

Kessel has taught literature and writing at North Carolina State University, where he helped found the MFA program in creative writing. He lives with his wife, the novelist Therese Anne Fowler, in Raleigh.

Naomi Kritzer has been writing science fiction and fantasy for more than twenty years; her fiction has won the Hugo Award, the Lodestar Award, the Edgar Award, and the Minnesota Book Award. Her newest book is *Chaos on CatNet*, which is a sequel to *Catfishing on CatNet*, and is set in Minneapolis. She lives in St. Paul, Minnesota, with her spouse, two kids (when the college kid is home from college), and four cats. The number of cats is subject to change without notice.

David Langford has been publishing and writing about science fiction since 1975. Novels include *The Space Eater* and *The Leaky Establishment*; there are many collections of his reviews, criticism, and humorous commentary. His twenty-nine Hugo awards span several categories: fanzine and semiprozine for the science fiction newsletter *Ansible* (1979–), short story for "Different Kinds of Darkness" (2000), and related work in 2012 for the online *Encyclopedia of Science Fiction* (with John Clute and Peter Nicholls), of which he remains a principal editor. In his spare time he runs the small press Ansible Editions and (occasionally) sleeps.

Arthur Liu (杨枫) is a Chinese science fiction writer and translator based in Beijing. His works have been published in *Science Fiction World*, *Non-Exist*, and *SF Stave*, among other Chinese science fiction magazines. As a computer engineer, he founded the Chinese Science Fiction Database, serving as its chief administrator. He wishes to be a cyber crawler.

Ken Liu is an American author of speculative fiction. A winner of Nebula, Hugo, and World Fantasy awards, he wrote the Dandelion Dynasty, a silkpunk epic fantasy series (starting with *The Grace of Kings*), as well as short story collections *The Paper Menagerie and Other Stories* and *The Hidden Girl and Other Stories*. He also penned the Star Wars novel *The Legends of Luke Skywalker*.

Prior to becoming a full-time writer, Liu worked as a software engineer, corporate lawyer, and litigation consultant. Liu frequently speaks at conferences and universities on a variety of topics, including futurism, cryptocurrency, history of technology, bookmaking, narrative futures, and the mathematics of origami.

Steven S. Long is a writer and game designer who's worked primarily in the tabletop role-playing game field for the past twenty-five-some years, during which he's written or cowritten approximately two hundred books. He's best known for his work with Champions and the HERO System but has worked for many other RPG companies. In recent years he's focused more on writing fiction and has had numerous short stories published. His Master Plan for World Domination has reached Stage 64-Omicron.

James Lovegrove is the author of more than sixty books, including *The Hope*, *Days*, *Untied Kingdom*, *Provender Gleed*, and the *New York Times* bestselling Pantheon series. His work has been translated into fifteen languages. He has written eight Sherlock Holmes novels, a collection of Holmes short stories, and a Conan Doyle/Lovecraft mashup trilogy, the Cthulhu Casebooks. He has also written four tie-in novels for the TV show *Firefly*, one of which, *The Ghost Machine*, won the 2020 Dragon Award for Best Media Tie-in Novel. He contributes two regular fiction-review columns to the *Financial Times* and lives with his wife, two sons, and tiny dog in Eastbourne, not far from the site of the "small farm upon the South Downs" to which Sherlock Holmes retired.

Ken MacLeod lives in Gourock on the west coast of Scotland. He has degrees in biological sciences, worked in IT, and is now a full-time writer. He is the author of nineteen novels, from *The Star Fraction* to *Beyond the Reach of Earth*, and many articles and short stories.

Nick Mamatas is the author of several novels, including *The Second Shooter* and *I Am Providence*. His short fiction has appeared in *Best American Mystery Stories*, *Year's Best Science Fiction & Fantasy*, *Asimov's*, Tor.com, and many other venues. Nick is also an anthologist: his most recent compilation is *Wonder and Glory Forever: Awe-Inspiring Lovecraftian Fiction*. His fiction and editorial work has been variously edited for the Hugo, World Fantasy, Shirley Jackson, and Bram Stoker awards.

Lisa Mason has published eleven novels, including *Summer of Love* (a Philip K. Dick Award Finalist) and *The Gilded Age* (a *New York Times* Notable Book), and two collections, *Strange Ladies: 7 Stories* and *Oddities: 22 Stories*. Her OMNI story, "Tomorrow's Child," sold to Universal Pictures.

Her latest science fiction novel, *Chrome*, was published in 2020. *Publishers Weekly* said, "Mason entertains and elicits fascinating questions about human nature in this fast-paced, action-packed science fiction adventure." Forthcoming is *Spyder*, book three in the Arachne Trilogy.

Tim Maughan is an author and journalist using both fiction and nonfiction to explore issues around cities, class, culture, technology, and the future. His work has appeared on the BBC, *New Scientist*, *MIT Technology Review*, One Zero, and Motherboard. His debut novel, *Infinite Detail*, was selected by the *Guardian* as their science fiction and fantasy book of the year and was shortlisted for the Locus Magazine Award for Best First Novel. Maughan also uses fiction to help clients as diverse as IKEA and the World Health Organization to think critically about the future. He currently lives in Canada.

Paul J. McAuley is the author of more than twenty novels, several collections of short stories, a Doctor Who novella, and a BFI Film Classic monograph on Terry Gilliam's film *Brazil*. His fiction has won the Philip K. Dick Memorial Award, the Arthur C. Clarke Award, the John W. Campbell Memorial Award, the Sidewise Award, the British Fantasy Award, and the Theodore Sturgeon Memorial Award. His latest novel is *Beyond the Burn Line*.

Misha's first novel, *Red Spider White Web*, published in England, won the 1990 ReaderCon Award, and was a finalist for the Arthur C. Clarke Award. Her prose has appeared in Germany, Austria, Australia, Japan, America, and Canada. Her piece "Tsuki Mangetsu" was used in a dynamic performance by two Australian composers and won the 1989 Prix d'Italia. She was formerly the editor of *New Pathways* magazine, and her review column "Points of Impact" carried through three magazines: *New Pathways*, published by Mike Adkisson; *Ice River*, edited by David Memmott; and *Science Fiction Eye*, edited by Steve Brown.

Janelle Monáe is an American singer, songwriter, rapper, and actor. They are signed to Atlantic Records, as well as to their own imprint, the Wondaland Arts Society. Monáe has received eight Grammy Award nominations. Monáe won an MTV Video Music Award and the ASCAP Vanguard Award in 2010.

Michael W. Moss writes cyberpunk, fantasy, and hard-boiled noir fiction. He also designs typefaces, one of which was used in an episode of *Doctor Who*. Michael lives in Portland, Oregon, with his significant other, two cats, and dog, Eddie.

T. R. Napper is a multiple award-winning science fiction author. His short fiction has appeared in *Asimov's*, *Interzone*, *The Magazine of Fantasy & Science Fiction*, and numerous others, and has been translated into Hebrew, German, French, and Vietnamese. He received a creative writing doctorate for his thesis: *Noir, Cyberpunk, and Asian Modernity*. Before turning to writing, T. R. Napper was an aid worker, implementing humanitarian programs in Southeast Asia for a decade. During this period, he received a commendation from the Government of Laos for his work with the poor. These days he has returned to his home country of Australia, where he works as a Dungeon Master, running campaigns for young people with autism for a local charity.

Mandisi Nkomo is a South African writer, drummer, composer, and producer. He currently resides in Hartbeespoort, South Africa. His fiction has been published in the likes of *Afrosf: Science Fiction by African Writers*, *AfroSF V3*, and *Omenana*. His poetry has been published in *The Coinage Book One* and *Shoreline of Infinity*. His academic work has been published in *The Thinker*. His works have been longlisted for the Nommo Award for African

Speculative Fiction. He has been shortlisted for the Toyin Falola Short Story Prize. He is also a member of the African Speculative Fiction Society.

Brandon O'Brien is a writer, performance poet, teaching artist, and game designer from Trinidad and Tobago. His work has been published in *Uncanny* magazine, *Fireside Magazine*, *Strange Horizons*, *Reckoning*, and *New Worlds, Old Ways: Speculative Tales from the Caribbean*, among others. He is the former poetry editor of the Hugo Award–winning magazine *FIYAH*. His debut poetry collection, *Can You Sign My Tentacle?*, is available now.

Craig Padawer's fiction has appeared in several journals and anthologies including *Conjunctions*, *The Dalhousie Review*, *After Yesterday's Crash: The Avant-Pop Anthology*, and *The Weird: A Compendium of Dark and Strange Stories*. He lives in New York, where he is a film professor.

Victor Pelevin is one of the most popular contemporary Russian-language writers. He won the Small Booker Prize, the National Bestseller Prize, and many other accolades for his works, which have also been translated into many languages and turned into films. He established himself as a major voice in the 1990s with his early novels, which included *Omon Ra* and *Generation P*. His most recent novel, *TRANSHUMANISM, INC.*, was published in 2021. The motion picture based on his novel *Empire V* was released in 2022.

Gerardo Horacio Porcayo is a Mexican writer, born May 10, 1966, in Cuernavaca, Morelos. Nowadays he lives in the city of Jojutla. He has a master's degree in Iberoamerican literature from the Universidad Ibero Puebla.

He has won many short story awards: *Axón Electrónico Primordial* (Argentina, 1992), *Puebla* (1993), *Kalpa* (1993), *Más Allá* (Argentina, 1994), *Sizigias* (Many Authors Anthology category, 2002), and *Sizigias* (Best Published Novel category, 2004). He also won the XXIX Concurso Magdalena Mondragón 2013 (Essay category). He has received an honorific mention of the Premio Internacional de Narrativa Ignacio Manuel Altamirano 2015.

He is considered the introducer of cyberpunk to Hispanic American literature with the publication of his first novel, *La primera calle de la soledad*, and the first (and only) Mexican cyberpunk anthology: *Silicio en la memoria*. He is also considered a fundamental figure inside Mexican Neogothic for his literary works in this genre, and for his editorial development with *Azoth* fanzine.

He has published twelve novels, three short story compilations, and three science fiction anthologies.

In 2018 he attended Worldcon 76 as a panelist, in San Jose, California, as a member of the Mexicanx Initiative.

In 2021 he was included in *The Best of World SF Volume 1*, edited by Lavie Tidhar, with his short story "Rue Chair," and in *Shadow Atlas: Dark Landscapes of The Americas*, edited by Carina Bissett, Hillary Dodge, and Joshua Viola, with his poem "The Hollow Place," originally written in English.

Yurei Raita is a name comprising the kanji for "spirit" and "rain" or "thunder" (as the phonetic transcription of the English word *writer*): *ghost writer*. The software that wrote this story worked within structural parameters gleaned from more than one thousand short stories and how-to-write essays written by Hoshi Shinichi. The software was developed in 2015 by the Sato-Matsuzaki Laboratory, a research team based at Nagoya University.

Rudy Rucker has published about forty books, both pop science and science fiction novels in the cyberpunk and transreal styles. He received Philip K. Dick awards for his *Software* and *Wetware*. He earned a PhD in higher mathematics. He worked as a professor of computer science in Silicon Valley. He paints works relating to his tales. His latest novel, *Juicy Ghosts*, is about telepathy, immortality, and an evil, insane president who has stolen an election.

Nisi Shawl is the multiple award-winning author and editor of *Filter House*, *Talk Like a Man*, *New Suns: Original Speculative Fiction by People of Color*, and *Everfair*—an example of the steamfunk offshoot of the steampunk offshoot of cyberpunk. Shawl's work on diversity in the imaginative genres includes cofounding the Carl Brandon Society and cowriting *Writing the Other: A Practical Approach*, the basis of their ongoing in-person and online classes. A new story collection, *Fruiting Bodies*, is available. In early 2023, their first middle grade novel appeared: a historical fantasy titled *Speculation*.

Lewis Shiner is the author of *Outside the Gates Of Eden*, the cyberpunk classic *Frontera*, and the award-winning *Glimpses*, among other novels. He's also published short story collections, journalism, and comics. Virtually all his work is available online for free.

Alex Shvartsman is the author of *The Middling Affliction* and *Eridani's Crown* fantasy novels. More than 120 of his stories have appeared in *Analog*, *Nature*, *Strange Horizons*, etc. He won the WSFA Small Press Award for Short Fiction (2014) and was a two-time finalist (2015, 2017) for the Canopus Award for Excellence in Interstellar Fiction. His translations from Russian have appeared in *The Magazine of Fiction & Science Fiction*, *Clarkesworld*, Tor.com, *Asimov's*, etc. Alex has edited over a dozen anthologies, including the long-running Unidentified Funny Objects series. He's the editor in chief of *Future Science Fiction Digest*. Alex resides in Brooklyn, New York.

Marissa Skeels is a Melbourne-based translator who has lived in Fukushima, Kyoto, and Tokyo. Her translations of Japanese stories have appeared in various literary journals.

Neal Stephenson is the bestselling author of the novels *Reamde*, *Anathem*, *The System of the World*, *The Confusion*, *Quicksilver*, *Cryptonomicon*, *The*

Diamond Age, *Snow Crash*, *Zodiac*, and *Termination Shock*. He lives in Seattle, Washington.

Bruce Sterling, author, journalist, editor, and critic, was born in 1954. Best known for his ten science fiction novels, he also writes short stories, book reviews, design criticism, opinion columns, and introductions for books ranging from Ernst Juenger to Jules Verne. His nonfiction works include *The Hacker Crackdown: Law And Disorder on the Electronic Frontier*, *Tomorrow Now: Envisioning The Next Fifty Years*, *Shaping Things*, and *The Epic Struggle of the Internet of Things*. His most recent book is a fiction collection, *Robot Artists and Black Swans: The Italian Fantascienza Stories*.

During 2005, he was the "visionary in residence" at Art Center College of Design in Pasadena. In 2008, he was the guest curator for the Share Festival of Digital Art and Culture in Torino, Italy, and the visionary in residence at the Sandberg Instituut in Amsterdam. In 2011, he returned to Art Center as visionary in residence to run a special project on Augmented Reality. In 2013, he was the visionary in residence at the Center for Science and the Imagination at Arizona State University. In 2015, he was the curator of the "Casa Jasmina" project at the Torino Fab Lab. In 2016, he was visionary in residence at the Arthur C. Clarke Center for Human Imagination.

He has appeared on ABC's *Nightline*, BBC's *The Late Show*, CBC's *Morningside*, MTV, and TechTV, and in *Time*, *Newsweek*, the *Wall Street Journal*, the *New York Times*, *Fortune*, *Nature*, *I.D.*, *Metropolis*, *Technology Review*, *Der Spiegel*, *La Stampa*, *La Repubblica*, and many other venues. He lives in Belgrade, Austin, Turin, and Ibiza.

Wole Talabi is an engineer, writer, and editor from Nigeria. His stories have appeared in *Asimov's*, *Lightspeed*, *The Magazine of Fantasy & Science Fiction*, and several other places. He has edited three anthologies: *Africanfuturism* (nominated for the Locus Award), *Lights Out: Resurrection*, and *These Words Expose Us*. He has been a finalist for several awards, including the prestigious Caine Prize, the Jim Baen Memorial Award, and the Nommo Award, which he won in 2018 and 2020. His collection *Incomplete Solutions* is available in print and audio. He likes scuba diving, elegant equations, and oddly shaped things.

K. A. Teryna is an award-winning author and illustrator. Her fiction has been translated from Russian into six languages. English translations of her stories have appeared in *Asimov's*, *Apex*, *The Magazine of Fantasy & Science Fiction*, *Strange Horizons*, *Samovar*, *Podcastle*, *Galaxy's Edge*, and elsewhere.

Jeffrey Thomas is the author of such novels as *Deadstock*, *Blue War*, and *The American*, and his short story collections include *Punktown*, *The Unnamed Country*, and *Carrion Men*. His stories have been reprinted in *The Year's Best Horror Stories XXII* (edited by Karl Edward Wagner), *The Year's Best*

Fantasy and Horror #14 (edited by Ellen Datlow and Terri Windling), and *Year's Best Weird Fiction #1* (edited by Laird Barron and Michael Kelly). Thomas lives in Massachusetts.

Vauhini Vara's debut novel, *The Immortal King Rao*, was a *New York Times* Editors' Choice and was named a best book of the year by NPR and *Esquire*. Her story collection *This Is Salvaged* is forthcoming. She has written and edited journalism for the *New Yorker*, the *New York Times Magazine*, the *Atlantic*, and other publications; her short stories have appeared in *McSweeney's*, *Tin House*, and elsewhere. Her essay "Ghosts," originally published in the *Believer* and anthologized here, was also honored in *Best American Essays 2022*. She has won an O. Henry Award for her writing, along with other honors from the Rona Jaffe Foundation, Yaddo, MacDowell, and others. She is the secretary for Periplus, a mentorship collective serving writers of color.

Yudhanjaya Wijeratne is a writer, data scientist, and general tinkerer. He lives and works in Sri Lanka. He cofounded and helps run Appendix.tech, a media and technology operation that fights misinformation (Watchdog Sri Lanka), builds software to help in times of crisis (Watchdog Elixir), and fills information gaps between people and the government.

He also works with the SciFi Economics Lab, architecting societies based on viable alternate economic structures, and with LIRNEasia, a think tank working across the Global South, on the intersection between data, algorithms, and government policy. His science fiction has been nominated for Nebula and IGF awards, published on ForeignPolicy, *Wired*, and Slate, and has appeared on bestseller lists.

E. Lily Yu is the author of *On Fragile Waves* and the librettist of *Stars Between*, with composer Steven K. Tran, for the Seattle Opera's 2021 Jane Lang Creation Lab. She received the Artist Trust LaSalle Storyteller Award in 2017 and the Astounding Award for Best New Writer in 2012. More than thirty of her stories have appeared in venues from *McSweeney's* to Tor.com, as well as twelve best-of-the-year anthologies, and have been finalists for Hugo, Nebula, Locus, Sturgeon, and World Fantasy awards.

Yun Ko-eun began her writing career when she won the Daesan Literary Award for her 2003 short story "Piercing." Her short story collections include *Table for One*, *Aloha*, *The Old Car and the Hitchhiker*, and *If Pyongyang Were on Monopoly*. She has authored the novels *Zero-gravity Syndrome*, *The Disaster Tourist*, *A Pirated Copy*, and *Library Runway*, as well as the collection of essays *The Warmth of the Void*. She is a recipient of the Hankyoreh Literary Award, the Lee Hyo-seok Literary Award, and the CWA Crime Fiction in Translation Dagger.

ABOUT THE EDITOR

Jared Shurin's previous anthologies include *The Outcast Hours* and *The Djinn Falls in Love* (both with Mahvesh Murad and both finalists for the World Fantasy Award). He has also been a finalist for the Shirley Jackson Award (twice), the British Science Fiction Association Award (twice), and the Hugo Award (twice) and won the British Fantasy Award (twice).

Alongside Anne C. Perry, he founded and edited the "brilliantly brutal" (the *Guardian*) pop culture website *Pornokitsch* for ten years, responsible for many of its most irritating and exuberant articles. Together, they also cofounded the Kitschies, the prize for progressive, intelligent, and entertaining speculative and fantastic fiction, and Jurassic London, an award-winning, not-for-profit small press.

His other projects have included the *Best of British Fantasy* and *Speculative Fiction* series and anthologies of mummies, weird Westerns, and Dickensian London. A frequent reviewer, he has also written articles on topics as diverse as *Gossip Girl* and *Deadwood*.

Jared is a certified BBQ judge.

ACKNOWLEDGMENTS

No one does a better job of standing on the shoulders of giants than an anthology editor.

I owe a debt of gratitude not only to the authors and translators whose work appears in this volume, but also the many editors who initially discovered and published those stories. These include, but are not limited to: Victoria Blake, Bill Campbell, Sarah Champion, Neil Clarke, Ellen Datlow,* Milton Davis, Eileen Gunn, Jason Heller, Karie Jacobson, Maxim Jakubowski, Richard Jones, James Patrick Kelly, Larry McCaffery, Rudy Rucker, Bruce Sterling, Jonathan Strahan, Joshua Viola, and Stephen Zision. These editors—and many others—created, fueled, and sustained this fragile genre: thank you all.

Navigating the twin worlds of cyberpunk and permissions presented a challenge, but I met some expert guides along the way. A special thanks to Richard Curtis, Vaughne Hanson, Simon Kavanagh, John Shirley, Paul Graham Raven, Robin Moger, Nisi Shawl, Marissa Skeels, Ganzeer and the kind people at the SFWA for going above and beyond in their help.

Much support (literary, emotional, physical, occupational, or culinary) was provided by Vicky, Sam, Becky, Syima, Patrick, CFM, Mahvesh, Matt M, Arin, Rich, The Good George, the Garlic Club, and my 'waffle-loving' Discord friends. Many of whom don't even like cyberpunk . . . but still got behind this project and helped every step of the way.

Much tolerance was also provided by my wonderful family, who have heard me talk about nothing besides cyberpunk for several years. A special shout out to

* In the introduction to *Mirrorshades*, Bruce Sterling refers to Ellen Datlow as "a shades-packing sister in the vanguard of the ideologically correct." This is the single coolest description ever and is entirely merited.

Sophia, George, and Nathaniel, shaping up to be three of the best *-punks* the world has ever seen.

David Holden, Lavie Tidhar, and Alex Shvartsman were terrific traveling companions, providing support, guidance, and good humor across time zones and digital platforms.

I had never met Ann VanderMeer before this project began. She steered me in the right direction at the outset (and provided impromptu therapy), and has been gracious with her time and her advice throughout. She is a role model both as an editor and a human being.

The Big Book of Cyberpunk would not have been possible without the hard work and dedication (and patience and creativity and chutzpah) of Ron Eckel, Anna Kaufman and Nick Skidmore. Thank you both so very, very much. The transatlantic team at Vintage Books has been brilliant. Turning a two-thousand-plus-page Word file into the beautiful objects you see before you is an amazing achievement. Thank you so much to production editor Kayla Overbey; copy editor Kathy Strickman; proofreaders Lyn Rosen, Karen Niersbach, and Melissa Holbrook Pierson; designer Nicholas Alguire; publicist Jordan Rodman; and marketer Sophie Normil for making magic. In the UK, thanks to managing editor Rhiannon Roy; proofreader Saxon Bullock; marketer Hannah Shorten; publicist Maya Koffi; production controller Konrad Kirkham; and cover designer Yeti Lambregts.

Anne C. Perry and Goblin: You may have 631,002 cyberpunk walruses and one tiger. You've earned them.

PERMISSIONS ACKNOWLEDGMENTS

Madeline Ashby: "Be Seeing You" by Madeline Ashby, © 2015 by Madeline Ashby. Originally published in *Pwning Tomorrow: An Anthology of Short Fiction from the Electronic Frontier* (2015), edited by Dave Maass. Reprinted by permission of the author.

Ryuko Azuma: "2045 Dystopia" by Ryuko Azuma, © 2018, 2023 by Ryuko Azuma. Originally appeared on Twitter. English translation copyright © 2018 by Marissa Skeels. This first English publication by permission of the author and translator.

Bruce Bethke: "Cyberpunk" by Bruce Bethke, © 1983 by Bruce Bethke. Originally published in *Amazing Science Fiction Stories* (November 1983). Reprinted by permission of the author.

Lauren Beukes: "Branded" by Lauren Beukes, © 2003 by Lauren Beukes. Originally published in *SL Magazine* (2003). Reprinted by permission of the author.

Maurice Broaddus: "I Can Transform You" by Maurice Broaddus, © 2013 by Maurice Broaddus. Originally published as *I Can Transform You* (2013) by Apex Publications. Reprinted by permission of the author.

Myra Çakan: "Spider's Nest" by Myra Çakan, © 2004 by Myra Çakan. Originally published in German as "Im Netz der Silberspinnexx" in *Der Atem Gottes und andere Visionen 2004*, edited by Helmuth W. Mommers. Reprinted by permission of the author.

Samuel R. Delany: "Time Considered as a Helix of Semiprecious Stones" by Samuel R. Delany, © 1968 by Samuel R. Delany. First published in *New Worlds* (December 1968). Reprinted here by permission of the author and his agents, Henry Morrison, Inc.

Philip K. Dick: "We Can Remember It for You Wholesale" by Philip K. Dick, currently collected in *The Philip K. Dick Reader*. Copyright © 2001 by Philip

K. Dick, reprinted here by permission of The Wylie Agency LLC and the author's estate. The story first appeared in *The Magazine of Fantasy and Science Fiction* (April, 1966).

Greg Egan: "Axiomatic" by Greg Egan, © 1990 by Greg Egan. First published in *Interzone* #41 (November 1990). Reprinted by permission of the author.

Minister Faust: "Somatosensory Cortex Dog Mess You Up Big Time, You Sick Sack of S**t" by Minister Faust, © 2021 by Minister Faust. First published in *Cyberfunk!* (2021), edited by Milton Davis. Reprinted by permission of the author.

Fabio Fernandes: "Wi-Fi Dreams" by Fabio Fernandes, © 2019 by Fabio Fernandes. First published as "Sonhos wifi" in *Cyberpunk: Registros Recuperados De Futuros Proibidos* (2019), edited by Erick Santos Cardoso and Cirilo S. Lemos. The first English translation appeared in *Love. An Archaeology* (Luna Press Publishing, 2021). Reprinted by permission of the author.

Bernardo Fernández, *Bef*: "Wonderama" by Bef, © 1998 by Bernardo Fernández, *Bef.* First published in *BZZZZZZT!! Ciudad interfase* (1998). This first English-language translation published by permission of the author.

Taiyo Fujii: "Violation of the TrueNet Security Act" by Taiyo Fujii © 2013 by Taiyo Fujii. Originally published in *SF Magazine*. English translation ©VIZ Media. Translated by Jim Hubbert. Reprinted by permission of the author and translator.

Ganzeer: "CRISPR Than You" by Ganzeer, © 2018–2021 by Ganzeer. First published on the author's website as "Staying Crisp," revised by the author for this edition. Illustrated by the author. Reprinted by permission of the author.

Eileen Gunn: "Computer Friendly" by Eileen Gunn, © 1989 by Eileen Gunn. First published in *Isaac Asimov's Science Fiction Magazine* (June 1989). Reprinted by permission of the author.

Saad Hossain: "The Endless" by Saad Hossain, © 2020 by Saad Hossain. First appeared in *Made to Order: Robots and Revolution* (2020), edited by Jonathan Strahan. Reprinted by permission of the author.

Khalid Kaki: "Operation Daniel" by Khalid Kaki, © 2018 by Khalid Kaki. First published in *Iraq +100* (2016), edited by Hassan Blasim. English-language translation by Adam Talib. Reprinted by permission of the author and Comma Press.

James Patrick Kelly: "Rat" by James Patrick Kelly, © 1986 by James Patrick Kelly. First published in *The Magazine of Fantasy and Science Fiction* (June 1986). Reprinted by permission of the author.

John Kessel: "The Last American" by John Kessel, © 2007 by John Kessel. Originally appeared in *Foundation* (Summer 2007). Reprinted by permission of the author.

Naomi Kritzer: "Cat Pictures Please" by Naomi Kritzer, © 2015 by Naomi Kritzer. First appeared in *Clarkesworld* (January 2015). Reprinted by permission of the author.

David Langford: "COMP.BASILISK.FAQ" by David Langford, © 1999, 2004 by David Langford. First published in *Nature* (December 1999). Reprinted by permission of the author.

Arthur Liu: "The Life Cycle of the Cyber Bar" by Arthur Liu © 2021 by Arthur Liu. English translation by Nathan Faries. Original publication in *Future Science Fiction Digest* (September 2021). Reprinted by permission of the author and translator.

Ken Liu: "Thoughts and Prayers" by Ken Liu, © 2019 by Ken Liu. First published in *Slate: Future Tense* (2019). Reprinted by permission of the author and the author's agents, Scovil Galen Ghosh Literary Agency, Inc.

Steven S. Long: "Keeping Up with Mr. Johnson" by Steven S. Long, © 2016 by The Topps Company Inc. All Rights Reserved. First published in *World of Shadows* (2016), edited by John Helfers. Shadowrun & Matrix are registered trademarks and/or trademarks of The Topps Company Inc., in the United States and/or other countries. Catalyst Game Labs and the Catalyst Game Labs logo are trademarks of InMediaRes Productions LLC. Reprinted by permission of Catalyst Game Labs.

James Lovegrove: "Britworld™" by James Lovegrove, © 1992 by James Lovegrove. First published in *Interzone* (December 1992) and reprinted in *Imagined Slights* (2002). Reprinted by permission of the author.

Ken MacLeod: "Earth Hour" by Ken MacLeod, © 2011 by Ken MacLeod. First published on Tor.com (June 2011). Reprinted by permission of the author.

Nick Mamatas: "Time of Day" by Nick Mamatas, © 2002 by Nick Mamatas. First published on Strange Horizons (January 2002). Reprinted by permission of the author.

Lisa Mason: "Arachne" by Lisa Mason, © 1987 by Lisa Mason. First published in *Omni* (December 1987). Basis of the novel *Arachne* (1990), published by William Morrow. Reprinted by permission of the author.

Tim Maughan: "Flyover Country" by Tim Maughan, © 2016 by Tim Maughan. First published in *Terraform* (November 2016). Reprinted by permission of the author.

Paul J. McAuley: "Gene Wars" by Paul J. McAuley, © 1991 by Paul J. McAuley. First published, in a slightly different form, as "Evan's Progress" in *New Internationalist* (March 1991). Reprinted by permission of the author.

Misha: "Speed" by Misha, © 1988 by Misha. First appeared in *Prayers of Steel* (1988), published by Wordcraft. Reprinted by permission of the author.

Janelle Monáe and Alaya Dawn Johnson: "The Memory Librarian" by Janelle Monáe and Alaya Dawn Johnson, © 2022 by Jane Lee LLC. First published in *The Memory Librarian* (2022) by Janelle Monáe. Used by permission of HarperCollins Publishers.

Michael W. Moss: "Keep Portland Wired" by Michael W. Moss, © 2020 by Michael W. Moss. First published in *The Trench Coat Minotaur* (2020). Reprinted by permission of the author.

T. R. Napper: "Twelve Minutes to Vinh Quang" by T. R. Napper, © 2015 by T. R. Napper. First published in *Writers of the Future: Volume 31* (2015). Reprinted by permission of the author.

Mandisi Nkomo: "Do Androids Dream of Capitalism and Slavery?" by Mandisi Nkomo, © 2020 by Mandisi Nkomo. First published in *Omenana* (August 2020). Reprinted by permission of the author.

Brendan O'Brien: "fallenangel.dll" by Brendan O'Brien, © 2016 by Brendan O'Brien. First published in *New Worlds, Old Ways: Speculative Tales from the Caribbean* (2016), edited by Karen Lord, published by Peekash Press. Reprinted by permission of the author.

Craig Padawer: "Hostile Takeover" by Craig Padawer, © 1995 by Craig Padawer. First published in *After Yesterday's Crash: The Avant-Pop Anthology* (1995), edited by Larry McCaffery, published by Penguin. Reprinted by permission of the author.

Victor Pelevin: "The Yuletide Cyberpunk Yarn, or Christmas Eve-117.DIR" by Victor Pelevin, © 1996 by Victor Pelevin. All rights reserved. English translation © 2022 by Alex Shvartsman. This first English-language publication by arrangement with the author's agents, FTM Agency Ltd., and translator.

Gerardo Horacio Porcayo: "Ripped Imaged, Rusted Dreams" by Gerardo Horacio Porcayo, © 1995, 2023 by Gerardo Horacio Porcayo. First published in the Antología de Jóvenes Escritores Morelenses, *Palabras Pendientes* (1995), by the Government of the State of Morales. English-language translation by the author. This first English-language publication by arrangement with the author.

Yurei Raita: "The Day a Computer Wrote a Novel" by Yurei Raita, © 2015 by Satoshi Sato and Sato-Matsuzaki Laboratory, Nagoya University. English translation © 2019 by Marissa Skeels. English translation first published in *Big Echo* (October 2019). Reprinted by permission of the author and translator.

Rudy Rucker: "Juicy Ghost" by Rudy Rucker, © 2019, 2023 by Rudy Rucker. First published in *Big Echo* (October 2019). Afterword first published in this volume. Later expanded to *Juicy Ghosts* (2021), from Transreal Books. Reprinted by permission of the author.

Nisi Shawl: "I Was a Teenage Genetic Engineer" by Nisi Shaw, © 1989 by Nisi Shaw. First published in *Semiotext(e) SF* (1989), edited by Rudy Rucker, Peter Lamborn Wilson, and Robert Anton Wilson. Reprinted by permission of the author.

Lewis Shiner: "The Gene Drain" by Lewis Shiner, © 1989 by Lewis Shiner. First published in *Semiotext(e) SF* (1989), edited by Rudy Rucker, Peter Lamborn Wilson, and Robert Anton Wilson. Reprinted by permission of the author.

Neal Stephenson: "The Great Simoleon Caper" by Neal Stephenson, © 1995 by Neal Stephenson. First published in *Time* (Spring 1995). Reprinted by permission of the author and Darhansoff & Verrill Literary Agents.

Bruce Sterling: "Deep Eddy" by Bruce Sterling, © 1993 by Bruce Sterling. Originally published in *Isaac Asimov's Science Fiction Magazine* (August 1993). Collected in *A Good Old-Fashioned Future* (1999), published by Spectra. Reprinted by permission of Writers House LLC acting as agent for the author.

Wole Talabi: "Abeokuta52" by Wole Talabi, © 2019 by Wole Talabi. First appeared in *Omenana* (October 2019). Reprinted by permission of the author.

K. A. Teryna: "The Tin Pilot" by K. A. Teryna, © 2022 by K. A. Teryna. English translation by Alex Shvartsman. First English-language publication in *Isaac Asimov's Science Fiction Magazine* (August 2022). Reprinted by permission of the author and translator.

Jeffrey Thomas: "Immolation" by Jeffrey Thomas, © 2000 by Jeffrey Thomas. First appeared in *Punktown* (2000), from the Ministry of Whimsy Press. Reprinted by permission of the author.

Vauhini Vara: "Ghosts" by Vauhini Vara, © 2021 by Vauhini Vara. First published in *The Believer* (August 2021). Reprinted by permission of the author.

Yudhanjaya Wijeratne: "The State Machine" by Yudhanjaya Wijeratne, © 2020 by Yudhanjaya Wijeratne. First published on Slate.com (September 2020). Reprinted by permission of the author.

E. Lily Yu: "Darkout" by E. Lily Yu, © 2016 by E. Lily Yu. First published in *CyberWorld* (2016), edited by Josh Viola and Jason Heller. Reprinted by permission of the author.

Yun Ko-eun: "P" by Yun Ko-eun, © 2014 by Yun Ko-eun. All rights reserved. Originally published in Korea by Changbi Publishers Inc. English translation copyright © 2022 by Sean Lin Halbert. This first English-language publication in arrangement with Changbi Publishers Inc. and with permission of the translator.

FURTHER READING

The Big Book of Cyberpunk is, despite its obvious heft, not an exhaustive review of this fascinating genre. As noted previously, it is also limited to short fiction, while cyberpunk thrives across many different formats.

The recommendations below are not intended to be a 'best of' list or a definitive bibliography. Instead, these are works that I, personally, enjoyed, and would suggest to those who wish to keep exploring what cyberpunk has to offer.

For the sake of variety, I have tried, except where unavoidable, to exclude works by authors who appear within this anthology. As always, my selection is personal and whimsical.

ALBUMS

1. *Beyond the Valley of 1984* (1981) by The Plasmatics
2. *Power, Corruption & Lies* (1983) by New Order
3. *The Initial Command* (1987) by Front Line Assembly
4. *Outside* (1995) by David Bowie
5. *Interstellar Fugitives* (1998) by Underground Resistance
6. *Gorillaz* (2001) by Gorillaz
7. *Year Zero* (2007) by Nine Inch Nails
8. *ArchAndroid* (2010) by Janelle Monae
9. *Terror 404* (2012) by Perturbator
10. *Simulation Theory* (2018) by Muse

FILM AND TELEVISION*

1. *Escape from New York* (1981)
2. *Outland* (1981)
3. *Scanners* (1981)
4. *Blade Runner* (1982)
5. *Videodrome* (1983)
6. *Max Headroom* (1985)

* For sanity's sake, I've not included sequels. But you can safely assume that *Blade Runner 2049* is also, indeed, cyberpunk.

7. *The Running Man* (1987)
8. *Akira* (1988)
9. *Robocop* (1987 and 2014)
10. *Demolition Man* (1993)
11. *Wild Palms* (1993)
12. *Strange Days* (1995)
13. *Johnny Mnemonic* (1995)
14. *Hackers* (1995)
15. *Lawnmower Man* (1996)
16. *Batman Beyond* (1999)
17. *eXistenZ* (1999)
18. *The Matrix* (1999)
19. *The Cell* (2000)
20. *Black Mirror* (2011)
21. *Ex Machina* (2014)
22. *Sense8* (2015)
23. *Mr Robot* (2015)
24. *Westworld* (2016)
25. *Severance* (2022)

VIDEO AND TABLETOP GAMES*

1. *2400 AD* (1988)
2. *Cyberpunk* (1988)
3. *Mean Streets* (1989)
4. *Shadowrun* (1989)
5. *Corporation* (1990)
6. *GURPS Cyberpunk* (1990)†
7. *Kult* (1991)
8. *Syndicate* (1993)
9. *Beneath a Steel Sky* (1994)
10. *Hell: A Cyberpunk Thriller* (1994)‡
11. *System Shock* (1994)
12. *Heresy: Kingdom Come* (1995)§
13. *Netrunner* (1996)
14. *Deus Ex* (2000)
15. *868-HACK* (2013)
16. *Watch Dogs* (2013)
17. *Satellite Reign* (2015)
18. *Cyberpunk 2077* (2020)
19. *CY_BORG* (2022)

ANTHOLOGIES

1. *Mirrorshades* (1986), edited by Bruce Sterling
2. *Semiotext(e) SF* (1989), edited by Rudy Rucker, Paul Lamborn Wilson and Robert Anton Wilson
3. *Storming the Reality Studio* (1991), edited by Larry McCaffery
4. *FutureCrime* (1992), edited by Cynthia Manson and Charles Ardai
5. *Simulations* (1993), edited by Karie Jacobson
6. *Cybersex* (1996), edited by Richard Jones

---

* I've listed franchises, not individual games, and dated to the first installment therein; excluding sequels, reboots, new editions or other expansions. With many thanks to George Osborn and James Long for their help.

† Perhaps less notable as a game than as a moment in cyberpunk history, *GURPS Cyberpunk* was the cause of the ill-fated Secret Service raid of Steve Jackson Games, demonstrating, amongst other things, the heightened confusion and paranoia at the time.

‡ With apologies to the fine people at Take-Two Interactive Software, this game is truly terrible - notoriously so. It is from the generation of *Myst*-like games, wherein the player does a lot of precise mouse-clicking to solve puzzles and 'earn' the reward of grainy video cut-scenes. In the case of *Hell*, the puzzles were (inadvertently, due to flaws in the code) impossible and the video cut-scenes included Dennis Hopper and Grace Jones. *Hell: A Cyberpunk Thriller* is, in and of itself, cyberpunk.

§ This obscure but fabulous game mostly exists in a shoebox under my bed.

7. *Disco 2000* (1996), edited by Sarah Champion
8. *Hackers* (1996), edited by Gardner Dozois
9. *Future on Ice* (1998), edited by Orson Scott Card
10. *The Ultimate Cyberpunk* (2002), edited by Pat Cadigan
11. *Rewired: The Post-Cyberpunk Anthology* (2007), edited by James Patrick Kelly and John Kessel
12. *Cyberpunk: Stories of Hardware, Software, Wetware, Revolution and Evolution* (2013), edited by Victoria Blake
13. *CyberWorld: Tales of Humanity's Tomorrow* (2016), edited by Jason Heller and Joshua Viola
14. *A Punk Rock Future* (2019), edited by Steve Zision
15. *Cyberfunk!* (2021), edited by Milton Davis

COMIC BOOKS AND GRAPHIC NOVELS*

1. *The Long Tomorrow* (1976) by Dan O'Bannon and Moebius
2. *Judge Dredd* (1977) by John Wagner and Carlos Ezquerra
3. *The Incal* (1981) by Alejandro Jodorowsky and Moebius
4. *American Flagg* (1983) by Howard Chaykin
5. *Ghost in the Shell* (1989) by Masamune Shirow
6. *Battle Angel Alita* (1990) by Yukito Kishiro
7. *20/20 Visions* (1997) by Jamie Delano, Frank Quitely, Warren Peece, James Romberger and Steve Pugh
8. *Transmetropolitan* (1997) by Warren Ellis and Darick Robertson
9. *The True Lives of the Fabulous Killjoys* (2013) by Gerard Way, Shaun Simon, and Becky Cloonen
10. *Vision* (2015) by Tom King and Gabriel Hernandez Walta

* To spare my sanity and yours, I've only listed the first publication date. As any reader of comics knows, continuity is tenuous at the best of times.

NON-FICTION

1. *The Media is the Massage: An Inventory of Effects* (1967) by Marshall McLuhan
2. *Future Shock* (1970) by Alvin Toffler
3. *Simulacra and Simulation* (1981) by Jean Baudrillard
4. "The Neuromantics" (1986) by Norman Spinrad (*Isaac Asimov's Science Fiction Magazine*)
5. "High Tech - High Life: William Gibson and Timothy Leary in Conversation" (1989) (*Mondo 2000)*
6. *Cyborg Manifesto* (1991) by Donna Haraway
7. "A Cypherpunk's Manifesto" (1993) by Eric Hughes
8. *The Posthuman* (2013) by Rosi Braidotti
9. *CCRU: Writings, 1997-2003* (2017)
10. "Heavenly Bodies: Why It Matters That Cyborgs Have Always Been About Disability, Mental Health, and Marginalization" (2019) by Damien Williams

Two excellent volumes that cover the breadth of the genre are *The Routledge Companion to Cyberpunk Culture* (2020) and *Fifty Key Figures in Cyberpunk Culture* (2022), both by Anna McFarlane, Graham J. Murphy and Lars Shmeink.

NOVELS, NOVELLAS AND COLLECTIONS*

Precursors

1. *The Long Good-bye* (1953) by Raymond Chandler
2. *The Stars My Destination / Tiger, Tiger* (1956) by Alfred Bester
3. *The Soft Machine* (1961) by William S. Burroughs
4. *A Clockwork Orange* (1962) by Anthony Burgess
5. *Crash (1973) by J.G. Ballard*
6. *Shockwave Rider* (1975) by John Brunner
7. *Home is the Hangman* (1975) by Roger Zelazny
8. *Blood and Guts in High School* (1978) by Kathy Acker
9. *True Names* (1981) by Vernor Vinge
10. "Press Enter_" (1984) by John Varley

Cyberpunk

11. *Street Lethal* (1983) by Steven Barnes
12. *Hardwired* (1986) by Walter John Williams
13. *Dark Toys and Consumer Goods* (1989) by Lawrence Staig
14. *Santa Clara Poltergeist* (1990) by Fausto Fawcett
15. *The Illegal Rebirth of Billy the Kid* (1991) by Rebecca Ore
16. *High Aztech* (1992) by Ernest Hogan
17. *Down and Out in the Year 2000* (1992) by Kim Stanley Robinson
18. *Destroying Angel* (1992) by Richard Paul Russo
19. *Trouble and her Friends* (1994) by Melissa Scott
20. *Clipjoint* (1996) by Wilhemina Baird
21. *Brown Girl in the Ring* (1998) by Nalo Hopkinson
22. *Noir* (1998) by K.W. Jeter
23. *Pashazade* (2001) by Jon Courtenay Grimwood
24. *Market Forces* (2004) by Richard Morgan
25. *Kung Fu High School* (2005) by Ryan Gattis
26. *Cyclonopedia* (2008) by Reza Negarestani
27. *Slum Online* (2010) by Hiroshi Sakurazaka
28. *The Stories of Ibis* (2011) by Hiroshi Yamamoto
29. *Self-Reference ENGINE* (2013) by Toh Enjoe
30. *The Red* (2015) by Linda Nagata
31. *Infomocracy* (2016) by Malka Older
32. *Otared* (2016) by Mohammed Rabie
33. *The Goldblum Variations* (2018) by Helen McClory
34. *The Tiger Flu* (2018) by Larissa Lai
35. *Autonomous* (2018) by Annalee Newitz
36. *Sweet Harmony* (2020) by Claire North

* A reminder that I've deliberately chosen not to include works by those authors who otherwise appear in *The Big Book of Cyberpunk*. However, for the sake of the historical record: 'I officially recommend them all.'

37. *Noor* (2021) by Nnedi Okorafor
38. *Immersion* (2022) by Gemma Amor
39. *Mindwalker* (2022) by Kate Dylan
40. *Cyberpunk 2077: No Coincidence* (2023) by Rafal Kosil

*Post-cyberpunk**

41. *Microserfs* (1995) by Douglas Coupland
42. *Maul* (2003) by Tricia Sullivan
43. *Harmony* (2010) by Project Itoh
44. *Machine Man* (2011) by Max Barry
45. *The Mall* (2011) by S.L. Grey
46. *Bleeding Edge* (2013) by Thomas Pynchon
47. *Sad Sack: Collected Writing* (2019) by Sophia Al-Maria
48. *XX* (2020) by Rian Hughes
49. *Prompt: Conversations with Artificial Intelligence* (2022) by Dave McKean
50. *Red Earth* (2023) by Michael Salu

* At the risk of lobbing another definitional grenade into the fray, 'post-cyberpunk' in this case stands for works that are in conversation with (or otherwise informed by) cyberpunk, but in some way - thematically, aesthetically or topically - radically and distinctly depart from the movement.

VINTAGE CLASSICS

Vintage launched in the United Kingdom in 1990, and was originally the paperback home for the Random House Group's literary authors. Now, Vintage comprises some of London's oldest and most prestigious literary houses, including Chatto & Windus (1855), Hogarth (1917), Jonathan Cape (1921) and Secker & Warburg (1935), alongside the newer or relaunched hardback and paperback imprints: The Bodley Head, Harvill Secker, Yellow Jersey, Square Peg, Vintage Paperbacks and Vintage Classics.

From Angela Carter, Graham Greene and Aldous Huxley to Toni Morrison, Haruki Murakami and Virginia Woolf, Vintage Classics is renowned for publishing some of the greatest writers and thinkers from around the world and across the ages – all complemented by our beautiful, stylish approach to design. Vintage Classics' authors have won many of the world's most revered literary prizes, including the Nobel, the Booker, the Prix Goncourt and the Pulitzer, and through their writing they continue to capture imaginations, inspire new perspectives and incite curiosity.

In 2007 Vintage Classics introduced its distinctive red spine design, and in 2012 Vintage Children's Classics was launched to include the much-loved authors of our childhood. Random House joined forces with the Penguin Group in 2013 to become Penguin Random House, making it the largest trade publisher in the United Kingdom.

@vintagebooks

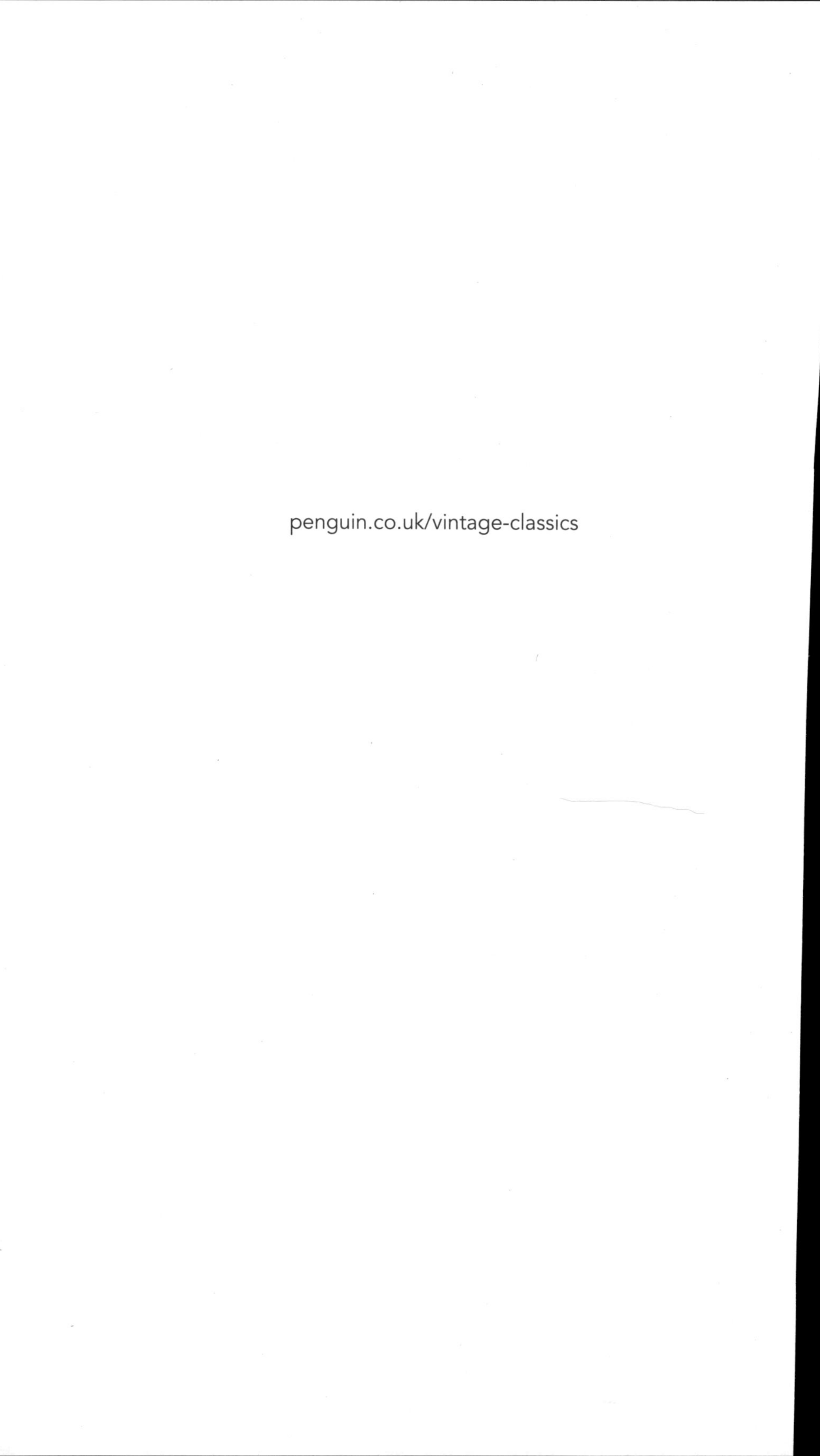